FIRMAMENTS

BOOK I *of the* TEMPEST TRILOGY

by

NATASHA KENNEDY

Beauty without kindneſs dies unenjoyed, and
undelighting. *Samuel Johnſon*, LL. D.

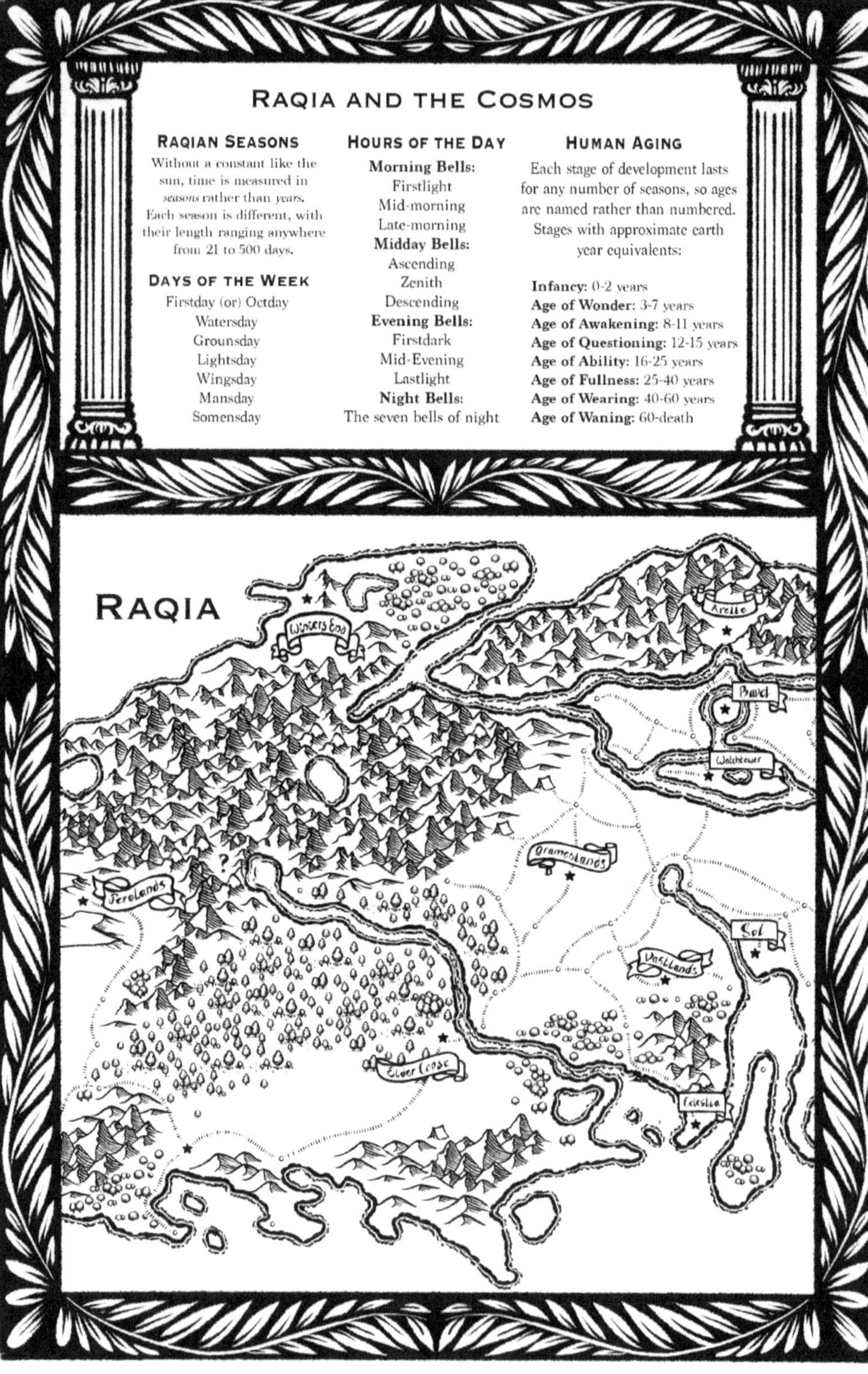

RAQIA AND THE COSMOS

RAQIAN SEASONS
Without a constant like the sun, time is measured in *seasons* rather than *years*. Each season is different, with their length ranging anywhere from 21 to 500 days.

DAYS OF THE WEEK
Firstday (or) Octday
Watersday
Grounsday
Lightsday
Wingsday
Mansday
Somensday

HOURS OF THE DAY
Morning Bells:
Firstlight
Mid-morning
Late-morning
Midday Bells:
Ascending
Zenith
Descending
Evening Bells:
Firstdark
Mid-Evening
Lastlight
Night Bells:
The seven bells of night

HUMAN AGING
Each stage of development lasts for any number of seasons, so ages are named rather than numbered. Stages with approximate earth year equivalents:

Infancy: 0-2 years
Age of Wonder: 3-7 years
Age of Awakening: 8-11 years
Age of Questioning: 12-15 years
Age of Ability: 16-25 years
Age of Fullness: 25-40 years
Age of Wearing: 40-60 years
Age of Waning: 60-death

RAQIA
Winter's End
Arelle
Bavel
Watchtower
Perolands
Gravenlands
Sol
Vastlands
Elder Cross
Celestia

HIGHEST HEAVENS
WATERS ABOVE
GLASSY SEA
RAQIA
SPACE
EARTH
AND THE
LOWLANDS
WATERS BELOW
HADES

TABLE *of* CONTENTS

Prologue

WHEN IS IT RIGHT TO KILL THE KING?"

King Sol blinked. He stared at the toaster who held up his goblet with a playful smile, swirling it in his hand while he rose from his chair. A stiff silence hovered above the room of noble party guests, then a couple of the more inebriated Faeries laughed. Right—this was one of those *comical* toasts. But who was this man? Sol didn't remember inviting him to the private celebration.

"Is it when he has reigned too long?" The speech-giving Faerie continued his monologue with that same, knowing smile. "Is it when he has failed to lead his people? Or is it when he has led them down a wrong path?"

King Sol gripped the arms of his throne. Other party guests began to lower their goblets. "Fae Dezmund—who is this man?" he demanded.

A nervous quiver of motion moved through the throne room as Faeries rose from their chairs. Dishes clinked and cloth napkins dropped to the floor. Fae Dezmund drew his sword, holding his position beside the king's throne.

"I ask again," the man with the goblet said, his voice crescendoing as he took a step closer to the king's lofty seat. "When is it the right thing to do to kill the king?"

King Sol's eyes snapped sideways as his ears detected the snapping sound of a bowstring tightening. "There!" he barked, pointing toward the back of the hall. "A human points a weapon at me!"

"No weapon can kill the Faerie King," Dezmund whispered from beside the king. "Don't panic, Sire."

"Who in Hades are you?" King Sol demanded. He pointed a lavishly gloved hand at the toaster. "I've never seen this Faerie before. What's he doing in my—?"

"Never seen me before..." the Faerie with the goblet shook his head. Then his smile morphed into a bitter expression, featuring a pearly white set of snarling teeth. "Are you quite sure?"

King Sol's hand twitched. Recognition seized him like an attacker from behind; he knew he recognized the man, but he didn't know *how*. He carefully reached for his scepter, which sat idly on the table beside him.

"Sire..." Dezmund hissed, "Don't move."

Sol glanced up at his bodyguard, the Faerie of War. "You *just* said that no weapon can kill me... why wouldn't I—?"

"That man back there holds Orion's Bow, Sire," Dezmund said from the side of his mouth. Few people could recognize a weapon such as Orion's Bow, but both Sol and Dezmund were two who could.

"Ah," the Faerie who still held his position at the center of the room nodded his glass in King Sol's direction. A portentous splash of red vino spilled down the rim and onto the floor. "Realization dawns. Perhaps *now* I may have your undivided attention?"

The select number of party guests inside the throne room for King Sol's Firstday Feast stood petrified like a display of statues. If the king gave his attention, they would too. If the king was scared, then so were they.

"I ask a third time," said the man with the goblet. He strode forward toward the throne. His heels clicked against the marble floors, and his black hair seemed to float with a life all of its own. "When is it *right* to kill the king?" The man had presence. He had the sort of presence that could make one want to hear everything he said, even if he had a legendary weapon pointed right at one's heart—which he did. Then his face finally registered in the Faerie King's mind. Somenus, this was *Somenus*!

"How?" King Sol demanded, "How did you return?"

"It is never right to kill the king," Fae Dezmund finally responded. "It is never right for a Faerie to kill *anyone*." His voice boomed like a war drum. "Which is precisely why Faeries are incapable of killing!"

Somenus swirled his glass again, spilling more vino onto the white floor. "I would say that there *is* a right time to kill a king," he said, "And that is when the king has stopped leading his people. If a king neglects to lead, what choice do his subjects have but to rebel?"

Sol and Somenus held one another's gaze. All others in the room seemed to disappear as the two ancient rivals studied one another. How? How had Somenus managed to return? Surely it was impossible! Had... had *Aorist* helped him return?

"You think I have misled my people," King Sol said loud enough for all to hear, "And you think you could do better?"

"You haven't led your people at all," replied Somenus. He cast his goblet onto the floor, and a brasslike clang resounded as vino splattered widely across the marble. "You have them all believing they are useless—existing just to exist."

King Sol snorted. "Once again you try to force The Question upon me, as if I have some responsibility to answer it—as if I have some hidden *knowledge* I am keeping from the Fae."

Somenus tipped his head back as he let out a soft laugh, sounding as pleasant and benign as the coo of a dove. King Sol reached for his scepter. Somenus snapped his head back up, glaring with clenched teeth. Sol recoiled his hand, defenseless.

"How delightful it must be," Somenus said as he swiveled to regard the others in the room, "to have your entire family with you on this auspicious day."

Sol's fists clenched. Perspiration crept down his temples. "No..." the word barely escaped his lips audibly. He turned his attention to the back of the hall where the human stood, holding back the string of the bow. So, this was it? *This* was the end? Well, Sol wasn't going to go down without a fight, not when his wife and children were also in danger.

Sol dove sideways to seize the scepter. At the same time, a weight hit his chest. The scepter dropped to the floor and rolled. As Sol clung to his bleeding chest, he caught a glimpse of Somenus out of the corner of his eye. Somenus knelt down to pluck the scepter from the floor. He turned it in his hand pensively, then looked up at Sol.

"Kill them all," cried Somenus, "Not a single Faerie leaves this room alive!"

Sol slumped into his throne; pain and shock prevented him from any sort of retaliation. He looked up helplessly; Somenus stepped toward him.

Screams and cries could be heard as Somenus' bowman took down every Faerie in the hall, one by one. Sol's entire family was being murdered right before his eyes. How could this have happened?

Rather than finding strength in his final moments, Sol felt himself growing into a helpless child again. Long-forgotten memories played at the back of his mind, reminding him that he had never been truly safe. Death and annihilation surrounded him on every side. Faeries turned to stone everywhere he looked. Where was his protection? Where was his guardian?

Where was Aorist?

—— Leo ——

Through the Firmaments

I WAS GETTING USED TO LONG FLIGHTS; that cramped feeling of my knees brushing the seat in front of me didn't seem so tortuous anymore, and I was even growing fond of sitting in one place for hours on end, staring at the top of a stranger's head—just thinking about existence. Is that what happens when a person is uprooted and aimless for too long? Do we begin to question our very presence on the Earth, as if by floating in the air too long, away from the solid ground, we suddenly wonder if we belong there? Or was it just me?

Earth: my spherical world twisting round and round, trapped in an endless, cyclical rhythm of day and night, life and death, waking and sleeping. What was this strange cycle in which I was trapped, where every morning I was born into a new life and every night I died? Is that not what sleep was—a kind of death? Every morning at waking, I had to remember who I was and what I was supposed to do; and every night I would surrender to my heavy eyes and enter the spirit world inside my head.

I would have kept going on in this cycle of life and death forever if I had not been abruptly interrupted like a record part-way through a song. I would have kept circling the sun on my ever-spinning earth, just like my plane circled the globe, searching tirelessly for someone I didn't actually want to find. I, Leonard Levi, a mediocre seminary drop-out and part-time ambulance driver, would be the lucky, though undeserving, one to leave the death-bound cycle of the Earth and stare into the chaotic world beyond.

Thankfully, it only took a little over an hour to get from Melbourne, Australia to Hobart, Tasmania. It would be the final leg of my journey—at least, I hoped so.

"What time is it?" Lydia asked from beside me. She had a sleep mask over her eyes, though it never did help her sleep. She wore it mostly to provide herself with an illusion of privacy. The poor introvert was withering away with all this global travel. I did my best not to talk to her when she had that thing on, but since she initiated the conversation, I replied.

"Hell, I don't know." I checked my watch, though I couldn't remember if it was set to local Melbourne time, or Singapore time. "Have you managed to sleep at all?"

"No," she said in a weary voice. She lifted the mask up, resting it against her forehead, and gave me a dozy smile. Man—she was pretty. With short, blonde hair, bright blue eyes, and a kind soul, she was everything a woman could be in my estimation. I'd been in love with Lydia since I was old enough to care about that sort of thing, but never had she thought about me as more than a brother. I was used to that by now. The long hours of travel and hardship together in the last several weeks tested my honor a fair bit, but I like to think I did alright. No, she would not see me as more than a brother, especially when her own brother had abandoned her so thoughtlessly.

"We will land pretty soon," I said, "I think we will catch up with him this time. He's only two days ahead of us this time! I am positive we will find him at the Bay of Fires."

"I know," Lydia said through a yawn, "I don't know how I am supposed to feel about it, though."

I nodded slowly. It had been such an arduous, pain-staking journey for us both, and I was definitely dreading facing my credit card debt after all this madness. Benji had led us on a wild, Carmen San Diego goose chase all over the world, and we weren't thrilled about it.

"What are you hoping for... when we find him?" I asked.

"That's what I don't know," she said. Her smile faded. "He has no idea we are looking for him. What if he... what if he isn't glad to see us—to see *me*?"

I sighed. "Benji is always glad to see us, Lydia," I said, "I am sure that once he explains to us why he abandoned his studies at Oxford, we will understand what all this is about. Something really big must have happened. There *has* to be a reason for all this!" Through the tone in my own voice, I was beginning to realize that it wasn't only Lydia who was feeling insecure about her relationship with her brother Benji. I, too, had felt abandoned by my best friend.

Why had he suddenly dropped out of his doctorate program and dashed away into the Alps? Lydia and I had hoped to surprise him by flying to the UK to see him, but instead he surprised us. Two years he had been at Oxford, without a single trip back to Seattle to visit us. We had hoped to find out why. Well, no *wonder* he wasn't getting our letters—he was gone!

One lead led us to another. I could write an entire book of all the places we went, people we met, disappointments we felt as we searched for Benji. We followed leads through the Alps, which led us to Hungary, which led us to Ukraine, which led us into Siberia, where we found he had gone to India. As we went thousands and thousands of dollars into debt, we followed his trail from India to Singapore, Singapore to Australia, and now to Tasmania. But why? Where on Earth was he going?

"Americans, eh?" asked a deep voice. I turned my head 180 degrees to see a middle-aged gentleman, sitting beside me with a book open in his lap.

"Yes," I said with a courteous smile.

"Vacation?" he asked.

"No, *um*—" I had so many conversations like this one, why could I *still* not think of how to explain what we were doing in one short sentence? "We are meeting a friend." That was good enough.

"Americans," he snorted, "Skipping across the world like you own the place."

I chuckled nervously; I had heard that one a lot, too. "Well, it's pretty great being able to see other places, and experience other cultures." I would do anything to stay out of an argument, so I tried to take his comment as graciously as I could.

"What makes you all think you are the ones who should be in charge?" he asked, pointing a finger at my face.

"I..." I drew out the pronoun, searching for the most ingratiating response. "I really don't see myself as *in charge*, sir. I am merely a guest."

"Quite right," he said, lowering his finger.

"Do you get a lot of—um—*Americans* visiting around here?" I asked, trying to keep the conversation light.

The man grunted. "I've met plenty of kids like yourselves traveling and tasting and searching, kids talking about *finding* themselves and all that. *Losing* themselves, more like!"

"Heh, heh," I maintained a smile. I wasn't traveling for pleasure! *Hell*, I would have preferred to be home right about then! "Yeah, it has been kind of a trend for my generation to travel and all that—see the world. But that's not what I..." I paused. Surely that's not what *Benji* was doing, was it? Just traveling for his own amusement? No... no, this had to be bigger than that.

"Trends die for a reason," said the man as he closed his book. I frowned inwardly. Every time someone beside me actually went so far as to close their book, I knew the conversation would carry on indefinitely. "Pretty soon, your generation will get so lost, there won't be any of you left."

"I... that's..." How was I supposed to respond to that? What a pessimistic perspective! "I mean, I am sure that's not true of everyone who travels the world. I think there is a lot of good that can come from seeing other places, and seeing how others live. It makes one not think the world revolves around themselves, like many of us 'Americans', no doubt, do," I said, "But I am sure you are seeing something as well. Are you implying that the trend to travel and wander is an overall *bad* thing for a young person?"

"It's an illusion," he said, "You leave your homes thinking you will find yourself, when really you have left yourself behind."

"Tell me what you mean," I said. I pulled out my little quote book and pencil. One thing I *did* think was pretty awesome about all the world travel was acquiring unique perspectives and wisdom from the various characters I met.

"Who are you?" he asked. "What makes you *you*?"

I sensed the philosophical challenge and took it. "Well," I said, bobbing my head with a nod, "My name is Leo. I am an ambulance driver, and... part-time seminary student?"

The man winced, then chuckled. "Well met, Leo. I am Virgil. Now, Leo: by your own description of yourself, have you become less of yourself since you left home?"

"I...." I stammered.

"Well, are you driving ambulances right now? Saving lives?" he asked provocatively.

"Well, not at the moment."

"So, even by your own estimation, you have become less of yourself," he said with a smug smile.

"But Leo is more than an ambulance driver," said Lydia, popping her head into the man's view. "He is a kind man. He is a listener. He is someone who draws people out. He has not become less of that since he left home."

I blinked in astonishment, then beamed. "Well, what *she* said!"

"It is true what you say," said Virgil, "A man's character comes with him. But like it or not, his identity is changing. Much of who we are is who we are to others. Are you a husband? A father?" he asked.

I chuckled nervously, "Well... not yet!"

"Are you a son? A brother?"

I glanced at Lydia, then back at Virgil. I was an only child, but at the moment, I *was* a brother. "I am both," I said.

"But how are you being a son when you are not with your family? How are you being a brother without your sister? How are you an Ambulance driver without an ambulance?" He leaned back into his chair. "It is alright to travel for a time, but to completely disentangle yourself from your community *is* to lose yourself. To find yourself again will take a rebirth into a new community; and usually those of you who choose to do this, only grow tired of their new community, and therefore seek another rebirth. It is an illusion to think one can reinvent themselves completely, because as *you* have so perceptively pointed out," he gestured toward Lydia, "a person's character always travels with them."

The conversation would become more relevant later, though in the moment it didn't seem too pertinent. When we did find Benji, only a few hours later, those words echoed through my ears: *A person's character always travels with them.*

The moment we found Benji was not unlike the moment Henry Morton Stanley found David Livingston in the depths of Africa: surreal. It had been like chasing the ghost of our long-lost brother, and there he was: sitting right at the tip of an outcropping of rock, overlooking the Bay of Fires. He was bent over it crookedly, poking at a rock below himself with a stick. I noted evidence of a bushy beard jetting out from either side of his head and for a moment, I wondered if I had been pointed in the right direction. No, the man at the hostel had been explicit: Benjamin Lee had gone out to see the Bay of Fires. This was the only guy around; this *had* to be him!

I stepped forward, motioning for Lydia to stay where she was.

"I'll make sure it's him," I said, "Then call you over."

"Thanks," she said in a nervous voice. More than once Lydia and I *thought* we had found Benji, and I didn't want her to go through that kind of disappointment again. I wandered over to the outcropping, feeling the crunch of gravel beneath my now-destroyed Jordans. The man turned slightly, just enough to see me coming, then returned his gaze to the horizon line.

I walked until I was directly behind him and asked, "May I join you here, friend?"

"Welcome, stranger," came his voice. It was both familiar and unrecognizable, like finding an old childhood photograph you forgot existed. I could see a little brown book in his hands. "Sit with me."

He turned his head slowly to find my face. A mighty beard did its best to distract me, but his eyes betrayed the guise; it was Benji. Recognition illuminated his face, and the sides of his mouth turned upwards into a playful smile.

"Leo," he said, grinning.

"Hey, you old hobo," I said, returning the grin. I sat down beside him, rubbing my shoulder against his. This was our way: to pretend like there was no time or space between the last time we were together.

"Look at that," Benji said, pointing out toward the horizon line. The sun was beginning to set, hovering over the top of the waters, casting an orange reflection.

"Bay of Fires," I said, observing how the colors made it look like the sea was ignited.

"Yeah," Benji said as he stared out at it, nodding. Then he turned to me, punched my shoulder, and crunched me in a quick, manly hug. I gave him a few hard slaps on the back in return. It was hard to be annoyed at him in a moment like this. I finally found him! I turned my head to find Lydia and nodded her over. I saw her begin to run toward us.

"Lydia is here too," I said quickly, pulling back.

"Ah," Benji turned to see her approaching, then looked back at me with a cringe. "I suppose you both have been wondering where I... went."

"Sort of, yeah," I said with a smile.

Benji stood dutifully, and caught Lydia in his arms as she came running, erupting with tears. He gave me an amused look out of the corner of his eye while he patted her back, saying, "It's alright, hell—Lydia. I'm fine. Alright? It's good to see you."

I shook my head at him, arms crossed.

"Alright," Benji said, pushing Lydia back gently. "This is definitely a surprise. What are you two *doing* all the way out here?"

Lydia and I looked at each other.

"Well," I said, "We actually went to Oxford to surprise you for Christmas."

"Oh!" Benji bit his lip, "Damn."

"Yeah," Lydia wiped her eyes, "Benji, why didn't you tell us you left?"

Benji shrugged. "Hell, I didn't think I needed to."

"Because..." I cleared my throat twice, "Because you thought we didn't care where you were?"

"Oh, Leo," Benji swung a playful fist at me, "You *know* that's not why. I just... I've been independent for quite some time now. I'm not used to *writing home*, and all that. I was eventually going to tell you guys everything, but I've been working on something really important."

"Oh!" Lydia made a big sigh of relief, placing her hand on her chest. "Oh, that's what we hoped—*erm*—figured! Does this have to do with your doctorate?"

Benji shook his head. "No. No, I did leave that behind. I've been following a much more important lead. I think... I think I might have found what I have been searching for all my life."

I raised my eyebrows. I knew what he meant; it was a loaded statement. Since we were lads, Benji always told me he knew there was something big he was supposed to do with his life, though he could never figure out what it was. He was so gifted; everything he touched seemed to turn to gold. It was no surprise when he ended up studying philosophy—when he could have chosen to do *anything*—his search always came back to questions: *deep* questions. And what do you study when all you have are questions? Philosophy.

"You... you think you found the answer to your question?" I asked, "Way out here, on the other side of the world?"

Benji gave me his classic, knowing smile. It had been *years* since I had seen him, and yet some things were still the exact same.

"You two came out this far to find me," he said, "you are true friends. Thank you."

Lydia brightened, then threw herself into his arms again, holding him tightly. Benji laughed, ruffling her hair with his hand.

"We really were worried about you, Benj. We lost you, and we couldn't find you. No phone, no note... what happened?" I asked.

Benji patted Lydia on the back, then shoved his hands into his pockets. "Hell, guys—I don't think it's something I can explain in one sentence."

"Well," I said, "Let's sit down and watch the sun set, and see how far we get."

"Sounds good to me," Benji said, giving me that same boyish grin.

"Wait a minute, you guys." Lydia exclaimed, "How can you act so blasé about all this? Benji! We have been chasing you for weeks! We've racked up enormous debt; nearly got robbed several times and—"

Benji patted her back again.

"Sis," he said, "Sit. All will come out."

She let out a deep, frustrated breath, then nodded. The three of us sat there together, side by side, with our feet dangling off of the rock ledge. Benji sat sandwiched between us and leaned back on his hands.

"It didn't take long at Oxford before I realized it wasn't the place for me," he said. I felt my heart sink into my chest. That I had heard before... many, *many* times. He may have been gifted, but he struggled with perseverance—with *finishing* things. "The things my mentor had me reading and studying," he shook his head, "It was like... like I knew more than he did why it was all wrong. And I tried, Leo, I really tried to push through with it. I actually stayed the course, remembering what you told me: *Keep going, Benji. How you feel doesn't matter, just do it. Once you have your PhD, you can make your own rules.*"

I chuckled. Well, at least he remembered *some* of the things I said! And... well... I couldn't exactly fault him when I myself had dropped out of my masters program to get a stable job.

"So, what happened?" asked Lydia, who was leaning her head on his shoulder.

"I met someone. He—He gave me this book," Benji passed me the small brown book. I took it and turned it in my hands. "Rasselas" was written on the spine. I cracked it open carefully, noting it was an old copy. The copyright dated back to 1759; it was a first edition. The pages had browned, and it smelled old and dusty. It honestly was just my kind of smell.

"Pretty," I said.

"Did you know Samuel Johnson wrote fiction?" Benji asked, turning to look me in the eyes.

"No," I said, "Didn't he write dictionaries?"

"He was so much more than a dictionary-writer," Benji said with a chuckle, "But yes. This was his only work of fiction, written to pay for his mother's funeral."

"Who gave it to you?" asked Lydia; I could tell she was eager to move the story forward. Benji and I could sit there talking about books all day and all night—this she knew well.

"A man I met on one of my walks through the countryside," Benji said, "It was... I can't explain it, guys. It was special. He gave me this book, and he told me that if it stirred something up in me, I should meet him in Zurich."

"Zurich?" I laughed. I knew Benji too well to think he would ever turn something as random and intriguing as an impromptu trip to Zurich down.

"Did the book... do what he said?" asked Lydia patiently.

"Yeah," Benji said, stretching his arms into the air. "Yeah, it did. It's about privilege. A man, like me, with all the earthly gifts in the world. He was discontent in his paradise, so he left it, searching. I knew in my heart that Rasselas was *me*. This man I met, he told me that there was something more than the world that I knew. So I went. I went to Switzerland."

"Was he there?" Lydia asked.

"Sort of," Benji said with a sigh. "What I found was a trail of breadcrumbs. It was like... like a test of sorts: a puzzle."

"Yeah," I said, "The leads we chased trying to find you felt very... random."

Benji chuckled. "I can't *believe* you guys chased me this far. That's... that's insane!"

Lydia and I exchanged glances; we were annoyed, yes, but we also felt proud. That journey had not been easy for either of us.

"Anyway," Benji said, pointing at the book in my hands. "I've been slowly reading that book while following him. And... here on this ledge, I was about to read the end."

"You mean," I turned the book sideways; this book was so small! "You mean, you haven't finished it yet? You don't know how it ends? I could read this in an hour!"

Benji laughed, "I know, I know. But it's all part of the journey, you see. I was supposed to read the marked spot *here*, it was the final stage of my test before I met him again."

"The man who gave you the book, you're supposed to meet him... *here*?" Lydia asked, sounding doubtful.

"Yeah..." Benji said in a whisper as he raised his eyes to the horizon, "Just as the sun set."

He turned his head slowly and looked at me, searching.

"Leo..." he said slowly, "oh my God..."

"What?" I asked, blinking.

"Leo, I was supposed to meet *you* here all along, wasn't I?"

I chuckled nervously, "Uh... no, Benji. I don't think so."

Benji nodded slowly, investigating my face, as if checking for a lie. "Alright," he said carefully, then his mouth cracked into a smile again. "Alright, then. Then, I am glad you two are here with me: here at the end of my journey."

"Well, the sun is setting, Benji," Lydia said in a short tone, "Where is the man?"

Lydia and I looked around; there was not a person in sight—not in any direction. Benji kept his eyes on the horizon.

"He will be here," he said, "I *know* he will."

I looked down at my hands where the book lay and opened it to the last page. "Have you read this yet?" I asked.

Benji looked at me. "No," he said, "I was about to... and then you two showed up. Why don't you do the honors, Leo? Turn to the marked page, that's what I'm supposed to start as the sun sets."

"Well," I cleared my throat, then stood. Benji and Lydia, scooted back, giving me space as I posed there, right on the tip of the rock, and raised my free hand in the air, as I imagined old Shakespearean actors would when they read their lines. Benji raised his eyes to me, looking—for the first time in his life—content.

"Flatter not yourself," I said in my jazzed-up reading voice, "with contrarieties of pleasure. Of the blessings set before you make your choice, and be content. No man can taste the fruits of autumn while he is delighting his scent with the flowers of spring:" I cleared my throat as a strange sensation fluttered across my skin, then continued, "no man can, at the same time, fill his cup from the source and from the mouth of the... Nile." I tried to swallow. My throat suddenly felt quite dry. I coughed.

Benji lurched forward suddenly, pointing at me, "Leo!" he gasped.

I opened my mouth to speak, but I could not. My body felt frozen, electrified with a bluish glow. All I could move were my eyes. They darted around, searching.

"Leo, no!" Benji cried, rising to his feet. I saw him dive toward me, but before our bodies touched, he was gone. No... no *I* was gone!

<hr>

I remember blackness, and then swirling color mixed with feelings and sensations. I felt happy. I felt unexplainably and unwaveringly at peace.

My existence felt both instant and eternal as I floated, weightless, through a colorful tunnel of stars. Where was I?

I felt myself moving up. Yes... up—higher and higher, passing the emptiness of space and continuing on as if into the divine realms.

I don't know how to describe what I felt as my body passed between the barriers of the cosmos. It was as if my life was no longer spread across years of time, but was all-existing in one single moment. I was both young and old; mature and innocent; dead and alive; all at the same time. All of me existed at once in that journey; I felt both love for people I didn't yet know, and sadness for things I hadn't yet experienced. My spirit was awake in full.

How can I describe that fully for you? I can't. But something happened to me on that trip,

Something important.

Then, like paint splashed against a canvas, the world took form around me again. My body found itself in a dark, domed room. When I eventually opened my eyes, I was on my back, staring at a circular stained-glass window, designed to look like some sort of sun. As I moved my fingers, I sensed dust gathering between them.

I blinked my hazy eyes open and closed, endeavoring to focus. As my vision cleared, I could see the figure of a person standing before me. Someone very tall was looking down at me with their hands placed determinedly on their hips. The person was silhouetted against a blue backdrop. From where I lay, it looked like a glowing ocean hanging vertically behind them.

"What..." I spoke in a raspy, drunken voice.

"*Of the blessings set before you make your choice,*" said a rich and steady male voice, "*and be content.* This is my final lesson. Yes, I give you a choice—to come with me, to see what no other human in your generation has ever seen. To look, like the man in the Flammarion Engraving, past the fabric of your world, and stare into the naked Cosmos. But what have you learned as you have traveled the world, boy? What have you *seen*?"

I endeavored to sit up. My body was sore. Had I fallen? The ground beneath me was cold, and I grimaced at the sensation of slightly damp trousers against my legs. The words spoken to me took a minute to reach my ears.

"Say, *what*?" I asked, gazing up at the figure. Lights and shapes began to crystalize before me as my surroundings grew more and more lucid, as if I were waking from a dream.

"You, like Rasselas, have seen many lives, many people," he said in an eloquent tone, "You must let the desire for *more* die to be content. Only then can you see more; only then can you—" the voice halted. "I say—are you *listening* to a word I am saying?"

I crawled onto my feet and rose, then stretched my back. I still couldn't tell if I was dreaming or awake, but I tried very hard to concentrate on the speaker.

"What have I seen?" I asked. "You mean... all the travel?"

"Through the Alps; the Himalayas, the seas, and more," said the man as he raised his hand dramatically into the air, shaming my poor performance as I read from the book earlier. My eyes focused on his face.

He had an ageless countenance: not young, and not old, though his silver hair seemed to suggest he was in his mature years. He was clean-shaven, with shoulder length wavy locks, and a prominent, furrowed brow. His most surprising feature, however, was his set of long, pointy ears, cleft in two. I stared at them with my mouth half open, trying to remember what on Earth brought me to this moment.

"You have done everything I asked of you;" he said, "you have trusted me, and proved to me your perseverance. And now? Now, I will finally give you what I have promised. I give you the opportunity of a lifetime: to be my apprentice. Yes, Benjamin, I chose *you*."

I rubbed my eyes, cranking my wrists back and forth like a sleepy toddler, then crossed my arms.

"Damn," I said, "I think you've got the wrong guy."

The man's already crinkled brow hardened further. "I say," he said slowly, then exclaimed, "I *say*!"

"Hi," I waved slowly with my hand, "I'm Leo."

"Oh, damn," the man dropped his arms to his sides. "Damn—*who* are you?"

"Uh... *heh heh*..." I chuckled nervously, "I think maybe I should ask: who are *you*? Oh yeah, and *where* am I?" The foggy memory of the blue lights and strange disappearance swelled within my mind. I knew something mystical had happened—I just wasn't sure *what*!

"Oh *Hades*," The man cursed, shoving his hand into his pocket and retrieving some sort of fancy-looking pocket watch, "Damn, damn, damn..." It was like watching a mad scientist try to figure out where he went wrong after some embarrassing explosion. "I don't want to have to explain this all to some..." he glanced up at me, "accident."

"You thought I was Benji, didn't you? You're the man who..."

"I don't have time for this," he muttered as he fiddled with his watch, completely ignoring my questions. It was like I wasn't even there!

"Hey," I stepped closer to him, "Hey, can you please answer me? Can you please tell me what on Earth is going on?" Maybe it was just another fault with my personality that is constantly avoiding conflict, but I tried to confront the stranger as courteously as possible. And in all honesty, even though it was I who had been dragged suddenly from my previous existence, I felt guilty. It was clear to me now: Benji should have been the one standing there in that mysterious, windowless chamber. "Please?" I asked quietly, "Can you tell me what's going—?"

The man started. "*What*? Oh." He bit his lip as he eyed me, up and down, condescendingly. "Look, I'll send you back and you can forget any of this ever happened. Alright? You're not... *Hades*," he cursed, "You're not prepared to actually *know* anything, son. It's better if I just send you back and let you think this was all a dream, alright? You're dreaming—*understand*?"

"*Son*?"

"Anyway, it's Benjamin I am after. Benjamin—have you heard of him? Damn, I still don't know where I went wrong." He stroked his chin with his thumb thoughtfully, then blew air out of his lips.

"Yeah, I have heard of him," I frowned, "I'm his best friend."

"Oh," He cringed, "*Leo*, you said?"

"Y—*Yes*? Dude, can you tell me what's going on?" I asked. "I *know* I am not dreaming!"

"Yes, you are!" He snapped, taking a step away from me. "Now, keep your distance. You'll be home in a minute."

The man wasn't giving me answers, so I kept my mouth closed and turned to take in my surroundings. The chamber, constructed entirely of rustic grey stone and mosaic floors, was about as large as an old English church sanctuary, though round, with a perfect dome at the top. There was a circular table at the center of the room, with a map painted upon its surface, and—I whirled around—there was not a door in sight. That is, the only thing remotely akin to a door was that big wall of vertical blue water, swirling within an iron black frame. It was at least ten feet high, and eight feet wide.

I definitely *wasn't* in Tasmania anymore. I scratched my head with a vocal yawn. I had this messy, untamed matt of auburn curls that lived like a sort of animal companion on my head; it shed a few flakes as I lowered my hand and shoved it in my pocket. What time was it? I was pretty used to not knowing what time it was by this point, and even more used to seeing new places. But this? This was a whole new kind of different. Even the air didn't smell right. Where *was* I?

"There!" Exclaimed the mysterious stranger. "There, I think I found him."

I looked over at him expectantly, shoving my hands into my pockets. "I am guessing you're not going to explain it to me?" I said dryly.

"Look," he said, pointing to the blue waters. I gasped. Inside the waters was a vision of Lydia and Benji, arguing with one another, back in Tasmania.

He made an irritated groan. "I am going to send you back home, then bring Benji here—happy?"

Oh... he *had* actually explained it to me! But where *was* here? "Uh... yeah!" I said, "Where exactly—*erm*—Where are we?"

He groaned again. "You would never understand. Leave that sort of thing to Benjamin, alright? Just..." he stalled, "just remember you're dreaming, alright? *Dreaming.*"

"Yeah, yeah," I said unenthusiastically, "I got it. So... can I at least ask your name?"

The man gazed up at the heavens, as if begging for mercy, then looked at me with tired eyes and said, "Momentum."

"Momentum..." I said slowly, "...is your name?"

The man snapped his head to the side, like a dog spotting a mailman by the door.

"What was that?" he asked himself—I mean—he definitely wasn't asking *me.*

"What?" I looked at the random wall he seemed to be studying. I could feel a slight tremor beneath my shoes. The little bits of dust and gravel, which at first had lain quietly upon the ground, began to rise like steam.

Momentum's eyes grew fearful, searching the room. "No..." he mumbled, "No, he can't."

The tremors grew. And turning to look at the wall opposite the big blue water door, I saw one of the stones shifting. I walked toward it curiously, reaching out my hand to touch it.

"Don't!" Momentum gasped. "Lad—get back!"

I felt the man yank against the back of my jacket. I flew backwards into his body. Then, before I could even stumble onto the ground, the wall, quite literally, exploded.

All I could hear was a ringing sound... and then some muffled voices as I lay on the marble, covered in debris. I pushed myself up to my feet and coughed violently, groping for a wall to lean on, then fell back down.

Words were being spoken in the room , muffled, booming, indistinguishable sounds—and yet—I could understand every word perfectly in my mind.

"So, here you are," said the voice. My body began to shake uncontrollably, as if *it* were more scared than my mind was. Who was talking? I blinked frantically, searching the dust for a source. A black shape seemed to emerge from the now-apparent hole in the wall. "I finally found you."

"Stay back," I heard Momentum say. There was a shuffling motion beside me where he was clamoring to his feet.

"Don't you dare make demands of me!" the booming voice said. I couldn't move; terror took me, though I couldn't think of a reason why. "You have hidden from me long enough. Turn over the Gate! It belongs to the throne!"

I felt Momentum pull me up by the shoulder. He dragged me backwards.

"It does not," Momentum shouted as he pulled me backwards. Then he lowered his voice. "Don't look at him," I heard him whisper into my ear, "Close your eyes."

"Why?" I wanted to ask, but my mouth didn't work. I did as he said, I closed my eyes.

"Stay away from that door!" The voice screamed, and the whole room began to grow dark. "Hand over your Imperium, I order you!"

Momentum made a great roar, as if in pain, then grabbed my torso with both arms from behind, holding me in a tight body lock. Then I felt him jump backwards. And together, we fell.

This was my second time in what was called the "Flammarion Tunnel": the gateway through the Cosmos. Down was the direction I felt this time—then sideways. Momentum's vice-like arms held their bond around me, and—regrettably—I opened my eyes. I saw two glowing eyes looking back at me, floating in a mist of indistinguishable shapes and colors. Then a hand reached out to me. I screamed. Whoever had found us was entering the tunnel.

One of Momentum's hands let go of me, and I saw it fumble with the golden watch. He held it in his hand, then crunched it with a single grip. Just as he did, a burst of red fire erupted from where the glowing eyes floated. I heard a deathly scream.

Then, a world of brightness and green colors swirled around me, taking form. I felt a thud. Momentum gasped as I landed directly on top of him, on the ground. I could see a blue window above me, tightening closed. Within it, fire seemed to burst, and debris began to rain down on us from it. Just before much else could escape, it shut itself. Then, all was silent.

I stared up at the sky above me. Blurry green branches hung overhead, covering the glow of a gentle, cloud-covered sky. Momentum pushed me off of himself, and I found my face hitting a hard—though grassy—patch of earth. Then I gasped. There, laying right beside my face, was a hand.

I scrambled backwards, making an embarrassing sort of squawk as I pointed at the thing. It was gloved, bloodless, and motionless. But still, it was a severed hand! I turned to look at Momentum who lay there, with his foggy eyes staring upwards where the portal had just closed.

"There's a hand of... of..." I stammered. My hands were shaking; my whole body was shaking. "Who... who..."

"It's... gone," he whispered mysteriously.

My eyes darted back to the hand. "Uh... Momentum, was it? What the *hell*?" I said in a quivering voice.

"It's gone, lad," he said quietly, "It's over."

I looked around, seeing the familiar sight of trees and grass. "You brought us back to Earth?" I asked quickly, "Where's Benji? Where's Lydia?"

"Gone," he said, "It is gone."

"Are we back in Tasmania?" I asked, growing fearful. Was I stranded once again? How long would it take to find Benji *this* time?

"Tasmania? *Earth*?" He turned his head lazily to look at me, though his body remained lifeless. "No," he said, "No, not Earth." he mumbled, "We're still on Raqia."

I flattened my mouth into a line. "Dude," I said, "What the hell is going on?"

"What the hell?" Momentum blinked, then made a defeated chuckling noise. "*What the hell*, indeed."

"Dude!" I yelled, thumping the ground with my fist. "*Talk* to me!"

"Why tell you?" He asked in a distant voice, "You will be so much sadder when you hear."

I bit my lip until it nearly bled. It was the hardest moment in the world to be a calm, respectful guy.

"Tell me," I said.

"The Gate is destroyed," he replied, "That's it: gone. It was the only way I could travel to the lowlands—where you come from. You're stuck here... forever."

—— Clover ——

An Impossible Task

NOTHING YOU DO REALLY MATTERS—or that's what Clover thought, anyway. Did it matter if he didn't tip the barman? Sure, it could make a momentary impact; but even if got him thrown in the stocks—did it really matter? He wouldn't mind if it did matter; he liked the idea of things mattering. What would it feel like to care about such things? That's what he was here to find out: if he could care. And where was "here"? "Here" was nowhere.

"Are you going to drink something or not?"

Clover glanced upwards at the dusty barman who stood there with the look of a man who was restraining himself from scratching a terrible itch.

"Do you serve anything... unique?" asked Clover.

"Unique?" The barman snorted. "I serve ale and mead. Oh—and well water."

Clover glanced down at his lap where his coin pouch sat. Would he spend his last coin on a drink? That did sound like a foolish thing to do—what would become of him? Would he be forced to live in poverty? Would he be thrown in the stocks for sleeping on the streets of this remote village? Yes... that might cause him to care about something; it might make him *feel* something.

"Floods above!" The barman exclaimed. Clover glanced back up at the bearded man to see him gaping wide-eyed down at his pointy ears. "You're an Elf?"

Clover blinked. "And?"

"By the floods, boy," The barman looked side to side excitedly, searching for a witness. When he saw that no one else of note was sitting nearby, he turned back to Clover, "What are you doing way out here?"

"Absolutely nothing," said Clover. He wasn't being impertinent; he was entirely honest in his response. Therefore, it confused him when the barman drew back with a frown.

"Something's going on, isn't it? I've never even *heard* of an Elf journeying west of the Elder Copse. What are you doing this far into the Woodlands?"

"I told you," Clover said with half-open eyes, "Nothing."

The barman pulled his lips into his mouth and stared at the Elf with a calculating glare. "Fine then," he said, "keep your business to yourself. But I know something strange is going on around here. I have seen more than one stranger in my tavern in the last week, and no one travels this far out into the Woodlands for no reason!"

"Not *no one*," Clover retorted.

The barman raised an eyebrow. "What?"

"Not no one," Clover said again, "You see, that is *exactly* the reason why I traveled out here."

"What is?"

"No reason."

The barman rolled his eyes and turned away, grunting to himself.

"Wait," Clover lurched forward, holding out his last gold chip, "A mead please, barman?"

The barman turned back, then couldn't help but chuckle.

"They call me Sam," he said, "and it costs you only a silver chip."

"This is all I have," Clover said with a blank face.

Sam held out his hand and took the chip. "I'll get you change."

"No!" Clover said quickly, "No—no change."

Sam furrowed his brow. "Didn't you say this is all you have, boy? That's quite a hefty tip, and it won't get you much around here."

"Yes," said Clover, "It's all I have."

Sam studied Clover for a moment longer, then amusedly sauntered back to his barkeep, chuckling to himself.

Well, he was destitute now. Now, he would have to live off the fruit of the land; now, the cold, hard ground would be his only bed; now, he would be sure to feel different. He didn't feel any different being coinless *yet*, but he was sure something would change soon. He turned to the side and peered out the little lead-paned window; it granted a quaint view of the one street this town had. It was the *only* town marked on his map of the Raqian Woodlands, and it couldn't have housed more than a hundred citizens.

He had hoped to find strange and mysterious things here, but instead, the only passers-by he witnessed on those streets were simple country folk. They hadn't been averse to seeing strangers like himself, but he could tell that it was pretty uncommon for someone to venture by. Sam the barman had mentioned other strangers passing through this little town of Nemus; perhaps Clover would find out who they were... or perhaps not. What did it matter, anyway?

Sam returned with a glass of mead, slamming it down on the table gracelessly.

"A mead for a gold chip," he said in a teasing voice, "For an Elf—hah!"

Clover examined the glass, which looked flawed, as if when hand blown, the maker crafted without attempting to match its brothers. The mead had a rich, gold color. Clover brought the glass to his nose, sniffed, then turned to smile at Sam.

"Thank you," he said, "This is exactly the sort of thing I am looking for."

"Oh, is it?" Sam placed his hands on his hips and shook his head. "Who knew that all it would take was a glass of expensive mead to make the blank boy smile!"

"Indeed," Clover said, then he sipped the rim of the glass, taking only a taste into his mouth. He brightened. "Thank you, Sam. This is very nice."

Sam continued to shake his head, chuckling. "I am glad it pleases you, Elf. Floods—what a strange day."

"I say," Clover cleared his throat as he set his glass down upon the table, "You don't suppose you could point me to the next town? I'm traveling westward... or southward... or anywhere but eastward."

Sam blinked. "Son," he said, "I've not heard of any towns west of here; it's nothing but strange, unmappable wilderness. And anyone who has ever left in that direction has never come back."

Clover straightened his back. "Really?" he asked, "So you're *really* the only town out here?"

"Floods if I know!" Sam said. "The only life I've known has been in this part of the wood, and I've never had reason to wander or wonder."

"You and I are similar," Clover said with a distant look in his eyes, "I never had reason to wander from the only home I ever knew... until... well... until now!"

"No wonder you look so lost," Sam said with a look of compassion, as if he were consoling a child who couldn't figure out how to whistle. "Son, you should go back home—to wherever you came from."

"But why?" Clover asked, "Why—in fact—should I do anything at all?"

Sam sniffed. "You're not going to get philosophical on me, are you? I have no time for that sort of—"

"No," Clover said as he sagged into his chair, "If I wanted to have a philosophical conversation I could have just stayed in the Elder Copse," he turned his focus to the barman, who was growing more impatient to escape the conversation by the minute, "I was actually hoping to *experience* things, rather than talk about them."

"Mmm," Sam nodded, "Well, son, good luck with that."

Clover watched the barman plod away, back to his place behind the counter. He posed there, polishing already-clean glasses, as if all he needed to be happy was to take his place in his world. There he was: the barman of Nemus. How content he was to just *be*.

Clover could have been content to just *be*, he supposed, back in the Elder Copse. But he had gotten some sort of itch—an itch that couldn't be scratched there in the home of the Woodland Elves. It was an itch for meaning. Or perhaps—an itch to feel something. Other people seemed to feel things just fine, but there Clover always sat, observing others and their various emotive interactions. Other people had ambitions; other people had sadness; other people had purpose.

What was the purpose of a son who had been raised to one day take his father's place—knowing that his father would never die? He was as useless as a chair with no legs; a pitcher with no spout; an aurochs with no horns—a king with no throne.

Clover sat, drinking his mead slowly for an indeterminable amount of time. There was no bell tower in the little town of Nemus, and no sign of a skydeacon to keep track of the time. So instead of counting clicks or listening for hour changes, the people here just lived intuitively, letting the day change at its own pace. In a world with no sun and moon; no spinning stars; no constants and no clocks, a day could be as long or as short as it wanted. Did it matter if time passed as Clover drank his mead? Did it matter how long it took? Out there it sure didn't.

By the time he had finished, the daylight outside began to change from a warm yellow to a natural green, lighting up the various leaves and foliage with a soft glow. The outdoors called to him, he thought. So he rose, taking his spear in hand, and walked out.

It took only a few steps to leave the little town; and soon it was far behind him. Soon, he was as lost as a shipwreck, surrounded by a silent audience of tall, looming pine trees. The bottom halves of their trunks, reaching fifty feet into the sky, were bare. But way up at their tops, they were so thick with branches, that they created their own sort of night sky. Little openings between their pine-clustered twigs showed glimpses of the daylight sky, giving off the illusion of stars. A mist hung in the air, just over Clover's head, like a gentle covering of warmth and color.

As he walked, Clover used his great spear, which was one and a half times as tall as he was, as a walking stick. From tip to base, the ornamental weapon was adorned in pure gold, frosted with green filigree. A gift from his grandfather, this spear was the only possession Clover chose to take with him, aside from his little coin purse. He didn't exactly plan on fighting anyone, but it happened to be the only thing in his hands in the moment that he decided to leave his home. And so, it came with him.

Clover stopped. There was a curious scurrying sound approaching him through the foliage behind him. He turned, watching as a little creature emerged from the bushes. Clover frowned; this sort of creature was not unfamiliar to him. It was no taller than his knee, with a head too big for his body, long pointy ears protruding out from either side of his head, and a dusty, though carefully sewn, outfit. The thing looked like a doll, with its tiny boots and long, billowy scarf. Upon his head was a floppy red cap. He had a flat, catlike face, with large blue eyes, and a wide smile. A single pointy tooth refused to stay inside his mouth, and therefore popped out the side of his mouth like a toothpick.

He was holding something. That something was very familiar. Clover knelt down before the creature, setting his spear upon the ground.

"Give it here," Clover said as he held out his hand, palm up.

The thing scurried closer like a squirrel sniffing for nuts.

"Come on," said the Elf, "Put it here."

The little creature blinked its round eyes up at Clover, and his pupils contracted into slits. Its little mittened hands held out a single gold chip. The coin's shape was cut eloquently, with a symbol of a fern on its face.

"Put it here," Clover said again. The little creature placed it upon his hands. Yes, it was the coin Clover had given to the barman. Clover snatched the thing into his hand quickly and pocketed it, startling the little being. "Did you steal this?" Clover asked, rising.

The thing drew back, hiding behind a fallen leaf.

"Thieving scumbag!" Clover snapped, kicking his boot in the thing's direction. Garden gnomes like these lived around the outskirts of the Elder Copse, and no doubt many of them made homes in these dense, chaotic Woodlands. Anytime some little trinket or small item of clothing went missing, these tiresome pests were almost always to blame. Who could know why they stole what they stole—it was always at random, and very often the items would reappear in unexpected places. It was almost as if the creatures thought they were being helpful. That was almost never the case.

The most infuriating thing about the little wordless garden gnomes was how charming many seemed to think they were. They had the most imitative and innocent ways of trying to make friends with the Elves, giving off the appearance of intelligence and even personality. But all this ever meant was that they were never rightfully penalized or eradicated from the Copse, and Clover was constantly forced to chase them out of his perfectly organized spaces. The pests—they always found the tiniest and most insignificant ways to ruin one's day.

"Now that man is going to think I stole this back!" Clover said spitefully, "Why did you—?" He groaned to himself and turned away, ignoring the little thief. It scurried away into the bushes, and Clover gladly left him behind.

It was a good while later when Clover found a sort of beaten down path. He followed it, thinking it could have been made by some mysterious beast. A moose? A bear? He clutched his spear tighter, feeling a growing excitement within himself.

He heard voices ahead and paused to listen. There was one very loud man, and a second, submissive sort of man arguing over directions. Clover stepped closer, popping his head around a tree to look at them. One of the men was alarmingly taller than the other, curling down to meet the smaller man's eye level. It was like watching a father trying to fit himself into his children's playhouse.

"He has to be somewhere around here," said the giant, "He came to the Valley in search of assistance, that is what the scout said."

"No one in the town could tell me where to find the Valley. No one knows how to get there," said the second man timidly.

"Keep searching," barked the giant, "I'll wait for you in the tavern. Give me the bags."

The smaller—though still bulkier and gruffer than Clover—man pulled aside his travel sack. And opening it, he pulled out two leather pouches. At first Clover thought they might be water skins, but their lack of weight seemed to indicate they were empty. The giant took the pouches quickly and tied them against his belt. Then, the two parted ways.

Clover wondered momentarily who those two men might have been, or what could have been in those little pouches, but then the wonderment passed, and he no longer felt interested. This is how it always went for Clover, nothing ever seemed to interest him for long.

He wandered on. He had no real inclination of where he wanted to go, or what he wanted to find; he simply wandered.

A fallen tree, leaning over a gentle stream caught the Elf's eye. He approached it and crossed it like a bridge. He then followed the edge of the water, walking upstream. For a moment, Clover felt the relief of his solitude. How pleasant it was to be free of the constant chattering and babbling of the other Elves! There was no one bothering him, no one urging him to improve how he spent his time. Out here, he could be as aimless as he felt.

The stream led to a waterfall, cascading down a rocky cliff. Clover lifted his eyes to see how high it rose, but the thick tree covering above obscured the cliff's top. Clover felt a pang of disappointment at reaching the river's end, and stood there motionless, wondering what he should do next. Should he just stay there forever? What did it matter?

A strange noise sounded from the waterfall. Clover blinked.

"Hallo?" he said, peering around. The sound called again. It was something akin to a child's laugh. Clover took his long spear and thrust its tip into the falling waters. The spear's parting presence made a sort of window, and Clover could see that, on the other side, there was an empty space. Well, it could be just a little space under an outcropping of rock, but it was enough of a space that Clover thought he should at least try to fit inside it. He threw his spear through the waterfall. It disappeared.

The Elf nodded to himself, then dove into the water. He sputtered and choked for a moment, startled at the force of the current just under the waterfall, but pulled his head back under the water, and swam forward. On the other side, the current grew still, and Clover's head surfaced inside a blue-lit cave. It wasn't easy pulling his soaking body, with a now-heavier green cape, from the pool. But with a few grunts he found himself on dry land. Or was it dry? Clover yelped in surprise as he stared face-to-face with another man.

The man had pale skin and a handsome face; he would only just have reached the age of fullness. His wet, brown hair, though short on the sides, fell messily down over his brow in longer locks. Clover turned his head side to side, observing his own reflection. He was gazing into the surface of a black reflective rock. Turning, he observed that all the cave walls seemed to be made of this reflective material. He could see hundreds of Elves standing there, peering about like a child caught searching for food in the kitchen.

"Hallo?" Clover said. His voice echoed throughout the cave. There was no response. Clover glanced down at his wet self with a grimace. His white tunic suctioned itself against his body, granting him the appearance of a wet hound. He stepped from one foot to the other, creating a sloshing sound with his knee-high boots as he made a puddle on the ground where he stood.

The laughing noise sounded again, and Clover whirled his head to the side, slapping some of his wet hair against his forehead, to see a small beast standing there. It was some sort of ovis, he decided, similar to the goats his people kept. Only this thing has a thick, shaggy coat, and a longer bushy tail. The ovis was white in color, with patches of brown. He wasn't at all an attractive animal, but his uniqueness intrigued Clover. It bleated again, shaking his head at the Elf.

"Do you speak?" Clover asked. Clover knew better than to ask such a thing of a strange animal; he knew well that animals could only be understood by people who had taken the time and care to make a special bond with them. "Hallo—do you speak?"

Bah, it said, for it really was only a sheep. Then it began to trot happily deeper into the cave. Feeling that the beast was no doubt as aimless and careless as himself, Clover followed it.

The reflective passageway curled through the center of some sort of mountain pass, and Clover's world grew darker as he followed the animal deeper and deeper into its belly. Before long, his path grew a little steeper, venturing upwards toward a glowing light. Soon, he and the sheep came to an exit, framed in draping greenery, like a bride's veil.

Clover stepped through the vines to find himself inside the concave bowl of a lusciously green valley. He was surrounded on all sides by towering mountain peaks, covered with thousands of tall pine trees jetting upward like spikes on a porcupine's back. The place was erupting with life and color, with soft, grassy topography rolling about at the center. It was like stepping inside a snow globe. A lone house sat on the far side of the valley, no more than a half-mile walk away. The ovis trotted out into the valley, transforming in Clover's eyes, into a little white cotton bud as he ventured further and further away, joining other little cotton buds which dusted the valley in white.

A gust of wind blew past Clover, catching in his cloak. The force pushed against him, and he stumbled forward a few steps. His wet clothes clung to his damp skin, and he began to feel—perhaps for the first time in his life—cold. He wrapped one of his arms around himself, then charged forward with his spear in hand. If anyone lived in that little house, they would be sure to have a fire. Yes, there was a little smoke snake swirling up out of the house's chimney. He would head there.

Clover walked deeper into the Valley and began to shake from the cold. The sky above began to turn to colder, bluer colors. It was Firstnight, the moment when day became night on the world of Raqia, where there is no setting sun. One never knew when exactly it would arrive, but when it did, it was unmistakable. A person grew tired and experienced an intense pull to quiet and warm places.

Clover began parting his way through a particularly dense cluster of white sheep. They all seemed to be meandering in one direction, so Clover found himself moving with them like a fish riding a gentle current. There was a sort of satisfying pleasure to wandering like a herd animal; he need not think for himself in that moment, he need only follow the others, trusting that whoever was at the front knew where they were going.

"This way," called a voice. Then came a whistle.

Clover found himself quickening his pace as the herd around him did so. He lifted his eyes to see a woman standing beside a gate, holding up a wooden staff. Her face was veiled by the darkening night, but Clover could see the silhouette of her body, like a statue in a city square, calling all to herself.

She lowered her staff as she noticed Clover's obvious presence, juxtaposed against the cluster of animals.

"Hello?" she asked, "Who goes there?"

Clover walked until he came right to the gate. The sheep parted around him like water, continuing on into their pen while he stood there not three feet from the woman. He placed the butt of his spear against the ground and looked into her face.

Clover dropped down onto his knee and felt his chest. His heart seemed to stop beating altogether. It was as if time itself had stopped to hold its breath—watching as Clover's eyes studied what must have been the source of all beauty. Had he found it? The stairway to heaven? The doorway to Eden? Who was she? Who was this woman?

"Beatrice," said Clover, "Eve; Lady of the Garden—tell me who you are." He gazed upwards at her face; it was like the shining light of the Morningstar, whose beauty cannot be veiled by either day or night.

The woman pursed her lips suspiciously, studying Clover, then chuckled.

"Oh, get up," she said, kicking the toe of her shoe against his shin. She laughed. "You heard me—get up!"

"Who could stand before such beauty?" he said in a voice as serious as a dying breath, "who could stand before such perfection!"

The woman dramatically rolled her eyes, then turned to shut the small gate to her sheep's pen.

"Fine," she said with her back turned, "Stay there then."

Clover started, gasping with fear as she began to leave, charging off into the darkness.

"Wait!" he called as he scrambled to his feet. "Wait, Beatrice!"

"Nope!" she said in a distant voice. Then he heard her laugh.

"Wait!" Clover called again and rushed after her with wet sloshy steps. "Eve? Tell me who you are!"

She laughed again, even louder, then stopped to turn and study Clover with a condescending stare.

"You had better follow me," she said, "Papa will want to know there's a wulf in the fold."

"A wulf?" Clover started, "No! I—I'm an Elf!"

"Well, I can see *that*," she said as she placed one of her delicate, caramel hands on her hip, "And whether wulf, Elf, or man—*no one* is allowed in Paradise Valley."

"Aye," Clover said as he placed his hand over his heart, "Aye—I can see why. No man should be allowed to lay his eyes on you; most wonderful, beautiful—"

"You had better stop adding to your list of sins," she said with a grin, "I tell Papa everything, you know."

Clover blinked. "I... I am so sorry. Yes," he said, "Yes, I should be sent away. Surely, I am not holy enough to be here!"

The woman smirked. "By the stars," she said with a sigh, "You're a funny one. Come on, you and your little friend had better come this way—Papa will want to speak to you before he sends you away."

"My—?" Clover froze, then turned around to see two glowing eyes peering from behind him. He scowled. "That—" he bit his lip, then turned back to the woman, "That's not mine, he's just a thieving—"

"Come along," she said. She was already moving back toward the house, whose glowing windows grew brighter against the darkening night.

Clover huffed, then ran to catch up. He could hear a hurried pattering from behind, so he turned swiftly to snatch the gnome by the arm.

"Stop following me!" he hissed. The gnome's eyes grew as wide as circles, then he wiggled to get free. Clover noticed him now carrying a large bundle, nearly as large as himself. "What have you got there?" Clover asked as he yanked the thing out of the gnome's hands. He dropped the critter onto the ground, and it hurriedly scrambled behind his boot.

Clover recognized the bundle; it was one of the leather sacks that the giant had been carrying. Clover groaned.

"You can't just *steal* things!" he barked.

"Come on!" the woman called after him.

Clover kicked the gnome free of his boot, fastened the sack against his belt, and raced after his new obsession.

As they reached the house, the night was as dark as a windowless closet. They ventured around to the back door where a large lantern lit a cobblestone courtyard. There, shirtless and sweaty, a man was chopping wood.

"Papa," the young woman said as she leaned her arm against the doorframe of the house, "Papa, someone found the Valley."

The man, with skin as rich a caramel color as the woman's—though alarmingly more scarred—plunged his ax into a chunk of fallen tree, then turned to inspect Clover. He furrowed his thick brow and crossed his arms.

"An Elf?" he asked, "What in Hades?"

Clover felt suddenly aware of his disheveled, wet state, and pulled his hands innocently behind his back, joining them together.

"Hallo," Clover said, "I am Clover."

"Clover?" The man snorted, stepping closer, "That doesn't sound like an Elven name to me."

"Well, it's not my given name," Clover said blankly, "But it is the thing I like to be called." He felt himself grow smaller as the man drew himself up to full height. He was at least a whole head taller than Clover, and his arms three times as thick. Judging by the old battle scars gashed across his face and body, Clover guessed this man had seen war, and a lot of it. One of his eyes looked vacant, encased in a white glaze.

"Oh," said the man, "Are you the sort of boy who finds need to abandon the gifts of your parents? Even the name they gave you?"

"Well," Clover said, rubbing one of his ankles against the other, "Sort of. You see—it was my mother who first called me Clover, you know. She thought a simpler name suited me. But in another sense, I think you are right. I left my home and family behind on this journey without their consent or knowledge."

The man glanced at his daughter, then back at Clover, with a look that asked, *Can you believe this?*

"I found him wandering around with the sheep; drenched like that and everything," she said, pointing at Clover's sorry state.

"He must have found the water passage," the man said, walking back over to where his ax waited. He plucked the thing effortlessly from its place and held it up to Clover. The lantern light reflected off its polished edge.

"I would guess so," said the woman. She crossed her arms and leaned against the side of the house, watching with amusement.

"Sir," Clover said bravely, refusing to flinch at the sight of the ax, "Sir—I would like to ask about your daughter."

The woman chuckled.

"Oh, this should be good," said the man with a grin. "Yes? What have you got to ask, boy?"

"Is your..." Clover hesitated, glancing bashfully at the woman, then back at her father, "Is your daughter free to marry?"

"Hah!" The man barked a laugh. "Are you joking?"

"Why would I joke about such a thing?" Clover asked, looking from face to face between the woman and her father. "I say—do you think I am *joking*? I have never been more serious in my life!"

"Oh dear," the man's smile faded, "he's serious?"

"I am as surprised as you are, Papa," said the girl.

"I know that I am a stranger, a nobody, a nothing... but please, if you would just give me a chance! I would be your slave for an eternity if it meant a shot at that woman being mine."

"My *name* is Isabella," she said sharply.

"Don't tell him your name," the man grunted.

"Well, you're going to make him forget everything anyway," she said with a wave of her hand.

"Forget?" Clover gasped. "No!"

"Sorry, son," said the man, "No one can know where Paradise Valley is— and no exceptions."

"No, please!" Clover cried, "Send me away if you must, but do not take her face from me!" This was it! He was *feeling* something! "I could live the rest of my life content if I just had the memory of her face!"

The woman blinked, as if surprised by what she heard. There was silence in the courtyard.

"I mean, Papa," she said, turning to look at her father, "Do you *have* to take his memories? He looks pretty harmless to me." Clover chose not to take offense at that, though he was tempted.

"Isabella," said her father cautiously, "You know the rules."

"Fine," Clover said determinedly, "Take my memory if you must, but first, give me dinner and a place to lay my head for the night. Give me a warm fire, and a meal to share with the woman I love. Then—yes—you can take it all away from me again."

The man studied Clover, looking bemused. "Alright," he said, "Deal." He held out his hard, calloused hand to the Elf.

Clover eagerly took it, gripping it firmly in with a single shake.

"Joel," said the man, "You can call me Joel."

"Clover," said Clover as he took his hand back to himself.

"I know that you didn't just come here asking for my daughter's hand," Joel said solemnly. "You have another reason, don't you?"

Clover shook his head, "I have never had reason in my life to do *anything* until this very night when I met the lovely Isabella."

"You're lying," said Joel.

"I'm not."

"Then what have you got there? Tell me that *bag* means nothing to you," said the man as he thrust a finger at the pouch which hung on Clover's belt.

"Oh, that's not mine," Clover said flatly.

Joel's face hardened. "I am showing you hospitality, boy; don't be obstinate with me."

"I'm not!" Clover retorted. "Why won't you believe me? This thing isn't mine!"

Isabella watched on the sidelines with a look of amusement. "Well, where did you get it?" she asked.

"The thieving scumbag!" Clover said, pointing his finger into the darkness. "There's a felling garden gnome hanging around here!"

"No need to swear," Joel said, trusting his ax back into the log, "You don't have to tell me where you got the bag, just..." his voice trailed off, then he began to walk into the house.

"I am telling the truth!" Clover said angrily, looking to Isabella for support. "The gnome stole it, you see."

She chuckled. "Alright," she said with a shrug, then pointed at an outdoor hearth which burned brightly. "Hang your cloak there. Papa won't want you dripping on the furniture. And leave your boots by the door. You can dry the rest of yourself by the fire inside."

Clover watched silently as Isabella turned and went into the house. His heart leapt within his chest. He had found her; he had found the only thing in the world that mattered. Isabella was her name, and he had *found* her.

Clover was disappointed to see four places set at the table. Isabella had drawn up a stool for the gnome, who looked equally as damp as Clover himself, holding a fork like a sword in both hands excitedly. Clover seated himself across from Isabella, thankful for the opportunity to gaze into her face, and combed his floppy hair back to smile at her.

She smirked, then turned to watch her father who seated himself at the small table's head.

"It's nice to have someone in Hanz' spot again," said Isabella with a voice as bright as a bell.

Her father grunted. "Yes," he admitted, then placed his hands on the table. Clover bowed his head as Joel spoke the words of prayer, thanking the Lights for their meal. It was a relief for Clover when Isabella lifted the lid of the lone pot on the table to reveal a vegetation stew. He had heard rumors that humans ate meat; thankfully these particular souls were more virtuous.

"Alright," Joel said, raising his eyes to Clover as Isabella served them each a bowl of stew. "Where did you get the bag?"

Clover sighed, then pointed at the gnome. The gnome blanched, then dashed to hide under the table.

"He's really sweet," Isabella said, "Is he a creature you have bonded with? Does he speak to you?"

Clover balked. "Speak? *Bonded*?"

"Do the Elves bond with animals, Papa?" Isabella asked her father as she ladled his food.

Joel nodded. "They do," he said.

"It's not that I don't know how to befriend an animal," Clover said dryly, "I just have no desire to befriend a garden gnome. They're thieves, you know."

"They're not thieves," Joel said, leaning back in his chair, "they're imitative."

"You've *seen* one of those things before, Papa?" Isabella asked with excitement as she seated herself.

"Many seasons ago; long before you were born," said Joel, "Anyway, he probably saw *you* stealing, and copied you."

Clover flattened his mouth into a line. "Hades knows why the thing keeps bringing me stolen things," he said as he plopped the bag onto the table, "You can have this, for all I care."

Joel eyed the sack. "Do you know what that is, Elf?"

"How many times do I have to say it?" Clover asked impatiently, "No."

Joel nodded to himself.

"What is it, Papa?" Isabella asked her father with a fading smile. There was a breeze of tension between them.

"I'll open it for you, if you wish it," Clover said, locking eyes with Isabella. She seemed, for a moment, to blush under his gaze, then her eyes flashed with excitement.

"Yes!" she said, "Open it!"

"No," said Joel, raising a hand into the air, "Not now."

"Do it!" Isabella said quickly.

Clover found it impossible to refuse the woman he claimed to love, so he opened it.

Light emanated from the mouth of the sack. Then, to Clover's great surprise, a pair of reflective, metallic gold wings sprung forth from it, and a small man rose from within. The pair of wings, attached to his back, fluttered, stretching out. The man, who was no larger than the palm of Clover's hand, looked around, examining the faces of those at the table.

"A faerie?" Isabella gasped. She turned to look at her father with confusion. "Papa, did you know a faerie was in there?"

The faerie, with perfectly white, short hair, cleft pointy ears, and a trim red coat, paused at the sight of Joel's face. His expression was one of recognition, and shock.

"Timbre Wulf?" he asked. "Flood waters—he's brought me to Timbre Wulf?"

Joel sighed, slouching into his chair.

"Dezmund, is it?" Joel asked with weary eyes.

"Papa?" Isabella asked slowly, "Why is he calling you Timbre Wulf?"

"Are you working with Korbin?" Dezmund demanded. "Floods—tell me you're not working with Korbin!"

"I'm not working with anyone," Joel said in a dark tone, "I am done with the fae; how many times do I have to tell you that?"

Dezmund sniffed. "Korbin abducted me not two days ago. So, how did I get here?"

Joel glanced up at Clover, then back at the little faerie. "I do not know who Korbin is."

"He is a lackey of King Somenus," Dezmund the faerie said. "He's hunting those of us who fled."

Joel glanced up at his daughter, "Isabella," he said quietly, "Please wait outside."

"Outside?" Isabella lurched forward urgently. "No! No, I am staying right here!"

"You are not ready to... you do not need to hear any of this," he said, his tone hardening.

"Papa!" Isabella rose to her feet. "Please! I am grown now; whether you like it or not, I am going to find things out! Now *explain* to me what is happening!"

"You may not give me orders," her father said firmly. "Now both of you—out!"

Isabella slammed her fists on the table, then turned, breathing heavily to herself as she cooled her temper. Clover rose slowly to his feet, taking his wooden bowl of stew with him.

"You want us outside?" he asked innocently, leaping inwardly at the idea of some time alone with his love.

"Out!" Joel yelled, losing his patience.

Clover and Isabella stepped out into the night air. It wasn't quite as cold now that Clover's clothes had mostly dried, but he still grabbed his cloak from the outdoor fire. It was toasty warm, though it smelled of smoke. Isabella passed him by, throwing her own, floor length cloak over her shoulders. She paced quickly into the fields where her pasture was, climbing up onto one of the stone walls.

She sat on the top of the short pen wall, with her legs dangling inside where the sheep were sleeping, and slumped defeatedly. Clover walked up behind her and leaned his arms against the wall's ledge beside her, looking up at her face. Her long, black hair, lit with a silver glow from the star light, cascaded down past her shoulder, resting down beside where Clover's elbow rested. He was tempted to lean over and smell it, but refrained.

"I am growing so tired of this," she said quietly.

"Who could grow tired of living *here*?" Clover asked wistfully, "It's like you live inside a painting."

Isabella glanced down at Clover, "No," she said, "It's not living here that I am tired of—though I wouldn't *mind* a change," she looked back out at her flock, "I was talking about my father. He... he will not tell me certain things."

"You didn't know your father was Timbre Wulf?" Clover asked.

Isabella shot him a glare. "What do you mean?" She pressed.

Clover shrugged, "That faerie called him Timbre Wulf. You didn't know your father was Timbre Wulf?"

"Who is Timbre Wulf?" she asked sharply. "Do *you* know who that is?"

"Well of *course* I do," Clover said blankly, "Everybody does."

Isabella swung her legs over the side of the wall and jumped down beside Clover, she drew close to his face with a scowl and jabbed her finger at him.

"Tell me! Tell me right now!" said she.

Clover stuttered. He could hardly think with the love of his life standing so close to him! "Tell you what?"

"You said everybody has heard of Timbre Wulf. Well? I live out in the middle of the woods, and I have never traveled further than Nemus! So, tell me what it is that *everybody* but me knows!"

"Sure," Clover said, taking a step back, "I'll tell you. I'll tell you anything you want. I'll tell you how much I love you, if you ask; I'll tell you how many stars I would pluck from the seas to marry you."

Isabella stuttered, then shook her head. "Tell me who *Timbre Wulf* is."

"He's a..." Clover hesitated.

"He's a *what*? Why are you stalling?" Isabella stamped her foot on the ground.

"Who is Hanz?" Clover asked.

"What?" Isabella drew back. "He's my brother—why?"

"The faerie named Dezmund seems to know who Hanz is," Clover responded casually.

"What do you mean? How do you know that?"

"I can hear him," Clover said, "...'*It is Hanz who is rallying faeries in the Woodlands, I thought it was you who had sent him*,'" he mumbled, recounting the words he had just heard.

"You can hear them?" Isabella asked, hitting Clover's chest with a mighty shove with both her hands. Stunned, he stumbled back.

"Yes!" he said, "Are you angry?"

"No!" she whispered excitedly, "How can you hear what they're saying from all the way over here?"

Clover tapped his pointy ear proudly. "Elf, remember? Anyway, it's easy to pick out voices from this far away when there's no other people around."

"Tell me what they are saying!" she said excitedly. Clover blushed as she stepped closer, offering him a playful smile. He swallowed loudly, then nodded.

"Alright," he said, "The faeric says: Somenus is imprisoning all of us who have fled, and all of us who will not take part in the Rites."

"Who is Somenus?" Isabella asked.

"Uh," Clover found himself gazing absently into her bright, brown eyes. Her lashes were like spider's legs, and when she blinked, he felt drawn into some sort of trance. "Who?"

"Somenus," she said, tapping his chest impatiently with her hand.

"You don't know?" Clover furrowed his brow. "Seriously?"

"Hades, Clover!" she snapped, "Haven't I said this already? I don't know anything about what happens outside of the Woodlands."

"Have you heard of the Nightmare Faerie?" Clover asked.

She started. "Well... yes! He's sort of a myth though, isn't he?"

Clover shrugged. "There's a real dream faerie, and his name is Somenus, the second of his Kind. He's been around for thousands of seasons. Anyway, people call him the Nightmare Faerie because—"

"Because he visits people in their *dreams*?" she asked in a suspenseful whisper. "That's what Hanz used to say when we were kids!"

"Yeah, I guess so," Clover said, "Anyway, he usurped the Faerie throne in Arelle two seasons ago. He is the new Faerie King."

"Oh," Isabella said, looking down as she processed. "*Two* seasons ago, you said?"

Clover nodded. "Somenus took the throne at the end of the season of Daybreaking."

"Yes..." Isabella mumbled, "Yes, something happened here at the end of Daybreaking." She looked up quickly at Clover, "I heard my father talking to some people outside. He would not let me hear. I was younger then, still in the age of questioning."

"I think your father is talking about that day," said Clover, looking up toward the homestead.

"Tell me what he is saying!"

"He says: Hanz took my staff without my permission. Two of you already came to me after the plot to kill the late king. I told them Timbre Wulf was no longer a Friend of the Fae."

"Friend of the Fae?" Isabella asked herself.

"It's just when a faerie..." Clover began to explain.

"Keep telling me what Papa is saying!" Isabella said urgently, stepping closer to Clover as she rested her hand against his shoulder. It was almost as if she thought *she* could hear better when she was closer to him. Clover didn't mind at all.

Clover cleared his throat, "'They asked for my help to kill Somenus, and I told them I would not,' your father says, 'Why?' Dezmund is asking—he sounds angry. He asks, 'Why have you abandoned us?' Now your father is saying, 'It was you who betrayed me; I have lost my wife and now son to your wars; I will not help you. If my son wishes to throw away his life for you, that is his choice. I will not stop him, though I begged him not to go.'"

"What?" Isabella gasped. "Hanz left... to help the faeries... because Father *refused* to help them?"

"That's what it sounds like," Clover said, "When did your brother leave?"

"He left shortly after that night," Isabella said with sadness in her voice, "I never knew why. He told me... he told me he had something important to do." She sighed.

"Dezmund is telling your father that he met with Hanz. They came here to the Valley in search of you."

"*Me*?" Isabella gasped. "What? Tell me what they are saying!"

"'Stay away from Isabella,' your father says, 'I do not want her involved in your schemes.' Now Dezmund is talking. He says, 'We need her help in order to kill the Nightmare Faerie. Hanz says we can trust her; he says we need her. We risked coming back all this way to find her; I risked being abducted by Korbin to find her!'"

"Really?" Isabella asked in astonishment. "Hanz came back to find me? Clover—" she gripped Clover's shoulders tightly with both her hands, "Clover, is he still *here*?"

"Uh..." Clover hesitated, "'Okay, your father says, 'I don't care what Hanz says, and I am sorry he risked the safety of others to come here, but it is fruitless. I will not let Isabella be tainted by your darkness.' Now your father asks what they wanted you to do... alright, Dezmund doesn't know, but he trusts Hanz' plan. Hanz is waiting for you in Nemus. Now Dezmund is saying that there is a weapon that can kill the... kill the..." Clover blinked, realizing Isabella was no longer standing beside him. "Isabella?" he called. He saw her dark figure disappearing into the blackness. He chased after her, finding her rummaging around in a woodshed.

"I'm sorry, Clover," she said breathlessly, fitting a lantern against the end of a walking stick. "I cannot stand around here anymore and do nothing. If Hanz came to find me, I *must* speak with him!"

"But!" Clover gasped, "But, Isabella! Your father thinks it's dangerous for you!"

"My brother knows me well," she said sternly as she pushed past Clover to grab a traveling sack. "If he thinks I can handle myself out there, then I can! Father taught me enough about fighting for me to defend myself," she turned to look Clover in the eyes, "And Clover—I need to know why he left! I know now for sure that my father will never tell me about his mysterious past, and he will never let me leave the Valley. Don't you see? This is my only chance to escape! Now, are you coming or not?"

Clover hesitated. "You—you want me to come with you?"

She shrugged. "I am leaving that up to you. But like it or not, I am leaving. And we had better leave now!" This all seemed so sudden. Only just earlier that day she had seemed so content in this valley; so happy to be here!

"It sounds like this Korbin character—the one Dezmund was talking about—is out to get Hanz and possibly *you*; perhaps I should come with you, to keep you safe and all that."

"Do whatever you want," she said.

"Isabella," Clover said urgently, taking one of her hands in his. "I would do anything for you; I *love* you!"

Isabella bit her lip, doing her best not to laugh. "Clover..." she said with a sigh, "I am sorry, but you don't love me."

"Yes, I do."

"No, you don't."

"How can you know that?" Clover asked with concern in his voice, "I never say things I don't mean. *Never*!"

Isabella blew air through her lips impatiently. "Clover," she said in a short tone, "You cannot love someone—not *really*—without knowing anything about them. We just met. Our friendship is as shallow as a plate. You couldn't possibly love me, not the real me."

"I..." Clover shook his head, "No, that is not how love works at all!"

"Oh really?" she crossed her arms. "Enlighten me, then. How *does* love work, Clover?"

"Love is constant," Clover said, "It will not waver. It is a choice made. To love someone truly is to never stop."

"See?" she said, holding out her hand toward him, "See—true love is tested by *time*!"

"True love may be *tested* by time, but it can still be just as pure and as true at the beginning of its journey as it is at its end. It may grow and develop, but just because it is new doesn't mean it isn't true! Give me a chance to prove myself to you—and you will see. My love for you will never waver."

Isabella barked a laugh. "Hefty promises. Are you sure you want to make them?"

"I have never made a promise I was more sure I could keep," Clover said fervently. "I love you, Isabella."

"Whatever you say!" She laughed, then hoisted her sack over her shoulder. Clover courteously passed her the lantern staff, then followed as she marched out of the shed.

They hiked out to the edge of the valley, out to the same cave passage where Clover had entered through.

Isabella poked her head inside the cave and looked around cautiously.

"Everything alright?" Clover asked, stepping up beside her.

"I don't usually come out here at night; it will be dark, I suppose."

"I'll protect you!" Clover said virtuously, stamping the end of his spear onto the rocky ground. The sound reverberated through the caves.

"Thanks," Isabella said with a hint of sarcasm in her voice.

"This is where I saw one of those goats of yours; he led me to the Valley, you know," Clover said as they started walking inside.

"They're sheep, not goats," Isabella said as she walked. "They are very special, you know. These are the only sheep left on this side of the mountains, my father says."

"Really?" Clover asked, "Sheep—like in faerie stories?" The outlandish books the faeries liked to read, and sometimes distribute, told a lot of stories involving sheep, Clover thought. He himself had only read a few, and he was pretty sure they *all* referenced sheep at some point.

"Yes," said Isabella, "They—"

Clover jumped as she whirled around, gasping in horror.

"What?" Clover asked hurriedly, "What happened?"

"My sheep!" Isabella cried. Clover could see true fear in her face.

"They're fine," Clover said, shrugging, "Your father will—"

"No!" She gasped, "Father will come looking for me once I am missed; I *know* he will! The sheep will be left unattended. Clover—Clover, I can't just leave them alone!"

"Then... you're going to stay after all?" he asked, feeling a little relieved.

"No," she said, crossing her arms. She began to tap her index finger against her elbow rhythmically, and then a smile crept up the side of her mouth.

A sinking feeling pulled against Clover's heart. "No..." he said.

"You said you loved me? You said you wanted to *prove* it to me?" she asked, moving closer to him.

"Isabella..." Clover groaned, "You can't ask me to—"

"If you love me," she said in a honey-like voice, stepping so close he could smell her, "You will watch my sheep, won't you, Clover?"

Clover clenched his jaw. "Yes," he answered through his teeth.

"Don't let them out of your sight, alright?" she said, tapping his shoulder.

"How long?"

She shrugged, "Until I am back?"

Clover sighed. "But what about the... the Nightmare Faerie, and all that? What if you're gone a long time?"

She smirked. "Then we will see just how *constant* your love really is, Clover."

"You think you are calling my bluff," Clover said soberly, "But you will see. I *will* do this for you."

Her face seemed to change, as if she were tempted, just for a moment, to believe him.

"Sure, Clover," she said casually, turning back toward the caves, "I appreciate it."

"Watching these sheep will be the greatest thing I ever did," Clover said as she walked away. "Even if I never see you again."

"Alright!" Isabella called out, then waved without even turning around to look at him.

He watched until her dark shape disappeared into nothingness, then raced back to the pen of sleeping animals. He meant what he said: he would do this for her.

⚬

Clover woke to a kick in the stomach. He lurched, groaning as the boot drove itself back into his ribs again.

"Hey!" he mumbled, scrambling to his feet. He had fallen asleep while leaning against the door to the sheep's pen.

"Where is she?" Joel asked darkly, "Where is Isabella? Damn—we talked too long, didn't we? Where is she?"

Clover cradled his stomach. "That hurt!" he said, pulling his spear from the ground. Joel kicked the spear out of his hand with lightning speed. Clover backed against the wall of the pen in terror at the sight of Joel's eyes. He was like a roused bear. "I... I..."

"I asked you where she is, damn it!" Joel yelled, throwing the sack at the Elf. Clover caught the sack and looked down at it.

"Is—is that faerie still in here?"

"Well, *I* don't have the power to get him out of there!" Joel said, stepping close enough to run his finger across Clover's neck threateningly. "Elf," he said, "Where is she? If I find out you were trying to romance her under my nose—"

"No!" Clover swatted his hand away, "She left!"

Joel froze, studying Clover for the truth. Then he seized the Elf by the throat and lifted him into the air. Clover wheezed helplessly, clinging onto Joel's wrists.

"*Why?*" Clover begged.

"She *left?*" Joel roared, "Left the Valley, at *night?*"

It wasn't in Clover's nature to lie, so he said, "She went to find her brother, Hanz."

"*What?* How did she—?" He hesitated, then tightened his grip around Clover's throat. "You overheard us, *didn't* you, you felling Elf?"

Clover couldn't speak, so Joel dropped him to the ground, waiting as Clover coughed and sputtered, rubbing his neck frantically.

"Sorry," Joel said, letting out a deep, hot breath, "My temper, when roused, is..." he glanced at Clover. "Listen, dangerous men are after Hanz and anyone with him. I need to go find Isabella before she gets wrapped up in all this. Take that sack."

Clover looked down at the leather pouch, then up at the man. "Why?"

"Because I don't want it. Now—get out of the Valley, and never come back."

"But I can't!" Clover said desperately, scrambling to his feet.

"You can and you will," Joel pointed at Clover with a threatening finger.

"No!" Clover cried, "No, I promised Isabella!"

"*What*?" Joel gritted his teeth. "Promised her *what*?"

"I promised I would care for her sheep! She asked me to prove my love by—"

"You've got to be kidding me," Joel cradled his forehead in his fingers. "Look, you can't stay here, Elf. I am sorry. No one but my family is allowed in the Valley."

"But I promised," Clover said, "I will not break my promise."

"Then the sheep are yours," Joel said with a wave of his hand, "Take them."

Clover froze, stunned. "But I—!"

"You cannot stay in the Valley," Joel said firmly. "Take the sheep if you wish, but you *must* leave."

Clover turned to look at the cluster of sleeping sheep, then back at the menacing man. This man was Timbre Wulf; the great faerie killer; the keeper of the Beatus staff; Clover couldn't exactly say 'no' to *him*!

"Now?" Clover asked weakly, "I have to leave *now*?"

Joel nodded.

Clover sighed, then picked up his spear. He turned to open the gate of the sheep's pen, then glanced back to see Joel watching him.

"Well," he mumbled to himself, "I guess I found something to care about."

3

— Lola —

The Crimson Gate

"FATHER, YOU HAD BETTER GET ME MARRIED OFF—and quickly!" Lolette said in a scolding tone.

King Antecus lifted his eyes wearily from his book.

"What did you say, seashell?" he asked, pinching his concerned eyebrows together just above the nose. It was one of his only expressions that made him actually look old. The king had lived for thousands of seasons; but who could tell?

"I said, you had better get me married off. I mean it." She stamped her foot upon the ground impatiently.

"Oh." He reluctantly closed his book and leaned back in his wicker chair. His light, airy hair moved, caught in the sea breeze which always blew tenderly up there in the Warmwinds Tower. "I was hoping that *wasn't* what you said."

"Father!" Lolette exclaimed, "Take me seriously for once!"

"I do take you seriously, child," he said softly, crossing one of his knees over the other, "I take this sort of thing very seriously. There is no reason to get you married right now."

"Ah *hah*!" She pointed at the ash-haired Elf accusingly with her finger, "You are quite wrong there. I can tell you a reason."

He moaned to himself, "Elves do not *need* to marry, my seashell, and you have only just passed the age of questioning—there is no hurry. You know when I married your mother, she had lived over a thousand seasons. And... well... at times I *still* wonder if it was the right choice."

"Father!" Lolette gasped. "Do not say such things!"

"Lolette," King Antecus said as he drummed his fingertips against the hard shell of his tome, "I have already looked about for a husband for you—at your request. It would not be good to rush this conversation. Now, the Faerie delegation from Arelle arrives today; you had better go ready yourself."

"But this is my problem," said the princess as she placed her hands on her hips, "Your lack of urgency will not do. I fear—well, I fear I am becoming quite a problem for you!"

Antecus tried to hide his amusement by rubbing his mouth thoughtfully with his hand.

"Hmm," he hummed, "How so?"

"Well," Lolette moved across the terrace and sat on the wicker chair across from her father with a sort of graceful, though childlike, plop. "The only way to live well on this world is to love goodness, truth, and beauty, as you know, and I rather think I am... *straying* a bit. I am trying to be good by waiting for you and all that, but I find myself... sort of..." she winced, as if embarrassed to say the word, "*Longing*."

"Longing?" Antecus repeated the word, "Seashell... that's hardly..."

"Longing!" Lolette swiped her finger into the air emphatically. "And... I think that before I go and get carried away with falling in love with somebody, you had better get me married." She nodded to herself with a sense of finality, then smiled widely. She had done well, she thought.

King Antecus placed his book on the table next to himself, then leaned forward with his elbows on his knees.

"Have you *already* gone and fallen in love with someone?" he asked in a leading tone.

"No," Lolette said quickly. Then she paused. "Well, I might have done, but I can't be sure. At first, when I met Trefolian of the Elder Copse, I was sure I was in love." She shook her head to herself, "but he didn't seem to care two petals about me! And then there was... erm... someone *else*," she shook her head again, quicker this time, "But he will not do either."

Antecus' face perfectly captured a look of anguish. "Lola," he said, "I am not sure what to say... your mother might have..." his voice trailed off.

Lolette bit her lip. He was thinking about her mother again, wondering how different things might have been if she were there. Oh dear—she had done it again; she had put her father in a position where he felt inadequate without her mother by his side. This was why she was trying to *help him out*!

"Oh, Father," Lola said with a smile, reaching over to touch his hand. She held it tightly. He moved his eyes to look at her, and his pained expression seemed to ease. "You're doing everything right. All I am asking is that you just... *hurry it up* a little. Then you won't have to worry so much about me!"

"I don't really want you married yet," he said mournfully, "I like your presence in the Palace. Besides, it is a good thing to be content with one's state before they get married."

Lola pursed her lips. Her father knew to use the word *good* when trying to convince her of something. He knew her devotion to that word.

"But that's just it, Father," she said, still squeezing his hand, "I am not content! And it bothers me. That is... I am content," she looked to the side, deliberating within herself, "but I also find myself *longing* at times." She peered into her father's eyes. "Have you ever found yourself *longing*, father?" She really stressed the word *longing*.

"I..." he looked around awkwardly, at anything but her face, "I am not sure."

"I am sure you *are* sure!" she said quickly, "I am sure you have found yourself *longing* before."

"Lola..."

"Anyway, I don't think it can be good for a girl like me to sit around longing all day. I just keep thinking about how wonderful it will be to be in love—and to have someone good and true and... beautiful... to spend my life with." She said that last statement with a look of wandering excitement, then she focused her eyes back on her father determinedly. "I don't think I am *meant* to be single for seasons on end. So, can you find someone for me to marry? You know, someone—"

"Good," her father finished her sentence, then his mouth softened into a smile. "I'll see what I can do, Lola," he said, "If you really want this."

Lola stood, ringing her hands with excitement. "Oh, *thank* you, father! I promise I will do my best to be patient! But... oh please," She leaned down to grasp his hands in hers, "please don't take *too* long!"

The king pulled the corner of his mouth to the side. "You know, I *had* thought that raising a willful daughter would mean trouble *convincing* you to get married when the time came. Who knew *I* would be the reluctant one when the time came? But..." he sighed, "if you really want this, you will let me do it in my way and my time."

"Of course, of course," Lola said, stepping back, offering repeated bows with her head. "I will give you time to... erm... Father?"

"Yes, seashell?"

"It would be nice if you picked someone... sort of..." she cringed, "dashing?"

King Antecus blinked. "I... will do my best, seashell. Now, please go get ready for the delegation. It..." his eyes seemed to glaze over, "Well, I think it will be important to make as good an impression as we can this time."

Lola raised her eyebrows. "You don't think... Father, do you think King Somenus will go to *war* with us?"

"No, no, surely not," he shook his head, but Lola could tell he was not being entirely truthful. "I don't think he would dare."

Lola backed away from her father, observing him as he reached for his book. She had disturbed him long enough. She would go now.

Lolette was coming down the narrow spiral staircase, holding up the train of her dress cautiously, when Lady Fernhazel found her.

"Princess!" Fernhazel called from the bottom of the stairs, "There you are! Come, I have been looking everywhere for you!"

"Oh, I am coming," Lola said as she skipped the final step, landing on the floor with a bounce.

"The delegation will be here soon," said the court lady, "You're not half dressed!"

"I am plenty dressed," Lola retorted, looking down at herself. She was wearing her green, embroidered gown, which flowed fabulously behind her whenever she walked in a straight line.

"Not for Northerners, you aren't. Let's go." Lady Fernhazel said, taking Lola by the wrist. How bossy Fernhazel always was, especially whenever Northerners visited!

Lola let herself be led through the castle grounds, all the way to her own bedchambers. But as she walked, she let her mind wander. So, her father would find her a husband after all. Yes, love would no longer be a fantasy, but a reality! But who? Who would this man *be*?

As they rushed through the open-air skybridge, Lola spotted the sea. Its colors were a deep, dark blue today. What could that mean? Did she have enough time to visit the skydeacons before the delegates came? The sea air smelled extra salty. What could *that* mean? Latimer had told her something about saltiness— what was it again?

"Stop daydreaming and hurry!" Fernhazel said, yanking Lola by the arm. Lola trod after her in an uneven stride as she gazed around at the misty air. Celestia was aglow with mysterious weather today. Did no one but her notice?

Once they arrived in Lola's chambers, Fernhazel began barking orders at the maids. They made quick work, unlacing Lola's clothes and preparing her special outfit. She could hardly focus on them when her mind was wandering like this, though. She gazed upwards with a smile as chaos whipped and buzzed around her. She would get married. It *would* happen.

"What's inside your head today?" Fernhazel asked. The frank manner in which she asked the question startled Lola from her reveries.

"Sorry?" Lola asked, blinking.

"You're more distracted than usual. What's going on?" Fernhazel was standing a few paces away, watching as the maids attached layer after layer of billowy skirts to the princess.

"Why do we have to dress like this when delegations come?" Lola asked, wishing to keep her thoughts private. "So many skirts, I feel as though I might fall over!"

"The humans in the north have a different sense of modesty," Fernhazel said, "You know this."

"Yes, but," Lola huffed, "the *Faeries* don't. I've heard they wear cross-robes and togas and... and women even show their legs in Arelle! So, I don't see the need for—"

"It's just our policy for all delegations, Lolette," Fernhazel said, sounding impatient. "Plus, humans often accompany the Faeries when they come, remember? We don't want any of them gawking at our princess!"

"Do you think Leck will come this time?" Lola asked, turning to look behind her as a maid pulled the drawstring against her waist just a tad too tight.

"You shouldn't call a Faerie by their first name," said Fernhazel with a sigh, "Lolette, you should be careful befriending the Fae. They... they're a bad sort."

"Not all of them are bad!" Lola said, turning to frown at the court lady. "Leck has been very kind, and he is trying to help father work out a good relationship with the... the new Faerex." Lola shuddered inwardly at the thought of the new Faerie King. No one liked to think about the fact that the dreaded *Nightmare Faerie*, as many liked to call him, was now on the throne of Arelle.

"The *Messenger* Faerie," Fernhazel said, refusing to call him by his first name, "*works* for the Faerex. You should keep your distance." There was warning in her voice.

The maids stepped away from Lola, studying her so as to be sure they had done their job well. Lola turned to face her large oval mirror. She looked like a doll wearing that huge skirt and tiny bodice. Her bright auburn hair fell loosely over her shoulders in waves, its length reaching down to her mid back. She had bright green eyes, and a little nose. The white, strapless bodice juxtaposed against the large skirt made her frame look quite small, and she was already rather short for an Elf! She turned herself side to side, sighing.

"Well," she said, "Hopefully I am not meeting my future husband today dressed like *this*."

"Future husband?" Fernhazel sniffed. "Back to this again?"

Lola turned quickly to face the brown-haired Elf. "Please, don't dampen my mood," she said, "I think marriage is a good, true, and beautiful thing. It's not a bad thing to desire!"

Fernhazel didn't look impressed. "The Transcendentals are pursuits, not ideals. You had better get your head out of the clouds if you think marriage is filled with goodness, truth, and beauty, Lolette. Plus... something tells me it's your own fantasies and not the Transcendentals that make you want marriage so badly."

Lola hated talking with Fernhazel about such things; the woman was so confident in her own logic and intellect, yet she never actually did anything with it. Her life was as boring as a blank sheet of paper!

"I don't think you understand what I mean," Lola said with her chin turned upwards. "I merely mean to say that there is nothing wrong with wanting to get married, is there? Is it so bad to long for a... sort of... *friendship* that is so deep and profound, it makes one want to—"

"No." Fernhazel said quickly, holding up her palm as if to ward away evil. "I find *romance*—if that is what you are describing—to be a terrible mirage. It is the very essence of emptiness; it promises happiness, leads its victims on a path of hope, then ends in misery. Lola," she used Lolette's more familiar name as an olive branch, "Don't follow that scent; it leads to madness."

Lola felt an inward rage rising within her, like a forceful tide. "That is not what I mean at *all*!" she snapped, "I am not longing for empty feelings and shallow romance; that is the exact opposite of what I want!"

Fernhazel raised one of her eyebrows. "Oh?" she asked. "How?"

"I wish to indulge in the *deepest* of friendships, with a person of character who would love me as truly as I love them!"

Fernhazel snorted. "Then you had better not look for it in marriage." She pointed across the room at Lola's bedside table which housed a stack of little faerie novels. "You read too much romance; it's filling your head with fantasies."

Lola felt the urge to slap Fernhazel across the face, then quickly cooled her rage by closing her eyes and taking in a deep breath.

"Lady Fernhazel," she said, opening her eyes with renewed calm, "I see no reason why one cannot find profound friendship in marriage. And I will prove it to you! I will marry such a person, and make the whole world see that such things are not fantasies. And if such a man truly cannot be found, then—you just watch—I will *never* marry!"

Lady Fernhazel had an amused smile on her face. "I would love to be proven wrong," she said with a sigh, "But be ready to be unmarried for a long, long time, Princess Lolette. For, I fear, you have *grossly* overestimated what virtues can be found in men."

Lola stood beside her father's throne with her hands folded together, resting just above her waist. She found it hard to take her deep, calming breaths when she wore such a tight dress, and so she found herself growing more nervous than usual. She was always excited when delegations came to the Elven kingdom of Celestia; outsiders brought in so many interesting smells and cultures. But for most of Lola's life, they had always been from the human kingdoms, or the Elder Copse. Ever since Somenus usurped the Faerie throne, however, the faeries had begun to send delegations. Faerex Somenus ruled Arelle differently to his predecessors; he *liked* being involved in Raqian politics.

And if her father was right, he was *too* involved.

"There's two of them," Sir Thorne, one of the honor knights, whispered into King Antecus' ear. "The Messenger, and another, new Faerie."

Lola glanced to the side, watching her father's face. He was nervous. Maybe no one else could see it, but *she* could; she knew him too well. Her gaze floated back to the scene before her. She could see the whole ceremonial hall from where she stood. Elves from noble families lined the sides, but down the center of the room ran a silver carpet, marking the way for the delegates.

The faeries always arrived in style. If Faerex Somenus had done anything right, Lola thought, it was that he had a lot of pomp and pride, and his people made such grand entrances. As their procession glided into the room, following that silver carpet, they paraded all sorts of banners and flutists. They played faerie music, which did something magikal, Lola thought, to its listeners. It bent everyone's moods, giving an air of optimism.

Two faeries led the procession. One was Leck; Lola knew him well. With his slick black hair pulled back into a bun, and those thin, discerning eyes, he was hard to miss. She lifted a finger, tempted to wave when she met his eyes, but resisted. No, she reminded herself, he would not be a good man to fall in love with. For one thing, he was a faerie, and she knew her father would never allow a marriage with a faerie. And secondly, he worked for the Faerex. As handsome and honest as he seemed to be, she could not trust a man who would serve someone as evil as Somenus. Leck did not smile when he saw her; he kept his face stoic. That seemed odd.

The other faerie she had never seen before. Everything about his countenance was dark, aside from his pale, almost colorless skin. His black hair framed his face in wavy locks, and his black tunic, belted at the waist with reflective onyx, added to the look. But it was that dark, shadowy aura around him that really added to his villainous vibe; it was as if his hidden wings couldn't stand being unseen, so they left a shadow of their presence, casting a dreariness over the entire room.

One of the humans in the procession, wearing plate armor, stepped forward and cried out in a voice louder than necessary: "His holiness, the Faerex of Raqia, King Somenus, has sent his servants: Leck the X Messenger, and Felix the II of Sight."

Lola refrained from a gasp. Faerex of *Raqia*? No one debated that he was King of the Faeries and of Arelle—but of *Raqia*? —the whole *world*? Lola glanced at her father, half-expecting him to contradict the statement.

"Peace to you, King Antecus," said Felix, the dark Faerie, stepping forward. He placed a foot on the bottom step leading up to her father's throne.

"Well met, Felix of Sight; it is an honor," said her father. "Welcome to Celestia."

"Let's get right to it," Felix said with half-open eyes. It was as if he were reluctantly forced to get out of bed to be there! "Somenus has graciously given you two full seasons, a total of eight hundred and forty days, to think about it, and now he wants an answer: will you ally with him or not? Will you submit to his authority over the land?"

This was different from past interactions; this was *very* different. Lola snuck a glance at her father; there was anger on his face.

"We haven't been *mulling over* a decision for two seasons," King Antecus replied firmly, "we already told the Faerex our decision. We do not make military alliances, and we do not submit to his rule over us! The Elves have always stayed autonomous from the Fae, and we plan to keep it that way!"

"Do you deny that the Faerex reigns over the ground beneath your feet? Do you ask the Faerex to put this to the test? You may think this land is yours, but the second he desires it, King Somenus can ask it to turn to dust beneath your feet. Famine, King Antecus. Are your people ready to face *famine*?"

King Antecus rose from his throne with gritted teeth. "Your threats will not persuade me into giving Somenus my warriors or my submission!"

Lola didn't think she had ever heard her father yell before. It was a voice she couldn't even recognize.

Felix drew back, holding his chin high. "I see," he said, "Your words have been recorded. I will take them to the king. Good day, King Antecus of Celestia. We will depart before Firstlight."

King Antecus scoffed loudly and fell back upon his throne gracelessly. Lola rushed to his side, placing an encouraging hand upon his shoulder. He reached up to touch her fingers with his, sighing as the faeries turned and left.

"Leck bought us some time," he said quietly, "but I fear things really will change now."

"Is it true what he said?" Lola asked, "Can the Faerex really cause famine here?"

Her father nodded slowly. "All the soil belongs to the throne."

Lola started. "So... so he really *is* king of Raqia?"

"No," her father said sharply, "He is not. He may be a steward of the land, but he is not King of all governments!"

She patted her father's shoulder. His anger was near a boiling point, and she knew it would be unkind to aggravate him further.

"You are strong," she said to him, "and a good King. You will lead us well through a time of famine."

"Elves may be immortal like the fae," her father said, "but unlike them, we *do* need to eat to survive. I fear..." his voice drifted into silence.

"*Whatever is true; whatever is beautiful,*" Lola said, reciting her mother's words, "*whatever is good—pursue these things, and it will bring fullness.* Even in a time of famine, those words will be true, will they not? If they will not sustain us in times of trial as well as plenty, then they are meaningless."

Antecus chuckled, then cranked his head upwards to find her face. "Yes, seashell," he said fondly, "I think you are right."

"Is it wrong that I feel *glad* for an opportunity to be tested?" she asked, smiling warmly at her father.

He pulled the corner of his mouth to the side. "I suppose it's not wrong, though perhaps a tad strange." He chuckled, then patted his hand against hers. "You are so much like your mother. You... you immortalize her by remembering her words, Lola."

There was a pang of sadness in her heart, but she would not show it on her face. No, not when her father needed to see her strength in her. There were times when she could share her sadness with him, but it was not this moment. This moment was one no king ever wanted to face, when he made a decision that would hurt everyone. And if there was anything a king needed in a moment like that, it was a smile from someone who trusted him.

<hr>

Lola sat in the sand, chuckling at how unfitting her big, blue skirt was for her surroundings. There, in her private little lagoon, she waited. The Firstdark bell was ringing; night had come to her coastal paradise. A tapestry of purple colors wove through the sky, reflected like a mirror against the black sea waters. The tide splashed against the rocks by her feet. It was such a wild coast, yet such a gentle shore.

Her life, and the road before her, felt like the Sea—ever changing but never changing. How like the waves her heart swelled and receded as she waited for things to just *happen* to her. How lonely it was.

To be lonely is to have a disconnected and discontented heart with one's community. That is what her father always said. She did believe him, but couldn't one be content and yet long for something *more* at the same time? Her father also liked to say: *in nuance there is truth*. So, wasn't there nuance in the tension between contentedness and longing?

That longing she felt—it was so strong! Was it so bad to yearn to share these thoughts with another? To bind herself to another soul in such an unbreakable way that she was no longer one person, but two? Or that they would no longer be two people, but one? This was a bond stronger than neighbor to neighbor, or father to daughter, that she wanted. She wanted it, and she wasn't ashamed of it. And for it she would wait, even if it never came. That—she thought—was the nuance of discontent contentedness.

There was a burst of light on the horizon. It lit up both the sea and the sky in a blaze of purple fire. This was what the skydeacons called the Nightbreak. Those who lived by the sea knew to watch for it, especially the Elves. Every night was different; it never looked the same. *The weather is soaked in meaning*, the skydeacons would say, *and if you learn to interpret the skies, you might be able to see it*.

And nothing could be more true. For the skies of Raqia are nothing like the atmosphere down in the Lowlands like Earth and his sisters. No, the skies of Raqia are like a reflective window, barring the way—though giving a glimpse into—the Heavens above. The Lights lived there, on the other side of the glass: ever shining and ever present, since before the Cosmos was ever made.

The Nightbreak sent a cold wave across Lola's little coastal nook. She drew her arms around herself and stood to peer around. Leck always met her here at Nightbreak. It had been their little tradition to exchange books whenever he visited. She knew it was a bit of a childish fancy to secretly meet a faerie in a remote place, but really, she comforted herself, it was for *books*! She may have entertained a bit of affection for the Messenger Faerie at one time, but her friendship with him had matured since she had grown in the last two seasons. He was a friend, and nothing more.

And there he was! Like one of her father's mighty birds, Leck's wings flapped into view as he flew down to their meeting place. The wings of the Messenger Faerie were spotted, white and brown, and feathered like a great owl. It was a magnificent sight to see a faerie flying like that; so before she went plodding through the sand to catch up to him, she took a moment to watch him land.

The two hurried to meet each other, and Lola found herself laughing as she tripped over more than one rock racing through the uneven beach in her ridiculous ten-layered skirt. Leck had a mischievous smile on his face when he met her.

He bowed then said, "It is an unhappy day, but it gives me joy to see you smiling, nonetheless. I fear there is no stopping the storm anymore. The king is determined to get your father on his side."

"Oh," Lola said as she tried to tame her windblown hair, pulling it behind one of her pointed ears. "Yes, I fear so. But I am so glad you found time to meet me. Did you bring any books this time?"

"Just one," said the faerie. He pulled aside his linen bag, the one he always carried, and opened it. He produced from within a little green book, then passed it to the princess.

Lola excitedly opened it to read the title page.

"Phantastes," she read aloud. "A Faerie Romance for Men and Women." She felt a little flutter within her heart as she read the subtitle. Another romance... a *faerie* romance! Was this... was this an offer of... *love*?

"I thought you'd like this one," Leck said as he crossed his arms, "I found it in the old library in Arelle. Took me about a day to read it."

"A day!" Lola exclaimed. "Oh, Leck. I wish I had that luxury. I have to try and make a book last as long as I possibly can... then I find myself rereading it, and rereading it, and rereading—"

Leck broke into a laugh. "I wish I had that sort of passion," his eyes twinkled, "You, uh... you have such an inspiring way of finding joy in small things."

Lola blushed. "Thank you, friend," she said. She hoped that by saying the word *friend*, she might discourage any thoughts of romance on his end. By the look on his face, it didn't seem to have any effect. "Well," she said, "I expect I won't see as much of you anymore, now that father has made an enemy of the Faerex."

Leck turned his gaze toward the horizon and grimaced. "Things are definitely going to change. I think Felix has—" he cut himself off, jerking in surprise.

"What?" Lola asked, "What is it?"

She followed his gaze. Then she gasped, placing her hand over her mouth. It was like something out of a nightmare. Four spider-like bat wings, as large as a building, came flapping down toward them. At their center was Felix, the Faerie of Sight. His feet hit the ground with a spray of sand, only a few paces away from them. His eyes were fixed on Leck.

"So," he said, marching forward. Four wings—he had *four* wings? "The plot thickens."

"Felix!" Leck exclaimed, turning to face the other Fae. "This... this..."

"*This isn't what it looks like?*" Felix guessed, "*This is a surprise?*" He sighed as if already bored by the conversation. "Leck, I know what's been going on with you. I've known all along." He gestured with his finger at the two of them.

"What do you mean, sir?" Lola asked, feeling offended, "What do you mean by *going on*?" Was he insinuating that there was a secret *romance* between them?

Leck zipped his mouth closed, then stepped between Lola and Felix.

"Yes, I knew you were befriending the Elves, Leck. *He* knows as well," Felix said as he began to walk around the two of them, circling like a wulf rounding up his victims.

Leck scoffed, "Knows what? I've only ever done what I have been asked! Was I not *supposed* to befriend the Elves?"

"Liar," Felix said with a shake of his head. "We were friends, Leck, how could you betray me like this?"

"Betray *you*?" Leck scoffed. "Look, I brought the princess books. That's all. Whatever else you think me guilty of—"

"I *know*, Leck," Felix said, lowering his voice. "I am the Faerie of Sight, remember? You think I haven't watched you? Do you really think you could do this without me knowing?"

Leck's eyes flashed; his cheeks grew hot. "You..."

"Show me your arm, Leck," Felix said, "Take off your cuff."

Leck looked down at his left arm where one of his decorative gold cuffs was clasped. He sighed.

"Take it off." Felix repeated. Leck did so, and dropped the ornate cuff to the ground. Lola breathed in sharply at what she saw. There, on the underside of Leck's wrist was a purple symbol, glowing brightly. And there was shame on Leck's face.

"What... what is that, Leck?" Lola asked quietly. Felix's sharp eyes darted to Lola, like an eagle spotting bigger prey.

"I've been watching for a long time, Leck," he said, keeping his gaze locked on the princess. It was almost too much to bear. What did it mean for the Faerie of *Sight* to look at her? It was as if she was completely and utterly exposed. "...Since before you even came here," he continued. "Somenus has had plans for King Antecus." He finally freed Lola of his intense stare and turned his cloudy blue eyes back at the Messenger Faerie. "It... I..." he fought for the right words, "I did not expect to find out you were in the Purple Order. That is... it's quite a blow."

Leck spat upon the ground. "Don't you speak to me about betrayal, Felix!" he seethed, "You betrayed *us* first!"

"Us?" Felix raised his eyebrows, "And who is *us*?"

"The Fae!" Leck shouted, "The true King!"

Felix blinked, then pulled something from his belt. It was a silver cuff, attached by a little chain to a brown pouch of sorts.

"I wish I didn't have to do this," said Felix, "I wish you had not... Oh Hades," he shook his head, then reached out and took Leck by the arm. Leck did not fight him, he only turned to look at Lola with sorrowful eyes.

"I'm sorry," he said. Felix clasped the cuff around Leck's arm, and then there was a burst of light. Lola gasped; Leck was gone! Felix pulled the sack closed by its drawstrings, then hung it upon his belt. He looked at Lola with the most vacant, deadening stare.

"What have you done to him?" she asked fearfully, pulling her little green novel to her chest. "What... why?"

"*I'm* sorry, Lolette," Felix said. It seemed like a genuine apology, though she didn't know what for. Something around Felix's neck flashed. It was then that she noticed his monocle dangling from a long chain. Her eyes focused on it as it began to glow. Then, Lola's world went black.

When Lola awoke, she did exactly what a woman *should* do when she finds herself waking up in some strange, dark place: she screamed.

"Woman!" The man sitting in the chair at the center of the round chamber jolted and turned his head to glare at her. It was Felix, looking particularly moody.

"Help!" Lola shouted. A useless word, but it was the first one she could think to say. She was sitting on some sort of rickety cot in the corner of a dark, stony dome-like room. The entire place was lit with an eerie red glow. The source of the scarlet color was a large, oval porthole on the side of the chamber, encasing what appeared to be a vertical wall of rippling red water. Felix was sitting at the room's center, his body facing that wall of water, though at the present, his face was turned in her direction.

"Oh, stop," he mumbled, then turned away from her.

"You... you...!" Lola rose unsteadily and pointed a shaking finger at him. "You *abducted* me!"

"Yes," Felix said with his back still turned. "Now, shut up."

"No!" she screeched, "No, *you* don't get to tell *me* to shut up! You have done a villainous thing by abducting a poor girl from her home—a princess, no less!"

That seemed to give reason for Felix to turn and glance at her again. He examined her, then snickered to himself. "*Villainous?*"

"Tell me at *once* where I am!" Lola demanded with a stomp.

Felix rose from his chair and turned to face her. Lola suddenly regretted confronting the Faerie; he was so much more intimidating when he was looking directly at her. His eyes were like endless oceans, vacant and yet full.

"The Crimson Gate," he said in a monotone.

"The—" Lola blinked, then her eyes shifted to the red water. "*That?*"

"Yes," Felix said.

"But *why* have you brought me here?" she asked, shrinking under his gaze.

"Because I wasn't going to fly you all the way to Arelle in that felling skirt," he pointed. "You're as heavy as an aurochs with that thing on."

Lola looked down at herself, then back up at the faerie with a look of disgust. "You *flew* me here?" She wasn't sure why the idea offended her so; in most cases, she would have been thrilled at the idea of a faerie flying her somewhere. Perhaps it was the indecency of it all. It was wrong for him to do this—yes—*wrong*!

"I'll take you to Arelle at Firstlight," he said in response, "So get some sleep while you can."

"Sleep?" Lola scoffed, "*Sleep*? How am I supposed to sleep when—" she cut herself off, "Did you say you're going to fly me to *Arelle*?"

"No," he said, "I am going to *take* you there. It's not the same thing. I told you; it's too far to fly."

"You..." she stammered, growing confused.

Felix pointed at the red water. "That," he said, "is a gate. We will take it in the morning. There, have I said enough? Go to sleep."

"But why are you taking me to Arelle?" she asked, noticing that the wall of water seemed to have an image within it. She narrowed her eyes, forgetting that she had just asked a question. What was that she could see within the water? Was it Celestia? Her home?

"I have been told to bring you there," he said.

"By whom?"

"By the only person who I take orders from: the king." Felix looked at her with a blank stare, standing motionless in the middle of the room.

Lola's eyes widened. "Really?" she asked, growing fearful. "So, this... *this* is why you came to Celestia? To take my father's only child to... to use me as ransom?"

Felix gave no response to the question. Instead, he turned to sit back on his chair.

"Your felling book is on the bed," he mumbled from where he sat, "Something to do if you can't sleep."

The image in the portal began to change. Lola watched silently from where she still stood, half stunned. Like a reflection in the vertical water, scenes began to flash by, and from what Lola could tell, it was like seeing from a bird's perspective if he were flying through the air over Raqia. It made her feel a bit sick, if she were honest.

"It's a magikal gate," she said quietly.

"Wasn't that obvious?" Felix responded, still gazing at the waters.

"So, anyone can look into it... and look at real places?" she asked. "Is that what you are doing, Sight Faerie? Looking around at the world?"

Felix made a loud sigh, as if to inform her he wasn't pleased by being asked another question.

"You're partially correct," he said as the image in the water paused before a great white city, with pointy spires and high walls. "Yes, this is a gate to anywhere I look. But it will not work for just anyone, *I* am its keeper: the Faerie of Sight. Only I can use it." He turned around to shoot a glare at her, "So don't try escaping anywhere with it while I am sleeping; it won't work, you see?"

Lola nodded slowly, and her eyes began to grow damp. She was scared. She stepped back timidly until the backs of her knees hit the side of the little cot. She sat upon it and drew her legs up toward her chest. Thankful, for once, for the huge billowy skirt, Lola buried her face into her knees and began to sob as quietly as she could.

The Faerie of Sight was good enough to leave her be. The room became eerily silent. And after a time, the images in the mirror faded into nothingness. Felix fell asleep.

When his head dropped onto the back of his chair, and Lola was sure Felix would not wake, she laid down upon her little bed and opened her book.

She took in a deep breath, then let it out, opening to the first chapter.

"*I awoke one morning,*" she whispered to herself as she began to read the first line, "*with the usual perplexity of mind, which accompanies the return of consciousness.*" Then, in that dark, lonely corner, Lola's face lit up with the faintest of smiles.

⁕

It was probably morning, but who could tell in a windowless room? Lola had no idea where this place was that Felix had brought her, only that he had mentioned it was a "tower". She sat patiently on the little bed, trying to comb her messy hair with her fingers while Felix sat lifelessly in his chair. He was awake now, scanning his eyes across various landscapes in that magikal Crimson Gate.

She was recounting to herself the conversation she had with her father only the day before.

Whatever is true; whatever is beautiful, Lola had said, reciting her mother's words, *whatever is good—pursue these things, and it will bring fullness.* Even in a dismal place like this, torn away from her people and her family—those words must still be true, mustn't they? If they would not sustain her in times of trial as well as plenty, then they were meaningless.

This was a test, she told herself. She had no idea what was coming, but one thing was for sure: she was a prisoner. Sitting on Lola's lap was her book from Leck. *It was a gift for this very unexpected time,* she thought. It was a reminder that she could still find joy in beauty even in the midst of her captivity. She had only read one chapter, but already the story seemed to resonate with her. Anodos, a man who had just come of age, found himself in a land of faeries and magik. It was apparently more pertinent than even Leck could have anticipated!

"Did you sleep?" Felix asked as he stood to stretch. He yawned, straightened his tunic, then said to himself, "Oh, fell beasts. What do I care?"

"I did," Lola said in a polite tone, though her face showed her displeasure.

"Well, get up," said the Faerie. "It's time to go."

Lola rose to her feet hesitantly. "We are going to go... through *that*?" She pointed warily at the portal.

"I already told you that," Felix said in a short tone, turning to face her. "Weren't you listening, woman?"

"Don't call me *woman*," Lola snapped, "It's rude."

Felix blinked, then sniffed. "Sorry," he said.

"An apology!" Lola remarked unenthusiastically, "How kind."

"Do I need to drag you through?" he asked lazily. "Let's go."

Lola shuffled one foot in front of the other, making her way toward the water. "Will I be able to... to *breathe* in there?"

Felix turned to look at the portal. "Oh," he said, "Yes, I think so. Just go in, you'll be fine. You might—uh—*see* things in there... but that's normal."

"See things?" Lola swallowed, "Scary things? What do you mean?"

"Oh, nothing; just get in there!" Felix impatiently pushed against her back, and the princess found herself falling forward, hands outstretched, into the face of the waters.

⸻ • ⸻

Traveling through the Crimson Gate was like walking into a living painting. Colors and images flashed and danced around Lola like tempestuous winds. She felt herself floating forwards, though she knew not where. It was as if she were everywhere and nowhere, all at the same time. Felix said she might see things, and there inside the portal of Sight, see things, she did.

She saw moments in her life that she had long forgotten; they flashed before her eyes in an instant. She saw things that she had no idea she had ever seen; from the glowing red world when her eyes first discovered sight, to the first time she saw her mother's face. And more than that, she saw things that she thought she should not see: things which she was pretty sure had not yet happened.

"Beloved," she heard herself say. No, it did not come from her mouth, it came from an image. She tried to focus her eyes on it, it was playing seemingly in a loop. She stared as intently as she could at the vision, capturing it in her mind, concerned it would vanish like all the others. There, she saw a man in white. He had a silver helm covering his face, but she could hear him speaking.

"Lola," he said. There was compassion in his voice. "What have they done to you?"

The image seemed to shift and change, and she thought she saw herself in his arms.

"Beloved," she said, with her own lips this time. She knew him—it was *him*! It was...

The world began to take shape around Lola once more, and the vision dissipated.

4

—— Isabella ——

The Rites Come to Paradise

*A*LL THIS TIME, *I*'VE BEEN LEFT IN THE DARK, Isabella thought as she journeyed boldly toward Nemus in the thick, woodsy night. *It is time for answers.*

She felt a little bad about leaving that poor love-sick Elf behind. But honestly—he would have been a tiresome traveling companion. Sending him back to watch her sheep seemed to be the only surefire way to get her father to take care of him. She didn't *like* when her father used his enchanted ring to make people forget about the Valley, but she appreciated its usefulness. Before long, Clover will have forgotten all about his ridiculous crush.

There was a part of her that didn't want him to forget her, but she was pretty sure that was her vanity. No, it was best to release the poor fish back into the river—let him swim freely again.

"Right," Isabella whispered to herself as she spotted the brazier glowing from the town's unimpressive watchtower. "Time to stay focused."

Hanz came to Nemus hoping to meet with her, so whatever happened next, she needed to know why! Her father and her brother seemed to disagree on whatever it was the Faeries wanted—why? What did they know that she didn't know? And why did her father never tell her the truth of his past?

Isabella stepped up to the watch tower and waved at the watchman who was sitting on the ground, smoking. He jostled awkwardly to his feet once he saw her shadowy figure approaching.

"Who goes there?" he asked in a shaky voice.

"It's me, Ed—Isabella," She stepped close to the small fire pit that Ed, the night watch, was perched beside.

"Oh, *Hades*, Isabella," Ed wiped his brow with his sweat-covered handkerchief; the thing hadn't been white for a very long time. "It's just you."

"Who else would I be?" She chuckled.

Ed tried to feign courage with a laugh, but it was unconvincing. "Well," he wiped the side of his face with the cloth, then drew in a deep puff of tobacco. "We've gotten a lot of visitors today," he said, "Some—*erm*—some soldiers moving through, and everything."

"Soldiers?" Isabella leaned sideways, peering down the town's one street. Yes, Clover had overheard something about Hanz being chased by someone... "Ed—have you seen my brother in town?"

"Your *brother*?" Ed blinked. "Yeah, lots of people looking for him. I haven't seen him, though. Isabella," he stepped closer, lowering his voice, "I don't know if it's the best idea—you coming to town at night without your father—these men looking for Hanz, they..." he peered side to side, then dropped his voice so low, she could barely make out his words, "They seem like a bad sort. And they—they're setting up a shrine in the town square. A *shrine*!"

"A shrine?" Isabella drew back. Ed was trembling. He wasn't the bravest man in the watch, but it wasn't like him to rattle in his boots like this. "To... the Lights?"

"No," Ed straightened, then took a quick rallying puff on his tab, "To the Faerex."

Isabella scowled. She had heard that the Faerex was forcing cities to put up shrines to faeries—but she never expected that sort of thing to make it this far into the Woodlands!

"Well," she said slowly, "Don't mention to anyone that Hanz is my brother, alright? I'll keep my head down." She took a step toward the village road. Ed caught her arm.

"Isabella!" He said cautiously, "There's a lot of soldiers in there—are... are you *sure* you want to go in? They really aren't the sort of people who—"

"I'll be fine!" She yanked her arm free of the man. Really! Sure, she was a woman, but she wasn't defenseless! She strode confidently into the village, then quickly began to regret it.

She had never seen Nemus at night, so she expected things to look different. What she *didn't* expect was to see so many lights on. From the glowing windows to the excessive outdoor torchlight, the village was bustling with activity. She could see people moving around, whether in alleyways or clustered into groups in the main village square. In all her life, Isabella had never seen the town so crowded. Was this what it was like in cities outside of the Woodlands? Were the streets just *filled* with people?

She pulled her hood over her head protectively as she approached the square. Oh dear—Ed was right! There, mounted beside the town's notice board, were two polished stone monoliths, one larger than the other. A brass bowl lay before each one, containing freshly burned incense.

She leaned closer, reading the inscriptions chiseled onto the stone. The larger stone read: *Somenus, III Faerex and II Faerie of Dreams*; and the smaller: *Everwood, XVI Faerie of Craftsmanship.* Lights above—she knew there were strange cults that engaged in faerie worship, but this? This was right in the middle of the Village square! Surely the chieftain didn't approve this.

Isabella took a step back as a couple of villagers approached. She pulled the side of her hood close, watching.

"There—that's it, right there," said one of them, gesturing to the monoliths. Isabella didn't need to see his face to know who it was; she recognized his voice. It was Prax, the stonemason. He had his wife Maise on his arm.

"What, *those*?" she asked, pointing toward the shrines with her index finger. "You brought me out here, at this time of night—with all these strangers mulling about—to show me some *rocks*?"

"I didn't put those there," Prax said defensively, "Someone *else* did. Some of the soldiers did."

"Well, what's the problem?" she asked, tugging his arm in the direction of their front door, which hung ajar only a stone's throw away. "Other people are allowed to do stonework, you know."

"Yeah, but," Prax cleared his throat uncomfortably. "They look... *religious*. Maisy, you don't think *this* is what the town meeting tomorrow is about, do you? What's Father Beeminder going to think about this?"

"Town meeting?" Isabella made her presence known by taking a step closer. Both husband and wife clutched each other in surprise, then relaxed when they saw her face.

"It's just me," Isabella smiled. "Goodness—why is everyone so jumpy?"

"Isabella!" Prax exclaimed, "What are you doing in town at this hour? And unattended, too!"

"Go home, child," Maise said as she waved her lacy handkerchief in Isabella's vicinity. "A young woman like yourself shouldn't be out this late without protection. There's men from the East in town!"

"I'm not alone," Isabella lied. "Father will be along shortly."

"Oh," Prax nodded, "Well good. He can probably get the chieftain to come out and explain *this*, then!" The stonemason kicked the tip of his boot against one of the stones. "I don't like the look of what's going on around here. I know stonework, and these things reek of strange religion, I can promise you that."

"They're shrines," Isabella said, "to Faeries."

"What?" Maise peered sideways at her husband, "Is that true?"

"Those words written on the front," Isabella said, knowing Maise couldn't read, "they are the names of faeries."

"But no faeries live out here," she retorted quickly, "I don't see why we should—"

"They're *religious*, aren't they, Isabella?" Prax asked, lowering his voice.

"Yeah, I think so," she said hesitantly, "I've heard of stuff like this. Faeries gain magik through certain things... I think these shrines are places where people can come to help patron Faeries gain power—and I suppose they're meant to get something in return."

"Praying," Maise said sharply, "That's called *praying*!"

"Something like that," Isabella mumbled, kneeling down to inspect the larger shrine. "I think this one is for King Somenus—he's empowered when people think about him, I think…"

"You seem to know a lot about faeries," Prax said in a wary voice. Isabella turned her head sharply to peer up at the man.

"So?" She raised an eyebrow.

Prax shrugged innocently, then exchanged a knowing look with his wife. Isabella pursed her lips suspiciously.

"The soldiers are looking for your brother," Maise said.

"And?" Isabella rose to her feet and faced the couple.

Prax shrugged again. "People are wondering if your family is what brought the soldiers to Nemus."

"We aren't *wondering*," Maise said coldly, "It's obvious! These men are looking for your brother—and your father, too."

"You should probably go home, Isabella—or at least stay by your father's side," said the stonemason. Isabella didn't hold their suspicion toward her against them; they were scared. Something was happening, and her family really *was* at the center of it, it seemed.

"I will," she said with a smile. "And don't worry about the shrines; I am sure the chieftain will have them removed as soon as the soldiers leave town."

"If they ever leave town," Maise whispered to her husband. She tugged at his arm, then the two of them retreated back into their house. Isabella watched them slam the door, bolting it tightly. She tucked her loose hair behind her ear, sighed, then made her way toward the inn. If Hanz was in town, Sam would know about it.

Isabella turned the iron ring handle to the tavern door and pulled it open. She blinked a few times as her eyes adjusted from the cold blue night to the warm orange interiors of the torchlit tavern. Never had she seen the place so full, with every chair occupied and bodies stuffed close together between tables. The din of loud voices and drinking men instantly ceased when she stepped through the door. All faces turned toward her in an instant, and then—as if the movement were planned—they all lowered their gazes in unison to look at her feet. Good grief—what could they have against her *feet*?

Isabella rubbed one ankle against the other, then strode in, disregarding the rude and leering stares. Sam was standing behind the bar, as he always did, with an empty glass in hand. His mouth dropped open once he recognized her, and he seemed to grow tense as she approached. The faces followed her all the way until she leaned against the bar. She felt the back of her neck begin to itch; the stares were becoming oppressive. Perhaps she *shouldn't* have sent Clover away...

"Evening, Sam," she said brightly, masking any sign of timidity. The surrounding voices began to chatter again, no doubt discussing her presence.

"Miss," Sam leaned forward, shifting his eyes from right to left. "This isn't the hour for young ladies to—"

"Well, I heard women showed their ankles out here," slurred a drunk from beside her; he was leaning over the bar and reaching toward her with an unsteady hand. "I just didn't expect to see them on a—*augh*!"

Isabella was pulling the man's pinky finger at a backwards angle, debilitating his hand for a moment.

"I'd suggest you not finish that sentence, sir," she said with a hiss, then released him with a flick of her hand. "And if you like your fingers, then keep those hands to yourself."

The drunk snapped his arm against his side protectively, then impatiently slammed his glass on the bar. Those nearby snickered at the show of confidence, but no one actually seemed intimidated.

Isabella exhaled slowly, refocusing. She wasn't sure what to make of the man's comment, but she was quickly beginning to realize why it might have been a bad idea to come in here alone. No—she was fine. Everyone saw her as a defenseless, weak woman; little did they know she could probably handle an attack better than most of the *men* in her town! Isabella bit her lip. Sure, she could handle herself if one person tried to assault her—but fifty armed men in a tavern? This... was not something she had completely thought through.

She refocused on Sam, the innkeeper. He was the backbone of the town, and a close friend of her family's. If anyone could give her an idea of what was going on, he could. It was therefore unsettling to see such a strong and steady man hiding fear behind his eyes.

"Sam?" she asked, "Can I ask you—"

"Miss," Sam spoke to her with the nervous calm of a dying parent, "Go home. *Please.*"

It was the '*please*' that made Isabella's heart begin to pound. That 'please' sent her one, clear message: danger.

This was a bad idea, Isabella thought to herself as she backed away from the counter. Sam nodded slowly. His eyes screamed: *get out of here.*

This was a really bad idea, she thought. Why had she done this? Everyone else had seemed so scared, why hadn't she been scared? Was it because she had never actually been in danger before? Every time she came to town, Isabella's father had been at her side, making her feel invincible. Was she invincible? How could she know unless she put it to the test? Well—this wasn't the moment to try taking on fifty soldiers; this was probably the time to make herself scarce.

Isabella continued to step backwards, then watched as Sam's eyes widened until they had more white than color. Then his gaze moved upward, peering above her head. Isabella's back hit something, and she froze. Something deep and primal inside her told her not to turn around.

She did, anyway; she turned. At eye level, she saw a belt. Isabella lifted her chin, following the buttons on the front of the man's jerkin, until finally—when she didn't think her head could crank back any further—she found a face. Standing crookedly over her, bent out of shape like a raven trying to fit itself into a wrenhouse, was something that could almost be described as a man. Well—he *must* have been a man; he had all the necessary physical attributes and accouterments to *be* a man; but there was something... *off* about him. He had a long, bony face and black goatee, framed with some tatty, shoulder length hair. The man wore a mirthless smile with a judging, confident set of brown eyes.

"Uh," Isabella stuttered, "Excuse me, sorry." She turned to pass him. His hand caught her shoulder. That hand—it was large enough to wrap around her head like a helmet!

"Just a moment, miss," he said in a voice as thick and congested as mud.

Isabella lifted her eyes once more to look into the man's haunting face. "Yes?" she asked bravely.

"Walk with me," he said, rotating her by the shoulder to face the door. She was as helpless as a doll in his clutch. Without being given a choice, she found herself walking beside the man. He led her out the front door, back into the village square.

"Can I do something for you?" she asked. Her hope was to appear confident, but her voice betrayed her; it was small and trembling. They stood just outside the tavern in the night air. The streets were beginning to clear, and she suddenly felt very alone.

"Yes," he said smoothly, "I couldn't help but overhear—you are the sister of the man Hanz, who grew up in these parts?"

Isabella swallowed. He had heard that? How? *When?*

"I... I..." she searched for excuses.

"What is your name, child?"

"I..."

"Isabella? Is that what I heard?" he turned her to face him, then bent down to peer into her eyes.

She nodded silently, like a child caught in a lie. This was the man looking for her brother—she had walked right into his reach. How foolish! What could she do now? Her eyes scanned the street. Should she *run*?

"Well, you're a pretty little thing, aren't you? Quite unspoiled, I think."

Isabella pulled the corner of her mouth to the side. No one had ever dared to speak to her like that... save Clover, perhaps. But still, this was different. Something about his words felt slimy. *No,* she thought, *I am not some helpless village girl—I can get out of this one. I just need to stay calm.*

"Have you seen your brother?" he asked slowly.

"I..." her mind raced. *Think, Isabella—think!* "Yes," she said, "I have."

The man's eyes flashed. "Well, could you tell me where?" His fingers kneaded her shoulder, ruffling the side of her heavy cape. Her eyes shot to the side, examining his knobby hand.

"I was going to meet him," she said quietly, then pointed down an alleyway. The man lifted his head back into the clouds, gazing toward the alley like a predator catching a scent. Well, there was one thing Isabella had that she hoped this giant of a human didn't have, and that was speed. She ducked, activating his reflexes; he snapped his hand closed tightly. She pulled her shoulder back, then slipped her head through the cape, leaving him standing there clutching an empty garment. Then she dashed. He roared, casting the clothing aside, then pounded after her with his long, thick legs.

Bolting down a side street, Isabella ran faster than she ever thought possible; she ran so hard, her shoe flew off. She cursed. These were the wrong kinds of shoes! Isabella could hear the man shouting, his voice howling like a wulf.

"Get her, damn it! After her! That bitch is Hanz' sister!" He called. Isabella could hear commotion from all sides of the village. Dread came splashing down on her like a heavy rain as she skidded to a stop. Each direction she turned, she could see the glow of moving torch light. She was surrounded. She moved to duck behind a large barrel, but yelped when a pair of arms snatched her and threw her against the side of a stone wall. She let out a muffled scream as a gloved hand clasped over her mouth. She shook, then reached for her hidden dagger.

"Quiet," whispered a familiar voice, "Hold still—it's me!"

She shifted her gaze to the side, then gasped. There he was: Hanz.

5

— Leo —

Over the Stars

I HAD PROBABLY LAIN IN THE GRASS for an hour before I finally figured out what felt so wrong with the sky.

"Hey," I said, breaking the silence. "Where is the sun?"

Momentum, who was lying beside me like a corpse, turned his head to look at me. With eyes half open, he said, "There isn't one."

Neither of us had spoken up until this point. About an hour earlier, this guy had just told me that the "gate" to Earth—or whatever—had been destroyed. What did that even mean? He had done nothing but lie there, sulking, and I had done nothing but lie there, sulking; and the two of us made a pretty boring pair as we lay there, sulking, with neither of us having an idea of what to do next. What is someone supposed to say after they are dragged away from everything they know, then told they can never go back? Was I supposed to just take this guy's word for it?

No, all I could think to do was lie there, processing. But that sunless sky... that got me talking.

"What do you mean, *there isn't one?*" I asked suspiciously.

Momentum sighed loudly, no doubt for my benefit. "Didn't I tell you you're not in the Lowlands anymore?"

"Well, how the hell am I supposed to know what that means?" I snapped.

"Oh, I don't care."

I turned onto my shoulder in the grass, glaring at him. He turned his head away from me passive-aggressively, gazing back up at the sky. "Look—*you* brought me here, so the least you can do is talk to me!"

"I didn't mean to bring *you* here," he said wistfully, "Benjamin was the one who—"

"It's not my fault you made a mistake!" I said, "So you can stop bringing that up!"

Momentum scoffed to himself.

I held my breath for a moment; my pushiness wasn't working on him, so I did my best to draw him out.

"So are we..." I said slowly, "...in your land now? The place where you—erm—*pointy-eared* people come from?"

His eye rolled into its corner, giving me a look, but his head stayed pointing up to the heavens. "Pointy-eared people?"

"Look," I laced some grass between my fingers where my hand laid against the earth, "You said I am stuck here forever, right? So, could you just be cool for a sec and tell me what's going on? Are you like," I cringed at my own ignorance, "an Elf or something?"

Momentum sat up, then snapped his face in my direction. "No, not an Elf. Please, don't call me an Elf."

"Right," I sat up with a groan, "stupid of me to guess that—sorry."

"No, Elves have smaller ears," he rubbed the side of his head, pulling back his hair a bit, "See, us Fairies have a cleft."

"Uh... *faeries*?" It took every ounce of self-control I had not to snicker.

Sensing my childish reaction, Momentum frowned. "If you are going to make any wise cracks about—"

"No, no!" I waved my hands defensively, "Faeries—that's cool. So, you're, uh... a *faerie*. Cool, cool, cool..."

"Well, anyway," he sighed, "You're in another plane. It's not like the Lowlands; there aren't celestial bodies like stars and suns ruling the hours of the days and nights."

My eyes blinked unresponsively, like a browser failing to load a page. "Huh?"

Momentum stared at me blankly, then groaned. "Look—this is why I spent *years* preparing Benjamin before bringing him up here! It's not easy to comprehend."

"No, no," my competitiveness with my very-talented best friend kicked in, "I can take it. Explain!"

The Faerie didn't seem convinced, but he shrugged and said, "So it helps if you just think phenomenologically."

I made that blinking, lost face again.

Momentum dropped his head, sighing, then lifted it, saying, "That just means—you see the world from your own perspective. You were taught that the sun revolves around the Earth, right?"

"Actually, I was taught that the Earth revolves around the sun..."

"Well, anyway," he huffed, "something is revolving around something, *right*?"

"Well, yeah," I raised an eyebrow.

"But *phenomenologically*, the Sun rises, crosses over you, then sets, right? It goes up then down."

"Well, that's how it appears, but it's not actually what happens," I said.

"Exactly," Momentum pointed at me, "It's how it *appears*."

"So..."

"So anyway," he shrugged, "Your generation is all about science, and the whole *'how'* everything works."

"Mhmm...?" I narrowed my eyes skeptically. If he was one of those weird flat-earthers...

"But up here, *how* something works doesn't matter as much. It's all about *why*. If something has meaning, then it is true. See? So, we don't *need* a sun!" He looked pleased with himself.

"I... you lost me."

The Faerie deflated. "Look!" he snapped, "Your Earth—and other lands like it—it's down here," he drew a line in the dirt. "This line is the sea, and *here* is your land," he drew a little island on the line, "Got it?"

"Sure."

"And here above the land is the sky," he made a squiggly line for the clouds, "And above that is the emptiness, where all the celestial bodies are." He started making dots in the space above the land.

"So, space?"

"Sure—space, with stars and sun and moon. But *above* the emptiness, there is an impassable barrier."

"*Above* space?" My mind had trouble wrapping around that one.

"Forget about looking through telescopes. Just think: impassable barrier. So, no matter how hard you try to get beyond the stars, or how far you try to look, you cannot pass it."

"Right... impassable," I mumbled.

Momentum drew a hard line above the stars. "That is called Raqia: the canopy that holds up the Heavens. It's the great separation between the Heavens and the rest of creation, way back when everything was made."

"Oh!" I stared down at the drawing. Here, I thought I was getting a science lesson. Suddenly, my seminary studies came parading back into my mind, and I realized I was gazing down at an Ancient Near Eastern map of the Cosmos. "This is a map of the Cosmos! I learned about this in seminary!" I exclaimed. "And— I suppose the underworld is down there," I pointed underneath the sea line, at the bottom of the map.

"You're smarter than you look," he said, then nodded. "Yes, Hades is down, and the Heavens are up. Encased inside a protective shell is the world of you mortals," he tapped his finger against the island which symbolized Earth in his map. "Get it?"

"So... we are..." I reached, "In *Heaven*?"

"Oh, Hades—no!" The Faerie pointed back at the canopy barrier. "Here, we are here."

"Where, the separation line?"

"Yes," Momentum smiled proudly, "Suspended above the stars, scraping against the top of the shell is Raqia. We are the shell, I guess. Like a ceiling above your universe, held up on four pillars, like a table."

"Uh..." I smiled innocently, "Seriously?"

"So, no," he said flatly, "We don't have a sun. But we do have days and nights."

"How can you have days and nights without a sun?" I asked doubtfully.

"Well," he crossed his arms smugly, "You went to seminary; were there days and nights before the sun and moon were created?"

Damn—he had me there. "I guess, if you're going by the ancient Hebrew creation account," I said slowly, "Then yes: there were days and nights before the sun and moon were made."

"And do you know *why*? Remember, Leon—*why* is very important."

"It's Leo..."

"Because Light came first!" He shot his finger upwards towards the sky. "The Lights were always there, and they made day and night. Up here on Raqia, the passing of time isn't constant like it is down there; our days and nights come and go as they please. Above us is a glass sky, holding up the Glassy Sea. And sitting up there on top of the sea is the Highest Heavens. That's where the Lights live."

"Uh..." My eyes must have glossed over because Momentum ceased his speech and hissed.

"Look, it's very hard to explain to someone who has been.... *educated!*" he said, as if it were an insult. He rose to his feet. "And speaking of time passing—night *is* going to come at some point, and we need to figure out where we are!"

Oh—he was moving! I scrambled to my feet. "You mean... you don't know where we are?"

"Well, I have an *idea* of where we are—we were supposed to be back in my home," he straightened his coattails, "But when the portal exploded, it spat us out... somewhere."

I gazed up at the sky. Was it really made of *glass* up there? It did seem to have some sort of texture, but there were also clouds and wind, just like any other atmosphere. The daylight above didn't seem to have a single source. It looked something like a cluster of colored lanterns inside a cloudy glass shower. There was movement to the lights; gentle movement.

"So... what time is it?" I asked absentmindedly.

Momentum barked a laugh, then said, "Let's go this way." He began to march through the trees.

"Wait for me!" I said, using the famous line reserved for the smallest kid in the group.

"Ah!" Momentum halted, then whirled to face me. "Wait!"

"What!" I skidded to a stop.

"Go get it," he pointed. My eyes followed his finger, back behind me, then down at the ground. I gasped.

"What—*that*?" The hand lay there.

"Yes, that. Get it."

"No way!"

"Get it, *now*!" He growled.

"*You* get it! I am not touching a severed body part!"

"Pick it up, or I am leaving you behind," he demanded. Well—I couldn't argue with that one. As infuriating as this guy was, he was my lifeline here. I stomped over to where the hand lay, picked it up, then shoved it into my hoodie pocket. I certainly didn't want to touch it directly with my hands for long. It was creepy—and more than that—it was *warm*!

I mumbled silent complaints to myself as my one and only acquaintance on this world marched forward into the trees.

I followed dutifully.

"So... this world is called Raqia?" I asked as we walked. I wasn't fond of awkward silences.

"Didn't I say that?" said the faerie without so much as turning around to look at me. He was swinging his hands side to side, parting branches and foliage to blaze a way forward.

"And..." I flinched as a branch snapped against my face, "You people who live up here... are Faeries?"

"Yes," he said, then I heard him mumbling to himself.

"What? I missed that," I called.

"There's humans here, too," he called back to me.

"Really?" I brightened. Alright, so I wasn't *totally* out of my depth in this place.

"Not originally," he said, "But there are now. Faeries are the original inhabitants."

"Do you... have wings?"

I heard him mumble under his breath again.

"*What*?"

"Nothing! I wasn't talking to you!" He paused, then turned to look at me. "Yes," he said blankly, "We have wings."

"Where are they?"

"Well, they aren't visible all the time. We don't have to show them. Sort of like your emotions—do you wear them on your sleeve all the time?"

"Uh..." No, I definitely didn't. "So, your wings are more like an idea than reality?"

"Oh, don't be ridiculous," he continued forward again, letting a branch swing toward my face. "Of course they're real."

"So, are they—?"

"Shh!" Momentum was crouching down in the grass. I ducked unenthusiastically.

"What is it, now?" I whispered.

"Quiet!" he shushed, then pointed. I leaned my head to the side to see past his body. There was a clearing in the trees ahead, and I could see the side of a short stone fence.

"Have we found civilization?" I asked softly.

Momentum glanced toward me, "Yeah, a town. I just am not sure which one..."

"Why are we hiding?" I whispered, "Aren't they friendly?"

"Well, faeries aren't exactly *liked* in every village," he whispered.

"Oh," I blinked, "They're not?"

"No!" he whispered, "And besides... we are sort of..." he blew air through his lips, as if deliberating. "It's complicated."

"Does this have to do with the guy who destroyed the portal?" I asked, leaning toward his ear. Whoa—his ear definitely *was* odd!

"He didn't destroy it," he hissed back, "*I* did."

"Why?" I returned, feeling somewhat shocked. Momentum had seemed so depressed about it!

"Because I didn't want *him* to get access to it—or the Lowlands!"

"But who *is* he?" I asked, doing my best to maintain a whisper as I pressed.

The faerie shot me a glare. "He—" his eyes studied me, "He's the Faerie King."

"What? Seriously?"

The two of us hunched lower as voices approached. Two men, dressed in somewhat feudal attire, strolled past us on a dirt path.

"I think with the wind blowing from the east, we had better get the cattle moving. I don't want to be caught out here in the dark," one said as they passed.

I tugged on Momentum's sleeve. He responded by driving an elbow into my side. I tugged at him again.

"*What?*" He hissed.

"They speak English here?"

Momentum dropped his head in defeat, comforting himself with a groan.

"What?" I tugged at him again. "*Do* they?"

"No!" he snapped, "You're the only one speaking English. Now hush—"

"I saw two wrens in the tree back there, we have a bit of time," said the other man.

"Linus," Momentum whispered, "I need you to—"

"It's Leo."

"*Quiet*! I need you to go talk to them."

"What? *Me*?" I swallowed. "Why?"

"Because I need to know if they are sympathetic to the Faerie King," he returned. "I am not going to show my face unless I know they're not going to call the city watch."

"Do you *want* them to be sympathetic to the Faerie King?" I asked.

"Good question... just—just ask them if they have seen any faeries around and see how they respond."

"And *then* what?" I was sweating nervously now, "Won't they be suspicious of *me*?"

"They probably will," he shrugged.

"Then why don't we both go?" I asked weakly, "I don't want to just stroll out of the bushes and scare these farmers!"

"They're not farmers."

"Well, whatever! I don't want to—"

"Go now, or I'll push you!" he snapped.

"Fine!" I rose, dusted myself off, then marched out onto the path.

The men were a few yards ahead of me, strolling with walking sticks in hand. From where I was standing, I could spot evidence of a city up ahead through the trees.

"Uh, hello!" I called, waving. The two turned sharply toward me, holding up their sticks in alarm. "Hey, I'm Leo!"

They looked at each other, then at me, then watched hesitantly as I jogged up to them. If I hadn't gotten so used to asking strangers for directions during my travels prior to this, I probably never would have had the confidence to dive in like this, but thankfully—I had.

"Hello, Leo," said one of the men. His eyes were traveling across my body like a pinball machine. No doubt my attire confused more than impressed him.

"Hi! Just, uh..." I blubbered, "heading down the road!"

"That's nice," said the other man. He was chewing on an unlit cigar that protruded out from his thick beard.

"So!" I said, joining my hands together behind my back. I rocked back and forth on my heels awkwardly, "Seen any Faeries out here on your... uh... *walk*?"

"What?" The first of the two to speak to me rubbed his bald head. "Faeries?"

"Yeah! You know—Faeries? Interesting, um... people."

"Are you trying to be funny?" Asked the bearded fellow.

"Hah hah..." I cringed. "I don't know."

"Look," the bald one began to turn away, "Bother someone else, son."

"Uh," I glanced toward the bushes where Momentum was shaking his head at me. "Strange people—faeries. Hmm?"

"Look, son," the bearded man stepped toward me, pulled his cigar from his lips and pointed its wet, eroded tip at me, "I don't know where you come from, but around here we don't joke about faeries. The skydeacons don't like it. They say it's irreverent. Here in Greenridge we try to be respectful toward their... type. Now, I don't like it any more than the next man, but I sure as Hades don't want the Faerex finding any reason to poke around here with his soldiers, alright? So perhaps you should take your... *joking* somewhere else."

"Oh!" I shook my head nervously, "Yeah—no... yeah... joking! No, I definitely won't do that. Uh, The *Faerex*?"

The two glanced at each other then back at me.

"Right! Oh, *right*... the Faerex!" I nodded slowly, "Yes, I definitely know who that is."

"The Faerie King?" The bald guy said bluntly.

"Right!" I chuckled nervously, nodding like an idiot, "Of *course*—I knew that!"

"Well," the bearded man had a compassionate look in his eyes, "Take care of yourself, son." They turned and left me standing there, walking back toward the city.

"*Ow!*" I rubbed my throbbing head, sucking in air. "Why did you *hit* me?"

"That was the most embarrassing display I ever—" Momentum slapped the back of my head again. "You're *terrible*!"

"Hey—you're the one who pushed me out there! What was I *supposed* to say? I have no idea what's going on!"

"Well, if I had known you were a complete imbecile—"

"Look, did you find out what you wanted to find out?" I asked sulkily.

"Yes." He was brushing twigs from his coat. "We aren't liked here, but we won't be attacked by any mobs, I don't think." He turned, giving me a funny look.

"What?"

"Let's switch coats."

"*Why?*"

"Because you have a hood."

"Does that mean you'll carry the hand now?"

"No!"

⎯⎯⎯ • ⎯⎯⎯

We strolled into town looking like a couple of jesters. With Momentum in my orange hoodie, looking like a convict, and me in his buttoned coat looking like a LARPer, we attracted a lot of suspicious stares.

The city of Greenridge looked something like a pile of spilled mosaic glass on the side of a green, rocky slope. The ridge was a slanted grass-covered piece of land, jetting up into the sky on an angle, and the city built upon it, with its pointed little buildings, was splashed with bright, pastel colors. The surrounding topography was mostly rolling farmland, cut into grids with low stone walls, and further off in the distance I could see rough-cut mountains painting the skylines. It was hard to believe this place wasn't on the Earth, except for how colorful everything was. It didn't feel natural; but it was definitely beautiful.

"Greenridge," Momentum whispered to me, "Damn... Winter's End is *mountains* away!"

"Winter's End?"

"Shh."

"Where are we going now?" I asked, growing nervous under the gathering stares.

"The bell tower," Momentum whispered back, "The skydeacons there can provide me with some maps... I hope."

"So that you can find your way—uh—home?" I asked, doing my best to keep my hands out of my pockets. That lifeless hand filled up my pocket and I was finding it hard to not think about it constantly.

"Yes," said Momentum. He pointed further up the road at a whitewashed tower. "There, that's where they'll be."

We approached the small orange door at the base of the tower. It had a pretty little silver bell hanging just above its knob. Momentum flicked the bell with his fingers, then turned to look at me.

"This time, let me do all the talking, alright?"

"Gladly!" I crossed my arms.

The door swung inwards, and a face popped out. He was a young man about my age with jet black hair pulled up into a topknot. His eyes shot quickly back and forth looking at us from face to face, then said,

"Can I help you?"

"Yes," said Momentum as he lowered his hood, "I am here on behalf of King Somenus—can I speak to whoever is in charge?"

The young man choked on his own saliva, then slapped his chest in an attempt to breathe again.

"Oh dear," he coughed, "We had no idea you were coming so *soon*! You must be the Faerie of Vows!"

"Mmhmm..." Momentum glanced toward me in warning. I got the message and kept my mouth closed... but of course, I said,

"And I'm Leo!"

"One moment," said the man nervously, offering us repeated bows, "I will get my master."

We waited there by the door as we listened to his hurried footsteps ascending the tower stairs within.

"*Are* you the Faerie of Vows?" I whispered.

"Of course not! Now, shut up!"

"Are you the Faerie... *of* something?" I asked in ignorance.

"Of course I am! Liam—shut *up*!"

"It's Leo..."

We both straightened as the clambering footsteps returned. The door swung open once more, only this time *two* men in grey robes stood there, panting.

"I am Winke," said the young man in the topknot through labored breaths, "and this is my Master, Forewinds."

Forewinds was standing there with his chin held high, doing his best to look proud while he himself was out of breath.

"Hello," said Momentum flatly, "You going to let us in, or...?"

"It is a pleasure to receive you, Endring," Forewinds, the more important man out of the two said to Momentum, "Please, come in. We were not expecting you as of yet, but we do have something we think you will be pleased by."

Forewinds motioned for us to duck as he led us inside the tower. Its insides were nowhere near as pretty as its outsides. Within, the tower was nothing but a hollow cylinder, lined with patchy wood stairs. Forewinds was chattering nervously as he ascended, and we followed slowly.

"Yes, we got your message about keeping an eye out for faerie outlaws—and what do you think? Not two bells ago, one showed up in Greenridge, right in the middle of the street!"

Faerie outlaws? I eyed Momentum, but he didn't look at me.

"Yes, well it seems you're not completely incompetent," he said, stepping seamlessly into his role, "And what did you do with him?"

"We put her in the wine cellar. I... well... What *else* were we supposed to do?" Stammered Winke, who was a few steps below us, "We don't know how to trap faeries! Well—we half expected her to disappear again, but she is still there, you will be pleased to hear!"

"Disappear?" Momentum cranked his head to stare at Winke with a doubtful eye. "Faeries don't *disappear*."

"Of course, uh, sorry—sir," Winke gulped audibly.

We crested the top of the stairs, and Forewinds pushed open a set of double doors. Our world got much brighter again as we stepped into the circular room. It was something like the top of a lighthouse, with glass windows on all sides, and an open-air balcony. At the center of the room was a dangling rope. My guess was that it was attached to a bell up above. It was—after all—called a bell tower!

"This place is so pretty!" I exclaimed.

"Yes, shut up, Liam," Momentum waved a dismissive hand toward me, then turned to Forewinds. "Now—I will need a place to stay for me and my... bodyguard... and some maps, and paper."

"Of course!" Forewinds bowed, "I... Endring—I understood you had a *message* for us from the Faerex. He... he has agreed not to withhold our food?"

Momentum stared lifelessly into the man's eyes. "Have you set up shrines in your city for him?"

"Yes! Yes, we have!"

"Well, then," Momentum shrugged, "I am sure he will."

The two skydeacons looked at each other with blustering smiles, "Thank you—*thank you*, Endring!"

"Don't thank me," Momentum snapped. "I've got nothing to do with it. Now: lodging, maps, paper, ink..."

"Yes, yes," Forewinds poked Winke who bowed several times, then dashed off to rustle through some papers on the other side of the room.

"We live in the floors under the tower, where it is cool," said Forewinds, "Will you mind if we put you up in some of our empty rooms? I'm afraid there's no windows down there..."

"That's fine," Momentum said.

"Then we will bring what you have asked for to your room. We will be ringing the Lastlight bell, soon," he added, "Is there anything you will want before dark?"

"Just some food for my human," Momentum gestured toward me, "And some water for me."

"So, uh," I said, opening my mouth once I realized someone was looking at me, "What time did you say it was?"

Forewinds blinked a few times, glanced at Momentum, then back at me and said, "I just said we will ring the Lastlight bell soon."

"Uh, ok..." I smiled through my teeth.

"Don't mind him," Momentum said through a sigh, "He's... simple."

Forewinds nodded knowingly. "Right," he said, "Well, come with me then."

He led Momentum back to the door, and they began to descend. I disobediently wandered over to where Winke was shuffling around at a messy desk.

"Can I help?" I asked. He passed me a stack of rolled up maps without even looking.

"Here," he said, "you can carry these." Then he paused his rustling and turned to peer at me in the eyes. "What's it... like?"

"What's *what* like?" I asked, adjusting my arms to hold the pile of maps.

"Working for—you know—" he lowered his voice, "The *Nightmare Faerie*?"

The Nightmare Faerie? Who on Earth was the— "You mean the Faerie King?" I asked.

He nodded slowly, "I know we aren't supposed to call him that anymore... but..." his eyes shifted to the side, "But that's what he is, isn't it? Is he scary?"

An image flashed through my mind of those glowing eyes I saw in the portal, then the realization hit me that I had the man's very *hand* in my pocket. The Faerie King; the Nightmare Faerie; the man in the portal; were they all one and the same?

"Uh... yeah. He is."

Winke searched my face. "You're terrified, aren't you? *Hades*," he shuddered, "I can't imagine working close to him. Thankfully I'm not high up enough in the Fellowship to make the seasonal pilgrimage to Arelle, but... I guess one day I'll have to meet him in person! That is, if I want to advance."

I had no idea what the man was talking about. "So, uh," I sucked my lower lip into my mouth in hesitancy, then asked, "What *is* a skydeacon, anyway?"

Winke stared at me with his mouth half open and his head cocked to the side. He was trying to figure out if I was sincere, I think. "Do you honestly not know what a skydeacon is?"

"Uh, I forgot..."

Winke squinted his eyes, "Are you teasing me?"

"Nope."

"How... but don't you work for the Faeries?"

"Sure," I tapped my foot nervously, "But uh—I am just a bodyguard; they don't tell me much."

Winke blew air out the side of his mouth.

"I'm simple," I added, hoping it might help my case.

"Well," Winke shrugged, "We interpret the skies. You know... we ring the bell towers? We predict the time of day?" He gave an encouraging smile, "...and the seasons?"

"Oh! Right, right," I pretended to remember. *Predict* the time of day?

"Well," Winke picked up a stack of paper and a little wood box. "We had better head down to your master. He will be wanting these things."

I followed Winke precariously, carrying my stack of scrolls down the stairs. He led me down to the ground level, then opened another door which led further down. For being underground, the stairs we descended were well lit, with glowing lanterns set into the walls like stained glass artwork.

"Why do you guys live underground?" I asked as I examined the glowing illustrations on the walls.

"Greenridge gets a lot of high winds," Winke said, stopping on a landing. He pointed to the door beside him. "Here are your quarters. Yes—yes, very windy here. It's safer to sleep underground, and cooler too! The very windy days can be quite hot."

"Oh, cool," I smiled, then nodded for him to open the door. He led me into a generous chamber, lined with stone walls. More mosaic lightwork ran through the walls like gold veins in a mine. There was Momentum, sitting at a desk tapping his foot impatiently.

"Where have you been?" he asked, directing his question at me.

"I was just helping Winke," I said innocently and dropped the stack of maps on the desk in front of him. "Have you got something against me helping people, *master*?"

Momentum sniffed. "You can leave us, Winke."

"D—did you want to see the faerie in the cellar?" He stuttered nervously.

"Not now," Momentum barked. "Leave us!"

Winke bowed politely to Momentum, then to me, and then left.

I turned to the faerie and smiled, scratching my head. "Man!" I whispered, "Are we *lying* to these guys about who we are?"

"I'm afraid it's necessary," Momentum mumbled, rolling open a map. He seemed displeased with it, casting it aside, and opened another. "If I told them who I really was, I'd be in the wine cellar with the other poor faerie they apprehended."

I looked around the room. There were four tidy beds that were looking pretty inviting right about then. I was dog tired. "Yeah... is that because you're a faerie outlaw, or something?"

Momentum made a non-committal noise, "*Meh*, I guess. I haven't actually broken the law or anything—but I'm definitely on Somenus' list of most-wanted."

I plopped myself on a bed, kicked off my Jordans and laid down. "Oh yeah? What'd you do?"

Momentum glanced at me. "I... I think I scare him."

I shifted, looking at him with surprise. "Scare him? Why?"

He shrugged.

"You said you were the Faerie of *something*... are you the faerie of something, uh... special?"

I heard him chuckle. He leaned back in his chair, dropping the map to the desk and looked up at the ceiling. "*Every* faerie's title is special, Leon."

"Leo."

"So yeah, of course my title is special."

"Every faerie has a title?"

He nodded. "Faeries are different to humans like you. There's a set number of titles: a thousand. So only a thousand faeries can exist at a time, each taking up a title. So, like, Endring is the seventh Faerie of Vows. That means there were six other Vow Faeries before him."

"Wait... so there's only a thousand faeries alive in the world?"

"Less," Momentum said as he trilled his fingers on the desk. "I don't remember the last time all thousand were filled at once. Faeries are immortal, as in, we can live forever, but people don't really like us. We are hunted and hated in many places. But if there are vacant titles, then if a faerie child is born, they take up one of those titles. Get it?"

"I think so," I laid my head back. "So, the Faerie King... Winke called him the Nightmare Faerie. Is that his title?"

Momentum chuckled. "No. That's like a human folk name for him. He's been alive a *long* time." Momentum's eyes grew distant, as if calling back old memories. "Anyway, he's actually the II Dream Faerie—or Faerie of Affection, actually—but no one really uses that title anymore. Archaic, I guess."

"Dream Faerie..." I mumbled. Then my eyes widened as I became suddenly aware of that bulk of flesh stuffed into my pocket, pressed disturbingly against my body. I sat up in bed, unfastening the buttons on my coat as quickly as I could. I threw the coat onto the other side of the room. I heard Momentum exhale through his lips.

"Liam," he said dryly, "Don't throw my coat. It's one-of-a—"

"It's *Leo*!" I yelled. "And I'm *sorry*! I... that hand!"

Momentum leaned forward to examine his map.

"It's like it's still alive," I said quietly, "Why are you making me carry it?"

"Of course it's alive," Momentum said, "It's still part of him."

I snapped my head toward him. "You..."

"He's a *faerie*, Leon. He's got flesh like a human, but his life force doesn't come from blood; it comes from magik. While magik still flows through him, his body will remain alive. So that hand is just as much a part of him as it ever was."

I gawked. "Are you telling me that he can still... feel with that hand? Like—when I touch him?"

"Yes."

"Then why are you making me carry it around!" I bellowed.

"Will you please pipe down?" He slammed a fist on the table, "I am trying to concentrate! And I don't want you drawing attention to us!"

"Can he like—*hear* everything we are saying?" I stared across the room at the coat fearfully.

"It's a hand, not an ear!" Momentum scoffed. "Will you calm down?"

"*You're* scared of it, too!" I pointed an accusatory finger at him, "That's why you're making *me* carry it!"

He glanced at me out of the corner of his eye. "Look," he said, "It would be a very bad idea for me to carry it, but we can't leave it behind."

There was a knock on the door. Momentum motioned at the coat which laid on the floor, right in the main walkway. I reluctantly hopped off the bed, grabbed the coat, then held it as the door opened.

"I've got that food you asked for," Winke said with a smile. He was holding a tray of fruit.

"Fine," Momentum barked, "Put it on the table."

Winke trotted into the room and placed the tray on the desk. He peered over Momentum's shoulder curiously.

"Ah," he said, "Heading west from here?"

"Please mind your own business," Momentum mumbled.

"Of course. Uh," he backed away slowly, "Anything else you will be needing, my lord?"

Momentum looked up in my direction, then back at Winke. "Yeah—could you get a tailor to come here in the morning? My servant needs some... help."

Winke peered sidelong at me, then nodded. "Of course, yes. It will be done." Be bowed and left.

"You got something against my *clothes* now?" The bed made a creaking sound as I sat back down on it.

"I just don't want you drawing attention to us."

"I happen to like my jeans."

"You'll live." He turned back to his work.

I placed the jacket-covered hand at the foot of my bed, then laid down again.

"So, I'm a *servant* now? I thought I was your bodyguard."

"I demoted you."

"Hey," I sat up quickly, "If every Faerie has a title, what's yours?"

I saw the faintest hint of a smile creep up the side of his mouth. "Well," he said modestly, "I don't usually share that information with..."

"Come on!"

He leaned back with a grunt, then turned to me with a look of pride. "I guess you could call me the Faerie of Time."

"Faerie of Time?" I raised my eyebrows. Well, that sounded important. "Which, *uh...* number are you?"

He smirked. "My dear Leon," he said, "I am the *only* Faerie of Time."

6

——— Clover ———

The Fero Lands

Clover had wandered aimlessly for two days, with a herd of about thirty sheep in tow. He had taken a western path out of the Valley, as directed by Isabella's father, and that had taken him out of the Raqian Woodlands altogether. Two days in the belly of the mountains—they were dark and disorientating.

Halfway through the third day, Clover finally saw evidence of daylight in the distance. The sheep rushed ahead of him, glad for evidence of life. Sure, there had been food in the mountain tunnels. This was Raqia, after all: a land uncursed by Death. Food grew *everywhere*. But beasts like sheep craved the free air, and Clover could tell they were feeling lost with their new leader.

No doubt Isabella had worked for years to build a bond with them. Clover? Well—he was ashamed to admit—he had never made a bond with an animal in all his life! Other Elves did it all the time, but he never seemed to have that knack for getting beasts to trust him. It was a miracle the sheep followed him at all; Clover assumed they did so because Isabella—his angelic muse— taught them so well.

Clover used his spear to direct the ever-chaotic mass of sheep out of the tunnel, and into a circle under the bare sky. The geography was like nothing he had seen or even heard of. Clover had grown up in the Elder Copse, where one could barely even see the sky when encased in a world of thick trees. Here, there was almost nothing *but* sky. Red, sandy earth stretched out before him. The landscape in the distance was geometric and squarish, as if cut out by a brick plasterer. Two words could be used to describe the world Clover was in: dusty and red.

The sheep mulled around aimlessly, searching the ground for grass. Where was all the *grass*?

"Where *am* I?" Clover mumbled. He scratched his head helplessly; why wasn't there any life around? There wasn't supposed to be *any* part of Raqia without life!

One of the sheep plodded up to the Elf and peered at him. Andrew, the fat one; it was the only sheep Clover had thought to name, and that was only because he always hung around at the back, struggling to keep up.

"Do you know where we are?" Clover asked him, kneeling down. The sheep blinked its black eyes at him. No—Clover had never in his life heard an animal's voice. What would it even sound like when it happened? He didn't know. The garden gnome, who had followed along like a scavenger, raced up to Andrew's side and waved up at Clover.

"What do *you* want?" Clover grimaced. "Do *you* know where we are?"

The gnome tried to climb up Clover's leg but was kicked aside.

"No, don't," Clover snapped, "No free rides. If you want to come with us, you have to pull your own weight!" The creature admittedly didn't have any weight, but it was the principle of the thing! "Now... where do I go from here?"

The gnome did its best to try and jump, pointing fervently up at something on Clover's body. The Elf looked down, noticing the sack on his belt.

"Oh," he mumbled, "I guess I could ask that faerie for directions..." He reached for the pouch and pulled it open. There inside, curled up into the fetal position, was the sleeping Fae. His wings wrapped around himself like a blanket, and a silver chain, no thicker than that of a necklace, was attached to his ankle. Clover poked him.

The little Faerie grumbled, then sat up with a scowl.

"How long has it been?" he asked groggily.

"Since what?" said Clover.

"Since Timbre Wulf!"

"Oh. Two days?"

"You waited two days to open me up again? What's *wrong* with you?" The Faerie rose to his feet angrily.

"Was I supposed to open you?" Clover asked flatly.

"Yes! Any decent person would have thought, 'Oh, I have a living being in my possession. I should check to see if they are alright'!"

"Are you alright?"

"Well," he straightened his coat defensively, "Yes, I am fine. But really, you should be more considerate."

"Sorry."

"It's fine…" The Faerie, whose name Clover was pretty sure was Dezmund, looked around. "Where are we?"

"I was hoping you could tell me that," Clover said weakly.

"Right," Dezmund rubbed his chin. "The topography looks like the Fero Lands… but where's all the grass?"

"The Fero Lands?" Clover raised his eyebrows. "Where the Horse People live?"

"I don't think they like being called *the Horse People*," Dezmund said as he peered around, "But, yes."

"Are there really *horses* around here?" Clover asked excitedly. He had heard about the legendary beasts since he was a lad: they were the rarest beasts on their world.

"I don't know," the Faerie said, "Look. Why don't you head due west? I bet we can find the Fero City before long. Then, I can speak with their chieftain."

"What am I—your ox?" Clover pouted, "Just carting you around wherever you want to go?"

"Yes!" The little voice did its best to yell, "I am Dezmund: the XXIV Faerie of War! I'm probably the most important person you've even spoken to in your *life*! So, you will do what I command!"

"I hardly think that's true," Clover said blankly, "I just met Timbre Wulf," he gestured behind himself with his thumb, "And my father is King of the Elder Copse, you know."

Dezmund, taken aback, flinched. "Oh... well... *he is?*"

"Yeah."

"Well, *Hades,*" he tried to comb his hair back with his hand. "I'd rather speak with him than the Fero King. Why don't you take me to your home, uh—Prince?"

"I'm Clover," said Clover, "And no—I am not going back there. I left so that I could go on an adventure."

Dezmund stared hopelessly up at the Elf. "*Adventure?* Oh, Hades... you're one of *those*, are you?"

"Yes," Clover said proudly, "Whatever 'those' are. Anyway, I've got to watch these sheep for my true love. And I can't go back to the Valley..." Clover's voice trailed off as the realization hit him that he didn't know when he would see her again.

"...and?" Dezmund placed his hands on his hips.

"And... I don't know," said the Elf, "I'm sort of stuck not knowing what to do next. Isabella went to go find her brother Hanz, and—"

"Wait—Isabella? *She* is your, uh... true love?"

"Yes."

"Right," Dezmund rubbed his hands together, then mumbled, "I can work with this. Yes!" He clapped his hands together, "Clover—you want to see Isabella again, do you?" He had the same voice as a man coaxing a dog with a ball.

"Yes!" It worked like a charm.

"Well—listen up. I *work* with her brother Hanz, alright? And Hanz has a special task for her. Would you want to—erm—help her out?"

"Yes!" Clover said virtuously, "I would do *anything* for her!"

"Good, good," the Faerie rubbed his hands together, thinking. "Right. So, take me to the Fero Lord, alright? He can help us out. I just need to speak with him. Then we can help Isabella with her.... Quest."

"What's her quest?" Clover asked, holding up the little sack containing the Faerie closer to his face.

"We are part of the group of Faeries who are trying to overthrow the Nightmare Faerie, Clover. Isabella is going to help us bring him down."

"Oh!" Clover raised his eyebrows. "But what do they need *her* for?" Something deep inside the Elf felt angry at the idea of anyone pulling Isabella away from her safe and perfect Valley.

"Don't worry about that; just take me west and pull me out when you find the Fero Lord."

"But there's no food out here!" Clover said quickly, "Won't my sheep starve out here?"

"*Sheep?*" Dezmund looked around wearily at the flock. "*Hades*, Clover. Why have you got all this livestock?"

"Isabella asked me to—"

"Look, whatever," the faerie dismissed Clover with a wave, "Just take us to the Fero City. They'll have food."

⚬

Clover marched diligently westward, smiling to himself all the way. He was back on track! Isabella: the only thing that mattered. He would help her with her quest! He didn't exactly feel any personal need to take down the Nightmare Faerie, although from what he had heard, the man was definitely a despot. But if Isabella found reason to be a part of this plan, Clover might as well be a part of it as well.

The further west Clover traveled, the dustier and the redder everything got. Before long, he found what appeared to be a wayfinders tower. By the time their lumbering party reached it, night was setting in. At its base, there was a storage house stuffed with food.

"Oh, thank the Lights!" Clover said when he opened a hatch containing oats. He cupped his hands and fished some out, then turned to offer it to the clustering sheep. They took their turns eating from his hands. By the time Clover thought he had fed everyone, the supply of oats had greatly decreased. Clover, not wanting to be accused of theft, tossed his gold coin into the pile of oats, then shut the hatch.

The Elf walked a large circle around his flock, pushing them into a bundle with his staff. He had no idea if he had lost anyone, but he counted thirty heads, and that was how many he had started with. Once he was sure they were all lying down, bundled together like a big fluffy cloud, he ran up the spiral steps of the wayfinders tower.

From the top of the tower, Clover took in the landscape. Eastward, Clover could see the green mass of trees which was the Raqian Woodlands. Running through the center of that forest was a black, spiked mountain range. Somewhere amongst those peaks must be Paradise Valley. He turned his gaze westward, toward the wild lands. Not many ever journeyed this far. Amidst a cluster of umber mesas and winding plateaus, Clover spotted evidence of a city carved into the cliff walls. That must be the Fero City! He wasn't too far; it would take less than a day to walk there at his flock's pace.

Clover descended the tower then folded himself into the mound of sheep like butter in pastry, craving their warmth as the cool night set in. Once again, Clover was cold. What a strange feeling—to be cold!

The Elf stared up at the night sky. At its center, there weren't many star reflections; it glowed mostly of the same red that dusted the Fero Lands. The stars could only be seen where the Glassy Sea reflected the stars below Raqia, and that tended to be around the outer edges of the sky. Sometimes they could be seen directly above, but Clover didn't know why; his guess was that it tended to make a difference where you were geographically. For example, the one time he had visited Celestia, the night sky was completely covered with the starlight reflections. The sea—now that was a glorious sight. One day, he thought to himself, he would take Isabella there.

⚬

Clover opened his eyes to a dull, hazy, morning light. There was movement around him in his little sheep's nest, as the beasts began to wake. The gnome was curled up into a catlike ball on his stomach.

"Hey!" Clover barked, "Off!" The thing lazily rose, then slid down his leg just as Clover rose to his feet. "Alright, everybody up," Clover began to rouse his sheep, kicking them one by one. Where was his spear? "Time to go. Move. We are going to find the—"

Just as Clover turned westward, he came face to face with the disturbing perspective of the point of an arrow, aimed directly at his face.

"Stand down," said a voice. An archer stood, cranking back his bow and aiming at Clover point blank, in the face.

"What's wrong with you?" Clover grabbed the arrowhead and shoved it aside. The archer swung his bow back into place, stepping back.

"Hold still—I'll shoot!" he demanded. Clover took a step back and studied the soldier with a vacant and unthreatened expression. The man was a whole head taller than Clover, with a mighty build and heroically thick arms. With darkly tanned skin, and deep brown hair, the man was exactly how Clover had imagined a Fero man to look. He couldn't think why the man would want to run around on a chilly morning without a shirt on; the archer was clothed with only a cloth wrap around his waist, made up of strips of colored fabric. His face was stern, reducing Clover down to ashes with a deep glare. His jaw was wide and square, and clean shaven; and his eyes framed with a set of gentle crow's feet.

"What have you got against me?" Clover asked defensively, "We were just sleeping! Is no one allowed to rest at a wayfinder's point?"

"Thief!" the man barked, "You stole our food!"

Clover squinted in confusion, then said, "Well, I threw a gold coin in there; did that not cover it?"

"I didn't see a gold coin! Now put your hands high where I can see them!"

"Did you look in the hatch?" Clover asked angrily, "I threw it right—" his eyes caught a glimpse of the gnome, sitting on the ground, carving circles into the dirt with the same gold coin. "Damn."

"I said hands where I can see them!" The archer was speaking in a language Clover had never heard before. The Elf cocked his head to the side, listening, then raised his hands.

"I suppose you will need to take me to your leader?" he asked.

"Hah," The archer lowered his bow, hooking it over his shoulder. Rather than sheathing he arrow, he held it in his hand like a dagger pointing it directly at Cover. The red ribbon tied at the end of the arrow flapped in the wind. "I am the highest leader you are ever going to speak with, Thief! You're going to prison."

"What? No!" Clover reached out for the arrow, taking it by its shaft. "I need to speak with the Fero Lord!"

The archer yanked the arrow back, but Clover held fast. "Let go, or your sentence will worsen!"

Clover pulled back on the arrow, knocking the archer off balance. The man stumbled forward, giving Clover enough time to leap over one of the doodling sheep and grab his spear. He turned, holding fast to his weapon, then lifted his eyes in time to see the black frame of the archer's silhouette flying down at him from the air.

Clover struck the man's side with the length of his spear, hoping to spare him any injury. The man came at him from the side, tackling him to the ground.

"*Agh*—stop!" Clover complained as the man's body, which was twice the mass of his own, pressed him into the ground. Red dust began to rise around them as they wrestled against each other. Clover kneed the man's stomach, then wiggled out from under him and dashed away.

"Get back here, you little coyote!" the archer called, gazing around at the thick fog of earthen dust. Clover disguised himself as best he could in the disturbed atmosphere, searching with his eyes for his spear. "Come out—I've got your beast."

Clover's heart felt a surge of worry. "Which beast?" He called from the dust cloud.

"The one in the red hat."

"Joke's on you; I don't *care* about that one!"

"You want to put that to the test? I've got a knife to its throat!"

The archer was threatening an *animal*? How barbaric! "Fine!" Clover snapped, stepping forward with his hands raised high.

The archer was holding the gnome in his arm with a smirk. He had his arrow pointing back at Clover's neck.

"Come with me—you and all your..." he glanced at the surrounding herd, "livestock."

"Fine," Clover shrugged.

The archer picked up Clover's elegant, glistening spear and rotated it, watching as the morning light reflected off its golden bladed tip. Then he slammed its butt against the ground and said,

"Alright, let's go."

Clover and company were led down a path of dry, cracked earth. It occurred to Clover, after about a bell's worth of walking, that the gully in which they were treading had once been a river bed. Where had the water gone?

Before long, the Fero City came into view. Like towering skyscrapers above, jagged cliffs towered overhead, with windows and doors cut into their sides.

Clover's escort was joined by other warriors as they entered the city. The scene was spectacular. Ladders and bridges stretched across the maze of mesas, creating an intricate community of beautiful design. For a desert, it was quite colorful. Green plants, flowers and vibrant paint embellished the front of all the terraced residences and walkways, capturing the feeling of a secret walled garden.

As the archer led Clover into the city, they attracted a crowd of curious onlookers. Some peeked their heads out of the windows from above, while others came out their doors, lining the main stretch of road.

"Everybody looks so worried," Clover remarked as he studied the faces who watched him.

"Pipe down," The archer barked. He was leading Clover to some sort of pavilion, a circular plaza at the center of the city, paved with intricate sandstone designs.

"I need to see the Fero Lord," Clover said under his breath. More crowds seemed to be gathering as word no doubt spread about the strange visitors.

"You might get your wish," said the archer. He motioned to a few of the soldiers who began to round Clover's sheep up, leading them away.

"No!" Clover gasped. His heart pounded with anxiety—now *that* was a new feeling! "They need to stay with me!"

"They'll be fine," said the archer who took Clover by the forearm and yanked him forward. He threw the Elf on the ground, right at the center of the plaza. Clover's palms skidded against the rough stony ground. He looked up, watching as three other Fero people approached. Their faces were covered by clay masks, with circles cut out at the eyes.

"Hallo?" Clover snapped one of his feet onto the ground but remained in a one-legged kneel. "Are one of you people the Fero Lord? Please, I just want to speak to the Fero—"

"Who are you?" Asked one of the masks; it was blue, and behind it came a female voice.

"I—" Clover peered around. There were hundreds of people watching him now. "I'm Clover."

"You're an *Elf*?" The next mask asked; it was red. He didn't sound impressed.

"Well, yeah!" Clover huffed, "Is that... a problem?" Why on the table did everyone always act so surprised when they realized he was an Elf?

"Why have you come to our lands, Elf?" Asked the third, white mask. This was also a male, and he stood at the center, looking like the leader of the three. Was *this* the Fero Lord? What even *was* a Fero Lord?

"Uh..." Clover felt a little out of his depth, "I've got a Faerie who wants to speak to the Fero Lord."

There was an eruption of angry voices from those around him. He could actually hear the white-masked man gnashing his teeth.

"How many times do we have to tell Somenus' messengers: we will not bow to him?" The white mask roared.

Clover blinked. "Well," he said blankly, "I don't think my Faerie *likes* Somenus, if that helps."

The white mask glanced at the blue mask, then aimed itself back at Clover.

"What do you mean?"

"I mean," Clover refrained from an eye roll. "I think my Faerie wants to... sort of... *destroy* Somenus—or something."

"You *think*?" cried the white mask. "Where *is* this faerie, anyway?"

Clover reached for the sack on his belt. The sound of a thousand knives being drawn was pretty, but unnerving. Clover looked around peevishly, "It's just a bag," he said, "Can I open it?"

The white mask nodded, raising his hand in a command for his warriors to lower their arms. The archer kept a tight grip against Clover's shoulder, keeping him low.

Clover opened the bag. Dezmund popped out, shielding the blaring light from his eyes.

"Well," Clover said to Dezmund dryly, "I don't know if this guy is the Fero Lord, but I did my best."

Dezmund turned, finding the surface of the white mask, then cowered slightly. As menacing as it was to Clover, it must have looked apocalyptic to the tiny Faerie.

"Well?" The white mask asked, crossing his arms. "Who are you?"

Dezmund straightened, flinging out his wings triumphantly. Sadly, it wasn't as magnificent as it would have been, had he been his full size.

"I am Dezmund," he yelled, barely audible to the three masks, "the XXIV Faerie of War! I am a member of the Purple Order: the faeries who refuse to bow to Somenus' reign!"

The white mask and the blue mask exchanged some empty mask looks, then turned their attention back to Dezmund.

"Is that so?" asked the white mask. "And why have you come this far west—to us?"

Dezmund seemed to rally himself, tightening his little fists, "We plan to kill Somenus, and I need *your* help!"

This got a reaction from the three. They seemed to jostle with curiosity.

"Somenus has drained the life from our lands," said the white mask. "He has sentenced our people to death."

Clover's eyes widened. Was *that* why the archer was so protective of the food?

"Uncle!" The archer said suddenly. Clover jolted in surprise.

"Quiet, Yuma," The man in the white mask lifted his hand.

"If that is true, then you would be wise to help me!" Dezmund said, "We plan to put a new King on the throne: a good King. Once Somenus is dead, life will return to you; you will see water and crops again!"

"You have not said what it is you want from *us*, Dezmund of War."

"I need an army," Dezmund said darkly, "Faeries cannot kill—it is forbidden of us. I need a human army to combat Somenus' human army. Once we breach the Faerie city of Arelle, we can kill Somenus."

"Uncle!" The Archer said again, even more earnestly. The white mask wagged back and forth.

"And once you get into the Faerie city," the white mask said cautiously, "How do you expect to kill the man who—they say—can never be killed."

"A Faerie King *can* be killed, even one as strong as Somenus," said Dezmund bravely, "How do you think Somenus killed the *last* king, two seasons ago?"

"I am agog to know," the white mask said flatly.

Dezmund cleared his throat, "He had a weapon: a weaponed blessed by the first faeries. It is a bow that can kill anyone."

"And you plan to find that bow... and use it to kill Somenus?"

"Uncle!" The archer cried urgently.

"Yuma—wait!" The white mask slammed his foot against the ground. Clover could feel the restlessness emanating from the archer. He desperately wanted to speak.

"Please," Dezmund said, "Send an army with me, and we can give you back your lands!"

The man in the white mask bowed his head. "I cannot give you an army, small Faerie. I do not have an army to spare. We are a small nation, and I fear our numbers cannot compare to those of Somenus' army."

"Uncle!" The archer stepped forward, "There are those of us who do wish to fight. Send us—send us to attack Arelle!"

"Yuma..." The white mask sighed.

"We've watched our people fade for two long seasons of famine; I will not stand by and wait while there is something to be done!" Yuma the archer said firmly.

"As I said," the white mask directed his words toward Dezmund, "We do not have an *army* to send—but we may be able to send help. If it is an army you wish for, then you should seek out some of the stronger kingdoms which have resisted Somenus' rule."

"But most of the human kingdoms are giving in to him, and the Elves are refusing to engage!" said Dezmund.

"Not all of the human kingdoms have given in," the white mask said. He then took hold of the large, clay thing and lowered it from his face. The man behind the mask looked like an older, wrinklier version of Yuma, with two thick plaits running down his shoulders. His expression was weary, like someone who had grown accustomed to sorrow. "There is one place we thought to go to for help."

"Who?" Dezmund asked, then his eyes flashed. "Not... not *Bavel*!"

The man before him—the Fero Lord—nodded gravely.

"You sent an emissary to Bavel?" the Faerie asked in astonishment. Clover couldn't tell if he was horrified or impressed—perhaps both.

"Not yet," said the Fero Lord, turning to glance at the blue mask beside himself. "But we are down to our last few stores of food—we won't last much longer. We *will* starve. Bavel is the only other human kingdom we know of that hasn't bowed down to the Faeries. We thought perhaps they might help us."

"Bavel won't help anyone but themselves," Dezmund said coldly.

"Perhaps not," said the Fero Lord. He was watching Yuma carefully as he spoke. "But perhaps, with your help, we might be able to offer *them* something. If it is true that you know how to find a weapon that could kill the Faerie King, they might be willing to help. And as I am sure you already know, Faerie of War, no one on Raqia has a greater army than Bavel."

Clover watched for Dezmund's reaction with curiosity. Bavel was the greatest and strongest of all human nations, but they absolutely despised the Fae. Would Dezmund be desperate enough to go to *them* for help?

The little Faerie sighed. "My Lord," he said, "What you say is true. They do have the greatest army, and they do hate Somenus; but I am a Faerie, and Faeries are forbidden entry into Bavel. Since the city was first made, the gates of

Bavel were enchanted by the Faerie of Magik, preventing any magikal beings or items from entering it."

"Would it help you..." The Fero Lord spoke slowly; there was dread in his eyes, "if we sent someone with you... to act on your behalf."

"Uncle!" The archer could hold his tongue no longer, he knelt beside Clover, placing his hand over his heart, and said, "Please—send me! I have told you many times that I will not stay and watch our people die. I *must* go!"

The Fero Lord eyed his nephew. "You wish to... act as an emissary for this Faerie?"

"I wish to kill Somenus," was the man's reply.

Clover raised his eyebrows and peered around to see how the others reacted. The faces of those who actually heard Yuma's words were predominantly solemn. Dezmund turned his head sharply to stare at Yuma.

"I do not need you to do *that*," Dezmund said hastily, "We already have someone who is going to—*erm*—kill the king. But I do need someone to—"

"No!" Yuma barked. "I will kill Somenus; I will end my peoples' suffering."

Dezmund studied Yuma, then turned back toward the Fero Lord with a sigh. "If he is willing to take my message into Bavel, I will not hesitate letting him... kill Somenus."

Clover felt about as useful as the fifth leg on a table. He was holding the Faerie—so that was *something*—but he felt pretty superfluous. Perhaps table legs were undervalued, after all, he was able to be a part of something that sure *seemed* important, without having to do anything but kneel. But how was any of this helping Isabella with her quest? Dezmund had said they had someone picked out to kill Somenus. He didn't mean Isabella, did he?

"Well," The Fero Lord closed his eyes, speaking loud enough for all to hear, "Yuma, if you want to take up this charge to set our people free of Somenus' oppression, you may go with our blessing."

"Thank you, Uncle," Yuma said reverently, bowing his head low.

"Come," said the Fero Lord. He motioned for Clover to rise. "We will discuss the details inside." He looked around at those who had gathered. Hundreds of his citizens were watching anxiously. Clover wondered what it must feel like to be that man: to be the one leading a multitude of people toward death. Clover's stomach churned with something akin to nausea: it was guilt. It was not a feeling he ever wanted to experience again, and at the same time, he wondered if he would ever be free of it. Why had he fed his sheep all those oats? How many meals had he stolen from the stomachs of starving people?

Clover found himself pondering very dark things as he followed the Fero Lord into his hut. Starvation wasn't something he had ever given thought to. And why would he? Who could starve on a world like Raqia where food grew plentifully without coaxing? Everyone knew that the Faerie King could control the land of Raqia—but no one had ever dreamed he would use that power to destroy!

Yuma, Dezmund, the Fero Lord, and a few other important-looking Fero people sat around in a circle discussing plans. Clover, who quickly realized he was more ornamental than anything, found himself wandering around the outskirts of the room, examining the artwork painted on the clay walls. The homes in the Fero City seemed to be made of an orange, claylike plaster.

In this particular room, which was rounded and dome-like in its shape, the walls were lined with a narrative of drawings, sketched with white chalk. He walked a slow circle around the room, eavesdropping here and there on Dezmund and the rest, trying his best to understand the flow of the narrative of the wall paintings. There was farming; then some battles; then a whole bunch of swirls. Clover narrowed his eyes, looking closer at a particular character who seemed to show up pretty often in the story. He had a white mask, not unlike the Fero Lord's, and six lines emanating out from his center like six points in a star. There was another character, similar, with the six-star points, but it had a blue mask.

Something small scurried past Clover's feet. Looking down, the Elf spotted the gnome hiding behind his boot.

"Hey!" Clover whispered. He leaned down and snatched the thing into his arms. "Give me that coin!" He fished through the creature's mittened hands and yanked out his gold chip. There it was: clean as anything.

"Right!" The Fero Lord snapped his hands against his thighs, "Then I think we have an arrangement."

Clover watched as those in the circle rose from their kneeling positions and exchanged hugs and handshakes. Clover dropped the gnome, who dashed off into a corner. Dezmund, whose sack sat on the floor, turned to wave at Clover. The Elf plodded over and looked at the sack.

"Alright," Dezmund said through a long, drawn out, yawn. "Come on; pick me up."

Clover did as the Faerie asked, holding the sack up toward his face.

"Did you all make a... a plan?" Clover asked.

"Yes," Dezmund was rubbing his eyes.

"Are you sleepy?"

Dezmund snapped a look up at the Elf's face. "I'm not *sleepy*—I am drained!"

Clover's eyes narrowed into slits. "Are you going to explain the difference to me?"

"Don't you know what this bag *is*?" The Faerie pointed downwards emphatically.

"How on the table would I know?" Clover asked blandly.

Dezmund dropped his arms, exhaustion washing over him like a heavy rain. "It's a..." he yawned, "It's a prison. It's draining my... my magik."

Clover cocked his head to the side curiously. "It drains your magik? Does that mean you're dying?"

Dezmund rubbed his eyes again, like a toddler who is *sure* they're not sleepy. "Sort of," he said through another catlike yawn, "Yes. It will drain me to the point before death... I think; I hope."

"Can you..." Clover poked at the sack, "Can you *breathe* in there?"

"I'm not awake when I am inside," Dezmund said as he sat down cross-legged. "A person would go mad if they could be awake in one of these. But yes, I guess I can breathe."

"Can..." Clover looked side to side, as if he were about to ask about a forbidden subject, "Can Faeries *live* without breathing?"

Dezmund blinked. "I... I don't know! I can't think of anyone who has put it to the test. We can live without eating; I know *that.*"

Clover nodded slowly. "Well, that's nice."

"Well, look," Dezmund prodded the fabric beneath him, as if testing its comfort level, "It uses up my remaining magik staying awake, so you had better close up the sack and only open it when you absolutely *need* to."

"When will that be?"

"Whenever you get to the king of Bavel," Dezmund hesitated, "Or I guess... whenever you get out of Bavel. You can tell me what he said... or..." he stopped to yawn again, "or whatever."

"So, I am supposed to take you to the Labyrinth City?" Clover asked.

"Labyrinth?" Dezmund sniffed, "Oh. Oh yes, Bavel... yes."

"How am I supposed to get inside?" Clover asked with a furrowed brow, "Don't you need special invitations to get in?"

"Speak to Yuma," Dezmund was lying down, waving his arm dismissively at Clover, "He'll tell you the plan. He's to take you to someone who..." his eyes were closed now, his mouth barely moving, "Someone who..."

Clover closed the sack by pulling the drawstrings tight. He fastened the thing onto his belt and looked up to see Yuma, that stubborn archer, standing before him with his thick arms crossed.

"Well?" Yuma lifted his chin slightly, as a reminder that it was a privilege for Clover to be able to meet his eyes.

"Yes?" Clover shifted his weight from one leg to the other.

"We leave in the morning. Did you..." Yuma's lips pursed tightly, "Did you pay attention?"

"To what?"

"To our conversation; to the plan."

"Oh... no."

"What?" Yuma dropped his arms to his sides. Somehow, he seemed to grow taller. It was less intimidating than it was impressive. As much as Yuma seemed to want to make Clover shrink into his skin, Clover instead found himself wanting to admire the man. "You weren't *listening*?"

"No."

"Elf—don't you *care* about what's happening?"

Clover glanced to the left. "Care?" he asked. "I... *care* is a very strong word."

Yuma lunged forward, poking his nose condescendingly down at Clover. "My people are dying, and you don't *care*?"

Clover didn't flinch. "I didn't mean to cause offense; I was simply trying to be truthful. And truthfully, I care about almost nothing. It's a flaw, I think, but at the very least I try to be honest about that."

Yuma stared. "You—*what*?"

"Regardless of my emotions," Clover said blankly, "I am going to help you. I am going to *do* things; isn't that enough?"

Yuma shook his head, "What a depressing life you live, Elf."

"My name is Clover."

"That's even more depressing."

"Well," Clover shrugged, "Do you want my help or not?"

"Not really."

"Oh..." Clover glanced to the side. "Well, you see... I would *like* to come help you."

"Why?"

Clover suddenly felt himself standing on the outside of the house on a rainy day, looking in through a window. "Because... Because I want to."

"Listen," Yuma placed a hand on Clover's shoulder. Clover glanced at the calloused fingers which gripped him tightly, then back up at the archer's face which was bending toward him. "Has it ever occurred to you that your ability to not *care* about things is a privilege?"

"Um..."

"The fact that you've been able to live such a careless and uneventful life: do you know how privileged that is?"

Clover shook his head slowly from side to side.

Yuma sighed. "Clover, I don't need you to care about what's happening to my people. I just want to know that you are committed enough to go with us all the way, or I am not going to take you with me."

"I am," Clover said bravely, "I've got this girl that I—"

Yuma's face twisted with disgust. "A *girl*? Oh, lad…"

"What? You've got your people, and I have a girl. Isn't that… isn't that enough?"

Yuma withdrew his hand from Clover's shoulder and smirked, bobbing his head knowingly. "So, you've got a lass who wants you to what—perform a great deed or something?"

"Not exactly," Clover shrugged, "Well… maybe. She's gone on a quest to help bring down Somenus… I think."

Yuma was doing his best to keep a straight face. "Sure. And, *erm,* the sheep?"

"She's asked me to watch out for them, to prove my love, that it is constant."

"Mm," Yuma was stroking his mouth. "And you, *erm*… you think she was… you think she isn't messing with you?"

"Messing—?" Clover's mouth snapped open in horror. "What? *No*! Isabella is as pure as the Crystal Seas! She would never *mess* with someone; especially not someone who was deeply in love with her."

"Mhmm… Clover?"

"What?"

"Have you, *erm*… have you pursued many women?"

"No," the Elf crossed his arms defensively. "I've never been interested up until now."

"I see," Yuma had a look of jovial sympathy in his eyes. "Well. Clover, I am sorry you got dragged into all this—by a *woman,* no less—are you sure you want to continue, even if this woman isn't waiting for you on the other end?"

"What would be the point of proving my constancy if it could waver simply by the idea of being disappointed? Of course I'll do it!" Clover said ragefully.

Yuma's eyes sharpened, and he nodded. "Well, at least you're devoted, I'll give you that—poor lad."

"Don't *poor lad* me," Clover snapped, "I'm not a prisoner to my promise! I'm a very *willing* captive!"

"Fine, fine," Yuma turned, "Look, we will speak with the prophet tomorrow. He can confirm whether or not you are needed on our quest."

"Prophet?" Clover started. "You... you know a prophet?"

"I know a few," Yuma said, placing his hands on his hips.

"Really?" Clover took a step toward the archer. "Can I talk to him—or her?"

"I just said that we would," Yuma glanced at Clover sidelong, "What's gotten you so... Clover," he sighed, "Prophets are not fortune tellers: they are truth speakers. You're not planning about... asking about your *romantic interests*, are you? Clover, this is a very serious—!"

"I know," Clover said quietly, "I know it's serious; I just..."

"You just *what*?"

"I've always wanted to meet a truth speaker."

"Oh. Well..." Yuma hesitated, "Well, you're in luck. Tomorrow, we will set out and meet him. My companion knows how to find him."

"Your companion?" Clover asked, then blinked when he realized Yuma had walked out of the hut. He glanced around the room, then spotted the Fero Lord standing by a wall, gazing at the historic depictions. Clover meandered over to the chieftain timidly, walking aimlessly as he worked up the courage to talk to the man. Finally, the chieftain turned and offered Clover a smile.

"Yes?" asked the Fero Lord, "Did you want to speak with me?" The man had a kind face, and judging by his leathery skin, it had seen many seasons.

"Hallo," Clover said bashfully, walking in a crooked line toward the Lord. "I wanted to... *give* you something."

The chieftain raised his eyebrows with a smile. "Oh, yes? What is it, lad?"

Clover held out is one gold coin open on his palm. "I know it isn't much... but I took some food when I—"

The Fero Lord smiled widely and took the coin from Clover's hand.

"There's not much we can trade for out here, young Elf," he said, "But I thank you for the kindness. Kindness is something I never turn away."

Clover found himself smiling. "Well... anyway."

"Thank you for helping our people, Clover. You have brought hope to our dying lands; that is no small thing."

Clover's eyes brightened. "Really?"

The chieftain nodded. "You're doing a good thing by helping us. From what I know of the Elves, they do not get involved in human affairs."

"That's true," Clover said, "We mostly keep to ourselves."

"You are a credit to your race, then. Please—take care of my nephew," The chieftain seemed to gaze out into empty space, "He is the last symbol of strength our people have."

Clover peered curiously into the chieftain's face. "Aside from you?"

The man turned to regard Clover, blinking with surprise. "Oh... No...I'm not..."

Clover smiled. "It probably doesn't mean much coming from me," he said, "But I think you *are*."

7

—— Lola ——

The Vineyard Palace

Lola's body took shape in the physical world once more and she gasped, as if breathing air for the first time. The words from her vision—words spoken by her beloved—rang repeatedly in her ears like a reverberating bell.

Lola, he had said, *What have they done to you?*

Lola peered around at the startling scenery; her skin was glowing with a radiant warmth. She looked up toward the sky—there was no large celestial body shining down on her; no, it was the city which emanated light. It was Arelle, the Light City, whose buildings and architecture glowed like the stars, and it was beautiful. The flat, polished stone surface on which she stood must have been high, for as she looked around at Arelle's magnificence, it was mostly spires and clouds that she saw. Before her was a white, marble palace, shining like the Morningstar.

She was standing at the end of a long, rimless bridge. Lola turned to look for Felix, but neither he, nor evidence of the red portal were there. There was nothing but empty sky. She was standing at the edge of a drop off. In a City designed for Faeries, it must be a normal thing to have high landing platforms for winged, flying beings—but for an Elf like her, it was terrifying. Lola gasped and recoiled backwards, colliding into another body.

"*Hades!*" A woman cried, swinging her arms to find her balance.

"I am sorry!" Lola snatched the woman's arm, then held her steady. "Oh," Lola gazed at the woman's ear, "You're a human!"

"So?" The woman, dressed in a floor-length blue toga, snapped her arm free of Lola's touch.

"I'm sorry," Lola tucked her arm against her side, "I was expecting only Faeries to be here."

"Oh, Lights!" The aging woman gawked, "You're an Elf!"

"...Yes?" Lola looked side to side nervously, "I'm sorry, someone just pushed me through a glowing gate and—"

"Come on, girl." The woman seized Lola by the wrist and yanked her in the direction of the palace. "Let's get you inside." Lola stamped unevenly after the woman.

"Excuse me," Lola said, watching as the long braids dangling off the woman's wig swung behind her, "Where are we—"

"Let's get you inside, and I'll explain everything," the woman said without so much as turning her head.

Lola was led through an open-air pavilion. They weaved swiftly between massive pillars, and Lola noticed sculptures dotted throughout the scene, mounted up on pedestals. She stared, open mouthed, at the lifelike statues. There must have been at least twenty of them, striking unique poses, and painted in full color. Lola was surprised to see that they all had round human ears. Hadn't she just walked into the kingdom of the Faeries?

"Beautiful!" Lola said, pointing, as she passed one statuette. The frozen woman was draped in an orange toga with fabric that seemed to run down the pedestal and drape onto the floor. "So lifelike!"

The woman who had been trying to drag Lola through the pavilion sighed defeatedly, watching as the Elven Princess stepped up to the monument. The statue's eye shifted, gazing down at the princess. Lola gasped, stumbling backwards.

"It's not him," said the statue—who turned out to be an actual woman. She dropped her arms from their petrified pose and placed her hands haughtily on her hips. "It's just another tramp." She stepped off her pedestal and scowled, eyeing Lola with suspicion.

The hall seemed to erupt with motion as all the other figures came to life, climbing off their mounts.

"Oh," Lola smiled, chuckling to herself, "I thought you were statues, dear, me!"

The woman in orange snorted. "Don't you know where you are?"

"No!" Lola cried earnestly, "I don't!"

"Playing the innocent card?" Another voice said. Lola turned to see a woman in emerald green stepping up to her side, straightening the jewels on her cascading necklace. "An interesting tactic."

"Look, she's an Elf," said the woman in orange.

"What?" The green-clad woman balked, then stepped up to touch Lola's ear. The Princess cupped her hand over her ear protectively, shying back.

"I'm Lolette, Lola," she said cautiously, watching as the women clustered around her in curiosity, "I just arrived."

"Welcome to the Vineyard Palace," the woman in orange said with a smirk, "I am Lady Fayne of the Sapphire house, Fifth Level of Bavel."

"Oh, Lights!" Lola gasped, "You're a lady of Bavel? Were you abducted, too?"

Lady Fayne turned amusedly to those beside her and exchanged some jeering laughs.

"Where did you get this one, Alabaster?" Lady Fayne asked, turning to Lola's escort who was fidgeting with something in her belt. "She seems like a real card."

"What?" Alabaster, the wigged woman in her wearing years started, then sneered, "Oh, she was just standing on the landing. The watchman must have dropped her off. She's an Elf—look!" She pointed a long, painted nail at the Princess.

"I—" Lola eyed the crooked fingernail; it had chew marks on the tip. Had no one taught this woman how rude it is to point at someone's face? "I am from Celestia," she said bravely, "It a small coastal colony—"

"*Celestia*?" Lady Fayne started, "We know what Celestia is, girl! *Hades*— I didn't think the king was sending out as far as the southern coast!"

"I think King Somenus wants to govern all of Raqia," Lola said quietly, "Don't you?"

Lady Fayne raised an eyebrow as she studied Lola.

"Ladies," she said in a commanding voice, "Let's get this girl... assimilated."

Lola felt herself practically lifted off the floor as the group of two dozen or so women led her forward. She was carried through the palace, gliding down a long hallway, until she was brought into a large dressing room of sorts. A row of oval mirrors lined one wall, while a line of velvet-laced platforms lined another. The princess found herself placed at the center of one of the platforms, and gazed side to side as a few of the women surrounded her to examine her skirt.

"She's wearing a seven-layered Gramenlands design, with a Tradesmeet bustle," Alabaster remarked through her teeth; she had a smoldering cigarette sticking out of her mouth.

"Well, you're in Arelle now, *Lola*," Fayne was saying, standing a few paces back like the head of the pack that she was. "There's no need for layers when it comes to Faeries. They haven't got the same ideas about fashion and women's legs."

"Oh," Lola blushed, "Well, we don't worry too much about layers either—"

"And anyway," Lady Fayne cut her off; she was twirling some of her loose brown hair around her index finger, "Human men aren't allowed in the Vineyard Palace, so you don't have to worry about that. Only Faeries attend the banquets."

"Banquets?" Lola asked, turning hastily to the side in surprise as two of the other richly-adorned women began to dismantle her skirt. "What banquets? Where is the Vineyard Palace? Is this where the king lives?" Lola turned side to side, then found Lady Fayne's face in the cluster of women once more.

Fayne seemed to be pursing her lips in a calculating glare. "You can stop playing the fool with us, *Lola*, it won't work here."

"No, but," Lola felt her body grow lighter as the final layer of thick, billowy skirt was removed from her person. She stood there in nothing but her strapless white slip, feeling rather exposed. "But I really *don't* know where I am!"

"What did your father tell you," Fayne asked sharply, "when he explained where you were going?"

"What? He didn't! Father didn't send me away!"

Fayne stepped up to Lola fiercely, the others stepped aside quickly, parting the way for her.

"Like it or not," Lady Fayne hissed, "Your father sent you here. Deal with it: we all have! I know it might *hurt* to think of your old, caring man taking money and a title to be rid of you, but there it is! Life is disappointing."

Lola shook her head gravely, "No! I wasn't... *exchanged*... I was kidnapped!"

Fayne snorted. "Oh, stop. Stop your virtuous, innocent act. It'll only make enemies here. Now, every nobleman on Raqia is dying to get the invitation to send their daughter here; don't try and tell me your father is above it all."

"But my father hates King Somenus! He swears our kingdom will never unite with the Nightmare Faerie!"

A hushed reverberation of horrified whispers washed through the room. Lady's Fayne's face was one of sheer terror.

"Lola," she whispered, her eyes darting around hastily, "We don't call him that here."

Lola blinked. "I..."

Lady Fayne stepped up so close, Lola could smell her thick, floral perfume. "Who *is* your father, Lola?"

"He's..." Lola couldn't think of a reason not to be truthful, "My Father is King Antecus."

More suspenseful murmuring echoed throughout the room. Fayne's glare sharpened, and she stepped back.

"It's not fair!" a golden-haired girl on Lola's right pouted, "I've been waiting for weeks to be noticed, and now we have an Elven *Princess* to compete with?"

Fayne glanced toward the complainer with a grunt. "That's life, Garnet," she said, "Then again, it's not like you stood a chance before Lolette got here."

"Are you talking about competing for *Somenus'* attention?" Lola's eyes widened, "If so, you don't have to worry about competing with me! I have *no* interest in that man whatsoever!"

Fayne scoffed. "Oh, stop."

"I mean it!" Lola said firmly, "I've already got my heart set on the kind of man I want to fall in love with, and I can promise you; Somenus falls short!"

This got a reaction out of the listening crowd. They huddled closer to Lola in a snickering mass, with Fayne at their center. She had a predatory grin.

"Oh, *well*," she said mockingly, "Do tell us what sort of man you want to... *fall in love* with."

Lola could sense the woman's bullying nature.

"Someone..." Lola said courageously, "...worthy..." she paused; Fayne was yawning. Lola rallied herself, "And anyway, I want to marry someone who only has eyes for me—Somenus has multiple wives!"

"Oh, Lola," Fayne blinked lazily, "All men have wandering eyes."

Lola scowled, "Not all men have multiple wives!"

"What makes you think Somenus isn't worthy?" The golden-haired girl named Garnet asked from the sidelines defensively. Fayne snorted, shaking her head.

"He's a bully," Lola said sharply, "And a usurper... and he's been threatening my father for two seasons now; I want nothing to do with the man!" Silence followed as Lola stopped to take a breath.

"Well," Fayne broke the quiet with a yawn, "That's probably for the best."

Lola found Fayne's face with her eyes. "What? *What* is?"

"It is probably for the best that you keep your distance from King Somenus."

"Why?" Lola asked, watching Fayne's expression.

"Because the rest of us are fighting for his attention, and you just became the tallest poppy in the field. If you value your skin, you'd do best to stay back when he next comes."

Lola stepped off her pedestal and peered around at the women. "But why? Why are you all fighting for his attention? Isn't he... scary? Isn't he?"

"Lola," Fayne barked, "He's the king—of the *world*! He comes to dine here several times a week and selects *wives* from among us. Who cares if he's got other wives," she sneered, "but believe it or not, NO! He's not *scary*."

"He's *amazing*," Garnet said with glossy eyes.

Lola felt her face grow pale. "*What* did you say?" she whispered. "He selects wives from among us?"

"Lola," Fayne sighed, crossing her arms tightly, "Don't you know? The Vineyard Palace is a *harem*!"

A *harem*? Lola's mind grew foggy. She had been brought to a... a harem?

She felt herself staggering backwards. A few helpful hands caught her before she fell onto her backside.

"Oh gods," Fayne gasped, "She *didn't* know."

"I... I..." Lola stuttered. Her knees buckled helplessly. "I don't want to be here..." she mumbled incoherently. She fell backwards, losing the strength in her legs. There were a few yelps of surprise as the women watched her collapse onto the ground. At least five of them pulled out their fans and began to wave them at her as Lola touched her head gently with her fingers.

"Just breathe," Fayne said coldly, watching from above with her arms still folded together. "Damn."

"I–I–I want to go home," Lola's voice trembled.

"You can't," Fayne said dully, "I know it's hard to believe; but your father sent you here. Alright?"

"I want to go home," Lola said again, blinking out tears helplessly. She gazed up at Lady Fayne. The woman had her brown ringlet curls tied up into a beehive on the top of her head and two circular brass earrings framing either side of her face. She was staring coldly at the princess, shaking her head.

"Look," she said with a sigh, "We will help you settle in, alright? If you promise to stay away from Somenus, we will take care of you."

"You don't have to worry about that," Lola said wearily, "I want nothing to do with that man; I can promise you, Lady Fayne: you will not have to worry about me."

Lady Fayne closed her eyes, exhaling deeply. "Alright," she announced, "Ladies, let's get the princess dressed."

⸺ ◆ ⸺

Lola watched the evening unfold from a distance. She was sitting up in a private alcove which overlooked the main pavilion of the Vineyard Palace. It was like a thick bird's nest, woven together with the same vino vines that adorned the Palace like lace on a wedding gown. The Vineyard Palace was topographically the highest elevation in the kingdom of Arelle. What was once a white slab of pure stone, the tip of the lone mountain at the center of Arelle had been carved into a grand home. It was Greco-Roman in style, with flat ceilings, round, ribbed pillars, and shallow steps, descending into the rest of the city.

Its elevation was so high, that those who dwelled there could barely see the rest of the city, and seemingly dwelt among the clouds. Up there, where the light is pure and the glassy sky is close, the First Faerie of the Vine grew his vineyards. This Palace, which was once the lavish home of the first Faerie of the Vine, was now where Somenus threw his frivolous banquets and parties. Up there, where he kept his potential wives, sent as gifts from the Raqian nations, only his most trusted fae were allowed to go.

There were only two ways to enter the Vineyard Palace. The first was through the long, arduous length of steps which wove in endless switchbacks up the side of the white mountain; but hardly anyone ever attempted such a tedious climb. The second way, and really the only practical way, to enter the Palace was through flight. So, Lady Fayne wasn't wrong when she said humans never really went up there. Throughout Lola's time in the lofty, glowing halls of the Vineyard Palace, other than the human women who had been brought there, Lola would only ever see Faeries coming to visit. Why then, she wondered, did she not see Faerie women within the harem? Aside from herself, they were *all* human.

There was a long, bare sky bridge which jetted out of the Palace pavilion, suspended in the clouds. That was the landing platform, and that was the place where when the king did come to visit he always landed.

From where she sat, Lola had a good view of the landing platform, along with the main pavilion. Her legs were crossed at the knees as she leaned back into her wicker chair, and her little novella was cracked open in her lap. The other women in the harem had dressed her in a faerie dress, which seemed to be nothing but an unsewn length of white fabric, tied over one shoulder, and clasped together with a few brass clips; some at the waist, and some on the arms. Her hair had been pulled to the side in a loose plait and was woven with gold cords. They had tried to embellish her face with some of their glamorous paints and powders, but she had refused, believing the practice to be an exercise in worshiping beauty at the expense of truth.

The women of the Vineyard Palace were posed way down there on their pedestals, waiting for the king to arrive. There was to be a banquet on this Wingsday night—apparently there was *always* a banquet. Sometimes the king came, sometimes he didn't. Lola didn't personally want to meet Somenus, but she was definitely curious to see what he looked like. She peered around the sky, noting the little spires from the tops of towers which climbed high enough to be seen from Lola's elevation. She wondered what the rest of Arelle even looked like!

Lola gasped, clutching her book close to her chest as she spotted what appeared to be a black creature sitting on one of the tower spires, with four sail-like wings curling out from its center.

"What is that?" she asked, fearfully pointing a shaking finger toward it.

Alabaster, who was sitting beside Lola, slumped in another chair, pulled a cigarette from her mouth, turned it to peer at the dog-end, then flicked it over the railing. She blew out a cloud of vapor.

"Who, the watchman?" she asked, raising an eyebrow.

"That's *Felix*, isn't it?" Lola said in astonishment. Yes, she recognized those wings from the beach, where she was first abducted.

"You're on first-name terms with the watchman?" Alabaster spat a brown lump of saliva gracelessly onto the floor, then sat back.

"I, uh…" Lola turned, observing Alabaster cautiously as the woman pulled off her wig and scratched at her prickly, balding head. "Sort of."

"Gives me the creeps, that Faerie. Him and his… daemon wings." Alabaster flopped her wig back onto her head and smiled cheerlessly through her grey teeth.

"Does he ever come to the banquets?" Lola asked.

"*Hades*, no. And thank the fortunes he don't! Then we'd have to be civil to him!"

Lola wondered momentarily how a woman like Alabaster came to be in her current position, then redirected her thoughts toward more pleasant places.

"When does the king usually arrive?" Lola asked. "And why does everyone pose like that?" Lola stood, gazing down at the array of women. Really, they looked exactly like a bunch of statues!

"He comes when he comes," Alabaster said. Even when Lola was leaning over the edge, on the opposite side of the alcove, she could *still* smell the woman's breath. "And the ladies is like…" she hesitated, "…*Are* like pretty dolls. You know, the king can see who he fancies to have on his arm for the evening, and then they go with him into the banquet." She shrugged.

"So not everyone is invited to the banquet?" Lola asked, looking back at the maid… or chaperone, or whatever Alabaster was supposed to be.

Alabaster shook her head. "No. Being in the king's harem gives these women a *chance* to be noticed, but it's never guaranteed he's going to marry any of them." She poked her newly lit cigarette in Lola's direction, "I hope your father knew that when he made the deal! There's no *promise* of becoming one of the king's wives!"

"Well, I don't *care* to be one of his wives!" Lola said with a scowl, "So you can let that thought rest!"

Alabaster made a shrug that said, *As if I care.*

Lola sat back down on her wicker chair, braving the cloud of scent that seemed to hover around Alabaster's person, and cracked her book back open.

"She came forward within a yard of me," Lola read aloud, "and said, in a voice that strangely recalled a sensation of twilight, and reedy river banks, and a low wind, even in this deathly room, 'Anodos, you never saw such a little creature before, did you?'"

"Wait, who said that?" Alabaster asked after pulling deeply at her tab.

"The Faerie," Lola said impatiently, dropping her book into her lap.

"Wait—the one in the drawer?"

"Yes! Now, you need to listen if you are going to get the full effect of the story!" Said Lola. Alabaster was probably the last person to appreciate a good Faerie novel, but beggars, Lola reminded herself, could not be choosers; and she preferred reading aloud than in her mind when others were present.

"Who is Anodos?" asked the leathery woman.

"He's the main character!"

"What kind of a name is Anodos, anyway?" Alabaster leaned forward to spit again, adding to the growing puddle between her sandals.

"'No,' said I; 'and indeed I hardly believe I do now!'" Lola continued determinedly, "Ah! That is always the way with you men; you believe nothing the first time; and it is foolish enough to let mere repetition convince you of what you consider in itself unbelievable. I am not going to argue with you, however, but to grant you a wish."

"Grant *who* a wish?" Alabaster whined.

Lola leapt to her feet, gasping excitedly. "Look!" She pointed. A flutter of four graceful wings sprung into view from below the clouds. Daylight seemed to reflect off his black, luminous wings. Though spiny and batlike, there was a surprising element of beauty to them. "Is that him? Is that the Faerie King?"

Alabaster spat loudly, then stood, peering. "Yeah, that's him."

Lola was reluctant to admit to herself that even from afar, there was a certain elegance to the king. She couldn't make out his face from this distance, but the way he walked, and the pace of his stride: there was a glory to him.

The princess watched intently as other faeries flew to the landing place, then strode down the runway. The king, leading the party, meandered around the colorful statutes, seemingly browsing. For a moment, Lola thought he was looking for something he couldn't find. He walked from one row of statues to another, and then back again. Then he stood, motionless, for a moment, running his hand through his black hair. What expression was he making? He began pacing again.

Lola saw him stop by Fayne's pedestal and hold out his hand. She stepped down gracefully and walked beside him into the inner palace.

"So... is she going to marry him?" Lola found herself asking.

Alabaster snorted. "What? Hades if I know!"

"But he took her to the banquet!" Lola turned, regarding the woman.

"That just means he's *interested*. If he takes her back to the Eight Stones, then I guess that counts as..." she snickered, "*marriage*."

Lola wrinkled her nose squeamishly. She didn't like what the woman was implying. Somenus was said to have over a hundred wives—had he never actually *married* any of them?

"Are you saying that he...?" Lola found she didn't want to finish her question.

"What do you *think* a king does with his concubines?"

Lola blanched, then turned away. "I really couldn't say," she mumbled.

"Well, I can tell you—"

"Please!" Lola snapped her head back, glaring at the woman. "Let's leave the discussion there, shall we?"

Alabaster shrugged, then continued to smoke as if there were no need to breathe tomorrow.

Well, what now? Lola wondered to herself helplessly, What am I supposed to do?

⁘ ⁘

That evening Lola finally found sleep in her quiet, windy chambers. The women of the Vineyard Palace slept in generous private quarters, with large open pillar-lined balconies. Arelle had a perfectly warm and comfortable climate, even way up in the clouds where Lola's room was, so she didn't mind the breeze washing over her, lulling her to sleep.

The princess sat up suddenly in her bed, waking to a voice calling from outside.

"Lola!" She heard it again. It was the voice of a man; the most familiar voice she had ever heard, and yet she could not place who it was. She leapt out of her bed; she could not stop herself. It was as if she could not control her own body. Arms shaking, she ran towards her large open window. There was nothing but a drop off before her. The voice called again. "Lola! Are you there?"

"It's you!" she cried back, as if reciting lines she did not remember memorizing. A feeling of overwhelming relief filled her being. Yes, it was the voice of her beloved; if only she could remember who he was! Lola dropped down onto her knees and peered over the edge of the cliff-like drop. A figure was climbing up the side of the wall. If she could just see his face, she knew she would remember him fully.

"Beloved!" she cried, "I'm here!"

She knelt by the window, reaching her arms down toward the figure who seemed to struggle in the dark, missing a foothold. "Just a bit further, beloved!" she cried, "Just a bit further, and I will see your face!"

He lifted his head, and just as the light seemed to begin to illuminate it, she heard another voice. This voice—this unfamiliar, comforting voice—came from behind her.

She stopped for a moment, feeling suddenly chilled, and turned around. There was nothing but darkness behind her. She thought it had said her name. She looked around, searching for its source, then quickly chose to forget it. She thrust herself back toward the window shouting, "Beloved, beloved!"

❦

Lola sat up suddenly in her bed, drenched in sweat. She looked around hurriedly, barely acknowledging that what she had just experienced was a dream. No, it was too real. She bolted toward her window and cried out at the top of her lungs, her throat aching, "Beloved! Just a bit further, and I will see your face!"

There was no response. Her eyes darted around, desperately searching the darkness. Lola flung one of her legs over the side of the drop off, then bit her lip. *What am I doing?* she thought. *It was a dream!*

Before Lola could even think to pull her leg back up, a gust of wind suddenly blew hard against her. She tried to lift her head to see what caused it, but the presence was quicker than she was. She felt a tight grip wrap itself around her arm which suddenly lifted her, as if weightless, and threw her across her room and onto her bed.

Lola cried out in shock as she lifted her head to see none other than Felix, the Faerie of Sight, standing in the large opening of her window.

"Felix!" she gasped angrily, "Why did you—?"

"—save your life?" The Fae said blankly. "You would have died instantly if you had fallen off that height. What in Hades were you doing?"

"I thought someone was down there," she hesitated, realizing how foolish it sounded. "I mean..."

He pulled the corner of his mouth to the side. "No one is there. As I am sure you could guess, it's pretty impossible to climb a wall of solid polished stone. You were dreaming."

"Well, I know that now." Lola hugged her body with her arms, feeling suddenly exposed. There was a man in her room! "Can you please leave?"

"Fine," Felix turned and marched toward the ledge, priming to leap.

"Wait!" Lola reached out her hand.

"What?" Felix turned slightly, whipping his ratty black locks to the side.

"Why did you bring me here?" she asked timidly, lowering her hand. Felix turned to face her head on.

"I was told to."

"By Somenus?"

"Yes."

Lola bit her lip. "You can fly... could you... take me back home?"

Felix made no facial reaction to the question; he simply said, "No."

Lola felt foolish for asking. She turned her head to the side, avoiding eye contact. "Felix?"

"What?"

"I think I... I think I saw things when I went through the portal." She stole a glance at his face. His eyes seemed to glow with curiosity.

"What did you see?" he asked.

"Is it possible to see the future?"

Felix drew his chin high into the air so that she could not see his eyes. "I... am not sure."

"Is it possible to see someone you haven't met yet?"

Felix lowered his eyes and studied the princess. "Yes. What did you see?"

Lola sniffed primly and turned her eyes away from the faerie. "None of your business."

"Look," Felix sighed, taking a step back toward the window's ledge. "You might get..." he hesitated, "...*dreams* here. Don't pay too much attention to them. And stay away from the window's ledge."

"Fine," Lola said sharply, still keeping her gaze to the side.

"And Lola?" Felix said darkly.

"*What*?" She snapped her face toward the man.

"Don't miss any more banquets."

"What?" she frowned. "Why do *you* care?"

"It's not about me," Felix snapped, "Just be there next time, that's an order!"

"Well, what if I don't?" She threatened childishly.

Felix shook his head. "Please," he said, "Don't test me."

Then he was gone.

8

—— Isabella ——

The Purple Order

Y ou still haven't told me where we are going!" Isabella whispered. She was huddled close behind her brother Hanz, holding tightly onto a bit of his cloak as if it were a lifeline in a raging sea.

"I'll explain everything soon," Hanz said confidently as he raced through the trees. Everything around them was dark, but Isabella could see a faint purple light glowing from the top of Hanz' staff. That staff. She recognized it; it was her father's staff.

"How did we escape the village?" Isabella couldn't help but ask, "How did no one see us?"

"Everything will be known."

They were trudging through a little stream, running along its length and splashing as they went; Isabella's feet were drenched and growing cold. Isabella wasn't sure why Hanz chose to run only in the shallow waters, rather than the dry earth; surely it didn't mask their footsteps enough to be untrackable!

After some length of time, when the night seemed to be reaching its darkest point, Hanz came to a halt. He passed Isabella his staff.

"Hold this," he said, "Keep the light low so I can see."

Isabella reverently held the black, slick staff. It seemed to be nothing more than a blank black pole, as it always had been, but that purple light at the end—that was new! She held the tip low to the ground as Hanz pushed a pile of dead leaves to the side, unveiling a trap door.

"Here," he mumbled, yanking open the hatch. "Get inside."

Isabella peered behind her into the darkness. "Are you sure we haven't been followed? That... that man..."

"Get in! We're not being followed," Hanz said in a hasty whisper. "In!"

Isabella ducked low, then carefully climbed into the hatch. She slipped, skidding down the first few steps on her backside.

"Careful!" she heard her brother call from above as he closed the hatch. They were in a dank, narrow stone stairwell. Isabella clung to the damp steps, watching as the staff clanked down below. Its purple light dimly illuminated a long, eerie descent.

"Where are you taking me?" she asked fearfully.

"Don't worry, Ella," Hanz touched her shoulder, scooting down toward her. She flinched, then relaxed into his touch. Staring down at the ominous staircase, watching as the purple light continued to drop, Isabella sighed.

"Hanz," she whispered, "I think I'm scared."

"Me, too," said her brother, "But the worst is over."

"Who was that man?" she asked. She could not get the image out of her mind of that gigantic beast of a man standing there in her village square at night.

Hanz was silent for a moment, then he said, "Do you mean Korbin?"

"I mean the giant," Isabella said with a tremble.

"Come on," Hanz found her hand in the darkness, "Let's get down the steps and talk about everything in the light. These are the kinds of conversations better *not* had in darkness."

Isabella set her jaw then nodded.

"Right," she said bravely, "Let's go."

She carefully rose to her feet and began to descend. It was one of those mind-over-matter things, where Isabella had to convince herself that, no, she was not descending a staircase into the empty bottom of the table, and no, there were not worse evils waiting for her once she reached the bottom.

When they finally reached a landing, Hanz pushed open a door. And there was light within!

Isabella gasped with excitement as she burst into the room. They seemed to be standing in an old cellar of sorts, with arched ceilings and domed passageways. The air was thick, and Isabella guessed there wasn't much ventilation in a place as low as this, but there were plenty of torches lit and lining the walls, so there was definitely air!

"It's me!" Hanz announced as he entered the chamber. He pulled his heavy hood off of his face. He was holding his staff now; Isabella guessed he had procured it from the bottom of the stairs where she had dropped it. She gazed at her elder brother in wonder; he looked so much like her father when he was holding that staff. And when had he grown so tall? His wavy black hair was tied back in a tail, and his brown skin glistened in the warm lighting. His face—he was handsome, with a strong jaw, and that signature crooked nose, though without his father's beard, he looked a great deal younger. It had been two seasons since she had seen him; she had grown too. Isabella blinked, realizing that he was studying her as well.

"Isabella," he said softly, "You're a woman now."

Isabella was embarrassed to find herself blushing. "Hanz," she murmured, tucking some stray hair behind her ear. "Stop."

Her brother sniffed awkwardly, turning to the side. "I am sorry to have dragged you away from the Valley. I didn't know if Dezmund got the message to you..."

"He didn't *really*," Isabella tightened her teeth together nervously, "Some Elf had him in a bag and—"

"A *bag*?" Hanz gasped, "You mean he was captured?"

Isabella shrugged her shoulders. "Hanz, I have no idea. I am in the dark, as always! I need you to explain to me what's happening; why are we here? Why did you come back for me? Why did you leave two seasons ago?" She was quickening the pace of her questions faster than a peddler on the verge of losing a sale.

"Isabella," Hanz chuckled, reaching toward her with an open hand, "Slow down! Come, come in," he turned motioning to a table in the room. Isabella blanched, realizing there were others in the room. She felt herself growing smaller as she shuffled forward, with Hanz guiding her, his hand against her back. Three other conspicuous characters seemed to be sitting around a low wooden table. "Don't be shy, these are friends," Hanz said in that confident, older-brother tone.

"I'm not shy," Isabella whispered, her cheeks growing hotter. No! She wasn't just the *little sister* anymore; she was a grown woman! She straightened her back and managed to make the last few steps toward the table solid and defined.

"Isabella," Hanz said in a wide smile, "These are some *very* good friends. Friends," Hanz addressed the table, "This is she: this is Isabella, my incredibly talented and *beautiful* sister!" Isabella didn't love the introduction, but it was nice to hear her brother praise her so. Hanz, he was always so charismatic. She glanced at her brother's smiling face; he could charm a pack of wulves!

The three figures rose, pulling down their hoods in a single, seemingly-choreographed motion. Isabella recoiled slightly, noting that all three of the others were faeries, with long pointy cleft ears. There were two men and one woman. They all seemed to study Isabella with judging eyes.

"Isabella," Hanz said encouragingly, "We are the Purple Order. Sit, sit!" He pulled out a rickety chair and patted its dusty base. Isabella sat warily. Hanz sat beside her, leaning forward onto the table eagerly. "Right. Introductions!"

Isabella peered around at the three faeries. At first, she feared they might pounce on her, but as she calmed herself with some steady breaths, she came to realize that it was they who were more afraid of *her*.

"This," Hanz reached across the table and tapped the hand of the first male Faerie, "is Tristan. He's the Eleventh Faerie of Water, eleventh of his kind— you know how that works?"

Isabella nodded slowly. "Yes," she said quietly, "I think so."

Tristan, Faerie of Water, lifted a timid hand to wave and rocked it back and forth in Isabella's direction. His stunned eyes seemed to look past her rather than at her. He had pale skin and colorless shoulder-length hair, pulled to the side, with crystal blue eyes. "Hallo, Isabella," he said in a voice like a perfectly still lake.

"Hello, Tristan," Isabella smiled. If Hanz could be calm and confident, so could she!

"Tristan helped us get here without being tracked," Hanz said proudly, slapping the Faerie jovially on the shoulder. "He's a master, and *truly* one of the greats! Tristan was there in Arelle, right in the middle of the Eight Stones when Somenus took the throne, weren't you, Tristan?"

"I, uh... well," Tristan sputtered modestly.

"And this is Angel, the twentieth Faerie of Sound. He was also *invaluable* in getting us to and from Nemus without being tracked," Hanz said emphatically, slamming his palm on the table several times. Angel, a trim, brown-haired faerie with a face that seemed to always gravitate towards a smile shook his head amusedly.

"Oh Hanz, will you stop?" He winked at Isabella. "Hello, child. Welcome to the Order."

Isabella examined the man curiously. "Hello..."

"And *this*..." Hanz grinned across the table at the woman who shook her head knowingly at Hanz. "This woman is the pride of the Order, and quite possibly the most *impossible* Faerie I've ever met," he belted a laugh, "Isabella, this is Riah. She is the third Faerie of Illusion. You can't trust a thing this woman says," He winked across the table at her, "And yet there is no one else I trust more on this entire, *felling* table of a world."

Riah nodded at Isabella silently. She had eyes of an indistinct color, but they seemed to glow. Her dark hair rolled down her left shoulder like a waterfall, and Isabella thought to herself that despite this woman seeming a tad unsettling, she was, by all accounts, lovely in appearance.

"So," Isabella said, turning to Hanz, "The Purple Order. There are four of you?"

Hanz laughed. "No, no. This is our scouting team. Well..." his countenance fell, "minus Dezmund."

"Where's Dezmund?" Angel asked sharply.

Hanz turned to Isabella. "Did you say he had been put in an Exilium Prison?"

"What?" Isabella blushed at the attention. "I... I don't know what that is, but when I saw him, he was in a little bag."

There was a murmur of discomfort at the table as the Faeries exchanged whispers.

"He said that someone named Korbin had taken him," Isabella added.

"Wait—" Tristan, the cautious one, leaned forward, "If Korbin took him, then how did you speak with him?"

Isabella glanced at Hanz who nodded, signaling for her to be truthful. "Well," Isabella said, "An Elf said he found the bag, and he had brought it into the Valley, where my family lives."

"So, Dezmund *isn't* with Korbin?" Riah, the silent female Faerie asked.

Isabella shook her head. "I don't think so," she said, "He is with my father."

"Then he is in good hands," Hanz said with an air of finality. "We can discuss Dezmund's part of the plan later. Right now, we need to focus on the task at *hand*!"

"The girl's barely gotten here," Tristan said, "Are you sure you want to—"

"Isabella has lots of questions," Hanz said quickly, "Don't you, Ella? So I think we should all do her a favor and answer them. Then we can give her some time to... think about what she wants to do."

Tristan leaned back with a shrug. "You're the boss."

"So," Isabella said cautiously, "The Purple Order?"

"Right!" Hanz stood, thrusting his hands on his hips. "Isabella:, we are the Purple Order, the Faeries who have refused to bow the knee to Somenus, the usurper. Those who defy him are being hunted and killed. So! We have banded together to fight for survival, and to bring down this evil reign!"

"But you're not a Faerie," Isabella said dryly, gazing up at her brother. "Why are you in the Purple Order?"

"Hanz isn't in the Purple Order," Riah said, "He *is* the Purple Order."

Isabella turned to regard Riah, who seemed to stare indistinctly at her. "What do you—?"

"Two seasons ago," Riah said in a voice both soft and sharp at the same time, "Somenus came to the Eight Stones with a human warrior at his side. They had a legendary weapon, and with it they killed King Sol the II. I was there. Tristan was there," she pointed to the Faerie on her right, "And as they killed everyone there, one by one, we fled."

"Eight Stones?" Isabella asked timidly.

"That's the Faerie King's House," Hanz informed her kindly, "Sort of the main Palace in Arelle."

Isabella nodded slowly, "If Somenus is so powerful, and he killed so many with this... legendary weapon. How did you escape?"

"Somenus didn't kill," Riah said darkly, "His human warrior killed, Faeries can't kill. Don't you know that, human?"

Isabella raised an eyebrow at the feistiness. "Sorry for the confusion," she said coolly, "I do know that. So—how did you escape? And the human warrior," she glanced toward Hanz, "That wasn't... Korbin, was it?"

Hanz nodded gravely. "You are spot on, sis," he said, "Korbin came wielding an ancient bow."

"Orion's Bow," Riah added, "I *know* it was Orion's Bow."

Isabella wanted to ask what on the table Orion's Bow was, but Hanz spoke too quickly.

"Now here is the odd thing, Isabella," he said, "Somenus apparently died a thousand seasons ago, in a famous Faerie war where he tried to seize the throne. And he almost did take the throne all that time ago. But he lost. Can you guess how?"

Isabella shook her head. "I don't know much about Faerie wars," she said.

"It's a shame," Hanz said darkly, "Do you know why? Because a thousand seasons ago, King Sol II had his own human hero, and *his* name was Timbre Wulf."

Isabella looked side to side in disbelief. "Wait—you're not saying... *Papa*?"

"Papa is Timbre Wulf," Hanz said, "One of the oldest and greatest of Raqian warriors."

"But he's human!" Isabella said in disbelief. "No. There's no way he could live a *thousand* seasons!"

"He can if he is a Friend of the Fae," Angel said matter-of-factly, "A Friend of the Fae can live as long as his protecting Faerie lives."

Isabella turned her head sharply in Angel's direction. "You mean, father has a Faerie's protection?"

"He had many," Hanz said, placing his hand on Isabella's. This action seemed to ground her. It was a lot to take in, but she could handle it! "Papa isn't protected anymore; he asked to be free and live his own life after a time. He made a home in the Valley, got married, hence *us*."

"And he never told us any of this..." Isabella muttered to herself.

"Well," Hanz sighed, "I can't exactly blame him; he wanted to be free of his past. But his past came and found him again." Hanz glanced at Riah, signaling for her to continue the narrative.

"Tristan and I survived because of my powers of illusion," Riah said, "and when we escaped Arelle, we went directly to find Timbre Wulf. He was the only human who had ever fought Somenus and survived."

Isabella's eyes widened. "So, two seasons ago... when I saw Papa speaking with some mysterious visitors..."

"That was us," Riah said, "He turned us away. In the time of our greatest need, he turned us away."

Isabella glanced at Hanz. His eyes were staring off into the indistinct air.

"I was there," Hanz said, "Papa explained to me that he had made a vow never to kill for the Faeries again. I... it felt wrong to me, to leave the Faeries with no human help."

"So, what did you do?" Isabella asked in anticipation.

Hanz exhaled slowly. "Well, I took Papa's staff. It was a weapon given to him by the Fae. Blessed by the Fae. I told him that if he would no longer take up the name of Timbre Wulf, then *I* would... He did not stop me. I left with Tristan and Riah that night."

"Why didn't you tell me?" Isabella asked, feeling an old anger surface unexpectedly, "Why did you leave without saying *goodbye*?"

Hanz turned to regard his sister with a look of sorrow. "Ella," he said, "You were still in the age of questioning at the time; Papa didn't think you were ready to know about all this. I felt it would be easier for you if—"

"Well, it wasn't!" Isabella snapped, "It *wasn't* easier!"

Hanz sat there silently. "One day," he finally said, "I will ask for your forgiveness. But first, I must transgress you further."

Isabella leaned back in her creaking chair, "I guess that is the big question," she said, "Why have you come back for me?"

"Well," Hanz glanced at the other Faeries. "Here is the thing. Riah, Tristan, and I—with the help of Papa's staff—have made it our mission to round up and protect all the Fae who have fled Somenus. Together, we plan to kill Somenus and put a good king on the throne."

"How many Faeries are in the Order?" Isabella asked.

"Almost a hundred now," Hanz said excitedly.

"And they... they all follow *you*, Hanz?"

"We follow *Timbre Wulf*," Riah interjected. "He is a symbol of strength to the Fae. He is the warrior who destroyed Somenus the first time, and he will do it again."

Isabella gazed at her brother. "Hanz," she said quickly, "*You* are going to kill Somenus?"

Hanz smiled proudly, then nodded. "Yes, Ella. I am."

"With Father's staff?"

"No," Hanz sighed, seating himself in his chair. "No. It's not that easy killing a Faerie King. He's got the Faerie crown powering him, and everything. No, we need something really powerful in order to kill him."

Isabella pursed her lips. "Right," she said, "that legendary bow, I'm guessing?"

All four of the Purple Order members nodded together unevenly.

"That's where *you* come in," Hanz said, growing tense. She could tell by his face that he was going to ask something impossible of her; it was a look she had seen him make many times in their youth when he was about to get her into trouble.

"Alright," Isabella shook her head, grinning, "Let me have it: what do you want from me, Hanz?"

Hanz leaned across the table; he gazed intently into his sister's hazel eyes.

"I need that bow," he said fervently as he peered seemingly into her soul.

"And... I am supposed to get it for you, somehow?" Isabella asked with an eyebrow suspiciously raised.

Hanz rotated his head to look at Riah, then nodded once. Riah rose and left the room.

Hanz straightened to his feet and strolled around the table to Isabella's side.

"We've been trying and trying to get that bow, but everyone we send to steal it from Korbin never comes back. He somehow always finds our spies. No—he is too suspicious of Faeries!"

Isabella didn't like where this was going; she already hated Korbin, and she would be glad if she never thought about him, much less *saw* him again!

"I don't think..." she began.

"Just let me finish," Hanz spun to face her, "Just... hear us out."

Isabella stood in alarm as Riah dragged a lifeless body into the room.

"Who is that?" Isabella asked fearfully. She watched as Riah dropped the body of a female woman onto the floor. She wasn't stiff enough to be dead, but she was definitely unconscious. Isabela crept toward her hesitantly. The woman laid there in a crooked state, dressed in charcoal black leather armor. Her black hair was pulled into a high tail, and she wore—to Isabella's shock—*trousers*, with long, knee-high boots.

"This," Hanz said as he walked to where the woman lay, "is a bounty hunter."

Tristan and Angel joined their circle, gazing down at the unconscious body. Isabella noticed three of the sacks—just like the one Dezmund was in—attached to the woman's belt.

"Bounty hunter?" Isabella looked to Hanz for answers.

"Korbin has been hiring humans to hunt down Faeries. This one captured three of us before we managed to bring her down. Riah, show her." Hanz gestured to Riah the Illusion Faerie.

Riah knelt down and pulled open the woman's knapsack. Out of it she took a letter, and a round gold seal. She passed the seal to Isabella who examined it. A crest was impressed upon it, with three stars at the center. A thick, red tassel hung off the seal, dangling down Isabella's hand.

"What is this?" Isabella finally asked.

"That letter is from Korbin himself, tasking this woman—Scarlet Wingsday—with apprehending four key Faeries. In this letter he says that if she brings all four of them to Arelle, he will make her an officer."

Isabella took the letter gingerly; she acted as though she was reading it, but her eyes glossed over, crossing the letters on the page into indistinct scribbles.

"Uh," she folded the letter, "What does this have to do with..."

"Look," Hanz pointed down at the lifeless woman. "Look at her."

Isabella's heart felt an uncomfortable pressure. The woman did look a bit like herself; was *that* what they wanted her to say?

"Look at her!" Riah said with a jeer, pointing at Isabella with her finger. "She's just a terrified little peasant girl. We can't expect her to play the role of a spy—much less a Bounty Hunter!"

"Give her a second," Hanz said patiently, watching Isabella's eyes, "She's stronger than you'd think."

Isabella's eyes shot in Hanz' direction. "*That's* what this is about? You want me to... to become this woman?"

"We need this to work," Hanz said in a low, hopeful voice, "We need someone we can trust, someone sharp and talented. We need *you*, Isabella."

Isabella dropped the letter, letting it float gracefully down onto Scarlet Wingsday's body like a snowflake. She chuckled.

"Hanz," she said, "This can't work."

"Yes, it can!" Hanz said quickly, "I've thought through *everything*!"

"Have you thought through the fact that Korbin has met me before? ...That he will *recognize* me? And Scarlet Wingsday is supposed to bring in Four Faeries—have you thought about *that*? Plus, how am I supposed to even begin to *find* the weapon? And let's say I do find it, how am I supposed to get it out of Arelle? This whole plan, it—"

"She's smarter than she looks," Riah said, nudging Hanz.

Hanz nodded proudly. "We've got answers for all those questions, Ella. But there's only one question you need to answer, and that is if you'll help us. Isabella, will *you* join the Purple Order?"

Isabella felt the pressure press down harder on her heart as all four of the Purple Order members stared unblinkingly at her. Was she supposed to make up her mind *now*?

"Answer my questions first," Isabella said cautiously, "And I will give you my answer."

Hanz nodded. "Alright—well, for starters, Scarlet Wingsday already captured three of our order in those bags," he pointed down at the body, "Only the Faerie King can get Faeries out of their exile bags, so we have no hope of rescuing them anyway. The last Faerie on her list," Hanz glanced at one of his companions, "Is Angel."

Angel nodded soberly, "I've already made up my mind, miss Isabella," he said with a smile, "I'll gladly go into exile for the Order."

Isabella gaped in horror at the idea. She shook her head.

"Then," Hanz folded his hands together, "There's the problem of your identity. Well, fear not. We have the masterful Faerie of Illusion on our side! Riah will put a spell on you, masking your true identity. No human, nor faerie, nor Elf—or any other living thing on this table—can recognize you until the spell is broken. And as far as getting the weapon *out* of Arelle once you find it?" Hanz glanced at Tristan.

"We have one spy in the city that we've managed to keep hidden from the Nightmare Faerie," Tristan said, "He is the Messenger Faerie, and he can find us, no matter where we are. You will get it to him, and he will bring it to us."

"But how will he know to trust me?" Isabella asked, sweat beading her forehead.

"We will explain all that, sister," Hanz said in a calming voice, taking a step toward her with his hand outstretched. "I know this is a lot to take in, but I need you to be strong for me. "Look, here," He showed her his arm and turned it so that the soft side of his wrist was visible. There, a strange purple symbol glowed like a luminous tattoo. "Everyone in the Purple Order has one of these, it connects us all to the staff—lets us send out for help if we need it. When you find the bow, you can just activate it, and not only the Messenger Faerie, but all of us will know where you are."

Isabella looked face to face at those who watched her.

"This is it, isn't it?" she asked aloud, "This is the moment I have been waiting for, the moment where I am asked to do something... big."

Something about her words made Tristan grimace, she didn't know what.

"This... this isn't right," he said, stepping back from the circle.

"Don't do this now, Tristan," Hanz said wearily, rushing to the faerie's side. "Don't... don't give into the doubts!"

Isabella watched as Hanz chased Tristan into a corner. The two seemed to whisper angrily at each other.

"What do you think?" Isabella asked, turning to face Riah. Riah seemed surprised to be the focus of Isabella's question.

"*Me*?" Riah asked defensively.

"Yes, you," Isabella crossed her arms. "You're the most skeptical out of the lot, it seems. So, I'll get the most truth from you. Hanz could convince a poison-maker to drink his own brew, so of course he can make this plan sound creditable. But what about you? Do you think this will work?"

Riah blew a stray strand of hair away from her eye. She glanced at Angel, who shrugged, then back at Isabella.

"Hades," she said, "Our hopes have been foolish from the start. Somenus has already laid a strong foundation for his reign, and he's one of the most powerful Faeries in existence. But I've seen Hanz do the impossible over and over again. There's almost a hundred Faeries who would be dead or imprisoned if Hanz hadn't come to our rescue. So, in one sense, no, I don't think this will work. But in another?" She sighed, glancing over to the corner where Hanz was speaking fervently with Tristan. "I think that if we *don't* try, then we really are giving in to our deaths anyway. There is a fool's chance that this plan will work," she looked back at Isabella, "and if you have Hanz' blood, and the blood of Timbre Wulf, in you, then this just might work."

Hanz and Tristan walked back to the circle. Hanz had his hand encouragingly on the Faerie's back.

"Tristan has something he wants to say," said Hanz.

"Well," Tristan cleared his throat, then bowed his head reverently toward Isabella. "I think I will never forgive myself if I do not speak the truth to you, young girl."

Isabella smiled at the Faerie. "Alright," she said, "what is it?"

"Your brother is very... *optimistic...* about what we are asking you to do," he said, "I think neither you nor he have an idea of just *what* is being asked of you. You are brave, and you seem quick-witted as well, but still, you are young and naive. This man, Korbin, if he found you out..." he trailed off, looking to the side, "No, it doesn't feel right sending you to your doom like this."

"If I don't go," Isabella responded, "Then I send all of *you* to your doom."

Tristan's eyes snapped up to meet hers. "It's not the same."

"It is, for me," Isabella said, turning to connect eyes with her brother. He gazed at her proudly, nodding. "If I shy away from helping those in need, when the opportunity comes my way, then I am as evil as Somenus, surely!"

"No," Tristan shook his head, "You are not counting the full cost of your sacrifice. There is an almost certain future where you fail! It is wrong of *us* to ask this of you! You are a sweet, innocent girl; you shouldn't be—be—" he glanced down at the unconscious body of Scarlet Wingsday, "You shouldn't be taking on the identity of a murderer, walking straight into the jaws of Hades, only to..."

"I'm *not* just a sweet, innocent girl!" Isabella cried, her eyes flashing like fire. "And if you think it is wrong to ask this of me, then fine! Do not ask me. But you *cannot* stop me from going if I wish to go!"

"There's my sister," Hanz said proudly, nodding to the group. "Look at her; she can do *anything*. She's got the blood of Timbre Wulf pumping through her veins. Don't you *dare* try and stop her!"

9

—— Leo ——

Cymbeline

I woke up drenched in sweat. I could hear myself yelling, though my voice sounded far away. No, I wasn't yelling; I was screaming. I was screaming like a child in the night who couldn't distinguish his terrors from reality. I couldn't stop.

There were hands touching me. I flinched, looking side to side to see Winke and another skydeacon trying to steady me. Where was I? They shook me violently until I finally coughed for breath.

"It's alright, Leo," Winke was saying as he gripped my arm tightly. "You're awake now."

"What?" I tried to say, but my voice was so hoarse that nothing really came out.

"Let's get him to sit down," said the other skydeacon. I felt them lower me down to a chair. I looked around hurriedly.

"Where am I?" I asked weakly.

"In the tower," Winke said, stepping in front of my view. He was trying to console me with a confident smile.

"*What*?" I shook my head. "How? Why?"

"Leo," Winke said slowly, "Why don't you put it down."

"What? Put *what* down?"

"That..." Winke's eyes dropped down toward my lap. I looked down to see myself grasping the gloved hand of Somenus with both my hands tightly. I looked back up at him.

"Oh," I muttered, "Uh... I don't think I'm allowed to put it down..." My hands wouldn't let go.

Winke looked at his companion with concern, then back at me. "Were you having a nightmare?" he asked.

"I..." Something inside me didn't want to remember. "I don't know."

"Come on," said the other skydeacon, "Let's get him back to his master."

I was too stunned to argue. I walked vacantly between them as they led me carefully down the wood steps of the bell tower.

"Imagine having to work for Somenus?" Winke whispered to his friend, behaving as though I couldn't really hear them. "Look what it does to people."

"Poor lad," said the other.

They led me down to the quarters where Momentum and I had been staying and knocked. Momentum didn't look pleased to be disturbed in the middle of the night but changed his tone when he saw me standing there.

"Get him in bed," Momentum said quickly. They led me to my bed and sat me down. Winke turned to whisper something to Momentum, pointing at the hand I was holding. Momentum nodded, then sent them away. He walked over to my bed, sighed, then sat beside me. He touched my arm, then waited silently. I felt my muscles begin to relax, and when my grip on the hand finally loosened, he whacked the appendage onto the ground.

I sighed deeply, then shut my eyes. Momentum sat by my side until morning.

⚬

I sat up and looked around. Rather than sleep granting me rest, I felt spent. I didn't see Momentum anywhere, but I wasn't alone. My eyes found the hand, resting vacantly on the middle of the floor. I knew him—I saw him, though I couldn't fully remember what I had seen.

I rose unsteadily from the bed and walked a semicircle around the hand. Was I supposed to pick it up? I couldn't just leave him there, could I? He... he couldn't be left unattended.

The door to the room flung open, and I yelped as Momentum stepped in.

"Oh, you're awake," he remarked, then glided across the room to his spot by the desk.

"You startled me," I said in defense of the womanly noise I had made a second earlier.

"Hey, don't leave that there," Momentum glanced over at the hand, "I don't want the skydeacons picking it up."

"What—are you worried they might... get horrifying nightmares, or something?" I asked passive-aggressively.

Momentum shot me a sideways glance, "Have you got something to say, Leeland?" He had a gold pocket watch of sorts in his hand, and he was repeatedly popping it open then snapping it shut in a loop.

"It's *Leo*!" I snapped, "And—!" I cut myself short, blinking in surprise. There was the faintest evidence of a smile hiding in the corner of his mouth. "Oh my god," I crossed my arms. He was teasing me. "You are the worst."

Momentum leaned back in his chair and observed me silently.

"Are you going to tell me why you can't just hold him?" I asked.

"*Him*?" Momentum raised an eyebrow, then sighed, "I can't afford to be compromised."

"Oh, and *I* can?"

"Leo," Momentum sighed, "Can you just hang onto it a *little* bit longer? I'm... I just need a little more time to figure out what I am going to do with it. I'm *trusting* you with it, Leo."

I sighed; he got me there. He made me feel... *special*. It made me want to rise to the task.

"Fine," I snapped. "But I don't like... touching it. Can you get me a—a bag or something?"

"The tailor will be here soon," Momentum said lazily, "we can ask him to get you one."

"A tailor?" I huffed, plopping myself back on the bed, "How long are we going to *be* here?"

"Not long," Momentum said with the tip of a pencil in his mouth; he was peering down at a map, marking lines on it here and there.

"So, you're saying a *tailor*," I glanced down at my jeans, "Is going to make me clothes—from *scratch*?"

"No," Momentum said in his pencil-biting mumble, "He's just coming to take some measurements, then he can make something fit you. No," he leaned back, glancing my way, "We will probably leave before the day is out."

"That's probably for the best," I muttered. *He* knew where we were.

Momentum narrowed his eyes. "What makes you say that?"

"I...." I drew out the word cautiously, peering down at the appendage. "I think he knows we are here."

Momentum groaned like a tree in the wind. "Great," he said sarcastically. "So... he spoke to you then?"

"I don't remember," I said, feeling a chill ride up my spine, "I just have this... feeling."

"Right, well," Momentum rubbed his forehead, "Then let's leave as soon as we can."

"What about the tailor?" I asked, feeling suddenly disappointed. As much as I liked my Levis, I was getting sort of used to the idea of getting a... well... a costume to fit the vibe of the place I was in.

"Forget the felling tailor," Momentum was standing now. "We just need to leave... quietly... without causing suspicion."

The door swung open.

"My lord!" Winke said excitedly as he poked his head in, "May we enter?"

Momentum and I found each other cautiously with our eyes; he seemed to silently communicate the words: *just act natural.* I smiled nervously.

"Heh, heh, sure!" I said eagerly, "C'mon in!"

Momentum lowered himself slowly onto his chair, watching suspiciously as Winke led a guest inside.

"I've got a real *treat* for you," Winke made eye contact with me, as if trying to silently communicate his own message that said something like: *please be nice to this guy.* I nodded politely at him, smiling through my teeth.

Then, a rickety, stick-legged skeleton-of-a-person jostled into the room. The tailor, who had more wrinkles than he did hair, looked as though the only place he truly belonged was in a museum. His legs seemed to bend in any and every direction at the knees like a flamingo, with his proportions appearing tampered with; his torso, to name another, was about as short as his head; and his neck—well—he didn't appear to *have* one.

The character clambered over toward me, waggling an unsteady finger.

"Is this the lad?" he asked in a voice as unstable as a three-legged horse, "Oh gods—is he... is he *alright*?"

I blinked at the man, caught in a daze of sheer amusement. "I... uh..." I glanced toward Momentum, who only stared unblinkingly at the scene. I smiled at the man. "Yes, I am fine. Um... how are you?"

"This is Wharf!" Winke said in a booming voice, nodding in my direction. "He's our tailor!" Winke then lowered his voice and leaned toward me. "He's a bit hard of hearing—so you'll need to speak nice and loud with him, alright?"

I glanced back at Momentum who shrugged.

"Nice to meet you, Wharf," I projected, "I'm Leo!"

"Take off yer trousers!" The old man said as he began to fish through his large, canvas bag.

"I—what?" I eyed Momentum. He was rubbing his mouth thoughtfully. "I, heh, heh," I gazed around the room, waiting for everyone to politely leave. No one did, and the door remained hanging open. "Uh," I tried to speak loudly for dear old Wharf, "Did I hear you right?"

"Do as he says, Leo," Momentum said from behind his hand. I shot him a glare. His mouth did its best to hide its smile, but his eyes betrayed him.

"Wharf really is the best," Winke said brightly from the other side of the room, "Just do as he says."

I had no idea what was normal in this world for men's fashion, so I sighed and began to unfasten my jeans.

"Floods above!" Wharf exclaimed, reaching for his exceptionally large magnifying glass. He held it to his eye and leaned toward my knee, examining the pant leg. I froze, hoping he might compel me to stay clothed. "What sort of—by the Lights! This is a very *tight* weave," He prodded my knee. I looked up toward the ceiling helplessly, wondering if there would ever come a time in my life where I was *not* about to undress in front of this curious old turtle. Weren't we supposed to be running *away* from here right now? Hell—if the Nightmare Faerie did happen to show up here, I'd be damned if I wasn't wearing any—

"Didn't I tell you to take these off?" Wharf waved his hand before my face.

"Fine, fine," I mumbled, then yanked my jeans down to the ankles.

"What in *Hades*?" Wharf was using his magnifying glass in the one area of my body that *nobody* wants one of those used. It was the entire reason I didn't want to be doing this with witnesses present.

"They're uh... koalas..." I said shyly. I had been mighty proud of these boxers when I purchased them off a street vendor in Singapore. I had never dreamed of... of showing them off to anyone! Momentum turned to the side, hiding his face from my view. I could see his shoulders shaking slightly. "Look!" I barked, "I got these from—"

He waved a silencing hand at me, refusing to look my way.

"Now, see here!" Wharf held up a stretch of measuring tape with arms trembling like an earthquake, "Let's just get you measured so we can... dress you properly."

"Fine," I said loudly, rolling my eyes.

"Now," Wharf wrapped the tape around my waist, "Do you dress right or left?"

I glanced helplessly down at the man. "I... *what*?"

"Right or left?" The mass of wrinkles demanded. I blanched, then glanced at Momentum, whose face was now buried in his arms on his desk.

"Uh... left..." I mumbled.

"I'm sorry, lad," Wharf croaked, "My ears aren't good—did you say left or right?"

"Left!" I screamed, red in the face. "And shut up, you ass!" I crowed at Momentum who was now shaking with restrained laughter. "Have you got what you need now—Wharf?" I yelled at the man impatiently.

"Yes, yes," The man tapped me against the ankle. Damn, his hands were surprisingly soft! "Put ye trousers back on, lad; go on—get them up."

"I am, sheesh!" I said, hot-cheeked and humiliated; I snapped myself back up defensively. Wharf silently continued to measure my chest, shoulders, arms, and wrists—all the while failing to notice the gloved hand lying on the ground beside him. It was probably the weirdest, tensest moment of my life, waiting for that man to finish his business so that Momentum and I could hurry up and get out of there.

"Uh, sir," Winke said, strolling over to Momentum, who had managed to compose himself.

"What?" Momentum shifted, eyeing the young skydeacon.

"I was wondering if you wanted to—*erm*—" He lowered his voice, "See that Faerie I was talking about? I... we..."

"What—spit it out," Momentum said impatiently.

"We were told that if we apprehended someone from the list, there would be an—erm—*reward*."

Momentum and I caught each other's eyes for a moment.

"Uh," Momentum folded his hands together, "*Did* you get someone from the list?"

"I am not sure," Winke whispered, "But she has... had—erm—she's got..."

"What, man?" Momentum slapped the desk with his palm, "What has she got?"

"Four wings, Sir," said Winke. Momentum's face grew vacant. I couldn't tell what he was thinking, and of course, I had no idea what the significance of *four wings* meant, whatsoever.

"Right, then," Wharf was packing his things back into his little sack. "I'll have ye some clothes by the end of the day. Some—" he gave me a wary look, "*proper* clothes."

"Have you got a knapsack or something I could use?" I asked quickly.

"Eh? *What*?" Wharf leaned his ear toward me.

"Have you got a knapsack or something I could use?" I repeated in a loud, spiritless voice.

"*Agh*," Wharf scoffed, then fished open his bag again. He threw a small bag at me, with an over-the-shoulder strap attached to it. "Take it," he said, then began to plod over to the door. Winke rushed to let the man out, then turned expectantly toward Momentum.

"Um, sir?" he asked from the door.

"My servant will go with you," Momentum said with a wave of his hand. I frowned, then marched over to the Faerie's side. I leaned down to whisper in his ear.

"Me? Why me? What am I supposed to *do*?"

"Look—I just want you to find out who she is, then come and tell me. I need to grab a few things from the tower before we go, and I don't want anyone following me."

"Are we," I glanced to the side, "Are we going to *rescue* her?"

"What?" Momentum flinched.

"I mean... it sounds like they're going to turn her in to the Nightmare Faerie... that's bad... right?"

Momentum sighed, "Leo—we aren't going on rescue missions right now. Just... just go with the man and find out who she is, then we can talk about," he groaned to himself, "how to get out of here before Somenus..." he glanced at the hand.

I followed his gaze, then looked back at him. "If we have his hand, won't he *always* be able to find us?"

Momentum was silent for a moment.

"Sir?" Winke called from the door.

"One moment!" Momentum called, then eyed me. "There's a place we can go," he whispered, "Where he won't be able to trace us. Just... go with the man and keep him busy for a few clicks."

"Fine," I tested my fly, just to be *sure* it was up, then turned and ran toward the door.

"Leo," Momentum sang, "The *hand*."

I skidded to a stop, then grabbed both the hand and the satchel that Wharf had given me. I slung the bag over my shoulder then stuffed the hand inside and ran to meet Winke.

I closed Momentum's door behind me and smiled at Winke who stood waiting in the hall.

"Wharf is a great tailor," Winke said blankly.

"Uh... cool!" I scratched my nose. "That's... nice."

Winke glanced to the side, "Uh, Leo?"

"Yeah?"

"Is the Nightmare Fa—" he paled, "I mean... is the Faerie King," he gulped, "Is he... evil?"

I didn't know how to respond. "I don't... know."

Winke nodded, brushing out his grey, floor length robe absentmindedly.

"Is everything alright?" I asked, sensing unspoken words.

Winke sighed. "This faerie girl... is he going to...?"

"Look," I shoved my hands into my pockets. "I don't know about the Faerie King, but I do my best to look out for people. I am an EM—" I paused, "I am a... *doctor*... of sorts, and I always try to take care of people. So, I assure you, if you put this girl in my care, I'll take care of her." As the words were coming out of my mouth, I remembered how little power I had to back them up. Well, it was too late to take them back, and Winke was looking at me with wide, hopeful eyes.

"Alright," he said quickly, "Come with me!"

I was led further down the curling stone stairs, down into the wine cellar. Winke opened the door with a key, then stood aside to let me pass him. I ventured in, peering around cautiously, half expecting to get jumped. Winke followed me in.

"Back there," he said, pointing. There was a set of bars, sectioning off the back of the wine cellar. Old barrels seemed to be kept back there.

"Is it normal for people to have dungeons in their cellars?" I asked curiously as I crept forward.

"No," Winke chuckled, "this is just where we keep our most prized vintages."

I saw a body huddled in the corner, shrouded in shadows. I didn't see any wings.

"That's the faerie?" I asked, pointing. "Where's her wings?"

"They're gone now. I don't know how to make them come back—but I swear there were four."

"Fine, fine," I swatted him away. "Step back—I don't want to scare her. Uh... have you got a key?"

"You're going to go *in* there?" He asked fearfully.

"Well, yeah!" I shot him a glance. "Key?"

Winke passed me a large iron key. I bounced the thing in my hand, admiring its weight, then clanked it into its home and turned the lock. The satisfying sound of a bolt moving into place reverberated around the cellar, and I stepped in.

I made myself lower, moving toward the girl on my knees with my hands low toward the ground as a sign of peace.

"Hey," I said softly, "My name is Leo—I'm coming over to you."

"Stay back," she said. She sounded tired. I heard her sniff.

"I'm a friend," I said confidently, "I don't hurt people. I help people. Alright? I am coming over." I inched closer.

"Come any closer and I'll rip out your eyes!" she hissed.

"That's alright," I said calmly, lowering myself into a kneeling position. "I'll stay right here until you're ready for me to come closer. Why don't you come out where I can see you. I'm Leo."

Silence.

I turned to see Winke watching in suspense.

"Why don't you leave us, Winke," I said, "I don't think she likes you. Wait just outside the door." Winke started, then dashed off out of the room. I turned back to where the woman was sitting; her knees were tucked protectively up toward her chest. I could see her bare feet curled into each other just a couple feet away from me. Her skin was a deep, dark brown.

"Who are you?" she asked.

"Leo."

"I know, but... are you one of... *them?*"

"Uh," I scratched my head, "I don't know. I am just a guy, and I don't like—work for anyone. Well, I sort of work for this guy. He told me to come find out which faerie you are. We might..." I lowered my voice. "We might be able to rescue you."

"*Rescue* me?" Her voice sounded hopeful. "You mean... take me back home?"

"I don't know where your home is," I said, "But I think we might be able to get you out of this cellar."

"I was just in my room... and then... I was here! Or, there... or in some street, or something!" she said quickly.

"The people who took you... they said you were a Faerie." I said, "Is that true?"

"Look—I don't even know what a Faerie *is*! I... I didn't even know I had wings!"

I drew back. "What? *Really?*"

The woman climbed out of the shadows and peered into my face. Her eyes were yellow, and she wore her hair in white dreads, pulled back in a low tail.

"Listen," she whispered, "Don't lie to me—are you really here to help me?" She searched my countenance with fierce eyes.

"Yes," I said firmly. "I am. My master and I are about to leave this place, and we will take you with us, if you cooperate."

"*Cooperate?*" She grimaced, "I don't like that word."

I sighed. "I just mean that we are in a tricky situation, so you would have to like... play it cool."

She rotated her head like a cat contemplating an attack. "Fine," she said softly. "I'll go with you."

"You have to pretend like we are taking you prisoner... or something..." I said, biting my lip. "The king of the Faeries is after us, and after you too. And we are trying to..." I knew I was probably getting the narrative wrong, but I had to give her *something,* "We are trying to get to a place where he can't find us."

She nodded in slow motion. "Alright," she said. "Are we leaving... now?"

"I... uh...." I looked left then right, "I don't know. Let me go speak with my master. I'll... I'll be back!"

I stood, walked out of the little cell, and locked it behind me. I found Winke hiding outside the door.

"Dude—are you scared of her?" I asked, observing the man cowering there.

"I... uh..." Winke straightened. "Aren't *you* scared of Faeries? Oh—Hades, no. You work with them all the time, don't you?" He tried to straighten out wrinkles that weren't present in his garment.

"Dude, it's fine. Chill," I patted his shoulder. "Of course I get scared."

Winke eyed me. "Well, what are you going to do with her?"

"I am going to speak with my master, and then I think we are going to take her with us. Believe it or not, she wants to, um... serve Somenus."

"Oh!" Winke looked shocked. "Oh, right."

"Can you take me back to my master?"

"Yes!" Winke rushed up the stairs.

I followed him, hoping I had done right. I found Momentum in the same place I had left him. Once alone, I strolled up to him, whistling.

"Why do I get the feeling you've done something to annoy me?" Momentum asked with his arm leaning against the desk.

"Have you already done what you wanted to do?" I asked.

"Yes."

"Wow, you're quick."

"So are you," he said dryly, "Now come on. What happened? Who is she?"

"Well, I don't know much..." I rocked back and forth on my heels. "I mean... she's a girl, and she's black..."

"She's a dark Faerie?" Momentum asked with a head tilt, "How can you tell?"

"No," I blinked, "I mean she had like... dark skin."

"Oh," Momentum shrugged, "Well that doesn't narrow things down hugely. Did she have four wings?"

"I don't know. Her wings were invisible, I think. And she said she didn't even know she was a Faerie; she said she didn't even know she had wings."

"*What*?" Momentum rose to his feet. "She's lying then."

"I don't think so," I slid my hands into my back pockets. "No, I can usually tell when someone is lying."

"How can she not know she is a Faerie?" Momentum asked haughtily.

"I don't know," I shrugged, "She just said one second she was in her room, and then she was in the street with wings on."

Momentum stared at the wall for a moment.

"What?" I asked, "You've got an idea, don't you?"

"I just..." he mumbled, "It sort of might line up with..."

"With what?" I asked, leaning my face sideways into his field of vision. He caught my eyes with his.

"When the Lapis Gate was destroyed," he said vaguely.

"The portal?" I asked, straightening. "Why would she appear here when the portal was destroyed?"

"That's what I am wondering..." Momentum mumbled.

"Anyway, I told her she could come with us."

"You, *what*?" Momentum rose to his feet commandingly. "No—Leo! We... we have to get out of here now. We can't drag around a—"

"Dude," I said with a solemn shake of my head, "I am not budging on this one. She's coming with us."

Momentum exhaled hot, frustrated air through his nostrils. "Fine," he said, "But we are leaving *now*." He grabbed a single map from the table and shoved it in his inner jacket pocket.

We exited the room together and ascended the steps to the ground floor. There, we saw Winke standing dutifully beside Forewinds, the head skydeacon.

"I hear you are taking the...*faerie girl*... with you?" Forewinds questioned.

"Erm, yes," Momentum glanced toward me, "Can you bring her up here?"

"We were promised a reward if we turned in any of the greats," Forewinds said, tapping his chin thoughtfully. "You can't just... *take* her."

"We can and we will!" I said, stepping forward. The skydeacons regarded me. "If you want a reward, then you had better do as we ask!"

Winke flinched. "Shall I fetch her, Fellow Forewinds?"

Forewinds held up a foreboding hand. "I want a promise that our city will benefit from our cooperation."

Momentum pulled his lips into his mouth and nodded. "Sure," he said, "I *promise* you will benefit from handing us the girl."

"Shall I fetch her *now*, Fellow Forewinds?" Winke asked.

"Quiet, Fellow," Forewinds hissed, then he turned to Momentum with chin held high. "I will give her to you—but I want something in return."

"What is it?" Momentum asked through a lazy sigh.

Forewinds produced a spyglass from his deep robe pocket and held it forth reverently.

"This was passed down to me by my father, and his father before him," he said. Momentum took the glass and turned it in his hands. He took a moment to peer through the eye hole.

"This is for spotting color changes," Momentum said, then passed it back. "A chromoscope."

"Yes," Forewinds said brightly, "You seem to know your equipment. Well—I was wondering if you might..." his cheeks flushed with embarrassment. "Is it too much to ask for you to bless it?"

"I'm the Faerie of Vows," Momentum said impatiently, "What could you possibly expect me to do with it?"

Forewinds swayed back and forth bashfully, "Well, I hadn't thought that far. Perhaps you could think of something useful to a skydeacon?"

Momentum rolled his eyes. "Fine," he said, then took the thing in his hands. I half expected him to utter some made up words and was surprised when the item began to glow. Momentum passed it back to the skydeacon, who examined it excitedly.

"What... what did you *do*?"

"Look through it," Momentum said dryly, "And you'll know. Now, get the girl."

"Get her for them," Forewinds nudged Winke, then turned to race up to the tower to test out his blessed instrument. Winke raced downstairs while Forewinds raced up.

"What did you do?" I whispered.

"More than he deserves," Momentum mumbled. "Now, listen. A faerie could have flown here by now, if Somenus really knows where we are. We need to run."

"If I've got his hand, then won't he be able to follow us?" I asked, feeling sweat beads forming on my head.

"He can really only locate you while you're sleeping. He's the *Dream* Faerie, Leo. Remember that."

"Okay..." I turned quickly, hearing approaching footsteps. Winke was there, holding a lead tied to the faerie woman's hands. She was examining Momentum and me one by one. Momentum was staring, open mouthed at her, looking horrified.

"Thanks Winke," I said, taking the lead from him. "We'll be off, then!"

"We are *not* taking her with us," Momentum hissed through his teeth.

"Yes, we *are*!" I said in a sing-song voice, jabbing Momentum in the side.

"No." Momentum marched out of the tower, then began racing down the hill.

"Come on!" I tugged urgently on the woman's lead and she followed me. Winke watched us scramble down the hill after Momentum.

"Wait for us!" I called, panting. The woman was grunting angrily, trying to keep up as she tripped over her long, cumbersome dress.

"Why is he running away from us?" she asked.

"Come on!" It was all I could think to say as I hunted Momentum down. "Wait for me!" I called, "Or I am chucking this hand into the street!"

I saw Momentum skid to a halt up ahead, right where the city's street met the forest's edge. He turned to face me as I bounded up to him.

"Leo!" he bellowed, "She is *not* coming with us!"

The three of us cowered as a great, black shadow passed over us. I gazed up into the sky, and then my face lost all its color. A great winged figure glided through the sky on four monstrous black wings, straight for the bell tower.

"Is that Somenus?" I asked.

"Let's not find out," Momentum said with voice cracking. "Follow me!"

I followed Momentum, and the woman reluctantly followed me. He led us into the forest, craving the protective cover of the trees. It would not take long for them to find us, I was sure. We ran and ran, until Momentum came to a panting halt inside a little quiet copse of birch trees. He keeled over, gasping for air, as did the rest of us.

"This is insane," I croaked, "Momentum, what is going *on?*"

"What's going *on?*" The Time Faerie tried to rise into a standing position, fighting for breath. He pointed a heavy arm toward the woman. "*She* is lying to you!"

"What?" The woman crowed. "What are you talking about?"

"I know who you are, and you know who I am!" Momentum, in an uncharacteristic state or rage, cried with foam jetting from his mouth.

"*What?*" The woman yanked the lead out of my hands. I stared at Momentum, then at her, then back at him in confusion. "I've never seen you before in my *life!*"

"*Liar!*" Momentum shrieked, "I swore if you ever showed your face to me again I would kill you—*kill* you!"

"Who in the *depths* do you think you are?" The woman marched up toward him, pointing her bound hands toward him threateningly. Momentum stumbled away from her in terror, falling onto his backside.

"How did you get back here? How did you get *through?*" he asked, groping the dirt with his hands.

"Guys," I raised my hands slowly, one pointed at each of them, "Please, calm down. Somenus is going to be here soon; if we don't calm down, we are all dead."

"Shut up, Leo!" Momentum yapped, "This is between me and Temmy. You stay out of this, you little..."

"*Temmy?*" The woman balked. "Is that what this is about? My *mother?*" She scoffed, looking up toward the sky. "Look, I have *had* it with men berating me and shaming me and—"

"Mother?" Momentum rose to his feet. "No... *what?*"

"If my mother has hurt you, I am sorry. Join the mass of the *many* people she has terrorized," the woman said spitefully, "Well. I hope it pleases you to hear she is dead. There! Are you *happy*?"

I shot a glance at Momentum who was frozen in a state of dumb-struck shock.

"Guys," I said, breaking the silence cautiously, "What is going on?"

"How did you get here?" Momentum finally asked, "How did you...?"

"I don't know! Why will no one *believe* me?" She stamped her bare foot on the ground.

"What's your name?" Momentum asked; his temper seemed to be cooling.

She was panting violently, glaring. "Why should I tell you?"

"Please," I chimed in, "Tell us your name."

She snapped a look at me, then softened slightly. "Cymbeline," she said. "My name is Cymbeline."

"Cymbeline," Momentum said in a low voice. "Your wings... did they show up when you found yourself... here?"

She nodded. "Yes."

"And your mother never told you that you were a faerie?" He asked.

"No."

"Can you make your wings appear again?" Momentum asked. I could see a look of suspense in his eyes.

"I am not sure..."

"Yes, you can," Momentum said, taking a wary step closer to her. He seemed... *afraid* of her. "Once a faerie finds their wings, they can always find them again. Go on, *show* them to me."

Cymbeline lowered her hands slowly. "Why?"

"Just do as he says," I said, hoping I was right.

Cymbeline closed her eyes.

10

—— Clover ——

The Truth Faerie

Clover watched at a distance as Yuma said his goodbyes. Standing vacantly, with one hand on his spear, and another resting on the head of Andrew, the fat sheep, Clover wondered to himself what those in the Elder Copse thought about his own disappearance, if they thought about it at all. He wasn't exactly *liked* in the Copse, despite being the son of someone important. Dozens of people waited their turn to embrace Yuma and wish him well with tearful words. Yuma was clearly a man deeply loved by his community; Clover envied that somewhat. Not that he envied the attention Yuma seemed to get from others, no. What he wanted was to *be* someone worth missing—and that, he knew, he was not.

Yuma met Clover there by the Archstone, at the entrance to the Fero City. He glanced around with mild curiosity at the sheep.

"So, they're... coming with us?" asked the warrior. Yuma was dressed better for a journey, with sturdy trousers, calf-high boots, and a rucksack slung over his back. A red ribbon, tied to the end of Yuma's single arrow, which was strapped to the sack, blew in the wind.

"Well, yes," Clover said blankly, "I promised Isabella that—"

"Isabella is her name?" Yuma turned slightly to regard Clover with a look of amusement.

"Yes." Clover felt a pang of protective anger at the sound of her name coming from someone else's lips. "I promised her that I wouldn't let them out of my sight."

"And I suppose you take that promise quite literally," Yuma said.

"Well, of course I do. What are words for if you can't take them *literally*?"

Yuma nodded, "If the whole world thought the way you do, it would probably be a better place. Alright, come on." The warrior began to march out of the city.

"So," Clover jogged to catch up, swinging his spear to coax his sheep along. "Where are we going now?"

"We are meeting the last member of our party," Yuma said casually, "I'll let *him* break the bad news to you."

"Bad news?" Clover said, panting as he lifted Andrew from the ground. Yuma was walking too quickly for all the sheep to keep up. "What bad news?"

Yuma stopped walking and stood before the open, red desert. He cupped his hands over his mouth, then made an impressive bird call with his lips. Clover placed the sheep back on the ground and knelt beside him, watching curiously.

"It's a beast, isn't it?" Clover asked. "Your companion?"

Yuma turned to look down where Clover was kneeling. "Yes. He's a prophetic beast, so we are going to let him lead the party."

"What—really?" Clover looked side to side, wondering from which corner the beast would emerge.

"And Clover," Yuma said as he turned back toward the desert, "If he tells me to leave you and your sheep behind, I will."

Clover pulled the corner of his mouth to the side. "You're expecting him to say that, aren't you?"

Yuma made the same bird call again, then dropped his hands. "Yes," he said, "You're a lovesick kid who's carting around a couple dozen sheep. I fear it would be cruel to drag you along, honestly."

"But *I'm* the one who was going in the first place!" Clover said, rising to his feet. "I brought the faerie here, and I—" The Elf's words died in his mouth as a figure came bounding toward them from the distant plains.

Yuma turned to grin proudly at Clover.

"A horse?" Clover gasped, "Your companion is a *horse*?"

"Well, I don't like to brag," Yuma said amusedly. The muscular black stallion charged up to Yuma, rearing itself on its hind legs with a cry. The warrior lifted his hands, taking the horse by the snout as the beast excitedly lowered his head.

Clover watched in amazement as the two, man and horse, greeted each other. Yuma rubbed his hands playfully along the beast's mane and whispered in his ear. The horse eagerly walked circles around him, trotting like a foal.

"Can I..." Clover mumbled, "Touch it?"

The beast turned and pointed its glistening black eyes at Clover. Yuma, with his arms wrapped around the horse's neck, smiled at the Elf.

"Clover, come over here," he said.

Clover tiptoed forward cautiously, clutching his spear fearfully.

"Lower your weapon," Yuma warned, holding out his hand, palm down.

The horse snorted hot air through his nostrils and stamped the ground. Clover flinched.

"It's alright," said Yuma, "He's not mad, he's excited. He likes you."

Clover raised his eyebrows, then crept closer.

"Hallo," said the Elf, "I am Clover."

The horse kept his head steady, waiting as Clover neared it.

Yuma rubbed the side of the beast's neck. "Alright," he said, "Come, let him smell your hand."

Clover reached out a palm, then gritted his teeth as he approached the animal. It smelled him. Clover's mouth curled upwards into a smile.

"He... you said he likes me?" Clover asked weakly.

"Yes," Yuma said, "Unfortunately."

"You can... hear his voice?" Clover lifted his gaze, running it along the beast's long nose, then found one of its round, marble eyes.

"Yes," said Yuma; his own smile was fading. "Clover, this is Waiting For the Day."

Clover leaned forward and smelled the beast's fur. He leaned back again, keeping his palm just below Waiting For the Day's mouth.

"Why did you name him that?" Clover asked.

"I didn't name him," Yuma said, "He told me his name."

"I thought animals didn't have names until people gave them," Clover said.

"That is usually true," said Yuma as he ran his hand along Waiting For the Day's back. "Either this beast is special, or someone long before me named him, and he remembered."

"Horses are said to be the rarest animals on the table," Clover said reverently, "How did you find him?"

"He found me," said Yuma, looking somewhat protective. "After the famine started. Oh, maybe a season ago?"

Clover nodded. "He's going to come with us?"

Yuma and Waiting For the Day looked at each other.

"What do you think, Day?" Yuma asked softly, "Will you come with me?"

The horse didn't seem to move, and Clover definitely couldn't hear an audible voice. But he was thankful for the chance to see a creature communicating with its bonded human. What was it like to hear an animal's voice?

"Yes, but," Yuma said, looking at the horse. "But what about the—" he glanced at Clover, then back at his beast.

Clover waited patiently, watching with curiosity.

Yuma bowed his head to the horse, sighed, then looked over at Clover.

"Look," said the warrior, "You can come... but..."

"But what?" Clover glanced at Waiting For the Day. "But I have to leave my sheep behind? Please, Sir Horse—I made a promise to watch over them. Please, you can't ask me to leave them behind!"

"You can stop trying to appeal to my beast," Yuma grumbled, "He's already made up his mind."

Clover waited expectantly with round, hopeful eyes.

Yuma sighed. "Your felling sheep can come, too. But *look*," He held up his hand in warning, "We are not going far; we are heading into the Woodlands to meet with the Truth Faerie. That is *all* I am promising."

"The Truth Faerie?" Clover asked with a head shake, "Why?"

"It's what we talked about yesterday when you weren't listening," Yuma said spitefully, "Remember? We are going there to ask for counsel. Waiting For the Day knows where to find him."

"Right," Clover nodded, "So the Truth Faerie... is real?"

"Of course he is real," Yuma turned to Face Clover. "Now, come on." Yuma mounted the horse with a single, swift leap. Clover peered upwards, admiring.

"You want me to climb up, too?" he asked.

"No!" Yuma snapped, then began to ride eastwards in a slow trot.

Clover swung his spear at the herd of confused sheep.

"Come on," he yelled, "Let's go, let's go. Isabella is this way!" The wooly beasts mulled about aimlessly. "Not this again," Clover complained, "Come on—move in one direction!"

Yuma rounded his horse, accelerating into a canter, then ran a circle around the sheep. They made some noises of alarm, then began to trot fearfully forward.

"Thank you," Clover said enthusiastically as he watched his sheep move in the right direction. Yuma ignored him, racing forward to lead the pack.

⁂

Clover wasn't thrilled to be back in the Woodlands. He had hoped that by embarking on this new adventure, he would be able to see new places. Now, it felt like he was retracing old steps. But to his delight, this northern ridge of the forest seemed to be remarkably different from where he had ventured through before. The trees were predominantly oak and birch, with leafy branches, rather than the standard pine. This made the ground harder to traverse, however, since the oak trees had bigger and messier roots, and they lined the forest floor like a thick tangle of spilled yarn.

The sheep had trouble stepping through such uneven terrain, and that slowed the pace of the party greatly. Yuma thought they could have reached the Truth Faerie's location by late morning, but it was already past the midday zenith, and he was a great deal more than frustrated.

"If your *felling* sheep hadn't been here, we would have been there by now!" The warrior snapped.

Clover leaned against a knobby oak stump, panting. "What's the rush?" Clover asked breathlessly, "We will get there when we get there." Upon Yuma's demand, Clover had carried Andrew all morning, hoping to quicken the pace. Waiting For the Day was waiting at the front of the pack, looking back expectantly toward them.

"*What's the rush*?" Yuma balked, "Are you *joking*?"

"No."

"My people are rationing meals, starving day by day—dying!"

"Alright, alright," Clover snapped, "Well, my sheep are still sheep. Let them go at their pace!"

"If they weren't here—"

"Well, they *are* here!" Clover yelled, "So, will you just... let them be what they are?"

Clover and Yuma exchanged silent glares. A tug roused Clover from his anger. He looked down to see the gnome pulling at the back of his tunic excitedly.

"What? What do you want?" Clover asked impatiently. Yuma grunted in annoyance, then marched off to speak with his beast. Clover knelt before the little creature who was rocking back and forth on his heels bashfully. His little shoes—their design was so detailed, so fine! Clover sighed. "Alright, I can tell you have something behind your back; what is it?"

The gnome seemed to blush, then he held out his treasure before Clover with his little mittened hands. Clover was both enraged, and yet somehow not surprised to see his shiny gold coin, there in the thing's hands.

"You thieving scumbag!" Clover barked, snatching the coin from his paws. He shook it violently before the creature's wide face. "This was a gift—a *gift*! Now, you've made me look like a... a...You've made it look like I don't care about these people!" Clover dropped his head defeatedly, and the gnome seemed to take that motion as an invitation to climb up on his shoulder.

"Come on," Yuma called from up ahead, "There's a stream here. Let's water the flock then keep moving."

Clover was too tired to force the lazy sheep to drink; he merely watched as the sheep closest to the stream wetted their hooves and quenched their thirst. He noticed Waiting For the Day wandering around, poking his snout down amongst the herd, as if communicating. He wondered what a horse could have to say to a sheep in a circumstance like this.

"Clover," Yuma said after clearing his throat. Clover glanced sidewards from where he leaned against his tree to see Yuma squatting beside Andrew, stroking his head.

"Hmm?"

"I'm sorry for my temper," said the man.

"Oh," Clover turned his head back to its resting position. "No need to apologize."

"No, there is," Yuma said quietly. "It's important that I..." the man hesitated, "slow down, I think."

Clover blew some of his stray hair off his forehead. "Sure," he said, "Whatever you say."

"I'm trying to apologize," Yuma snapped, "You don't have to be so cold shouldered!"

Clover turned his head toward Yuma again. "What?"

"Stop being so passive!" Yuma barked, "I know you're upset."

"Yuma," Clover said dryly, "Believe it or not, I am not upset. I am just thinking."

Yuma flattened his mouth, observing the Elf. He couldn't easily read someone as plain spoken as Clover. Did he really just... *mean* what he said? Yuma sat upon the ground.

"Fine," he said, "What are you thinking about?"

"Well," Clover said absently, "I am just wondering if my presence is strengthening or worsening the chances of our success; and that got me wondering what success even looks like in a venture like ours; then I was trying to remember what we are actually trying to accomplish—killing the Nightmare Faerie? Is that it? Then I was thinking that perhaps my reasons for coming along are selfish. But then... I thought they were *not* selfish because I was coming in support of Isabella. Then," he sighed a wistful sigh, "that got me thinking about Isabella, and her lovely face."

"Floods above," Yuma shook his head, "Alright... so you really were just thinking."

"Am I right?" Clover asked quickly, "Are we trying to kill the Nightmare Faerie?"

"Uh... yes, Clover. That is what we are doing," Yuma said.

"Why?"

Yuma blinked, "Because he is destroying my people by draining life from our lands."

Clover nodded, "But it's not like I've got a personal reason to... kill the Faerie King."

"So then why are you here, Clover?" Yuma asked sincerely.

Clover gazed silently at the sheep for a moment. "I think..." he began, then grew quiet again.

"Does it have to do with Isabella—this girl?"

"Yes," Clover said, looking back at Yuma, "I've sort of... never cared about anything before. Then I met her and it was like... like an artist picking up a pen for the first time; or a river otter taking its first swim; or an eagle taking its first flight—it was like I saw the thing I was always supposed to see, but I didn't know why it was important. When I saw her face, it was like nothing else in the world mattered but her. I didn't need her for myself, I just needed her to *be*—to exist in the world, untouched and untarnished. She was so perfect, so lovely; like a daybreak flash, or a first laugh, or a dying breath."

Yuma stared silently.

"My life is complete knowing that she is in the world," he said, "and if all I do with my idle years is to live and die for her, I think I would be happy. The Elves call this our passion: the thing we devote our lives to. I never thought I would find one... and now I know why they say it can make people go mad."

"But," Yuma broke his silence, "but she's a woman, Clover. She will break your heart, and then what?"

Clover raised an eyebrow. "Break my heart? How?"

"Well, let's say you live and die—and all the rest—for her, then she turns you away? What then?"

Clover blinked. "I don't think you understand what I am saying," Clover said with a consoling voice, "I don't need her to need *me*, that would be pretty presumptuous. But Hades—" his eyes seemed to glow, "If she *did* love me..."

"So where is she?" Yuma asked flatly.

Clover shook himself from his daze. "I don't know," he said, "She's gone to find her brother; I think she's involved in the plot to kill the Nightmare Faerie. So—I figure I should be involved too, and I might be able to, I don't know... help out—Hey! What are you doing?"

"What?"

"Watch out! The thieving scumbag is—" Clover pointed. Yuma looked down to see the gnome fishing through his rucksack. Yuma smirked and reached out to touch the creature's back. The thing squeaked, then gazed fearfully up at the man.

"It's alright," Yuma said as he slowly reached into the rucksack. He pulled out a little pouch and opened it, revealing a little cluster of colorful clay beads. The gnome curiously scurried up to the pouch and peered inside. He placed his hands into the bag and rolled them around amongst the beads, excited by the clinking sounds they made.

"He'll steal from you," Clover warned, "He's a little pest—followed me all the way from the Elder Copse."

"What did you say his name was?" Yuma glanced over at Clover curiously.

"I told you—he's a thieving scumbag! He doesn't have a name!"

"Careful," Yuma chuckled, "Or that name is going to stick."

"He's—" Clover froze, "He's not *bonded* with me!"

"How do you know?" asked Yuma, who was now scratching the critter's head. "He sure seems like he is."

"'Cause I can't hear his voice," Clover said quietly. "I thought you could understand animals if they bond with you."

"Maybe he's just not talking," Yuma said helpfully.

Clover blinked. "You… you think he's…"

"Where did you get this outfit?" Yuma chuckled, lifting up a length of the gnome's billowy scarf.

"I didn't dress it," Clover mumbled, "He came like that."

"Do you think he belongs to someone else?" Yuma asked.

"Felled if I know!" Clover shrugged in defense, "I think he dressed himself."

Waiting For the Day trotted up to Yuma, wagging his head jovially.

"What is it?" Yuma asked, rising to greet his beast.

I'd rather bond with a horse than a… Clover glanced down at the thieving scumbag who scurried between his feet, fearful of the horse.

"Clover," Yuma said urgently, "Clover, he's here! He's found *us*!"

"Who?" Clover pushed himself off the tree, "*Somenus*?"

"No!" Yuma whispered, "The Truth Faerie!"

Clover looked side to side, half expecting a glowing angel to appear before them. "Where?"

Yuma and Waiting For the Day were both gazing in the same direction, further down the stream. Clover followed their eyes and was surprised to see no one but a child walking aimlessly toward them. He was a boy, somewhere in the age of awakening, when a child's age is marked by their ability to see outside themselves. He had soft, gold hair, curled up into ringlets, and a round face. His faerie ears jetted out sideways, giving him a gnome-like appearance, and he wore a simple white tunic. His wings were hidden, so if his ears hadn't been so obvious, one could hardly know he was a faerie.

He had a stick in his hand and was dragging it through the stream idly, whistling as he walked.

"Hallo!" he said, lifting a hand to wave when he met Clover's eyes.

Clover and Yuma scurried to attention, rushing to stand by each other's sides. Waiting For the Day trotted up to the boy and lowered his snout in deference.

"Oh, Day!" said the boy in a cheery voice. He kissed the horse between its nostrils. "Who have you brought here?" he asked, then looked up at the two gentlemen. "A grand quest, indeed," he remarked, studying them with his round, green eyes. "Look, that one's glowing a whole lot!" he pointed, but Clover and Yuma couldn't tell who at.

The horse rotated its head to face Yuma.

"Hello, I am Yuma," said the warrior. He knelt down on one knee to match the boy's height, "I come from the Fero Lands. I'm a friend of Waiting For the Day's."

"I'm Clover," said Clover, remaining in his blank, standing pose.

The boy looked from Yuma to Clover, then back again. "I suppose you're wanting a prophecy?"

"Can you just..." Clover remarked, "hand out prophecies whenever you want?"

Yuma shot Clover a glare.

The boy laughed heartily, then tapped his chest with his hand. "I'm Lija, I am a Truth Faerie, the seven hundred and seventh, I think. And yes, Clover of the Elder Copse: I can! All truth is prophecy, and I suppose one of the ups and downs of being me is that I can only speak truth." He grinned proudly, holding his stick straight up in the air like a baton.

"Seven Hundred and Seven?" Clover asked, "Why so many?"

Yuma nudged him, muttering, "Can't you guess?"

Lija laughed again. "Oh, it's no secret!" he said quickly. "The truth is scary—and prophets get killed a lot. Now, come on, let's meet everyone!"

Clover and Yuma shuffled nervously about as Lija strolled from sheep to sheep, greeting each one personally. To Clover's great annoyance and frustration, Lija asked him the name of every single animal, despite Clover saying each time, "I don't know." It wasn't until Lija came to the last sheep, that Clover was relieved to finally say, "*Andrew*!" And which point, Lija said,

"I don't think that's right..."

Yuma finally managed to get Lija to sit down, and the three of them made a small circle by the stream.

"Ooh, what about this one?" Lija pointed excitedly at the gnome. "What's his name?"

"I don't know," Clover glanced at Yuma, "Thieving Scumbag, or something."

"Aw," Lija picked up the critter and placed it in his lap. "Now, I suppose you both want to talk to me."

Clover and Yuma exchanged uneven glances.

"We are setting out to kill the Nightmare Faerie," Yuma said in a confident tone, "This Faerie, Dezmund, says we need to get an army. We thought we should try Bavel, the kingdom of Men; they have an army, and they don't like Somenus."

Lija listened intently. "And what are you wanting to ask me?"

"Well," Yuma cleared his throat, "Should we... do that?"

Lija nodded. "Yes."

Yuma swayed side to side, "Uh... really? Just, yes? We should go to Bavel?"

"Yes."

Clover sniffed. "Why do you look so surprised?"

"I just didn't expect him to say we *should* do anything," Yuma muttered, "I expected him to be more... cryptic."

"No," Lija said with a bob of his head, "You should go to Bavel."

"Both of us?" Asked Clover.

"Yes."

Silence.

"Erm," Clover's throat felt suddenly dry. "And... we should kill the Nightmare Faerie?"

Lija looked from Yuma's face to Clover's. "Yes."

"And..." Yuma said uneasily, "Are we going to succeed?"

"Did you know there is a curse on whoever kills a Faerie King?" Lija said.

Clover and Yuma both shook their heads.

"Yes," Lija said with a little sigh, "It's a law, written on the table of Raqia like a scroll—whoever kills the Faerie King dies: always."

Yuma's face grew hard. Clover turned slowly to observe him. He seemed to be deliberating within himself.

"Alright," Yuma said in a low voice, "I am prepared for that."

Astonished, Clover turned to see the Truth Faerie's reaction.

"There are just two problems," Lija said, "The Faerie of Affection is already powerful, but now that he is the king, he is almost impossible to destroy."

"Faerie of Affection?" Clover asked confusedly.

"That's his name," Lija said with a smile, "The Dream Faerie's *real* title. Anyway, Yuma, the first problem is this: The Faerex is full of magik, so he's hard to kill. You'll need to find a weapon that can match that power."

"Where will we find it?" Yuma asked quickly.

Lija thought for a moment. "Well... it will come to you, when the time is right."

Yuma nodded. "What is the second problem?"

"Well," Lija sighed, "Somenus can fill up the mind of anyone in his presence. Whether filled with obsession or fear, you will not be able to resist letting him into your head. The more that you fear, the more attached to him you become. This... makes it pretty impossible to—shall we say—point an arrow at him and kill him."

"So, what am I supposed to do?" asked Yuma intently.

Lija seemed to deliberate. "Well," he tucked his feet under himself and knelt, "It's simple, really. You have to love something more than you love him."

Yuma snorted, "Well that's easy; I *hate* him."

Lija shook his head, "Let me put it this way: you have to love something more than you love yourself."

Yuma pulled his lips into his mouth.

"Does Yuma love something more than he—*ow!*" Clover rubbed his aching rib where Yuma elbowed him.

Lija sighed, shaking his head. "I will tell you this, Yuma: younger brother."

Yuma drew back, listening with suspense. Clover, sensing tension, turned to drawing circles in the dirt with his finger.

"When it comes to killing the ancient evil one," Lija said gravely, "It will not be you, Yuma, but Clover."

Clover's finger paused mid circle. He snapped his head up to stare unblinkingly at Lija; then Yuma; then at Lija again.

"*What?*" Yuma lunged. "No!"

"Why does it need to be *you?*" Lija asked skeptically. Yuma sniffed.

"It doesn't *have* to be me—I..."

Clover swallowed, then rose to his feet. Lija looked up at him expectantly.

"Why Clover, though?" Yuma asked with a sense of urgency.

"Isabella?" Clover asked softly.

"What—" Yuma scoffed, "Are you saying that because he has some useless obsession with a woman he barely knows—?" Yuma's words died in his throat as Clover turned and wandered off into the woods.

11

— Lola —

Dream within a Dream

It was Somensday, the seventh and last day of the week. Lola had been in the Vineyard Palace for two days, and while she was starting to find her bearings, she still felt completely overwhelmed by the situation she found herself in. She was determined, however, to conquer her trial, and hold fast to her ideals. What was her passion worth if it could not see her through the darkest of times? This test, this upset to her life, was an opportunity to prove to herself and to the world that the transcendentals were not just philosophical ideals, but forces that could shape one's very soul. Yes, they would protect her; like enchanted charms, they would shield her from this chaotic world.

"Reading that book again?"

Lola glanced up from her reading spot and stared across the room at Lady Fayne. She was taking her daily stroll around the palace with Alabaster close behind, fanning her with a feathery plume.

"Oh," Lola rubbed one of her eyes, "No, I was lost in my thoughts."

"Is that the book you were telling me about?" Fayne asked Alabaster, who leaned forward to glance at Lola.

"Yes," she said dryly, "That's it. It's about faeries and romance, and some felling man."

"Give it to me," Fayne said as she thrust out her hand toward Lola. Lola observed her hand.

"I am sorry, but no," Lola said.

Fayne scowled. "Hand it over—I want to read it!"

"I'll read it to you if you like," Lola said politely, "But this is my book; it was a gift from a friend and I am not going to give it away just because someone tried to bully me."

Fayne scoffed. She crossed her arms and looked to her side where Alabaster was plucking a feather from the fan. "Alabaster—take that book."

"You will not take this book," Lola said gently but firmly, "Lady Fayne, would you like me to read it to you?"

Fayne lurched forward and snatched the book from Lola's hands. Aghast, Lola turned to stare at the woman in shock.

"Are you... a *child*?" Lola asked with disappointment in her voice. "Why would you behave like this?"

Fayne snorted, waving the book victoriously before Lola's face. "I'm going to enjoy *not* reading this!"

Lola sighed. "Lady Fayne," she said, turning from her reading nook to place her feet on the ground, "Your unkindness toward me will get you nothing. But just think—imagine if you had found a friend in me. I doubt your imagination could fully grasp how beautiful that could be. Like a cup of water in a desert land, or a plate of food in a famine; a friendship in a den of enemies can make the difference between life and death." She rose to her feet and took a step closer to Fayne, "So please, take my book—my one joy in this empty place— and do what you like with it; and nothing will change. But do *one* good thing to someone else—hand it back—and *everything* might change." Lola held out her hand expectantly, then waited.

Lady Fayne studied Lola. She breathed in and out slowly, searching with her eyes. She slowly passed the book back.

"Thank you," Lola said as she carefully took the book. She smiled. "Now will you sit? I can read you the beginning."

Lola found her spot once more, tucking her feet up onto the ledge of the window. Fayne sat primly beside her, flicking her hand to dismiss Alabaster from her side.

"Right," Lola opened the book, licking her fingers before finding the first page, "The book starts with the most beautiful sentence... It's so pretty and inviting—oh! The title: we must always start with the title. There... *Phantastes: a faerie romance for—*"

"Lola..." Fayne said, resting her hands daintily on her lap.

Lola peered up from her pages. "Hmm?"

"Is it true you were brought here... against your will? I mean—against your father's will?"

Lola hesitated, then nodded. "Yes," she said, "Father has been refusing to let Somenus set up the Faerie Rites in Celestia. He never would have sent me here."

Fayne nodded to herself. "I am from Bavel, as you know, and we don't practice the Rites either."

"Were you abducted, too?" Lola whispered.

"No, my father sent me here. He sees the benefit in making friends in high places. Couldn't hurt to have an alliance with the Faerie King," she said distantly, with her head turned away from Lola.

"Lady Fayne, are you... glad to be here?"

The woman pulled one of her curly locks loose from her braid and began to twirl it around her finger. "Yes, I think so."

"Why?"

"Lola, I don't know what it is like where you come from, but in Bavel, a nobleman's daughter has only one real future: to be married off in the most beneficial way to her family's house. So, being sent somewhere new, with a chance at becoming a queen? Of *course,* I prefer to be here than in Bavel."

"A chance at being queen?" Lola raised her eyebrows. "Of *Arelle*?"

Fayne sniffed. "Well, if somebody actually provides Somenus with a son, they no doubt will be made queen."

"Oh..." Lola's eyes dropped back down toward her book.

"Listen, you seem like a nice girl. I..." Fayne shifted in her seat, "I see no reason why we can't be civil to one another. Just..."

"Yes?"

"Somenus has shown some interest in me," she said with a flutter of pride in her eyes, "Just don't get in the way."

Lola flattened her mouth. "I told you before, I have no interest in the Faerie King."

"You say that now," Fayne had a wild look in her eye, "But after you meet him, it will be different. He has a... a *way* with people—a way of grabbing your attention one way or another. He fills all your thoughts..." the woman's words drifted off into silence and she seemed to stare into a blank space.

"Well," Lola sighed sympathetically, "Have you ever heard what people say about Elves?"

Fayne turned curiously, then shook her head.

"Well, we can be very single-minded about things, fixating on one passion until it takes over. So, I know what it is like for something to *fill up my mind*—it is very hard to think about anything else once something like that takes over! So, I appreciate the warning."

Fayne focused back on Lola's face. "Lola," she said, "I need him."

Lola's smile faded. That look on Fayne's face—that look of blind obsession—it was just like the face of the man who killed her mother. "Fayne," Lola said softly, "He will not satisfy the... the hole you feel inside yourself."

Fayne turned sharply. "*What*? What do you know of what I feel? Nothing!"

"Somenus is a man of *many* wives, Fayne. Do not give him your heart. He will... break it."

"I don't care about that!" Fayne scoffed, "All I need is to be *one* of his women; that would be enough for me."

It was shocking to hear a woman speak that way. Lola wondered what life this woman had lived before coming here. She sighed.

"I will do my best to keep my distance at the banquet tonight," Lola said, withdrawing her forces, "Hopefully he will notice you again."

"I thought you said you weren't going to attend the banquets!" Fayne said quickly.

"I got in trouble for staying away," Lola said quietly, remembering Felix's words. "I think I need to at least show up. You must understand..."

"Fine," Fayne waved her hand dismissively, "But if you get selected, I want you—"

"Lady Fayne," Lola said firmly, "How many times must I tell you? I will *not* be encouraging Somenus!"

<hr>

The Somensday banquet was the nightcap of the week; it was that night when the king rewarded himself for all his hard work and held an exceptionally large feast at the Vineyard Palace. This Somensday, he had invited the Faerie of the Vine as his honored guest, who very proudly arrived early, strolling around the array of posed women with his finger against his chin.

He had dusty blonde hair combed back in a wave, and eternally squinting eyes. His wings resembled the wings of a bird, though the feathers appeared to be made of a cloudy purple glass. While Lola had chosen a perch far on the outskirts of the pavilion, she ended up getting a good look at the Vine Faerie when he came to inspect the grapes growing along the palace wall beside her. She was told to remain perfectly still, and that her beauty could be better observed when she wasn't talking, but she wasn't sure if it was actually a rule.

"Did you grow those vines?" she asked in a whisper. The Faerie of the Vine whirled around, looking side to side.

"I say—who said that?" he asked as he brushed out his clothing.

"I did," said Lola. The Faerie gazed up at her.

"Oh, hello," he said with a smile. He stepped closer and placed his hands on his hips. "Aren't you supposed to..." he wasn't sure how to finish that sentence.

"I don't know," Lola shrugged, "It's my first day doing this, so I figure I should make all my mistakes. Plus—the king isn't here yet, is he? I'm Lola, by the way."

"I say," he chuckled, "You're a funny one. Nice—erm—outfit."

Lola glanced down at herself. She had chosen to wear white, hoping it would attract less notice than the other women wearing bright colors.

"Thanks," she said. She was maintaining her pose, which was simply to stand square on both feet with her hands folded at the waist. "What's your name?"

The Faerie grinned. "I don't think you're allowed to ask me that—but since it's your first day, and you're making all your mistakes—my name is Veritas," he bowed jovially, "XI Faerie of the Vine."

"Oh, Veritas!" Lola clapped her hands gently together, "That means truth!"

"Yes," he laughed, "It does. And to answer your previous question: no, I did not grow these vines." He glided over to one budding stem and touched a cluster of grapes. "No, these vines were planted by the first of my kind—thousands of seasons ago. A special place, this."

"Oh!" Lola exclaimed, "Do you make vino with them?"

"Why, yes," Veritas spun on his heel to grin at her, "I'll be pouring some tonight! A vintage from the season of Azure Rivets—eight seasons ago, now," he said while thoughtfully rubbing his thumbs together.

"You make vino for King Somenus?"

"I make vino—yes, yes—for Arelle." He turned his head to gaze out at the sky. "Ah, here he comes."

"The king?"

"Yes, Somenus himself!"

"Erm—Veritas? Can I ask you something?"

The Faerie turned to regard her curiously. "Hades—you're chatty."

"Yes, I've been told that many times. Um... can I ask you..."

"Yes?" he squinted.

"What do you think of the Faerie Rites?"

"Hades!" Veritas laughed. "Politics? At a Somensday banquet? You're breaking *all* the rules, aren't you, girl?"

"Yes, well," she batted her eyes innocently, "It is my first day, after all."

Veritas snorted. "Well—what do I *think* about the Rites? Not a very *narrow* question, is it? I could just say: I think they work."

"Do you think it is right? The Faeries being... worshiped? Like gods?" she asked cautiously.

"Well, define *gods*," Veritas said lazily, "We are greater beings, we were made before the mortals, and we have gifts to bestow. Why wouldn't we set up a system that works for everybody? Somenus has done a good thing by going and answering the Great Question; and I am not going to complain. King Sol sat on his laurels for thousands of seasons, just humming and hawing over the Question—acting as though it didn't even matter! Somenus has gone and done something about it."

Lola smiled courteously, trying to piece together what she thought the faerie might be talking about. "The Great Question?"

"Oh, dear, little harlot! Best not inquire into Faerie politics if you don't really know much about them. Ah, well, here he comes," he turned toward the landing platform where Somenus was cresting, his mighty four wings stretched out with a span as wide as a building. He marched down the catwalk with the confidence of a lion, then hid his wings just before walking between the first set of pillars.

Lola hurriedly resumed her pose. Veritas observed her with a chuckle.

"I just realized you're an Elf; no wonder you don't think the rules apply to you," he said in a low voice.

"Don't draw attention to me," she whispered, trying to keep her face from moving, "I'm not exactly wanting to meet the king just yet."

Veritas peered upwards. "Well, *now* you've gone and made me curious!"

"Please," Lola hissed, "go walk somewhere else so he doesn't—" she froze, shooting her eyes away from Somenus as he came gliding over.

Veritas bowed low, with a flamboyant swing of his arm, then rose.

"Sir Veritas," Somenus said with an easy smile, "Welcome." Lola was surprised to hear a voice so gentle coming from the man who had been called *The Nightmare Faerie*. It was deep, yes, but soft. Lola, trying to keep herself from being noticed, refused to steal a glance at the king, as curious as she was to see what he looked like up close.

"Ah, yes, Sire, thank you for the party, it's such an honor, and all that," Veritas said with that signature lisp the upper classes seemed to use when they wanted to appear haughty. "Pretty ladies, pretty ladies," he said, twirling a finger in the air.

"Are you easy to please?" Somenus asked amusedly, "Come on, have you found somebody you fancy?"

"Not for myself, no," Veritas feigned a yawn, fanning his mouth, "I wouldn't dare pick a favorite among *your* possessions, Sire. Never!"

Somenus chuckled. "Well, I—" his voice went silent. Lola, eavesdropping from up on her pedestal, grew nervous at the sudden absence of noise. The silence lengthened indefinitely. Then she saw motion in her peripheral vision, and Somenus walked into view. He looked up into her eyes with an expressionless stare. He said no words; he simply studied her face.

"Hello," she said.

"Hello," he replied.

"Ah, that one is an Elf, Sire," Veritas said, stepping up to the king's side. Veritas winked up at her. "She...erm...she's *chatty*."

"Lolette?" Somenus asked. With his black wavy hair and green eyes—yes, it was true what others had said, Somenus was a very attractive man.

"Yes," Lola said with as much civility as she could muster. Yes, he knew exactly who she was. Of *course* he did! He had her kidnapped!

"What do you think, Veritas?" Somenus asked, keeping eye contact with the princess, "Should I bring her along?"

"I say—" Veritas straightened his sleeves, "Do. She's dashed entertaining."

Somenus held up his hand to Lola. She couldn't think of anything else to do but take it. He helped her down. Lola first scanned the scene for Fayne, dreading her reaction. When she didn't find her, she turned back to the king and placed her hand on his arm, following him as he began to walk forward. His clothes didn't match the rest of the scene. While everyone else was draped in togas and loose robes, Somenus wore a suit, with tight trousers and gold buttons, just like the human noblemen. He kept one of his hands behind his back, tucked under his heavy, trailing robe, and the other he held firmly to the side, like a supportive rail for Lola to lean on.

Veritas stood on the king's other side, talking as he walked.

"And anyway, the two barrels I've had opened tonight are from the *Azure Rivets*, you know, one red, and one white. I think you're really going to appreciate the tartness of the white, knowing how much you love tartness, and we are having it cooled just to the—"

"Welcome to Arelle," Somenus said under his breath. Lola blinked, then turned to look at the man's face. She didn't feel that overwhelming obsession that everyone talked about when she looked at him, but she definitely felt there was something... *extraordinary* about his looks.

Welcome? she scoffed. He dragged her here against her will, and then says, *welcome?*

Somenus led her into the banquet hall. It was bustling with activity. The table had been set with tall candlesticks and polished silver settings. Other Faerie guests were already here, standing around with important looks and smug faces, all wearing gold bands around their heads. Servants walked here and there, holding trays of vino glasses, offering tastes to those in attendance. Lola turned away the glass offered to her.

"*Ah, ah, ah,*" Veritas chased down the servant holding the tray and snatched a glass from it. "No—Lola, I won't let you turn this away. It's a palate cleanser I've prepared. Go on," he pushed the drink into her hand. Lola glanced at her host who watched her with a vacant smile.

"Thank you, Veritas, I—"

"Drink, drink!" He clapped his hands. "Let's see what the lady thinks of my vino!"

Lola sipped. Her eyes sparkled. "Oh," she said quickly, "That's lovely!"

Somenus made a courteous chuckle. "Let me try," he said, then took her glass carefully from her fingers, still keeping his left hand behind his back. Lola watched as he sipped from the small, tasting crystal glass. He held the liquid in his mouth and seemed to swish his mouth side to side with a perplexed look on his face.

"Mmm," he nodded, "Not bad."

"Thank you—*thank you*, Sire," Veritas bowed three times, each with accelerated speed.

"I'm looking forward to the main event," Somenus said as he passed the mostly-full glass to a ready servant. "Come, Lolette, let's find our seats."

They broke away from where Veritas was talking animatedly about his vintages to whoever would listen and made their way toward the head of the banquet table.

"Well," the king said, "I suppose you want to ask me why I brought you here."

"I—" Lola turned to gaze up at him. "Yes!"

Somenus led her by the hand to her chair. A servant pulled it out for her, and she sat. Somenus sat beside her at the table's head, tossing his cape to his side. Lola gasped, noticing a stub where his left hand should have been. Somenus leaned back in his chair and stared at her blankly; he didn't seem to appreciate the reaction.

"That is..." Lola cleared her throat and crossed her legs at the ankles, "I wanted to ask..." she found herself struggling for words. *This* was the man that everyone was so afraid of? He was intimidating, for sure, but he seemed so calm... so understated!

"Princess Lolette," Somenus interjected, "Let me explain. I've ruled Raqia for over two seasons, now, and in all that time, I have sent delegations, hoping to make a peaceful alliance with Celestia, and your father."

"But you rule the Faeries, not the Elves!" Lola said bravely, "Why should we have to—"

Somenus held up his hand defensively, "Please," he chuckled, "Allow me to finish. I don't expect you to agree with everything I am doing, young one, I simply wanted to give you the honor of knowing the details. Yes, your father refused to allow any faerie influence to enter Celestia. He wouldn't so much as allow a single Faerie shrine to be placed within his borders, even though there are many within who wish to partake in the Rites. Now, I know you have been taught that every race should rule themselves, but you must understand *my* burden, princess: the burden of the *land*. Before humans ever came to Raqia, and before the Elves were made, we Faeries were given rulership of this land. And the Faerie king was given the throne—a throne that grants authority over all the soil, including the land of Celestia."

"But..." Lola's eyes seemed to gloss over. If that were true, then *did* her father have the right to shut out the Faerie King from their lands?

"A disobedient child may bar their parents from their bedroom," Somenus said, "But the parents still rule the house, and it is their *responsibility* to discipline their child."

"So, you took me... to *punish* my father?" Lola scowled.

"Believe it or not, Lolette, I took you out of kindness. I could have just gone to war with your father, but instead I am offering a..." he hesitated, his eyes drifting to the side, "A third option."

"Which would that be?" Lola asked bluntly, "Ransom or marriage?"

Somenus shifted his eyes back to her face, then smirked. "Well, either, depending on how things play out."

"Well, let me clear the air then," Lola raised her chin, "Marriage will not be an option."

Somenus snapped his mouth closed and leaned back, looking amused. He nodded.

"What?" Lola huffed, "Why are you making that face?"

Somenus shrugged.

"I really have my heart set on marrying a *different* sort of man, you know," she said quickly.

He nodded.

"For starters, I would never even *consider* marrying someone who already—" her face flushed, "...who already has wives!"

He nodded again.

Lola felt herself growing embarrassed, though she didn't know why. She cleared her throat nervously. Was she refusing a man who had never actually proposed to her? No, he had only just implied that he...

"Someone fill these empty glasses!" Veritas appeared on Somenus' other side and was waving his hands excitedly. "We are pouring the red—the *red*!"

Lola leaned back in her chair and lifted her napkin to her face. Why was she blushing?

"Lola," Veritas plopped himself on his chair gracelessly. "This red is going to," he paused to conceal a belch, "By the floods! It's going to send you to the Glassy Sea and back!"

Lola leaned to the side as a servant filled her glass to its rim. Her eyes shifted back to Somenus, who was still silently watching her with a lazy smirk. The king was provided a much larger goblet, but it was only filled to its halfway point. He took it in his one hand and sniffed it, finally turning to look at someone else.

"What's this one called, Veritas?" he asked the Vine Faerie.

"I told you, Sire," Veritas was standing now, swishing his vino in his glass, "Azure Rivets—red!"

"Oh," Somenus sipped quietly. "Yes, lovely," he said, then turned back to Lola. "What do you think, Princess?"

Lola had never had more than one sip of strong drink in one sitting. Nervous about losing her edge, she took the smallest of tastes. The drink filled her with unimaginable warmth, and she found herself smiling, despite her nervous discomfort.

"Beautiful," she said.

"Why thank you, thank you, thank you!" Veritas bowed three times, spilling vino onto the table with each movement.

"Sit down, Veritas," Somenus said, placing his jeweled goblet on the table. Veritas bumbled into a heap of apologies before scooting down the table to see how others reacted to his vino. It seemed that the only thing this man enjoyed more than his own vino was to hear others compliment it. The king exhaled softly through his nostrils, focusing his eyes on his goblet as he rotated it counterclockwise.

"So, what sort of man, then?" he asked.

"What?" Lola turned.

"You said you had your heart set on a certain sort of man. What sort of man is that?" His eyes remained fixed on his cup.

"Someone good, honest, and beautiful," Lola said automatically. She blushed. Those words sounded so weak, so meaningless when she said them out loud to him.

Somenus nodded. "The Transcendentals," he said.

"Yes," Lola was surprised to receive more than the usual blank stare.

"Did you know," Somenus continued to rotate his goblet, "that some used to say that those were the names of the Lights: the good, the true, and the beautiful?"

Lola's eyes widened in astonishment. "I—I hadn't heard that before."

Somenus' head bobbed thoughtfully. "Yes, there are many who believe those things are the source of magik, too."

"What?" Lola leaned forward, "Really?"

Somenus released his grip on his glass and leaned back to look at the princess blankly.

"No one is truly good," he said.

"I agree," said Lola, "But I'd like to be with someone who at least... tries."

"And how will you know?" he asked, "If someone is trying?"

Lola's mouth opened and closed wordlessly.

"I think it's nice," he shrugged, turning back to finger his cup, "To put an ideal before your own preferences. I think you're an exceptional person for doing that."

Lola's mouth still hung open. This was not the person she expected to meet when she sat down with the Nightmare Faerie.

"You make me jealous, actually," Somenus said absently.

"What?" Lola finally said, twisting her eyebrows curiously.

"You make me jealous," he said again, turning to regard her, "of The Transcendentals."

"What do you mean?"

"You've got a lot of..." he paused, searching for the word he wanted, "*affection*, Lolette. A man would be lucky to get it."

Lola felt herself blushing. "Well, I am flattered..."

"I'll speak with your father," Somenus said, straightening up in his chair, "Let's see if he takes the ransom. I won't force a marriage, of course."

"You... won't?" Lola asked with surprise.

"No," said the king. He motioned for a servant to serve food onto his plate. "But I hope to have the pleasure of your company again," he said as he snapped his napkin into place on his lap.

"Of course," Lola said politely. She couldn't exactly refuse, could she?

"Right, well," Somenus cleared his throat, "Honored guests!" He projected, "Let us eat!"

⁕

Lola was dreaming about the man from her vision again. It had left such a strong imprint on her mind; she had seen someone that she had not yet seen. How was that even possible? It was both real and fantasy at the same time. In her dream, she was sitting on the side of her balcony with her feet dangling off the edge, peering down at the man as he tried to scale the wall.

There he was, wearing a white tunic and a helmet covering his head, just like he was in the vision.

"Are you coming up here to save me from this place?" she was asking as she swung her ankles side to side. "I'm a princess locked away in this high tower—and here you are climbing up here to rescue me." Everything suddenly made sense; dreams were so helpful in that way.

"If I could just make it to the ledge," he said, "Then sure! I'd love to rescue you. *Erm*—what is it you need rescuing from?"

"The Nightmare Faerie," she said wistfully.

She saw his hand fumble on the balcony's ledge. "Nearly there," he said with a grunt, then his chin popped up to the ledge. She observed his dented helmet. "Hey!" he said in a friendly greeting, "What's your name?"

She laughed, "I'm Lola. And you are my Beloved. I saw you in a vision."

"Lola," said a voice. This voice came from behind her. She turned her gaze, but only saw darkness. When she whirled back to face her beloved, he was gone. She sighed in disappointment.

Someone else emerged from the shadows behind her and sat beside her on the ledge, his feet resting on the inward side of her room. She was both surprised and yet not surprised to see King Somenus there. It was a dream, after all, and nothing is ever really surprising in the dream plane.

"Who was that?" Somenus asked softly.

"He was…" Lola found that she could not remember, not when she was gazing into those clear, celadon eyes. Somenus—the man had been named after Somensday, the day of rest. With eyes like those, who couldn't find rest looking into them?

"Yes?" he asked, smiling faintly.

"I'm dreaming…" she said, her conscious mind suddenly pressing itself in, sensing something that didn't belong in a world of dreams.

"Yes," he said, his smile widening.

"But you… you're not a dream," she said, though she wasn't sure what she meant.

He raised an eyebrow playfully. "True," he said, "*I* am real."

Lola shook her head quickly, then gazed back toward the balcony. Who was it she had seen moments before? Wasn't there someone else?

12

—— Isabella ——

The Light City

I t had been two full weeks since Isabella split ways with her brother and the rest of the Purple Order. They had traveled out of the woodlands with her for a time, but Hanz had business that took him in the opposite direction to Arelle, so Isabella had traveled alone. Well—she wasn't *exactly* alone; she had four faerie companions, stuffed into little magikal bags. In all of those empty days, traversing the surface of the Table by her lonesome, Isabella could have opened one, but something deep inside her resisted. Though she knew the Faeries within were either willing or helpless, she still felt guilty. Here she was: dressed as Scarlet Wingsday, and taking them to their doom.

Arelle. Isabella lifted her eyes gently; there it was, the Light City—the kingdom of the Fae. Isabella was sitting on a rugged hill which provided a fantastic view of her surroundings. There were many places like this throughout Raqia; they were called Wayfinders Towers. Built apparently by the first skydeacons on level places of higher elevation, reachable by a level path, they were meant to be resting places for travelers. Constructed of white stone, the buildings were easy to spot from a distance, looking like little glowing temples.

Like a large gazebo, it was made of six pillars and a domed roof. There was a fire pit in the middle of the covered area, along with a striking steel and a pile of wood. An ever-burning torch was hung at the entrance, next to a stone-carved sign which read: Wayfinder's Respite, with a little golden seal underneath it. It read: *Maintained by the LXX Faerie over the Traveler*. Isabella sighed—that was one of the Faerie titles on Scarlet Wingsday's paper.

Isabella leaned against one of the pillars with her feet pointed at the little fire she had made. The lookout granted her a spectacular aspect of Arelle five miles to the Northeast. She could also make out the Labyrinth City of Bavel which stuck out of the skyline like a massive single mountain about fifty miles to the southwest. She exhaled loudly, relaxing herself. She hadn't realized she was so tense. She had lived a long quiet life in Paradise Valley, always surrounded by tall cliffs or dense trees. Seeing a view like this from a Wayfinders Tower was enough to take her breath away. She had no idea Raqia was so big!

It had been three weeks since she had agreed to her mission, but most of her time since had been arduous travel. Now that she was able to see Arelle up close—she could see with her own eyes why people called it "the Light City". It finally started to feel real.

Isabella had been given much advice and commentary on how she was to act and speak as Scarlet Wingsday, the infamous bounty hunter—but that sure didn't mean she felt ready. She was dressed for the part though, wearing a slick, black leather suit of armor, complete with an eye mask. Her long, dark hair was now wound on top of her head in a pristinely tidy top knot, clasped with a black leather band. She had blackened the outer edges of her eyes with a smudgy layer of eyeliner and her lips were touched with deep rouge.

Isabella wagged her knees back and forth, listening as the leather squeaked. Pants—she was wearing *pants*! She couldn't help but grow red in the face, knowing that someone would eventually see her dressed like this. It was one thing for her brother to see her—but men she didn't know?

Clothing is a magikal thing; it is like a temporary transformation. By changing what is on the outside, the inside is wooed to follow in the act. Isabella felt different, she walked differently—she simply *was* different, when she wore this outfit. Its maker had designed it for a purpose, and it did its work on her.

She felt powerful. She felt independent. She no longer looked like the innocent forest maiden—no—she no longer *was* the innocent forest maiden. She had an office to fill—to become—and that office was Scarlet Wingsday: the thief who would steal Orion's Bow.

She didn't feel all that new *yet*, but the costume seemed to give her just enough of a barrier between herself and the rest of the world to make her feel brave enough to walk through the gates of Arelle with enough confidence to lie.

"Scarlet," she said to herself in a whisper, reminding herself of her new name. She gazed down at her forearms which were tightly gloved. Then, she slowly pulled off the glove on her left hand and gazed at her inner forearm. It *looked* untouched, but it was only an illusion.

Isabella's mind drifted back, recounting a conversation with Hanz three weeks prior.

"The mark of the Purple Order," Hanz had said. He had used the Beatus Staff to imprint her arm with the glowing symbol. The tattoo looked like a stylized set of butterfly wings. It glowed so bright that it lit up the dark cellar. "This acts like a beacon, Isabella. With this, we can find you no matter where you are."

"Surely Korbin will notice this," she gazed at it apprehensively.

"Most of us keep our arms covered so that we can remain hidden. But for you, I think that will not be enough."

"No," Riah shook her head slowly, "Anyone working closely with Korbin will need more protection. But my spell will be perfect for that." She rubbed her hands together, causing black and purple sparks to emit from her pendant necklace.

"Spell?" Isabella pursed her lips.

"Nothing bad," Hanz shook his sister's shoulder boyishly, "Remember we said we would put a spell on you that would keep anyone from recognizing you? Well, this spell will act as a covering for you, hiding anything *recognizable* such as your face and the Purple Mark."

"Are you *sure* that will keep him from knowing I am your sister?" She still felt scared.

"Not Faerie, nor human, nor beast, nor Elf could see through this spell, Isabella. Even *we* will struggle to see you as you are." Riah assured her.

"But everything will change when you find Urbis, the ancient bow." Hanz warned her, growing solemn.

"Urbis?" Isabella asked, growing overwhelmed.

"That's the name of Orion's Bow," Hanz said. "Once you find it, that's when you need to break the spell. Otherwise, we will never be able to find you, and neither will our contact, the Messenger Faerie. The illusion spell hides the mark, therefore rendering it useless to us. So, once you find the bow, and you know you are safe—you must activate the mark, which will cause the illusion to dissipate. So, you must make sure you are secure. Then, Leck will come."

Isabella's mind drifted back to the present. Would this spell really be enough to shield her from being found out?

You must make sure you are secure. The words echoed in her mind as she gazed down at her arm. She observed the Light City once more, noting its towering walls. Would Leck really be able to come get her out of there when the time was right? She was going into the mouth of the lion, and without any assurance that her lifeline would remain viable. Tristan's warnings began to seem more sobering now that she was really alone.

So... The plan, she thought. As Scarlet Wingsday, Isabella was meant to bring her four Exilium Prison bags to Korbin, claiming her reward as one of his officers. Inside were four Fae who had apparently given themselves up as prisoners to be able to complete this task. In all this time, Isabella had convinced herself that the task would be easier done if she never spoke with the Faeries, but the closer she got to Arelle, the more the guilt weighed on her. Perhaps if she could just hear from their own lips that they were willing to do this, she wouldn't feel so bad?

She reluctantly opened one of the sacks.

Inside was a small, palm-sized Faerie with silver dragonfly wings. He stretched his back and shielded his eyes from the sudden burst of light. He yawned, then peered up at Isabella. Seeing the masked woman, he chuckled to himself. "Just had to gloat once more?" He observed his surroundings. "We aren't even in Arelle yet."

"What's your name?" she asked softly. He narrowed his eyes.

"You *know* my name."

She shook her head. "I am Isabella, remember? I am the sister of Hanz."

His eyes widened. "Oh! I forgot..." he scratched his head, no doubt trying to remember his timeline. "These damn bags make everything so confusing. Your spell is powerful," he examined her closely, "I thought you were Scarlet Wingsday."

"I suppose that's a good thing," she shrugged. "So, what is your name?"

"I am Via." He bowed unceremoniously, tripping over a fold in her skin. "I am the LXX Faerie over the Traveler."

"Oh!" She glanced over at the wayfinder placard then back at him. "You made this place?"

He grinned proudly. "No, I did not make it, but I maintain it. *Erm...*" his face fell. "I used to, anyway."

"You bless the traveler?" she asked curiously. Growing up in the Valley, her father had told her some details about the Fae, but she never had much experience with them.

"I look out for them, yes, yes—and they look out for me." He closed his eyes as if trying to remember a past life. "How long have I been in this bag?" He looked fatigued.

"I don't know," she sighed. "But it has been three weeks since I set out."

He nodded. "Next is Arelle?"

"Yes." She frowned. "I am afraid I am taking you to General Korbin."

He smiled encouragingly at her, hiding his own fears. "Yes, it is something I agreed to. Your brother seems to have a plan."

"What will he do to you? Korbin, that is," she asked hesitantly.

Via sat down on her hand, looking increasingly drained. "I am not sure. No one really knows what he does with those of us he manages to get his hands on. I can only imagine he imprisons us for life."

"Will he try to get you to serve the new King?" she asked.

"I am sure he will try—but who can know? Any of us who have fled the new rule are in hiding. We don't know much."

"How many of you refused to join the Faerie Rites?"

"It's hard to know, but probably more than the Faerex wants to admit, and less than Hanz wants to claim."

"Via..." Isabella gazed sorrowfully at the beautiful creature sitting serenely on her hand.

"Yes?"

"I don't think I can do this to you—take you to Korbin, that is." She felt herself wavering. "It doesn't feel right."

"Well," he laid back into her palm, resting his hands behind his head. "We all already made our choice, didn't we? Once I am exiled in one of these bags, only the Faerie King can let me out. Did you know that? So, my only hope here is a new King, isn't it?" He closed his eyes.

"I suppose so," said Isabella sadly, "But it still doesn't feel right! Is this really the only way I can..."

Via was asleep. This was the sad yet merciful effect of the Exilium Prisons, Hanz had told her. The bags slowly drained the Faerie's Magik, taking all power away from them, with only enough for them to stay alive. This made them tired and dormant. It was barely an existence.

Isabella lovingly slipped him back into the bag and pulled the drawstrings tight, allowing him to find some rest from his imprisonment. It felt like such a tragedy trapping someone so influential and important in a little bag, keeping them from their life's purpose. But Isabella reminded herself that she was *not* Scarlet Wingsday—not the old one, anyway—she wasn't the villain who had imprisoned this Fae. She was the one who would free him from this bag, she promised herself.

"I must do this," she told herself, kicking ash over the small fire with her leather boot. She gathered up her traveler's sack, wrapped her black cloak around her shoulders and drew the hood over her face. Then she turned her face toward Arelle and descended the hill.

—•—————•—————•—

A couple hour's walk brought Scarlet Wingsday to the mighty gates of Arelle. A long stone bridge led her over a wide but still river and up to the entrance of the Faerie City. The city was surrounded by walls fifty stories high, and if there were any guards stationed atop them, no one could tell. From down under the looming white gates, she stared hopelessly at them. How was one supposed to get in?

How would Scarlet Wingsday act? she asked herself, trying her best to remain fearless, if that were at all possible. She pulled the gold, palm-sized seal out of her cloak. Its fat, silky tassel hung off it swinging, saturated with bright red dye. She let the light flash off the gold for a moment, holding the thing tightly with authority. She *did* have permission to enter.

Just then, a shadow passed over her. Isabella looked up to see four jagged silhouetted wings descending over her. She felt an urge to scream as a thing of nightmares soared toward her, but she held her nerve.

A dark-haired Fae with pale skin and glassy eyes landed in front of her, holding out his hand. She froze for a moment, unsure of what to do, then she realized he was asking for her seal. She passed it to him.

The Fae glanced down at it, then looked up at her, narrowing his eyes. "I am Felix, II Faerie of Sight," he said.

"I am…"

"Scarlet Wingsday." He looked back at the seal. "I know who you are."

The spell seemed to be working, but Isabella still felt petrified with doubt.

"I am here to…" she began, endeavoring to remain confident.

"I know why you're here; show me the bags." He passed the seal back to her and crossed his arms.

Isabella forced herself to keep her chin high, despite how nervous she was, and pulled a cluster of Exilium Prisons out of her satchel. Then she passed him the letter from Korbin, detailing the exact Fae she was asked to apprehend. Felix raised his eyebrows and nodded slowly.

"Impressive," he said, though his face showed no emotion. He opened one of the bags and peeked inside, then quickly closed it again. "Well!" He bowed his head to her slightly. "Let's get you inside."

Turning around to face the gates, Felix held up his hand and they began to creak open. Isabella took in a deep breath, then let it out determinedly as she followed Felix into the Light City.

She could not believe the beauty of the place. Every stone, every tree, every work of architecture in Arelle was both ancient and perfect. There was no crack of rock, no tarnished metal, no blemish in sight. It was a perfectly kept city with a design that felt both planned and unpredictable at the same time. No two buildings were alike in design, though everything was made of polished white marble. Color, however, splashed across the scene by way of trees and plants, some dangling over rooftops, some springing out of roadsides. It had the appeal of a wild garden, but was, in every way, shape, and form, neatly kept.

Isabella couldn't help but smile as she passed through the city, knowing she was one of few humans who had ever been allowed to do so. Unlike the average human metropolis, this place was not bustling with foot traffic and busy streets. It was quiet, serene, with only a few dotted Faeries who seemed to be taking daily strolls.

Felix led her through the main city square, where there did seem to be more Fae out and about, perhaps twenty at most, but then the scene seemed to change as they walked down a side street which sloped upwards. As she lifted her eyes, Isabella could see a building of more squarish and geometric proportions, jetting into the sky. Though it was made of the same white marble as the rest of Arelle, it seemed to emanate gloom.

Felix stopped to gaze at it.

"Fort Axes," he said, "General Korbin rules here."

Rules? It was a strong word to use for a military leader, wasn't it?

Felix pressed forward, signaling Isabella to follow him up a steep climb of wide stairs. As she came to the entrance to the Fort, she read the carved inscription over the portcullis which was one of the only indications of vandalism she had seen since entering the city. Carvings in the stone read: *Fort Axes*, and underneath, *General Dezmund, XXIV Faerie of War*. A dark crusty layer of black paint had been used to cover up the War Faerie's name, though it was still easily read. Isabella wondered why, after two seasons, Korbin wouldn't just replace the inscription with a new one.

They passed under the iron portcullis, and once inside, the mood of their surroundings changed drastically. The shiny-white marble that made the rest of the city glow was messily splashed with the same blackish paint which stained

Dezmund's name. Blackness was smeared throughout the entire interior of Fort Axes. And what's more, it stunk. Isabella's mind was cast back to childhood memories of broken legs and scuffed knees. She knew what her senses were detecting—it was blood she smelled. Old blood.

Her skin began to crawl as they made their way through the courtyard, and her mind began to reluctantly calculate the amount of blood it would require to cover an area this large. Once she could no longer stomach thinking about it, she locked her eyes on the back of Felix's wings which seemed to be the only untarnished thing in her sight. Isabella thought she might vomit as the stench attacked her senses in waves each time she dared to breathe.

The courtyard was filled with human soldiers. They loitered about, leaning on their spears, and talking amongst themselves with gruff, unhurried voices. The army of bandits didn't seem like something that belonged in Arelle, but they did seem to belong here in the blood-stained Fort Axes. One of the burly soldiers poked the man next to him, pointing over at Isabella as she passed. Moments later, she was serenaded by a chorus of catcalls and filthy remarks; she could practically feel splashes of ugliness hitting her, like the blood on the glorious white marble within Fort Axes.

Was this horrid place to be her new residence?

There was a manor house within the fortress, and Felix hid his wings in order to enter the place. Isabella followed along.

"Do you... work for Korbin?" Isabella asked, endeavoring to break the tense silence.

Felix of Sight shot her a glance, then faced forward again, continuing his march. "No," he said, "I serve the king."

"Sure," Isabella mumbled. What else could she possibly ask him, now? Do you like it here? What's it like serving a usurper? Would you mind telling me where Orion's Bow is kept?

"You're the first hunter to come back with the required Faeries," Felix said at length, "So... I have a feeling Korbin will be pleased."

He was trying to encourage her; somehow it made her feel worse.

"Oh yeah?" she asked, "No one else came back?"

"No, we've had a lot of Faeries turned in. I am just surprised you actually grabbed them... *all*."

Isabella suddenly felt the desperate need to swallow; but swallowing now would only make her seem as suspicious as she was! She let the saliva collect in her mouth nervously. Did this Felix Faerie *suspect* her?

Once inside the building, her world grew even darker. Few torches or lamps were lit, so the only thing she could really see was the carpeted floor that led her through some sort of foyer and into a dark, cave-like room. If she didn't actually witness herself walking through the front door, Isabella would have guessed that she was inside some sort of underground cellar. The black stone walls were greasy with moisture and there was hardly a single piece of furniture. A large stone table stood at the center of the room, and sitting on the other side of it was a crooked figure, lurched over and shrouded in thick shadows.

"Scarlet Wingsday, my Lord." Felix bowed reverently. Isabella curtsied, hoping it wasn't too ladylike for a bounty hunter.

The figure moved. In the darkness, its shapelessness seemed to slide into the form of a human figure. Isabella could hear the sounds of popping joints and cracking bones as he rose into a towering silhouette. His hands dropped down onto the table where one of the few torches shed some dreary light; she could see his long fingers spreading.

"Scarlet," he said in a deep, honey-like voice. "Welcome."

The voice was all too familiar, and Isabella felt like she was back in the tavern, cornered by the monstrous, seven-foot villain.

"Light the lamps," he yawned.

Felix took hold of a torch and walked around the room, lighting things up. Isabella winced, expecting Korbin to look more like a monster than a man as the light shone on him. Surprisingly, though bony and crooked, he looked very much like the human she had met in the tavern. He stood there, pale as death, as if he had spent too much time indoors.

"Let's see what you brought," he said, holding his palms out to her. His arms were so long that though he was standing, he still needed to bend his elbows sharply in order to rest the backs of his hands on the table.

Isabella boldly dropped the bags, the letter, and the seal all onto the stone table. Korbin grinned widely.

"Well!" He sucked air in through his gritted teeth with delight as he picked up the letter, reminding himself which Fae he had asked her to collect. "This is quite the haul."

"I did what you asked," she replied, "nothing more, nothing less." She said the line just how she had practiced a hundred times before this.

"I see that," he said, making eye contact with her. He paused, raising both his eyebrows. "I say," he paused and walked crookedly around the table until he came face to face, looming over her. "Take off the mask." She did so, looking up at his under-nose confidently. "You look..." his eyes studied her face for what felt like an eternity.

This was the moment of truth—or lies, one could say—Did he know who she was?

"Well, you're a pretty little thing, aren't you?" he said, tapping his chin with a sinister grin, "Quite unspoiled, I think." He then leaned on the table with one of his hands, cackling to himself.

Was she overthinking things, or were those the exact same words he had said to her in the village of Nemus? Her heart began to race. He knew who she was—*surely*. Unless, of course, he used the same lines with just about any woman he came into contact with.

He straightened, ending his cackling with a clearing of his throat. "Anyway, Wingsday, I did not expect you to be so *dainty*. Thank you for that momentary distraction."

"Oh, please," she rolled her eyes, allowing some of her sass to make an appearance. "Are you done?"

Korbin chuckled in response. "For now."

"Is she staying?" Felix asked impatiently, reminding the two of them of his presence. Korbin grinned widely again.

"Yes, she is staying. You may return to your post."

Felix scoffed. "I'll go where I please," he said, "I don't answer to you."

Korbin turned to sneer at the Faerie.

Felix bowed to Korbin then nodded his head at Isabella before he left the room. Isabella felt a jolt of fear as he left, realizing she would be alone with the monster. *No*, she would have to get used to this. She needed to stick it out through this meeting, then hopefully, once she got her position, she wouldn't have to talk to him very much.

"Come with me, Wingsday," Korbin said, his volume rising as he marched toward the door. Isabella jolted to attention. "And take those bags with you."

She gathered up the four faerie bags and skipped after Korbin as he swiftly exited the room. The two of them left the manor house and crossed the blood-stained courtyard. The abusive voices assaulted her once more, getting a rise out of Korbin who seemed thoroughly entertained by the mess of disorganized soldiers. She kept her eyes on Korbin, unwilling to look at the rabble rousers, and followed the general as he descended into an underground level of the fortress.

"You could hardly call this an army," she muttered, "your dim-witted soldiers seem useless." She allowed herself to be vocal, telling herself that it was part of the role she was playing.

Korbin laughed again, clasping his hands behind his back as he descended the stairs in rickety thuds. "Dim-witted, *yes*, that is how I like them. They are worms."

"I suppose as long as they take your orders, you don't care how they carry themselves?" she asked skeptically.

"Care?" He chuckled again, "About *worms*?"

They descended into the dark underbelly of Fort Axes. It had the appeal of an old Roman Sewer system. The architecture was, in its way, pretty, with curving passageways and keystoned archways, it felt like a labyrinth to someone like Isabella who had never been there. She wondered what could be down there.

It did not take too long to find out. As they walked the main, wide strip, she began to realize that many of the archways on either side were laced with iron bars. It was a dungeon of sorts. Each barred enclosure seemed to be empty, right up until they came to the very end of the hall. There were two points of interest.

Firstly, there was one big cell here at the end of the strip, as large as a schoolroom. One lone prisoner stood within, looming like a shade. Secondly, there was a bookshelf of sorts, built into the wall, containing several rows of Exilium Bags.

"Put them there," Korbin pointed his elongated index finger toward the bags, "And remember this," he moved his hand to point at the bottom shelf. "See those dusty ones?"

"Training another minion?" A voice spoke from the darkness. Isabella glanced at the cell to see a lanky, long-haired faerie leaning against the bars, peering at her with deep purple eyes.

"Silence, worm," Korbin grumbled in annoyance. Isabella wondered momentarily who the prisoner was. Korbin continued, "The dusty ones, see their color?"

"Yes," she observed.

"Those have been," he paused to give her a toothy grin, "*drained*."

"You mean they have run out of Magik?" she asked, remembering what Hanz had told her. The bags drained the Fae of their lifeforce.

"Just about," he said.

"These are the Faeries who oppose the king? Somenus keeps them here?" she asked.

The caged fairy scoffed. Korbin shot a glare at him, then looked back at Isabella. "Yes, this is the place for his enemies."

"Why isn't *he* in a bag, then?" she asked, nodding in the direction of the cell. Korbin didn't answer. He simply pointed back at the shelves, reminding her to place the bags there. She began to shelve the faeries, feeling a growing sense of doom. These four Faeries had entrusted themselves to her; now she was putting them here, in this dank prison, just to be drained of all life?

"He's afraid of me," the faerie in the cell said, laughing, as if the very idea was ridiculous.

Korbin groaned. "Wingsday, collect the drained bags from the bottom shelf."

Isabella apprehensively picked up the bags.

"And those, get those empty bags there." He pointed to a pile of empty Exilium Prisons.

Korbin nodded in satisfaction, then set off back the way they came, saying, "Follow."

She trailed after him, but not without taking a backward glance at the mysterious faerie. He was still staring at her through the bars.

Korbin led her down an alternate passageway, mumbling for her to remember which one. She hurriedly shot her eyes around, looking for some sort of recognizable marker. She didn't see one, so she told herself to watch on the way back.

"General," she said, "who was that?"

"He's a worm." *Worm*—he loved that word. He seemed all too familiar with it, like someone who had spent far too much time with them; and perhaps he had.

Before long, they came to the end of the passageway where there was nothing but a lone iron door. Korbin stopped at the door, turning to her with a smirk. "Give me the bags," he said.

She passed them to him.

"At the top of the stairs," he said, pointing back where they had come from, "Captain Banther will be stationed there. Tell him to take you to the Craftsman to return whatever empty bags you have."

"You...are not coming?" She stared down at the drained bags, wondering what he was going to do with them.

He grinned. "Eager to stay by my side?"

She grimaced. "No. But you promised to make me an officer if I did what you asked."

He laughed openly, leaning back against the iron door drunkenly. "*Major Wingsday*," he raised his eyebrows twice, "how is that?" She nodded slowly, feeling relieved at least that the beginning of her plan seemed to be working. "Alright, *Major*. Return the bags to the Craftsman and then we can make arrangements for you to stay."

"Alright," she said, stepping away from him.

"I will see you soon," he reassured her.

It wasn't a comfort.

When she ascended the stairs and came back into contact with the light, it was barely a momentary relief before the stench of old blood accosted her. She glanced around, scanning for "Captain Banther". There was a human soldier with silver pins on both shoulders, indicating some sort of rank. She marched up to him confidently.

"Captain?" she asked. The man turned to her, eyeing her up and down with condescension.

"Who are you, wench?" he asked dismissively.

"That's *Major*, to you." She flaunted her superior title. "The general said you'd know where the Craftsman is."

The captain spat on the ground. "*Major*, huh? Good for you."

"Take me," she ordered.

"I am not taking orders from you," he stretched out his arms, "I am only doing this 'cause the boss asked me to."

Surprising even herself, Isabella reached for her obsidian dagger and thrust it, unsheathed, under the captain's throat. "Disrespect me again, and I'll paint this place some more." He yelped like a disobedient dog, offering her apologetic eyes.

"This way," he held up his hands with a whimper. "Major!"

She sheathed her dagger and followed as the man skipped ahead, leading her out of Fort Axes.

That felt too easy, she chuckled to herself. Perhaps playing the tough girl role wouldn't be the hardest thing about this mission. It came pretty easily, ordering low-lifes around; she wasn't sure if she should be more pleased or disappointed with herself.

It was a relief to leave Fort Axes and walk amongst the white marble once more. This time, however, she felt like *she* was the dirty presence whose footsteps tarnished the pretty place. After the sticky, blood-stained Fort Axes, the city looked all the more reflective to her.

Reflections were something new in Isabella's world. Growing up in the Valley, with the shiniest objects being that of rippling ponds, foggy matte glass, and black hammered iron, Isabella had never so much as seen her own face's distinguishable traits on a smooth surface. She knew she was pretty—based on others' remarks—but witnessing it in a mirror wasn't something she had ever been burdened with. Now, in the dazzling faerie capital, where even polished marble pillars cast off some sort of reflective light, she saw herself often—only rather than seeing herself as that young, bright eyed village girl, she only saw a dark-clad villain. Scarlet Wingsday, a woman whose beauty was still evident, but whose innocence was shrouded.

Captain Banther led her through a little gate into one of the residential grounds inside the Light City. He pointed up at the house which sat happily within.

"The Craftsman lives here," he said. "I trust you know how to get back?"

"Go," she said.

What a pretty little house! She felt like an imposter to its peaceful existence, but pressed on knowing she had the authority to be there. Walking through the front door, she witnessed a quaint little workshop within. A lone Faerie sat bent over a desk, sewing tiny stitches into a piece of fabric while staring through a bubbly magnifying glass. He had an ancient look about him, though his face appeared young. Sandy brown hair was pulled delicately behind his head in a single braid.

"Hello," she said politely, not wishing to disrupt his work. The Craftsman peered up at her, past his large magnifying glass. He sighed defeatedly at the sight of her.

"What is it?" he asked.

"I'm Major Wingsday," she said—owning it, "I've got some bags for you."

He looked a little fearful after hearing the 'Major' in her title, and stood quickly, holding out both hands.

"Of course," he said hastily, "please hand them over!"

She placed her satchel on the ground and pulled out three unused Exilium prisons. He took them carefully, examining them closely.

"What is your name?" she asked. He glanced over, surprised at her interest.

"Why," he cleared his throat proudly, "I am Everwood, XVI Faerie of Craftsmanship."

"Ah," she raised her eyebrows, remembering the shrine she saw in her hometown. "Nemus?" she asked.

He started, blinking continuously in surprise. "What about it?"

"It's a village in the Raqian Woodlands. I—erm—I passed through there," she said, "I saw you have a shrine there now."

"Yes, well," he blustered with hot red cheeks. "I suppose you must have."

She sat herself on an empty chair without being asked and put her boot up on a table, leaning a little heavily into her role. "So what, you get a shrine, humans pray to you, then you get magik?"

He bristled at the brashness of her question.

"I," he began to stutter, "Not exactly, no. The shrine is there to give humans the chance to get aid. I can't exactly draw magik from this far away, you know. Now," he held up a hand defensively, "The Faerie Rites are new, and they will take getting used to," he cleared his throat uncomfortably, "but King Somenus at least has answered the Question for us. I will not argue with that."

"*Question*?" She frowned. "What question?"

"Miss," he bowed his head politely, then began to neatly fold the bags and place them in a chest, "I do not imagine you would know about the Question, or what it is, but it is very important to the Fae—something King Sol neglected to solve. Somenus, well, he has answered it for us."

"I see," she didn't feel satisfied by the cagey response, but she didn't press him further. "So, you make these bags, don't you? These—Exilium Prisons?" She kept up her tough act, when in reality she was just motivated by curiosity.

"I do," he said with a blank expression. "My King has requested this of me. I am the only one who can make them. Tricky thing, imprisoning a Faeie."

"And I see you're making more," she glanced at a roll of fabric, similar to that of the bags she had just handed him, resting on the cutting table.

He nodded solemnly. "I am."

"Why?"

"Well, I suppose the king wants to be prepared."

"Looks like you've made quite a few," she said, standing. She walked across the room and opened the chest he had placed her bags in. She raised her eyebrows. Inside there must have been hundreds. "Everwood," she turned, "How *many* did the king ask you to make?"

"P–please, if I am not making them fast enough," he said, shaking. Hades—he was terrified! He knelt before her. "Is this why you have come? Am I... have I done wrong?"

Isabella was horrified at the show of submission. "Please, get up!" She panicked.

The Faerie rose to his feet and bowed again, trembling. "Miss, are you here to kill me?"

Isabella didn't know what to do, her heart pumped guilt through to the rest of her body, and she was frozen for a moment, thinking of what to say.

"No," she mumbled, trying to remain calm. "But I asked you, how many have you been asked to make?"

"Well," he glanced over at the chest, touching his fingertips slowly as if adding up numbers in his head.

"Just how many does the king want?" she pressed, unsure as to why the answer felt so important to her.

"Nine hundred and ninety-nine," he blurted, fearful that she might threaten him if he didn't give her an answer.

"Nine hundred and..." she stammered, "Aren't there a thousand Faerie titles, Everwood?" she asked.

"Well, yes, that's right," he answered.

"Everwood," she sighed, "Why would you think I was here to kill you?"

He blinked. "Isn't that..." he hesitated, "Isn't that what you humans are here for?"

"Is it?" she asked weakly. "I only just arrived."

Everwood nodded gravely. "Miss," he said, "humans carry death with them. Before Korbin's army came in here, the only way a Faerie could die was through the command of the king, and he almost never used the scepter."

"Humans didn't come into Arelle before Somenus?"

"But rarely," he said.

She nodded. "Look, I am sorry for scaring you. I was only sent to drop off the bags, alright? You're doing... fine."

It was becoming clear exactly what it meant to the Faeries to have human soldiers galivanting around in their capital. It meant death. These immortal beings, who had reigned over Raqia for thousands of years, hardly ever letting humans set foot in their holy city, now had bullies marching around their homes, constantly threatening them with their life's end. Everwood, Isabella guessed, had been worn down until he had no more will. Here he was, sewing day after day, using his gift of craftsmanship to enslave an entire generation of Faeries, most likely including himself, and all he was scared of in this moment was her.

"Thank you for your time," she said, unable to keep herself from leaving him with some sort of polite remark. There, in his mess of meaningless monotony, she left him.

Once she was outside, she stopped to take in a breath of the clean air.

"These people," Korbin said from behind her. Isabella turned to see him leaning against a shadowy wall, as if clinging to the only lightless corner of Arelle. "The Faeries, such sad little beings, aren't they?"

13

Winter's End

Cymbeline's wings appeared in a brilliant flash of brightness. Four perfectly white feathered wings glistened, flapping victoriously, as if thankful to have the chance to stretch themselves out. Cymbeline opened her eyes.

"Oh my god," I exclaimed as I rubbed my head in amazement. "That's so cool!"

Momentum was silent, half stunned as he took in the sight. He began to nod slowly to himself.

"Right, I see," he said, "Cymbeline—do you see anything odd?"

Cymbeline focused her sights on him suspiciously. "Aside from you?"

"Work with me," he said in a calming voice, "Just focus, and look around. Is anything... glowing?"

Cymbeline's face softened and she took in a deep breath. "Glowing, you say?"

"Yes," Momentum shifted his eyes up toward the sky, then back at her. I knew he was concerned about the same thing that was gnawing at the back of my own mind: was the Nightmare Faerie about to find us? "Is there anything that you see that looks different now that your wings are out. Anything that has a particular glow to it?"

Cymbeline exhaled. "I think so," she said, looking a bit unsure of herself. "But I mean... I think everything has a glow."

"Everything?" Momentum pressed, "Are you sure?"

"Well," Cymbeline gazed around at the scenery. "The tree branches... and the..." she was mumbling, "The wind—I can see the wind."

"What about this?" Momentum waved his arm in the air, "How about my arm?"

"Yes, it's glowing. Am I answering these questions right?"

Momentum dropped his arm, then glanced at me. "I know who she is," he said.

"Is it... bad?" I whispered. There was dread in his eyes.

"No," he said hesitantly, "No, I think it's good."

"Then why have you got that look on your face?" I whispered even lower. He pushed me away from him by the shoulder.

"Listen, Cymbeline," Momentum said, raising his voice. "We haven't got much time. I am going to ask you to help us, but it is going to be quite draining on you. I don't have time to explain everything, but what I can tell you is that it will save us all from a dreadful future. Are you... will you trust me?"

Cymbeline's eyes widened. "What? That's—that sounds ominous."

Momentum walked up to her, then knelt. "Please," he said, "we need your help. Will you please help us?"

I marched up to the two of them and placed a hand on Cymbeline's shoulder.

"You can trust him," I said, "Please. Someone evil is chasing us. Will you do as he says?"

"Fine," she said, stepping back. "Will you please get up now?"

Momentum rose to his feet. "Right," he said, "We don't have much time. Leo," he held out his hand toward me. I took it. He held out his other hand toward Cymbeline, and she took it cautiously.

Catching the hint, I glanced at her, smiling warmly as I held out my hand. Her eyes studied me for a moment, then she took my hand.

"Alright," I said, clearing my throat, "We are all in a circle now... so..."

Momentum had his eyes closed, and I felt him tighten the grip around my hand. Then, I felt wind whirring violently around me.

I blinked. We were suddenly indoors. I felt Cymbeline's grip on my hand loosen into lifelessness and reacted quickly enough to turn and dampen her fall as she wilted to the ground. Momentum grabbed her from the other side, and we found ourselves all sitting on the floor. I gazed down at Cymbeline; she seemed to have lost all her color. And no, I don't mean she was pale—I mean she actually looked colorless, like an old black and white movie.

"Momentum!" I gasped, touching her forehead. Then I felt her wrist for a pulse. "What's happened to her?"

"She's alright," he said, panting. I lifted my eyes to observe him; he seemed spent, too.

"What did you *do*?" I asked as I pulled her limp body up to prop her head on my lap.

He sighed and wiped some sweat from his brow. "I—that is—*she*, saved us. I just helped her along. She's the Transport Faerie."

"You knew which faerie she was... just by looking at her wings?" I asked.

He nodded. "I'd know those wings anywhere," he said ominously.

I raised an eyebrow. "And the whole *glowing* thing?"

"It's a faerie thing," he said, shrugging, "She pulls magik from movement, so I was checking to see if she could see movement around her."

"Pulls magik?" I asked.

"Come on," he rose to his feet with a grunt, "Let's get her somewhere quiet so she can recover. Don't worry, it won't take long. She's more powerful than she looks."

I hoisted Cymbeline up into my arms, then rose to my feet. Being a first responder in my life before Raqia, I had carried my fair share of limp bodies, so Cymbeline's small frame was an easy thing to manage. I stood beside Momentum and took a moment to gaze around.

"Where are we, Momentum?" I asked. We were standing at the center of the large hall. The reflective tiles beneath our feet were arranged in a circular mosaic pattern, in which we were at the center. The room was octagonal, with doors on four of the walls. On the four other walls hung four massive tapestries. Torches lined the room, burning brightly.

Momentum was dusting himself off and fixing the buttons on his coat so that they were all right-side-up.

"Is this the place you said where Somenus couldn't track us?" I asked.

He finally turned to me and offered a subdued yet proud smile. He nodded. "Yes," he said, "This is Winter's End: my home. Come on!"

He moved toward one of the doors. Above the door's frame was a placard imprinted with the symbol of a leaf. He walked through it and I followed, carrying the unconscious Cymbeline along.

"This is the Autumn wing," Momentum mumbled as we passed through a covered sky bridge. Rows of leaded windows provided a glimpse at the nearby scenery, which looked mostly of grey mist. We moved quickly through it, entering the Autumn wing. Rustic grey stone walls adorned a decent sized sitting room.

"This place is huge," I finally said as we crossed through the room. Momentum was marching toward a hallway. "Do you live in a *castle* or something?"

"I call it a house," Momentum said casually. He led me down the long hall, lined with closed doors. He opened the first one and led me inside. It was a bedroom. Simple but elegant, it had a bed, a washing table, a writing desk, and a wardrobe. Black iron candelabras lit the place warmly, as did a gentle fireplace.

"You left all your candles burning?" I asked as I peered around. "Isn't that a fire hazard?"

Momentum snorted. "Leo," he said, "I've been around long enough to acquire some everburns." He pointed at the bed. "Put her there."

I walked over to the bed and carefully placed Cymbeline down upon it. Already, her color seemed to be returning. She cracked her eyes open to look at me just as I slipped my arms out from under her. She gave me a weak smile.

"Leo," she groaned, "Where am I?"

"We're at Momentum's..." I glanced toward Momentum, then back at her, "*House*. You're safe. Just rest."

"How did we get here?" she asked weakly.

"Uh, *you* brought us here, Cymbeline—with Momentum's help."

"What?" Her eyes blinked repeatedly. "I..." she searched my face, "I can... *go* places, can't I?"

I nodded, "I think so. I think you can travel wherever you want." I turned to Momentum for confirmation. He nodded once.

"That explains..." her eyes grew heavy, "a lot."

"Just rest here," I said, "We'll be back to check on you. Momentum says you'll get stronger nice and quick."

I moved away from her bedside as her eyes drifted closed and walked to Momentum's side. "Hey—if movement gives her power, shouldn't we like... bring her somewhere where there's, uh... movement?"

He chuckled. "Leo," he said, "Firstly, we are by the sea. She can't get more movement than that. But secondly, she could be in a desert and still gain magik; she's one of the most," his eyes drifted to the side, "*powerful* Faeries on the world."

"Is that why she has four wings?" I asked, "Does that mean she's powerful, or something?"

"No," he moved to leave the room. I followed along by his side. "No, that has to do with her numeric title."

"What do you mean?"

Momentum led me back down the hall and into the sitting room. "I mean that every Faerie takes up a vacant title, right? So...if I died, then the title for the Faerie of Time would be vacant. So, if a faerie child was born, taking my title, they would be called the II Faerie of Time."

He took a place by a large window and gazed through it. I stood beside him, following his gaze. There was a heavy mist hanging in the air, but I could barely make out a foamy grey sea.

"So, what does that have to do with the number of wings?" I asked.

"Well," he slipped his hands into his pockets, "The first Faeries ever made have six wings, three on each side. A thousand titles—a thousand Faeries. Then, as death came to our world, many died. So, faeries began to marry and procreate," he cleared his throat, "and all that—and anyway, then we started seeing old titles return. But the second time a title was given, the faerie had four wings instead of six. And after that? Only two."

"So... most faeries only have two wings now?" I asked.

"Yes. Cymbeline is a Second. That's pretty rare," he said vacantly.

"Somenus is a Second," I said.

Momentum turned to observe me. "Yes."

"I've seen his wings," I muttered. My mind couldn't help but recall a vision from my dream the night before. Yes, I remembered his wings—like shades of death hanging over me.

Momentum glanced down at the sack I was carrying. "Anyway," he mumbled, "I can find a place to put that hand, now."

I jolted, remembering the thing's presence on my person. "So—he won't be able to find us here?"

"He is still present in his hand, I think," Momentum said cautiously, "but no, an old spell protects this place."

"What spell is that?" I asked.

Momentum turned to face me. "When any of the firsts made a spell, it can never be broken. We were creators, the Firsts. So, the things we made became a part of the land—a part of Raqia. The first Faerie of Illusion blessed this place," he gestured around to the building. "Winter's End. No one can find it unless they have been here before, and no one can see it from afar. There's a sort of protective atmosphere around it. And believe me, I am careful of who I invite here, so Somenus doesn't know where it is."

I stared at him. "Momentum," I said, "Are you the only First left?"

He twitched, blinking at me as if affronted by the question.

"You don't have to answer me," I said with a shrug, "I just... it must be pretty lonely, if it's true."

"Oh," he turned to look out the window, avoiding eye contact. "Well, don't worry about that. Faeries don't get lonely, you see. We like being alone."

It seemed like a convincing lie, but I didn't believe it. "So you are, aren't you? The last of the Firsts?"

He exhaled, keeping his eyes on the sea. "Yes," he said.

"And you recognized Cymbeline's wings pretty easily. You knew the Faerie who came before her…"

"Yes."

"Friend or foe?"

"Friend."

I nodded. "And Cymbeline's mother? Who was *she*?"

Momentum turned to give me a startling sneer. "Don't," he said sharply, "Don't go there."

"Sorry." I turned to try and find the sea through the fog. It seemed to be lifting slightly. "Hey. it's pretty cool living by the sea. I *love* the sea."

"Me, too," said Momentum. "You'll like living here; it's a special place."

I turned quickly. "You mean…?"

"What?" he sniffed, regarding me skeptically.

I found myself smiling. "You're going to let me live here with you?"

"Well, where else would you go?"

"I know—I just… thank you!"

"Don't mention it," he said dryly, turning back to the window. "Anyway, there's a second hall on the other side of the lounge; you can find a room there. The turret room is the best, honestly."

"Did a lot of Faeries used to live here?" I asked. "This place is huge."

"Not *really*," he said, "But I used to get a lot of visitors. Not so much anymore, though. I keep to myself mostly."

"Momentum?"

"Hmm?"

"You said that the First faeries, like… made things. That blue portal… was that something *you* made?"

He sniffed. "Mm… sort of."

"Is it one of those things that… can't be broken?"

"Unfortunately, it's one of those things that *can* be broken," he said, eyeing me sidelong, "but never fully broken. Perhaps one day it could be remade… but that's a question for another day."

"So, what now?" I asked, "We got here. Now we just… what?"

"Well," Momentum bent his back and I heard a subtle pop. "For now, just make yourself at home. I am sorry to say, but I am a pretty boring housemate. So, feel free to explore. I'll come find you later with some dinner, how does that sound?"

"Sounds great!" I said.

"Fine," he cupped his mouth with a yawn. "Alright, well, I'll be in the Winter Wing."

"You named the wings after the four seasons?" I asked, peering around.

"After *Earth's* seasons," Momentum said in a correcting tone.

"You haven't got winter in Raqia?" I asked, "Really?"

"How can we have the four seasons if we don't have a sun?" He turned to face me with arms crossed.

I blinked. "Oh... so it's just... always the same? How do you keep track of years, and all that?"

"We don't *have* years," he said flatly.

"Then..." my eyes shifted side to side. "Wait, so... what are your constants?"

A grin rose up the side of Momentum's mouth. He huffed a laugh. "We don't have constants. Well, we have day and night, but they are fickle and changeable. And we do have seven-day weeks. There, are you happy?"

I laughed. "No, I am definitely confused. You don't have *years*?"

He sighed. "This is going to take time," he said dismissively, "You'll get it all eventually." He turned and made his way toward the sky bridge. I jogged after him.

"How do you keep track of time if you don't have years?" I asked quickly.

"We have seasons," he said as he walked, "They range in length, but they are sort of like our version of years."

"How do you keep track of those?" I asked. We were back in the octagonal central chamber. He passed through a door marked by a snowflake pattern.

"There are signs and weather changes marking season changes. We name each season uniquely. Leo—that's what the skydeacons do, remember? They are the Sky interpreters, they manage time and determine hours, and all that." We were passing through a skybridge identical to one leading to the Autumn Wing, only the scenery was different, with the sea on the other side.

"Oh, I see. So, they're like scientists?"

"*No*, Leo," he scoffed. We came into the winter lounge. It had a simplistic design, with an array of hanging plants, and a fire pit at the center of the room. Rather than couches and armchairs, there were rugs and pillows strewn across the floors. "Science is observation. *Skydeaconry* is interpretation. There's a difference."

There was a large stairwell leading upwards at the back end of the lounge. Momentum began to ascend.

"Okay, but... language. You said I am the only person speaking English; what did you—?"

"Leo," Momentum paused, halfway up the stairs and turned to look at me. I had one foot on the bottom step, ready to follow him up.

"Yeah?"

"I want to be alone for a bit. Do you mind?"

I twiddled my hands together in embarrassment. "Oh, sure, sure, of course. So sorry!"

"I'll find you in the Autumn Wing at dinner time?"

"Yes! Sounds great! Yeah... questions can wait..."

He sighed. "Language is different here," he said with a tired smile, paused there on the steps, "It's not a barrier as much as it is an identifier. We may be speaking in different languages, but we can all understand one another. You'll get used to it, soon you'll be able to hear the actual words people are saying, rather than just their meaning. It'll sound like people speaking," he thought for a moment, "in different accents."

I gazed in wonderment. "You mean... I can understand *all* languages?"

He nodded.

"Seriously? Have you got a Septuagint lying around here anywhere?"

"Leo," he turned to continue his ascent, "Good *bye*."

"Right, right... bye!" I waved, watching as he disappeared up the stairs. My heart was thumping with excitement. Sure, I wasn't thrilled about everything that had happened thus far, but the newness of everything was enough to put a wide smile on my face.

I wandered aimlessly about for a bit, observing little things like candlesticks and rug tassels. There was so much newness that I could barely absorb any of it. This place was my new home. These walls, the rugs, the dreary fog, the many doors—would they all become familiar to me? Over the last several weeks, I had seen many new things, knowing I would probably never see them again. But this place, this quiet house with its many rooms and halls, this would remain. I would see it again and again, until I took its beauty and stillness for granted. This was my home, and yet it was the newest, most unfamiliar place in the world to me. How strange.

I found that hall that Momentum told me about, in the Autumn wing lounge opposite the hall which led to Cymbeline's room. I peeked through each door, each time growing more excited at the idea that I was selecting my own quarters. I experienced the same thrill that I felt when I was a freshy at seminary, moving into my dorm. Down at the end of the hall, I found what Momentum had called the turret room. It was bigger than the rest, with a king size four-poster bed, a dressing room, and a circular turret area, with tall, skinny windows. A large fireplace was the centerpiece of the room, a hefty log ablaze with warmth.

"Yes," I said proudly, with hands on hips, Peter Pan style. I pulled the bag containing Somenus' hand off my shoulder and threw it upon the bed. Then I wandered around the room, inspecting the furniture. I ran my hands along the smooth surface of the writing desk. No dust. I opened a drawer. Blank paper sat in a neat stack. I imagined sitting there, writing. Would that be a part of my new life? Writing? I had always dreamed of finding time to write.

I moved across the room and peered out the window. It was too foggy to see anything, so I undid the latch and threw it open. I had expected a burst of frigid air, but instead, it was pleasantly cool, stimulating. It smelled salty, and I could hear the sound of roaring waves. It was a wild ocean, and it called to me.

I soon found myself outside, walking through the uneven sand in a trance. For once, I wasn't running; for once, I wasn't searching; for once, I could just *be*. It was as if I had died. The old Leo had things to do, and life to live. The old Leo had a good life. But this Leo—well—I didn't know this Leo much yet, but he was at peace. The old Leo had died, and a new Leo was born. He was born there at the sea—there at the edge of the world.

The tempestuous ocean screamed at me, throwing spit and heavy mist my way. I stood right at the line where the waves stopped, and only small ripples of water touched my bare feet. Amazing how mere elevation could keep something as monstrous and terrifying as the sea at bay. It would swallow me if it could, but all I had to do was stand there and watch it try, only inches away from its motion.

I had stripped down to my koalas. Who wouldn't when they had an entire beach to themselves? While grey and windy, this beach wasn't cold. I could dip my feet in the cool waters without so much as a shiver. Now *that* was different to the beaches I grew up visiting in the Pacific Northwest!

I got an itch. It was an itch to swim. I had no idea if these waters would kill me or not, but I couldn't help it—I dove in. It was like skydiving, throwing myself into those beastly waves, letting them do their worst. They threw me around like a mouse in the paws of a lion, but they didn't devour me. I found the surface, and soon began to flow with the waves rather than against them.

After a time, I let the sea spit me out onto the shore, and I lay there on my back, basking in the sand. I couldn't believe how strange it felt to just exist, without a care. It was my new beginning, lying naked like a newborn on the shores of a new life.

I rolled onto my stomach and rose, sand covered, to my feet. I sloshed, step by step, to a higher elevation where the sand turned to little pebbles. I sat, making a sort of nest in a mess of smooth rocks and began to comb through them with my fingers. I picked up a pile and sorted through them until I found one I liked. It was a red stone, shaped like a teardrop. I dropped the rest of the stones and clutched the thing in my hand, rising to wander around some more.

Before long I found the place where I had left my clothes. I was mostly dry now, so I slid on my jeans, then continued bare foot back toward the house. *House*, I laughed, *it could hardly be called a house.* It was as big as a castle, or a fancy mansion. As I strode up a cobblestone stair, I could see someone standing up at the top, waving at me. I continued slowly, waving in return. It was Cymbeline. She trotted down the stairs and met me halfway.

"Hey," I said with a beaming smile.

She made a prim face when she noticed my half-dressed and sandy state. "Been swimming?" she asked.

"Yup," I held out my fist. "Here."

She stared at my hand hesitantly. "What?"

"Hold out your hand."

She did so gingerly. I dropped my pebble into it.

"Check it out," I said, "Found that on the beach."

"That's... nice." She wiped the sand off of it, turning it in the light.

"Nice place, this," I said, placing my hand back on my hip.

"This is where you and... uh... *Momentum* live?" she asked, raising her eyes to observe the sea behind me.

"Well," I chuckled, "Honestly, this is my first time here. You know, I think you and I arrived here in Raqia at the same time."

Her eyes found me, and she made a perplexed face. "Really?"

"Yeah. And I am sure that in time, we will understand the *why* behind it all, but for now—want to check out the castle with me?"

"Castle?" she looked behind herself.

"Er, house...or whatever."

"Alright," she said, throwing her long, loose dreadlocks behind her shoulder.

"Well, come on, then!" I said, and I ran past her. I shook the sand out of my shirt and pulled it over myself, then called, "Let's get ourselves lost!"

Winter's End was designed in the shape of a plus sign. The center of the house was called the Solstice, and inside there was the landing hall, where we had first arrived. Then the four wings spread out from the center, like four points of a compass. I ran through the halls, yelling and howling barefoot like a teenager, and Cymbeline followed along, observing the place quietly. There wasn't a single room that I didn't pop my head in and say, "hello", just to see how much it echoed. It was a perfectly maintained, and yet perfectly *empty* living space. The only place we didn't go was the Winter Wing, and that was because Momentum had expressed the desire to be alone.

"How can this place be so clean without any servants?" Cymbeline asked as we poked our heads into the kitchens within the Summer Wing.

"Beats me," I said, "but this place is definitely big enough to house servants. Do you think Momentum was like... a King or something?"

Cymbeline turned to me with a raised eyebrow. "*A king?*"

"I don't know," I shrugged, "Like in a past life?"

"A past life?"

"Yes," I said, "He's like thousands of years old, I think."

"Thousands?" her eyes flashed.

"Say," I turned to her. "Do you have, like... *years* where you come from?"

" *What?*"

"You know, years. Like, with a sun in your sky? And a moon?"

"What's a moon?"

I blinked. "You know, the big white ball in the sky at night?"

"We have a sun," she said matter-of-factly, "of course we have a sun."

"There's no sun here," I said, whispering as if it were a secret. "Wait—you haven't got a moon? Where do you come from, then?"

She sniffed, turning her chin slightly as if to say, *I do not wish to discuss the topic.*

"So, uh... Momentum says you get more power from movement," I remarked.

She blinked. "Really?"

"Yeah, like... he says that you can see movement glowing cause you get like... magik from it, or something."

"Right," she nodded slowly, "...*right...*"

"So, when I run, I make you more powerful?" I asked with a boyish smile.

She pulled the corner of her mouth to the side. "I..."

I dashed off down an unexplored hallway, howling like a wolf. Cymbeline followed unenthusiastically.

She found me panting at the end of the hallway. "How do you feel..." I gasped to catch my breath, "*now?*"

"The same."

"Ah, darn," I laughed, wiping my brow.

"It's getting dim outside," she remarked, "Any idea where we can find some food?"

"Oh!" I scratched my head, moving my mess of wide curls from side to side. "Momentum said to meet us in Autumn for dinner."

"Oh," she crossed her arms, "This is news to me."

"Come on," I primed to leap off into another sprint, but she caught my arm.

"Leo," she snapped, "Can you just…"

I glanced puppyishly, "Huh?"

"Can you just *walk* for a minute?"

"Oh," I relaxed, "Sure."

We walked side by side in the direction of the Solstice.

"Leo, can I ask you… who exactly *is* Momentum?" she asked thoughtfully, interlacing her fingers together behind her back.

"Right, uh," I used the front of my shirt to wipe sweat off my face. "He's a faerie."

"Yes, I knew that, but what sort of man is he? He lives in this big house, all alone…"

"I don't know," I said as I tucked my hands into my pockets. "I think he's sort of a hermit, to be honest."

"You said he's lived thousands of years. How is that possible?"

"I think Faeries don't die," I hesitated, "Unless they're killed."

Cymbeline halted, staring down at the floor.

"Are you alright?" I asked, tapping her shoulder softly.

She glanced at my hand, then at my face. "So, I won't… die?"

I raised my eyebrows. "I don't know," I said, "Probably not for a long time…"

She stared deeply into my face, as if looking for answers. "Leo…"

"Yeah?"

"I'm never going back there, am I?"

I exhaled slowly, then shook my head. "I don't think so. I mean… I guess if you wanted to go back… you might be able to teleport again?"

"But I could stay here, you think?"

"Yeah...?" I said in a questioning voice.

Cymbeline's mouth spread out into a smile. "Really? You think so?"

I nodded. "Why not?" I shrugged, "It's not like Momentum hasn't got any room. But, *erm*, Cymbeline... you don't *want* to go home?"

Her face paled, and she shook her head quickly.

"Ah," I nodded, "So home wasn't a... happy place?"

"Let's not talk about that," she said briskly, "Come on. You said there would be supper!"

"Oh, yeah!" I smiled. "Come on!"

Momentum was waiting for us in the lounge, standing by that same window he seemed to favor the last time. Once he saw us, he gestured to a small table with some fresh fruit and sliced vegetables. The three of us sat together, munching silently for a bit until Momentum said,

"Went swimming, I see?"

I grinned proudly through my teeth, halfway through a bite. "How'd you guess?"

"You've got sand in your hair," he said.

"Can't believe I get to live on the beach! Erm..." I fished through the plate, searching for a protein, "Is there a town, or anything, nearby?"

"No," he said, leaning back.

"What, nothing?" I asked, glancing up from the food.

"No."

"Like... *nothing*? Not even a—?"

"Wait, so," Cymbeline chimed in, looking worried, "Are you saying that just the three of us live here... and there's no one else around?"

"Not for a hundred miles," Momentum said lazily as he popped a grape into his mouth. Cymbeline and I exchanged hesitant looks.

"Do you ever get... visitors?" I asked.

"Mm," he hummed, "Sometimes. Maybe once or twice a season?"

"And uh," I tapped the table with my fingers. "How long is the average season here?"

"Mmmm," Momentum closed his eyes, "About three hundred days?"

Cymbeline groaned. "You weren't exaggerating when you said he's a hermit," she mumbled to me.

"Most faeries are hermits, if by hermits you mean that we like to live alone and away from the rest of the world. Cymbeline, you were raised around humans, so you have never had the opportunity, but I am sure that you gravitated toward silence and privacy, no?"

She bobbed her head to the side agreeably. "Well, yes…"

"Well, I *am* human!" I said emphatically, "And I *like* people!"

"Good for you," came Momentum.

"I mean… It's great living by the seaside and everything, but there's got to be *community* of some sort! I can't live in a world where there's nobody to talk to!"

"There's not *nobody*," Cymbeline mumbled.

"Well, once she's started figuring out how to store magik," Momentum gestured to Cymbeline, "She can take you anywhere you like."

"Hasn't she already figured that out?" I asked, "Look, she's already looking more like herself."

"No, I mean," Momentum sighed, slumping somewhat into his chair, "Storing magik is different from just passively soaking it up."

"Storing *what*?" Cymbeline shook her head.

"Alright," Momentum placed his hands flat on the table, "I'll only explain this once, so listen up." I leaned forward eagerly, while Cymbeline leaned back skeptically.

He raised his chin pompously, then cleared his throat. "Right: magik. Magik is the lifeforce for all of the Fae, and only the Fae can see it. If we didn't exist, no one else would even know it was there, at least they would know it differently. Magik is essentially glory. To Faeries, it looks like light. And there are two kinds of magik, alright? There's dark magik and light magik."

"Kind of like good and evil?" I asked helpfully.

"No," he sniffed, "Please don't interrupt. It is more like opposites—like positive and negative. Actually, a more accurate comparison would be like night and day. In the old days, we used to call the two types of magik daylight and nightlight; we believed that magik was leftover glory from when the Lights created the world. Anyway, there is glory of all kinds, and depending on a faeries title, they can see different things. So, Cymbeline here," he pointed to her, "She's a light faerie, so she sees more of a bright white glow. And what glows, in your eyes, Cymbeline?" he asked in that professor tone of voice.

"Movement?" she ventured.

"Yes. You see the glory of movement. And so, you can draw from it. It gives you life. Now, Faeries store magik in their beings, right? In our bodies."

Cymbeline and I nodded dutifully.

"But our bodies can only hold so much. And when we use magik to do things like travel great distances—like Cymbeline did, it uses up that stored magik, and drains our life force. So, if a Faerie wants to use magik regularly, without pulling from their own life force, they must have something like *this*."

Momentum reached into his pocket and pulled out a shiny gold pocket watch. He turned it one way, then the other. "This is my imperium," he said. "It's a faerie's most precious item, where we store our magik. If you've got an imperium, Cymbeline," he said, making eye contact with her, "You can soak up as much of that pretty movement glory as you like and store it in here. The more you save, the more you can do things like teleport and fly, and whatever."

"*Fly?*" Cymbeline's face froze.

"Well, you've got wings, haven't you?" Momentum said casually as he shoved his watch back in his pocket.

"So, you're the Time Faerie," I said, "What kind of, *erm... glory* do you see?"

He eyed me. "Mm. Good question."

"Are you being mysterious on purpose?" I asked, feeling a little disappointed. "Come on. Do you, like... get magik from time passing?"

He sighed. "It's hard to explain, Leo," he said as he crossed his arms protectively. The question seemed to make him nervous, as if I were asking him what salary he made.

"What, are you like... super powerful?"

He shrugged. "I see the glory in moments," he said.

"So," Cymbeline interjected, "When you helped me transport us all here from... *wherever we were before*, I had enough magik to do that, just in my body?"

"*Nnnngh*," Momentum shifted uncomfortably, "Sort of. I helped power you. Otherwise, you probably would have died. No, to do that kind of travel probably would have killed you if you did it on your own. See, you need to learn to *store* magik, Cymbeline." He tapped the table emphatically with his hand.

"So, faeries can just share magik?" I asked curiously, "Like a... like a blood transfusion or something?"

"Eh, I guess," Momentum said, "But only if the two faeries use the same sort of magik. A dark Faerie can't power a light faerie, for example."

"So, Faeries can't see both types of magik, then?" I asked, fishing through the plate of food some more. Really? There was *no* protein, and I was hungry!

Momentum shook his head gravely, "No. No, well...." he blew a raspberry through his lips. "I suppose there was one Faerie who could, but there has only ever been one of him, and I don't think that title will ever be filled again."

"Why not?" Cymbeline asked, "Who was he?"

"Well," Momentum sighed. "He was the Faerie of Magik—or the Faerie of Glory, some called him. He was the only one who could see both."

"Wow," I looked up from the food. "He must have been pretty powerful."

"He wasn't powerful," Momentum said with distant eyes, "He *was* power. That was the problem."

"Did he..." I lowered my voice, "Go bad, or something?"

Momentum exhaled through his nostrils. "When he did finally die," he said, as if skipping to the end of a long story, "we knew there would never be another one of him. Anyway!" He brightened, "Some titles are best filled only once."

"Hey, uh," I was scratching the edge of the plate nervously with my finger.

"What?" Momentum snapped, "You don't like my food?"

"Just wondering if there's any... probably not any meat or," I held my breath as I watched the rage form on Momentum's face.

"I'm only going to say this once," the man said with a body quaking with tension. "No meat. Not here, not ever—not ever again. If you are going to live in my house: no *meat*!"

"I—" I gulped.

"Death is all very normal down where you come from, and that's fine—that's how it all *works* down there," Down there? It was like I lived in Hell! "But up here, we do not kill to eat—we do not need to kill to eat. Do you understand? *Killing* and *butchering* are despicable, *ugly* acts, and I will not tolerate them, understand?"

"I..."

"Now," he seemed to soften, "If you like eggs, I have got some chickens and all that. But don't you dare ever *think* about eating any of them!"

"...the eggs?"

"No—the chickens! You can eat the eggs, they aren't fertilized."

Cymbeline had shrunk silently into her chair at the sight of the angry Momentum, and she was slowly uncoiling. "Well," she said timidly, "I am glad to hear you don't like killing, to be honest. Don't worry, sir, we won't ask for meat." She was talking like a submissive child. Where had that tall, confident woman gone? It was like the mere sight of an angry man made her free spirit retreat.

"Vegetarian for life then," I said quickly, "That's me!"

Momentum smirked. "Good man," he said, "And that's another thing to remember, Cymbeline," he said, turning his focus to her. "There is a law, written on the soul of every Faerie—a law we cannot break, even if we wish to."

"What's that?" she asked.

"We cannot kill."

* * *

"Leo, wake up!" Momentum was shouting, his face inches from mine. I felt him slap my face. I could hear myself screaming. "Wake up, Leo! Let go of it!"

He slapped me again. My dry eyes blinked rapidly. I gasped.

"I *can't*," I croaked, but no voice came out.

"Just let him go!" Momentum shouted.

"I can't," I mouthed. Still no sound. He whacked my hands forcefully, and Somenus' hand flung across the room, landing on the floor with a plunk.

My body was petrified; I tried to move my fingers but couldn't. At least I had stopped screaming. My eyes found Momentum's face; he was looking down at me pensively. He placed a hand on my head, then closed his eyes and mumbled something.

After a time, I felt myself relax. My hands dropped lifelessly to my sides and I stared blankly up at the Faerie. He sighed, shaking his head.

"Momentum," I croaked through my dry lips.

"Leo," he said, "You alright? That was a bad one."

"Did you put a spell on me?" I asked softly.

"*What?*" He narrowed his brow.

"I saw you whispering," I said. I still couldn't move my limbs.

He smiled weakly. "I was praying," he said. "What happened?"

"I don't know," I said, closing my eyes. "You tell me."

"You came in here screaming," he said, leaning back.

"I..." visions from my nightmare flashed through my mind. I whimpered.

"Hey," Momentum placed his hand on my chest. "Just rest. We can talk in the morning."

<hr>

I sat up and looked around the room. Where was I? I threw off the blanket and placed my feet on the ground. The bedroom was large, with several adjoining rooms. The bed was at the top of a raised platform, shielded partway by some drapery. To the right I could see a sitting area. Momentum was reclining in an armchair there, reading beside an open window.

"Momentum?" I asked. Well, I would have asked that, if I had had a voice. I tried speaking again. No, my voice was gone. I rubbed my sore throat pitifully. *Oh, that's right*, I thought, *I had a dream... and I came here.* Was this Momentum's quarters?

"Morning," he said from across the room. I rose, then descended the steps to where Momentum was sitting, giving the hand lying in the middle of the floor a wide berth.

I waved with my hand and mouthed the words, *Good Morning*.

"Lost your voice?" he smirked.

I nodded.

"Well," he sighed, turning his face toward the morning light that poured from the window, "At least *something* good came out of last night. I should be able to have a little break from all your questions."

I gave him a flat look.

"There's some tea here," he tapped a steel teapot. "It'll help the old—" he tapped his esophagus helpfully.

I nodded, then offered him a thumbs up.

"And there's some toast—*with* eggs!" He gestured proudly to a plate, "Made by yours truly."

I smiled. I don't know if he was taking pity on me or not, but he was being awfully nice.

"Now Leo," he said with a sigh, "We will find a place for that hand, now that we are here. You don't have to hang onto it anymore, alright? No more nightmares."

My smile faded.

Momentum raised an eyebrow. "Leo..." he said, "That's *good* news, isn't it?"

"Hello?" Cymbeline's voice called distantly from another room.

"In here," Momentum called, then dashed off to the door.

"Where's Leo?" I heard her asking from outside the room.

"He slept here last night," Momentum said, barring the way into the room. I picked up my fork and pressed it into the egg. It was soft boiled, just how I liked it.

"What, with you?" Cymbeline asked.

"Got a problem with that?" Momentum asked.

"I heard him screaming last night," she said in a lower voice. "I just wanted to check that he's alright. I tried to talk to him but he just ran away."

"I'm fine!" I tried to yell, but only a wheeze came out. I sighed, then took a helpless sip of tea.

"He's fine," Momentum said, as if picking up my cue. "Just a bad dream. He's eating breakfast."

"Can I come and see him?"

I perked up, feeling a little rosy that everybody seemed to be *worrying* over me.

Momentum groaned, then moved away from the door, letting her walk in. Cymbeline crept inside, then smiled at the sight of me. She waved. I waved back.

"Leo, how are you feeling?" she asked as she walked over.

I rolled my eyes and shook my head. Why was everybody tiptoeing around me? It was starting to get a little embarrassing.

"I'm *fine*," I mouthed, then gave another thumbs up.

Cymbeline sat at the little breakfast table, taking Momentum's spot. He stood a few paces back with his arms crossed, clearly peeved at the second interruption to his quiet morning.

"I see you found some eggs," she said with a teasing smile and picked up the plate.

There was a sudden booming noise, like the pounding of a war drum. Cymbeline yelped, dropping the plate of food onto the ground with a noisy clank. Momentum and I both mourned the sight of the spoiled breakfast.

"What was *that*?" She shrieked.

"Oh, calm down," he said, stamping his boot on the brass tray to stop its ringing, "It's just the door."

"Someone's... knocking on the door?" I mouthed.

"Yes," Momentum said, discerning my question.

"Which door?" Cymbeline asked nervously. "And why is it so loud?"

"The front door," Momentum yawned. "And I made it loud enough to be heard from anywhere in the house."

I rose to my feet excitedly, a childish smile on my face. Momentum sighed.

"I suppose you'll want to go and see who it is?" he asked, eyeing us both.

I nodded frantically, then shook two thumbs up.

Momentum spun on his heel and strolled unenthusiastically toward the door. "And just when I was starting to get some quiet around here," he mumbled.

Cymbeline and I followed as Momentum led us to the front door. It was at the Winter Wing foyer; I hadn't been there yet. The front door—or *doors*, to be precise—were large and looming. I wondered how someone was even supposed to open them when they were the size of a portcullis. The pounding reverberated again. Someone was definitely knocking from the other side.

Momentum stroked his chin.

"Are you going to answer it?" Cymbeline asked. "Are you expecting anyone?"

I had my own questions, but Momentum continued to benefit from my lack of voice with an extra moment of silence as we waited for his response. He turned around to look at us for a second.

"Momentum," Cymbeline finally said, "Who is at the door?"

"I don't know," he said passively. We all twitched as the knocking resumed.

"Open the door, Aorist!" A strong male voice called out from the other side. Cymbeline and I looked at each other, then back at Momentum.

He raised his eyebrows.

The pounding continued. "Please, Aorist," the voice called again, "Answer the Question!"

14

— Clover —

In the Shadows

"If my map is right, and my reading is right," Yuma said, turning his map sideways, "We will be out of the Woodlands by tomorrow morning. Then we will be in the far edges of the Gramenlands."

"Why wouldn't your map be right?" Clover asked from the ground. He was reclining against an apple tree, savoring one of its fruits.

Yuma sighed silently to himself.

"Yuma," Clover said with a mouth full of apple, "Why wouldn't your map be—"

"It's *right*, alright?" Yuma snapped. He crumpled the map up and shoved it into his rucksack.

"Well, I won't mind being out of the trees. I'm tired of trees," Clover said in a gloomy voice.

Yuma knelt down in front of their campfire. "How's the apple?"

"It's nice," Clover said after a hefty swallow. "Want one?"

"No."

Clover tippled his apple hand back pensively. "Yuma?"

"What?"

"Why aren't you eating?"

"I am eating. I eat at mealtime," the warrior said stubbornly.

Clover's eyelids closed halfway. "Yeah, but... you eat almost nothing only once a day. There's food everywhere out here, you know."

"I *know* there's food everywhere," Yuma snapped. "That's the problem."

Clover glanced at his apple core, then chucked it into a bush. "I see."

Yuma leaned back to sit cross-legged on the ground.

"You aren't eating more than your people are eating?" Clover asked.

Yuma grunted.

"Should I do that, too?"

"No," Yuma snapped. Then he seemed to soften. "Clover, I... this is a private matter for me."

Clover nodded. "So, why don't you wear a shirt?"

"*What*?" Yuma whirred his head in Clover's direction. "What kind of a question is that?"

Clover shrugged, plucking a second apple from his pile.

"Why do *you* wear a shirt?" Yuma retorted, "It's not like it's cold out here."

"Because then it would be improper," Clover said.

"*That's* culture," Yuma said, pointing accusingly. "It's not improper for me, so leave me alone about it."

"I wasn't trying to judge..." Clover said innocently, "I was just curious."

"Well, keep your curiosity to yourself."

Silence.

"Why have you been so angry since we met with the Truth Faerie?" Clover asked.

Yuma stared aggressively at the fire.

"Yuma?"

"Why *haven't* you been angry since the Truth Faerie?" Yuma returned.

"Why would I be angry?"

"Because he said you're going to *die*!" Yuma said in a raised voice. The word 'die' seemed to echo throughout their little camp ominously.

Clover looked down at his boots and grew silent.

There was more silence.

Thieving Scumbag jostled up to Clover holding an apple, added it to the little pile, then scurried off again.

Yuma bowed his head. "Clover..."

"Why would I be angry about that?" asked Clover.

Yuma glanced at him. "It doesn't make you angry?"

Clover shook his head.

"Well, how *do* you feel about it, then? Are you... are you going to do it?" asked Yuma.

"Do what?"

"Kill the Nightmare Faerie."

"Well, the Truth Faerie said I would, so I am sure I will," Clover said with a blank expression.

"Is that how it works? He says it, so it's true?"

"Isn't that how truth works?" Clover asked.

Yuma huffed. "And you're just... fine with it?"

"I..." Clover hesitated, "I'm not sure what I feel. I am just thinking about it."

"Is that why you've been so quiet for the last few weeks?" Yuma asked as he added a log to the fire. "You're *thinking*?"

"Yes."

Yuma paused, adjusting the logs, then reluctantly asked. "And what are you thinking about?"

"Isabella."

The warrior nodded. "I should have guessed that."

"I'm thinking about how the only way for her to succeed in her mission is for me to die. I think... I think that would be a worthy thing for me to do, but it makes me sad, 'cause..."

"Because you'll never have the chance to find out if she will love you back?"

Clover nodded. "I suppose it is the greatest test of my love," he said.

Yuma turned to regard Clover with a look of admiration. "Hmm," he nodded. "That's true."

"Hey," Clover sat forward.

"What?"

"What do the humans in the Gramenlands think about people not wearing shirts?"

Yuma rose and walked off into the trees.

"Well?" Clover called.

"I am sure the humans care less than the Elves do about that," he yelled back.

"Where are you going?"

"To find more firewood!" Yuma's distant voice said.

Clover hopped to his feet and sauntered over to the cluster of white fluff where his sheep had gathered together to sleep. He walked around them in a circle, rubbing some of their heads as he went.

"Three, four, five," he counted, bouncing his finger in the air. "Fifteen, sixteen," he nodded to himself. "All here." They had grown used to his leadership by now. Though none of them had spoken to him yet, they listened to him, and obeyed his commands. It was now at the point where they naturally followed him wherever he walked, and that meant they traveled much faster. It had taken weeks to journey through the great Raqian Woodlands, but they were nearly done. Once in the Gramenlands, a human territory, they would be able to travel by road. That made things both safer and also more complicated.

Humans. Clover shuddered. They scared him. Those wild, warmongering, meat-eating people. The humans in the Woodlands, from what he had heard, were supposed to be more docile and nature-fearing. And the humans in the Fero Lands didn't seem too bad, either. But humans in the East, where their numbers were concentrated and their culture strong? Clover didn't love the idea of meeting them. The Gramenlands would have plenty of humans, but they were mostly country folk: farmers, lumberjacks, miners. But Bavel— they were headed to *Bavel*! It was the crown of all human achievement, their pride and glory. The epitome of human snobbery could be found there, that's what everyone knew about the place; and that was Clover's destination. He dreaded it more than he dreaded killing the Nightmare Faerie.

Andrew made a stressed bleat. Clover knelt beside him and patted his head.

"Why are you so worried?" Clover asked, "Will you speak to me, big Andrew?"

The sheep's eyes partially closed, and he made another sound.

"I'll carry you again tomorrow if you wish," Clover said. He felt bad; the long travel seemed to be hard on the heavy sheep's shaky legs. Andrew rested his chin on Clover's knee.

"Clover," Yuma returned with a pile of fallen branches. He dropped them in a heap by the fire.

"Over here," Clover said, still patting Andrew's head.

"Clover, I've seen some concerning tracks. I think we should keep moving."

Clover shook his head. "My sheep need sleep," he said, "They can't walk through the night. Today was hard for them already."

Yuma nodded. "Fine," he said, "but we need to keep careful watch tonight."

"What kind of tracks did you see?"

Yuma stepped up behind Clover. "A pack of some kind."

Clover's eyes flashed. "Wulves?"

"Maybe. Are there wulves around here?"

Clover nodded soberly. Perhaps they *should* walk through the night. No. His sheep simply wouldn't do it. They were too tired—but still... Raqian Wulves, animals that humans had tried to train for battle, but were intelligent enough to break away and form their own tribes. They were the *last* beasts Clover would ever want to meet when herding a bundle of aimless sheep.

"I think you might be right," Clover said quietly. "Where were these tracks? How close to us? How fresh?"

"Twenty yards or so, and they looked pretty fresh, to me. But I am not used to tracking in the forest, so I could be off."

Clover stood. "We may already be too late..."

"Really?" Yuma tensed. "What—you think they're aware of us?"

"Oh, I am sure they are," Clover said as he found his spear. "Let's get moving. How far did you say the forest's edge was?"

Yuma thrust his rucksack over his shoulder and readied his bow.

Clover's nostrils flared. "Why is it you only carry one arrow, Yuma? There's going to be a *lot* of them!"

"You choose *this* moment to ask me?" Yuma snapped as he kicked dirt over the fire and separated the logs. "It's not for fighting wulves—it's for something *else*. I've got daggers, too, you know."

"Come on, up," Clover was poking his sheep with the blunt end of his spear. "Danger! Up!" The animals roused nervously at the tone of his voice. They ambled to their feet and began bleating noisily. "Shush!" Clover hissed. "Damn, we're going to be easy to track. *Damn*!" Clover knelt down and hoisted up Andrew over his shoulders, who seemed to have grown even heavier than the day before.

"I've never seen you this agitated," Yuma whispered, "Are they that bad?"

"Yes, yes," Clover said through his teeth, "Now get your damn map out." Night was deepening. It was the worst time to be running from a pack of wulves. "Just pray to the Lights they haven't already spotted us, or we are *dead*." Clover felt Thieving Scumbag, or TSB as he had begun to call him, climb up fearfully onto his shoulder.

"They're *that* bad?" Yuma asked again. "Clover, I can handle a few—"

"Let's go." Clover was charging forward, whacking his animals urgently. "Stay quiet, lads, that's it, no sheep noises."

Yuma ran ahead of the pack and pulled out his map. He touched the sides of the trees, confirming north by the placement of the moss, then led Clover forward with a wave of his hand.

"Let's head due north," Yuma whispered, "It'll be the surest way out of the Woodlands."

"You lead the front and I'll guard the back," Clover said, "If any sheep start lagging behind, I may need help."

"*Why* you had to bring these cursed—" Yuma mumbled under his breath. "Just *move*!"

Clover ushered his sheep forward, whacking their backsides mercilessly. They stamped forward in a rampage, terrified of being terrified. Clover panted under his burden; it wasn't easy carrying a live load while running after a long day of travel.

They made some good progress, but Clover's keen ears soon heard hurried footsteps.

"Damn it all!" Clover hissed.

Yuma turned urgently. "They coming?"

"Yes! Ready your weapons!" Clover turned his staff, then rounded his sheep into a circle. "They're surrounding us."

"How do you know?" Yuma ran up to Clover with his two daggers drawn.

"I can hear them," Clover said, placing Andrew down at the center of the fold. "You guard the sheep and I'll fight them off.

"You guard the sheep, and *I'll* fight them off!" Yuma said through gritted teeth.

"Listen." Clover stepped up close to the man's face. "I've fought these kinds of beasts before—I have experience. You defend, I'll attack. Some will be on the offensive, and others will steal the sheep. We've got to have a plan, or we're *dead*!"

"Fine," Yuma barked, twirling his daggers hungrily. "Let them come."

"Oh, they'll come," Clover turned and stepped forward, watching as gleaming yellow eyes formed in the darkness.

A tense silence stirred around them as more and more eyes appeared. Clover could hear the snarls communicating dark words to each other. He heard the thumping of at least eight heartbeats. *Eight*—there were too many.

Yuma yelped in the darkness. Clover turned sharply to see him slashing at a dark shape that had seized him by the ankle. Before Clover could shift his focus back to the head attackers, he was knocked to the ground. Clover's reflexes had served him well; he had managed to hold up his spear with both hands, blocking the attacker from sinking its jaws into his neck. Clover struggled against the beast who was at least three times his own size. He pressed his spear's length into the wulf's mouth, gritting his teeth as spittle dripped down onto his face. Howls sounded from all around, and then, the horrifying call of screaming sheep. It was a sound Clover wished he had never heard: so shrill; so weak; so pitiful—so *many*.

He plunged his knee into the wulf's belly, then rolled free. Then he thrust his spear into the thing's heart. It yelped before falling dead to the ground. Before Clover could yank the spear free, he was attacked from behind. Clover cried out in pain as an iron set of jaws clamped down on his shoulder. Heavy paws stamped down on his body as he pulled hard at his spear. Finally, he yanked it free of the dead wulf, then swung it against his attacker's body. The wulf yelped as it dashed aside, giving Clover just enough time to rise onto one knee. He could see four wulves circling around them. One mercy was that wulves tended to attack one by one; he had a chance, if he could just stay *alive*.

"This isn't where I die!" Clover growled, swinging his spear side to side, spinning in a circle as the wulves hesitated. He locked eyes with one, tempting it with a roar. "Come on—let me have it!" It lunged at him.

Clover pierced it through the eye with lightning speed, then withdrew his spear in a flash. Yes, he was gaining momentum now. He could do this. The disturbing nose of the wailing sheep caught his ear again. He turned to eye the fold for only a moment, but it was a moment he couldn't spare. A wulf leapt upon him from behind, slamming him down on his face. It knocked the wind out of him. Teeth met with that same shoulder wound. Clover screamed but couldn't find a way to break free. Then the jaws released him, and the pressure against his body vanished.

Clover raised shakily to his feet, then watched as Yuma slashed the wulf down with his knives.

"No," Clover gasped, clinging to his shoulder, "Defend the sheep, not *me!*"

"It's too late for that, Clover," Yuma said, panting. They were standing back to back, rotating reactively as the wulves encircled them. The beasts were mangy and grey, with long, knobby legs and high shoulders. Wulves the size of cows—and there were four of them.

Clover clung to his bleeding shoulder with one hand and his spear with the other. Whatever had become of his sheep, Clover's goal was simpler now: stay alive. If he died, everyone died.

"Run!" Clover crowed, "We've killed half your pack. *Run* if you want to live!"

One of the wulves, with lighter fur stepped forward, teeth gnashing. He was somewhat bigger than the rest. It growled discerningly.

"It's talking," Clover said, "Can you understand it?"

"No," Yuma said through labored breaths.

"This is your last chance!" Clover yelled, "I don't kill lightly, but I *will* kill you if you do not flee! I'm Prince of the Elder Copse, and I have killed many of your kind—run while you can: you face a legend this night!"

Yuma stole a surprised glance at Clover.

The wulf spread its quivering gums, boasting its menacing mandibles. Then it lifted its head and howled.

"Get ready," Clover whispered, "It's on."

Clover didn't wait for them to strike first. He leapt into the air, aiming straight for the alpha and landed on his back. The scene stirred into a blur of movement. Clover landed successfully on the alpha's back, but not before it seized his spear in its mouth. It threw the spear aside, then jumped, throwing its back end side to side and bucking to shake Clover loose. Clover held fast to its ears, trying his hardest to keep the fangs away from his body. His shoulder throbbed, and he could feel his tunic growing drenched in blood, but he held on.

"Yuma!" Clover cried. He tightened his thighs against the beast's back. He was only clicks away from being thrown aside. "Yuma—throw me a dagger if you can spare one!"

"Just a second!" Yuma's struggling voice sounded from nearby.

"Please," Clover held on desperately as the alpha reared upwards. "Now!"

"Heads up!"

Clover dared to release a hand and reached up into the air. He could hear the whirring sound of the knife spinning toward him. His ears were his only guide as he kept his gaze fixed on the wulf's head. Clover caught the dagger partially by the blade and winced. He was sure he had sliced a finger, but he couldn't waste a click. He readjusted the knife in his hand then slashed it against the wulf's neck. The beast howled, then thrashed again, knocking Clover to the ground. The wind left his body, and he laid there, unable to breathe as the beast stepped over him. Blood dripped from its head down onto Clover's face. He had hit it, but not perfectly enough.

Clover gasped, seizing air. Then, just as the wulf dove its snout down towards Clover's throat, Clover's arm swung in a flash, beating it to the kill. He sliced the thing's throat open. It made a pitiful nose, then shrunk back in pain. It toppled over lifelessly.

The other remaining wulves howled nervously at the sight of their felled captain and ran in uneven circles.

Clover rose shakily to his feet.

"Get away, run!" He cried in a hoarse voice. "I killed your king—and I'll kill you next. *Go!*"

The wulves rushed away, whining pitifully.

Clover stood, hunched over, with his wounded hand against his wounded shoulder. He panted, listening to his raging heartbeat. He was alive—but was anyone else?

"Yuma?" he called. "Yuma, where are you?"

"Here."

Clover turned to see Yuma kneeling beside the body of a dead wulf. His dagger was embedded into its skull.

"I'm too tired," he panted, "to pull it out."

Clover plodded unevenly to Yuma's side, then rested a heavy hand on his shoulder.

"We," he strived for breaths, "did it."

Yuma shook his head. "No," he said, "We didn't."

Clover turned his head, dreading what he would see. He trudged over to the silent scene of white mixed with red. There was nothing but stillness. Clover's boots splatted against moisture as he moved through the pool of blood at the center of his herd. Dead... *all* dead?

"I'm sorry," Yuma's voice came from behind him. "I tried..."

Clover lifted a silencing hand. He wandered around the bodies, counting, then losing count; counting, then losing count.

"No," his voice was practically nonexistent.

"Have none survived?" Yuma asked, kneeling down beside one of the corpses.

Movement stirred. Clover turned sharply to see one of the sheep's bodies twitching. He rushed to its side and knelt before it.

"Andrew?" he pleaded, finding the fat sheep vibrating wildly. "Andrew," he said again with a trembling voice. His lip quivered as he pulled the sheep's seizing body onto his knees. He hugged it tightly.

"Clover," Yuma knelt beside him.

"Silence!" Clover barked in a wet voice. Tears streamed from his eyes and he began to rock back and forth with a moan. "Andrew..."

Yuma sighed.

"Did you see him?" Clover asked weakly.

"What?" Yuma asked in a soft voice, "Who?"

"TSB... did you see him?"

Yuma shook his head. Clover's ear twitched, and he loosened his hold on Andrew's body to peer around.

"TSB—is that you?" he called. The little gnome's body scurried forward, then leapt onto his lap. Clover took him roughly and held him to his chest; then he sobbed.

Clover and Yuma remained there, waiting as Andrew continued to shake mindlessly. Clover held the sheep tightly with one arm, and the gnome in the other, crying like a grieving mother. After a time, Yuma finally spoke.

"You should put him out of his misery. He's already dead."

"No," Clover said sharply. His own body was shaking now, not from the tears, but from the pain of his wounds. "No. We wait with him."

"But he's—"

"No," Clover snapped, "We wait."

More time passed. Eventually, Andrew did die. Clover's shaking stopped, and he held his breath, gazing down at the creature's open eye. He exhaled slowly. Yuma sighed deeply as well. Clover released his hold on the animal and let it slip down onto the ground.

Clover felt Yuma's hand on his back.

"We bury them all," said Clover, "I'll be felled if any of their bodies get taken by those daemons."

"Thank you," said Yuma.

Clover turned to look at the man, confused by his response. "What?"

"Thank you."

"For what?"

"For not killing Andrew," said Yuma.

Clover searched his face. "Why?"

Yuma nodded. "I think..." his hand slid down off of Clover's back. "I think it's important to be with someone when they die. To be patient in their suffering."

Clover turned his head to look back at Andrew. Had it really made a difference to the creature that Clover *hadn't* killed him? Who could know?

The little gnome pulled himself free of Clover's arm and crept forward, rubbing his hands against Andrew's soft wool.

"He's dead, little thief," Clover said with a sniff. The gnome turned to gaze up at him with his large circular eyes. He looked expectant. "He's dead," said Clover, "We will bury him."

"Clover," Yuma tensed, "Look!"

Clover gazed down where Yuma was pointing, at Andrew's belly. Clover gasped. He could see movement rippling within.

"No way," Clover whispered. "Yuma, pass me your knife."

Yuma dashed off with renewed adrenaline and pulled the knife free of the wulf's skull with a loud crunch. He ran back and handed it to Clover. The Elf wiped the blade against his tunic, then sliced a clean line across Andrew's abdomen. Out spilled a red, rippling sac of blood. Clover rubbed the membranes with his fingers until the sac broke open, spilling wetness out onto Clover's lap. The shaking body of a tiny lamb lay there. Clover pulled his cloak forward and wrapped the thing up, rubbing it quickly to stimulate life. It began to cry.

Clover looked up at Yuma, smiling widely. "Yuma!"

"I see it," Yuma sighed.

Clover gazed lovingly down at the thing and held it to his chest.

"Well," Yuma wiped his brow. "I guess *Andrew* was a girl."

15

A Beneficial Relationship

Lola sat in the morning room, reading her novel. A half a dozen or so other court ladies were sitting nearby, playing cards around a table. The Princess licked a finger, then turned a page.

"Good morning," said Fayne as she placed herself elegantly by Lola's side. Lola looked up.

"Oh, you're speaking to me now?"

"I figure two full days of silence is enough," Fayne said with a magnanimous turn of her head.

Lola flipped her book closed, but left a finger tucked inside, marking her page. "You know," she said, "I've never understood the idea of silence when things are resolved more quickly through open conversations."

"You've never understood?" Fayne's eyes flashed, "You've never understood the idea that some people need time for their *anger* to cool?"

Lola licked her lips. "Lady Fayne... why were you angry with me? You know that I had nothing to do with Somenus taking me to the banquet, and if you had given me the chance to speak before now, I could have told you that I was very explicit with him. I told him I am *not* interested!"

Lady Fayne snorted. "Is any of that supposed to console me? You've got him *chasing* you now. So your disinterest is only going to stoke his fire!"

"Please," Lola said with sincerity, "I am trying to make friends with you! What do I need to do?"

Fayne scoffed, turning her head away.

"Is there something you think I could be doing differently?" Lola pressed, sliding her finger free of her novel, and placing the book on the table.

"Well," Fayne shifted side to side, warming to the pandering. "Listen—we need to ask why he is so interested in you."

Lola straightened her back. "Well, it could be that he is not actually *romantically* interested, you know. At the banquet he really just wanted to catch me up on his conversations with my father."

Fayne didn't look impressed. "Romance has nothing to do with it. He's *interested*—that's the key word. Why? He doesn't have to explain to his prisoner why he abducted her over a cup of vino. No, he's after something."

Lola cocked her head to the side. It was hard to know if Fayne's insights had any ground; this woman had more social experience, that was for sure. But was she as wise as she thought herself to be?

"What could he possibly be after?" asked Lola.

"What do you think? He comes here for entertainment—and for," she leaned forward and whispered, "*magik.*"

Magik. The lifeforce for Faeries. They all apparently had different ways of acquiring it, but Lola knew little of how it all worked. Who did? Faeries were always so private about their ways; they never bothered to share intimate details with the rest of the world. How did someone like Lady Fayne know any more than the next person?

"Surely the king doesn't *need* magik," Lola matched Fayne's volume, "And how could he get it from *here*?"

"Faeries are greedy," Fayne said, "They always want more. And what do you think? Somenus gains power when people *think* about him. He comes here to get women to fall in love with him—that's what I think. So, why is he after *you*? I can only guess you are thinking about him quite a lot," she leaned back, looking pleased with herself, "Tell me I am wrong!"

Lola frowned. "On the contrary," she said, "If he gets more powerful from people who think about him a great deal, he would do better pursuing someone like you. I am too busy reading my novel to care two shells about what Somenus is up to. And tell me, how do you know he gets magik from people thinking about him? Did *he* tell you that?"

Fayne's mouth dropped open, affronted by the insinuation. "I am sharing valuable information with you about the king, and you—you dare to *question* it?"

"It's not an insult to question new information," Lola said, refusing to buckle under the pressure, "I am simply trying to understand."

Fayne scoffed.

"Listen," Lola folded her hands together, "I can't control King Somenus, or whether or not he seeks me out. But I can tell you this: I am not going to sit here feeling guilty because *you* are jealous of something I seem to have that you don't. I am done dancing circles around your whims, Fayne. I am sorry if that makes an enemy out of you. It's not how I would want it, but there it is."

Lady Fayne drew back, studying Lola with darting eyes. Then she smirked.

"Well," she said, nodding, "So, you *do* have a backbone."

Lola refrained from an eye roll.

Fayne patted Lola's knee condescendingly. "Very well, little Princess," she said, then she rose and left.

⸺ ◆ ⸺

Lola received more than one dirty look that night from the other women when King Somenus made a beeline for her. She hadn't seen him for three days, but there he was, at the very next banquet, coming to find her. She sighed inwardly, then turned to Lady Fayne with an apologetic shrug. Fayne wagged her head side to side disapprovingly.

"Evening, Princess Lolette," Somenus said cheerily as he held his hand up to where she posed.

"Evening, Sire," she said.

"Aren't you coming down?" he asked, "Are you going to leave the king standing here with his hand out?"

She pursed her lips. "Are you sure you don't want to take anyone else about tonight? I've already expressed to you that I am not interested in courting you."

He snorted. "Come on down, Princess," he said with a smile, "I can tell you what I have heard from your father's messengers; how does that sound?"

"Oh!" She took his hand quickly and hopped down. "Well just so long as *everybody* knows," she said loudly, "I am only coming along because you *asked* me to."

King Somenus looked side to side with his eyes, then cleared his throat. "Are you finished?"

"Yes," she smiled politely, then took his offered arm.

Lola was surprised to see hardly anyone else in attendance at the party. When they came into the banquet hall, only a small table was set, with eight seats.

"Where is everybody?" she asked. She turned to see Somenus studying her intently. "*Erm,*" she flushed, "Sire?"

"Ah," he said dryly, "Only Somensday banquets are that large. Most times I come here with a quiet party. I'm dining with my..." he paused to think of the best description, "my *inner circle* tonight. Arelle's finest."

Lola raised her eyebrows. "Oh, *really?*"

"Evening, Princess," said a familiar voice. Lola turned sharply to see Felix of Sight strolling up to her with a goblet in hand. He looked surprisingly upper class, dressed in a buttoned suit, similar to Somenus'. He had neglected, however, to comb his hair, so he still seemed slightly out of place.

Lola tightened her mouth angrily. "Felix," she nodded civilly.

"Evening Felix of Sight," Somenus said with a gracious smile. "How did your little chase go yesterday, hmm?"

Felix bowed his head to Somenus, then straightened with a snap. "I'm afraid I lost them, as I am sure you are aware..." Felix's eyes drifted down to Somenus' missing hand. Lola looked side to side awkwardly.

"So," she said, doing her best to hide her sass, "Are you some sort of pet dog—running errands for the king?"

Felix rotated his body to face her and blinked blankly.

"Princess Lolette," Somenus said with a slight melody in his voice, "Felix is the most important Faerie in Arelle, second to me. I think you owe him an apology."

Lola blushed. She did feel a little ashamed of herself; not because Felix didn't deserve such a slight, but because she was usually above slander. No. She would not let her time among these villains make her lose her virtue!

"I am sorry, Felix of Sight," she said with a look of true remorse, "I forgot myself."

"Think nothing of it," Felix said quickly, snapping his head into a bow.

"I didn't realize you were," she glanced at the king for confirmation, "Second in command."

"Second in command?" A loud voice bellowed. Lola jumped, then searched for its source. Felix stepped to the side to allow an addition to their circle. Lola saw evidence of a man, that is to say, she saw his waistcoat. Somenus chuckled, watching as she searched the skies for his head. The lengthy human had an angular, bony face, a tidy beard, and shoulder length hair. He stood there crookedly in a suit, which must have required a fleet of seamstresses to make, and he looked about as unnatural as a rabid hound wearing a pink silk ribbon.

"I'll be felled," he said through a sinister grin, "if old Sight boy is called *second in command!*"

"A harmless mistake," Somenus said with a look of annoyance, "Princess, this is general Korbin, my *second* in command."

The general bent over to inspect her, his ears no doubt popping from the change in elevation. His eyes seemed to trespass her privacy as they traveled down then up her person.

"What a pretty whore you have there tonight," he said in his deep voice.

Lola flushed with embarrassment and took a timid step back. Hadn't Alabaster said human men wouldn't come up to the Vineyard Palace?

"I–I–I'm not a–a–" she stuttered.

"Korbin, please," Somenus said in an uncharacteristically casual tone, "You're scaring her, like you do everybody."

Korbin chuckled, shaking his shoulders back and forth unevenly. His laugh was interrupted with a congested cough.

"She the Elf King's bitch?" Korbin asked Somenus.

"Yes," said the king.

"Well, he giving his armies to us or not?"

"Korbin…" Somenus hissed through his teeth.

"Will you ever felling shut up?" Felix asked from behind his goblet, mid sip. Korbin turned his heavy gaze to the Faerie of Sight.

"You sassing *me*, peon?" the general yapped.

"Gentlemen!" Somenus snapped. "Will you both leave my side if you can't behave like noblemen? This is a *banquet*. No work talk. I'm here to play!"

Korbin and Felix turned away from each other silently. Somenus sighed, turning to Lola.

"Shall we find our seats?"

Lola nodded, knowing she had little say in the matter either way. Somenus led the way to the table and sat beside her. She looked around nervously, hoping that the tall human general wasn't anywhere nearby.

"Sorry about that," Somenus said unapologetically as he snapped his napkin into place. "Korbin can be so… *human* sometimes."

If that's what humans are like, Lola thought to herself, I'll be glad not to know any more of them.

"Sire," Lola leaned forward in a whisper. "Can I ask you something?"

Somenus' brilliant green eyes brightened. He leaned forward to match her tone. "Of course, Princess."

Lola squinted; why was he being so… *friendly* to her?

"I… I have an odd question to ask," she said.

"Ask me," he replied eagerly.

"You are the Dream Faerie, are you not?"

He nodded. "That is one of my titles," he said.

"Does that mean you can," her eyes shifted to the side, "You can make people dream about you?"

He smirked. "Why are you asking me this? Did *you* dream about me, Princess?"

She flattened her lips. "Sire," she said, "Did *you* dream about *me*?"

He chuckled, leaning back. "I am not sure what you mean."

"I saw you the other night," she said.

"At the banquet?"

"In my dream. I saw *you*, Sire." Her eyes narrowed. "Did you... come into my mind?"

"Your mind?" He shook his head, "No, I didn't do that. I merely... *peeked*."

"*Why?*" She frowned.

"I visit lots of people's dreams," he said with a shrug, "It isn't all that surprising. I don't take over, or anything. I just... visit."

"Well, please leave me alone in the future," she said with a turned up chin. "I don't appreciate *visits*."

He snorted. "I'll do whatever I please, princess."

She closed her eyes, composing herself. She opened them. "Sire, I—"

"Who was that man?"

She started. "What?"

"In your dream; who was he?"

She blushed angrily. "I don't know what you're—why would you *care*?"

"Who *is* he?" He asked in a cool voice, but there was urgency behind his eyes.

"I—"

"Well," Felix pulled out the chair across from Lola and sat gracelessly. "Am I interrupting?"

Somenus leaned back into his chair and plucked his goblet from the table. His eyes stirred with tension.

"No," Lola turned to the Faerie of Sight. "So, tell me, *Felix*, how long have you been Arelle's, *erm*..."

"Watchman?"

"Mm... yes, *Watchman*," she did her best to put on her polite voice. It was hard when she was encircled by those she hated. "How long have you been 'watchman' here?"

"Two thousand seasons, give or take," he said bluntly.

Lola twitched. "Oh! Two thou—*really*?"

"Yes."

"You served the late King, then?" she asked, glancing at Somenus who seemed to shift in discomfort at the mention of the last Faerie monarch.

"Yes."

"And now you serve... Somenus?" she asked slowly.

"Well, he's the king now, isn't he?" Felix asked bluntly, slamming his goblet down on the table.

"Gentlemen!" a Faerie with a jovial smile glided up to the table and pulled out the chair to Lola's left. "Evening, evening, evening!"

Lola looked to her side to see a Faerie with tanned skin and wavy brown hair sitting beside her, flipping his coattails behind him with a flourish.

"What a beautiful spread," he said, eyeing the table. He turned to regard Lola. "Hello, hello, hello!"

"Hello," she smiled politely.

"What a pretty—oh! Elf!" He slammed his palm against the table excitedly. "This must be the girl from Celestia! Lolette, is it?" He reached for her hand. She held it out and watched skeptically as he kissed it. He was a charmer, if she ever saw one.

"Yes..."

"Endring, at your service!" He said, still holding her hand. She pulled it back with a courteous nod.

"He's the Faerie of Vows," Somenus said lazily, pointing with his favorite studded goblet, "My main emissary."

"Yes, yes, Faerie of Vows," he said with a flutter of his eyelashes, "And Hades—I'll vow right *now* that I've never seen anybody so pretty!"

"Oh, *please*," Felix mumbled into his cup.

"Well," Endring slapped the table again, "I can't say I've had the pleasure of ever having traveled to Celestia, but I have heard she's a gorgeous city. Leck always had the honor of going there, well," he coughed into his hand, "A shame about all that."

"Leck?" Lola turned to Somenus. "Whatever did happen to him? Oh, please tell me!"

All heads at the table turned to Somenus.

"He's around," Somenus said, "Anyway, didn't I say no *business* talk tonight?"

"Well, you did tell me you heard from my father's messengers," Lola said bravely. "What did they say?"

"Ah," Somenus smiled unconvincingly, "Yes. Well, so far, your father hasn't said anything about paying a ransom."

Lola's heart fell. "What? Really?"

"Not yet.... But, let's give him time, Princess."

Lola looked down at her plate with a dismal sigh. Why hadn't her father offered any ransom? Didn't he *care* that she was here?

Korbin took his place at the table. Lola looked up fearfully at the giant. He looked like a father sitting at his children's pretend tea party, looming head and shoulders above the rest at the table.

"What have I missed?" he asked as he reached across the table to grab a bread roll. Lola watched in fascination as he continued to pile food onto his plate. Surely he wasn't going to eat *all* of that!

"I say, General," Endring said quickly, "Hungry?"

Korbin looked up to smile widely. Lola couldn't be sure, but it almost looked like he had too many teeth. "Always," he said with glistening eyes.

Endring seemed to retreat into his clothes. "Ah, hah, hah," he looked down at his lap and grew silent.

Lola picked up her own goblet and sipped, feeling the need, for the first time in her life, to experience the calming buzz of the spirits.

"Tell me, *Elf woman*," Korbin turned his focus to Lola.

Lola swallowed a large gulp of vino reactively. *Here we go*, she thought as she placed the cup on the table.

"Yes, General?"

"How large exactly is your father's army? Has he got archers? Spearmen? How *many*?"

Lola coughed. "I..." she glanced toward Somenus. "I don't think of our men as an army, General. *All* Elf men learn to fight, I suppose."

"How many men have you got?" he asked with a mouth full of food.

Lola paused, waiting for Somenus to come to her rescue. When he didn't, she replied, "I really couldn't say."

"Ah!" a spray of crumbs ejaculated from his mouth, "That's what women say when they are being missish. Loosen that trap, woman! Tell me!"

Lola's cheeks grew hot with rage.

"Korbin, I'll eject you from this table if you can't act like a human being!" Somenus yelled. His voice filled the air like a thick smoke. The table grew quiet, and all but Korbin seemed to retreat like turtles into their protective shells.

Korbin chuckled through a wet cough. "Sorry, *Sire*," he said in a mocking voice, "I'll *behave*."

Lola glanced at the king, giving him a weak, thankful smile. He nodded at her. Lola turned to see Felix staring blankly. What an unsettling person, Felix, Always staring, never speaking.

Korbin then turned and rose to greet three others who seemed to arrive late to the party. Lola relaxed a little. Finally, that menace was gone—for the moment, at least!

"Lola," Somenus leaned toward her, "Is it alright if I call you that?"

She turned. "Hmm? Oh—I guess so."

"Lola, I've a confession to make."

She blinked. "...yes?"

"I'm a little—well," he shifted in his chair, as if it suddenly grew as hot as an oven, "Well..."

"Goodness," she hovered her hand over her heart, "What is it? Are you alright?"

He laughed at himself with a shake of his head. "I'm fine, I'm fine. Lola... I have to be honest with you..."

Lola stared intently at him, trying her best to concentrate. She didn't expect the vino to hit her so *quickly*; she could barely see straight!

"I have to admit," he said, leaning closer in a whisper, "I'm a little disappointed."

"By what?" she asked, restraining a hiccup.

He tried to conceal a modest smile behind his napkin. "I'm disappointed that you're not... more open to a diplomatic marriage."

She hiccupped loudly, then shot her napkin up over her mouth in shame. "*What*?" she asked weakly.

He laughed heartily. "Lola," he said, "I like you, I'm drawn to you."

"What?" She retreated further behind her napkin, holding it up to her nose. Was it the vino, or did he just tell her he...

"Really," he said, "I wish you'd just swallow your prejudice and court me, Lola."

She hiccupped again, then covered her face completely in the napkin, hiding shamefully. She could hear Somenus chucking.

"Oh, please don't hide, Lola. I'm sorry. I didn't mean to embarrass you."

She lowered the silk napkin slightly, just enough to see Felix staring blankly at her. She shifted her gaze to see Somenus grinning.

"Forgive me," said the king, "I upset you."

"No," she said meekly, lowering the napkin. "No, no. I'm sorry. I took a rather large sip of that vino, and I'm afraid it—" she hiccupped again.

"Well," Somenus said, still in a low voice, "I'd betray my feelings if I didn't say something. Would you at least.... *Reconsider* your last resolution on the subject? I've rather got my heart set on you, Lola."

I've rather got my heart set on you, Lola. Those words...they could have come straight from one of her novels. By the Lights—she could have written them herself in her journal as the very words she wished someone like him would say to her one day!

She gazed confusedly at the king, studying his sincere eyes. *Why* was she so against marrying him? What had he done that was so terrible?

"Somenus," she said in a low voice. "Is courting you a way to... bridge the gap between you and my father—between the Fae and the Elves?"

Somenus bobbed his head to the side, "Well, yes..."

She nodded to herself. "I'll think about what you've said," she replied. She wasn't actually considering courting the Faerie King, but she would be a fool to turn him down on the spot *again*, wouldn't she? And yet, what if marriage was about more than affection? What if it was an opportunity to protect her people from war?

Somenus scooted back suddenly in his chair. He gazed down at where his missing hand should have been.

"Felix," he snapped.

"Sire?" Felix stood to attention.

"Felix, I..." Somenus rose from his chair and looked around. "I need to go. Will you—" he turned to observe Lola, "Will you walk her back tonight? I—I need to..." He ran out of the banquet hall.

"Oh, what a shame," Korbin said as he approached the table once more. "Seems like I'll have to found the feast tonight, or whatever it is you people like to do."

Lola turned, white faced, to stare with pleading eyes at Felix who was still standing, gazing toward where the king had left. He turned to her, then raised his eyebrows. She waved a timid hand. He raised one eyebrow higher than the other.

"Felix," she whispered.

He walked around the table, stood by her side, then leaned down.

"Can you take me *now*?" she whispered, eyeing Korbin who was currently sculling his third goblet of vino.

"Oh," Felix nodded quickly.

"Since the king seems to have moved on, I don't really see the need to stay."

"Right you are," Felix said, "Come on." He held out his hand.

Lola looked at it, surprised by the sudden genteel attitude, and placed her palm on top of it. He pulled her away from the table.

"Where are you two going?" Korbin demanded. "I'm the king of the feast now, and I want *things* to look at!"

Felix didn't flinch. "Somenus told me to escort her back."

"You can do that after I've finished," his eyes focused on Lola, "*Eating*."

"No," said the Faerie of Sight. He turned and led the Princess out of the banquet hall, ignoring the general's eruption of insults.

It was a mostly silent walk back to Lola's quarters. There was an outdoor stair which led from the back of the banquet hall, up to the third floor of the

Palace where most of the bedrooms were. The night was deep and black now, with a gentle twinkling of reflected stars above.

"Felix," Lola finally asked, as they were halfway up the stairs.

"What?"

"Is Somenus a... a *good* King?"

Felix flattened his mouth but couldn't think of a response.

"Is he good to his wives?" she asked, trying another question.

Felix's mouth pulled into an even tighter line.

Lola sighed. "*Does* he have any wives? Or does he just have a lot of... women?"

Felix stopped, then turned to look at her. "He has a lot of concubines," he said, "Back at the Eight Stones. From what I can tell, he treats them well."

Lola nodded. "Is that the life he is offering me?"

Felix sniffed. "I am not sure."

"Some of the women here think he pursues all these relationships because he wants, *erm*, Magik. Is that true? Is that why he comes here?"

Felix let out a long, drawn out, sigh. "I think ultimately what the king wants is an heir. If you could give him that, he might marry you."

Lola blanched. "All those concubines...and *no* children?"

Felix shook his head. "It's rare for a Faerie to be born." He turned and continued up the stairs. She walked beside him, thinking. They came up to a circular landing, crowned in grapevines.

"Felix," Lola stopped him again by the arm. He looked at her blankly, as he always did. "Does Somenus acquire magik by... by making people think about him?"

Felix folded his arms. "Not exactly," he said, "He's the Faerie of Affection, technically. So, I think he is especially empowered by passion towards him."

"Passion towards him? Like—love?"

Felix blew air out the side of his mouth. "Love, fear, hate... any sort of obsession."

"Is *that* why he wants to court me? Because... I don't think I—"

"Don't worry about that," Felix said quickly, "Don't... don't fixate on him, or try to piece together what's going on in his mind. That's—that's how it all starts."

Lola's eyes widened. Felix seemed to be speaking from experience. "I see."

"Just find beauty in other things, things other than him," Felix said.

"Beauty?" Lola scoffed, shaking her head. "And what do *you* know about beauty?"

"More than most, I think," Felix said dryly.

Lola's curiosity won out over her prejudice, if only for a moment. "What do you mean?"

"I'm the Faerie of Sight," he said, "What do you think I draw power from?"

Lola thought for a moment. "*Erm...seeing* things?"

Felix nodded. "Yes," he said, "But some things shine more than others," he turned to gaze at the clouds which hovered over the top of Arelle. "Beauty...it has a certain... glow. Anyway," he turned back to her, "Somenus has a lot of it. But other things do, too."

"Somenus has beauty?" Lola's eyes seemed to gloss over. "Yes, I suppose he does." She froze. "Felix..."

"What?"

"You get a lot of power from him, then...?"

"Yes, naturally."

"And he gets it from you?"

Felix shrugged. "A beneficial relationship."

"And yet, here you are telling me to find beauty elsewhere?" She raised an eyebrow. "Trying to warn me of a trap you yourself have fallen into?"

Felix shook his head. "I'm merely trying to answer your questions."

Lola narrowed her eyes. "You think I shouldn't court him, don't you?"

"I didn't say that."

Lola turned away from him in a huff.

"Come on," Felix pointed toward the doorway into the third level. "You should get to bed."

"You didn't answer my question, Felix," Lola turned.

"Which?"

"I asked earlier if Somenus is good; is he a *good* King?"

"Come on," Felix took her roughly by the arm and dragged her along. He practically pushed her through the doorway into her room. She turned to scowl.

"Good night, Felix of Sight," she said coldly, then slammed the door.

⚬

Lola dreamed of a place she had never seen that night. She dreamed of a small, pillared watchtower at the top of a mountain. It was the middle of the day, and yet stars dressed the sky like glittering fireflies. There were hanging vines draped from the ceiling, and blossom petals blowing in the wind. It was a safe place, far away from the Vineyard Palace and her many villains.

She was doing exactly what she wanted to be doing there: reclining on her stomach, reading her novel. In her dream, her book was filled not with words, but with pictures. She flipped through the pages, humming the tune of her mother's favorite song.

Then she heard a crack, like a blast of lightning. Lola sat up on her knees, then looked around. There was a man, standing on the other side of her little gazebo, panting. He wore a white tunic, black trousers, and a dented helmet. It was the man from her vision!

"Beloved!" she said, the word coming out of her mouth automatically.

He turned to observe her, then waved a hand.

"Hey," he said.

Her heart seemed to swell with memories she had no access to. This man—she *knew* him, if only she could remember how!

"Are you Somenus?" she asked quickly.

"What?" He looked side to side.

"Never mind," she waved her hands.

He plodded forward, gazing about, still breathing heavily. "Nice place," he said.

"It's my reading spot," she said matter-of-factly. As always, everything made sense in the Dream World.

"I suppose you're not needing to be rescued anymore?" he asked, sitting down onto his backside uneasily.

"No," she said, then she paused, remembering something about her waking life. "Well... maybe."

"What are you reading?" he asked, pointing to the book.

"A romance!" she said proudly, holding it up.

"About me?" he asked cheerily.

"I don't know," she said thoughtfully, "It's about a man named Anodos. He's going on an adventure in Faerie land."

"Sure sounds like me," Beloved said virtuously. He scooted beside her and leaned down to look at the book. Lola peered upwards.

"Beloved?" she asked.

"Hmm?"

"Can you take off that helmet?"

He reached up his arms and pulled, then shook his head. "I don't think so."

She sighed. "A pity. I'd like to see your face. *Erm*—Beloved?"

"Hmm?"

"Is it true that... that you," she felt herself blushing, "You love me?"

"I think I always have," he said. "If that's at all possible."

"Oh, good," she smiled, "I don't know why I doubted."

"Uh, silly question, but..." Beloved scratched his neck, "Do you, uh... you love me, too—right?"

"Of course!" she said, pushing herself up on her arms. Why, *of course*? Waking Lola wouldn't have approved of that reply, but this was a dream, after all.

Then the dream seemed to drift away, like a straying thought. Lola looked around the fog of her mind, trying to recall what she had seen. A voice spoke.

"Lola, there you are," he said.

She spun round, trying to find a form amongst the mist.

"Beloved?" she called. Her voice echoed endlessly.

"Here," the voice was close. She turned. There was Somenus, glowing like a lighthouse in a storm.

"I told you before," she said, a small ray of her conscious mind shining through, "I don't want you coming into my mind."

"*You* invited me here," he said.

"No, I didn't—!"

"You called me—I heard you calling my name," he said.

"That…" Lola looked around, hearing her own voice echoing around here. *Beloved*. "That's not you," she said with tightened fists.

"It is what I *could* be," he said, "If you would just give me a chance." He stepped back, moving away from her slowly. She watched him fade into the fog, and then he was gone.

—— Isabella ——

The True Master

Isabella—or rather, Scarlet Wingsday—was strolling down the main road on the east side of Arelle, right at the center of the Windsong Compound. Lower in elevation to the Eight Stones, it was where most of the Faeries lived. Unlike humans, the Fae seemed to prefer living alone, and they often resided in houses that never touched one another. Each home had its own unique touch of personality, and Isabella enjoyed trying to guess which Faerie might live in each place based on its quirks.

Three days into her new position, Isabella had been placed on door-knocking duty. It was pretty simple: walk through the Windsong Compound, knock on each door, and, as Korbin put it, *make sure everybody is where they are supposed to be.* It wasn't that the Faeries had been placed on house arrest—no, they seemed to be able to go places freely—it was more that Korbin, or perhaps the king, wanted to have a good idea of where all the Faeries were, and what they were up to.

She knocked on the door to the first house. It was narrow but stacked high with three stories. The top of the building seemed to be some sort of terrace, with a rain of foliage cascading down from it.

A voice called from up above, "Hallo?" Someone peeked her head over the corner of the roof. "Who is there?"

Isabella peered upwards. "Door checks!"

The woman mumbled for a moment to herself, then shouted. "Well, come on up, then. Front door is unlocked, as always!"

Isabella reached out for the door handle. It was a brass ring, molded into the shape of a wreath. She turned it, then entered. Inside the house, it smelled of spice and sap. As Isabella stepped forward, something crunched beneath her boot. She glanced down, lifting her sole to see a flaking pinecone. The house seemed to be pretty clean, aside from the odd pinecone littering the ground. It hardly felt like a house, Isabella thought, as the aesthetic of the place was closer to nature than it was to a home made of stones, as it appeared on the outside. The walls rippled with wood designs, akin to bark and roots. And the floor was tiled with polished tree rounds. Even the grouting seemed to be made of petrified pine needles.

Isabella spotted a spiral set of stairs, carved into what must have once been a massive tree trunk, about the size of an Elder Giant. As she climbed the stairs, movement rustled in the tree; birds had made nests within its cavernous knots.

She climbed a few flights until she came to the roof. To her surprise, the tree continued far above the house, towering over the city with pine-covered branches. As she stepped onto the terrace, she gazed upwards, marveling as the beast of a tree swayed contentedly in the wind.

"It's an Elder Giant!" she exclaimed.

"Good eye," said the Faerie. Isabella turned to see the woman sitting on the ground, scooping soil into little terracotta planters.

"Good day," Isabella said, straightening her armor. She stepped up to where the Faerie was sitting. She lifted her notebook and flipped to the first page. "Would you be..." she stretched out the word as she searched the list. "Faerie of Trees? The... fifth?"

"Xylo, at your service," the Faerie said flatly. "You're new."

Isabella lowered her notebook to inspect the Faerie. She was simply dressed in a cyan toga. Her brown hair was swirled messily in a bun on the top of her head, and her rosy cheeks were dusted with dirt marks.

"Yes, I am new," Isabella said, trying to look natural. She wasn't used to being seen as the muscle in a community. After being perceived as a weak, helpless woman for most of her life, there was something enjoyable about the contrast.

Xylo continued to scoop soil with her hands, placing it carefully into the next pot. "What do they call you?" she asked, keeping her eyes on her work.

"Scarlet. Scarlet Wingsday. I..." Isabella, shifted her weight, "Tell me, how did you get an Elder Giant way out here?"

"How did *I*?" Xylo looked up, smirked. "That tree is thousands of seasons old—*I* didn't put it there."

"Oh," Isabella turned to inspect the tree once more. As far as she knew, the Elder Giants only grew in a particular part of the Raqian Woodlands. They all belonged to the Elves, she thought.

"Every Tree Faerie has lived here in this house, you know," Xylo said, digging her hand back into her sack of compost. "I live under the shadow of many great Faeries."

Isabella turned. "How does it compare: living under King Somenus, versus King Sol?"

Xylo squinted. "That's... why are you asking me this? Is this some sort of test?"

Isabella shook her head. "No... I am new. I was just curious."

Xylo maintained a look of suspicion. "Honestly?" she said, "It doesn't make much difference to me. Somenus is King. I'll do what he asks, but he doesn't ask much. I suppose the only difference is having humans like you poking their nose into my world once a week, but I suppose I can stomach that."

This felt a little surprising to Isabella. Here she was, going undercover to help free the Faeries from a tyrannical king—and yet here was one of his subjects, nonchalantly planting seedlings.

"You wouldn't say Somenus is... a better or worse King?" Isabella asked.

Xylo rubbed her chin with her forearm. "Perhaps he's a little better than Sol. He answered the Question for us."

There it was again: The Question. What was this question all the Faeries seemed to care about?

"What question is that?" Isabella asked.

Xylo frowned. "Nothing humans would understand. Anyway, did I pass?"

"What?"

"Whatever you're trying to find out...?"

"Oh," Isabella tucked her notebook under her arm. "I was honestly just curious. Some Faeries I have encountered think Somenus is... evil."

Xylo nodded to herself. "Some of us thought Sol was evil, too," she said. Then she shrugged. "It's not for us to try and *fix* things, though. Sometimes in trying to fix broken things, we break them further."

"But Somenus is imprisoning all the Fae who won't participate in the Faerie Rites," Isabella said, forgetting herself.

Xylo cocked her head to the side. "Are you *trying* to get a rise out of me? Look—I don't like hearing of my brothers and sisters being punished, but it's up to the king how he deals with treason! It's my job to be the Tree Faerie, so that's what I am going to do! No one else is going to do it for me. So, I won't try to go and do the king's job—you understand?"

"Sorry," Isabella said quickly, stepping back.

"You've checked in, and now you can *go*," Xylo snapped.

Isabella made a little cross next to Xylo's name in the notebook, then beside it she wrote, *At home, planting seeds.*

"Thank you for your time," Isabella said, then turned about face, and left.

The house next door was a stark difference to the Tree Faerie's home. While the house itself was simple in design, plain, polished white sides, and cubic in shape, all around it were stacked piles and piles of, well, stuff. From broken pottery to ornate chests, to sacks of fodder, nothing seemed to belong there. She weaved carefully through a small path she found between fallen items before getting to the door. Then she knocked. The door swung ajar.

"Hello?" she called.

"Oh!" A voice within cried. "Oh, who is there? Quick! Come *in*!"

Isabella pushed the door open with a hesitant finger. The door clunked to a stop when only halfway. Something appeared to be blocking it. She squeezed through the crack, then stumbled over a crate. A startled chicken flapped out of a corner, squawking helplessly. Isabella jumped, falling onto a stack of books which toppled over.

"Oh, oh dear, don't do that!" A man peered out from a nest of tomes, crafted like an igloo around himself.

Isabella climbed to her feet, brushing some fishing net free of her shoulder.

"Sir," she snapped, pulling up her notebook to check, "Are you... Buz? Seventy-fifth Faerie of Epiphanies?"

"Oh!" he exclaimed, "Yes!" He rose to his feet and waved a skinny arm. It was the first time Isabella had seen a Faerie with a receding hairline. She was confused at first, thinking that Faeries did not age past the age of fullness, then realized that he was also missing his eyebrows.

Isabella made a cross beside his name, then wrote: *At home; making*, she paused to suck on the end of her pencil, *a mess.*

"Oh!" he said, scratching a missing eyebrow. "You're new!" He smiled proudly, as if he had just discovered the remains of an ancient empire.

"Yes," she said dryly. "Uh... I'll leave you then."

"Oh—wait!" He waved his arms, "Will you help me with something? I've got this idea... and I need you to hold something "

Two bells later, Isabella was finally leaving the house. She checked her list.

"Wait a minute," she mumbled. Leck the Messenger Faerie was next on the list, only his name had been crossed out. Leck—he was her contact! Why was he crossed out? Her heart thumped nervously. "I'm not... *alone* here, am I?" she mumbled. The notebook quaked in her hand. *Just continue the rounds,* she thought, *I'll find out what happened to Leck.*

"Right," she said aloud, trying to find her equanimity, "Who's next?"

Isabella walked door to door for two more bells, until she heard the Zenith bell ringing. She stopped to lean against a wall, checking her list.

"Only one left," she said, scanning to the bottom of the paper. Thankfully, she had only been assigned thirty Faeries. There were about a hundred more living in Arelle, but it would be someone else's job to check up on them. It was a strange thing to think that such a large city housed only about a hundred and fifty Faeries. Perhaps more had lived here at one time, but still, the place felt so bare and lifeless without people occupying the streets.

Sure, Korbin's human soldiers like herself wandered here and there, but they definitely didn't make the place feel inhabited, unless you called a vacant house filled with spiders *inhabited*.

Isabella climbed the long set of stairs that ascended the eastern wall. By the time she reached the top, she was huffing and puffing, and leaning against the wall for support. As fit as she was, it took more than a short hike to reach the top of Arelle's walls. Why did she have to come *all* the way up here? It was infuriating, but Korbin wanted her to *catch every Faerie in the moment.* It was important to him that they didn't know she was coming.

She glanced down at her paper again. *Wait in the watchhouse.* How long was she supposed to wait? She pulled up her pants at the belt, wiped the sweat from her brow with her sleeve, then marched to the watchhouse. It was a square, doorless building, built into the corner of the wall. Isabella ducked inside. Well, perhaps she wouldn't have to wait; there was Felix of Sight, sitting in a chair, looking out the window.

Hearing her footsteps, he turned his head briskly.

"Wingsday?" he asked, "What are you doing up here?"

"Uh..." she looked down at her notebook.

"Oh, floods," Felix cursed, "He's not put *me* on that list, has he?" He rose to his feet, arms shaking. "Listen here, lackey: no one *checks up* on me! Got it? If I see you up here again, I'll throw you off the south wall without a moment's hesitation!"

Isabella turned red in the face. "I was just following orders... *Sir...*"

Felix marched forward and snatched the list from her hand. He flipped through the pages, then sighed.

"Look," he said, "This isn't about you. He's just peeved at me after last night."

"What happened last night?"

Felix silenced her with his eyes.

Isabella gulped, then pointed at the notebook. "So... what should I write?"

"Give me your pencil," Felix held out his hand, then impatiently snatched it from her. He scribbled into the notebook. "There," he passed it back to her, "Just hand this to him."

Isabella glanced down at Felix's name in the book. *Fell off,* was written in the section for notes.

"I see," she said, then closed the notebook. She was beginning to sense a rivalry between the two of them: Somenus' head Faerie, and Somenus' head human. She looked up to see Felix studying her.

"You, uh," he cleared his throat, "You get that position he promised you?"

"Major," she said, placing her hand absentmindedly on the hilt of her sheathed sword.

He nodded. "You, uh... you gave him those exiled Faeries, I'm guessing?"

She nodded.

"And," his eyes shifted, "what did he do with them?"

Isabella blinked. "You... you don't know?"

"I don't have much jurisdiction over the exiles once Korbin gets them," Felix said, crossing his arms. "I'm merely curious."

"He keeps them in the dungeon," she said.

"Ah," he nodded, "Yes..." he turned his head slightly. "All of them?"

"Uh..." Isabella remembered Korbin taking the drained bags into the room with the iron door. Was she not supposed to talk about it? Did she care what Korbin told Felix? In her book, they were *both* the enemy! "I'm still learning the ropes," she said.

"Right."

"You don't like Korbin, do you?" she asked.

"Nobody likes him," Felix said unapologetically.

"So why does the king tolerate him?"

Felix narrowed his eyes. "Why are you asking this? You're human, you should know the answer."

Alarm bells sounded within Isabella's pounding heart. She was getting too careless; she was supposed to be playing the role of the greedy bounty hunter!

She sniffed, trying to play up some haughtiness, "Can't a girl ask a few questions?"

"She can ask," Felix said darkly, "At her own peril." He pointed to the door. "Don't come up here again, Wingsday."

"Yes, Sir," she said, hunching up her shoulders protectively.

"You work for Korbin," he shouted after her, "But he's not above me, you understand?"

"Yes, Sir." She left the watchhouse briskly, then sighed in relief once outside. She jolted, hearing a wet cackle. She turned to see Korbin leaning against a corner, hugging the shadow.

"Poor little dust worm," he said with mocking sympathy, "Hates to be reminded that he's just *one of them.*"

Isabella walked up to Korbin, but not very close.

"You talk like Faeries are inferior to humans," she said skeptically, "and yet you serve the Faerie King—a Faerie King who is spreading a religion that says Faeries should be *worshiped* by humans."

Korbin grinned humorlessly. "Oh, yes? Fancy that."

"Here," she passed him the notebook, "Everyone accounted for."

"Nothing... *suspicious*?" he asked as he procured it from her.

She shook her head. "Not unless you think Faeries being Faeries is suspicious."

"You sure have a lot of *questions*, don't you, Wingsday?" he asked.

Isabella stuttered. "I–I–I—*what*?"

"Lots of questions, yes," he straightened to a height that seemed to rival the Elder Giant. "Very curious girl, aren't you?"

"You were watching me today?" she asked, more as an accusation than a question.

He nodded. "Very curious. Very curious, indeed."

She stood there, waiting to be scolded. "And?"

"Well, I like to think you might make a good..." he tapped his chin, "*second in command,* one day. You have a mind of your own; that could serve me well."

She joined her hands behind her back, still waiting for the reprimand.

"*Lieutenant* Wingsday. How does that sound?"

She exhaled. "You'd promote me after only three days?"

"No, no," he laughed, "No, it's an incentive, Wingsday! I'm hoping you will work hard to please me. *Then* we can talk about a promotion to Lieutenant. Hmm? How does that sound?"

Isabella hated the idea of doing anything that might please a man like this, but it was her job to get close to him. How else was she going to find Orion's Bow?

"Sounds good," she said gruffly, "What do I need to do?"

Korbin laughed, tipping his stiff head back and placing his hand heavily on her shoulder.

"Well, for starters," he said, "I'll need you to start *trusting* me."

Korbin laughed to himself again, then plodded off down the stairs, back down to the city.

Isabella shuddered. There was something so hateful—so *unnatural* about that man. If her mission was to aid in killing him, she wouldn't mind. This whole business with killing the king, however... she scratched the back of her neck distractedly; she was struggling to fully understand why it was so important, when the Faeries who lived under his rule seemed so content. Surely, Hanz would not have sent her here unless it was dire. But it *was* strange: here at the center of it all, it all looked different. Did she not have the full picture? Or was it Hanz who didn't have the full picture?

Braving the Sight Faerie's displeasure, Isabella walked back into the watchhouse. Felix stood there with his arms crossed, watching her expectantly.

"Oh," she said, glancing behind herself momentarily, "You were watching us, weren't you?"

"It wasn't hard," he said flatly, "I didn't even have to read lips, I could *hear* you from over here."

"So, you can see whatever you want to see?" she asked, "As the Faerie of Sight?"

He stared blankly. "What do you want, Wingsday?"

"I have a question for you," she said bravely, "On my list... Leck the Messenger Faerie," she watched as Felix turned to roll his eyes, "Why was his name crossed off the list?"

"Don't you *know*?" he snapped, "He was exiled for being a member of the Purple Order. He's on that damn shelf in the prison."

Isabella blinked, her mind trying to process quickly how to respond. Did Scarlet Wingsday know who the Purple Order was? Should she sound pleased by the idea? Leck, her only contact she knew of in the city—*exiled*?

"I... the Purple Order?" she stuttered.

"A damn shame," Felix sighed, turning to look out his window. "We were friends."

"They're the Faeries who are fleeing from Somenus?" she asked, hoping she did right.

Felix shot her a glare. "They're the Faeries who are plotting to kill the king!"

"Why?" she asked, holding a vacant expression.

"Hades knows," he muttered, "Probably because they want to put their own King on the throne. Oh, they claim it's in defense of King Sol—but King Sol and his line are dead! What do they expect to achieve by killing the next King?"

Isabella's mouth opened and closed wordlessly. "I–I figured those in the Purple Order just didn't like the Faerie Rites, and that's why Somenus was having us hunt them."

Felix scoffed, rolling his eyes dramatically. "Somenus isn't forcing the Fae into the Rites," he said, "Now I know some Faeries don't like how he answered the Question, but that doesn't mean they should go and *kill* him for it!"

Isabella's mind swirled with confusion. Was this true? Was Somenus really only hunting the Purple Order because they were plotting to kill him?

"Why are you asking me all this, soldier?" Felix demanded, stepping close. He eyed her from above with condescension. She looked up his nose.

"I... I am merely interested in faeries," she said, her voice feeling small.

"Hah!" Felix laughed, somehow, without smiling. "You think I don't know who you are? Scarlet *Wingsday*? You think I haven't heard of you?"

"What?" she hesitated. What *had* he heard of her?

"Wingsday—you think I don't know why you call yourself that? Wingsday, the day the Faeries were made. You're the infamous Faerie killer, killing the Fae only on Wingsdays, boasting you're unmaking them on the day they should have never been made. You *hate* my kind. So, whatever your *sick* interest is, you can take it far away from me."

"I..." she felt sick, nauseous from the ups and downs of the conversation. She had no idea what emotion she was supposed to be feeling in the moment, and her body rebelled, twisting her stomach into knots. "I don't kill Faeries anymore," she said, "I just collect them for Somenus."

"You don't, do you?" Felix sniffed. "And I suppose the birds have stopped flying and the fish have stopped swimming?"

She turned away from him. "Thank you for your time, Felix," she said sternly, "I will bother you no more."

"I may tolerate Korbin, and the humans in Arelle," Felix said to her back as she began to walk out of the watch house. "But I hate it. I hate your filthy stain on my city."

Isabella stopped, then turned to glance at the dark Faerie. "Well," she said, "I am sorry to hear that."

She walked out onto the wall. Instead of descending, she thought she might make the best out of the trip and walk around the city from its highest point. She knew now that she probably wouldn't make the trip up here again any time soon, not when Felix was so hostile toward her.

The walls towered so high above Arelle, there were clouds beneath her. She wandered aimlessly, sliding rather than lifting her feet as she walked.

"What in Hades am I doing here?" she finally asked herself out loud. She turned to gaze out at the scenery outside of Arelle. In the distance, she could see an outline of a massive mountain, shrouded in the distant atmosphere. That would be Bavel. She was so far away from everybody, isolated. Somehow, when she was perched so high above the rest of the world, everything seemed different. It was such a stark contrast to how she felt in that cellar, when Hanz convinced her to join in his plot.

With Hanz, it was dark all around her, the air was close and thin, and everyone believed so strongly in her, she figured they must be right. Now... now, she was away from those influences, where the air was clear, the sky bright, and everybody seemed to doubt her—she felt so differently. She wasn't sure she *wanted* to be a part of a plot to kill the king anymore! No, she really didn't!

Killing a King. It was so... so big! Hanz had gotten her to do many things in their childhood that she later regretted; was this the same? Had she blindly rushed into one of his grand plans without stopping to get all the information?

She thought she had done better than that; she thought she had asked all the important questions; she thought she was on the right path. And perhaps she was! But no... things *had* changed. Leck, her contact, was exiled. If she did manage to find this legendary weapon, what would she even *do* with it? And if she wanted to give up on the mission, she couldn't exactly leave! *Felix* watched the only way in and out of the city. It was possible she could get Korbin to give her some kind of job that let her leave the city, but she would have to be careful. The second that man suspected her of treachery, there would be no mercy for someone like her.

No, she was stuck; stuck in Arelle, stuck as Scarlet Wingsday, and stuck serving Korbin. Well, she had time. She would use that time carefully and learn more about what was actually happening. Was Somenus forcing the Fae into the Rites? Was he hunting the Purple Order for good reason? Could she come and go within the city? Did Hanz have any more contacts in Arelle?

She sighed. She could do this. She could be Scarlet Wingsday, at least for a time.

17

— Leo —

Aorist's Boy

I woke up with a yawn, then sat up. Something heavy jostled against my legs. I looked to see the chest sitting there, locked tight. I must have tried to open it again in my sleep. When I had gone to bed the night before, the chest had been on the floor. Well, thank goodness Momentum kept the key, otherwise I might have opened it!

I shook it; the hand thumped within. I still dreamed about him, but Momentum was right. The nightmares weren't as bad when I couldn't directly touch him. I hopped out of my bed, then slid the chest under it. Letting out a long, drawn out, vocal yawn, I trudged over to my wardrobe and pulled it open. I dressed myself in something more befitting of someone in Raqia—trousers, a tunic, and a black belt—and shod myself in some ankle-high boots.

I hesitated, listening as muffled voices passed by my door. Well, I had gotten what I had wanted: there were *people* here at Winter's End. It had been two days since they had arrived. A whole big group of Faeries—nearly a hundred of them—had moved in. I opened my door and peeked down the hall. A couple of Faeries spotted me and one of them rushed over.

"Ah, Leo!" said one, "Any idea if we can see your master today or not?"

"Uh..." I scratched my curls, "Whisp, was it? Faerie of..." I had met so many Faeries in the last couple days, I was losing track of who was who.

"Voice," he said quickly, grinning proudly.

"Voice, right," I slid my hands awkwardly down my thighs, then blushed when they found no pockets. This outfit would take some getting used to. Perhaps I needed to learn to sew... I could make my own pockets...

"Leo?"

"Hmm?" I blinked. Whisp, a cheery, outgoing Faerie with short silver hair, was gazing expectantly at me. "Oh! I can go ask him."

"The boss is really hoping to speak with him," Whisp said, "Say—we missed you at breakfast!"

"Breakfast..." I mumbled. I must have slept in *again*—or was the night just shorter last night? I seemed to be the only one that found the non-cyclical days and nights confusing. "I'll, uh," I walked past him, "I'll speak with my... *master*." Why was everyone under the impression that I was a servant, anyway?

I walked down the hall on the men's side of the autumn wing. All the rooms were occupied now, and some faeries even had to share! Just as I walked into the lounge, another Faerie stopped me.

"You—Aorist's boy!"

Boy? I turned, forcing a tired smile. "Yes? Uh... oh," I racked my mind for his name, "Blink, was it?"

"*Brink*, actually," he said with a slightly turned up nose.

"Right... Faerie of... *numbers*?"

"Good memory. Say, would you take a message to your master? The boss is hoping to speak with him."

"Yes, I know," I mumbled. I spotted Cymbeline on the other side of the room, talking with their, as they called him, boss. "I'll speak with him. I'm on my way there now, actually."

Brink left before I could say any more. He dashed off somewhere, and I found myself walking over toward where Cymbeline was.

"Hey, Cym," I waved, hoping I could join the conversation. The man she was talking to turned to give me a charismatic smile.

"Ah, Leo! My only other fellow human, how fare you?" The man smiled through his perfectly white teeth.

"Morning, Timbre Wulf," I said, doing another idiotic slide of my hands against the fronts of my thighs. Damn, I was used to pockets protecting me from intimidating conversations!

"Oh, Leo," he laughed, slapping a manly hand against my shoulder. "Call me Hanz."

"Sure thing, Hanz," I said. I had no idea *why* I found the man so intimidating. Was it because he seemed perfect in just about every way?

"Your friend Cymbeline was just telling me that she is the *second* Faerie of Transport. Hades! How *amazing*!" He turned to Cymbeline, "You're a special Faerie. Do you know that?"

She shrugged. "I still hardly know what it means to be an *un*-special Faerie," she said. I had only known her a few days, but I could still pick up on a hidden sass in her voice that Hanz couldn't. Cymbeline, I had found, wasn't impressed by flattery.

"There's time for that," Hanz said, "And I am sure you are up to the task."

"You'll find that Cymbeline is a pretty cool gal," I said, "Second Faerie or not."

Cymbeline turned quickly to look at me, then smiled.

"Finally awake, Leo?" she asked. "Did you sleep alright?"

"Yeah," I nodded, "Slept much better, thanks."

"Say, Leo, you're Aorist's wing, aren't you?" Hanz asked, slapping my shoulder again.

"Wing?"

"Only I was just hoping he was ready to speak with me today. I've got something really important to ask him."

"Yes, I think he knows," I said, maintaining a courteous smile, "But I'll remind him. I'm on my way to the Winter Wing now."

Hanz squeezed my shoulder; it hurt. "Good lad," he said. He patted my back as I walked away. I yawned again, then left the Autumn Wing as quickly as I could before anyone else could stop me.

I found Momentum sitting in his armchair by the window. He looked up as I came in, squinting his eyes. It was always when I saw him like this, weary-eyed, with an old book in his lap, that I remembered just how old he was. I pictured a long, white beard trailing down his lap, and layers of wrinkles surrounding his eyes, with little, tiny spectacles resting on the tip of his nose. This picture helped me understand him, gave me some context for him. It was hard to grasp just how ancient he was when he wore the face of a man in his 40's.

"Leo," he said, closing his book partway, "How did you sleep?"

"Much better," I said, placing myself in the chair across from him.

"No... dreams?" If he had had those tiny spectacles, he would have taken them off and looked at me through his clear, ancient eyes.

"Oh, I had dreams," I shifted in my chair, "But nothing like the last few nights. I think it makes a difference when I don't touch the hand."

"Well, of *course* it does," he said hastily, "It's his body! Hades—Leo. Why you want to keep that hand in your room is beyond me. Let me lock it in the vault!"

"Uh, well it helped having it in the chest."

"You didn't... try to open the chest? In your sleep?" He narrowed his eyes suspiciously.

"Well," I smiled sheepishly, "I did, but *you* had the key! So, I couldn't."

Momentum sighed. "Leo..."

"Don't worry about it," I said quickly. "Anyway, Hanz is asking to speak with you again."

Momentum turned to look out the window. "Hmm."

"Hey, uh... what's a wing?"

He snapped his head back at me. "Are you trying to be funny?"

"No... somebody called me a—"

"Oh," he rolled his head in a circle, "*That* kind of wing. Right. It's just like a glorified valet, or something, a human thing."

Ah, so it *was* a slight. I sniffed.

"Well, Leo, if you're intent on keeping that hand with you at night—*Lights know why you would want to do something like that*—I don't know if it's a good idea to have you around all those Faeries."

"Oh, yeah?" I leaned forward. "Why?"

"Well, it's *Somenus'* hand. I can't imagine that they will be thrilled about the man they are trying to hide from being, well, *right under their noses!*" He sighed. "And anyway, I don't want you having your nightmares around them. So, you had better move in here."

I brightened, then looked around hesitantly. "In... your room?"

"In the Winter Wing! *Hades*, Leo," he rubbed his temples. "There's another room next to mine. Why don't you move in there."

A goofy smile appeared on my face.

"Oh, stop, it's not *that* special," he flung his tome back open.

"Momentum?"

"Hmm?" He was looking down at his book.

"Why do they call you Aorist?"

"You already asked me this."

I scratched my head. "Yeah, well... you didn't answer me."

"I didn't?" He looked up. "Curious." He looked back down.

"Is it just another name for you? 'Cause it doesn't have to be all that mysterious."

"Yes, Leo," he mumbled, "It's another name for me." He looked up, staring past me. "A name... from another age." His eyes found mine. "A man who no longer exists."

"What question do you think Hanz is going to ask you?" I asked.

"Hmm?" His face twitched, as if his mind was only just returning to the question.

"When they first arrived," I said, "Hanz said he had a question for Aorist."

"Not *a* question, Leo, *the* Question. It's to do with Faerie Philosophy."

"Oh!" I perked up. I liked philosophy!

Momentum blinked lazily. "Well, it's not all that exciting," he said, "Not after you've debated it for thousands and thousands of seasons."

"Well, what it is?"

"*For what reason,*" he said, suddenly shifting into a performative voice, twirling his hand in the air, "*were we made?*"

"For what reason were we made?" I repeated. "Who, Faeries?"

Momentum nodded. "Everything has a reason, a meaning. No one knows this more than Faeries. We know we were made on the fifth day—*the day before the Elves,*" he said with a swing of his hand, "And we know we were made after the spirits, but everybody disagrees on *why* we were made. We have these great gifts, these powers over creation. We see this magik that no one else can see, but why?"

"Can't you just... do whatever you want? Isn't that enough?" I asked.

Momentum blinked, then sighed defeatedly. "That's what Faeries have always done, Leo. We've just... existed," his eyes grew distant, then he shook himself back to attention. "Anyway, it is believed that the first Faeries were given a charge, a mission, so to speak. But no one seems to remember what it was."

"I can see the elephant in the room," I said with a smirk, "If you're a First, then you should apparently *know* the answer to the question."

Momentum nodded soberly.

"Do they know you're a First?"

"They know Aorist, the First Time Faerie, is a First... at least that's what I think they know."

"So, they came here hoping you could answer the question?"

Momentum slumped into his chair. "I suppose so. You know—this has a lot to do with Somenus."

"How so?"

"Well," Momentum scrunched his face thoughtfully, "All of these Faeries are here hiding from Somenus, claiming to have fled from his oppressive reign— at least, that's what I have surmised."

"That's what I have heard, too," I added.

"Now, do you know why most of the Faeries have *not* fled Somenus? Why most of them still follow him, even though he usurped the throne?"

I shook my head. "I didn't know that most of the Faeries still followed him."

"Yes," he said, "When Somenus took the throne, he officially 'answered the Question'."

"What was his answer?"

"He declared that Faeries were made to rule Raqia, plain and simple. He says Faeries are the superior beings, and they should be revered as such."

I nodded continuously, processing. "And... is he right?"

Momentum exhaled very, very slowly, blowing a silent raspberry through his lips.

"Momentum?"

"Hmm?"

"What's the answer to the question?"

There was silence between us, aside from a sudden, gentle gust of wind that blew through the room and rustled some papers on a nearby desk.

"Leo," he said.

"Yeah?"

"Let's tell Hanz that we can speak with him at the midday zenith bell. Until then, why don't you pack up and move next door?"

My heart swelled with pride. We—tell Hanz that *we* can speak with him at the midday Zenith bell. Even if no one else thought I was important, Momentum did.

I stood and stretched.

"Hey, Momentum?"

"Hmm?" He was looking down at his book again.

"Why have you waited so long to speak with Hanz?"

"*So long?*" He looked up angrily; I imagined the old man version of him whipping off his spectacles in a huff. "It's only been two days! Why is he in such a hurry? I told him I would house *all* eighty-seven of his refugees, then I fed them and gave them time to settle in, then promised him I would put some thought into his question. So, he's got no reason to *rush* me into an audience!"

"Sounds fair," I smiled widely, backing away towards the door.

"Oh, and Leo, tell Cymbeline not to tell anyone she is the II Transport Faerie I... Leo... Leo, I don't like that look on your... has she *already* told them?"

I nodded sheepishly. "Hanz is a pretty charismatic guy," I said, "He seems to have a way of... getting people to open up when he wants them to."

Momentum sighed. "Damn."

"Zenith bell?" I asked, inching toward the door. I was eager to check out my new *situation* next door.

"Yes, yes," he waved his hand in dismissal.

I rushed out of the room.

The 'situation' next door was pretty great. The room mirrored Momentum's, as if there were not one, but two master suites in the Winter Wing. I wondered who had lived here before me. My face flushed with curiosity—had Momentum had a *wife* at one time? A man who lived that long... he must have!

The room was set up nicely; everything was fresh, fresh bed linens, fluffy pillows. I opened the wardrobe—even fresh clothes! Had he done all this for *me*? I walked to the bed and tested its comfort level by belly-flopping onto it. Pillows bounced onto the floor. I looked up to see there was a photo on the bedside table. I blinked. I bounced up, then flung my feet over the side of the bed. I took the little picture in hand, then gazed, mouth open.

It was a picture of Momentum holding a little baby boy. Did Momentum... have a *son*? I squinted. The picture... something wasn't right about it. I turned the frame over and was surprised to see something that definitely didn't belong in this world: the old, scratched off sticker remains of a barcode. I pulled on the little tabs of the frame and removed the backing. Sure enough, it was a photo print; it could have only come from Earth! I pulled the photo closer to my eyes, peering closely at the date on the back. It said, *August 12th, 1990.*

"August twelve," I whispered, gazing up in amazement, "This is Benji's birthday." 1990—Benji would have turned one. I looked around the room, realization hitting me like a bug on a windshield. "Oh man..."

This room hadn't been prepared for me—it was supposed to be *Benji's* room. I suddenly found myself feeling like that kid who walked into the wrong class on his first day of school, leaving the room with my tail between my legs, wishing no one had noticed me. Momentum didn't want me; he wanted Benji!

I quietly reassembled the photo and placed it across the room on the desk. Something inside me didn't feel great about baby Benji watching me sleep at night. Then I noticed something else. A little brown book sat conspicuously on the desk. I picked it up. *Rasselas*, the spine read. It was the book I had been holding when I first transported to Raqia. I guessed that after I gave it back to Momentum, he left it here. I looked around. Was this place a sort of... *shrine* to what could have been?

I had about a hundred questions, but I thought I should probably do as Momentum asked and grab the chest with Somenus' hand in it.

"So, Momentum says... hey, hey! It's me, Leo. Hi. Momentum says," I sighed, waiting as Hanz turned to greet yet another passer-by.

"Yes, Oakland, good to see you, glad to see you settling in." Hanz turned to smile at me. "Yes, what were you saying?"

"I spoke to Momentum and—"

"Oh, Tristan! Tristan, come here," Hanz was waving to another Faerie across the room. He turned to me expectantly. "Yes? What did he say?"

"He wants to meet at the Zenith bell. A private audience, I think," I said as his friend Tristan strolled up to us.

"Oh, finally!" Hanz said, turning to Tristan with a wink. "Tristan, the wing here says Aorist will meet with us at the Zenith bell."

"Friend," I said, then coughed once, "And he asked for it to be *just* you, Hanz."

"I'm sorry," Hanz said sincerely, "I didn't realize you were a *friend*! Hades."

"You're a Friend of the Fae?" Tristan asked with wide eyes. Concern seemed to be a permanent feature on the Faerie's face.

Friend of the Fae? The way he used those words made them sound like some grand title. "Uh... yes?"

"What's in the box?" Hanz asked pleasantly.

I looked down at the locked wooden chest I had hoisted under my arm. "Just some stuff," I said, "I am moving out so that there's more room for Faeries."

"Oh, how kind," Tristan said, his eyebrows still twisted with endless concern, "Hanz, you should take his room; it's much nicer than the rest."

"Tell Aorist I'll see him at the Zenith bell," Hanz said, then he turned and left. I rotated to face Tristan the Water Faerie.

"So, *erm*, Hanz seems like a nice guy," I said.

"I've never known anyone like him," Tristan said with a face of admiration.

"Tristan," a female Faerie galloped up to us, her ponytail swinging behind her jovially, "Where's Hanz?"

"Ah, Rowyn, this is Leo, Aorist's *friend*." Tristan gestured toward me with a bow.

"Hi, Rowyn," I lifted a hand to wave.

"Oh, Lights!" she exclaimed, clapping her hands excitedly. She was a small, spirited woman with strawberry hair and round pleasant facial features. "You must be little Benji—oh!" She laughed at herself, "Not so *little* anymore!"

"Uh..."

"I met you when you were just a little thing! That gift you have of talking to *all* animals? Who do you think gave you *that*?" She beamed.

"You...I'm guessing?" I said, unsure of how to respond. Was Benji able to speak with *animals*?

"I'm an old friend of Momentum's," she said with a thumb-point to her chest, "Eighth Faerie of Fauna, at your service!"

"A pleasure to meet you," I said, "I'm Leo."

"Oh," she blinked, "*Not* Benji?"

My face flushed with embarrassment. *Not Benji.* Apparently, that's what I was to a *lot* of people.

"Rowyn was so good as to show us the way to Winter's End," Tristan said, heroically changing the subject.

"I confess, I am the one who was guilty of leading everyone here. I don't think Momentum is very pleased about it, but he is too good to turn us away." Rowyn sighed, "He knows Somenus hunts us."

"Wow," I said, "All Eighty-seven of you... are running from Somenus?"

She nodded soberly. "Some of us are on his exile list, while others run because they refuse to bow to him. Hanz found us all and brought us together. I don't know what I would do without the Purple Order."

"Purple Order?" My eyes shifted between Tristan and Rowyn.

"We're just thankful to be in Winter's End, finally," Tristan said, "There's no other place in Raqia where Faeries can hide from Somenus. He can't find this place. No, no."

I smiled encouragingly. "Well heck, I am thankful you're here, too! This place is pretty lonely without other people around. Hey! You guys know there's a *beach* here? Some good swimming."

"Swimming?" Tristan paled. "In the *sea*?"

"Yeah," I readjusted my grip on the slipping chest beneath my arm, "You're the Water Faerie. You must love a good swim!"

"Yes, but the Sea, lad..." he seemed to shiver, "What if you fell through the bottom?"

"Fell through the—" I blinked, "...Of the *sea*?"

"No, no," the Water Faerie shook his head fearfully, "Best not to go in the sea, lad. It's wild, has a mind of its own."

I nodded obediently, fully planning on a swim later that day. I was addicted.

I walked into Momentum's quarters just before the Zenith bell. Most people had no idea when the bell would sound—not unless they were a skydeacon who could read the signs in the skies. No, every hour was different, with a different number of seconds, or *clicks*, as Raqians called them. But it was handy having the Time Faerie as my friend. He gave me a watch that could anticipate the hours to help me adjust to Raqian life.

"How did the move go?" Momentum asked, peering up from his book. It was as if he hadn't moved since the last time I saw him, and perhaps he hadn't.

"Good," I said, gulping down the guilt I had for occupying Benji's precious space.

"What's that face?" Momentum narrowed his eyes. "What's wrong?"

"Nothing!" I said quickly.

His eyes narrowed further.

There was a knock on the door.

"Aorist?" Hanz' voice called from outside.

"Go let him in," Momentum sighed, "*despite* the fact that he's early." I moved toward the door but Hanz walked in anyway.

"Good day, Aorist," he said with a bright face, "I was sure it wasn't a problem if I arrived a few clicks early."

"You were sure, were you?" Momentum closed his book.

Hanz seated himself in my chair and then turned to me with an expectant look.

I looked back at him.

"Aorist, it would be good to speak with you *alone*, if possible," Hanz finally said.

"We are alone," Momentum said blankly.

Hanz bounced his head in my direction.

"Oh him?" Momentum waved his hand, "Just pretend he isn't here."

My heart sank. Ah—so it wasn't that I was special; it was that I didn't *matter*—that's why I was allowed to be there. Maybe I *was* just his wing. I plopped myself on the desk chair, sitting a couple yards away from them.

Hanz cleared his throat, then leaned forward.

"So," Momentum said quickly, taking up the chance to speak first, "You're calling yourself *Timbre Wulf?*"

"I *am* Timbre wulf," Hanz said, "The first Timbre Wulf was my father, and he has passed his weapon onto me."

"The Beatus Staff," Momentum raised an eyebrow. "He... passed it on?"

"Yes. I have made myself available to the Faeries in their time of need, just like my father did before me."

"Do you know...Hanz, just *what* your father used to do for the Fae?" Momentum leaned forward.

"He fought for them," Hanz said, "...Defended them."

"He *killed* for them, Hanz."

"Yes."

"Timbre Wulf isn't a figure of which I am proud of in my history, Hanz," Momentum said with a sigh, "I am not thrilled to see another one come into being."

"I don't need you to approve of me, Aorist," Hanz said, "That's not why I am here."

"Then why *are* you here?" Momentum asked, "...Aside from asking me to harbor refugees?"

"I need you to answer the question for my Faeries," Hanz said, staring deeply into Momentum's eyes.

"Why? Why now? Why so urgently?"

"I've told them all that Somenus is wrong, and that I would help them find the real answer."

"Oh, *have* you?" Momentum chuckled, "Have you, *indeed*? Well—how kind of you!"

"Why do you mock?" Hanz snapped. "Do you laugh at your people's plight?"

"I am laughing at your naivete!" Momentum slammed his fist on the arm of his chair. "Why did you promise those Faeries something you could not deliver!"

"I knew you had the answer," Hanz returned, slamming his own hand. "How? *Why?*"

"My father told me. He told me you were a First!" Hanz raised his voice.

Momentum leaned back. "*Did* he?"

"If you're really a First, then you know what happened in the beginning," Hanz eyes locked onto Momentum, fiercely. "I just need *something* to tell my Faeries, *something* to give them to hold onto!"

"How old are you?" Momentum raised an eyebrow.

"Age of fullness," Hanz said, thrown by the question.

"How many seasons?"

"Thirty..."

"And you dare to speak to me like this? To challenge me? If you *really* believe that I was *there* the day that the First Faeries were made—the day the first commands were given—" Momentum rose to his feet, "How can you demand *anything* of me?"

Hanz rose, matching Momentum's height. I watched, gritting my teeth; they were both such powerhouses! "Aorist," he said with shaking limbs, "I need your help... *please.*"

Momentum sat. He sighed. "Say I answer the question, what exactly do you plan to do for these Faeries?"

Hanz remained standing, looking down at the ancient Time Faerie. "They need a new King."

"Well," Momentum shrugged, "That's a shame." Then he froze, his eyes darting upwards. "By the Lights... you're not going to..."

Hanz nodded soberly. "Yes," he said, "I am going to kill Somenus."

Momentum paled. "But you can't!" he gasped. "He's the king!"

"He is an evil King, and he's killing my Faeries."

"Your—" Momentum scoffed, shaking his head in bewilderment, "*Your* Faeries?"

"Yes, *my* Faeries," Hanz yelled, "I have risked my life over and over to protect them, sheltering them, leading them. They were scattered; hunted; leaderless! I... I brought them here hoping *you* could help me!"

"You want to *kill* the king?" Momentum bellowed, sweat beading on his head. "*Kill* Somenus? Hanz, don't you know what happens to the person who kills the Faerie King?"

"Yes," Hanz said firmly, tightening his fists, "And I am prepared to lay down my life for my Faeries."

Momentum dropped his head into his hand. "And *then* what? Once he's dead—*then* what do you do?"

"We crown a new King. A King who can answer the question."

"Well, *who* in Hades—?" Momentum looked up, then paused.

I shot a glance at Hanz, then Momentum, then back at Hanz.

"You," said Hanz, "We would crown *you*, Aorist."

I carefully closed the door to Momentum's chambers, then turned to look at Hanz with a cringy smile.

"Man. He's scary when he's angry," I whispered.

Hanz began walking away before I even finished my sentence.

"I..." I muttered, "If it's any consolation, I think you're doing something really brave."

He stopped. He turned, eyeing me silently.

"You've saved a lot of lives, and it seems like you're trying to make the world a safer place for the Faeries..." I was just spouting whatever came to the top of my head. Momentum had so vehemently refused the idea of being made a King, I thought Hanz might have needed some cheering up.

"You should convince your master that he should support us," he said.

"I'm not sure I have that kind of... influence," I admitted.

Hanz left.

"*Pfft....*" I released some pent up pressure inside my chest. "Man." So, Hanz wanted to kill Somenus... and make *Momentum* King? Honestly, I didn't mind the idea very much.

I meandered through the Winter Wing, thinking. Momentum was so sure that killing the Nightmare Faerie was a bad idea, but *why?*

Before long, I found myself on the beach; I often seemed to gravitate there. I loosened my belt and cast it into the sand. I took hold of my tunic and began to pull it over my head, then froze at the sound of someone clearing their throat. I whirled, finding a figure sitting in the sand behind me.

"Hi, Leo," Cymbeline waved.

"Cymbeline!" I pulled my shirt back into place briskly, "What are you doing out here?"

"I figured I might find you here if I waited long enough," she said in a melancholy voice.

"Is everything alright?"

She shrugged. "I saw you moved out of the Autumn Wing."

"Oh... yeah..." I walked through the uneven sand, then sat next to her. "It's 'cause of the nightmares."

"Oh," she nodded. Her eyes didn't look my way, they drifted out to sea.

"Are you... alright?"

"Hanz told me I should make an imperium," she said.

"Oh yeah? What do you think about that?" I asked. I could tell something was wrong, but I wasn't going to press.

"Well, he said I needed to choose an object of value to me. I don't really have anything like that," she said with a look of angst.

I nodded. "I bet Momentum could give you something cool."

She snorted. "It has to be something of value to *me*," she said. She looked down at her hand; it was closed into a fist. "This was the only thing I could think of."

I looked at her hand, waiting expectantly. She opened her fist to reveal the pebble I gave her a few days before. I laughed.

"Well, that's not much of a valuable item," I said. "It's just a pebble I found here on the beach."

"I *know*," she snapped. "And I don't even know the first thing about how to store magik in it anyway. And why would I? It's not like I even *care* about being a Faerie."

I watched her carefully. She was pokier than a cactus. "Oh yeah?" I asked.

"Why is it you get to be in the Winter Wing, and I have to be left with all of the other Faeries?" she finally demanded.

"Ah," I nodded. "Well, you should ask Momentum."

She scoffed. "He doesn't talk to me like he talks to you. Sure, he's civil, but when you're not around, he won't even look at me! You don't see it because you're too nice. But Momentum doesn't like me, Leo. That's why he let you into the Winter Wing, and not me!"

I blinked. "I don't think he likes me as much as you think he does," I mumbled. "Haven't you noticed? I am basically like a servant, just someone to order around. Don't you see? You're special; you're a Faerie! I'm just a... a..." I huffed, "A *human*. And you can tell by how Momentum talks about humans, he thinks we're..."

"What?" she snapped.

"Lesser... I think." I shrugged. "I don't know. Humans kill, we do stuff that makes him mad."

Cymbeline rolled the pebble between her fingers. "I wish I was a human."

"*Why?*" I frowned.

"Hanz thinks it's important that I start storing magik," she said, changing the subject. "Do *you* think I should, Leo?"

"I... *me?*"

"Yes, *you*. What do you think?"

"I think it would be pretty cool for you to get excited about what you can do. I think you need to have a sort of," I blew air out of the side of my mouth, "...a *curiosity* about yourself. You need to find out why you are special, you know? Like... not cause Hanz or Momentum says you are. Just... start storing magik and see what happens."

Cymbeline was looking at me with searching eyes. "Do *you* think I am special?"

"Uh... I don't think it matters what *I* think."

"It does to me."

"Well," I smiled, "Then you *know* the answer, Cym. Anyway, what did Hanz say you had to do to store magik?"

"Well," she looked down at her stone, "Momentum said that once I found an imperium, I just had to hold it, and concentrate on the glowing things."

"Oh," I nodded, "Is that why you came to the sea? All the motion?"

She bobbed her head to the side noncommittally, "Maybe."

"Well, let me know how it goes," I said, "But that pebble might not be valuable enough to become an imperium. You should ask Momentum about it."

"I don't want to ask Momentum about it," she grumbled.

"Alright..." I rose, "Well, like I said, let me know how it goes."

• —— • —— •

That night, I knocked on Momentum's door and crept in. I saw him lying on his bed with his arm over his face, but his candles were still lit.

"Momentum?" I asked. There was no response. I crept a little closer. "Are you awake?"

"What do you want, Leo?" he said in a muffled voice.

I walked up to his bedside and sat on the edge. Momentum lifted his arm slightly, peeking at me.

"Had a bad dream?" he asked in a teasing voice.

"Hah, no," I shook my head.

"Sorry I sent you away earlier, I wanted some space." Momentum covered his face once more with his arm.

"What would be so bad about you being king?" I asked, remembering how violently he had been against the idea.

Momentum chuckled ironically. "Leo... no."

"If Somenus is so evil," I said slowly, "would it be so bad to kill him?"

Momentum groaned. "Leo... don't you remember what I said about Faeries? We are *forbidden* to kill."

"But it's not *you* killing Somenus, it's Hanz," I said.

Momentum threw his arm aside and glared at me. "And does a murderer go to prison, or does his knife?"

I sighed.

"Do you know who Timbre Wulf was? The first Timbre Wulf—the *real* Timbre Wulf?"

I shook my head.

"He was a knife, Leo. A very, very powerful knife, made by the Faeries." He turned his head away from me. "He was one of our greatest failures."

I bobbed my head up and down, listening.

"Leo, what's going on?" Momentum turned his head back to gaze at me with tired eyes. "Something is up with you."

I lifted my head to gaze off into the middle distance. "What's a Faerie Friend?"

"Oh," Momentum blew air through his lips. "It's what Timbre Wulf was. It's sort of..." he blew again, moving his head side to side, "Sort of a special friendship between a human and a Faerie."

"Oh yeah?" I asked, still staring at nothing.

"Yes, it's like... well, it's when a Faerie decides to protect a human. They put magik inside them, like an imperium. It keeps them alive, protects them, protects them from old age—from death. Of course, it can only last as long as the giving Faerie has magik. Once the Faerie dies, so does the gift."

I turned my head and looked down at him vacantly.

"Was Benji your Faerie Friend?"

Momentum blinked. "Is that what this is about?"

"One of the Faeries thought I was him," I shrugged, "And I saw this... this photo..."

"Yeah," Momentum's eyes shifted to the side.

"You've been preparing to bring him here for a long time, haven't you?" I asked.

He nodded.

"Why?"

He shrugged, exhaling wistfully, "It's hard to explain."

I nodded, dropping my head onto my chest. "Was he your Faerie Friend?"

"Well..." Momentum placed his arm over his face again. "He still is."

I raised my eyebrows. "You mean... he's immortal—still?"

"Yeah, I guess so," Momentum mumbled.

I turned my head away.

"Leo," Momentum sighed, "Don't worry."

"Worry?" I snapped my head back. "Why would I worry? Worry about *what*?"

Momentum slid his arm down to give me a lazy, half-baked smile. "I like you, Leo."

"I..." I turned away bashfully, "Hah—that's...funny. Thanks, I mean..."

"Good night, Leo," Momentum said, placing his arm back over his eyes.

"Oh," I jumped up to my feet, feeling a surge of excitement. It was amazing what one *tiny* affirmation could do for my self-esteem. "Sure, sure. I'll let you sleep, then!"

"Leo..." Momentum groaned.

"Right!" I raced toward the door. "Been a long day, I'll let you sleep!" I put one of my feet through the door then turned toward him again. "Uh... Momentum... I like you, too!"

"Leo!" he snapped. "Good *night*!"

18

— Clover —

Gatekeeper

How are we even supposed to get *in*?" Yuma asked as he stared out at the great city. From the view there on the wayfinders tower, Bavel looked like a giant mountain, blocking out half the sky. Its base was miles and miles wide, and its top was shrouded in clouds. Was the labyrinth city built on a mountain, or was the entire city the mountain? No one knew. It was as ancient as the Faeries.

"Aw...look!" Clover, sitting beside the fire, pointed excitedly at the lamb in his lap. "Solo is sucking on my finger!"

"He's hungry," Yuma said, turning to glance down at the odd pair.

"Little Thief," Clover whispered, "Get the milk!"

Clover's gnome fished through Clover's rucksack and produced a drink pouch.

"Clover..." Yuma turned his gaze back to the city. "We *have* to talk about a plan."

"Plan?" Clover squinted up at Yuma as he unscrewed the lid on his drink pouch. "The Truth Faerie said we should go in, so we are going to go in!"

"Yes, but..." Yuma sighed, dropping his head. "Isn't it supposed to be really hard to get into Bavel?"

"Oh, it's basically impossible," Clover said brightly, smiling as his lamb began to suckle on the milk. "Look, look!"

"I see it," Yuma stated.

"Little Solo," Clover said fondly as he stroked the lamb's soft back. It was such a tiny little thing. "What a good little—*agh*," Clover winced.

Yuma zipped his head around. "Clover?"

"It's nothing."

"It's your shoulder, isn't it?"

"It's fine," Clover said, petting his lamb again. It had been a few weeks now, and the wounds had finally begun to scar over. He might even be able to remove the stitches soon!

"You're in pain, I can tell," Yuma said, moving to kneel down by the fire.

"I told you," Clover's smile faded slightly, "I am fine. The lady in Lumbarg did a good job sewing things up. She's used to treating the tree-toppers, and they get worse wounds than this."

Yuma quietly stared at the fire.

Clover looked up. He could tell that it was worrying Yuma to not have a plan. Clover didn't feel the need to have one, but he supposed there was more than one opinion that mattered in the party.

"Well..." Clover said, "I am pretty sure to get in Bavel, you need a ring."

Yuma shot his head up, like a guard dog sensing movement. "What kind of ring?"

"They've got this really tight social system," Clover said, looking up at the looming city, "There are six levels to Bavel, each representing a social class. There are different rings indicating which levels you can access."

"Most important people on the top?" Yuma asked with a skeptical look in his eye.

Clover nodded. "And so only citizens get rings. And even getting a First Level ring is hard. There's a set number of citizens allowed per level. That keeps the city from being overpopulated. So, there's only a certain number of rings. And people *kill* for those rings, I've heard."

"You seem to know a lot about it," Yuma mumbled.

"Well, Father made me train to be a diplomat," Clover said off-handedly, "Anyway, there are such things as diplomat rings, but that's—"

"Let me stop you right there," Yuma held up a hand. "Who *is* your father, Clover?"

Clover blinked. "What? He's an Elf in the Elder Copse."

"Yes, I figured that. But back when we were fighting the wulves, you said something... about you being a prince."

"Oh... yeah," Clover looked down at Solo the lamb and scratched his head, "Have I not mentioned that?"

"No."

"Well, it's not like it changes much," Clover shrugged, "Anyway, the rings—"

"Clover," Yuma leaned forward, "It changes a *lot*! For example, aren't your people concerned about where you *are* right now?"

"They don't know where I am," Clover said casually, "and I don't think my absence makes much difference. It's not like there was anything for me to *do* there."

"What about training to be a diplomat?"

"*Eh*," Clover squirmed, "I did that already. But it's not like father ever sends delegations."

"I don't suppose you could have gotten access to one of those *diplomat rings*? Back at the Elder Copse?"

"Oh," Clover said melodically, "I suppose I could have..."

Yuma sighed. "This is why it helps to *talk* about a plan, Clover."

"Well, I don't think father would have given me his ring, anyway," Clover said, "He doesn't like Bavel, and he wouldn't have wanted me representing the Copse there. In fact, if he knew what we were up to, I am pretty sure he would lock me up before letting me go and kill the Faerie King."

"Oh," Yuma raised his brow, "Really?"

"Yeah," Clover nodded. "I, uh... I might be known as a bit of a rebel... back there."

Yuma smirked. "That doesn't surprise me."

"Anyway, Father and Somenus came to an agreement—they sort of tolerate each other. So, me going into Bavel to ask for an army to attack Arelle? Well…"

"I see," Yuma nodded soberly. "Are you sure you want to do this, Clover?"

"Of course!" Clover frowned. "Why do you keep asking me that? It's not like I am going to change my mind!"

"People change their minds all the time," Yuma said, leaning back.

"Well, *I* don't," Clover said with a pout. "What are promises worth if they can be broken?"

"Well, then how are we supposed to get into Bavel, Clover?"

"I figure we just…" Clover's eyes drifted around, "knock on the front gate. See what they say."

"You trained in diplomacy," Yuma said, "Does that sort of thing usually work?"

"Well… no…"

"What if you tell them you're the Prince of the Elder Copse?"

Clover gritted his teeth and shook his head. "No… they might send a falcon to my father to confirm—bad idea."

Yuma felt his chin thoughtfully. "Are there ways to get rings?"

"There's probably a black market in Shadowroots for citizen rings—but they'll be pretty pricey."

"Shadowroots, the city surrounding Bavel?"

"Yeah. All those who get ejected from Bavel due to overpopulation, they just made another city. They're all still basically Bavelonians, but they don't have rings."

"A city that won't take care of its own children," Yuma shook his head with a look of distaste. "Makes me sick."

"Our best bet," Clover said, staring into the fire as his thoughts came together, "Is to make a strategic friend. Someone who can get us in. There must be something we can offer someone in Bavel… something that makes us stand out."

Yuma shrugged.

"You're a decent archer, aren't you?" asked Clover, shifting his gaze to Yuma.

"Hmm? Well, of course I am."

"Maybe you could get a place as a Black Eagle."

"Bavel's legendary archers?" Yuma scoffed doubtfully. "I am sure they don't take recruits off the street."

"You never know," Clover said with wide eyes, "They can't easily recruit within the walls of Bavel, since citizens would have to give up their rings to join."

"The Black Eagles don't have rings?" Yuma asked doubtfully.

"No," Clover said quickly, "they sort of act like their own Kingdom. They don't live within the city; they live on top of the walls that run around the city like an ant hill."

"The Labyrinth City of Bavel," Yuma said distantly, reciting the name he had heard a hundred times, but had never known what it meant.

"Yes, they sort of have their own city up on the walls. They protect Bavel from invasions, I mean, *they're* the army we are trying to enlist, anyway!"

"So, what are you saying?"

"I'm just thinking out loud..." Clover mumbled, closing the lid on his sack of milk. "They probably don't take in new recruits often, but I bet there is someone in Shadowroots who knows when and where it happens."

"What are you saying? You want *me* to... to try and sign up to be a Black Eagle?"

"Well," Clover shrugged, "It would get us into the city. Maybe if you worked up trust with them, you might be able to speak with their general."

Yuma's face darkened. "This... Clover, this could take a long time."

Clover nodded. "The king of Bavel is the most inaccessible person on the world. It would be easier getting an audience with Somenus than it would him. This *has* to take some time."

Yuma turned his head quickly; Clover saw his jaw tense.

"Your people will hang in there," Clover said quietly, "We have some time."

Yuma continued to look away.

"Let's just go into Shadowroots and see what connections we can make; maybe this will all go by really quickly! Yuma…?"

"What about Dezmund?"

"What?"

"Dezmund. The Faerie in the bag." Yuma rotated his head back to face the fire. "Didn't you say Faeries can't enter Bavel?"

"Let's leave him with Waiting For the Day," Clover said, turning to look over the edge of the tower. Waiting For the Day was grazing in a nearby patch of grass. "He'll take good care of him while we're in the city."

"Day?" Yuma leaned back, growing concerned. "What… leave him *behind*?"

"Humans in the East eat animals, Yuma, you don't want to bring a big, huge horse into Bavel. It's just asking for trouble."

"What about *that?*" Yuma pointed at the lamb.

Clover held Solo close to his chest protectively, "I am not letting him out of my sight! He's small, I can protect him."

Yuma squinted. "You think there is any chance of the king of Bavel helping us, Clover?"

Clover thought for a moment, then said. "Well, I don't think the Truth Faerie would have sent us here only to fail."

"But really," Yuma insisted, "For what reason would the king of Bavel go to war with Somenus?"

"Well… I know the Bavelonians really wouldn't appreciate Somenus' new declaration that Faeries are supposed to be like the gods of Raqia. Bavelonians basically believe the opposite. They think humans are the ones to be worshiped. It's their whole system. The higher up in elevation you are, the more godlike you are. That's why they've built the city in the way that they have. It's a religion: worshiping those above you and oppressing those below you."

"Hades," Yuma scoffed. "And *these* are the people we are coming to for help?"

"Yeah…" Clover stared off into the middle distance.

Yuma sighed. "Clover?"

"Hmm?"

"You can talk to me, you know..."

"About what?"

"About," Yuma nervously shifted his weight back and forth on his knees. "The sheep."

Clover's face went blank.

"You didn't fail Isabella," Yuma said quietly, "Do you realize that?"

"I..." Clover's eyes became glossy surfaces. "I don't want to talk about it."

"You defended them bravely. You did everything you could. You were a good shep—"

"Yuma," Clover held up a hand, "Please... stop. I... I don't want to talk about it."

"Well," Yuma stood. "I'll speak with Day about what you have suggested. See if he has any advice."

"You mentioned him being a prophet," Clover said quickly, "Is he like the Truth Faerie? Can he tell us what to do?"

Yuma crossed the wayfinder's tower, heading for the stairs, "Not exactly... he just... never lies."

Clover watched Yuma leave, then he stretched out his legs, getting his toes closer to the fire. He then slid his hand out from under Solo and stretched out his arm, then groaned deeply. Hades, his shoulder hurt.

⸺·· ⸺⸺ ● ⸺⸺ ··⸺

Shadowroots. What was once a slum of Bavelonian rejects was now a metropolis, surrounding the mountain city like a dusty aura. The city stretched out for miles and miles, without any symmetry or evidence of city planning.

It took Clover and Yuma an entire day to find its center, and another day to find out where the Black Eagle's recruitment office was. By a small miracle, they found it, sitting in a ramshackle building nestled beside one of Bavel's four city gates. They had been told that the Eagles were turning people away, but they headed there anyway, hoping for a lead.

Clover leaned against a building opposite the street to the Recruitment Office, hiding Solo protectively under his arm. He kept his green cape wrapped over his front, and TSB sat quietly on his shoulder, nestled into Clover's hood.

Yuma had been in the office for two bells, and still he hadn't come out. Clover wondered if he should go in and check on him. No. No, if things were going *well*, he didn't want to interrupt!

"You look about as out of place as a woman in a smokeroom," said a nasally voice. "Hey—Faerie boy. I am talking to you. Hey!"

Clover turned his head. He started, seeing a heavy-set man in a hooded cloak walking towards him. "Who, *me*?"

"Who else would I be calling a Faerie boy?" he smiled, revealing the twinkling light of a metallic tooth in his mouth. His cloak was black, lined with ornate gold designs on the trim. There was evidence of a double-buttoned suit beneath the cape.

Clover looked side to side. "Well... I had *assumed* you were talking to a *Faerie*."

The man grinned through his curly beard. "You can't fool me, boy. I saw your pointy ear."

Clover frowned at him. "What do you want from me?" he asked suspiciously.

The man chuckled to himself. "I want to hear your story; that's all."

"Why?" Clover held his glare.

"Well, it is not every day I see a Faerie boy walking around in the Shadowroots with livestock under his arm," he said, "I find you very curious."

"I am not a Faerie," Clover cleared his throat.

The man chuckled again, nodding knowingly. "*Sure*, you aren't."

"Have you never *seen* a Faerie before?" Clover rolled his eyes.

"No, I haven't," his voice grew lower, "but your ears give you away."

Clover stood up straight, eyeing the man with an intimidating stare. The man's face was clean and his beard trimmed, unlike the other pedestrians he had witnessed. His skin was quite pale in comparison to the others as well, suggesting that he spent a lot of time indoors. It was the man's strange lisp, however, that gave him away. "You're a nobleman." Clover guessed.

The man raised his eyebrows. "You have a keen eye, Faerie."

"Elf." Clover said flatly.

"*Elf?*" The man raised his eyebrows in astonishment, running his eyes up and down Clover's body with fresh curiosity. "By the floods! I didn't think Elves were real!"

Clover snorted. Elves predated the humans on Raqia; what a ridiculous thing to say! "Well, now you know. So, tell me...Nobleman...what brings you to these streets?"

The man chuckled in amusement. "Shouldn't I be the one asking *you* questions?"

"I see no reason why we both can't get information," Clover shrugged, "Where does one get food around here?"

The man laughed heartily, then gestured for Clover to follow him into the nearby town square. Clover apprehensively followed the gentleman, glancing back once toward the Recruitment office, until they came to an outdoor restaurant.

The man procured a table for them and gestured for Clover to sit. The two sat cross legged across from one another on a raised platform while an old woman served them steamed buns and vino. Clover rested Solo the lamb in his lap and TSB nestled in next to him. The man raised his eyebrows in interest but said nothing, picking up his glass to toast.

"To an interesting conversation," he said.

"Sure," Clover held up his glass, tapping it against the man's. "What do I call you?"

"You may call me Patro," he gave Clover a squinty-eyed grin. "And you?"

"Clover."

"Well, *Clover,* tell me what brings an Elf to the Shadowroots."

"I am hoping to gain entrance into the city of Bavel," Clover said.

Patro responded with a hearty laugh. "So is everyone else. Why?"

"I need to speak with the king." Clover said flatly.

Patro's eyes widened, and he studied Clover's face for sincerity. "*Why?*"

"I cannot tell you," Clover said calmly, "but it is important."

"*No one* gets an audience from the king," he said with a face of reverence, "No one would dare."

"I have to do what I have to do," Clover shrugged. "So, why is a Nobleman wandering around outside the walls? Don't you belong in Bavel?"

Patro leaned back, inhaling deeply. "Yes, I am a Nobleman. I am out here looking for an..." he paused for effect, "*opportunity.*"

"For what?" Clover sensed an iceberg.

Patro only smiled. "How much for the lamb?" he asked bluntly.

Clover frowned. "Is *that* what this is about?"

"Oh, no," he laughed at Clover's seriousness, "I was just curious. Not here to sell it, then?"

"No."

"Anyway, I was actually just interested in you, *Clover.*" He raised his eyebrows twice.

"Why?"

"I am in a unique position." he said quietly, reaching into his pocket. Clover watched him cautiously, fearing an attack. Patro pulled his hand out of his cloak and opened it to reveal a small shiny object. Clover's eyes widened. It was an intricately designed gold ring with three sapphires set into it.

Clover leaned forward, lowering his voice to a whisper. "A citizen's ring?"

Patro nodded slowly, then placed the thing back into his pocket. "Yes— the very thing every person in this gods-forsaken city would kill for."

"Where did you get it?" Clover raised an eyebrow.

Patro chuckled to himself then leaned forward to whisper. "I recently married off one of my daughters and freed up a position in my household."

Clover thought for a moment silently then asked, "So you are looking for someone to fill the place? Why not save it?"

Patro snorted. "You have no idea how dangerous it is up there, Elf. I may be the head of the household, but there are many in my family vying for my place. Several attempts have already been made on my life. No, I won't find help inside the city. I am searching for a..." he searched for the right word.

"A bodyguard?" Clover guessed.

Patro nodded, grinning once more. "Yes." He drew out the 's' for effect.

"Are you considering asking me?" Clover beat him to the punch.

"Yes."

Clover looked around the city for a moment, letting his mind process this. "But didn't you think I was a Faerie?" Clover asked suspiciously. "I thought Bavelonians hated the Fae."

"They do," he replied, "though I am not like most Bavelonians. I have an interest in what happens elsewhere. I came out here hoping to make a connection with someone like you."

"I thought Faeries couldn't enter Bavel," said Clover.

"They can't. I was not considering offering you the position until I learned you were an Elf, if I'm honest. Something tells me this opportunity could benefit us both. I have heard," he leaned back, glancing away, "that the Elves are great warriors."

Clover shrugged.

Patro nodded gleefully. "I am sure you know what I mean."

Clover frowned. "I wouldn't call myself a warrior."

"Sure, sure!" Patro winked, taking a quick sip of his vino.

"So... what, are you offering me a position in your household?"

"Would you pledge to be my bodyguard?" Patro answered Clover's question with a question.

"Sure," Clover shrugged, seeing nothing wrong with protecting a life. "But only if you are alright with me seeking an audience with the king."

Patro's jolly grin turned to a scowl. "We can talk about that, but I don't want trouble being caused in my house."

"And my lamb?" Clover asked defensively. "He's not for eating!"

"Of course, of course!" Patro slapped the table, returning to his jolly self.

"Oh," Clover froze, realizing he was forgetting someone. "I have a traveling companion..."

"Ah," Patro held up his palm to Clover, shaking his head, "I only have one ring. I will take you, and your little pets if you so-wish, but no one else."

Clover sat there thinking quietly while Patro stuffed an entire steamed bun into his mouth. Clover wrinkled his nose; it smelled of meat.

So—just like that, he was offered a position on one of the highest levels of Bavel. He didn't like the idea of leaving Yuma behind, but this opportunity seemed too good to pass up!

"Can I have some time to consider your offer?" Clover asked, laying his hands on Solo and TSB.

"Very well," Patro said, smacking his lips as he licked his fingers clean. "You have until nightfall. I will wait at the Southern Gate until the lastlight bell rings. If you do not come by then, you will not see me again."

Clover nodded. "I will tell you my answer either way," he said.

"Grand," Patro stood, bowing his head to Clover slightly. "Until then, strange little Elf."

Clover waited, watching Patro leave. He then turned to glance at the table, realizing the man had neglected to pay for the food. He sighed, tossing his one gold coin on the table, then walked away. Well, he would probably end up getting it back eventually, anyway.

As he approached the Recruitment Office, he brightened at the sight of Yuma exiting the building. They made eye contact from across the street, and both rushed to meet one another.

"Well?" Clover asked, swinging his cape over his shoulder to hide Solo.

Yuma's face twisted with an effort to smile. "Hello, Clover."

"*Well*?" Clover stepped closer, "What happened?"

Yuma squished his mouth into a flat line.

"Did they send you away? What *happened*?" Clover asked excitedly.

Yuma exhaled. "Well, they want me to begin training in the morning."

"*What*?"

"Why are you smiling? It's... Clover, do you realize we will probably be separated for a while?"

Clover's smile weakened. "Well, yes, for a time. But Yuma, that's great!"

"You look like you've got something to tell me," Yuma looked down at the Elf, who was nearly a whole head shorter than himself. "You're practically bursting with anticipation."

"I've got a way into the city, too—as a bodyguard!"

Yuma blinked repeatedly. "What, already?"

"I think the Lights are watching out for us," Clover said, "All we had to do was just walk here, and this was just given to us!"

"That's... a pretty simplistic way of seeing things," Yuma mumbled.

"It's what happens when you're on the right path, isn't it? The way is cleared for you before you place your foot on the soil." Clover said, reciting an old Elven proverb.

"Not in my experience..."

"Why do you look so glum?" Clover asked, "Everything is going according to plan!"

"How's that shoulder?"

"Fine."

Yuma turned to gaze at the city gates. "That man waving at us... is he your... contact?"

Clover glanced sideways to see Patro waving.

"Oh, yes. He's the Nobleman I'm going to be protecting," Clover said, raising his hand to wave back.

"Well," Yuma sighed, "It's six weeks of training before I can even test for a posting. So, it'll probably be six weeks before you and I can connect again, at the earliest."

Clover nodded.

"You, uh... you think you can handle yourself in there?" Yuma asked as he crossed his arms.

"You saw me with the wulves," Clover said, feeling a little hurt, "of course I can handle myself!"

"These are a different kind of wulves, I think," Yuma said, shifting his eyes to the side.

"What do you mean?"

Yuma looked upwards. "Well... the Eagles seemed to imply that there's a lot of... *crime* in the city."

"What kind of crime?"

Yuma placed a hand on Clover's good shoulder. "Come on," he said, "Let's grab a bite, and we can talk over all the details."

⸺ ⸺ ◆ ⸺ ⸺

Patro laughed gleefully when he saw Clover arrive to meet him at the gates of Bavel. It was a little unsettling just how keen Patro seemed to be about Clover coming to work for him, but he told himself that all would be well if he kept his head.

"You must remain loyal to me," Patro said as he carefully pulled the ring from his pocket. Clover held his palm open, and Patro hovered the ring over it for a moment. "Elves are... *exotic*... like Faeries—Bavelonians will not like you. I am your protection and you are mine, so if I die, then you die, and if I live, you live."

"If you say so," Clover said. Patro dropped the ring into his hand. Clover placed the thing on his right middle finger and admired it for a moment as Patro began to walk toward the massive gates.

Just then, one of the Black Eagles dropped down in front of them, startling Clover. The soldier was dressed in a black tunic, trimmed with silver, and an emblem of an eagle on the chest.

"My Lord!" The Eagle bowed to Patro reverently. "Open the gates!" He turned to yell up at the barbican, then looked in Clover's direction. "And who is this? A *Faerie*?" He scowled.

"He is my bodyguard," Patro grabbed Clover's wrist and held up his hand, revealing the ring.

The Eagle held his glare, "My Lord, Faeries are forbidden from entering the city."

"He is not a Faerie," Patro chuckled, finding enjoyment in aggravating the guard. "He is an *Elf*."

"Elf?" The guard eyed Clover suspiciously. "Aren't they just another kind of Faerie?"

"If he is indeed one of the Fae," Patro said calmly, "Then the city gates will not let him in."

The guard nodded slowly, "Alright... you may enter."

Clover and Patro were watched closely as they entered the city, and to the guard's dismay, Clover did not disintegrate when he passed through the massive gates. A small palanquin was waiting for Patro on the other side, and a couple of servants bustled into action when they saw him arrive.

"This is my new bodyguard," Patro bellowed proudly to his servants, "He will be joining the Sapphire Household. The servants scowled at Clover, whispering to one another secretively once Patro was up on his Palanquin.

It took a few hours for the little party to ascend the city. Each new level of Bavel was guarded by yet another gate, and yet another uncomfortable encounter with a Black Eagle who judged Clover with suspicion. It was clear to Clover that only humans belonged in this city, and the higher they went, the more he wished he didn't ever have to enter.

Once finally in the Fifth Level, Clover felt a little bit more comfortable as there were almost no people on the streets. The population was miniscule compared to the lower levels, and it made the place quiet and palatable for a Woodland Elf like Clover, who was used to the tranquil life.

The sky was the most remarkable thing to Clover about the Fifth Level. It was so close. From the ground, the hard, glasslike Raqian sky reflected the land beneath it like a mirror. But when standing this close, a person could actually see the rippling texture of the hard sky like painted glass. It gave Clover chills to think he was so close to the flood waters, separated only by that thin—though unsurpassable—translucent canopy. No wonder the Bavelonians saw themselves as gods to be worshiped; they truly were as close to the divine as one could get.

The small procession came to a small private Gate within the Fifth Level; it was the grounds of the Sapphire House. The family seemed to own at least a mile of Fifth Level land, and within this walled community, there was an assortment of houses as well as an expansive garden network. The "household" was like a mini kingdom of which Patro was the king—and Clover would soon find out what it looked like to serve under him there.

"Here we are, Clover," Patro shouted down at Clover who was walking beside the Palanquin quietly, holding tightly onto Solo while TSB clung onto his good shoulder. "This is the Sapphire House, and your new home."

"Well," Clover said, gazing about blankly, "Alright."

19

— Lola —

In Vino Veritas

"This is demeaning," Lola whispered under her breath.

"At least we're not on the barrel crew," Lady Garnet whispered back, "They have to dump all the heavy grapes in. Look." She leaned with one arm against the wall, and with the other she pointed upwards. Lola was deep within the belly of a concave white basin made of marble. Gallons upon gallons of grapes were being dumped from above. It's true, the women tasked to throw the grapes inside looked exhausted; and yet Lola still would have preferred that job to smashing the grapes with her bare feet!

The princess leaned back against the side of the basin and wiped her brow.

"Can't they find servants to do this sort of work?" she asked, looking down at her feet. She was dressed in a white knee-high toga, with deep purple stains up to her knees. She was practically naked in here!

"The maids of the Vineyard Palace have always crushed the grapes for the seasonal vinos," Garnet said with a smile, "That's what Lady Fayne told me, anyway. But we only have to do it once a season, and I can't help but think we will probably all be married off to Somenus before the next season comes around. So just think, you only have to do this once!" She was faithfully stamping grapes, bouncing her knees up and down alternatingly.

Lola cringed. *We will probably all be married off to Somenus before the next season comes around.* That was a disturbing thought.

"Only ten-second breaks!" called a voice from above, "Keep those lovely feet moving, Princess!"

Lola gazed upwards. Veritas was sitting on a chair, watching with a goblet in hand.

"Doesn't it feel a bit demeaning being watched by that Faerie?" Lola whispered again.

Garnet shrugged. Then her blue eyes flashed with excitement. "Oh! Do you think Somenus might come to watch us? How romantic would *that* be?"

Lola blushed, shaking her head. "No. I don't think it would be."

"Lola!" Garnet pushed some of her golden hair over her shoulder. "Somenus has taken you back for the last eight banquets! It's been weeks, and he still only chooses you! You must feel special."

Lola exhaled quietly through her nostrils as she half-heartedly stamped some more grapes.

"Special..." she muttered, "I suppose that is how I am *supposed* to feel." Perhaps she did feel special. Perhaps that was her problem. Banquet after banquet, she saw Somenus the gentleman; and night after night, he visited her dreams. Why? Why *her*?

"It's strange he hasn't proposed to you yet, isn't it," Garnet said thoughtfully, "Usually when he finds a favorite, they're gone by the time the second banquet is up."

"Oh," Lola sighed. "Well..."

Garnet darted closer, grabbing Lola's arm. "*Has* he? Has he proposed to you?"

Lola gritted her teeth. "*Erm...*"

"Lola! Somenus has proposed to you? Well, what are you still *doing* here?" She jumped up and down excitedly, smashing a few grapes in the process.

"Shush!" Lola squeezed Garnet's shoulder. "Please... I don't want that fact advertised.

"Fayne!" Garnet yelled excitedly, waving her arm.

"*Garnet*!" Lola watched nervously as the alpha woman marched over from across the basin.

Lady Fayne stood with her hands on her hips, eyeing Lola and Garnet expectedly. "What? What is it?"

"Somenus has proposed to Lola!" Garnet clapped her hands.

Fayne bit her lip with suspicion. "No, that can't be right."

"Tell her, Lola!" Garnet tugged on Lola's sleeve.

"Keep those legs moving!" Veritas' voice bellowed from above. All three women began to stamp their feet, though Fayne kept the same, intense glare focused straight on Lola.

"I... I don't wish to talk about this," Lola muttered.

"Did he propose to you, Princess Lolette?" Fayne asked bluntly.

"I... yes..." Lola took a few stamping steps backwards.

"Then *why* are you still here?" Fayne demanded.

"I... I..."

"*Why*?" Fayne stamped closer.

"Because I told him... *No...* several times!"

Fayne gritted her teeth. "And how did he respond?"

Lola's eyes widened into circles. "He... he asked me again, and told me to... *think* about it..."

Fayne closed her eyes for a moment, trembling like a kettle about to boil over. She refocused her glare on Lola, her eyes lit with the greenish fire of jealousy. "So are you telling me... you could have been out of here weeks ago, and several of us could have been chosen by now. But you just want some... *time* to think it over?"

"Lady Fayne," Lola said weakly, "I don't *want* to marry him... I've told him this!"

"Listen," Fayne snapped, "He's got his sights set on you, Princess. He won't give up. So as long as you refuse him, we all have to stand around like bulls in a milkhouse! *You* are keeping him from us!"

"That—" Lola blinked, "That's not fair."

"You kept promising me you wouldn't get in the way," Fayne yelled, swinging an open hand at Lola. Lola dodged the attack, stumbling backwards. "And *all* you have done is get in the way! *Damn* you, Lolette!" She swung her arm again, and this time her hand landed a solid blow on the side of Lola's face. The Princess tumbled backwards.

"Ladies! What's going on down there?" Veritas called, then his laugh reverberated around the basin in echoes.

Lola splashed onto her backside. Her toga soaked up vino like a sponge.

"Fayne," Lola cried, "I didn't want any of this!"

"Oh, really?" Fayne thrust her foot into Lola's side. "You honestly want me to believe that you aren't just basking in the pleasure of Somenus' obsession? You have him *pining* for you!" Fayne turned waving over the other women. "Ladies, Princess Lolette has been willfully keeping Somenus from us. She has a proposal but won't leave the Vineyard Palace!"

The others crowded around, their voices joining together in an angry grumbling cloud.

"Ladies!" Veritas demanded, "Back to work!" He was hovering over the basin with his wings flapping.

Lola drew in a deep breath, just before Fayne shoved her down under the vino. She felt kicks and scratches accosting her from all sides. At first, she thought: just endure for a moment, and it will end. But the abuse continued, until she began to sputter and cough. She reached for the surface and managed to grab a breath of air before she was shoved beneath the vino again.

Fayne held her down by the neck, squeezing tightly. *Oh Lights,* Lola finally admitted, *they are going to kill me.*

She struggled for her life, taking hold of Fayne by the wrists and shaking. The woman held fast. Lola's breath was running out, and her lungs began to jolt in protest.

Clicks before Lola finally gave in, she felt herself pulled upwards by the arm. She coughed violently. Fayne's venomous face was the first thing she saw. The woman was diving toward her with nails drawn like claws. Lola rose swiftly into the air, then watched as the woman in the basin grew smaller and smaller. Lola continued to gasp for breath, clinging hard to the arms of her rescuer.

Moments later, she was dropped onto a private landing, somewhere in the Vineyard Palace where she had not been before. She sank into a puddle of vino on the ground, panting.

"Hades, woman, what did you do to get you into so much trouble down there?" Asked Veritas. Lola looked up to see the Faerie of the Vine wagging his head. "They nearly killed you!"

"Thank you..." she said through her labored breaths.

"Well," Veritas sniffed proudly, "Yes, I did rather save you, didn't I. But it was for my own skin you know—Somenus would have been pretty upset with me if his favorite drowned in my vino. Though..." his voice seemed to wander down a beaten path, "It would have made for a legendary vintage..."

Lola wiped vino off her face, then began to wring out her hair, making a little pond on the marble floor.

"And anyway," Veritas sighed, placing himself on a padded bench, "I like you, old thing. Don't like to see you scratched by the harpies."

Lola coughed again, then nodded with a weak smile. "You saved me," she said.

"I saved my vino, really." He chuckled, folding his hands. "Now what happened back there? How has someone as pleasant as you made so many enemies?"

"It's not my fault!" Lola complained, slapping the ground childishly with her hands. A red splash erupted around her. Veritas laughed heartily.

"Well," Veritas sighed, "Why don't you stay here for now. I don't think it's really safe for you at the Palace anymore. Hades—why Somenus hasn't just brought you back to the Eight Stones by now is beyond me!"

Lola tried not to grimace. "Where *is* here?" she asked, gazing about. She seemed to be in some sort of lavish living space.

"Why this is where I live, dearest," Veritas said with an animated sigh. "Faerie of the Vine has always lived in the Vineyard Palace, you know. Now Lola, I am going to go tell Somenus what's happened. I am sure he will take you back to the—"

"No!" Lola gasped. "No... I don't... Veritas..."

The Faerie stared at her confusedly. "Lola, what is it?"

"I've not been taken to his house because I've refused to marry him…" she said sheepishly.

"What? *Why?*" He rose to his feet. "He seems pretty keen on you, and, well, from what I have seen, you seem to like him, too. Don't you *want* to marry Somenus?"

"No!" She slammed her palms on the ground again. "I never wanted to come here at all!"

Veritas didn't look very sympathetic. "So? From what I have heard, he was planning on going to war with Celestia. In bringing you here, he probably spared your life. Besides, if you gave him an heir, you'd be made queen—you could *end* the war."

"He would make an *Elf* the queen of Arelle?" she asked doubtfully. No non-Faerie had ever sat on the throne in Faerie history, as far as she knew.

"You don't know much, do you?" Veritas sat down again, grabbing his glass of vino to take a generous sip. He then held it out to Lola. She looked at the glass hesitantly. He shook it before her.

"Go on," he said with a sigh, "It'll do you some good."

She took the glass and sipped. Her senses all seemed to gasp in unison. Whatever Veritas was drinking, it was much stronger than she had anticipated. She handed the goblet back, doing her best not to twist her face in revulsion to the drink.

"No." She smacked her lips, "Father never really told me much about Faerie politics."

"I see." Veritas nodded. "Little Lola," he said, "Don't you know that the Faerex has no heir?"

Felix had mentioned Somenus' lack of an heir. "Well, I did know that… but surely there's no urgency; he's only been King for two seasons."

"No, but you need to understand that the Faerie throne is protected by blood. Somenus' bloodline is now tied to the throne. So, while he or any other heirs remain alive, no one else can steal the throne from him. He knows that until he has an heir, others might question the permanency of his reign."

"So, he is trying to secure his throne?" Lola raised her eyebrows. Veritas nodded animatedly, feeling the effects of his own drink. "Well, he has many wives," she muttered, "I am sure he will get one soon enough."

Veritas sighed loudly. "Don't be so sure. Faeries are not conceived very often."

Felix had said that, too. "Is that so?" Lola glanced at the ground awkwardly, the child in her wondering if she was even allowed to take part in this conversation.

"No, little Lola," Veritas said, "There are only a thousand titles—only a thousand Faeries allowed to be alive at a time."

"How many titles are available?" She asked.

"I don't know—no one *really* knows. It must be hundreds though since many died in the war two seasons ago." The merry smile disappeared from the Faerie's face and he looked suddenly pale. "Anyway!" He broke from his trance and turned back to Lola with a smile again. "Yes, he has many wives... *erm,* if you can call them wives. So, there should have been plenty of chances to have a child."

"And so... no children?"

"Well after the first season, he saw that none of his Faerie wives would get pregnant, so he started bringing humans into the Vineyard Palace. Well, everybody knows that it's a hundred times more common for a human to fall pregnant than a Faerie!"

Lola grew more and more uncomfortable to hear about procreation being discussed so liberally in her presence, but she appreciated knowing more about her situation, so she endured the impropriety. "And even still he has had no heirs?" she asked.

"That's right, though he doesn't like anyone talking about that fact." He looked off to the side, as if the Faerex was hiding behind his shoulder. "So, I can only imagine..." his voice trailed off, shrugging innocently, "Well...that since humans are letting him down as well..."

"Oh," Lola blushed, tucking her knees up to her chest and hugging them protectively at the center of her puddle.

"Well, it couldn't *hurt* to try an Elf, could it? Anyway, I am sure it can't be that bad living in the Eight Stones—even *I* don't get to live there! Well, I mean, most of his concubines end up living in the Radiant Palace, but Hades! If you *stay* his favorite, you'll never have to leave the Eight Stones!"

Lola stood, biting her lip with a look of fatigued determination. "But... but what if I don't want to marry him, Veritas?"

"Lola..." Veritas' jolly smile faded, "Do you have a choice?"

"Yes!" She stamped. "He *told* me I did!"

"Well," sighed the Faerie, "Lola... it might be time to rethink your options. It's not safe for you in the Vineyard Palace. And, well, Somenus seems fond of you. Would it be *so* bad?"

Lola's resolve weakened. *Was* he so bad?

"Now," Veritas placed his goblet on a table, then straightened his robes. "I had better tell Felix what's happened here. Don't want Somenus thinking I planned any of this!"

He took a few steps toward his landing platform, spread his wings, then dove down into the clouds.

Lola sat back down in her puddle, afraid she might stain anything she touched. She hugged her knees and began to quake. Her lip quivered, and a tear escaped her eye.

"What is the right thing to do?" she asked herself meekly. When she was just a protected daughter in her father's house, marriage was simple: find a good man. But what if that wasn't an option? Was there a world in which attaching herself to the Nightmare Faerie was a *good* thing? Getting to know him personally over the last few weeks was confusing, to say the least. He had been so different to what she had been told. At this moment, in fact, she was having a hard time reminding herself of any reason why he wasn't good, aside from having her abducted. But this was a war—things like that happened in times of war, didn't they?

Besides, there was that *other* factor... Lola hated admitting it to herself, but she was beginning to look *forward* to seeing Somenus at the banquets. She was beginning to *like* Somenus.

A flash of flapping wings rose into the sky near Veritas' landing platform. Lola looked through the pillars to see Somenus himself cresting onto it. His wings vanished, then he bolted toward her.

Lola scrambled nervously to her feet, waving her hands in defense.

"I'm sorry," she began, "I didn't mean to start a—"

He pulled her into his arms and squeezed her tightly. Not even for a click did he recoil as her vino-covered clothes began to stain his suit.

"Lola," he said in a voice heroic enough to shame a stage actor, "You're safe now!"

She blinked, stiffly waiting for him to let her go. When he didn't, she relaxed into the embrace a little; well, it wasn't the *worst* thing to be this close to him—he had a nice scent. She sniffed, trying to keep herself from crying. Even though it was in the arms of her enemy, Lola felt she desperately needed comfort.

"I'll never let those *bitches* near you again," he hissed, squeezing her tighter. "To think I almost lost you!"

"I'm alright," she said in a muffled voice.

"No, you're not—look at you!" He pushed her back by the shoulders and gazed at her vino-soaked body. She blushed, realizing she was uncovered up to her knees. "You don't belong in the Vineyard Palace, Lola—you're a princess. You're *my* princess! It's time you came to the Eight Stones!"

"But, I—!" She jolted, "I'm not... not ready to..."

"Lola," Somenus closed his eyes, letting out a pressure-releasing sigh, "It is time."

"Time?" She glanced side to side nervously. "Time for what?"

"My heart can't take this anymore," he said, stepping back to wipe his hands across the stains on his coat, "I need an official answer from you... tonight."

"*Tonight*?" Lola swallowed. She hugged her shoulders with her hands.

Somenus nodded. "Lola, I am going to hold a dinner for you at the Eight Stones. I... I want your answer tonight—either way." He studied her with a melancholy expression. "I hope..." he cleared his throat, then straightened, "I hope you will not disappoint me."

Lola tried to smile. "I will give you an answer tonight. Thank you for giving me time."

"Pack your things... if you have any... Either way I'll not have you in the Vineyard Palace anymore. I thought it was the best place to house an unmarried woman, but I see now that it will not be safe for you." Somenus turned to look around the living space. "I'll, uh... I'll have Felix fetch you at the Lastlight bell."

"Thank you," she said, squeezing some more vino out of her hair.

He turned back to her, then tried to conceal a smile. "And, uh... why don't you bathe before tonight."

"That would be for the best, I think," she chuckled softly.

"Well," Somenus cleared his throat, then walked closer. He put an arm around her waist. "Step there, on my foot," he said, pointing downwards.

"What?" Red-cheeked, Lola peered down at Somenus' boot.

"Step on my foot," he said, "And hold on tight."

Lola yelped, clasping her arms tightly around the king's waist as his wings burst out at his sides. Then he flapped, rising quickly into the air. Lola was too frightened to enjoy the ride, she squeezed her eyes shut, then waited until she felt Somenus landing again.

"Alright," he said, tapping her shoulder. She opened her eyes; she was in her room.

"Oh," she looked around wearily. "Thank you."

"I'd suggest you let Alabaster escort you to the bath house; I don't want you alone around the other women," he said, taking a moment to examine her room.

"Thank you, Sire," she said.

"Not a problem," he turned to smile at her, then dove through the window. She rushed to the window and watched as his winged figure soared down through the clouds. Her heart flickered with a quickened pace. He really seemed to care about her! Perhaps he *was* the sort of man she had been waiting for.

—

Lola sat on her bed with her book resting in her lap. She was leaning back on her hands, staring up at the ceiling. The light outside was waning. She had to make up her mind. What was she going to say? For so long, she thought she had the answer. It was an easy answer. No! But so much had changed in the weeks she had been at the Vineyard Palace.

For one thing, her father had offered no ransom for her return! That told her two things: firstly, it told her that Somenus would most likely resort to war; and secondly, it told her she was on her own. She had trusted that her father would protect her and find her a good husband, but where was he? He was gone; he had abandoned her. Perhaps the ransom Somenus had requested was one he was unwilling to pay; there was a part of Lola that understood that. But still... she felt betrayed. So, what should she do?

She had always promised herself she would do the "right" thing, all the days of her life. But what was the "right" thing? *Was* there a "right" in a situation like this?

"I would have to share my husband with other women," she mumbled, shaking her head. "I've never wanted that..." She sighed. "On the other hand, he seems to really care about me. If I became queen, I would be different..." She frowned. No, that didn't seem to comfort her.

The view through her open-air balcony became obscured by what looked like black sails. Felix flapped into view, then landed on the window's ledge.

"You know," she muttered, "*Most* people go to the door, Felix. It's not very polite to just step into a girl's room."

Felix all but rolled his eyes. "I knew you were expecting me," he said defensively.

"You're *early*," she said primly, "I could have been dressing."

"I could see that you weren't," he said, then bit his lip when he realized how poor a defense it was.

"Yes, I am sure you could," she said, rising to her feet. She snapped her book closed, then tucked it under her arm.

"Are you... packed?" Felix asked as his eyes glanced around the room. The rest of him remained perfectly still.

"Well, I don't really *have* any possessions now, do I?" She sassed, then waved her book at him, "Aside from this."

"Have you..." Felix's voice trailed off.

"What was that?" Lola stepped closer, leaning her chin forward, "Did you have something to *say*, Felix?"

"Have you decided what you will say to the king?" His face was blank when he asked. His face was always blank.

Lola's sassiness waned with the darkening sky. She shrugged. "I... I don't *know*, Felix..." Her eyes flashed, locking with his. "What do *you* think?"

"What?"

"What do you think I should do?" She poked her finger at him. "Would *you* marry him, if you were me?"

Felix rolled his eyes to the side; he hesitated, mumbling until he could figure out a way to escape the question. "Well, I... Well, I'm not a... I'm not sure that..."

"Felix! Just 'yes', or 'no'—what would you do?"

He dropped his head, groaning. "Why are you asking *me*?"

She thrust her hands onto her hips. "Well, at first, I asked you because you were the only other person in the room—but now that I am thinking about it... you're a good person to ask because Somenus seems to trust you. You no doubt see a different side to him that I do at the banquets. So tell me. Is he a good man to marry?"

"That's a hard question to answer," his voice twisted like a struggling fishing line, "He's... well..."

"Felix," she pleaded, "Is he a *good* man?"

"Good?" Felix snorted, snapping to attention, "Lola, *nobody* is good. I am the Faerie of Sight: trust me. Nobody is *good*."

"Fine," she sighed, but took a step closer as she peered into his conflicted face. "Is he *evil*?"

"What?"

"People say he is evil... is that true?"

"That's... not an easy question to answer..."

"What's the worst thing you've seen of him," she demanded, "*Faerie of Sight*—what's the worst thing you've seen that might make me not want to marry him?"

Felix's face finally snapped out of its vacant prison. A look of sheer horror spread itself across his countenance like a clean white sheet. His eyes seemed to search an old memory; it was as if they couldn't look away from what they saw.

"Felix...?" Lola whispered, waving her hand in front of his eyes. No reaction. "*Felix...?*"

"Lola... I..." he mumbled, shaking his head.

"Felix," she touched his shoulder, tapping it a few times. "Felix, tell me."

His eyes shifted down toward her. He pursed his lips and shook his head.

"Tell me."

He shook his head again.

She sighed. "Felix... I am forced to make this decision tonight. Please— give me this *one* thing. If you have any compassion for me and the powerless position that I am in, then please, give me this. *Tell* me. I want to go in with my eyes open. Felix, what have you seen?"

Felix sat on the window's ledge with a thud. His shoulders slumped, and he stared defeatedly down at the ground between his feet.

"Fine," he said, "I'll tell you. But..." he turned his head sharply, muttering, "Oh why do I even care? You hate me anyway... it shouldn't make a difference if I tell you..."

Lola glided over to where he sat and placed herself on the floor by his feet. She leaned an elbow on the windowsill and rested her chin in her hand. She looked up at him, waiting patiently.

Felix glanced at her, then back down between his feet.

"I've been Arelle's watchman for a long time," he said, "It's a very honorable position here. It's always been reserved for the Faerie of Sight. My predecessor, the First Faerie of Sight, he built that Crimson Gate I took you to."

Lola nodded, giving Felix a little encouraging smile.

"The Crimson Gate is in a tower south of here, hidden on a little island in the middle of these two great rivers. Half my time I would spend here in Arelle, and the other half I would go to the tower to keep an eye on Arelle. It was what King Sol wanted me to do."

"Did he ask you to... spy on people?"

Felix nodded, "Different seasons brought different requests. But I was always obedient to him, always did as he asked. Then, a thousand seasons ago, there was a war. Somenus raised a human army and attacked Arelle, killing many of Sol's heirs. He nearly defeated him, but he wasn't strong enough to defeat him. So back then, Sol had Somenus executed—or so we thought. Anyway, King Sol became extremely paranoid after that. He was sure, for some reason, that Somenus would come back. So, he asked me to find something..."

"Find what?"

Felix shrugged. "Just a weapon... something he thought might protect him. Anyway, I couldn't find it. But that wasn't good enough for him. He wanted it. And more and more, he wouldn't let me come back to Arelle; he wanted me at the tower, *looking*." Felix scoffed, "Looking and looking, all the time. Never *doing*; always *looking*."

Lola frowned. "How long was it like that?"

Felix turned his head slightly. "How *long*?" His shoulder shook with a huff of a laugh, but his face remained like stone, "A *thousand* seasons, he made me look. Sure, he let me come back to Arelle from time to time, but every time I did, he would still scold me and berate me. He *needed* that weapon. Hades— after a time I would have loved to find that weapon, if it meant someone would *shoot* him with it!"

Lola's eyes widened.

Felix shook his head. "But I stayed loyal to him," he said, "I... I kept looking. But I got too good at looking, princess. I just looked and looked—and I sort of became... numb to the things I saw. Over the seasons, I searched harder and harder, trying to find more beauty. And when I couldn't find it, I looked for other things that gave me power... ugly things."

Lola leaned back, taking in a deep breath, then exhaled. "And then what?" At what point would Somenus step into this story?

"Well," Felix reached up and fingered the monocle that hung around his neck, "After all that looking and seeing," he held up the imperium, "I began to realize just how much power I had accumulated. I... and I..." his eyes lit up, as if remembering an old passion, "I realized I might be able to see things that no one else on Raqia could ever see. So, I looked *past* Raqia; I looked *down*—down under the stars."

"*What?*" Lola gasped. "Were the Lowlands down there?" The Lowlands...the Faeries had books, and plays, and stories about worlds under the stars, but no one knew if they were actually real!

Felix nodded. "Yes, there were other worlds, other things to see down there. I became so fixated," his pace quickened, "So obsessed. I stopped eating, stopped drinking. I stayed awake day and night, sleeping only when I couldn't keep my eyes open any longer. I think the world forgot about me for a time," he shook his head, "It was as if I didn't exist. Only the things I *saw* existed. And then I wanted more. My curiosity raged. What more could I find?"

Felix paused, taking a rallying breath. Lola shifted as both the night and the suspense thickened. "What more could there possibly be?" she finally asked.

"There was more," he rotated his head to look her in the eyes. "I looked lower."

"Lower... than the lowlands?" she asked, her throat feeling dry.

"I found the underworld, Lola. I saw Hades."

Lola's body grew stiff. The air around her felt cold. "The Underworld? You mean... Death?"

Felix nodded, holding her gaze. "Yes, I saw where Death reigns. I saw where the ancient spirits roam, and the disembodied souls wait. I saw a great city—a horrible city. And then—I found him."

Lola blinked. "Who—*Death*?"

"Somenus."

Lola started. "You saw... *Somenus*? In *Hades*?" Her voice crescendoed.

"Shades in Hades: there's nothing necessarily *off* about seeing that. Daemons in Hades: horrifying, but not unexpected. But a man—a *living* Faerie—in Hades? It wasn't right. But there was Somenus, *living* down there in the Underworld, holding the very weapon Sol was so desperate to find." Felix shook his head. "Somehow, Sol had imprisoned Somenus in the Underworld. Hades knows why he did it, but he did. So, I began to watch the Dream Faerie. I grew curious about a man making a home amongst the dead." He reached out a hand and touched Lola's shoulder. "He was thriving down there, Lola, ruling down there. I can't tell you what sort of things I saw, but I can tell you this: it was nothing good."

Lola's stomach was churning. She yanked her shoulder back, freeing it of Felix's cold touch. "You're telling me..." she said, "That Somenus lived... in *Hades*... for a thousand seasons?"

Felix nodded. "Yes."

"And..." she didn't want to know the answer to the question she was about to ask, but she asked anyway. "How did he get out?"

"Well," Felix shifted his weight side to side, "Funny thing about *doors*," he said, "They go both ways. So, I suppose after a time of me looking through my gate, watching that... that genius of a Faerie—one day—he just looked back at me."

Lola was biting her lip so hard, it nearly bled. "*You* let him in?"

Felix stared at her. "*Let* him in?" He shrugged, "He had walked through before I knew what was happening, but yes—I let him in."

"And you helped him kill King Sol?"

Felix stood. "I didn't stop him," he said, "So if you want to call that *helping* him, you may. Whatever story fits your narrative."

"What exactly has Somenus done to make you think I shouldn't marry him?" Lola asked, rising quickly. "You haven't actually *named* anything all that evil!"

"I *didn't* say I thought you shouldn't marry him. You asked me the worst thing I have seen," Felix snapped, "I suppose you want me to say something like: Lola, do not marry him, he murdered women in their sleep; Lola, do not marry him, he tortures innocents for pleasure. Well, I've seen plenty of men do things like that. I've seen King Sol do things like that. Any king you marry, any *man* you marry, might do something like that." His voice grew louder. "But you asked me the worst thing I have seen, and I told you. There is only *one* man I have ever seen—in all my seasons of watching this Lights-forsaken world—who *lived* in Hades like he belonged there."

He panted silently, watching her face with restless eyes.

"If he terrifies you so much," Lola said, "Why do you serve him?"

"Because," Felix's face darkened, "He's my king. I'm the watchman, and I serve the king. Without that, I am nothing."

Lola nodded. She wiggled her fingers, realizing they were losing circulation from the tense period of her clenching her fists. "Right," she sighed. "I see." She turned away and took a few steps toward her bedroom. "A moment of evil, or a sudden evil act... even a good man may do," she turned to look at Felix. "But a man acclimated to evil, that is worse?"

"I think it is," Felix said.

"Then by your own definition," she said spitefully, "You are more evil than Somenus."

Felix nodded. "I suppose I am," he said, "Since I'm the one who watched him—who watches him still."

"You could spare me this decision," Lola said, her heart growing heavy, "You could fly me away, right now. You could *do* just *one* good thing."

Felix shook his head. "The only good thing left I have to do is serve my king."

"Even if your king is..."

Felix nodded. The Lastlight bell began to ring.

Lola dropped her head. "Alright," she said, "You had better take me to the Eight Stones, then. It is time to give him my answer."

Lola was reluctant to be close to Felix after that conversation, but she sucked up her pride and stepped toward him, hugging his waist as he flung his wings out into view. He stuck out his foot expectantly, and she stepped on top of it. He put his arms around her and held on tightly.

"I suppose," Lola mumbled.

Felix looked down quickly, pausing before taking flight.

"I suppose Somenus let you come out of the tower," she said, "He gave you a life back in the light. He let you come back to Arelle. I guess we should grant him that."

"Yes," Felix said, "He did."

"Well..." She looked out toward the clouds, "Better take me to him."

They landed in front of a square building, lined with a hundred pillars. It had two levels, stacked symmetrically, with a network of levels and stairs swirling around it. Like the rest of Arelle, it was made of polished white marble, and glowed even in the night.

Felix dropped Lola there, then took a few steps forward.

"This way," he said, pointing toward the front entrance.

Lola clenched her fists, mustering up every ounce of courage she had. "If I love what is good," she whispered, "It will protect me."

Felix flattened his mouth, watching her with a look of dread.

"Well, come on," she marched past him, blazing through the doors.

"Lola!" Somenus waved, running to meet her on the other side of the door.

"Oh," she stuttered, weakening as he dove in to hug her. She closed her eyes for a moment, promising herself she would not back down.

Somenus leaned back to smile warmly. "You look so radiant, Princess! Come, come and sit," he pulled her by the arm, "I've had the most splendid meal prepared. You are going to *love* it—"

"Somenus..." she mumbled, but he talked over her.

Pillars and paintings whizzed past as Somenus dragged Lola through the Eight Stones. She could hardly take anything in; everything was happening so fast! They appeared inside an intimate dining room; only two places were set. Lola turned around to check for Felix, but he was gone.

"Sit, sit," Somenus pulled out her chair. She sat slowly, reaching nervously for her napkin. Somenus whipped his coattails back and sat beside her, grinning. He rested his arms on the table, and Lola did her best not to stare at the stump. She was getting used to it, but it still made her feel a little queasy.

"Somenus, thank you for going to all this effort," she said weakly.

"Of course," he snapped his fingers, motioning for a servant to serve the first course.

Lola cleared her throat. Why did he have to be in such a good mood? It would be a much further fall from a good mood than it would have been if he was already doubtful. Could she not stall for *one* more day?

"I've got an excellent room set up for you, right next to mine," he said, taking a glass of water in his hand. "Lola, I can't tell you how excited I—" he shook his head, "Oh, dear—I'm getting ahead of myself."

Lola gulped. "Yes, I probably should, *erm...*" She reached a trembling hand for her water glass and sipped.

"Hades, you look nervous," the king remarked. Some of the spark left his eyes. "Are you... alright? No one hurt you again, did they?"

"No, no," she set her wobbly cup back down on the table, then straightened her napkin for the third time. "I... Well, I..."

Somenus silently waited, maintaining a smile.

"Shall I say it, *erm—now?*"

He nodded.

Lola closed her eyes. To love what is good: that was her only path. It would light her way down this maze of blackness. She could only marry someone she was willing to love, she thought—and she was not willing to give this man her affection.

She opened her eyes, gazing softly at the Faerie before her. "No," she said. "I cannot marry you; I am sorry."

Somenus' face was frozen for a moment, with that blank smile plastered across it. "I'm sorry?" he blinked.

"No," she said again, "I cannot marry you; I am sorry."

"Are you sure?" The smile was fading.

Lola nodded.

"Because I will not ask again..." he said with a twitching eye.

Lola nodded. "I have made up my mind," she said, "My affections are engaged elsewhere."

"Your *affe—*" he started, then rose to his feet suddenly. Lola stared up at him. He looked side to side, his breathing accelerating. "I... I... I've been *patient* with you—given you *time* to... to..." saliva seemed to foam from his mouth, "I *romanced* you—I didn't *force* you to do anything..." It was like he was reading off a list. His arms quaked; then his whole body quaked.

Lola's chair made a squeaking sound as she scooted back a little, preparing to make a dash.

"What is it you *want*?" he finally screamed, "What do I have to *do* to make you... you... why won't you... *why won't you do what I want?*"

Lola shrieked as he dumped the table on its side with the use of his only hand. She rose swiftly from her chair, then dashed behind it.

"Somenus!" she cried, "I just can't love you—I'm sorry."

"You can!" he snapped, kicking a chair aside. It flew across the room. Lola inched backwards as Somenus moved toward her, stepping over fallen plates and cutlery. "*Anyone* can love me!"

Lola shook her head. "No," she said.

"You bitch!" Somenus lunged toward her and took her by the throat. "Even after your father refused to lend me his armies, I still offered you a marriage! You could have saved your *felling* colony!"

"Sire, please," she croaked, clawing at his arm. "Please, don't be angry!"

"*Everybody* gives in to me sooner or later." He snarled. "You think you're different?"

"I'm sorry," she said between strained breaths, "I can't stay here. I can't be with you, Somenus."

"Oh," he barked a laugh, "That, *Lola*," he released his grip and watched as she dropped to the floor, coughing, "is where you don't have a choice."

20

— Isabella —

Ashen Shoots

ll hear, all hear," cried the skydeacon. He was standing proudly on the crier's stage at the center of Pondus Square, holding his hands up towards the heavens. The center of Arelle was bustling with movement as all her residents gathered to welcome the new season.

Major Scarlet Wingsday was leaning against a shadowy wall, watching from the back of the crowd. Sure, it was her job to watch the crowd and protect the skydeacon during the announcement, but she was also curious. This would be her first time welcoming in a new season since coming to Arelle, and here she was, at the heart of it all.

Betterfly, Somenus' head skydeacon, cleared his throat emphatically as he rolled out a scroll and held it before himself in a ceremonial pose. "Tomorrow is the Firstday," he bellowed, "of Ashen Shoots." He paused, a small glint of a smile appearing on his face as the crowd murmured with excitement. "Yes," he continued, "the Fellowship, with the approval of King Somenus, is proud to announce that this new season is called Ashen Shoots. So ends the Season of

Seedgully. Seedgully was, as we predicted, a total of four hundred and twenty days, and a total of sixty weeks. With few showers and temperate winds…”

Wingsday raised her eyebrows in surprise. Seedgully was 420 days? Her first day in Arelle had been the 20th day of Seedgully. Had she really been in Arelle for 400 days—practically a whole season? It didn't feel as long as a season; her life had been so busy thus far. But four hundred days—that was a long time. Perhaps it *had* been that long! She felt like a different person, that was for sure.

“However, on this Firstday's Eve, I am proud to proclaim,” Betterfly continued, “That Ashen Shoots will be a time of color and fertility. We will see blooms from the golden cereus flowers, heavy rains, and new shoots from the Ashen trees within the valleys. Vermis root crops, which we have not seen flower since the season of Treeworms, will be plentiful, and we will see a return of the pink windlarks here in Arelle.”

“Oh, Lights!” Xylo, who was standing a few yards in front of Wingsday, turned to smile at her.

Scarlet shrugged. “What?” she asked in her usual unenthusiastic tone.

Xylo, the Faerie of Trees, jogged over to the wall and leaned against it. “Did you hear that?” she said, whispering over Betterfly's ramble about wind directions.

“Which part?” Scarlet asked.

“Ashen shoots in the valleys? That's… that's special!”

“Xylo,” another Faerie separated from the inside of the crowd and approached their private corner, “Did you hear what he said?”

“About the Ashen roots?” Xylo said with a clap of her hands.

“No—the golden cereus! Those haven't bloomed in over seven hundred seasons!” He rubbed his own hands together. “They're deeply symbolic—there's *deep* tradition behind their promises.”

“No, it's the *Ashen shoots* that are symbolic, Endring,” Xylo shook her head, “*I* am the Faerie of Trees—I know about these things.”

“And *I* am the Faerie of Vows,” hissed Endring, the other Faerie, “I know about these things!”

Scarlet smirked. Hades, it sure was different experiencing a season change around Faeries. When she was growing up, their little family celebrated with small traditions, and the town of Nemus welcomed in the New Season with a village feast, but the Faeries found all those strange details so meaningful. It was all about the symbolism for them, and the message *behind* the season.

"So, what's so special about the Ash trees?" Scarlet asked lazily, pulling out her dagger. It was one of those brainless time passers—running the blade's tip along the inside of her nails.

Endring and Xylo both turned their heads to regard her, leaning there with her back against the wall.

"Ash trees represent long-standing tradition. Ash shoots very *rarely* appear," Xylo said in a condescending informative tone, "There are only five hundred and sixteen Ash trees on Raqia, and they've been there longer than I have! New Ash? This—this..." she shook her head, scanning her mind for which details to share, "This is really special! And... in the valleys? Why in the *valleys*?"

"How do the skydeacons know this is going to happen anyway?" Scarlet asked dryly.

Both Xylo and Endring gave her confused looks.

"Well?" Scarlet shrugged. "If it hasn't happened in so long, how do they know it's going to happen *now*?"

"Major," Endring sighed, "You're asking birds about how fish know how to swim. We don't need to know. We just let them do it!"

"Sure, fine," Scarlet sheathed her dagger.

"Anyway, it's the golden cereus that's the *real* symbol," Endring said quickly, "There are few left on Raqia. To the untrained eye, they just look like rugged, spiny cacti! But when they bloom—"

"Can you pipe down?" Scarlet waved her hand, "I am trying to listen to the announcement! I want to hear how *long* the season is supposed to be."

Xylo and Endring both turned their heads, gazing up toward the podium where Betterfly was still reading from his scroll. Endring looked back at Scarlet.

"No one can know for sure how long the season will be, they will just give an estimate," Endring said.

"So why is a human the head of the skydeacons here?" Scarlet asked in a skeptical tone, "Isn't there like a Faerie of Weather... or Faerie of the Skies, or anything like that?"

Xylo squinted. "Don't you *know*, Major?"

"Know what?"

Endring sighed. "There are no Faerie titles given over seasons or weather. The skies are the *Lights'* territory. No one controls the skies. We can only listen and observe."

"I thought the Faerie King controlled the seasons," Scarlet said, shifting her position to stand free of the wall.

Xylo laughed. "The king commands the *land*, not the skies or the seasons."

"The Throne is his third imperium," Endring said proudly, "It gives him authority over the land. He can work with the season, and he can *help* the skydeacons interpret coming seasons with the knowledge the throne gives him over the land, but he can't actually change anything about the seasons. As Xylo said, only the Lights can do that."

"So, is that why the Faerie King is the head of the Skydeacons?" Scarlet asked. "He's got information that they don't have access to?"

"*And* authority," Endring said with a raised finger.

"But there are no Faerie skydeacons?"

Endring shook his head. "Aside from the king, no. The Faeries are too busy with their own titles to care about announcing the time of day, you know."

Scarlet shifted her attention back to Betterfly who seemed to be bringing his speech to a close.

"...and there will be a Firstday Feast tonight here at the square, come the Lastlight bell," he was saying, "We will begin the celebrations!"

Scarlet scrunched up her nose. "Firstday feast tonight? But the new season is *tomorrow*."

Endring snorted. "Wingsday, you *humans* might celebrate a new season the evening of the Firstday, but we Faeries believe a new season starts at the Lastlight."

"We always celebrate the new season the night before the humans," Xylo said in a less judgmental tone. "So, our feast is tonight. Will you..." the Faerie of Trees paused as the bell tower began to chime. The Mid-morning bell was ringing.

Out of habit, Scarlet reached into her pocket and reset her clicker as the last bell rang. Most of the Faeries didn't keep track of how many clicks were in an hour, but it was essential to the life of a soldier; just about everything they planned—from meetings to patrol lengths—relied on clicks.

Scarlet snapped herself into attention. Come to think of it, she was supposed to be meeting the head priest of the Faerie Rites 200 clicks after the Mid-morning bell!

"Sorry," she mumbled to the two Faeries beside her, "Got to run."

Scarlet Wingsday, dressed in her black leather armor, marched out of the square. Her crimson cloak, pinned valiantly to her shoulders by two large brass brooches, flapped behind her in the wind. She made her way down the north road and found the Temple of Rites down at its end. As she entered, Captain Banther rushed to her side.

"Major," he whispered, slamming his right fist against his left shoulder in a salute, "Good Firstday's Eve to you."

"Good Firstday's Eve," she mumbled spiritlessly. She checked her clicker; it was at 150 clicks. "Has the head priest come out yet?"

"Not yet, Major," said the captain. He cleared his throat and his eyes shifted side to side; there was clearly something he wanted to ask her.

"What *is* it, Banther?" Scarlet snapped.

"It's, ^..."

"*Hades*, Banther," she cocked her head to the side, "What's got you so jittery?"

"A favor, Major," he said sheepishly.

Scarlet frowned. "What *now*?"

"Trouble in the Eight Stones. I've been asked to... well... it might be better if *you*..."

"One moment, Banther," Scarlet sighed as she checked her clicker once more: 200 clicks. The Priest was late. "Where *is* that worm?"

"It's an area where you might have more expertise than I," Captain Banther whispered.

Scarlet looked up at him, shoving the silver clicker back in her pocket. "Oh," she said, "I see."

"I was hoping you might help me out... again..." mumbled the Captain.

"Ah—Wingsday!" A voice echoed through the temple as the head priest came gliding over towards them.

"Hold that thought," Scarlet whispered to the captain. She and Banther then turned to stand at attention as the Priest, clothed in his velvet red robes, held his hands out to them in greeting.

"*Thank you* for coming," he said magnanimously, "I... there is a..."

"Father Bintnoz," Scarlet Wingsday barked, and the priest recoiled his hands with a look of terror, "It has come to my attention," she continued, "That you and Father Kneelock have been engaging in *debates* in the Pondus Square again. Is this true?"

Father Bintnoz stammered, looking shocked. "I—I—debates? No, no. It is Father *Kneelock* who has been..."

"Look," she snapped, stepping forward as she placed her hands on her hips, "Korbin is sick of having to deal with your petty problems. If you two can't work this out, it will not be hard for him to find your replacements, do you *understand*?"

Father Bintnoz stood there, mouth hanging open. He shook himself. "I have no problem with the Priest of the Lights holding his services in his own temple. I have nothing against the Light Priests, but he thinks *he* is going to say the New Season prayer at the feast tonight, and I—"

"Listen," Scarlet hissed, "I don't care two petals about who prays at the Feast tonight. That's up to Fellow Betterfly. What he says, goes. But we can't have you and Father Kneelock fighting publicly. It sends the wrong message! There's no reason why your two religions can't—can't—" she stammered, "Work together!"

Something irritating tapped at the back of Scarlet's mind; it was Isabella. Could the Light priests and the Faerie Rites Priests *really* be able to reconcile their beliefs? Didn't the Priests of the Lights preach there is only one God, and the Faerie Rites taught there were many? Scarlet shook herself back to attention. What did she care about theology? She had a *job* to do!

"I am *trying* to work with Father Kneelock," Father Bintnoz sniffed, "I agree with you. There is no reason we both can't teach within Arelle, but he won't acknowledge me as legitimate!"

"*Forget* what he thinks," Scarlet said, "Somenus said you're legitimate, and that is all that matters."

"Speaking of Somenus," Father Bintnoz shifted his mood, looking a great deal stuffier, "I have been wondering why I haven't seen you in the temple on Octdays... you know that *all* the humans in Arelle are supposed to worship their patron Faerie at the start of each week."

Scarlet scowled. "Stay out of my private affairs," she growled.

Father Bintnoz waved his hands innocently. "I am not accusing. I simply want to remind you of your duty as a human living within Arelle."

"Only one person around here can tell me what my *duty* is," she snapped, "And that is Korbin. If you want to take this up with him, then be my guest!"

Father Bintnoz's eyes widened with a look of horror. "Oh, that...th-th-that," he stammered, "there is no need for that!"

"Good! Now stop fighting with Father Kneelock, or you'll both be executed!" Her commanding voice echoed through the temple, and all within turned to regard her fearfully. "Good Firstday's Eve to you!" she snapped.

"Good Firstday's Eve..." Father Bintnoz replied weakly.

Scarlet turned about face and marched out of the Temple, with Captain Banther following close behind.

"Well handled, Wingsday," the captain said as they stepped out on the road, "These religious folk give me a headache... I never know how to talk to them without getting some sort of guilt-inducing sermon."

"Banther," Scarlet turned, pulling out her clicker: 590 clicks passed the Mid-morning bell. "What's happening at the Eight Stones that you... don't want to have to deal with?"

"It's Somenus' *concubines*, Major," he said quietly, "There's a... a..."

Scarlet tipped her head back, groaning. "*More* drama with his concubines?" She hated having to deal with those useless, spoiled women, but she had better luck than the male soldiers did. Besides, it made the king uneasy when human men went into the Radiant Palace.

"Yes," Captain Banther stood a little straighter, "One of the concubines has left the Radiant Palace and moved into the Eight Stones..."

Scarlet blinked. "You mean..."

"She's moved into the *Queen's* room," he said.

Scarlet sighed. "The Queen's room?" The Queen's room was what they called it, even though Arelle didn't actually *have* a queen yet. It was the room where Somenus kept whoever his favorite woman was at the time. "Doesn't someone already live there?"

"It's vacant at the moment," said Banther, "And one of the concubines has just... moved herself in. The guards in the Eight Stones don't know what they're supposed to do, so they sent me to ask for help."

"Damn," Scarlet shook her head. "The king isn't going to be happy when he finds out..."

"For the girl's sake," said Banther, "we should get her out of there."

"We?" Scarlet chuckled, "You mean, *me?*"

He nodded soberly. "They say this one is..." he searched for a euphemism, "hard to say 'no' to."

"I see." Scarlet shoved her clicker in her pocket. "Well, then I'll need you to take over for me and go speak to Father Kneelock. Tell him the same thing I told Father Bintnoz."

Captain Banther groaned.

"Hey," she snapped, "Would you prefer to go and arm wrestle a concubine?"

"No," he kicked a pebble. "I'll go hear my sermon."

"You'll go and threaten that Priest!" she said, "You're a soldier! You don't need to stick around for his sermon."

"Yes, Major," he saluted, then marched off.

Wingsday pulled her pants up by the belt, spat on the ground, then marched toward the center of the city. It took 500 clicks just to walk from the bottom of the stairs to the top on the way to the entrance to the Eight Stones. Somenus' house... Scarlet always felt uneasy going in there.

She had never actually met the king, and she was fine with that. But every time she went into his house, she was reminded of the original reason she came to Arelle. She was supposed to help kill him. No—she shook herself back to attention. That was an old, foolish mission. She was someone else now; she was someone who could actually do some *good* in Arelle. Killing kings was for lawbreakers and revolutionists, and that was not her. Scarlet Wingsday was a keeper of the peace.

"Alright, what's going on?" she said as she walked through the guard's entrance to the Eight Stones. Captain Chinte, the head of the Eight Stones guard, stood to attention, placing his fist against his shoulder.

"Major Wingsday," he said with a weary look on his face, "I'm glad you've come."

"So, you just stood there and *let* a concubine walk into the Eight Stones and move into the Queen's room?" She demanded.

"We didn't know that she hadn't been invited," he said, "Somenus threw his favorite woman in the prison again about a week ago, so we just figured he wanted to fill her place!"

"What did she do this time?" Scarlet shook her head. This must have been at least the fourth time Somenus threw that same concubine in the prison.

"Don't know, Ma'am," said the captain, "But I checked with the Mistress of the Radiant Palace, and she confirmed that Somenus hasn't sent for any other women."

Scarlet's stomach turned. She hated having to deal with Somenus' private life—namely, all the women he seemed to have relations with.

"You want me to send her back then?" Scarlet asked as she crossed her arms.

"We thought..." he hesitated, "It would be better for a woman to deal with her, if she continues to refuse to go."

"What, you can't handle arresting a woman? Too strong for you?" Scarlet scoffed.

The captain cleared his throat. "It's *this* woman in particular…" he said, "…she's hard to say 'no' to."

"So I have heard." Isabella said as she turned to leave.

"Thank you, Major," the captain called from behind.

Scarlet grabbed a halberd from the weapon's safe within the Eight Stones guardroom and marched up the main stairs. She found her way to the Queen's room, which was just opposite the hall to the king's room. She stopped to peer through the half open door into the king's quarters; they were vacant at present. So—this is where Somenus lived. What would Hanz think if he knew she could get so close to him? She sighed, then turned to open the door to the Queen's room.

A vase flung past her head and smashed against the wall as she stepped into the room.

Scarlet slammed the butt of her halberd against the tiled floor and stared, unimpressed, at the woman who stood across the room.

There she was, the rebellious concubine. She was wearing a big, hefty skirt, like most of the women in the radiant palace did. Scarlet had learned by now that human modesty involved women hiding the shapes of their legs, but she seemed to be exempt from all that as the only female soldier in Arelle. She fit into a category of her own. The concubine, in her emerald green attire, had frizzy black hair and an angular, though attractive face. She was glaring, red-cheeked, at Scarlet, priming to throw another vase.

"I'm not leaving!" she bellowed, "Somenus needs comfort right now, and *I* am going to give it to him!"

"The only comfort you will be giving anyone is the relief I am going to feel when I drag you, kicking and screaming, out of this house," Scarlet said coolly.

"No," the concubine demanded as she threw herself against the bedpost. "You cannot make me leave! I *will* see Somenus—at least once!"

Scarlet took a step forward. "Don't make me use this," she said, "I will if I have to. *No one* is above the law here, you understand?"

"This room is empty," hissed the concubine, "What harm is it if I stay here? That bitch is in prison, and good riddance. She doesn't know how to please the king like I do; I give him *everything* he wants!"

Scarlet Wingsday grimaced, and Isabella the virgin inside her blushed. "Look," she said, "Somenus might have you killed for coming in here without being invited, I am trying to spare you."

"*Fine*," she replied, "I will die if it means a chance to be with him again!"

Scarlet closed her eyes, mustering her inner compassion. She opened them again. "What's your name?"

"Lady Fayne," said the concubine with a judging head turn.

"Lady Fayne," Scarlet said, taking another step closer. "I will be frank. If you do not leave willingly, and you do insist on being killed, it will all happen before you get a chance to see the king. If you really do want to see him, you should do as you're told. If you like, I will speak to my superiors about you. Maybe someone will mention your name to the king. That is the best I can offer you. Will you take it or not?"

Scarlet watched silently as Lady Fayne calculated her options. After a hundred clicks of her tossing her head side to side thoughtfully, she finally said, "No."

"No?" Scarlet scoffed. "Why?"

"I *know* you won't kill me," she said haughtily, "You wouldn't dare kill one of Somenus' wives without consulting him first, or you might be killed yourself! I am staying right here until Somenus *himself* tells me to leave!"

Scarlet stepped back, nodding. "Somenus doesn't *have* any wives, but fine," she said, "But you will regret making trouble here, woman. I guarantee that."

Scarlet heard another vase smash against the door as she left. What an irksome woman!

1200 clicks later, Scarlet was marching, huffing and puffing, into the watch house.

"Felix?" she called, looking around. Where was that damned Faerie of Sight? She poked her head out the city-facing window and yelled again. "Felix, where are you?"

"Wingsday?" A voice asked from behind her. She turned to see the Faerie standing in the middle of the watchhouse with his arms folded. "What brings you all the way up here?"

Scarlet stepped up to him. "It's a problem in the Eight Stones," she said, "I am not sure what to do…"

"Why don't you ask Korbin? He's in charge of you lot, not me."

"It's about… the king's concubines," she said nervously, "I thought it might be a good idea to leave Korbin *out* of this one."

"Oh…"

There was an awkward moment of silence as both Felix and Scarlet remembered the last time Korbin had found reason to walk into the Radiant Palace.

"Anyway," Scarlet coughed into her hand, "I thought it might make it easier for all of us if we didn't remind the general about how… *interesting* Somenus' concubines are."

"Well, what's happening?" Felix asked.

"Someone's moved into the Queen's room," Scarlet began to say, then hesitated when Felix's eyes flashed with worry.

"Somenus sent for another woman?" he asked.

"No…" Scarlet raised an eyebrow, "she just went and moved herself in without asking."

Felix relaxed. "Oh."

"Felix… What happened to his last concubine? I heard she got thrown in prison again."

"Oh," Felix joined his hands behind his back. "That is… I think they've quarreled. But she will be back, I am sure."

Scarlet tightened her mouth into a line; she didn't really *want* the details anyway. "Look," she said, "this concubine refuses to leave, and we don't want to be accused of roughing up the king's women. Will *you* deal with this?"

Felix frowned. "Fine."

The two of them turned their heads sharply at the sound of a trumpet's call in the distance.

Scarlet gasped. "Was that…?"

"The Fifth Legion's call," Felix answered her question, rushing to the south window. Felix and Scarlet peered out to see the remains of an army marching up to the gate. The trumpet repeated its melody.

"So few..." Scarlet whispered, "So few have returned."

"Yes," Felix sighed.

"What are you waiting for?" Scarlet slapped a hand on Felix's shoulder, "Open the gates!"

"I will," Felix said, yanking his shoulder away from her touch. He stepped away from the window and brushed out his tunic.

"Felix," Scarlet said, turning to him with a hesitant cringe.

"What?"

"Will you fly me down there?"

"You don't have permission to leave Arelle," he replied, giving her a calculating look.

"My friends are down there!" she said, "I'll enter the city with them, just let me greet them!"

"Fine," Felix said as he walked out of the watchhouse. Scarlet rushed after him, then stepped up close as he stopped on his landing platform. Only once or twice had Scarlet actually asked a Faerie to fly her anywhere, but she knew the basic protocol, just balance a foot on their instep and hold on tight. She wasn't sure why she felt more bashful this time, but she nearly blushed when Felix held out an arm and looked at her with his blank, expectant face. She climbed onto his foot, then held on with one arm.

She made an embarrassing yelp when the Faerie leapt off the top of the wall and soared down towards the army. She clung tightly onto Felix's shoulder, gritting her teeth as the ground came closer and closer at an alarming speed. Then, just feet from the ground, Felix slowed his flight, and dropped her gracefully onto the ground.

Instantly, she ran toward the gathered soldiers, who were still playing their trumpet song, announcing their return home.

"Major Twilight!" she called as she rushed to the front of the group.

A soldier dressed in red armor turned quickly at the sound of her voice. He smiled through his thick black beard. "Wingsday!" He saluted with a nod of his head.

She galloped up to his side, then slammed an open palm on his shoulder. "Victory?" she asked as she peered around at the tattered group of fighters. She counted fifteen.

Major Twilight shook his head. "No," he said with a twitching eye, "I'm afraid it was over before it started. Those Elves..." his eyes fogged over.

"How?" Isabella shook her head, "Are you truly all that's left?"

Twilight nodded soberly. She could see it in his eyes; his spirit was broken. Scarlet searched the cluster of faces for her friends who had left so excitedly for the battle, and she couldn't see anyone she recognized.

"Those pointy-eared bastards are touch fighters, I'll give 'em that," he said with a head shake.

"But we outnumber them ten to one," Scarlet said, "How can they *still* be standing after all this time?"

Major Twilight shrugged, "They are fighting for survival on their own home front. It will take some time. But fear not, Wingsday," he said, lifting up his hand to shake hers, "Celestia *will* fall... eventually."

"Why won't he just surrender?" she said as the gates of Arelle began to swing open at their snail-paced speed.

"King Antecus?" Major Twilight scratched his head, "I don't bother with politics, Wingsday. I just do what I am told. He's a brilliant war strategist, I'll give him that."

Scarlet shook her head, watching as the weary band of soldiers plodded into the city. "I don't understand," she said, "Why won't he just make friends with Arelle? All Somenus asks is that he set up at least *one* shrine in their city."

Major Twilight shrugged. "Like I said," he said, "I don't worry about the politics of it all. But if I have learned anything about the Elves, it's that they're stubborn as Hades."

Scarlet walked side by side with Twilight into the city.

"I do wish this war would end," he said, "We are losing so many men in this fight... and it takes a lot of time to train the new recruits."

"It's time for the rest of the world to just *accept* that Somenus is the new king," Scarlet said angrily, "They may not like how he rules, but he is the Lord of the Land—*all* the land! He's not perfect, but neither was the last king. Why does King Antecus take issue with him?"

"The last Faerie King sort of ignored the rest of the world," replied Major Twilight, "I don't know about you, but until Somenus' reign I had never even *seen* a Faerie before. I think it will take time for the rest of the world to get used to a Faerie King who actually *uses* his authority over the land."

"Where do you come from, Twilight?" she asked.

"Oh, not too far—not as far as some of the others, the Gramenlands."

Scarlet nodded. The king of the Gramenlands had been sending a lot of soldiers to Arelle to fight for King Somenus.

"Well," she sighed, "I'm glad you made it back alive."

Twilight cringed. "I... I am glad to get these boys home. Anyway, I'll see you in Fort Axes. I had better report back to the general."

Scarlet nodded, then reached absentmindedly for her clicker as the Late-morning bell began to ring from the bell tower. She and Twilight both reset their timepieces, then nodded to each other before parting ways.

Scarlet found an empty bench and sat. She pulled off her glove and stretched her fingers open and closed. She then turned her hand and gazed at the underside of her wrist. Was there really a purple mark hiding there, masked by a spell? Had she really pledged herself to the Purple Order a season ago? Was she *really* involved in a plot to kill the king? She looked up toward the sky, exhaling. She knew so much more now than she did then. If only she could go back and tell herself to wait and think before putting some non-removable tattoo on her body. If anyone here found it, it could be the death of her! She didn't *want* to have anything to do with the Purple Order anymore; she actually *liked* being Scarlet Wingsday.

Sure, working for someone like Korbin gave her constant anxiety, and yet, she was doing something with her life; she had authority. She had the power to make real changes. She was at the heart of world politics, and there were opportunities to do good there. Sure, she wasn't doing anything *big* like killing an evil king; but she had the chance to be involved in doing good on a more nuanced level. Because of her, women like Lady Fayne might be spared from shame and punishment. It was enough for her to simply be a part of things; she didn't need more than that.

21

— Leo —

The Moon Queen

I opened my eyes and let the physical world take shape around me as I left the world of dreams. I let out a tense breath, then loosened my hands' tight grip around the box. I had managed to keep the nightmares at bay that night, so I woke feeling more refreshed than usual.

"Happy Firstday," said a voice.

I lifted my head quickly from my pillow to see Momentum standing beside my bed, examining me with his arms folded.

"Dude!" I bashfully pulled my blanket up to my neck; it wasn't easy with the wooden box containing Somenus' hand sitting on my chest. "Why are you watching me sleep? That's creepy!"

The Time Faerie only raised an eyebrow slightly.

"Momentum?" I cleared my throat, "Why are you in here? And don't try to tell me it's some *Raqian Firstday tradition* to go watch other people sleep without them knowing about it!"

"It is," he replied.

I opened my mouth, then held my breath, thinking. I frowned. "No, it's not!"

Momentum snorted amusedly.

"Can you give me some privacy, please?"

"Leo..."

"*What*?"

Momentum pointed at the box on my chest.

"Uh..." I tried to think up a reasonable excuse for why I was sleeping with the Nightmare Faerie's hand.... *Again*. "I, uh..."

"I know what's going on, Leo," he said dryly.

I bit my lip. He had been mostly silent about my relationship with the hand and didn't even ask me 'why' when I told him I wanted to keep it in my room. For the most part, he seemed to be someone who let others do whatever they wanted without questions. But I *knew* that he knew something was up, and I was dreading the day when he finally confronted me about it.

"Going... *on*?" I swallowed.

Momentum sat at the foot of my bed and leaned back on his hand. I sat up, placing the chest beside me, then nodded.

"Alright," I sighed. "Let me have it."

"You don't realize just what you're messing with, Leo," he said in a voice less scolding than I was anticipating; it was more like a sympathetic parent. "Inside that box is Somenus' actual hand—his being, his powers, and his life force—they are all inside there."

"I know..."

"I don't think you do know, Leo. You're *using* his powers when you sleep. I don't know what exactly you are doing in the dreamscape, but you're effectively partaking in Somenus' abilities because of your access to his hand."

I blushed. He seemed to know quite a bit! I nodded sheepishly. "I know," I said, "I've known that for a while."

Momentum sighed. "Leo... this is dangerous territory, a human tapping into a Faerie's powers like this. And this isn't just any Faerie—this is Somenus. Leo, he *knows* you're doing this."

"I know..." my face went from red to white, and I grew cold. "He... he finds me sometimes."

Momentum nodded. "I am sure he does."

"It's not as bad when the hand is in the box, though," I said in a reassuring tone, "When I can't touch him, he doesn't have the same hold on me."

"That isn't much of a comfort," Momentum said darkly, "Leo, you can't possibly believe that you can do this, use his powers and meet him nearly every night and *not* become obsessed with him."

My heart began to pound. It was as if I were an alcoholic whose secret stash had been discovered. "I—I'm not obsessed with him. I hate him!"

Momentum's brow tightened. "Leo... he is the Faerie of Affection. It is nearly impossible to resist his pull. You are not above this."

"I..." What could I tell him? This felt so private—*too* private to share the intimate details. "Momentum, you have to believe me; I have a good reason for doing this."

He rotated his head slightly, looking at me from the side calculatingly. He wanted to believe me. "What is your reason, Leo?"

I shook my head quickly.

"You're not... *spying* for him, are you?"

"No!" I gasped. "No way! I am not lying when I say I hate him, Momentum. No... it's something really important. I... I can't tell you."

"Leo..." he stroked his forehead.

"Momentum, please believe me!"

"I can see it in your eyes, you are addicted to that hand—addicted to its power."

"It's not the power I'm addicted to, it's," I hesitated, "It's..."

"I'm not going to take it from you... yet," Momentum said cautiously, "But you need to start being honest with me about what you're doing in the dreamscape. You're walking in places no human has ever been allowed to walk."

"I know..."

"Leo, tell me where you go in there. Is it Earth? Is it that you miss home?" He placed a hand on my knee.

I shook my head. "No... I don't actually miss the Earth all that much, to be honest."

"Leo, you can tell me—I'm not going to take it away from you," he said. His eyes seemed to shine with sympathy.

I opened my mouth... and someone knocked on the door.

Momentum and I both turned our heads toward where the knock was sounding.

"Who is it?" I called.

"It's Cymbeline," came my friend's muffled voice.

"Uh..." I slapped Momentum's arm, then pointed at my tunic which lay on the floor. "Just a second!" Momentum looked down at the tunic judgmentally.

"Don't you know how to put your clothes *away*, Leo? You have a wardrobe, you know."

"Pass it to me!" I hissed.

He bent down to pick up the garment, then threw it my way. I flung it over my shoulders, then jumped out of bed, checking myself in the mirror. My curls had grown long over the past year or so that I had been at Winter's End. Parted messily on the side, they fell just below my ears. The length had tamed the frizziness slightly, but *only* slightly.

"Uh, come in!" I shouted.

The door creaked open, and Cymbeline popped her head inside. "Leo, uh... oh!" She noticed Momentum sitting there. "What's he doing here?"

"I could ask *you* the same question," Momentum said with a hint of annoyance. "Coming into a young man's bedchambers alone?"

Cymbeline balked, her mouth hanging open in horror.

"He's teasing you, Cym," I said, slapping the back of Momentum's shoulder. "Don't listen to the old coot."

Cymbeline exhaled through her nostrils, locking her offended eyes on Momentum's face.

"How is it going storing magik in that thing?" Momentum asked lazily, pointing to the pendant necklace around her neck. She had woven gold wire around the pebble I gave her and turned it into a piece of jewelry.

Cymbeline looked down at herself, then up at the Time Faerie. "What do *you* care?"

"Hey, he's just asking!" I said nervously, "no need to get... uh..."

Cymbeline's eyes shifted to me. "*What*?" she snapped, "no need to get what, *irrational*?"

"No, I didn't mean that!" I said, pacing toward her. She always seemed to get agitated around Momentum, though I could never really understand why. "Cym, want to tell me why you came here this morning?"

"Not with *him* around!" she snapped, pointing at Momentum.

"I'll leave happily," Momentum mumbled as he rose to his feet.

I groaned, watching him leave. They were like a cat and a dog with each other; I couldn't seem to bridge the gap between them. Maybe I was trying too hard!

Cymbeline stamped her foot on the floor. "That nuisance! Why does he have to be so infuriating?"

"Cym..." I walked to her side, "He's not that bad; maybe if you just—"

"You don't see it, do you, Leo? He hates me! He's all nice to you, but with me, he always assumes the worst! He shows you kindness and preference, but with me, it's all quips and jeers."

"I am sure that can't be true," I began.

"Leo!" she barked, "Stop taking his side!"

"Does there *have* to be sides?" I asked nervously, "Can't I just like you both?"

She sighed, shaking her head.

"Come on, Cym," I smiled encouragingly, "It's our first Firstday! Let's have some fun, alright?"

Cymbeline's eyes flashed as she suddenly remembered what brought her there in the first place. "Leo," she whispered, "I found something... in the Solstice."

I raised my eyebrows. Yeah, she knew how to get me excited. We lived in a big, ancient castle, and everybody knew I loved discovering any and all of its secrets.

"What did you *find*?" I rubbed my hands together excitedly.

"Come on, I'll show you," she said. With Momentum out of the room, the innocent, gentle side of her was resurfacing. It intimidated others when she got feisty, but not me. I knew that whatever her life was like before Winter's End, it had not been happy. Something about her upbringing had taught her to have her guard up all the time. She was someone who had been raised with the understanding that the world was not a safe place.

I spun back toward my mirror, checking to see if I was presentable enough to leave my room. Well, I looked a little lazy, but a belt would tie the outfit together enough. I grabbed the black belt off the end of my bed and threw it around myself as we exited the room.

Cymbeline ran ahead, and I followed. As suspicious and spunky as she was to most people, she was actually quite thoughtful towards me. She used to get annoyed at me for running around the castle, but now she initiated it, knowing how much I enjoyed it.

Once we reached the entrance to the Solstice, we slowed down. She was panting as she placed her hand over her heart.

"Didn't do much running in your life before all this?" I asked with a playful grin.

She pulled the corner of her mouth to the side.

"Come on, Cym, tell me one thing about your past life. Were you upper class? Be honest."

She snorted. "Of course I was," she said proudly, placing a hand on her hip. "Were you?"

"I've told you!" I laughed, "I was a... a..." I searched for words she could connect with, "... a healer training to be a scholar."

She nodded primly, "Yes, well, that makes sense."

"Hey, don't give me those judgmental looks!" I pointed teasingly, "There's nothing wrong with scholarship!"

"I didn't say there was," she said, "Where I come from, the religious scholars and the healers are one and the same. They are greatly respected in our culture," she paused, then mumbled, "regardless of what my *father* had to say about them."

Ah—a window into her past! "Who, uh..." I started to walk forward nonchalantly into the Solstice, the large dome-like hall at the center of Winter's End. "Who was your father? Somebody important?"

Cymbeline's face fell. She shook her head. "I... don't want to talk about him."

"Was he cruel to you, Cym?" I asked quietly.

She shot me a defensive look, then softened. She gave a single nod.

"I'm sorry..." It occurred to me at that moment that Momentum—the master of the house—might remind her of her father. Perhaps that was why she was so distrusting toward him. It didn't, however, explain why he was such a brat towards her.

"Leo," Cymbeline pointed up at the wall. "See all these big tapestries hanging on the walls?"

I followed her gaze. Tapestries so large one could barely see the tops, lined the walls of the great hall. They depicted historical events, it seemed. "Yeah," I said, "I sometimes come here just to study them. So beautiful. Momentum commissioned them from the Thread Faerie a *thousand* seasons ago. That's basically a thousand years!"

"Yes," Cymbeline said as her eyes wandered across the depictions, "I know... but Leo, what do you think was up on these walls *before* the tapestries?"

My eyes widened. This house was indeed more than seven thousand seasons old, according to Momentum. "Great question!"

"Well," the corner of her mouth curled up into a smile. "I sort of had this idea..." She walked over to one of the tapestries and pointed to its bottom rim. The tops and bottoms of each tapestry curled around golden poles, which were mounted to the wall to keep them in place. This tapestry, however, seemed to have been vandalized. The bottom pole had been pulled loose and was laying on the ground.

"Did *you* do this?" I asked, feeling both worried and impressed at the same time.

She nodded proudly. "Yes, well, I am sure he can put it back up again. Plus, he already hates me. So, why not give him a reason?"

I chuckled, "You sassy Faerie."

"Anyway, look," with some effort, she lifted the bottom of the tapestry to look beneath it. I stepped forward to help. We pulled at the tapestry far enough to see a bit of the dark, stone wall behind it. "Look," she said again, pointing at the wall.

I gasped. Carved into the wall was evidence of a painted stone mural, sculpted in intricate detail.

"Look," she brushed her hand against the stone, "Look at *this*."

As my eyes adjusted to the dark lighting under the tapestry, I could see that she was stroking what looked like a large foot. It was a deep black in color, adorned in toe rings and anklets. I raised my eyebrows.

"There's... other murals under here!" I said in astonishment.

"Momentum said he knew my mother," Cymbeline said urgently, "Look at that foot—could there be a picture of *her* under here?"

We dropped the tapestry, which was in truth quite heavy, and stepped back.

"I wonder why he would have covered it up," I mused. Were there other, older, historical events depicted behind the tapestries, ones Momentum was keen to forget?

"Well?" Cymbeline said as a dark gleam of mischievousness glowed from her eyes.

"Oh!" I stepped back, laughing nervously. "You're not going to..." the alarm bells manned by the 'good boy' inside me were ringing loudly inside my head.

"Come *on*, Leo!" Cymbeline tugged at my sleeve, "If my mother is behind there, I deserve to know who she was!"

"Didn't you *know* your mother, Cymbeline?"

"I know the woman who raised me, yes. But she was someone here before she ever came to my world. I need to know why Momentum hates me so much!"

I sighed. "Oh, what the hell," I shrugged. "Yeah, let's make the master of the house angry by vandalizing his hall, and uncovering old, painful memories." I meant it sarcastically, but Cymbeline responded with a joyful clap of her hands, anyway.

"Yes!" she exclaimed as her wings flew out into view. I jolted, stumbling back in surprise. It didn't matter how many Faeries lived in Winter's End, now, it still always shocked me when they showed their wings.

"What are you doing?" I asked, watching as she flew into the air.

"I am going to yank out that second pole!" She called as she moved toward the top of the tapestry.

I cranked my head back to watch her. "Be careful!"

"Leo, don't stand there, it could fall on you! It's heavy," she said as she pulled at one end of the pole.

I rushed backwards, hugging the opposite wall with my back. She was right. The massive pole falling from that height could kill me!

"Uh... are you sure this is a good idea? *Augh*!" I yelped as someone poked me in the side. I whipped my head sideways to see Momentum leaning against the wall beside me, watching Cymbeline silently. "Um, hey," I mumbled. Are you... are we going to get in trouble?"

"In trouble?" he snorted. "Sure."

We both turned our heads to watch as Cymbeline yanked the pole free of the wall. A tempestuous wave of wind hit us as the massive tapestry dropped like a tidal wave to the ground. As the pole hit the tile floor, a disturbing clank echoed around the hall. I was *sure* I heard something crack.

Momentum blinked lazily. "She broke my damn floor," he mumbled.

"Uh," I scratched my head. Why wasn't he yelling, or scolding—or even telling us to stop?

I turned toward Cymbeline as she floated down to the ground. I rushed to her side. I was about to tell her that Momentum was watching us but hesitated when I saw her face. She was gazing up at the wall with a look of awe. I turned and found myself doing the same.

Behind the tapestry had been hiding an ancient depiction, sculpted into the walls of the solstice, then painted in intricate detail. The woman at the center of the image did, indeed, look like Cymbeline, with her black skin, her white hair, her yellow eyes, and her striking beauty. She was a Faerie with six large wings; they were black feathered hawk's wings, mottled with brown spots. One of her arms was stretched out, holding a sword, and the other gently held a bundle of wheat. One side of her face looked angry, while the other looked kind. Under her feet was a hoard of people forming a pile on which she stood. Some were dead, and some were bowing to her happily. Behind her head was a bright white circle, resembling a halo.

Down near the bottom of the sculpture was an inscription, written in a language I didn't recognize, though being in Raqia where Language was no barrier, I could still understand it. The title read: *The Moon Queen*; and the subtitle: *Her reign will end.*

The image was disturbingly stupefying. I found myself entranced with her face. It was both lovely and terrifying, and I couldn't look away.

"She was... my friend," Momentum said. His voice came from between us.

"How could..." Cymbeline began, then her voice weakened into silence.

I turned to look at her; a tear was escaping her eye.

"I don't understand," she spoke again, "how anyone could call her their friend. Look at her; she's... evil."

"A long time ago," Momentum said softly, "my friend and I used to travel to Earth—the place that Leo comes from—to keep watch over it. I would bring back books, culture, plays, songs," he paused to sigh. "The Fae didn't know about the portal we had, and so the only way they could know anything about the Earth was if *I* told them. Temmy was just a kid when she started getting interested in Earth stories—of *Faerie Stories*, as most people call them."

"Temmy," I said, "Was that—?"

"My mother," Cymbeline said, her eyes still locked on the illustration.

"We would bring her trinkets and treasures," Momentum continued, "We would bring her story books that she liked, and she just *loved* them."

We? I thought, who was the 'we' in this story?

"We would put on these plays," he went on, "depicting historical events that happened on the Earth, and she became one of our lead actors. Of course, no one knew they were from a real place, They sort of assumed that we were making it all up. We became sort of popular as culture-setters in Arelle. Well," he shrugged, "We sort of took Temmy in under our wings. We felt bad for her. She was the first Faerie of her kind, but no one knew what her powers were; no one knew how to train her, or how she gained magik. She absorbed practically no Magik—just trickles—so all she had was enough to just exist. Any time other

Faeries would talk about the glowing lights they saw around things, we would always find her crying in a corner a short time later. But Earth things gave her something to get excited about. She *lived* for our plays and stories."

Cymbeline turned her head, making a face of confusion. She studied Momentum for sincerity. "My mother?" she asked, "*crying*?"

"Strange, right?" Momentum chuckled. "But yes, in the early days, she was a very tender girl, not unlike yourself."

Cymbeline flushed, taking the comment as an insult rather than a compliment.

"So, time went on," he said, looking back up at the mural, "and she became more and more like a sister to us. Eventually, she began to realize that Earth was a real place. She *begged* us to take her there. We said 'no' over and over again. We *knew* it was a slippery slope. If we took one Faerie to Earth, others would find out about it." Momentum let out a drawn out sigh. "But she wore us down. Like I said, we felt bad for her. She was a Faerie with no calling, no power." Momentum hesitated, pausing to rub his eyes. "Hell—why didn't we listen to ourselves?"

"What happened?" Cymbeline asked, gazing back up at the depiction with the pile of human bodies, some dead, some alive.

"We brought her to Earth," he said. "And then we realized which Faerie she was, and so did she."

I gazed at the glowing white circle behind her head, painted in a glossy, luminous white. "The Moon Faerie," I guessed.

"She was the first Moon Faerie." Momentum said solemnly. "Without access to the Earth, who could know it? All we ever see of the moon from up here is a glowing white light somewhere in the North Sea."

"What is the moon?" Cymbeline asked innocently. We both looked at her.

"It is like the sun," Momentum said, "but it shines at night, and not as bright."

"Didn't you tell me about this before?" she asked me. "It's like some sort of star?"

"No," said Momentum, "It's much, much bigger than a star. Anyway, the Moon is like the sun in that it rules over many things on the Earth. It affects oceans, harvests, seasons, and, well, it meant she could gain more power than she knew what to do with."

"So, what happened?" Cymbeline asked in suspense.

"We lost her." Momentum said in a distant voice. "She...she became obsessed. After a life of meaningless existence and ridicule from other Faeries, she found that she was like a deity on the Earth. The humans of the Earth, whom she had learned to love from all our stories and books, began to worship her. Finally—she found a purpose. All that power and worship. It destroyed the woman she once was. She lived there on the Earth, ruling and suppressing nations for *centuries*, and we couldn't stop her."

"Centuries?" I asked, realizing he was talking about *my* world. "Would I know her by name?"

"I don't know," he shrugged, "she had many names, and she ruled distantly, like a god of ancient times. But she did what no Faerie should ever do. She ruled humans. It took me so long to catch her, and when I finally did, I didn't know what to do with her so I..." he looked over at Cymbeline, "I trapped her in a world with no moon."

"I see," Cymbeline nodded, "Paidion."

"Yeah," Momentum nodded, "I told her to stay away from me, and I would stay away from her. I knew not what or who she became in Paidion. I can see now she married and had a family."

Cymbeline nodded. I could see anger appearing on her face. "Yes, she married." She sighed, turning to look at Momentum. "So, I am the child of your worst enemy?"

"Yes," he said blankly.

"And that is why you hate me?" she asked as if she already knew the answer.

"No," Momentum looked down at the ground as he folded his arms. "That is not why I hate you."

Cymbeline's mouth dropped open, gasping in offense. She shook her head side to side, looked at me for one, helpless moment, then ran off.

"Seriously?" I walked over and slapped him on the shoulder angrily. "Why did you have to be so mean? You've just told her something really hard to hear about her mother, and then—"

"Leo," Momentum patted my shoulder, "I'm sorry, just... leave me alone about this."

I opened my mouth to speak but hesitated as he walked silently away from me. Perhaps Cymbeline was right. Perhaps he did hate her, after all! But, *why?*

I found myself processing that event over and over in my mind as I helped the Faeries prepare for the second Firstday Feast. There had been a big party the night before, and now today, there would be another. It was their custom to celebrate every night on the first week of a season. It was pretty cool being a part of a community with such rich traditions; I felt like I was a part of something bigger than myself, like I was one of those little people painted into the background of a famous painting.

I was busy setting a table, with my mind dancing around like a kite in the wind, when Hanz approached me. He was wearing an attractive blue button-down suit, with long coattails and knee-high boots. His hair was tied in a knot atop his head, and his face perfectly shaven.

"Leo," he said in that strong, charismatic voice, "Good Firstday to you! How fare you, brother?"

"Ah, hi," I straightened. "Good Firstday!" He called me 'brother' because we were the only humans at Winter's End; it was a nice sentiment, and yet the term felt a little patronizing rather than endearing. I couldn't figure out why, but Hanz and I seemed to be like water and oil, we just couldn't jive with each other. "I, uh," I dropped a couple cloth napkins onto the floor, "I *fare*, uh—well. I fare thee—*erm*—well... Fare thee well!" I wilted. "I'm, uh... good?"

"Leo," Hanz leaned toward me from the other side of the table, resting his hands upon it. "How'd it go with Cymbeline?"

"Huh?" I blinked. How did he know about what happened with Cymbeline earlier that day? "How did—?"

"You know," he whispered, "You said you would talk to her about joining the Purple Order. How did it go? You *did* talk to her, didn't you? 'Cause I am really counting on you here, brother!"

I shrunk a little. "I didn't exactly say I would talk to her about that, Hanz," I began.

"Oh yes you did!" His muscles flexed, and for a moment the warrior flashed his brilliance threateningly at me. "You definitely said you would."

I definitely didn't, but I wasn't exactly going to contradict him point blank! "Hanz," I said meekly, "I am not sure it's the greatest idea for her to join your order."

"I told you yesterday, Leo," Hanz leaned even closer, his sharp eyes boring holes into mine. I dropped a few more napkins. "She is the felling Transport Faerie, and she could get us *into* Somenus' throne room! When my sister sends the signal that she's found the weapon, we could go! Hades—we could use her to sneak in and find the weapon ourselves!"

Use her—yes, he was reminding me why I didn't like the idea. I tried to appear a little large, puffing out my chest. "Hanz, she's still in a really fragile stage. She's only just started learning to store magik this last season! I don't think it's a good idea to—"

"She's the Faerie of *Movement*, Leo," Hanz said in a condescending tone, "She's probably already more powerful than every other Faerie here! Don't you know the Faerie of Movement is one of the Original Eight?"

"Hanz, this has nothing to do with how much magik she's got, it's about getting her to enlist in a war she doesn't understand!"

"Leo," he vocalized my name as if he were cursing, "You are a human, you don't understand the world of Faeries. Whether she understands or not, this *is* her war! If she didn't spend so much time with *you*, she probably wouldn't be so confused still! She needs to spend time with her own people."

I frowned. He always managed to spin my strengths as weaknesses. I had been proud of how I helped bridge the gap between her world and this one. I may not have been a Faerie, but we both were the only people who had not been raised in Raqia. Cymbeline was scared of the Faeries; I thought I was helping her warm up to them! Even so, the way Hanz spoke to me—I began to doubt myself.

"She does spend time with the Faeries," I said weakly.

"Not enough time," Hanz said as he straightened, "She's always wandering over to the Winter Wing. She seldom eats meals with the rest of us, and so far, she has been extremely guarded. Leo, you're like a dam, holding back her waters from joining in with ours. Let her go, set her free."

"What are you saying?" I snapped. "You don't want me to be friends with her? You want me to stay away?" I scoffed.

"Leo, I am just asking you to encourage her to join our order. She would greatly benefit from being a part of a bigger Faerie community. It would give her something to live for!"

I paused, thinking. He *could* be right. The Faeries in the Purple Order were amazingly noble and kind. Sure, some of them were odd, and I wasn't very fond of Hanz himself, but it would give her an identity that was tied to *this* world. Was my skepticism toward Hanz and his order preventing her from getting close to her own people?

"I do want her to make more friends here," I admitted, "But she doesn't *have* to join your order, does she?"

"Let me worry about that," he said as a smile appeared on his face. He had the look of victory emanating from him. "Just tell her that she should be a part of our mission. Tell her *you* think it's a good idea."

"That's not what I—"

"Thank you, brother!" he said brightly as he started to dash away, "I'll remember what you've promised, and I'll check in with you tomorrow!"

"I," I jumped, dropping the rest of the napkins, "I didn't say I would!" He was gone. I melted a little. *Man*, that guy really knew how to kill my confidence. Every conversation with him was like that; they always ended with me feeling like a cog in his machine that required some greasing.

"Leo, have you seen Cymbeline around?" Rowyn trotted up from behind. "Oh. I thought you would have finished the napkins by now."

"Oh!" I blustered as I looked around at my spilled pile. "I'm sorry!"

"Well, we can't use those now they've been on the ground," she shook her head. "Leo! What's got you so distracted today?"

"I..." I remembered Cymbeline, "I've been worried about someone..."

"Cymbeline?" she asked with her head cocked to the side.

"Huh? How did you know?"

She smiled sweetly. "I heard her crying in her room before she went for a walk on the beach."

"Oh..." my heart sighed. "Poor thing."

"What happened?" she asked, taking a step forward to touch my arm.

"Oh, Momentum told her some stuff about her past," I said vaguely, not wanting to trespass on her privacy.

Rowyn nodded. "You care for her, don't you?"

"Yeah, I do," I said distantly. Then I turned to see the smirk on the Fauna Faerie's face. "Oh! Oh, Rowyn! No, no, no, no... not like *that*!"

"*Mhmm*!" she hummed knowingly.

"No, seriously," I could feel myself perspiring, "Rowyn, I really care about her. But she's like a sister to me, I... I don't think about her like," I sighed, "Oh, *please* don't go spreading rumors that might hurt her!"

"Calm down, Leo," Rowyn laughed. "I won't say a word!"

"It's not that I—" I paused as my ears twitched. A loud booming sound was echoing throughout the Autumn dining hall where we were preparing for the Firstday Feast. The room grew still as everyone looked about excitedly. It was a knock on the front door.

"Do you think another Faerie has come to find shelter?" Rowyn asked excitedly.

"I don't know," I said as I moved involuntarily toward the sky bridge. "I better go find out."

It had become the custom that Momentum, Hanz and I went to the door whenever there was a knock. Originally, it had just been Momentum and I, since it was Momentum's house, and for some reason he liked my company, so I always tagged along. But as the head of the Purple Order, Hanz declared it was his own duty to be there in case a Faerie was coming in need of shelter. Just so as not to overwhelm whoever the visitor was at any given time, Momentum wouldn't allow anyone else to come when there was a knock.

As I approached the front doors, I could see Momentum was already standing there, waiting for us.

"Who do you think it is?" I asked, panting as I jogged to his side.

"It's not hard to guess," Momentum mumbled, "I'd know that voice anywhere."

"Voice?" I asked. My question was quickly answered as someone began to bellow from the other side.

"Let me in, damn you! I know you're in there, Aorist! What are you waiting for? Open the damn door!"

I raised my eyebrows.

Hanz quickly joined us. He stood on Momentum's left, straightening his clothes for a moment. "Is it a Faerie?" he asked.

"No," Momentum said, rubbing his mouth. Was I mistaken, or was that a grin he was hiding behind his hand?

"Who is it?" Hanz asked, eyeing both of us. I shrugged.

The pounding resumed, louder this time.

"Damn you, Aroist, open the door!" The man screamed.

To my surprise, Hanz' face paled with terror. His mouth opened and closed wordlessly. I turned back to Momentum.

"Momentum?" I whispered, "Who is it?"

22

— Clover —

What is Iniquity?

Clover was tired—and Elves seldom grow tired. He stood there swaying beside Patro's bed as the master of the house slept, feeling increasingly unsure if he would be able to keep himself awake. In the past, pulling an all-nighter wasn't a difficult thing for the Elf, but after months of being required to do so on a regular basis, the desperate need for slumber tormented him.

Since the last assassination attempt eight weeks ago, Patro had not only become more paranoid, but he had also gotten cocky—flaunting his expert bodyguard and requiring Clover to be by his side at all times. Clover seldom had time to himself, and when he did, he tried to use it to sleep. When Patro the head of the Sapphire House slept, Clover would stand beside the bed, listening to the hateful man snore, while keeping his ears alert for intruders. In the early weeks, when he began his service in the Sapphire House, Clover had slept at night like any other member of the household, but once Patro found out that his superhuman Elf could go for days without sleep, he had tested that fact regularly.

Clover stood there, wondering if falling asleep would be so bad. If someone assassinated the head of the house, he could finally get some shut eye!

Clover frowned, disappointed in himself for entertaining the idea. As much as he despised Patro, he was still determined to keep his word and protect the man so that he could find a way to speak with the king of Bavel.

Patro's steadily loud snores began to break as the man erupted into a gravelly coughing fit. Clover opened his eyes, watching the man who sat up suddenly, throwing his covers off of himself.

"Clover!" Patro gasped. Clover stared at the man silently. Patro turned to see him there. "Oh good, you're still here. I thought someone had..." he began to stand from his bed, stroking his neck with his fingers as if he had expected to find something there.

"Yes, I am still here." Clover said flatly. "You ordered me to be here."

Patro glanced at Clover. "I was sure Appius would make an attempt on my life in my sleep last night."

"You seem to be sure of that *every* night," said Clover.

Patro stood, ignoring Clover's insinuations that he was growing paranoid. "Have you noticed Florus lately? He seems to be finding excuses to be around me more and more. He is an assassin, you know. I hired him once or twice myself." Florus was the second son of Appius, Patro's younger brother.

"I do not spy for you, Patro." Clover said as he crossed his arms. "I will protect your life, but I will not take part in your family's political games."

"Political games?" Patro pulled his dressing robe over his shoulders angrily. "Protecting me from assassins in my own home isn't a game, Clover— it's my *life!*"

Clover restrained his annoyance in silence. "You are awake now," Clover said, "and alive. So, I am going to take some personal time."

Patro grunted anxiously. "Rejoin me at lunch," he said, "Appius is throwing the Firstday Feast at his house today, and I want you there." He turned away from Clover to wash his hands and face.

"I will be there," Clover said, pausing. "But Patro, there is something I must speak with you about first."

Clover didn't have to see Patro's face to know he was angry; he felt the intensity radiating off of the man. "If this is about your meeting with the—"

"You told me that if I served you well, you would help me get an audience with the king, Patro," Clover said firmly. "It has been a whole season since I came into your house, and I cannot wait any longer. You must help me now."

Patro splashed water onto his face aggressively, and Clover could hear his breathing grow heavier. "Boy, I told you that I would help you if I *could*. I still know of no way to get an audience with the king."

"Perhaps I could suggest something," Clover persisted, following the angry Patro who was now pacing to the other side of the room in search of his clothes.

"I really don't have time for—"

"I know that the king's birthday is being celebrated on Mansday, and all of the Fifth Level families are sending him gifts. Whosoever's gift is his favorite is invited to attend his birthday banquet," Clover continued, though he could hear Patro growling under his breath. "If you receive that invitation, I want you to include me in the party."

"Clover." Patro turned to the Elf and stared daggers into his eyes. "Why would I?"

"I have saved your life countless times, and I have served you well. I have always kept my word. You must keep yours. You must get me an audience with the king."

Patro sighed. "Let me think about it. I haven't even decided which gift I will give the king yet."

"Please decide by the Firstday feast today," Clover said calmly. "If you cannot help me, I will leave your service and leave Bavel."

Patro's eyes widened in astonishment. The two men looked at one another silently as Patro studied Clover for any signs of a bluff. No, he knew Clover too well by now; Clover never lied.

"You can't leave now—Appius will kill me for sure! I... I need more time."

"Very well," Clover said, "I will give you until the luncheon at Appius' House on Watersday. You have until then to decide. But if you do not aid me, I *will* resign." Without waiting for Patro's response, Clover left.

Clover didn't expect Patro to help him. After a season in the man's service, he had witnessed a disturbing character flaw. Patro did not use words for their meanings; he used them for their effects. He did not care about what was true or honorable; he cared about getting what he wanted and used others to his own advantage. Many times, Patro had promised or implied things to his family members when he never intended on fulfilling his word. Yet, he was always careful to keep those close to him trusting and hoping that he would one day come through. He was, after all, the head of the house who held all power. No one wanted to fall out of his graces, and so they forgave this flaw, hoping they could manipulate him in the same way. This dynamic gave birth to a manipulative and narcissistic family culture in which everyone was comfortable to live; everyone but Clover, that is.

Clover left Patro's residence and wandered over to his own little house which was nestled nearby. He groaned seeing a few other Sapphire family members waiting outside his door. No matter how many times he refused them, the other members of Patro's household seemed to see Clover as a tool to be used for their own schemes. He walked past the three who were standing there, ignoring their greetings, and unlocked his residence.

He could hear them calling his name, but he disregarded them, slamming the door behind him. Sighing, Clover looked around the little bungalow. He didn't have any possessions that were truly his own aside from the things he brought with him when he entered Bavel. Though he had a residence and a job, he continued to see himself as a nomad. He was still on a mission, and he did his best to stay vigilant.

Solo laid on his bed lazily. The ram had grown quite large, and his wool was long, though kept. Two enormous, curling horns protruded from his head giving him an elegance that made Clover think of him as royal. Clover dragged his feet over to the bed and sat down beside the ram, patting his head.

"Sorry I didn't come back last night; I hope you had enough food."

I did. Solo responded in a voice that only Clover could hear. *But I wondered where you were. I was afraid you would not come back.*

"I will always come back," Clover said firmly, though he didn't understand why his eyes were watering when he said it. He leaned forward and wrapped his arms around Solo's neck. His mind flashed back to when he had held Andrew, Solo's mother, as she died. The watery eyes turned into a gentle stream of tears. Clover shook away the feeling of sorrow and sat up, patting the ram's head once more. "You are so strong and beautiful," Clover said, "I know Isabella will be pleased with you."

You are pleased with me, said Solo, *that is all I care about.*

This made Clover smile. Then he felt a soft hand touch his arm. Turning to look beside him, he saw TSB, the little gnome, smiling.

"Have you brushed Solo today?" Clover asked, feeling the sheep's wool. The gnome shook his head, then ran across the bed to search for the comb. Clover chuckled to himself, then gazed at the bed, imagining how it would feel to lie on it. "I am afraid I will not get any sleep just yet," he said more to himself than to his companions. "It is an important day for me. I just gave Patro an ultimatum."

Solo lifted his head and gazed at Clover with wide eyes. *Really?*

"Remember I said that I would wait until the beginning of the new season, and no longer?" Clover said, "Well, today is the Firstday of Ashen Shoots. I can't wait any longer—it's time."

Solo's eyes closed halfway. *I am worried you will anger the head of the house.*

"So am I," Clover whispered.

It's my first Firstday, then? Solo tilted his head to the side, smiling in the way that ram's smile. *What does Ashen Shoots mean?*

"Not sure," Clover shrugged, "Patro hasn't really read the full announcement from the skydeacon yet; he's only told me the name. I'll find out more today at the feast. How has TSB been treating you?" Clover smirked as the gnome began to pull the comb through Solo's thick wool.

Little Thief is doing fine, said the ram, *though he pines when you are gone.*

Clover chuckled. "Does he? Hah, well... does he, *erm*," Clover cleared his throat, "Does he ever *talk* to you?"

Solo wagged his head back and forth. *I've told you this before, I don't hear his voice.*

Clover nodded. "Yeah..." He peered up at the ceiling thoughtfully.

Clover?

"Hmm?"

Why do you look so sad?

Clover glanced down at the ram. "Sad?" He sighed. "I don't know. It's this place, I think. I can't wait to get out of this den of iniquity, and yet if I leave without seeing the king, I will have failed."

Iniquity? Solo blinked, *What is iniquity?*

Clover smiled, reaching forward to stroke Solo's neck. "It's not something you would understand. It is when someone does something wrong, like scolding when one should praise, or killing when one should defend."

Solo dropped his eyes solemnly. *Is it like what happened to my family? They should have been with me, but instead they do not exist.*

"Yes…" Clover's heart squirmed within his chest. He hated explaining evil to such a pure and innocent thing. There wasn't a drop of evil in Solo's entire being. "Well, I need to go do something, and then I will come back for some sleep. Then we can all have some time together. Goodbye, little ones." As he said this, he placed his hands on the heads of his two companions and yawned.

TSB looked up at him with wide, longing eyes.

"I will see you soon," Clover assured him, "I promise."

As Clover left his house, his path was quickly blocked by a tall, opportunistic young man. It was Domitianus, the first son of Appius and Patro's nephew. He wore a yellow suit with blue trim and sapphire buckles, and his wavy brown hair was perfectly formed into a pulled back tail. Clover wanted to curse under his breath at the sight of him but contented himself with staring lifelessly into the man's eyes.

"Ah, Clover!" Domitianus smiled charismatically as if he had bumped into Clover by chance. "Just the man I was—"

"What?" Clover cut him short. It was no secret to everyone in the Sapphire House that Domitianus wanted Patro dead; the man, in fact, flaunted the fact.

"May I walk with you, to...*wherever* you..." Domitianus jogged quickly alongside Clover who had moved past him, marching toward the Sapphire House's main gate.

"You seem to be doing it without my permission anyway," Clover mumbled.

"Hah, humorous as always!" The charmer quickened his pace to match Clover's. "My good man, I was wondering if I could entice you with—"

"*What*?" Clover stopped walking and turned to face the young man. "You want to offer me *more* money this time to kill Patro in his sleep? Or stand idly by while your goons take care of him?"

"Not *money*," Domitianus lowered his voice and moved closer to Clover. "Something money can't buy!"

Clover leaned away from him, disturbed by the intimacy of his whispering. "I don't want to know what it is. The answer is '*No*.'"

"You will not let me say it," Domitianus chuckled nervously, then stepped close once more in determination, gripping Clover's wrist. "*Hadriana*."

"Your wife? What about her?" Clover paused, his stomach tightening like he was going to vomit. "No! Leave me alone!"

"She is known all over the Fifth Level for her beauty," Domitianus ran after Clover who tried to dash away, stepping in front of his path once more. "*Everybody* was jealous of me when I secured her as my wife. Now. She has agreed to please you, and she's excited by the idea, even!" He raised his eyebrows enticingly.

Clover waved his arms in front of his face, as if a swarm of bees were attacking him. "Will you please *stop*? You people make me sick!"

The nobleman grabbed Clover by the wrists and held him steadily for a moment, staring into his eyes intensely. "Do not insult me by telling me you are not interested in my wife. Be honest with yourself. Is she beautiful?"

Clover sighed, closing his eyes. "*Please*," he said quietly, "Stop."

Domitianus threw Clover back a few steps, growling angrily. "How dare you ask to sleep with my wife, you knave!" He crowed loudly, letting his voice be heard by the others who had been waiting to speak with him.

Clover shook his head. "You can revile me if you want to—*kill* me, even—but I will not be swayed by your words."

"I am sure that could be arranged," Domitianus growled.

"Arrange it then," Clover said with a stubborn stare.

Domitianus gritted his teeth in fury but said nothing. He eyed Clover from head to toe, as if studying him for any weakness. Clover had become accustomed to this. *Everyone* seemed to be looking for ways to manipulate one another, and he was very often the target, probably because he was the only one in the entire household who Patro seemed to trust. This made Clover's life in Bavel a living hell. Daily, he was battered with temptations and invitations to become like the rest of these people. And the worst part of it all was what he felt happening inside him. In the early weeks, he had stood his ground, blocking off his mind and heart to the futile offers. But as time went on, while he didn't give in, he gave *pause*. To Clover, that in itself was failure.

Even now, the image of Hadriana, Domitianus' beautiful wife, passed before his eyes. A thud hit his heart at the thought that she was actually being offered to him. He did not want her. He did not pursue her—but she was *available* to him. He had withstood these constant offers for some time, but he felt his heart growing tired of the constant bombardment.

It was time to leave.

Domitianus stormed away, leaving Clover free to press on towards the exit to the Sapphire Estate. The two others who had been waiting to speak with Clover caught up to him just as he was about to leave the grounds. Two women stopped on either side of him with their arms crossed. The first was Marcella. She was the wife of Agrippa, Patro's firstborn son, and therefore Patro's daughter-in-law. She had black eyes and black hair, reminding Clover of a Raven, always seeming to hover over recent death. The other was Decima. She was the unmarried daughter of Appius, and Patro's niece. She was young and pretty, but without the innocence which usually complements the former attribute. Clover looked back and forth between the two sadly, inwardly mourning what they could have been if they had been born into decent families.

"You two again?" Clover groaned. "I am going for a walk, please leave me to my peace."

"Where are you always running off to?" Decima asked suspiciously. "Do you have some sort of lover out there?"

"He probably is leveraging his position to get into the Ruby House." Marcella chuckled. The women stood before him, adorned in their big skirts and low-cut bodices, carefully studying Clover's expressions.

Clover stared blankly at them. "I'm not surprised at your insinuations," he said, "I don't expect you all to think well of me, for you see your own flaws in others."

"*Flaws?*" Marcella scoffed. "Get off your throne, *saint*." 'Saint', Clover had quickly learned, was an insult the Bavelonians used for those who found value in virtue, believing it to be weakness.

"What do you two schemers have to say to me today?" Clover asked in a tired voice. "Say it quickly so that I can go for my walk."

"Clover, you know better than *anyone* how evil Patro is, and how he rules this house with tricks and schemes," Marcella spoke in a commanding voice. "Agrippa is not like his father; he will lead this family to greater prosperity. Once Patro dies, will you have a position in this house? No. You will be sent from the city. But if you help us, as the wife of the future head of the house, I can make sure you have a comfortable future here."

"You have said this many times," Clover replied, "You are eager for Patro to die so you can make changes. And *you?*" Clover turned to Decima, "You want the same thing—for Patro to die—for he will not marry you off to the Ruby house as you desire."

"Am I wrong to hate the man who will not let me marry?" Decima huffed, crossing her arms. "Anyway, you have the power in your hands to end this misery for all of us! Work with us, and we will help you. We will give you anything you want—*anything*!"

"We will give you an audience with the king." Marcella said firmly, holding Clover's gaze. Clover closed his eyes once more, taking in a deep breath. There was nothing he wanted more than to just leave Bavel. If he could get an audience with the king, it would all be over.

"Please, don't offer me this." Clover sighed. The two women glanced at each other excitedly. This was the nearest sign of weakness they had seen in him yet. He was tempted, and they leapt on the opportunity.

"Clover, we all know it is the only thing you really want. *We* could make it happen for you. It would be so easy!" He knew not to believe her promises, but he still didn't respond.

"And Clover!" Decima chimed in. "You do not have to kill him. All you need to do is let me into his room while he sleeps. *No one* will blame you for that."

Clover hated himself for giving them an inch. He shook his head, No. They were lying. The only person with the power to give him an audience with the king was Patro himself. "Ladies," Clover said with his eyes half open, feeling fatigued in more ways than one, "Please do not ask me anymore. My answer will always be 'No.'"

Marcella and Decima glared hatefully at Clover, then each other.

"When we kill Patro, you will be the first to be burned with him." Decima venomed.

Clover nodded. "Alright."

"You pretend you are not afraid, but you *are*," Marcella said spitefully. "Inside that lifeless shell there is a scared little Faerie boy."

"I am an Elf."

"We *know* you are scared, Clover," Decima joined in on the hunt. "We know you cry yourself to sleep—when you *get* sleep, anyway."

Clover was accustomed to the jeering and mocking whenever he refused their offers, but today the words seemed to hurt somehow. He wasn't sure *why*, as he didn't think he was scared, and he didn't cry himself to sleep. But the words stung. Yes, his heart was growing weak. He didn't feel weak in his resolve to refuse them. No. It was that he didn't feel the strength to *hear* their offers anymore. He felt he would rather melt away into the dirt, passing into non-existence, rather than listen to their words anymore.

"I must go," he said quietly, turning away from their angered faces. He then opened the gate and left the Sapphire house.

Clover wandered down the Fifth Level Main Street. It was a circular road that ran the circumference of the Fifth Level of Bavel, with each family estate attached to it. The street was wide and paved with marble, and along the sides were rows of tall, pleasantly shaped Cypress trees. The Fifth Level was too high to tempt most birds, and so it was always eerily quiet, with only the sound of an occasional breeze flowing through the leafy trees. It was Clover's adopted ritual to circumnavigate the Main Street daily, but today he was too tired. Instead of wandering until he spotted his friend, he left the paved path, walked up to the edge of the city wall, and sat beside it.

Smelling the breeze, Clover leaned his head back against the wall and closed his eyes. Perhaps now, at least, he could slumber in peace. His mind replayed the events of the morning. He had done it. Yes—he had told Patro he was leaving. Even if he couldn't get the audience with the king, he could leave. The idea of leaving without an army somehow gave him more peace than getting the audience. He hated Bavel; he hated everything about it. He and his companions had survived there an entire season, but he feared for their lives the entire time. Yes, it was time to leave.

"Move along, loiterer!" A voice called from above loudly. Clover opened his eyes to gaze upwards above him where a Black Eagle was staring down at him from the top of the wall.

"*You* move along, I am trying to sleep." Clover said as closed his eyes again. Clover heard the Eagle drop down beside him gracefully into the grass.

"I said move along," the man said commandingly as he booted Clover in the side.

"Stop it!" Clover caught the man's heel quickly, then glared up into his eyes—Yuma.

Yuma grinned. Clover tugged on Yuma's foot roughly, toppling Yuma onto his back.

"Clover!" Yuma scrambled to his feet and dusted himself off. "I am on duty!"

Clover chuckled, closing his eyes again, pretending to return to his nap. "Then don't bother me."

Yuma paused for a moment, putting his hands on his hips. "I thought you came out here to talk to me."

Clover cracked an eye open. "Well, I guess I did."

"Then why are you ignoring me?" Yuma nudged Clover's side with the toe of his boot.

"Ow—*stop*!" Clover grabbed his foot again.

"*You* stop!" Yuma yanked his foot away then whacked Clover's head with his bow.

"*Ow*!" Clover stood angrily, lifting up his fists defensively. "Leave me alone, I am trying to sleep!"

"Sleep?" Yuma grinned. "What are you, a rough sleeper? This is a Noble Level. You shouldn't be sleeping outside." He pushed his bow forward, poking Clover's stomach with the tip. "I could have grounds to kick you out!

"I wish you would!" Clover shoved Yuma by the shoulders, knocking him to the ground. Yuma grunted as he hit the ground, then Clover leapt on him, grabbing his neck.

"Off me, Elf!" Yuma choked, grabbing onto Clover's wrists.

Clover grinned. "*Now* will you leave me alone?"

Yuma threw Clover aside easily, knocking his body gracelessly to the ground, then stood with a chuckle. "You think you're stronger than me?"

Clover stood slowly, dusting off his tunic. "I *know* I am...I am just tired."

"What is going on with you?" Yuma raised an eyebrow. "Why are you so moody today?"

The playfulness in Clover's face faded and he met Yuma's eyes with a look of sadness.

"What is it, Clover?" Yuma's face changed, and he stepped forward protectively. "Did something happen?" Clover shook his head, but his eyes grew glossy. "Clover, what *happened*?" Yuma pressed, growing concerned.

"Nothing!" Clover shrugged his shoulders. "Absolutely nothing. I just..." his voice trailed off, looking to the side. This was frustrating. Why did talking with Yuma make him feel like crying?

Yuma sighed and crossed his arms. "Alright, I believe you that nothing happened. Just tell me what you are feeling."

"I don't *know* what I am feeling." Clover said in a childish whine.

Yuma nodded slowly. "Are you sad?"

"Yes."

"Are you angry?"

"Yes."

"Alright, what made you sad?" Yuma asked, leaning on his longbow like a staff.

"I don't know. I think I am sad about who these people are," he gestured with his thumb back at the Sapphire House. "Or who they could have been."

"And what made you angry?" Yuma asked patiently.

"These people!" Clover exclaimed. "They keep trying to make me do, or listen to, all these horrible things!"

"Yeah," Yuma nodded solemnly. "Are they at it again? Trying to convince you to kill Patro?"

"They *always* are," Clover said defeatedly, "But today I just felt like... I felt like giving them what they want if it would mean they would stop."

Yuma's face changed, and he looked almost fearful. "*You*—giving in?"

"I know," Clover dropped his head to his chest and watched some of the tears fall from his eyes onto the ground like raindrops. "I am ashamed to say it."

"Oh, don't be." Yuma put his hand on Clover's shoulder. "I am proud of you, little brother. You still said 'No.'"

Those words were all Clover needed to hear. Though instead of making him feel happier, they seemed to strengthen his sadness. So, the teardrops continued. Something felt right about crying, so he reveled in it, seeing how long his tears would flow. It was a silent cry, however, like a gentle spring rain. Yuma cradled Clover's head under his arm and ruffled his hair playfully, chuckling.

"Ah, Clover. Only someone like you could live here for a season and still remain untouched."

"What do you mean?" Clover looked up with a swollen face. "Untouched? *Look* at me!"

Yuma chuckled again. "I just mean... most people acclimate themselves after a season passes. But you? You... you still act surprised when people here do the wrong thing. You are still so disturbed by their wickedness, even though you see it every day. But yes," he pointed at Clover's face, "you *do* look a mess."

Clover ventured a smile, letting himself find humor in his sorry state. A moment later, that smile was lost. "Yuma?"

"Yes?"

"I have given Patro an ultimatum."

Yuma raised his eyebrows. "*What*? What *kind* of ultimatum? Why didn't you tell me about it first?"

Clover shrugged. "I don't know, I just can't take it anymore. Anyway, all the nobles are preparing gifts for the king's birthday. If Patro's gift is the favored gift, he will be invited to the Birthday Banquet."

Yuma shook his head slowly. "Clover, it was not time to make a move yet. You should have waited for me. We could have planned this together!"

"I can't wait anymore, Yuma!" Clover broke into a yell. "I can't live there for one more *day*! You get to walk around above the walls, watching and observing. But I have to be *one* of them. I can feel myself becoming acclimated. I can't...I won't..."

"Alright, Clover," Yuma sighed, grabbing Clover's shoulder in a firm grip. "What is your plan, then?"

Clover straightened his back, meeting Yuma's eyes with confidence. "If he does not get me the audience, I will leave."

Yuma frowned. "That doesn't sound like a plan."

"It is not a plan, Yuma. It is a decision." Clover said firmly. "I will not stay here any longer."

"We cannot breach the gates of Arelle without an army, Clover."

"I don't care. I will not stay here a day longer—not if it changes me. I will *not* become one of them to get what I need. Do you remember the promise I made myself?"

Yuma widened his eyes, staring silently at Clover for a moment, then nodded. "I remember."

"I will not become evil to kill evil." Clover said.

"Neither will I, Clover."

"Patro will give me his answer by luncheon on Wingsday. When I hear from him, I'll meet you here at night to tell you what he said."

Yuma groaned, turning away to look up at the glassy heavens. "Clover I... from what you have told me about Patro, I don't expect him to give you an audience."

"I have to try," Clover shrugged.

"I know." Yuma leaned against the city wall, looking over toward the Fifth Level Barracks, one of the large buildings constructed along the top of the wall. "I've chatted with the general a few times about our plans. He is interested, though I am not ready to explicitly ask him for support. I would have wanted more time."

"Can you ask him anyway?" Clover stepped forward. Clover was so caught up in his own life, he had forgotten that Yuma had been working on his own plan.

"I will ask him. If he is on our side, it will really help. His pride would love to challenge Korbin's army, but he won't do anything without the support of the king."

Clover nodded. "Alright, well why don't you see if you can talk with him today." He began to walk back toward the Sapphire House with refreshed determination.

"Clover," Yuma grabbed him by the wrist, "What makes you think Patro will give the favored gift this year?"

Clover blinked thoughtlessly for a moment. "Um."

"Clover?"

"I didn't think about that," Clover said, "It was a gamble."

Yuma bowed his head with a groan. "Clover, if you are going to give an ultimatum, it needs to be..."

"Yuma!" Clover yelled, snapping Yuma into attention. "I gave it because *I* am done. Do you understand? I am done here!"

"Alright, Clover," Yuma sighed. "You have said enough. Go, then. I will be here at nightfall."

"Thanks," Clover mumbled, hobbling away hopelessly.

Yuma watched silently for a moment as the Elf plodded toward the Main Street, then exhaled loudly. "Clover?" he called.

Clover stopped walking to turn and give Yuma a depressed glance. "Yes?"

"I am sorry."

"For what?"

"I am sorry you've had to live there, I..." he looked to the side, "I hadn't thought very hard about what kind of pressure you were under there. I guess I just thought..."

"Thought what?" Clover asked blankly.

Yuma walked over to meet Clover, with his Black Eagle tunic and long thick hair flowing in the wind. "I thought of you as perfect."

Clover cocked his head to the side. "I don't understand."

"You are always so pure. I didn't think of you as someone who could be tempted or pressured by their kind of evil. I saw you as invincible."

"Why would you think that?"

"I," Yuma chuckled nervously, "I don't know. Anyway, I guess even someone as steadfast as you can become weary."

Clover rolled his eyes. "Why wouldn't living with people like this affect me? I am sorry to disappoint you, but I am *not* perfect."

"No," Yuma sighed, "Clover. I am trying to say something *nice* to you."

"Well, it doesn't *feel* like you are." Clover crossed his arms. "You are making me feel more guilty for being worn down by these people."

"I'm sorry," Yuma nodded. "I am trying to say I had false expectations of you. I didn't think about how hard this was for you. I think it makes me admire you more—to think you have stood firm in the midst of all this."

"But I am *not* firm, Yuma. That's what I am trying to tell you!" Clover suddenly waved his arms in the air. "They make me so angry, so out of control. They make me *feel* like killing! I hate it!"

"I am sorry," Yuma said again, putting his hands on Clover's shoulders. "We will get you out of here."

Clover froze, looking at his friend in the eyes. "Thank you. I—I am sorry I failed us."

Yuma shook his head. "You haven't failed. You're still trying. Let's just finish this day, and I promise you'll feel better than you do now."

Clover nodded, feeling lifted by that hopeful thought. "Okay."

"And hey—Happy Firstday!" Yuma smiled playfully. Clover tried to match his smile.

"Happy Firstday."

23

— Lola —

Hevel

I t's such an odd part of the story," Lola said cheerfully as she thumbed through her book, "I can't believe *that* is always the chapter you like to hear!"

"I find it compelling," Hevel said in his deep, melancholy voice. He was sitting cross-legged on the floor of his dreary, underground prison, with his back against a shadowy wall. As much as he liked it when Lola came to share his space, he felt it was gentlemanly to give her space. He usually kept to his own side of the cell, leaving Lola the more private end. That, however, didn't keep Lola from wandering over to his side whenever she felt social. And she felt social very often.

The Elven princess glided over to where Hevel was sitting with her book held high. Her long, tattered dress, which was essentially several layers of utilitarian front-cross robes, dragged behind her. Even when masking her figure with thick clothes, and her hair cut unevenly short, just below her ears, Lola still carried herself like an angelic, weightless princess.

"Let me see... Cosmo.... Cosmo..." Lola muttered, "Ah yes! Chapter XIII." The princess knelt beside Hevel, holding her book open in both hands. "I saw a ship sailing upon the sea, deeply laden as a ship could be; But not so deep as in love I am, For I care not whether I sink or swim." She paused. "From an Old Ballad." She then smiled as she read the second poem, "But Love is such a Mystery, I cannot find it out; For when I think I'm best Resolv'd, I then am most in doubt. By Sir John Suckling."

Hevel placed his hand on Lola's knee. She paused from her reading and looked up. "What is it, Hevel?"

Hevel, her gaunt Faerie cellmate, smiled. "When you asked me what my favorite chapter was, I didn't realize you were going to *read* it."

Lola blinked in surprise. "Well... then do you *not* want me to read it?"

Hevel chuckled. "Princess, you've read this same book to me every time they've sent you down here; I've heard it at least four times now!"

"Oh," Lola closed the book partway, leaving her thumb inside to keep her spot. "I'm afraid *Phantastes* in the only book I own, Hevel."

Hevel tilted his head to the side. "You're one of Somenus' household. You don't have access to more books?"

Lola's face brightened. "Oh! I had never thought to ask!"

Hevel chuckled. "That's because you're so fixated on that one story. What about it captures you so deeply? I'd love to know," he said sincerely. "Every time you come down here, you have that smile on your face. You don't make sense to me. It must be something about that book."

Lola turned the book in her hands. "I think..." her smile began to wane, "I think it's because it is a story of finding beauty and Romance—not for oneself, but for others. Anodos..." she paused, "Anodos *dies.*"

Hevel nodded thoughtfully. "And that... is a comfort to you?"

Lola looked up from her book suddenly, her bright eyes focusing on the Faerie in front of her. "Well, I think you should know better than anyone. Death is not always bad."

"You seem to be asking me more than telling me," Hevel said quietly as he rested his hands on his knees. "But yes, you are right: Death is not always bad. Bad death is bad, and good death is good."

"Yes," Lola said with resolve, "This book is about a good death. Anodos is in love, but he cannot be with the one he loves. Instead, he finds a greater way to love her."

Hevel narrowed his eyes. "Why do you think you are Anodos?"

"I think everyone is Anodos," Lola said with a shrug, but then her brow seemed to tighten with concern, "Though... perhaps me more than others."

"Tell me what you mean, child," said the Faerie. His purple eyes seemed to glow from his dark corner, and Lola thought she could see a glimpse of his wings, like transparent black curtains, surrounding them in a protective dome.

"I..." she lowered her voice to a whisper. "I just mean—I have had to learn to find beauty in a life where what I really wanted is withheld from me. And though I love someone, I cannot be with them because Somenus is my husband."

"Somenus isn't your husband," Hevel said. Lola's face grew pale. Hevel's comment hurt more than it helped. He sighed. "I am sorry, I didn't mean to make you feel shame."

"No, no," Lola said weakly, "Don't apologize." She sighed wistfully. "My life *is* shame now."

Hevel shook his head. "Do not say that, child. You have *nothing* to be ashamed of. Evil may have been done to you, but you have not let it *inside* you."

Lola jumped to her feet and dashed across the room.

"Lola!" Hevel rose unsteadily to his feet, "Lola, did I say something that hurt you?"

Lola faced her corner of the cell, sniffing with restrained tears. Hevel would not come closer if she did not want him to.

"Princess, what is it?"

Lola cleared her throat and combed her hair back with her fingers. She turned to face him, forcing a brave smile to spread itself up the corners of her mouth. "Not to worry, Hevel. I am myself again."

Hevel gazed at Lola from across the cell.

"Don't give me that mournful look," Lola marched back over to him, "It makes one feel so sad!"

"Lola," he sighed, "It is good to be sad sometimes, too."

"I don't disagree," she said as she tucked her book into one of her skirt pockets. "But now isn't the time to be sad. Now is when I get to be happy! It is the *Distancer* stage—it is when I am most free!"

Hevel raised one skeptical eyebrow. "*Distancer* stage?"

"Oh," Lola folded her hands together, "Didn't I tell you last time I was here? I've finally realized there are cycles to my husband's insanity." Husband—she still called Somenus that, even though he hadn't technically married her. Who was she if she wasn't his wife?

"Oh, yes?" Hevel brushed some of his long, wispy white hair behind his shoulder. "I haven't heard this yet. Go on."

"Well," Lola placed her fingertips together with a proud smile, "You see, he's become quite predictable. First, he is the Charmer, wooing and acting kind and thoughtful. He knows I like romance, so he always starts there. Then when I do not give him what he wants," she maintained her cheerfulness, but her eyes seemed to grow vacant, "He becomes the Villain, taking what he wants regardless of what I want. After the Villain is the best part, the Distancer. That is when he can barely stand to see me or even think of me, so he sends me far away. In the Distancer stage, I am the most free—and it tends to be when he sends me down here into the dungeons with you."

"Ah," Hevel nodded.

"After Distancer comes the Pining stage. That is when he still keeps me far away, but he begins to miss me and sends messengers to find out how I am doing. After that? It is back to the Charmer again." Lola sighed, dropping her hands, "And the cycle goes on, over and over."

"No wonder you are so cheery, even when you are in a dank, musty prison like this," Hevel said.

"Well, I also enjoy *your* company deeply!" Lola said earnestly, reaching out to place a hand on Hevel's arm.

The Faerie blanched at her touch. "Oh, Lola," he chuckled, "You don't have to say things like that just to flatter me. I am well aware of my effect on others."

"No!" Lola gasped, "You don't scare me at *all*!"

Hevel shook his head. "I know I do, Lola. It is my place on this world to scare people."

"Truly," Lola smiled sweetly, "If anything, I am *comforted* by your presence."

Hevel cringed, then wagged his head. "No, that's not exactly encouraging."

"Why not?"

"Because my presence becomes a comfort to those who are *dying*, Lola," Hevel said vacantly.

Lola paused for a moment, nodding silently, then said, "You once told me that only those who are dying could see your wings."

"That is true."

Lola exhaled as slowly as she could. "I see them sometimes, Hevel. I've known for some weeks now that I must be dying."

Hevel only stared at Lola silently.

"But surely you see now why this book is a comfort to me," she added, "Anodos is *free* in death, even after facing great evil!"

"I see," Hevel whispered. "You see Death as freedom, then? From Somenus?"

Lola's eyes widened into circles. "I..."

"Lola," Hevel reached forward to touch her cheek, "You said that you were like Anodos in that you could not be with the one you love. Who is it? Who is the one you love?"

Lola shook her head. "He isn't real."

"But who is it?"

"He," she glanced down at her feet, "he's a dream—a dream of someone who truly loves me; and someone who I truly love."

Hevel nodded. "Somenus?"

"What?" Lola gasped, shaking her head. "No! It is not like that. The king does come into my dreams sometimes, but this is different." A smile crept up her cheek. "He... he loves me so purely."

Hevel stroked Lola's cheek with his finger. "I am sorry for what has happened to you, child," he said. "But this does not have to be an end for you; you do not *have* to die."

Lola stared into the Death Faerie's deep eyes. "It is only a matter of time," she whispered, "I will die soon, Hevel. I know this for certain."

He shook his head. "It doesn't *have* to be."

Lola narrowed her eyes. Did he... *know*?

"Sorry to interrupt..."

Hevel and Lola turned their heads in unison to see Felix of Sight standing on the other side of the bars, arms crossed.

"What brings you down here?" Hevel asked in a lazy voice.

"Oh dear," Lola sighed, shaking her head. "He's sent you to ask after me?"

Felix shifted his eyes from Lola to Hevel, then back again. "Yes."

Lola dropped her head. "See?" she waved her hand defeatedly, "It's the Pining stage now."

Felix shifted his weight. "Pining stage?"

Lola walked up to the bars and peered through them at the Faerie of Sight. "He's pining, isn't he?"

Felix bobbed his head to the side. "Yes, I suppose he is."

"But I've hardly been down here a week!" Lola complained, "I don't want to go back to the Eight Stones just yet! I... I..."

"Calm down," Felix mumbled, "He's not sent for you yet."

"*...yet...*" Lola whispered, "But he will soon."

"Probably," Felix said.

"Is there any way to help him forget about me—just for a *little* while?" Lola pressed her face between the bars to gaze pleading eyes at Felix.

"You *want* to be down here?" Felix said with a hint of confusion in his voice. "With *him*? He sent you down here to punish you."

"I *like* Hevel," Lola said smugly, then gasped, "But *please* don't tell him that!"

"This whole thing would be a lot easier for you if you just stopped resisting him," Felix said.

"That's easy for you to say!" Lola frowned. "You aren't the one who..." she froze with her mouth still open, then shook her head. "No, I will not waste words on you. You will never understand."

"Well," Felix shifted his weight again, "What do you *want* me to tell him, then?"

"Tell him," Lola placed her finger on her lip, a sparkle forming in her eye, "Tell him I am wasting away down here, and that I am beginning to regret my indifference towards him."

"That might make him send for you sooner," Felix said dryly.

"Well," Lola cleared her throat, "That's why you need to say I am beginning to regret. You should make him think that the longer I am here, the better."

"I can't make him think anything," Felix said, turning away from her. "Don't overestimate my influence here."

"Felix," Lola said, losing the fire in her tone.

Felix turned back to face her. "What?"

"I can't be with him... anymore. Is there a way you could bring someone *else* to him? Surely there are new women at the Vineyard Palace!"

Felix shook his head. "Princess, he doesn't *want* anyone else. He's fixated on you."

"By *why*?" She clung to the bars desperately, "Why can't he leave me alone—just for a *little* while? It is important I get some space from him!"

"Why?" Felix narrowed his eyes.

"Please," Lola reached a hand through the bars and tugged against Felix's sleeve. "Will you ask him? Tell him if he gives me some space, I might warm to him. Just give me... a few weeks..."

Felix frowned. "I will ask him, but I would not get your hopes up."

"Tell him I asked personally—tell him it might endear him to me."

"Fine," Felix stepped back, tugging his garment loose of her clutch. He then eyed Hevel for a moment. The two of them exchanged silent looks. "Is he... bothering you, Princess?"

"I told you. I *like* Hevel!"

Felix snorted. "Alright." He stepped away from the cell and turned to leave.

"Felix?" Lola's weak voice echoed after him.

"What?" Felix turned.

"You could... you *could* get me out of here."

Felix closed his eyes with a defeated exhale and shook his head. "I can't betray my king like that."

"Please," she said with a quivering lip, "Please get me away from him."

Felix left.

"Lola," Hevel said as he touched her shoulder. "Don't waste your pleas on him."

Lola sniffed. "I can't let Somenus close to me anymore, Hevel."

Hevel nodded. "I don't think he will give you that choice."

"Well," Lola turned to face the Faerie of Death, "Last time he got angry with me, he didn't touch me. He just sent me here. Perhaps..." her voice trailed off. No, it was only a matter of time. He *would* come for her again.

"Don't be afraid, Princess," Hevel said quietly, "For now, you are safe. Why don't you lie down and rest. Get some of that sleep you find so comforting?"

Lola nodded to herself. "Yes... yes, that sounds good."

Hevel took her by the hand and walked her over to the small cot that had been placed in the cell for her. She sat upon it, groaning slightly. Her body was sore. Sleeping in the cell, while it kept her safe from Somenus, wasn't comfortable. It was taking a toll on her body. She lay down on her side, tucked her knees up toward her chest and closed her eyes.

She could hear Hevel whispering prayers over her. And after an indeterminable amount of time, she fell asleep.

Lola found herself in the safety of her remote, pillared watchtower. It was her safe place, the place where Somenus never found her. She wasn't sure where it was, but it was beautiful, with swinging vines and fragrant flowers. Her waking life was at times unbearable, but this place? This place had—

"Lola?" Beloved ran across the watchtower and pulled her into his arms. "You're here!"

She threw her arms around his waist and squeezed as tightly as she could. "Beloved," she whispered, "I am so glad to see you!"

He ran his fingers down her long, red hair, which in her dreams had not been butchered by an angry husband.

"Happy Firstday," he said.

Lola pulled away from his body and looked up at his helmeted head. "Oh!" she exclaimed, "I forgot it is a new season!"

"Ashen Shoots," Beloved said brightly, "It's supposed to symbolize new beginnings... or something."

"New beginnings," she mumbled, "Yes..."

"Lola, are you alright?" Beloved asked, reaching forward to tap her nose with his finger.

"I'm fine! I am always fine when I am with you," she said cheerily, "Shall we continue the book some more?"

Beloved laughed. "I would *love* that," he said, "Even though the ending is so depressing."

"Depressing," she tutted, shaking her head, "Not for me."

Lola moved away from her Beloved and sat on the floor of the tower. She was surprised to see a pile of feather pillows gracing the area.

"What do you think of the pillows?" Beloved ask proudly, as if he were the one who had put them there.

"They're nice," she smiled, patting the pillow beside where she sat, "Now, come sit!"

Beloved walked over and sat, making a long, drawn out sigh as he leaned his head back on the pillow.

"Now, what chapter were we in last?" she asked as she opened her book, which, waking or sleeping, was always with her.

"Lola," Beloved said lazily as he tucked an arm under his neck, "How can the ending not be depressing for you? Anodos *dies*."

"Anodos..." Lola lowered the book, gazing down at her Beloved's helmet, "He loved the white lady, even though he could not be with her."

"So...." Beloved turned to look at her through the slit in his helmet, "So *I* am Anodos, then?"

Lola reached forward and placed her hand on Beloved's warm chest. She could feel his heart beating. He felt so real. In her dreams, he *was* real!

"I thought I was Anodos," she said, "Because I am not free to love you."

"No," he shook his head, "*I* am Anodos, because you are married to Somenus, aren't you? Isn't that what you told me?"

Lola nodded soberly.

"Anodos had to watch while the knight took the white lady away—he couldn't be with the girl he loved. Doesn't that make *me* Anodos?"

"I had not thought of it that way..." Lola mumbled. "And here I thought I was the one who had to..."

"Don't stress, Lola," said Beloved, "You don't need to worry about me. I'll be fine. It's *you* I'm worried about. Does your..." he cleared his throat, turning his face slit away from her, "Does your *husband* treat you well?"

"I don't think so," Lola said softly.

"Do you... want to talk about it?" he asked.

"No, I don't think so," she said, sliding her hand up to touch his helmet. She gave it a slight tug; it didn't budge.

Beloved chuckled. "We've tried this many times; I can't take it off."

"Why not?" She moaned.

"I have some theories... but I am thinking it's for the best, anyway," he said.

"How could you *say* that?" She crossed her arms, "I have been dying to see your face!"

Beloved turned his head back in her direction. "I think if I didn't have this helmet on, I would have tried to kiss you by now. That's probably not the best idea if you're... *married*."

Lola sighed to herself. "I suppose you are right. Oh, *tides*," she huffed.

"What?" Beloved asked.

"You are *just* the sort of man I would have wanted to marry—the fact that you *care* about that sort of thing."

"Aw!" Beloved's helmet seemed to smile, though nothing visually changed about it. "That's about the best thing someone's ever said to me."

Lola laughed. It felt so good to laugh like that—so free and careless. There in her dream, everything seemed so easy! There was no Somenus, no cell, no pain in her body.

"Oh, look at us," Beloved said as he reached out to tug at a strand of her hair, "Star-crossed lovers, eh? We are just like characters in a sad novel."

"It's not sad, not if I am able to simply know you," Lola said as she tucked her knees up into herself. "I am always happy here."

"Yeah," Beloved said, "Me, too."

24

—— Isabella ——

Look to the West

How many soldiers have permission to leave Arelle for personal reasons?" Scarlet asked Major Twilight. The two soldiers were sitting in the highest tower in Fort Axes together, exchanging stories since Twilight's return from battle the day before. The tower, while still part of General Korbin's main fort, was high enough that one could not smell the stench of the lower levels as much. No one really spoke about it, but Korbin still would not let them wash clean the seemingly blood-stained interiors.

"I don't think there's anyone under the rank of colonel who can take leave outside of the city—not within Korbin's army, anyway," Twilight said as he puffed his cigar, "But we all knew that when we signed up to join the army."

"Why did you sign up to join Korbin's army?" asked Scarlet. She had her own cigarette resting between her fingers. She tried not to smoke much, but it always felt like the right thing to do with the war-battered veterans. It was a way of entering into their peace.

"Well," Twilight tapped his cigar against the ashtray, "I was serving in the Gramenlands' outer rim battles, growing bored. We were told that whoever joined the regiments that were sent to Arelle would be paid more, and it sounded exciting. Who had ever gone into the Light City before?"

"Do you regret it?"

"No," Major Twilight shook his head, "Not at all. I'll return home to my wife after my four-season service with much more money than before. We can buy some land."

Scarlet nodded thoughtfully. Twilight seemed to have an idea of life after Arelle. Did she have something like that? She didn't really have a desire to settle down, not when there was so much potential here in Arelle.

"Anyway, Major," Twilight cleared his throat, "I've heard that you're reaching for the position of colonel. Is that true?"

Scarlet shrugged modestly. "I would like to be given more authority. I think there's a lot of good to be done here. I wouldn't mind being sent out as a human ambassador to some of the places still resisting Somenus' rule. I feel like I could convince them better than anyone else why it would be good to ally with him."

"*Really*?" Twilight raised his eyebrows. "I didn't know you were so passionate about all the politics, Wingsday!"

"I am. Living in Arelle definitely brings some perspective. It is like living one's whole life in a forest, thinking that the world is nothing but trees, only to finally climb the highest tree and see that the forest is but a small copse in the middle of a vast city." Scarlet gazed past Twilight, out at Arelle's cityscape.

"Wow." Twilight blew a puff of smoke with a raise of his eyebrows. "I didn't realize you were such an intellectual."

Scarlet turned her gaze toward the Major slowly. "I care about Arelle—about Raqia."

Twilight nodded. "You have family out there, people you care about?"

"Yes."

"Well, it's a noble mission: convincing those outside Arelle to come to terms with Somenus' reign. Would you like to start small? I've got a project for you that might give you a leg up on a promotion with Korbin."

Scarlet leaned forward. *This* sounded interesting! "I'm listening."

Twilight chuckled. "On our way back from Celestia, we captured a Faerie just outside the borders of Arelle, some sort of spy. He bore the mark of the Purple Order. You know, the Faeries who are trying to kill the king?"

Scarlet's eyes flashed with suspense. "*Really?*"

"I bet if you were able to convince one of the Purple Order to renounce their vows and serve Somenus, it would get General Korbin's attention." Major Twilight flicked his flickering dog-end off the tower's ledge and watched it drop down into the city.

"Where is this Faerie?" she asked.

"We put him down in the dungeon, in the cell across from the Death Faerie. Feel free to visit him. I'd be curious to hear how it went." Twilight fished into his pocket and produced an iron key. He passed it to Scarlet who took it gingerly. Though she was intrigued by the opportunity, she wasn't exactly thrilled to be in close proximity to the Death Faerie. He gave her the chills.

"Thank you, Major," she said as she rose. "I'll let you know how it goes."

Scarlet checked her clicker as she trotted down the winding tower stairs. It was 3620 clicks after the late morning bell. She had plenty of time before she went officially on duty. Scarlet had grown accustomed to the stench of Fort Axes, so she didn't even hold her breath when she descended into its main level. She made her way lower, into the prison beneath the fort, and was thankful when the air, while still thick and damp, became a little cleaner.

She strolled down the length of the underground tunnel system's main stretch, until she came to the end where the largest cells were. She noticed that the place was more lit than usual. That was probably due to the concubine's presence. The place even *smelled* nicer!

Scarlet glanced left into the Death Faerie's cell. Why the concubine was always thrown in there with him, she had no idea. She peered around for a moment, wondering where the woman was. Scarlet gasped. The Death Faerie was standing right by the bars, gazing at her with his penetrating eyes.

"Hades!" Scarlet cursed, jumping back from the cell.

"Hades," the Death Faerie chuckled, "Just another name for Death, you know."

Scarlet's fingers felt cold. "Stay back, Worm!"

Death cocked his head to the side. "Why do you fear me?"

The question angered Scarlet. How dare he ask her that? "I said, stay back."

"It is *you* who came to me," said the Faerie, "I am merely standing where I have been standing all morning. Now, what can I do for you, Wingsday?"

"I didn't come to—"

"Wingsday?" a weak voice croaked from the cell behind her. "Did you say *Wingsday*?"

Scarlet turned. A Faerie was sitting on the floor at the center of the cell with his feet shackled to the ground. Ignoring the Death Faerie, Scarlet marched up to the cell and unlocked it. She crept inside slowly, then knelt down before the Faerie.

He looked as though he had been beaten, with a remarkably fat lip. His brown hair fell just below his shoulders, and his skin was a mellow, pleasant brown. He gazed at her with bright green eyes, smiling faintly.

"Are you Scarlet Wingsday?" he whispered.

Scarlet nodded slowly. Her heart began to increase its pace. "Yes," she whispered back.

"I came here to find you," he said, "Your brother sent me with a message."

Scarlet's eyes flashed. She felt her knuckles growing white from clenched fists. She loosened her fingers, trying to calm her nerves. "I see," she sighed. "What is your name?"

"I am West, Faerie of Finding," he said with a bow of his head. "I have been sent on this perilous journey to find you, to see if you are alright, Isabella!"

"Quiet," she hissed, "don't use that name here!"

"Sorry," West whispered, "I... I am so pleased you found me, and that I found you! And you are *alive*! Have you located the weapon?"

Scarlet exhaled slowly. "West, you said my brother had a message for me. What is it?"

West nodded excitedly. "He said that if I found you, I should activate my mark, which I have done. So Hanz knows you are alive, even now!"

Scarlet glanced down at West's arm with its glowing Purple Mark. Here was yet another Faerie who had given up his life for a futile mission. If she could not persuade him to join with Somenus, he would join the rest of the Faeries who sat on the shelf of Exilium Prisons. What became of the drained Faeries? She didn't know, and she didn't want to know.

"I see," she said, "Anything else?"

West leaned closer, lowering his voice even further. "Hanz has brought the Purple Order to the fortress of the Time Faerie. It is a place where Somenus can't find us. There, he has found the Faerie of *Transport*. He believes that once you find the weapon, she will be able to transport him here to kill the Nightmare Faerie."

Scarlet's face must have changed because West drew back with a look of confusion.

"Isabella," he said, "Is something wrong?"

"West..." she sighed, reaching forward to touch his arm. "I have learned much since coming to Arelle—things that might change the Purple Order's plans. I am trying to gain a promotion that will allow me to visit Hanz and tell him what I have learned."

"What have you learned?" he asked urgently, grasping her hand.

Scarlet cleared her throat. "West, I have come to realize that it would not be a good idea to kill the Faerie King."

West's look of suspense didn't change. He waited to hear her full explanation before he arrived at his own opinion. "Go on," he said.

"Somenus isn't forcing Faeries to partake in his Rites. He is simply setting up a system for them to live out their purpose on Raqia. While I might not agree with Faeries being gods, I do know that it is the Faerie King's job to rule over the land. The Faeries here in Arelle are honored and protected by their king, and they are content. The prior King was no saint either, and some believe his reign was even worse than Somenus'. Now Somenus isn't a good King—but should that come as a surprise? West, for a people to commit treason against their King, there has to be a very *good* reason, and so far, I haven't found one! It feels wrong to come into this place and plot an assassination when I am not even a Faerie, and neither is Hanz."

West took in a deep breath, then exhaled with a nod. "You are not the first in the Order to come to this conclusion."

Scarlet raised her eyebrows. "I'm not?"

"There are some whom Hanz rescued that feel it is wrong to commit regicide. Aorist himself is against it. He cites the Faerie law to not kill."

"Aorist?"

"He's the Time Faerie," West said with a look of awe, "he is still alive in his hidden fortress. Some even believe he is one of the Firsts."

Scarlet leaned back, processing. "One of the Firsts? Do you mean one of the first Faeries who were made? The Original Eight?"

West nodded. "He's given us shelter, but he won't support what the Order is doing."

It was as if West already had his doubts. This would make things easier. "West, how many have joined the Order now?"

"There's near a hundred and twenty," he said, looking up at the ceiling thoughtfully, "Though only a few will come on the mission to kill..." he paused to swallow, "...the Nightmare Faerie."

Scarlet wondered for a moment if it was easier for them to talk about killing him when they used his false title 'The Nightmare Faerie', rather than, 'The king'.

"West," Scarlet said with a sigh, "I do not think it would be good to kill the king. It would only upset things further. Arelle is stabilizing after three seasons of unrest, but if there were to be another insurrection, it could be devastating to world politics."

West's eyes widened. "Hanz believes Faeries will never be safe while Somenus is on the throne."

"The Faeries who are running from Somenus could reconcile with him. I am sure there is a way to figure this out! The Purple Order is only in danger because of their plot to kill the king! You don't have to be a traitor to Arelle, West, you could recant."

West blinked a few times, then shook his head. "I am sure they will not forgive what I have done."

"I will vouch for you," she said firmly, "Why don't we put this to the test! If you are to be exiled anyway, let us see if Somenus will receive you! But West, regardless of your fate—do you want to be a part of the movement that would kill the Faerie King, usurper or not?"

West gazed at her for a silent moment before he finally said, "You are Timbre Wulf's own sister... and yet you would move against him?"

"I am Timbre Wulf's *daughter*," she said with a subtle growl, "And I can tell you right now, my father firmly believes that humans like my brother and I shouldn't be meddling in Faerie affairs."

West closed his eyes and bowed his head. "You are tugging on the thoughts I have kept held back in my mind. I have worried over this very thing." He opened his eyes again. "But your brother is so *sure* this is the right thing to do! He says Somenus is preaching a false calling over the Faeries, and that it will destroy them!"

"Hanz may be right about that. Somenus may even be as evil as we all fear he is, but still—is it for *us* to take up the executioner's axe? West!" She grabbed the Faerie's shoulder, "If Faeries are *truly* not supposed to kill, would the ultimate crime not be killing your own *king*?"

West's mouth dropped open, and then wetness began to form around his eyes. His shoulders slumped, and he bobbed his head in sorrowful agreement. "Yes," he said, "You are right."

"It may be wrong for Somenus to hunt and kill other Faeries, like Hanz says that he does, but he *does* have the authority to do so. Besides, I don't actually think Somenus is trying to just arbitrarily kill Faeries who don't like his way of ruling. He is, however, trying to secure his reign while some still resist him. It may not be virtuous, but it is something every King must do when he steals a throne," she shrugged, "I don't condone it, but like I said, he does have the authority as the king."

"Authority," West said with a hint of irony in his voice. "Yes, it is something Hanz doesn't want us to believe Somenus has."

"He sits on the throne, doesn't he?" Scarlet said, "He holds the scepter. He wears the crown. He *is* your king, West."

"I wish to repent," West said, lifting up his clear, determined eyes. "Please, let me see my king."

Scarlet felt her heart racing with delight. "Truly?"

"Yes," said West. He had a look of relief about him. "I have run from him long enough. The Faerie of Finding will find his king, now."

Scarlet's excitement quickly turned to terror. What if she was wrong? West was involved in a plot to kill the king—was there *any* chance of clemency for him? Well, if that weren't the case, he would die either way.

"What will you do, Isabella?" West asked, touching her hand with his, "If you truly believe the Purple Order is in the wrong?"

"Well," she sighed, "I plan to get promoted high enough that I can come and go within Arelle. Then I will go and speak with my brother. I will tell him all that I have learned. He trusts me. He will listen."

"Good." West smiled weakly. "I can rest knowing that my conscience will be clear of my king's death." West drew in a sharp breath, then gazed past Scarlet excitedly. "*Shh*," he whispered, "Listen!"

"What?" Scarlet turned to look behind herself. She could hear the faint murmur of a woman's voice.

"It's the story," West said as he did his best to scoot closer to the bars, "I don't want to miss it."

Scarlet rose to her feet and waited for a moment while her legs regained their circulation. She stepped closer to the bars and listened. She could just make out the words of a story.

"Don't disturb her," West whispered, "I want to listen."

Scarlet nodded, then left the cell. She locked it behind herself and paused for a moment, listening.

"Meantime, how fared Cosmo?" said the soft voice, "As might be expected in one of his temperament, his interest has blossomed into love, and his love—shall I call it *ripened*, or—*withered* into passion. But, alas! He loved a shadow. He could not come near her, he could not speak to her, could not hear a sound from those sweet lips, to which his longing eyes would cling like bees to their honey-founts. Ever and anon, he sang to himself, '*I shall die for love of the maiden*.'"

It was at that moment, Scarlet realized she had been transported by the words. Her memories had taken her somewhere else—somewhere far away. She could see his face, the love of someone that foolish and desperate. What was his name? *Clover?*

Scarlet inched away from the scene, stepping as quietly as she could so as not to disturb West's story. She let out a silent gasp when her back came into contact with someone else. She whirled around, wide-eyed, to see Felix glaring down at her.

"Felix!"

"Such a stupid story," he remarked under his breath, "and yet one can't help but find themselves captivated by it. A woman in a mirror," he chuckled, "how fanciful."

Scarlet blinked. Had the lifeless, skeptical Sight Faerie been listening, too?

"What are you *doing* down here?" she asked in a low voice.

"I could ask you the same question," Felix said with narrowing eyes.

"I was speaking with the new prisoner. I've convinced him to renounce the Purple Order."

The Faerie of Sight blinked, indicating a level of subdued surprise. "*Really?*"

Scarlet lifted her chin a little higher. "Yes. I was just on my way to tell the general. I am hoping Somenus might grant West clemency."

Felix nodded. "I'm impressed, *Wingsday,* though I didn't think you were the type to try and save a Faerie's life. Come on. There's something else in this for you."

Scarlet glanced to the side. "I suppose I've changed since coming here. I happen to *like* Faeries now."

Felix snorted. "Come on—it's a *promotion* you want out of this."

He wasn't wrong. "A promotion wouldn't hurt." A smile crept up the side of her mouth.

Felix chuckled. "Good luck, Wingsday."

Good luck? Was he being *civil* to her?

"Well, thanks," she pushed past him and began to head toward the exit.

"Oh, Wingsday?" Felix caught her by the arm.

Scarlet swung her head to face him. "*What?*"

"Have you found out anything more about what Korbin does with the drained Faeries?" His eyes searched her face as he asked, watching for a reaction.

"I... no," she said. Her jaw clenched tightly. She hadn't asked. She hadn't *wanted* to ask.

Felix released the grip on her arm, and she recoiled with a scowl. "Next time, don't touch me," she snapped.

Felix strolled past her, disregarding her venom, and approached the Death Faerie's cell. Scarlet watched him for a moment as he stood by the bars, listening silently while the prisoners were still unaware of his presence. He had almost no charisma, and yet there was something striking about his angsty silhouette. Despite him being one of the most unlikeable people she had ever met, she did kind of like the Faerie of Sight.

Scarlet found Korbin sitting in his cave-like office. She hated speaking with him while he was in there. It was always as if he had become a part of the dank grime that laced the walls. The general seemed to pry himself loose from his chair, like a mass of wet bark from an old tree stump, rising reluctantly to his feet.

"Wingsday," he said in a voice with a swamp-like congestion, "How nice to look at you."

Scarlet held her breath for a moment, reminding herself that this man was her superior officer, and she probably shouldn't challenge his phrasing.

"Sir," she said as she snapped her heels together. "I've come to ask for a promotion."

Korbin raised his eyebrows with a look of amusement. "*Have* you? Well, well," he bobbed his head, "tell me more!"

Scarlet cleared her throat. "I am ready for you to make me a colonel, if it pleases you. If you were willing to grant permission, I think I could be a useful ambassador for you. I have managed to convince the Faerie of Finding to renounce the Purple Order, and he asks for an audience with the king. I think I could get other Faeries who have fled to return to Arelle."

"*Really?*" Korbin ran his index finger along the surface of his desk, creating a little trench in the mysterious film that seemed to coat the room. "You... you are *that* committed to the king?"

"I am," she said firmly, nodding inwardly.

"You are telling me," he tilted his head back, peering at her through slitted eyes, "that you are ready to be *trusted* more?"

"I am."

"Well," Korbin snapped his head upright, "That is very interesting, Wingsday." He trilled his fingers across the table. "A colonel is an honorable position—a position reserved for only my most trusted and loyal officers."

"Have I ever given you reason to doubt me?" she asked sharply.

Korbin turned his head slightly, studying her. "I suppose not," he said cautiously. "Now, you *do* know," he began to circle the desk and make his way toward her, "A colonel would be trusted with the army's most sensitive military secrets. You would carry a key to the King's Vault—are you prepared to carry that much responsibility?"

Scarlet's heart throbbed with anxiety. A key to the vault? *The* vault? The vault which no doubt held the cursed weapon that Hanz was searching for? *Could* she be trusted with that knowledge?

"Yes," she whispered. Her mouth barely moved when she spoke.

"And are you prepared to *prove* that loyalty to me?" Korbin was now inches away from her, peering down like a looming willow.

"Yes."

Korbin exhaled hot air through his nostrils; the warm draft wafted her face with an unidentifiable, smoky stench. "Well," he said, "Then I wish for you to join me on Wingsday. I will test your loyalty then."

Scarlet held her breath, hoping it would not be long before he took himself and his horrible breath somewhere else. "Fine," she wheezed.

"Alright," Korbin nodded. Then, he finally paced back to the other side of the room. Scarlet slowly released her breath.

"Sir?"

"Hmm?"

"Would it be possible for you to grant West an audience with—"

"I thank you for your hard work there," Korbin said, "your part is done, for now. I will take this matter to the king. And *thank you*, Wingsday, you have done well!"

Scarlet was surprised to feel herself growing proud, even though the compliment came from the inhuman general.

"Well," Korbin became one with his chair once more, "See you on Wingsday, Wingsday." He chuckled to himself.

Scarlet rolled her eyes and left.

25

— Leo —

Timbre Wulf

Am I going to get a chance to meet him?" I asked quietly.

Momentum peered around the door to his own personal chambers. I mimicked him, and the two of us caught a glimpse of the legendary warrior, sitting there in Momentum's favorite reading chair with his big boots up on the coffee table. Momentum and I exchanged glances.

"He's pretty cool," I whispered.

Momentum snorted. "He's ruining my furniture." We both returned our gazes toward the menacing, mesmerizing man.

Timbre Wulf—the *real* Timbre Wulf—had only been with us for a day, and already the mood of Winter's End had completely changed. Yes, Hanz' own father had found his way to Winter's End, and he had shut himself away with Momentum for the entire day. I could hear his shouts booming from the room all through the night as I tried to sleep.

He and Hanz didn't share a single word with each other when he had first entered the house, and since then, they had kept to opposite ends of the premises. The Purple Order followed Timbre Wulf, and yet here was the *original* Timbre Wulf, storming venomously onto the scene. Everybody was confused.

Momentum and I pulled back from the corner and faced each other.

"He's asked me to bring Hanz," said Momentum, "You can come along if you like."

"Wait, really? *Seriously*? Me?" I placed my hand over my heart.

"Oh stop," Momentum mumbled, "Don't make me *un*-invite you."

I nodded quickly, zipping my mouth closed.

"Why don't you bring Hanz here after the Lastlight bell. I think by then old Joel here will have calmed down a little more."

"M–me?" I gulped. "You want *me* to fetch Hanz?"

Momentum gave me an unimpressed head turn. "And?"

"Oh, uh—sure. I can do that," I stammered.

Momentum rolled his eyes. "Leo, he's just another human, just like you."

"Oh, he's not just like me," I said as I made an arm-thickening gesture around my bicep, "And anyway, I don't think he likes me very much."

Momentum scoffed.

"He doesn't!"

"Leo, it's *you* who doesn't like him. Admit it."

"Well," I bristled, "*You* don't like him either, do you?"

"I don't like him less than I like anybody else," Momentum said lazily, "It's his plan I am not fond of. But that's not a reason to *dis*like him, is it?"

"You tell me!" I crossed my arms in a pout.

"What is you don't like about him?" Momentum leaned against the wall with a subdued smirk.

"I don't dislike him!"

"Fine then," Momentum straightened. "Then will you *please* bring him here after the Lastlight bell?"

"Fine." I marched away, feeling uncharacteristically peeved. The fact was, it was a mystery to *myself* why I felt so weird around Hanz. I was the guy who found something to admire in anybody!

Well, there was nothing for it; whenever I felt this out of sorts, I found myself marching down to the coast. Before I could remember how I even got there, I found myself stripping down and throwing my body into the wild waves. I liked it—getting smacked around by those bullying tides; it was like getting into a wrestling match with your best friend after a bad day. I needed to get out my pent-up aggression.

The seas must have changed with the season because they treated me differently that morning. Before I had swum for very long, I found myself thrown upon the coast, coughing and sputtering, gripping the sands with fearful desperation. I lifted my head slowly and glanced back at the angry sea.

"What is your *problem*?" I yelled. For a moment, I thought I could hear the words echoed back to me. *What is your problem?*

I sighed and pushed myself up by the arm. Leaning my elbows on my knees, I tried to catch my breath. What *was* wrong with me? I *did* dislike Hanz. Why? Was I *jealous*?

"What is my problem?" I asked myself with a shake of the head. Hanz, whatever his faults, was a good man, yet for some reason, something in my gut twisted whenever he spoke to me. "Is it just my pride? Do I hate him for condescending to me?" I scoffed at myself. "Who *wouldn't* condescend? I'm just a..." my voice trailed off, stolen by a heavy gust of wind.

Once I found the strength, I jumped to my feet and pulled my trousers on. I meandered around for a while, making deep footprints in the sand as I flew my tunic behind me like a flag. It flapped around in the beach winds, making pleasurable snapping sounds.

I did a little hop when my foot stepped funny on a pebble in the sand. "Ow!" I hissed, grabbing my heel. "That hurt!" I gazed down at the soft grey sand where a single pebble lay. It stood out like a black eye. I narrowed my eyes. "No way," I whispered, "It can't be..."

I reached down and plucked the thing from the sand. It looked like a smooth, red teardrop. I rolled it between two of my fingers pensively. This was way too familiar.

"Now, what are you doing *here*?" I asked the little rock. "Don't you belong to Cymbeline?"

I looked up and gazed around the beach. I hadn't seen her since she ran away crying on Firstday. She had been hiding in her room ever since, though Rowyn did say she spotted her walking down toward the beach. I clutched the thing determinedly in my fist and ran back to the house.

I raced through the Autumn Wing, dodging Faeries and making quick apologies as I skidded toward Cymbeline's chambers. I nearly smashed onto my backside when someone caught me by the arm in a vice-like grip.

"*Agh*—hey!" I yelped as I tried to catch myself. I recovered gracelessly to my feet, then turned to see Hanz' smiling face gazing down at me. "Hanz!"

"Leo, could we talk?" His grip on my arm didn't loosen once he had my attention.

"Uh, sure," I said. *Not like you're giving me a choice...*

Hanz pulled me into the hall and lowered his voice. "Have you spoken to Cymbeline?"

I held back a groan. "I was just on my way there now. I haven't seen her since we last spoke."

Hanz nodded to himself. "There's been a *very* important development in our plan. I need to know she is on our side."

"Oh yeah? What development?" I was genuinely curious.

Hanz' mouth twisted as he deliberated on how much to tell me. "My sister has made contact. After all this time, she is secure in Arelle."

"Oh! That's great!"

"Anyway, I think we may move sooner than later, and I need to know that Cymbeline can transport us there. I need to rescue her, Leo," his grip tightened, "I need to get my sister out of that pit of Hades!"

My heart made a thud in my chest. "G–go to Arelle? Transport there to... rescue your sister?"

"Yes."

Suddenly, the idea didn't seem so horrible. He wanted to *rescue* someone, after all. I nodded vacantly. "Yes..." I murmured.

"Will you *please* convince Cymbeline?"

I lifted my eyes to Hanz. I studied his face. He wasn't a bad guy. I was just jealous—*intimidated* by him! Maybe I needed to just swallow my pride and work with him for once!

"Fine," I sighed, "I'll talk to her—really."

"*Thank* you, Leo," Hanz said, smiling. I felt the grip release, and blood began to flow back into my arm. I tensed and released my fingers.

"No problem..."

"You're a good kid." He ruffled my hair, then marched away.

I took some deep breaths to soften the anger. *Forget it. It's just the way he is. I don't need to let his arrogance control me.*

I turned to face Cymbeline's door and knocked.

"Go away!" her voice called from within.

"Cym, it's me." I called.

There was a pause, then she said, "Go away, Leo."

"Cym, I found it on the beach."

I waited, then the door flew open.

"*What*?" She wore anger on her face like a helmet.

"Cym," I leaned against the door frame, "Just let me in? Let's talk, like we always do."

I could see her softening slightly. "Leo..."

"Come on," I placed one foot inside the door, "I'm coming in, alright?"

She didn't stop me. She watched as I glided into the room and placed my pebble on her desk.

Cymbeline slammed the door closed and rushed over to gaze at it. "Leo! How did you *find* that?"

"What did you do?" I sat down on her desk chair, "Throw it in the sea?"

Cymbeline blanched. "I... how did you know?"

"Well," I chuckled, "I don't think this sea *likes* being treated like a waste bin. Besides—I don't think it's that easy for a Faerie to lose their Imperium; Momentum says they have ways of finding their way back to their owners."

Cymbeline groaned, then marched across the room and flung herself face-first onto her bed.

"Cymbeline, what happened? Why are you trying to abandon all your... your..." as the words were coming out of my mouth, I realized. "...power?"

Cymbeline lifted her face from the bed to shoot a glare at me.

"Right..." I sighed, "Your mother? You're afraid of becoming like her?"

"Don't you see?" She sat up with a huff. "Everyone talks about how powerful I am—and I am just like my mother. Suddenly in a new world with all this power I didn't know I had. What is going to stop me from becoming like her? Don't you see why Momentum hates me? He knows I will be just like *her*!"

"Ah, Cym," I shook my head, "Don't say that!"

"It's true! You *know* it's true!"

"It's not true." I picked up the pebble and held it in my fingers.

"You heard him yesterday. He said he hates me!" She cried.

"Well," I coughed, "He actually said your mother *isn't* why he hates you, if that's any consolation."

Cymbeline scoffed. "No, it's worse, because instead he hates me for some *other* reason—as if there is something *worse* about me that I don't even know yet!"

"*Cym!*" I barked, startling both her and myself by the anger in my voice. "You can't let other people's thoughts about you form your identity! Momentum has a chip on his shoulder—maybe a *few* chips—that's not your problem, and it's got nothing to do with your *character*!"

I walked over to the bed and sat on the end.

"Cymbeline," I sighed, softening my voice, "You are a kind and humble woman. You are noble and honest. Who cares what Momentum thinks of you, or Hanz—or *anybody* else? No one can take away the woman you have become despite your hard upbringing. You're not like your mom. She had an easy life, and when temptation and trial did come her way, it blew her over like a tent in a storm. But you have already seen your storm, Cym. You've come out of it clean and pure, without a hint of guile. Your mother was given power without any context. And like a tall tree without any roots, she fell over. But you—you've given power *after* your perseverance. You earned your roots before you were given your height." I passed her the pebble. "You've earned this power, Cym. You won't do evil with it, will you?"

Cymbeline stared at the rock. I waited and watched as she studied it, then clenched it in her fist.

"I believe what *you* say about me, Leo," she said, turning to look me in the eyes.

"I... okay," I smiled.

Cymbeline placed the pebble back into her necklace where she had pried it loose. "I suppose I can store power... for a little longer, but Leo?"

"Yeah?"

"If you ever see me growing dark from the magik, I want you to tell me. Tell me to throw it away." She stared at me so intently, so trusting.

"I will," I said. I knew I would never have to; if only she knew it for herself, too.

"Well," she rose to her feet, "I suppose only one question remains."

"What is that?" I said as I watched her move across the room and open her desk drawer.

"I heard Hanz talking to you outside my door," she said with a drooping head, "He wants you to convince me to transport him to Arelle—to rescue his sister and kill Somenus." She lifted her head and looked at me. "What should I do, Leo? I will do whatever *you* say."

My stomach formed into multiple knots. "Uh... I don't know if I want that much, uh... Cym, *I* can't make that call for you!"

"What would you do, Leo? If you were me? Would you go?"

I bit my lip. "Well... If it were me, I would go—*not* to kill the king, but because there's people there who need help. I might go to make sure everyone was ok. But this is *me* we are talking about. I don't like the idea of *you* being in danger, Cym."

"Would you?"

"Would I, what?"

"Would you go with me?"

I straightened my back. Me? Go to Arelle? "Yes," I said, with every ounce of sincerity in my being. "Yes, Cymbeline, I would go there."

"I will only go if you go, too," she said as she pulled something from the drawer. She walked over to where I was still sitting on the bed and held out a simple woven gold wire ring.

I blinked. "Uh, what's this?"

"It's from one of my lessons. Rowyn has been teaching me how to enchant items. This is my first successful item I ever made." She held the ring out to me in her palm.

I picked it up and looked at it. "What does it do?"

"It has a single-use teleportation enchantment. If you put it on, you can go anywhere you desire—only once."

"Wow!" I raised my eyebrows, gazing at the ring with a feeling of wonder. "It's amazing to think that for me, this is an unimaginable gift, and yet for you, you can do it anytime you want!"

Cymbeline chuckled to herself. "Yes... I know. Odd, isn't it?" She smiled at me. "Where would you go, if you could, Leo?"

I felt an unimaginable pressure press down on my chest. I knew exactly where I would go, but I couldn't tell *her*! I passed the ring back to her.

"I... uh..." I blushed.

Cymbeline narrowed her eyes. "You... you're *thinking* of someone, aren't you?"

"What?"

"Your face," she leaned away from me with a look of caution, "You love someone, don't you?"

I nodded slowly. "I do."

Cymbeline turned her face away from me, clamping her fist around the ring. "I see."

I let out a long-held breath. "Cymbeline..."

She rose quickly to her feet. "You can tell Hanz I will go with him—but I won't join his ridiculous cause."

There was a sudden shift in her attitude toward me. I was no idiot; she had been about to give me that ring. Damn... she liked me. I stood slowly and walked toward her.

"Cym," I reached out a hand and touched her sleeve.

"Leo," she recoiled from me quickly, "go away."

"Cymbeline," I sighed and pulled the bristling cactus toward me. I put my arms around her and listened as she melted into a whimpering cry. "Cymbeline, you'll always be like a sister to me; and I'll always be here for you whenever you need me."

"*Why?*" she sobbed, "Why won't you love me?"

"I *do* love you," I said, "I just can't... I just..." I groaned inwardly. No, I couldn't spare her from this kind of pain. I had to let her *feel* it; I had to let her heart break so that she could build it back up again. "I'm sorry."

⸺⸺•⸺⸺

"You seem pretty mopey for someone who just secured the lives of so many people," Hanz said as he slapped me encouragingly on the back. We were walking together through the Winter Wing, up to Momentum's chambers. Hanz's staff was making a repeated snapping sound every time he took a step forward.

"Huh? Oh, sorry," I shrugged. "It's been a weird day."

"You did the right thing," said Hanz, "She needs to experience actually doing something with her powers, seeing tangibly how she can help people."

I bobbed my head in agreement. He could be right, there.

"You look lovesick, brother," Hanz said through a laugh.

"Hah..." In a way, I was. I *always* was, though. Now, I was just love-nauseous, if that were a thing.

"Thanks for the escort, but I didn't need a *chaperone* on my way there, you know," Hanz said.

"Oh," I mumbled, "Nah, just tagging along 'cause Momentum asked me to."

Hanz glanced at me sidelong.

"There you two are," Momentum said as we approached. He was leaning against the wall with his watch in hand. He snapped it shut and squinted his eyes at me. "Leo?"

"Tell you later," I flapped my hand dismissively. I didn't want to talk about anything with Hanz there.

"Well," Momentum cleared his throat, "Let's do this."

Hanz crossed his arms. "I was hoping for a *private* audience with my father."

"Sorry," Momentum said unapologetically, "That's not what this is about. Now, come on."

Hanz and I walked into the room and I noticed a couple more chairs sitting around Momentum's breakfast table. Timbre Wulf was already there, sitting like a storm contained in a bottle. Momentum, Hanz, and I sat around the little table.

Hanz opened his mouth to speak first, but Joel, Timbre Wulf's common name, lifted his hand in a silencing gesture. And here I thought Hanz was the intimidating guy: Joel? He made you either want to run away and hide or beg him to let you join his army.

"Son," Joel said in a deep voice, "I will let you tell me your peace, and then you must let me speak mine. What are you doing? What is your end goal with all these Faeries?"

Hanz made a little sigh of relief, then leaned back in his chair, "Well, I—"

"But first," Joel lifted a finger, "Tell me where she is."

She—we all knew he meant Isabella, Hanz' sister.

"She joined the Purple Order last season," Hanz said in a wavering, though courageous voice, "and has gone to Arelle as an undercover spy."

Joel's face remained as still as stone, he just stared at his son, daring him to say more.

"She's... she's searching for Orion's bow."

Joel closed his eyes. His chest expanded and contracted as deep, hot breaths did their best to cool his inner fire. "You sent... my daughter... my treasure...into...?"

Momentum and I exchanged nervous looks. Was I about to witness that booming yell firsthand?

Hanz shot a glare my way, then leaned forward towards his father. "Isabella and I want to help the Faeries, even when you will *not*."

"*Help*?" Joel's eyes snapped open. "Hanz—help? You're not helping them. You're becoming a weapon for them! They are defiling you, and you are defiling them!" His voice crescendoed.

"Father!" Hanz slammed a fist on the table. "You said you would hear my peace *first*!"

Joel leaned back, exhaling through a crackling groan.

Hanz straightened a little. "The Purple Order is a gathering of Faeries who fled Somenus' insurrection. They are loyal members of King Sol's court, innocents—Faeries whom Somenus has chosen to hunt down and capture. They came to me, begging for help! Their king wants to kill them, and anyone else who will not listen to and submit to his rule. He claims to have answered the Great Question—telling Faeries that they are gods who need to be worshiped by humans. He plans to subdue Raqia under his leadership, and place Faeries over every city and kingdom in Raqia. He defies even the *Lights* by building temples to Faeries and encouraging humans to worship them to help them gain Magik!" Hanz stopped to catch his breath. He looked from face to face of those around the table.

Hanz continued. "He has gone to war with some of the Elves, he has withdrawn fertility from the land in cities that will not build temples to him, and—and Father, is it not the job of *this* staff," Hanz shook the black Beatus staff which he never let out of his sight, "to defend the Faeries in their time of need?"

"Do you know why that staff was made?" Joel pointed at the weapon. "It was made during the first of the Faerie wars. It was made to *defend* the Faerex, and those who were trying to kill him and his family."

I glanced at Momentum, curious if that were true. He was gazing off to the side, as if he wished to be suddenly absent from the conversation.

"Yes," Hanz replied, "And that family is now dead—the original royal line killed off by *Somenus*!"

"Son," Joel said with clenched fists, "Don't you know there is a *curse* on anyone who kills the Faerie King?"

"I know."

"If you do manage to kill Somenus, you will die!"

Hanz shook his head, "No, with enough powerful Faerie's pledging their lives to me, I will be strong enough to survive the burst of reflected Magik. I have at least 120 Faeries who have made me their Faerie Friend."

Momentum scoffed, turning his head back to the table. "Oh, please."

Joel, Hanz and I turned our heads to look at him expectantly.

"A hundred and twenty?" Momentum demanded, "They have *all* made you their...?" He shook his head.

"It's the same thing you Faeries did to my father!" Hanz returned, "It's what has kept him alive all these years!"

"It was a curse!" Joel barked.

"A hundred and Twenty Faeries?" Momentum cried, rising to his feet, "Don't you realize what will happen when you kill a Faerie King with *all* their lives pledged to you? They will *all* die!"

Hanz' eyes widened, then he shook his head. "No... no that's not..."

"They will *all* die!" Momentum bellowed. I had never seen him so angry.

"I—" Hanz opened his mouth.

"You told me you were going to die for the Faeries, Hanz! You didn't tell me you were going to use them as a *shield* against the curse!" Momentum slammed his hands on the table. "You didn't tell me they *all* pledged their lives to you!"

"Fine!" Hanz slammed his palm on the table. "I will die! I'll make them all renounce their vows—are you happy?"

"You can't *kill* the king!" Momentum's voice was more of a scream than a yell now. I pulled at his sleeve. He shot a glare at me, then sighed and sat down. "Whatever," he flicked his hand at Hanz, "Do what you want. You won't succeed, anyway."

Hanz snorted. "You two are so eager to keep Somenus as your king? Don't you know that he would kill you *both* if he knew where you were?"

"Of course, we know that," Joel returned, "But it's not putting murder in our hearts." Joel and Momentum glanced at one another. "We've been down that road, Son. It will change you into someone you don't recognize."

"It will not be murder, Father," Hanz said nobly, "This is a war."

Joel shook his head. "Son, if you would but *listen*..."

"No, *you* listen!" Hanz slammed Beatus onto the ground. "I will not be stopped! With Cymbeline working with me, and Isabella sending recent contact, I am going to move—soon. I am going to Arelle, and *no* one can stop me! Even if it kills me, I am going to find a safe home for these Faeries, and the real answer to their Question! I promised them this, and I will not take that promise back!"

"Surely it would be better for so many people if Somenus were dead," I said weakly, glancing toward Momentum sheepishly. Momentum dropped his chin to his chest, and Hanz turned to me with a look that said he was surprised to hear support coming from my side of the table. "Somenus may be King," I said, "but I think he is hurting people."

Momentum turned his head to narrow his brow at me. His glassy eyes seemed to be asking me, *What do you know?*

"It is evil for a king to hurt his people," Momentum said in a soft voice, "and it is evil for a people to hurt their king. But evil only begets evil, Hanz—if you kill Somenus, it will not end the bloodshed. It will beget more bloodshed."

Hanz stood. "I have heard your counsel, and I thank you for it. But you are both old and jaded. You are tired from old wars. But this is a new war—*my* war, and *my* Faeries."

"Wisdom ages like vino, dear son," Joel said with pleading eyes, "It does not weaken, but it *strengthens* with time. We are two men living with the consequences of decisions we have made—decisions you are about to make all over again. *Listen* to us!"

Hanz shook his head. "I *must* listen to my conscience."

"Hanz!" Joel jumped to his feet, then sighed as his son stormed out of the room. Joel collapsed back down onto the chair. Momentum made a loud sigh. I turned to look at them.

"If what Hanz wants to do is so bad, why don't you two just *stop* him?"

"You don't get it Leo," Momentum said as Joel shook his head. "We *can't* stop him."

"You... can't?" I looked back toward the door where Hanz left.

"The monster you made all those seasons ago begot another Monster, Aorist," said Joel. "I did my best to stop him, but the monster lives in his blood."

Momentum shook his head.

"Why can't you guys stop him?" I asked.

Momentum rose from his chair and stretched. "Leo, that staff he is carrying around? He could kill every single person in this house with it in a matter of clicks."

My mouth dropped open. "*What*? I thought it was like... a beacon or something."

"It is many things," said Joel in a dark voice, "Including being the second most powerful weapon in existence... that we know of."

"The only other people in this house who could wield that thing are you and Joel, here," Momentum said, pointing at me, "Because you're humans. Faeries can't kill. We can't use weapons like that. So Hanz is... well, he is someone who can't be stopped. Whether we like it or not, he overpowers us all. We just have to hope he doesn't..." Momentum glanced at Joel, "...turn against us."

"Could *you* take it from him?" I asked Joel.

"Even if I could—which I can't—I swore never to touch that thing again."

I nodded. "So, what are you going to..." my voice trailed off as Joel stood and left the room without so much as a 'good night'.

Momentum watched him leave, scratching the back of his head.

"Man," I blew air through my lips in a whistle. "That was intense." I looked up to see a glaring Time Faerie leaning down toward me. "*What?*" I pulled my feet up onto my chair.

"What do you *know*, Leo? Tell me!"

"What do *I* know?" I frowned, "Don't you mean, what do *you* know?"

"No," he leaned closer, shaking his finger at me, "Don't turn this around! Why are you suddenly on the side of killing Somenus?"

"I'm not!" I scooted the chair away from Momentum and jumped to my feet. I circled the room, keeping distance between us as Momentum moved toward me. "I don't want to kill him, I was just... Momentum! I am *with* you here—I am an Ambulance driver! I don't have a killing bone in my body!"

"No, but something made you say that! Where do you go in your sleep, Leo? I *know* you are using Somenus' powers!"

"*Leave me alone!*" I crowed, "I don't want to talk about this!"

Momentum pulled back, giving me a look of distaste.

"And anyway, *you're* the one who could probably fix all this by telling everyone the answer to the Question! Why won't you tell anyone?"

Momentum started to make the same snarling noises one might expect from a raging bull, ready to charge.

"Come *on*! Just tell me!" I cried.

"Go to bed, Leo!" Momentum pointed at the door.

"What, you're sending me to bed like a little *kid*?" I scoffed.

"Well, since sleeping is all you care about these days, anyway!" Momentum bellowed.

"Fine!" I returned, matching his volume, "I will!"

I stomped out of Momentum's room, inwardly asking myself why on Earth I was so angry, and slammed myself in my room. Like a proper teenager, I even turned to lock the door and shout an added insult toward the door. I tromped through my room and found my chest from under the bed, then threw myself onto the mattress, fully dressed, holding the chest closely to my person. And in moments, I was asleep.

❖

I sat up. I lifted up my hands and moved them around. They looked as clear and colorful as ever, but the rest of my surroundings were like a faint blue blur. I looked down at where I was sitting. I could see a faint outline of Somenus' sleeping body below me. I didn't know where his mind was at; it would be somewhere in the dreamscape. If I could stay away from it, he wouldn't be able to torment me—at least not *yet*.

How could I describe the dreamscape? It was like an x-ray view of the world. I could see faint outlines of rooms and furniture, like blueprints, with foggy images of bodies walking around.

My surroundings, however, did not indicate where my physical body was, but where Somenus' was. I had deduced that this place was Arelle. Here, in the dreamscape, I had found a connection to Somenus through his hand. While my sleeping body remained at Winter's End, my mind and soul were in Arelle—walking amongst the sleepers.

As I gazed around, I could see glowing bodies, lying in different places. In the dreamscape, those who were awake were essentially nonexistent, and those who were sleeping lit up like lamps. Some shined brighter than others, though I didn't know why.

I hopped out of Somenus' body outline and floated around the dreamscape, moving my legs as if I were walking. This was what Somenus, the Faerie of Dreams, saw whenever he was sleeping: he saw the lights of those whose minds had left their bodies to roam the spirit world. I had learned that by touching any of those bodies, I could see inside that person's mind—I could see into their dreams, just like Somenus could.

It made me sick to think that Somenus must use that very power to gain magik from the affections and thoughts of others. In order to set myself apart from him, I tried to disturb as few dreamers as possible.

I floated downwards, searching for the brightest light, and the only light I really cared about. Yes, there it was. It was way down under the city again. I hurried toward it desperately.

I stopped just beside the sleeping body. She was curled up on a little cot. I wished I could see the shape of her true form, but her body was more like a light with a human outline; no specific features could be seen very clearly, aside from her face.

I reached forward to touch it, running my finger along her jaw. Then the light seized me, and I felt myself sucked into her mind.

"Damn," I groaned, feeling the stupid helmet form around my face. "Why does this thing always have to—?"

"Beloved!" I heard her voice. I snapped my head in her direction, finding her beautiful face through the infuriatingly thin slit in my helmet. Lola: the love of my life—the girl of my dreams.

"Lola!" I laughed as her body hit me like a blow to the chest. She wrapped her arms around me, and I clutched her tightly, hating that there were moments in my life when we weren't this close. I felt her, and yet I didn't feel her. It was only a dream, after all.

"Oh, I have missed you," she said as she peered up toward me.

It was amazing—*she* was amazing. Everybody else in the dreamscape didn't *know* they were dreaming; they all start out in a place of—well—dreaminess. Their awareness and inhibitions are asleep with their bodies; instead of having discernment and clarity, the dreamer would accept everything they see, even if it makes no sense. It isn't until Somenus would touch them or alert them to his presence that they would seem to wake up *within* their dream. Lola was different; she *always* seemed to be awake within her dreams.

She placed her hands on the helmet and shook it.

"Ow."

"Why must you *wear* this?" she asked hopelessly.

"It's..." I stuttered. Would it even help if I told her my theory? "The only time something like this happens is if you have seen me before... and this is your only memory of me, so you can't actually see my face, because you don't know it. But that can't be possible since we have never met!" I had learned a lot by watching Somenus and studying his interactions with various dreamers; those who had met him before saw him differently than those who met him only in their dreams.

Lola squinted thoughtfully for a moment, then gasped. "But I *have* seen you before!"

I chuckled. "What... Do you mean *here*? In your dreams?"

"No," she shook her head, "In the Red Gate!"

"....What?" I pushed Lola back with my hands and stared into her face. "*What* Red Gate?" She had never mentioned *that* before!

"Oh, never mind that," she patted my shoulder. "I don't want to think about *those* things, I want to be with you! Even if you aren't real..." Her smile seemed to fade. The comment hit me like a knife to the heart. Still, she didn't think of me as a real person. If only I could tell her how desperately untrue that was.

"Why would you say that?" I asked, feeling that melancholy mopey mood from earlier that day creep up on me.

Lola brightened a little. "Oh! I didn't mean to upset you!"

"You didn't upset me," I lied, "Nothing you say could ever upset me."

"You are so sweet, Beloved," she sighed, walking over to the little nest of pillows I set up for her. "Shall we read?"

"Yes," I said, though I didn't really *want* to hear more about Anodos and his depressing singleness. Had Cymbeline really been about to confess her love to me? I shuddered, then pushed the thought from my mind. No—I was with Lola now; that was all that mattered. I lay down on the floor of the private temple and rested my head on a pillow.

Lola sat beside me and rubbed her fingers across my helmet. Even though she didn't even touch my skin, it sent chills down my spine. I longed to know how it felt when she ran her fingers through my hair—if only...

"Are you *really* married?" I asked wistfully.

Lola withdrew her hand from my helmet, as if the mere mention of the idea made her feel withdrawn.

"Uh... yes," she said in a weary voice.

"To Somenus?"

"Yes."

The hatred welled in my heart like an over-boiling pot. Why? *How?*

"Well," I said, feeling the empty sadness of Anodos watching his love walk away on the arm of another man, "Why don't you read the book, now."

I lay there, listening to the voice of the woman I loved. I couldn't describe how or why I loved her. It was a feeling as old as the world and as fresh as a newborn baby. I loved her with every atom of my being, even though I had only met her here in the dreamscape.

I stared up at her face as she read, studying her lips, her rosy cheeks, her glorious auburn hair. *I will find you,* I promised her inside my heart, *I am coming to Arelle, and I will get you out of there.*

I would have lain there all night, listening to her voice, until someone forced me to wake up, if the darkness had not alerted me. *He* was approaching.

I sat up quickly.

"What is it, Beloved?" she asked urgently. I could sense *him*. I could feel the hand growing closer to its consciousness; it longed to be reunited with him. Somenus' spirit was coming to enter Lola's dream. Well, there was only one way to protect her from him, and I knew it all too well. I did it every night. I distracted him.

I knew he was obsessed with her. I could feel it in his hand. I could feel it in his mind. I had some bond with him that told me such things. Yes, he was obsessed with her—and it drew him to her. Yet there was someone else who he might have been just a little bit more obsessed with; someone whose presence and obsession could tempt him even more than she could—that was *me*.

"Don't leave me again!" she cried, grabbing me by the arm. She knew I was about to disappear, as I always did.

"I have to," I said, "But I'll be back, I promise. Hang in there Lola, just remember, you're *never* alone."

"Wait!" she held onto me, refusing to let go.

"What is it, Beloved?" I asked, pausing to touch her face.

"What is your name, Beloved?"

I gritted my teeth. No—I couldn't tell her. If she found out, *he* could find out. And I... I couldn't face it if he knew my name. It was already hard to keep his words from my mind... his eyes. No, it was something I couldn't give her.

"My name..." I sighed, "...is Beloved." I couldn't wait any longer; I vanished from her mind.

26

—— Clover ——

House of Perfidy

Y ou're not allowed up here, you know," Yuma said, flicking an acorn down toward the ground. "Only Black Eagles are allowed up on the walls."

"I'm not on the walls," Clover said innocently, "I am in a tree."

Yuma snorted. "Still, Eagles get suspicious of anyone trying to get this high—you could be shot."

"Shot?" Clover raised an eyebrow. "Are you going to shoot me?"

"Maybe." Yuma leaned back on his hands. He was sitting on the edge of the wall with his feet dangling down toward the Fifth Level. Clover had climbed the old, twisty oak tree that graced the public courtyard at the north end of the Fifth Level. He was sitting on a branch, only a couple feet away from the wall, peeling a mango.

"It's like a whole other world up here, isn't it?" Clover asked as he gazed past the wall. There were houses, buildings, walkways—even gardens up on the walls where the Eagles lived. "That person over there doesn't look like an Eagle."

Clover pointed toward a woman in a simple dress, pulling water up from what appeared to be a well.

"Eagles are allowed to bring families up here. In a way you are right, Clover. It sort of is its own city up on the walls." Yuma turned to observe the woman. "She is Malbec, the wife of the Brigadier General."

"Do you know everyone by name?" Clover asked, flicking a peel to the ground.

"Most people, yes," Yuma said, "At least everyone who lives on the Fifth Level wall."

"Do you ever go to the other walls?"

"Yes, sometimes," Yuma crossed his legs. "But most of the time, soldiers keep to the Level of their posting."

Clover nodded. "It's been nice since you got posted up here. There was a long time when I didn't see you at *all*."

Yuma raised an eyebrow.

Clover took a bite of his mango. "What? Why are you making that face?"

Yuma cracked a smirk. "You *missed* me, huh?"

"Didn't I just say that?"

Yuma nodded. "In your way, I guess you did."

Clover thought for a moment, then said, "Did you miss me?"

"What a ridiculous question," Yuma said. He leaned forward to stretch his back, then stood. "How has it been with Patro? Has he given you an answer?"

"I can only guess he is stalling," Clover mumbled. He didn't *love* being reminded of his ultimatum with Patro. "But I told him he had until today at luncheon."

"I heard the households all sent their gifts to the king last night. Do you know what Patro sent?"

"No." Clover yawned. "I was up all night watching Patro, then I came out here to check in with you."

"Lights, Clover," Yuma whistled, "When do you ever *sleep*?"

"I don't know," Clover shrugged. "Once we leave, I can promise you. I am going to sleep for a *long* time."

"It is strange to think about leaving this place," said Yuma, "I can't believe I am saying this, but it has started to feel a bit like home to me."

Clover tilted his head slightly to study Yuma's facial expression. "You *like* being an Eagle, don't you, Yuma?"

Yuma flattened his mouth. "I guess so. I am a soldier, always have been. So, I fit in easily amongst other soldiers. But the Black Eagles are unique; they're like a whole community made only of soldiers and their families, with their own culture and social structure. A man like me can find a place in a community like this."

Clover finished chewing his current bite of mango, smacked his lips, and said, "Yuma, you make it sound like you didn't fit in before this. Didn't you come from a pretty tight-knit community?"

Yuma crossed his arms and looked down at his boots. "I am more like you than you think," he said in a low voice, "I may be the chieftain's nephew, but I still felt like an outsider. I suppose I could have found a place there if I had married and had children, but that was never my way." He looked up at Clover. "But here, there is a place for me regardless of marital status. I never realized that was something I needed until I came here."

"But aren't you the general of the Fero Army?" Clover asked.

Yuma sniffed. "Clover, our army is nothing but villagers with bows and swords. The only true warrior there was *me*."

"I guess we are kind of similar, then," Clover said with a nod. He tossed his mango seed out of the tree.

"Clover, you can't just litter like that."

"The gardeners will clean it up." Clover glanced down at his sticky hands. "Do you have a handkerchief?"

"Clover," Yuma mumbled, digging into his knapsack for a handkerchief, "Have you ever heard of *pockets*?"

Clover held out his hand and took the napkin. "Thanks."

"You nervous about today?"

Clover looked up from his hands as he did his best to wipe them clean. "Nervous? Yes... probably. I'm worried that we spent an entire season here, just to fail. What a waste."

"This hasn't been a waste, Clover," Yuma said. "None of life is a waste; whether its bells spent gazing at a wall on patrol, or eating a meal, or spending time with those you love. All life is good life. All time is good time."

Clover thought about that. "Hmm...Well," he nodded, "I suppose a life spent moving in one direction, regardless of how fast or slow it moves, is worthwhile if the end goal is worthy."

Yuma chuckled. "You're a bit deeper than me, Clover."

"I may have been standing in one place for an entire season, but at least it is still pointed in the direction of Isabella and serving her."

"Ah," Yuma's smile weakened, "Right—*her*. Still think about her, do you?"

Clover nodded. "Yes."

"Haven't your affections sort of...I don't know...*weakened* after all this time away from her?"

"Affections?" Clover straightened his back in offense. "Affections aren't strong enough to keep me on the same path for a lifetime! Affections are inconstant—they come and go. It's my *promise* that keeps me dedicated. A promise cannot be broken."

Yuma winced. "Why would you make a promise to someone you only met once—to someone who didn't even love you back."

Clover turned his head to gaze out toward the Sapphire House compound. *Why? What a ridiculous question.*

"Clover... what drew you to her. Was she just..." Yuma grunted, "Was she just really attractive?"

"I don't know," Clover said under his breath, still gazing out toward the compound, "It was like... my soul just lit on fire when I saw her. Maybe it was her beauty...maybe it was her soul." He turned to look Yuma in the eyes. "But something inside me broke, like a shell around my heart. She made me feel things: anger, longing, desire, loneliness—passion. She was the person who brought me to life when I thought I was dead. It wasn't anything she did or said to me, she just *was*. She existed. I... I don't need her to be anything more than that."

"Hades, Clover." Yuma sighed.

Clover nodded, smiling a little to himself. "I... I can see how I must sound to you."

"How is that?"

"Humans talk about how Elves are so single-minded. We fixate on something and can't let it go. I... I think I see how strange it must seem to you."

Yuma shook his head. "It's us who are strange, Clover. We are flighty and inconstant. We *break* our promises."

Clover filled his lungs deeply with air, then exhaled. Yes—humans break their promises. "Patro is going to break his promise to me, isn't he, Yuma?"

Yuma nodded soberly. "Yes, I think he is."

"Yuma?"

Yuma lifted his chin to Clover expectantly.

"Have you ever had your soul light on fire... like that?"

Yuma cocked his head, thinking of how to respond. "I..." he twisted his head slightly. "No—no, I don't think so."

"Are you sure?"

Yuma frowned. "What do you mean: *am I sure?*"

Clover shrugged. "I don't know...you just looked sort of sad just now."

"Clover," Yuma chuckled, "Don't try to guess other people's emotions; you're really bad at it, remember?"

"Right."

The Midday bell began to sound from a nearby bell tower. Clover sighed to himself as Yuma pulled out and reset his clicker.

"Well," Clover swung a leg over the side of his tree branch, "Time to go."

"Lights be with you, Clover," Yuma said with an encouraging nod, "You're doing the right thing."

"One can hope," Clover said, then dropped down to the ground, landing in a crouch.

He rose to his feet and jogged back to the Sapphire House's front gate. Once inside the compound, he glanced toward the side path that led to his bungalow. He wanted to see Solo and TSB before the luncheon, but there wasn't time. They would be missing him after he was away all night, but they would have to wait a little longer.

Clover jogged toward Appius' house. Patro was meant to be having lunch with his brother today, even though the two hated each other more than anything on the world.

Clover found Patro waiting for him by the landing at the bottom of the stairs.

"What took you so long, you lark!" Patro snarled.

"I'm here on time," Clover said blankly. "Did you remember my—?"

"Ah, Appius! My dear brother!" Patro belted, ignoring Clover, holding out his hands at the sight of Appius at the top of the stairs.

"Well," Appius shouted from above, "Get up here already!"

Clover sighed, following as Patro tromped up the steps. There at the top, Appius and his household stood, bowing and shaking hands in greeting. Everyone all but ignored Clover, and he liked it that way. He wouldn't know what to do with himself if someone tried to interact with him in their shallow way. These family meals gave the outward appearance of peace and friendship, but behind every comment and glance was hate and deception.

It wasn't any wonder that Patro didn't ever set foot in Appius' Residence without Clover; he constantly feared for his life. Everyone knew, if Patro died, the Estate would pass onto his son. Appius, however, believed that in the case of such events, he had enough influence in the family to take over control. Appius himself never tried to kill his brother, but he had enough hatred in his heart to do so, and this allowed his family to entertain schemes and intrigues of such a nature.

Even so, Clover and Patro, were greeted with smiles and compliments when they entered Appius' house. As much as Patro was reviled, he still held the family 'throne,' and thus, everyone bowed to him.

The family lunch was eaten on the ground in Appius' outdoor pavilion. Lavish rugs had been laid out on the flagstones and feather stuffed cushions provided places for the guests to recline. The group sat in a circle on the ground, and at their center were large platters of cold food to eat. Meat was regularly served at Bavelonian meals, making Clover often nauseous at meal times, so he never ate with the others.

Instead, Clover sat beside Patro on his knees, keeping an eye out for suspicious characters or glances. He was a bodyguard, not one of the party-goers; that distinction was the only thing that helped him stomach being present at such a sickening affair. Eating animals, how *despicable*.

After introductions and preliminary small talks had taken place, Clover cleared his throat in Patro's direction.

Patro scoffed under his breath. "Let me guess—straight to the point? As always?"

"I would like to know if you made your decision," Clover said in a steady voice.

Patro scoffed a second time, jolting his head back animatedly. "*Yes*, I made my decision."

Clover didn't like the attitude he was getting. "I am guessing you have decided not to help me," he said.

"I don't like people who try to push me around," Patro spoke with the same patronizing attitude he usually reserved for disobedient grandchildren. "So, I have decided I will just have to find another bodyguard who is willing to stay in his place."

"When have I *ever* not done what I was asked?" Clover asked calmly, maintaining his equanimity.

Patro gave Clover a slow head turn, pursing his lips tightly together. "The moment you gave me an ultimatum."

Clover blinked. "I—I don't see how that was stepping out of line." He was being honest, as always.

"That is *precisely* my problem with you, Elf boy." Patro forced a phony grin. "You just don't *see* things, do you?"

"If you are implying something," Clover said carefully, "I don't know what it is."

"*Exactly*," Patro sighed, acting sympathetic. "You cannot hear silent words."

Clover looked at the man quietly for a moment, then nodded. "I see what you are saying. You do not use words for their meanings; you use them for outcomes. You do not like that I ignore your hidden cues."

"Precisely." Patro leaned back on his arm and stuffed a chunk of meat into it, proceeding to talk as he chewed it. "In one sense, I like this about you. I never have to wonder if you are scheming. But it gets old, and," he paused, squinting his face as though thoughtful, "you will not let yourself be manipulated."

Clover chuckled uncharacteristically, shaking his head. "Well, that is the first time I have heard you admit to manipulation."

Patro frowned deeply and swallowed his food loudly before saying, "Clover, I will be taking my ring back before nightfall. You are no longer in my service."

Clover felt a weight lift from his heart, and he suddenly felt like he could breathe deeply. "Really?" he asked. "Are you sure?"

Patro chuckled to himself. "I am sure. And it is a shame, really." He reached into his vest pocket, pulling out a little scroll which was sealed in metallic gold wax. Clover stared in astonishment.

"Is that—?"

"*Yes*," Patro smiled slyly, "It is an invitation from the king himself."

"Your gift was favored?"

"Yes." He sniffed with a pompous face as he tucked the scroll away. "He was *very* impressed with my gift. The queen herself wrote to say it was delicious."

Clover looked down in defeat. "I see."

"You know Clover, I should thank you, because if you hadn't provoked me to anger over this, I would not have tried so *hard* with this gift." He grinned widely; his golden tooth sparkled like a star in the seas.

"I suppose there is no longer any reason for me to sit here protecting your life now, is there?" Clover stood.

Patro grunted. "Go, I don't care. Appius is pleased with me today because I told him he could come to the king's banquet with me on Mansday."

Clover didn't respond verbally. He gave Patro a lifeless stare, then turned to leave.

"Oh, Clover?" Patro called to him. Clover stopped, giving the man one last moment of attention.

"What?"

"Thank you."

Clover frowned. Patro *never* thanked people—not genuinely anyway. "For what?"

Patro laughed and turned back to his food, letting the words float meaninglessly around in the air between them.

Clover took the long way back to his house. Well, it was over. It was over, and he felt relieved. Perhaps it was for the best. Would the king be any different to Patro? Would Clover even be willing to ask for help from someone who led a kingdom like this? He was glad he wouldn't have to face that choice. Why the Truth Faerie told them to come here, he couldn't guess. Perhaps he would never know.

As he walked around one of the garden paths behind Appius' residence, he stopped to admire a patch of flowers which grew under a fruit tree. They were white.

"Isabella," he said softly, picking one of the flowers and smelling it. He often stopped to say her name, reminding himself why he had come to such a horrible, Lightless place.

A rustling sound shook Clover from his reveries. He glanced around, searching for its source. One of the thicker bits of foliage was quivering with movement. He studied it carefully. There were no wild animals in Bavel, so what could it be? He stepped forward, speaking softly.

"Come out," he said, "I will not harm you." Movement burst from the bush as Clover's little gnome attaché rushed at him. He thrust himself into Clover's arms and clutched him desperately, quaking with fear. "*TSB*?" Clover wrapped his arms protectively around the infant-sized creature. "What is it? How did you get out of the house?"

The gnome only trembled.

"What is it?" Clover asked, growing concerned. How had he escaped the house? Clover *always* locked the door.

Clover's eyes darted in the direction of his house, and a burst of adrenaline fueled him into action. He jumped to his feet, holding the gnome against his chest, and raced home.

"Oh please, Lights," he prayed, hoping he was wrong about what he would find.

Once he rounded the corner and his bungalow came into view, he gasped. The door to his little house had been smashed to pieces.

"Solo!" he cried. He rushed inside, scanning the apartment for his ram. There were signs of a struggle, but Solo wasn't there. "*Solo!*" he screamed falling to his knees, still clutching the gnome tightly. "Where are you?"

The sound of a satisfied chuckle sounded from behind Clover. The Elf whirled around to see Domitianus leaning against the wall with his arms crossed, looking very pleased with himself. Clover stood, shaking, and stepped toward him.

"Where is Solo?" he demanded.

"*Solo*? Is that what you call it?" Domitianus teased.

"Where *is* he?" Clover's eyes grew wild; an uncontrollable rage welled up inside him. Domitianus' face changed as he studied Clover.

"Now, now," The Nobleman took a step away from him, growing increasingly nervous. "It wasn't *me* who took him!"

"*Where is he?*" Clover screamed, his mouth foaming.

"He's gone!" Domitianus cowered as Clover cornered him. He had not seen Clover angry before—*no one* had—not like this. "Patro gave him to the king!"

"The..." Clover stammered, "K–*King*?"

Patro's ominous words rang through Clover's tumultuous mind. *The Queen herself wrote to say it was delicious.*

"No..." Clover whispered, falling down to his knees.

Domitianus backed away from Clover quickly, seizing his chance to escape the Elf's rageful focus. "I mean, you had it coming!" he laughed nervously.

Clover knelt there, shaking. Visions from the wulf attack accosted his mind. He couldn't stop them. Images of blood and gore played on repeat. He saw Andrew's torn throat; he saw her shaking.

"No," he whispered, "No... no, no, no..." he shook his head back and forth. "Not Solo—he was the one... who," his voice cracked, "The one who *lived.*" Clover's hands formed into fists. TSB pried himself loose of Clover's arms and dashed under the bed.

Then, the rage seized control. Clover no longer made decisions—he acted. It was as if his mind was floating above his body, watching himself march out of the building. He raced through the Estate ground swiftly and gracefully, until he came crashing into Appius' house. He could hear gasps and screams from shocked party guests as he grabbed Appius by the throat and lifted him into the air with alarming strength.

"Where is Patro?" he demanded in a voice too deep to be his own.

"He went home!" Appius cried. Clover dropped the man and turned to glance at all the fearful faces before racing out of the house.

He flew toward Patro's residence. He blazed through the doors and marched past a group of shocked family members. A chorus of voices asked him what he was doing or where he was going, but he ignored them, stampeding forward until he had all but torn down the door to Patro's room.

There was Patro, Master of the Sapphire House, standing in the middle of the room. At first, he looked smug, posed there on the rug with his arms behind his back, ready to feast on his newest victim's misery. Then he saw Clover. He saw his face...he saw the predatory eyes of vengeance.

"Clover!" Patro squawked, quaking. He cowered instantly onto the ground as Clover sprung toward him. Clover pushed Patro onto his back, knocking the wind out of him, and leapt onto his waist, pinning him down. Clover seized Patro's neck. "Clover," Patro wheezed, "you promised to protect me!"

"I am no longer in your service!" Clover growled. He wanted to snap the man's spine, but some small part of his sanity still remained, begging him to let go. He couldn't; he couldn't let go. Patro shook from side to side beneath him. Clover reacted quickly, tightening his grip.

"Please, Elf! Don't kill me!" Patro pleaded, straining for air.

"You took my friend!" Clover bellowed. "You killed him! He was *everything* to me!"

"I'm sorry!" Patro gasped. Clover growled. Sorry? Remorse was an emotion Patro wasn't capable of feeling.

"*Sorry*? Patro—you are not sorry. You stole *everything* from me!"

"Let me live!" Patro pleaded. "Please!"

"I can't!" Clover felt himself shaking. He wanted to kill. He needed to kill. "Isabella... I'm sorry." He closed his eyes, tightening his choke hold.

Patro's wide, terror-filled eyes suddenly lit up with hope at the sound of her name. "Isabella would not want you to kill me!" he said, having no idea who Isabella was. Even in crisis, Patro was a strategist; he would pull at any string he could find.

"Don't invoke her name!" Clover pleaded, though a tear pried itself free of his eye. "Damn you!" As wrong as Patro was about everything, he was right.

"Please!" Patro begged, "In the name of Isabella, don't kill me!"

"*You snake!*" Clover roared. He tipped his head back and looked up toward the ceiling breathing loudly for a moment. "I..." he whispered, "I am not..." He looked down at Patro, loosening his fingers slightly. "I am not like you people... I refuse to... to..."

"Clover!" Patro pleaded, "Take the scroll, you can come with me! I will take you to see the king! Alright? Please—just—*spare my life!*"

Clover looked up suddenly, growing aware of his surroundings. He had an audience. Every member of Patro's dysfunctional family was crowded around, waiting suspensefully.

"Oh, just do it!" Marcella yelled. "Stop hesitating!"

Patro turned his head slowly to see his family crowded around, watching. He chuckled ironically. "Look, Clover. Do you see? They all want me dead."

Clover studied the faces of those watching, frozen in his moment of decision. Would he really do the unforgivable act of murder that Patro's family had begged him to commit for the last four hundred days? Was he no different to them? Had the man angered *Clover* enough to cause him to seek the same vengeance?

Slowly, Clover pulled his hands free of Patro's throat. He stood, taking a step away from Patro's limp body. Patro rose quickly, running to cling to the wall opposite to where his family had been watching. Domitianus stepped forward.

"If you don't have the guts," he snarled, "just let me do it!"

"*Domitianus*!" Patro hissed through his teeth.

"No one touches him!" Clover yelled, startling the room. "If anyone lays a finger on him, I will kill you!"

All were silent. After a few moments, some of the family members left, while others stayed, watching curiously. Clover turned his gaze toward Patro and sighed.

"Take me to the king tomorrow."

"I will!" Patro nodded fervently. "I will take you."

"And my Friend."

"Your..." Patro looked around in confusion. "Of course, yes—and your friend."

Clover's heart grew too heavy for the weight of his anger. Grief overwhelmed him, and he looked around wearily at all the onlookers.

"You people are horrible," he mumbled to himself, then raised his voice, "You're all horrible!"

No one said anything as he stumbled slowly out of the room, walking like an animated corpse.

He plodded lifelessly until he reached the Sapphire gates, then pushed them open and left the Estate. TSB ran in front of him, gazing worriedly up at him. Clover ignored him, sliding one foot in front of the other until he reached the Fifth Level Main Street. The gnome followed him at a distance, as if trying to watch over him.

"*Clover*?" Yuma called from a distance. He raced toward Clover, then met him with a slap on the shoulder. "Clover, what happened? You look like you're going to be sick!"

"It's over," Clover mumbled through his numb lips, "Everything is over."

Yuma sighed. "He said 'No?'"

"No—It's *over*!" Clover swung his shoulder free of Yuma's hand. "I am *done*!"

Yuma narrowed his eyes. "Clover... what *happened*?"

TSB scurried from the sidelines and raced up the back of Yuma's clothes. He hopped onto his shoulder, then hid behind his braid.

"Little Thief," Yuma whispered, holding out his finger to the trembling gnome. He looked back at Clover, whose body was hunched over like a dying houseplant. "Clover... just talk to me."

Clover's gelatin legs wobbled, then dropped him to his knees. Yuma crouched beside him and put a hand on his shoulder. He squeezed it.

"Yuma..." Clover whispered. "He's gone—Solo is *gone*."

Yuma squeezed Clover's shoulder again; he couldn't think of what to say. "I..."

"Patro took him out of spite... the king..." his voice cracked, "*ate* him... just like the wulves."

"Oh, Clover..." Yuma sighed.

"What must he have thought? Did he think I *abandoned* him?"

"No," Yuma pulsed Clover's shoulder again, "Don't think like that, Clover. I am sure it was over quickly for him."

Clover coughed out a sob, then leaned forward, pressing his face into the grass. He stretched out his body on the ground, weeping without any care about how he looked. Yuma placed a hand on his back and waited.

"I don't want to go!" Clover said at length through his tears. "You can't make me. I won't see the man who *ate* my friend!"

"What?" Yuma rubbed Clover's back. "Clover, what are you talking about?"

"*You* go. I can't go!"

"Clover... go *where*?"

"The felling King!" Clover said, turning his face in the dirt. "I can't see him. I *won't* see him!"

"I thought..." Yuma leaned his face down towards Clover's so he could meet his eyes. "Clover, I thought you said it was over."

"We have an audience with the king... Mansday," Clover sniffed.

"Are you *serious*?"

"...yes."

"Clover, can you at least be happy about *that*?" Yuma said, straightening back up.

"I will never be happy again."

Yuma sighed. "Clover, you got us *in*! Think of Isabella!"

Clover rubbed his face in the dirt. "I am too ashamed to think about her. I killed her sheep!"

"Clover!" Yuma swatted Clover's back. "Get a hold of yourself! You didn't kill her sheep—*she* did!"

Clover pressed himself up, shooting a glare into Yuma's face. "*What* did you say?"

"*She* was the one who left her flock behind, Clover. She abandoned them. *You* didn't. Alright? Isabella—whoever she is—isn't perfect, and neither are you. Now, if you can forgive her for letting down her flock, then you should forgive yourself. You're the most dedicated man I've ever met. You couldn't have done more for Solo, could you? You did everything you could, and that's all a man can do."

Clover slid up into a kneeling position. "You think... she will forgive me?"

"If she doesn't," Yuma slapped a palm on Clover's shoulder, "I've got some words for her."

Clover tried to sniff up a smile. "Thanks."

"Clover, I'm *sorry*," Yuma said, pressing his face closer, "An evil thing was done to someone you love. But it's not over, you've got to press on from here. You're coming with me to speak with the king. I need you, and you need me. We are going to stick this out *together*, right?"

Clover nodded weakly. "Alright."

"You don't have to say anything, just stay by my side. Let's get this over with, and then we can get you felling *out* of here."

"Alright."

"Come on," Yuma sighed, pulling Clover to his feet. "You don't have to go back there tonight. Come up to the walls with me, we can tell the general of our audience with the king. Maybe it's time to get him on our side. You ready for a change of scene?"

"Yes," Clover said as he wiped his sleeve across his face, "That sounds nice. I never want to go back to that house again."

"You don't have to," Yuma said, leading Clover toward the walls. "Come on, I am sure it'll be alright taking you up there, just this once."

27

—— Lola ——

The Goblins

Lola sat on her cot quietly, watching Hevel pace back and forth. He seemed agitated. Something was clearly bothering him, but anytime she asked him about it, he shrugged it off. She found it strange that everyone else was so afraid of him. He really was a kind and humble person. Lola knew her time with him in the prison would likely be short. She hardly ever spent more than a couple weeks there before Somenus had her return to the Eight Stones.

Hevel turned swiftly toward her, as if stirred by a sudden thought.

"Lola?" he asked in his deep, cavernous voice.

"Yes, Hevel?" She sat up a bit straighter, welcoming his attention with a smile.

"Why did Somenus confine you down here this time?" His eyes watched her intently.

Lola squirmed inwardly. She didn't like talking about her relationship with Somenus. "I... well..."

"Come, child," he sighed, "It's safe to talk to me about him."

Lola laced her fingers together. "Well, a week or so ago, when he was playing the Charmer, we were dining regularly together."

"Yes?"

Lola shrugged her shoulders. "He asked me to read my book to him, so I did."

Hevel waited for her to continue. After a long pause, he said, "And?"

"Then we quarreled. He grew angry at me." Her face grew as vacant as a leaf of unmarked paper.

"And?" Hevel took a step forward. "He *hurt* you?"

Lola shook her head, pinning her lips closed.

"Lola, you can tell me if he hurt you. I *care* about you." Hevel stepped closer, reaching his hand forward, palm up.

Lola looked at his hand. "Hevel, he didn't hurt me. He just sent me away, down here."

"I can tell something is wrong," Hevel sighed, dropping his hand. "The way you move; the way you sit—you're in pain."

Lola's eyes shot up to his face. "Hevel, I'm fine! *Nothing* is wrong!"

"You admitted to me that you are dying," Hevel pressed, "Lola, I won't stand by and let it happen! At least *tell* Somenus that you're—"

"No!" Lola jumped to her feet, then yelped from a sudden pain within. She bent over, thrusting her hand against her back. Hevel reached forward and caught her before she toppled face first to the floor. "No," she panted, "*Please* don't tell Somenus."

"As twisted as he is, Lola, he clearly cares about you. I am sure he would not want you in pain!" Hevel said, helping her back onto the cot.

Lola scoffed under her breath.

"At least let me see the wounds; perhaps there is something I can do to help," Hevel pleaded. He knelt down before her on the cell floor and took her hands in his. "I hate seeing you—the only light in my life—in so much distress."

"It's not the pain that distresses me," Lola whispered. She bowed her head and her chopped red hair fell in front of her face like a veil. "It's..." A single tear dropped from her hidden eyes and landed on Hevel's hand. He squeezed her fingers.

"*Yes*, child?"

"I... I am so scared of him," she said through a quivering voice, "I am scared of when he... gets close to me."

Hevel closed his eyes with a sorrowful nod. "Does he force himself upon you, my child?"

Lola scoffed. "I don't know."

Hevel dropped his forehead onto her knees. Lola lifted her head, surprised to see him shaking.

"Hevel? Hevel don't cry!" She placed her palm on his head. It was so strange to see that tall, powerful Faerie of Death kneeling before her like a child. "Hevel, please don't cry!"

The Faerie didn't raise his head; he squeezed her fingers with both his hands and whimpered silently.

Lola stared down at him. She felt numb. How could he cry for her when she couldn't cry for herself—not like *that*. No, she didn't want to cry. She didn't want to admit that what had happened to her was real. And was it so bad? Every other woman in Somenus' Harem had been compelled to do whatever he asked; why did *she* feel so shaken?

Lola patted Hevel on the head. "Do not cry for me," she whispered, "It is not so bad. You are the one living in this prison. I live in a palace most of the time. I... I don't want you to cry for me."

Hevel lifted his head slowly, peering up at her with swollen eyes. "Child, I hate to think of him mistreating someone as pure as you."

"He hardly ever touches me!" she said firmly, pushing Hevel back by the shoulder. "He's only ever..." she cleared her throat, "We've not *been together* very many times—at least not for a while. He... Hevel, he is angry at me because I do not *want* to be close to him."

"So, he hurts you?" Hevel sniffed.

"No," she shook her head. *At least, not very much.* "No, I think he gets angry enough to hurt me, but that's why he throws me down here."

"Why did he cut your beautiful hair?" Hevel reached a hand forward, touching a lock that was a bit longer than the rest.

"I told you... he gets angry, but I think he tries not to hurt me. I suppose he cares about me..." she looked down, "In his way."

"You are strong," Hevel said, "But I know you are hurting."

"Please," Lola pushed Hevel back so that she could stand. She walked to the other side of the cell. "Hevel, I don't want to talk about him."

Hevel rose, turning towards her. "You are dying, child. I want to know *why*."

Lola placed a hand on the wall for support and bowed her head. She gritted her teeth tightly together. "I... I can't talk about it."

Hevel suddenly rushed toward Lola, standing in front of her protectively at the sound of loud voices approaching their cell. Lola peered over his shoulder to see Felix and General Korbin walking side by side.

"You should take him to the king. Somenus will want to know about his confession," said Felix.

"Don't tell me how to do my part, you Worm," Korbin growled. "Questioning *first*." The giant rattled some keys against the iron lock, then threw open the cell door. Lola listened to cries of protest, mixed with frantic shuffling, as Korbin dragged away the other mysterious Faerie prisoner.

"Goodbye, Lola," the Faerie prisoner belted frantically as he was pulled past her, "*I love you!*"

Lola took a step forward, but Hevel blocked her with his arm.

"Who was that?" she whispered.

"He was a Faerie captive," Hevel whispered back, "I think he liked your reading."

"Good day, Princess," Felix said as he stepped up to her cell bars.

Lola pushed past Hevel's protective arm and walked up to him. "Hello, Felix."

"I came to, *erm*..." Felix rocked back and forth on his heels.

Lola sighed. "Are you taking me back to the Eight Stones? Has he sent for me?"

Felix coughed nervously into his hand. "I came to warn you."

Lola raised her eyebrows. She could feel her body tightening with suspense. "...Well? What is it, Felix?"

"He's coming down here," Felix whispered. "He wants to see you."

Lola snorted. "Didn't I just *ask* him for some space?"

"I am not here to get involved," Felix mumbled, "I just thought you would want to know he is on his way down here."

Lola nodded, composing herself. "Thank you, Felix," she said. "Can you tell what sort of…" she hesitated, "What sort of *mood* he is in?"

Felix twisted his mouth to the side. "I am not sure…"

"Angry?"

"No."

Lola winced. "*Hopeful*?"

Felix nodded slowly. "Somewhat. I don't know, Princess. I don't understand him."

Lola sniffed. "Felix, we both know you understand him more than anyone else here does."

Felix narrowed his eyes. He stepped closer to the bars, leaning his face between two of them. "Princess," he whispered, "What I told you…"

Lola stepped up to him, only inches away, and peered up at his face. "I haven't told anyone, Felix," she whispered back, "And I wish I never knew it myself." She closed her eyes as a wave of breath warmed her face from his nostrils. She glared. "Why would you tell me such a thing *right* before I was to be brought into his household? Why would you tell me where he came from?"

"You asked me to," he replied coolly. "I didn't have to tell you."

Lola bit her lip as tears welled up in her eyes. "I wish I had never asked you."

"*Do* you? You would have preferred to believe the lies about him?"

She sniffed. "At least *then* I could try to love him."

"What happened to your devotion to truth and beauty?" Felix asked dryly. "Now, you wish to live a lie—because it would be easier to live with yourself?"

"You mock me?" Lola slammed her hand against the bar beside Felix's face. "You *mock* my pain?"

"Lola," Felix stepped away from the bars, "It was a simple question. You told me that you value truth more than comfort. Is it still true?"

Lola jolted. "I…"

"Felix," a voice echoed from further down the hall, "out! I want some privacy with her!" It was Somenus' voice. She could hear his peppy footsteps clomping closer.

"Felix!" Lola reached through the bars to catch his sleeve. "Don't leave!"

Felix took her by the wrist and pried her hand loose. He shook his head at her, then left.

Lola scrambled backwards as Somenus' person appeared in view. He threw himself against the bars.

"Lola!" he called, "Why do you recoil? Come back!"

Lola clung to the shadows. She felt Hevel's hand touch her shoulder.

I'm not alone, she told herself, *I am never alone*.

"Come over here, Beloved," Somenus pleaded. His voice was as soft as a lamb.

Lola mustered up what courage she had and moved towards the man who should have been her husband. She did her best not to limp, keeping her head high.

"Hello, Sire," she said coldly, "What a surprise to see you here."

"Why so cruel?" Somenus reached his one hand through the bars and held it out to her. "Come, touch me."

Lola fought against her terror and walked closer. She placed her hand in his. He rubbed the back of her hand with his thumb. Looking into his eyes, she was reminded of how beautiful he was.

"Somenus," she whispered, "I asked for some space from you. Could you not give me even one *day*?"

"Lola," he moaned weakly, "Just the mere thought of distance from you made my heart ache. I want to be close to you."

She shook her head. "I am not ready to be close to you."

"You are *never* ready!" he snapped. "You *never* warm to me!"

"So, let me go! There is an entire palace of women who long to be close to you—*two* if you count the Vineyard Palace. Go! Find someone who loves you."

"No! I don't *want* someone else! It's *you* I love!"

Lola closed her eyes, rallying herself with a deep breath. "Somenus, I will not *ever* love you in the way you want me to."

"No!" He yanked on her hand, and she stumbled closer. "There has to be a reason, something that can be fixed. It's my *hand*, isn't it? You cannot love me because I am incomplete!"

Lola shook her head. "Your hand is not the problem, Sire; I simply cannot love someone so cruel. I have no affection to give you."

"What, and you give it to *him*?" Somenus squeezed her hand. His pupils grew small, and his whites wide.

Lola shook her head. "Leave him out of this. This is between you and me. Somenus—you have taken *everything* I have to give, there is nothing more I can give you!"

"You have given me everything but the *one* thing I desire!" he cried, pulling her closer to the bars. She found herself pressed against them, face to face with him. "Lola there is only one thing I want from you—just give me your affection!" The king leaned forward and kissed her lips. She stood there frozen, unmoving, as she always was when he touched her. He leaned back with a face of disappointment. "Still..." he whispered, "You will not even *try* to love me?"

"Somenus, you must let go of me," she said softly, "Let me go. Let this *obsession* go."

"I can't!" he whispered.

"You must. We both know this cannot go on forever. We both know what will happen if you will not give up on me."

Somenus shook his head. "I cannot give up—not when there is a chance you will love me."

"You know there is no chance," she said firmly, "and when that reality truly hits you, we both know what you will do."

Somenus released his grip with a flash, stepping back from the cell. "I have no idea what you are talking about!" he barked. "You have until Mansday! Then I am sending for you to come back home. We will try this again, Beloved," he turned away, flinging his long cape behind himself, "I will not give up on you. I will prove to you that I am worth your love. You will see—When I am whole again, you will see."

Lola watched him march away, disappearing into the gloomy shadows. She caught herself against the bars as she nearly collapsed into a heap of panting.

"Lola!" Hevel appeared behind her, grabbing her arms as a support.

"I'm fine, I'm fine," she waved her hand at him. "I just need some rest."

"Come on," Hevel led her carefully back to the cot. "Lie down. Get some rest. You did well, my child—so *brave!*"

Lola lay on her side as she did her best to take in deep breaths. "I don't understand," she moaned, "I have given him everything, my body, my time, my *life!* Yet still, he won't leave me alone—not until I have given him the *one* last thing that is mine."

Hevel knelt beside her, taking her hand once more. "What Somenus wants from *everyone* is their sanity, Lola," he said, "He wants our worship, our obsession. He wants us to abandon our reason and our virtue, all in the name of letting him become our very life. Usually when someone denies this of him, he has them killed. But you?" He shook his head. "There is something different about you."

"No, there isn't," Lola mumbled as her heavy eyes began to close over, "He is more desperate with me, yes—but it will end the same. He *will* kill me, Hevel."

Hevel leaned back slightly. His body grew stiff.

"You can feel it, can't you, Hevel? Death is coming for me."

Hevel tipped his head forward and rested it on her cot. He stayed there silently until she fell asleep.

⊷————•————⊶

Lola paced the length of the hidden temple, reveling in the feeling of the wind blowing through her loose robe. Jagged yellow mountains surrounded the scene, bathed in the light of a setting sun. Yes, a sun—just exactly how she imagined it to be in her Faerie stories. At least *here* she could find some peace away from Somenus. For some reason, he never seemed to find her when she dreamed of the hidden temple.

"I suppose it would not be so bad to die," she said to herself as she picked a white, velvety flower off a vine. "It would be better than facing the life that is to come for me."

Lola turned to gaze about the little pillared structure. How quiet it was; rustic and yet safe. Cracks grew along the edges of the foundation, and moss coated the floor. There was the circle of luscious pillows—she gasped. Beloved was there, lying down amongst them with his hands behind his neck.

"What's all this talk of death?" he asked lazily, "It doesn't sound good."

"Beloved," she whispered. This time, instead of racing into his arms, Lola found herself shuffling lifelessly over to him. She knelt beside his body, then laid her head on his chest.

"Lola," Beloved said quickly, touching her back, "Are you alright?"

"I don't know," she mumbled.

"Lola, please tell me you're not *really* dying," he said urgently.

"Can we please think about something else?" She turned her head to the side, curling up into a ball beside him.

"No. You tell me what's wrong right now, and I will fix it for you."

"Beloved," her voice trembled, "I don't want to talk about it."

"Has someone *hurt* you?"

"I don't want to talk about it!"

Beloved let out a vocal sigh. "Alright..."

Silence came between them. Beloved stroked her back with his fingers. She listened intently to his beating heart.

"Want to read your book?" he asked at length.

"No."

"...Seriously?"

"I hate that story," she mumbled.

"Oh, come on," Beloved wrapped both his arms around her and squeezed, "That's not true."

"I *hate* it!" she crowed.

"...Alright... how about I tell *you* a story?"

Lola lifted her head slightly, then dropped it again. "Do you know any stories?"

Beloved chuckled. "Sure, I do. I've read other books by the same author who wrote Phantastes, you know."

"*What*?" This got Lola to push herself up for a moment. She gazed at Beloved's endearing helmet. "Really?"

"Sure," he said. He pulled her softly back against his chest and cleared his throat. "There's this one about a scared little Princess, living in a big, mysterious castle."

Lola sniffed up her restrained tears. "I like the beginning."

"Sure, yeah," he said, "It's a great start. So, this little princess lived in a land filled with these scary little monsters called goblins. One time, when she looked out her window, she saw the face of one of them. It scared her so much." Lola's gripped Beloved's tunic tightly, listening.

"Yes," she whispered, "He had a horrible face."

"But what do you think she did? Instead of staying inside her safe castle, she ran outside, into the very place the goblins were. What she wanted was protection, but instead, she was left exposed."

"She couldn't think straight," said Lola, "She was too scared."

"Yes," Beloved cleared his throat, "You are right."

"What happened next?"

"Well," Beloved paused for a moment, as if trying to remember the rest of the story, "After running far, far away from her home, she finally made her way back to the house, away from all the monsters. And back inside the house, she found a secret room that she had never seen before."

"What was inside?"

"A safe place," said Beloved, "Like this temple—except it was a little dark room, like the inside of a cottage. There, she found her kind grandmother."

"A safe place..."

"Her grandmother gave her a special ring. *Next time you get lost,* the grandmother said, *This ring has an invisible string that will always lead you back home.* Well, the next time the Princess found herself outside, she followed her string. And where do you think it took her?"

"Home."

"No. Well—not at first. Her string led her, instead, deep into the goblin's kingdom."

"But *why*?"

"She was scared, but she knew that beyond the next turn, her grandmother would *surely* be there. The string took her deep into the heart of darkness, until she found a boy, held prisoner by the goblins."

"What was he like?" Lola asked, peering up at the chin of his helmet.

"He was kind, and brave," said Beloved, "and she rescued him. Together, they followed the string all the way back home."

Beloved paused, and Lola waited silently for him to continue, listening still to the steady beating of his heart.

"Was that the end?" she asked at length.

Beloved made a thoughtful, groaning sound. "I can't remember entirely," he said, "but I do think the goblins tried to capture the princess and make her marry the goblin prince."

"And did she marry him?" she asked quickly.

"Of course not!" Beloved chuckled, "She married the boy, of course."

"Are *you* the boy?"

Beloved looked down at Lola. "*You* are the princess," he said, "Scared and frightened by truly ugly things."

Lola turned her face away.

"Instead of running to those who would help you," he said, "you are running away. If you wanted, you could tell me what's happened. Instead, you run away."

Lola shook her head. She didn't want to feel the pain; she didn't want to think about the monsters, let alone talk about them.

"You're on a dark road, Lola," he said, "following a thin, invisible trail of hope through the heart of darkness. But you *will* come out of this. You will find your way home."

"My hope is fading," she moaned. The tears would not stay in her eyes. Even in her dreams, she was crying what felt like real tears. "It's so frail, ready to snap."

"Hang on, Lola," Beloved pulled her toward himself and held her as tightly as he could, "I promise you—I am coming. Just hang *on*."

28

—— Felix ——

The Watchman

Felix sat in Somenus' armchair with his ankle resting on his knee. He was rotating his monocle in his fingers, making little reflections dance around the room. His body was there, sitting in the king's chambers, fiddling endlessly with his imperium, but his vision was somewhere else. His sight was down in the cellar, watching her sleep. The Death Faerie was kneeling by her side, with his head resting on the bed.

Her conversation with Somenus had gone how he had expected. Once again, Somenus vied for her affections, and once again, she could not give them to him. He could not hear anything, no—but Felix had been a watcher long enough to read lips. In his mind, he could even hear voices as they would sound if his entire body were present. But no, he was the Faerie of Sight, it was only his eyes that could witness faraway things.

She looked so peaceful when she slept. It was some of the only times Felix felt relaxed. Despite Somenus having access to her dreams, she still seemed to find solace there.

Noises alerted Felix to footsteps approaching where his body was sitting. His vision zoomed back to himself at the speed of light. He blinked, refocusing on the view from his own head.

Somenus opened the door to his chambers and blazed inside. He pulled at his cloak, ripping seams as he threw it from his shoulders.

"Damn her!" he cursed as he did the same to his coat, losing buttons left and right.

"How'd it go?" Felix asked lazily.

Somenus ripped off his clothes until only his trousers remained. "Were you watching?" He jumped, huffing and puffing onto his bed.

"No," Felix lied.

"She won't—*gaugh*!" Somenus picked up one of his pillows and threw it across the room.

"She won't come back?"

"No!" Somenus threw himself back into a feathery mound of pillows. He lay there motionless now, staring up at the ceiling. "*Why*?" he croaked.

Felix spun his monocle in circles against the end of his finger. "She's one of your concubines. You can have her any time you want, isn't that enough?"

Somenus moaned. "You don't get it. Haven't you *seen* her when we sleep together? She's lifeless—spiritless!"

Felix frowned. It was as if Somenus assumed Felix watched *everything* he did. Surprisingly, that was one of the things Felix found he *couldn't* watch.

Somenus let out a long, drawn out sigh. "Felix?"

"Yes, Sire?"

"Do you remember the first time you told me about her? Way back when you used to spy on Antecus for me?"

Felix closed his eyes. "Yes."

"Remember what you said, when I asked you about his daughter? '*She's beautiful*', you said, '*She has a glow*', you said. Do you remember that, Felix?"

Of *course*, he remembered saying it, and how he regretted it since! "Yes," he mumbled, "I remember."

"Naturally, I was intrigued. The Faerie of Sight knows beauty, doesn't he? A glow, you said," Somenus huffed, "Well, I see a different kind of light than you do, Faerie of Sight. You see beauty, but I see something else."

Felix dropped his propped up leg to the floor and leaned forward. "Oh yeah?" he asked, "What do you see, Sire?"

"Sometimes I see the glows in the day, but it is in the night when I see the true lights within people's souls. There, in the dreamscape—where no one can hide their true feelings—I see the affections of all. You were right about Lolette, Felix, she has a glow. She is like a star in the seas, or the Lights above. She glows like a beacon of glory. Hades, if only I could *show* you!"

Felix leaned back in his chair. "Yes," he said quietly, "She's a passionate person."

"She is *bursting* with passion, Felix. But no matter how close I get, I can't access her light. She won't *give* it to me!"

"She's strong," said Felix. "She's figured out how to resist you."

"All that time, when I was buried under creation like a shade..." Somenus' voice became timid, "It was so dark. No one glowed there, Felix... no one."

Felix felt his chest tighten. Somenus hardly ever talked about *those* days. Felix himself wished to forget what he had seen of the underworld. Still—his curiosity burned. "The spirits of the dead?"

"The shades... the daemons... they don't have passion; they don't have affection; they have something else." Somenus' eyes grew wide with terror. "They just hunger... endlessly."

Felix crossed his arms; the chill was almost more than he could bear. "Why are you telling me this?"

"When I was down there, I dreamed of finding a light again,...of seeing the light of people's affections and passions. When I became king, I could get as much light as I wanted. But it wasn't until I saw *her* that I knew what it was I needed."

"And what was that?"

"I needed just one light—one really bright light. Like a beacon showing me the way home, reminding me that I'm no longer trapped in Hades."

Felix could see Somenus' body trembling even from across the room.

"You're not in Hades anymore, Sire," Felix said in a lifeless voice, "You're free."

"No…" Somenus shook his head side to side. "I will never be free. Not while *he* is with me. He hangs on… like a leech. He taunts me—reminds me I could not get out without a price."

Felix rose and strode over to the king. He procured a heavy blanket from the foot of the large bed and tossed it on him.

"She thinks I'm going to kill her," Somenus said as he turned his head to look up at the Faerie of Sight.

"Are you?"

"I could never!"

"Even if she won't give you her light?"

Somenus turned his head away. "Never. She's my life."

Felix wasn't convinced. Somenus was like a child trying to force an insect into friendship. Once the creature resisted enough, it would wind up dead in the hands of its 'friend'. Just like the insect, Lola's wishes didn't matter in this sad relationship, and *that* was the problem. He *would* kill her, eventually.

"Sire, may I ask you something?"

Somenus blinked wearily. "What?"

"The exiled Faeries… what happens to them once they're drained?"

Somenus squinted. "Why are you asking me this?"

Felix shifted slightly. "You exile the Faeries who resist your reign instead of executing them… why?"

Somenus let out a forced yawn. "Do I have to explain my reasoning to you?"

"No, but I would like to hear, if you are willing to tell me."

Somenus pulled his blanket over his face. "The exile gives me time to decide what to do with them."

Felix cleared his throat. "And?"

"You have eyes," Somenus pulled his blanket down to glare at Felix, "Haven't you looked?"

"I have."

"So why are you *asking* me?"

"I didn't know if you knew."

Somenus sat up. "I can't lead Faeries who won't see me as their king!"

"I am not arguing with that..."

"And besides, the more free titles there are, the more chances there are for an heir to be conceived!" It was as if he were trying to rationalize it to himself.

"Yes, but why would Korbin—?"

"Felix," Somenus pointed toward the door, "That's quite enough! I don't want to *talk* about him!"

Felix nodded. He moved toward the door, but Somenus called after him. "Wait—Felix!"

The Faerie of Sight turned, eyeing the half-dressed king. "Yes, Sire?"

"I need my hand."

Felix nodded. "I am looking for it."

"Find it!" He barked, "*Find* him, damn you!"

Felix all but rolled his eyes. "I don't know where he *is*."

"*He's* the one keeping her from me!" Somenus swatted the bed with his hands. "He's... he's..." His eyes grew wild, darting side to side as if searching for answers. "He's in my *head*!"

"In *your* head?" Felix hesitated. "I thought you said I was looking for a human."

"He's got some hold on her. If *he* were dead... she might be able to see me for who I am!"

"If you had a description of some kind..." Felix sighed, "There's a lot of humans."

"I *told* you," Somenus screamed, "He's with that felling Time Faerie!"

Felix clenched his fists. "Aorist's House is impossible to find. I've tried. If he's with Aorist..."

"Just find him!"

Felix closed the door behind himself. He could still hear the king's loud rantings as he descended the stairs. Once outside of the Eight Stones, he spread his four black wings and sprung into the sky. He weaved amongst the spires and rooftops, admiring the familiarity of it all. Arelle, he could fly through her with his eyes closed. He circled the city a few times before landing on the south wall, just outside his watchhouse.

As he often did, Felix sent his sight into the watchhouse ahead of his body. He never liked entering a room without knowing who was and wasn't there. He groaned. What was *Wingsday* doing waiting for him in there?

"What do you want?" he asked as he walked through the door.

The woman turned quickly, surprised by his presence. He chuckled inwardly, noticing her hot cheeks of embarrassment. Startling her seemed to be one of those few entertaining things in his life.

"Felix," she said with a stiff back, "I have a question for you."

He walked a semicircle around the girl. She acted confident, but there was an innocence behind her eyes that didn't make any sense to him. She looked like a child wearing their father's armor; the look just didn't fit. Wingsday: the infamous Faerie killer. She wasn't what he had expected.

"Well?" he plopped himself on his chaise. It sat by the window, where he had a good view of the front gate.

Scarlet crept closer with her hands joined behind her back. "I wanted to ask you about West... the Faerie of Finding?"

"What about him?"

"Did he get his audience with the king?"

Felix glanced side to side. "Why are you asking *me*?"

Scarlet blinked. "Banther said he saw you down there earlier. Didn't you take him somewhere?"

"Korbin took him for questioning, I think."

Scarlet's face paled. "Oh... do you think he's...?"

This didn't make sense. Wingsday actually looked *concerned*! Was this all an act? Was she trying to convince him she wasn't an enemy to the Fae, just to mess with him? Or was she actually as kind as she seemed beneath those eyes. No—she worked closely with Korbin; there was no way she was innocent.

"I am sure Korbin will speak to the king about West's confession. I can't promise he won't end up in exile, though." Felix said. He propped his feet up on his chaise and leaned back.

Scarlet nodded, glancing to the side thoughtfully.

Felix sighed. "Hey, Wingsday?"

She shot him a look. "What?"

"What happens to the Faeries once they are drained?"

Scarlet scowled. "Why do you keep asking me this?"

"Do you know?"

She shrugged. "I have my guesses."

"And?"

Scarlet crossed her arms in an effort to look tough. "I... assume they are taken to the king? Or... they're not just executed, are they? *Hades,* if Somenus wanted to execute them, why drain them first?"

She *didn't* know. Felix nodded. "Like working for Korbin, do you?"

She tapped her foot nervously. "For Korbin? No. But I like my position."

"Hmm..."

"So, *erm...*" she coughed, "What *does* happen to the drained Faeries?"

"That's got nothing to do with me," he said, turning his face away from her. His vision, however, remained focused on his face. When she didn't think he was watching her, she looked more unsettled—more *uncertain* of herself. She was nodding to herself.

"Right," she said, "Well, I thank you for your time." She checked her clicker, then shoved it back in her pocket. She moved toward the door to leave.

"Do I hear congratulations are in order?" he called.

She paused just under the door and looked at him. "Uh... hopefully."

"Colonel, I hear?" he asked with his eyes closed.

"Yes."

"You'll be able to come and go from Arelle—how nice."

"Well," she cleared her throat, "We will see. Just a few more boxes to tick, I suppose."

Well, if she didn't know now, she would know soon enough.

29

—— Isabella ——

The Descent

G ood Wingsday, Wingsday!" Korbin called from below. Scarlet could hear him cackling to himself, amused by his own, weak pun. Scarlet descended the barrack's stairs, pocketing her hands in her double-breasted black coat. Her red cape was pinned at the shoulders, dragging behind her on the steps. Her hair was kept, as usual, in a neat, high top-knot. It was the only way she could keep it out of the way without cutting it. Perhaps eventually she would cut it; after all, she was a soldier now.

"Morning, Sir," she said as she reached the bottom. Korbin forced a smile, offering her a little bow of his head. He was wearing a similar uniform, though his cape seemed to be attached crookedly, and his coat unbuttoned. 'Unbuttoned' was a good word to describe how the general kept himself. His look was never quite complete.

"Are you ready for a day tailing your master?" The general asked as he folded his hands together, cracking about a hundred knuckles in the process.

Master? She squinted. "Come on, let's go, *Sir.*" She stood there, waiting for him to lead the way.

Korbin spun on his heel, then marched off. Scarlet had to scurry to follow. Though he was merely walking, his legs were so long that his stride was as wide as she was tall. Korbin meandered aimlessly through the city, and Scarlet began to wonder if he even knew where he wanted to go.

After a time of wandering the lower city, Korbin made his way up the stairs to the Inner city, where only the king and his noblemen's houses were. Originally, it was the first Eight Faeries whose estates were built here. In more recent times, they housed the Faeries who were the closest to the king. Scarlet was pretty sure one of these Estates must have belonged to the Faerie of Sight, but she only ever saw Felix up on the walls. Did he live somewhere around here?

Korbin kept walking, making a beeline for the king's compound. Up there, at the highest point of the city was the Eight stones, where the king lived, the Radiant Palace, where his wives lived, and the Vineyard Palace, where his entertainment took place.

"Where are we going first, Sir?" she finally asked. Korbin didn't reply. He continued on, marching in the direction of the Radiant Palace. Scarlet felt herself growing nervous; it didn't tend to go well whenever Korbin found reason to go there. She was a little relieved when he turned aside to the guards' entrance. They walked inside, and all present snapped to attention.

"Sir," The captain on duty stepped forward, "How can I help?"

"You can help," The general snarled, "by doing your job!" He struck the man across the face with his oar-of-a-hand. The captain went flying backwards until his back hit the wall. He coughed, holding his hand to his face. Scarlet lurched forward with concern, but refrained from speaking. She knew better than to get between Korbin and his victim. "One of your felling bitches got into the Eight Stones? How?"

The captain's eyes darted back and forth, then found Scarlet. They seemed to be requesting reinforcements.

"I've already dealt with this matter," Scarlet said bravely, "It's all resolved."

Korbin turned. "Oh, *have* you? And what sort of resolution did you make?"

"The woman is back where she belongs," Scarlet said, hoping it was true. In truth, she had passed this on to Felix, and she never went back to ask how it went.

Korbin raised an eyebrow, "And what kind of discipline did you enact on the men who let it happen?"

The room grew very quiet.

Scarlet straightened her back. "None was needed, Sir That was my judgment."

Korbin took a step closer to her. "None was needed?"

"No."

Korbin nodded to himself. "Alright, come, Wingsday." He had to crouch to get through the door as he exited the palace. Scarlet chased after him, feeling a little confused. Korbin left the Inner city and headed down the steps into the lower towns.

"Sir," Scarlet said breathlessly as she tried to keep up, "Was that—?"

"Authority is something I like to see in my officers," Korbin said, still keeping his face pointing forward. "I am glad to see you can make your own judgments without trying to figure out what it is I want."

This came as a surprise to her. Scarlet always thought of Korbin as someone who believed the only 'will' in the world was his, and everybody else needed to figure out what it was and obey it.

"Thank you, Sir."

"You passed the first test."

Scarlet tried not to grimace. The *first* test?

The general led her back into Fort Axes. She followed him down into the underground prison, and into a passageway she had not been down before. Even after living in Fort Axes for a whole season, there were still hundreds of places she had never been. The place was like a labyrinth.

Korbin unbolted a door and held his hand out to her, gesturing for her to move first. She entered the room with him and gasped. There was West, kneeling at the center of the room with his hands cuffed behind his back, and his head resting on the ground. His knees were stained from the blood-laced floor. Scarlet shot a glance at Korbin. He was smiling.

"This is the Faerie who has abandoned the Purple Order to serve Somenus!" she declared. West rose swiftly, gazing hopeful eyes at her. For a moment, she was afraid he would call out her old name. Thankfully, he kept his mouth shut.

"The little worm," Korbin snarled, "How *convenient* to have a sudden change of faith once he's been caught."

"I can vouch for this man, Sir," Scarlet stepped forward, "He really does want to serve his king."

"Good for him," Korbin spat on the Faerie's face, "He can serve his King by suffering the punishment for treason." West recoiled but said nothing. His bruised and battered body began to tremble.

Scarlet held her breath. Well, she couldn't exactly wipe away the fact that this man had been involved in a plot to kill Somenus; he *was* guilty—but so was she!

"What I did was wrong," West said weakly, "I must pay the penalty."

"He could be of use to the king," Scarlet said quickly, "He might have information!"

West's eyes drooped, and he shook his head at her.

"I have already extracted everything this man has to say," Korbin said. He lifted his leg and placed his boot upon West's head. He pressed his foot down until the Faerie's head was once more on the ground. "Here." The general passed her an empty Exilium Prison.

Scarlet took it slowly. "You want me to..."

"Go on," Korbin pointed a crooked finger at the prisoner, "Exile him."

Scarlet hesitated. "But..."

"Can you take an order, Major?" Korbin hissed, narrowing his eyes. "This is a traitor to the king. I want to see you do what must be done."

Scarlet swallowed as she opened the mouth of the sack. Inside was a thin bracelet attached to a cord connected to the inside of the bag. Once it was around West's wrist, he would be forced into his small form. She crept forward and knelt beside the prisoner. She laid a hand on his trembling body, and chose her words carefully.

"Thank you for your bravery. I am sorry I could not have done more for you."

West nodded, and a couple tears dripped to the ground.

"Well, go on then!" Korbin sniffed.

Scarlet clasped the bracelet around West's arm. After a short burst of light, he shrunk down and fell into the sack. Once he found his balance, West gazed up at her with a wave. He bowed his head to her in thanks, then laid down within the sack. Scarlet carefully pulled at the drawstrings, hoping that the prison would be a merciful place for him to spend his days. Faeries were less conscious in their Exilium Prisons; slumbering away their days and nights as if their existence had been paused.

Korbin cleared his congested throat. "Bring it this way," he said. Scarlet rallied herself, rushing to follow Korbin as he once more disappeared from sight. They walked together through the underground tunnel system, making echoing footsteps reverberate through the halls.

All the while, Scarlet clutched West's sack close to her chest. Here was yet another Faerie who had put himself in this position to keep *her* safe. Something felt so wrong about it. They had given their lives for a cause that *she* had abandoned. Guilt clung to her heart like a barnacle. But the cause was wrong—it was wrong for *any* of them to die for it!

"You did well," Korbin said in a surprisingly soft voice. "While I want you to have the courage to make your own decisions, I also need to know you will take my orders, no matter your personal biases."

Personal biases? Well, she did make it clear that she wanted clemency for this man. At the end of the day, perhaps Korbin was right: she was still a soldier, and soldiers need to take orders, regardless of their personal opinions. *West did commit treason*, she told herself. *And so did you*, said the guilty barnacle.

"Well," she said in the strongest voice she could muster, "I am, after all, a soldier."

"Right you are, Wingsday. You are *my* soldier—never forget that."

"I won't, Sir," she replied.

"Well," Korbin coughed when they reached the shelving full of Exilium Prisons. "Put him up at the top with the other fresh ones."

What happens to the Faeries once they are drained? Felix's voice rang in Scarlet's head from their earlier conversation. Why had he asked her?

"Pick up those drained bags from the bottom shelf," Korbin said, pointing downwards. Yes, it was Wingsday, the day Korbin always had her bring the drained bags to the mysterious iron door somewhere in the tunnel network.

Scarlet knelt down by the bottom shelf. There were two of them. "Sir, what happens to the Faeries once they—?"

Korbin chuckled. "Just rearrange the shelf and meet me at the door, Major. You will see soon enough."

The tall general swooped his cape to the side and marched away, leaving Scarlet kneeling there beside the shelves.

Scarlet did this every Wingsday; she rearranged the shelves so that if any bags had lost color, she would move them down a shelf.

"Hello, Wingsday," said a deep voice from the cell beside her.

Scarlet jumped. "*Hades*!" She cursed. "Why they had to put these next to *your* cell, I have no idea," she mumbled more to herself than the Death Faerie, who stood there watching her by the bars.

"Don't you?"

Scarlet shifted slightly, looking at the Faerie out of the corner of her eye. "...Are you implying there is a *reason* they keep you two together?"

"There is, child."

Scarlet braved looking at the Faerie of Death head on. "Well?"

Hevel, Faerie of Death, knelt down onto the ground to match her eye-line, though even when kneeling, he was a great deal taller than her.

"I am here because the king is afraid of killing me," he smiled slightly, "So he puts the dying Faeries near me, knowing they will give me power, and keep me alive."

"I've always wondered why you were his only Faerie prisoner he didn't keep in a bag," she remarked.

Hevel nodded. "Yes, he seems to be so afraid of killing me, he won't even risk an exile bag, even though they do not kill, they merely bring a Faerie to the point before death."

"Why would he be afraid to kill you?" she had to ask.

"The king is not the only one under the protection of an ancient curse. It is said that whoever kills the Faerie of Death dies. The king is afraid of killing me, even indirectly." He exhaled deeply. "So here I am, gaining power while my brothers and sisters die before my eyes."

Scarlet's face softened. Why—all this time—had she felt so wary of the Death Faerie. It was as if simply his *name* made her hate him. And here, he was mourning the imprisonment of all these Faeries that *she* had taken for granted.

"You gain power from people dying?" she asked.

"Isn't it sad?" Hevel tilted his head to the side, "To see the glory of Death—it is both an ugly and a beautiful thing."

Scarlet knelt there silently, letting the words wash over her mind. The glory... of *death*?

"Where do you take them, child?" Hevel asked. There was a hint of desperation in his steady voice.

Scarlet's eyes flashed. "What?"

"Every Wingsday, where do you take the ones who are ready to die?"

"I..." she shook her head. She didn't know, and yet something in her knew *something*.

"They never come back," Hevel said, "It hurts me to watch them die, only to abandon them in their moment of need."

"What?"

"It is my calling to be with those in their moment of death. In their last moment, what do they see? I wish to offer comfort, but instead, they are taken far away from me. Why? What happens to my kin, soldier?"

"I..." What could she say? "I don't know... yet..."

Hevel rose to his feet. "I see."

Scarlet took the two drained bags and held them close to her chest. She felt an impulse to open the bags and show them to the Death Faerie, but wouldn't that just scare them? She wasn't even dying, and she found him terrifying, even now! She stood and moved away from Hevel's cell.

She didn't know what to say, so she backed up silently, watching his gleaming purple eyes loom from the shadows. Death...she had no idea he could be so gentle.

Once the Death Faerie was out of sight, Scarlet took a moment to let out a deep breath of released tension. She shook her head to herself. *Hades!* That Faerie gave her the chills! She looked down at the two bags in her hands.

...In their last moment, what do they see? Something deep inside Scarlet knew that the Faeries were executed, but she had always put that thought from her mind. This was the first time, however, she had ever stopped to think about her involvement. Was she the one who carried them to their final moments? Could she have been offering comfort after all this time to those who had no idea what was coming for them?

No—it was too much. Could she really look at them in the eyes and try to offer kindness when she was the one bringing them to their end? But surely, something was better than nothing. Had she been selfish all this time, protecting herself from the ugliness of their situation?

Scarlet stood, frozen in an empty hall, stuck in a moment of confusion. She twitched, rubbing her finger against the drawstring of one of the sacks. She sighed.

"Oh, come on, Scarlet," she mumbled, pulling at the mouth of the bag, "just *open* it."

At the bottom of the sack was a Faerie, lying on his side, sleeping. Scarlet gasped; inside was a child!

Stirred by the sudden flash of light into his world, the little Faerie yawned and pushed himself up on his arm. He rubbed his eyes for a moment, then pushed a cluster of golden curly locks away from his face.

"Oh," he said in a pleasant, little voice, "Hallo, Isabella!"

Scarlet jolted. How did he know her name? "Do you..." she hunched her shoulders and brought the Faerie and the sack up closer to her face, "Do you *know* me? Are you in the Purple Order?"

"Purple Order?" The boy thought for a moment, "No... no Purple Order, but I do know your name—your *true* name, anyway."

She felt a surge of terror. Her *true* name? She shook herself. "What is your name, child?" she asked.

The boy smiled warmly. "My name is Lija—I'm the Truth Faerie."

The *Truth Faerie*? "But you're... you're just a child, what are you doing here?"

Lija looked confused for a moment. "I think I remember being abducted in the name of the king, yes... though I didn't do him any wrong. No, I am afraid the curse of the Truth Faerie still follows me."

"The curse of the Truth Faerie?" Scarlet asked softly.

"Well, that's what I call it anyway," he yawned, "I scare people."

"Scare people... like the Death Faerie?"

Lija laughed. "Yes, like him. Isn't it funny? How someone can be so scared of Death that they will not kill him, and yet so scared of Truth that they will try to kill me?"

"*Funny* isn't the word I would have chosen."

Lija's smile weakened. "Isabella, why do you look so sad? Are you going to kill me?"

Scarlet froze.

The Truth Faerie sighed. "Please, don't do this."

"I... I am not going to kill you," she stammered.

"Please," the boy reached his tiny arm out to touch her finger, "Do not do this to yourself. You are kind and beautiful—you should not kill Faeries. It will change you."

"I'm not killing Faeries..." she said unconvincingly.

"You should not kill."

"I..." she wanted to repeat her last statement but found she couldn't.

"So," the boy sighed, pulling his hand back to himself, "This is it. I am going to die."

"Perhaps you are not," Scarlet said weakly.

Lija gave her an unimpressed look. "How long will you go on fooling yourself, Isabella? How many people will have to die for you before you *do* something about it?"

"*What*?" Scarlet pulled the Faerie away from her, distancing his voice.

Lija shook his head. "To think that he loves you so much, to think he is willing to die for you, and you don't even remember him."

She frowned. "What are you talking about! Stop trying to provoke me with your words!" She pulled at the drawstrings quickly, silencing the Truth.

Her heart was pounding like a drum. This was too hard. Scarlet found that she did not have the strength to open the other bag, lest the next Faerie upset her more. She had a job to do, and she was only putting herself in danger by stalling.

She raced for the iron door, knowing that if she resisted any longer, she might not have the heart to go through with what she must do. As she turned the last corner, she could see Korbin's dark shadow waiting for her by the door.

These Faeries broke the law, she reminded herself, *The king has every right to execute them, I am merely a soldier following orders.*

"There you are," he said, pushing himself off the wall, "Come on." The general unbolted the iron door; it made a heavy churning sound of metal on metal as it opened. "Ladies first."

Scarlet held her breath, then walked past him, into a thick, musty darkness.

Once the iron door closed behind them, Korbin led Scarlet down a steep, dark stretch of stairs. She placed her hands on the walls on either side, wary of slipping. The feeling of dread grew as they descended lower. Korbin didn't bring a torch, so for a time they walked in complete darkness. Those few clicks in the darkness felt like an eternity. For a moment, Scarlet was reminded of her journey into the cellar with Hanz; was this descent similar? Was her life about to change again?

She sighed inwardly as Korbin pushed open a door at the bottom of the stairs, streaming light into their world. The two moved into the room ahead. It was a round chamber of stone, with similar architecture to the cellars above. On the ground, jagged symbols had been carved into the flagstones. At the back of the chamber was a large brass basin, about a meter in diameter. Etched all around it were patterns, like words in a language she couldn't understand. The basin held a ball of flame which seemed to hover at its center. Nothing was inside the large bowl; nothing was burning; the mystical flame seemed to live all on its own.

Scarlet stopped to scan the room, noticing scraps of fabric covering the ground. No, it wasn't just fabric; it was bags—Exilium bags.

"General?" she asked, unsure what to do with herself.

Korbin did not speak to her. He moved over toward the basin and stood in front of it, bowing his head. Then, with eyes closed, he began to chant in unintelligible words.

"Sir?" she stepped forward timidly. He did not acknowledge her. He continued his mumbling, then lifted his head suddenly, gazing at the flame.

"Bring me the first bag," he said in a low voice, his eyes still glued to the fire.

It was too late to turn back now. Scarlet passed him the bag she had not opened. Korbin snatched it, like a ravenous wolf, then forced it open. He dug his hand inside and pulled out the sleeping Faerie, holding it by its wing. Scarlet winced, watching the wing snap in half like a twig.

"What are you called?" Korbin asked in a predatory voice.

The Faerie twisted in pain, trying to find the source of the voice. He looked up at Korbin in confusion, then gaped.

"*Well*?" The general growled.

"I am Leck," he said in a groggy voice, "The Messenger Faerie."

Leck? Scarlet took a step back, hoping to avoid being seen. *This* was the Faerie she was supposed to make contact with?

"Messenger Faerie," Korbin said in a mocking voice, "What sort of glory do *you* taste of?"

"*What*?" Leck thrashed helplessly in the air, like a fly in a spider's web.

"Come on, what *felling* lights do you see?"

Scarlet cringed. She had lived amongst Faeries long enough to know now that he was asking a very *personal* question.

"Tell me, or I'll kill you!" Korbin howled.

Leck's eyes widened with terror, then he glanced down at the flame beneath him. "No!" he gasped, "Please!"

"*No*? You will *not* tell me?" Korbin grinned, pressing his fingers together and snapping the wing in a second place. Leck screamed in pain. Scarlet lurched forward, reaching out her hand. Korbin shot her a glance, eyeing her suspiciously. She stood down, looking away.

"Please give me mercy!" Leck said in a weak voice.

"What do you draw, Faerie?" Korbin pressed.

Leck dropped his head in defeat, "I… I cannot explain it to others. It is something only I can see."

"Well," the general twisted the Faerie slightly, "I will find out soon enough."

In an instant, Korbin dropped the Faerie into the hovering flame. Scarlet stifled a scream as she watched Leck burst into dust the second he made contact with the fire. She held her hand on her mouth, feeling her heart pound in her ears, and watched as his remaining sparkling dust collected in the bottom of the basin, just below the hovering flame.

"Give me the next one," Korbin turned to Scarlet, holding out his monstrous hand.

Scarlet held onto the bag containing the Truth Faerie tightly, frozen in indecision. What could she do?

"Give it to me." He hissed, pressing his hand closer. "*Wingsday*."

Wingsday. It was the name of the Faerie killer that Felix and so many others loathed so much. Is that who she was? Before she could think too hard about what she was doing, Scarlet passed the bag to the giant. He snatched it from her quickly, retrieving the Faerie from within. Out came the Truth Faerie, dangling by his wing, turning to look straight at Korbin in the eyes. The little Faerie froze in terror, his eyes widening with something akin to recognition.

Korbin snorted. "Who are you, boy?" he asked. The Faerie turned to look at Scarlet. Her heart seemed to stop. He tried to smile at her, but his eyes betrayed his true feeling of hopelessness. "Who *are* you?" Korbin pressed.

"I am the Truth Faerie, and you?" The boy's eyes narrowed, "I know who *you* are, and where you came from. You are—"

Korbin dropped him into the flames. In moments, he was nothing but dust.

Scarlet screamed, throwing her hands over her mouth. Tears streamed down her face as an eternal weight of guilt seized her heart. *I did this,* she thought, *I let this happen*. Korbin bent over crookedly, clutching the sides of the basin. He laughed as the sparkling ashes floated down into the base of the bowl. Scarlet couldn't escape the horrific condemnation of her guilt; it was like a layer of sticky dirt covering every inch of her body, inside and out. She was like the inside of Korbin's dripping, filth-covered quarters; she was like him, becoming *part* of the blood-stained grounds of Fort Axes. She was a part of this; she was a part of this! She began to shake.

What happened next horrified her beyond what she could have predicted. Korbin reached his hands into the flame, unperturbed by its scorching heat, and he cupped up the Faerie ashes like water from a pool. He pulled them carefully to his lips, then tipped his head back and drank them in, swallowing eagerly.

Scarlet stumbled backwards, her back slamming into the wall. She watched as the monster lowered his hands, eyes closed, and took in a deep breath of relief.

"What *are* you?" she asked, her voice quivering. "*Why* would you do this?"

Korbin straightened, then turned to her, scanning his eyes across her small frame. "I am your master," he replied. He threw aside the two empty sacks on the floor, then stepped forward. "For you have passed my final test. Are you mine, Wingsday? Have you finally and fully become mine?"

How was she to answer? Would she turn him down, only to see the same fate as those Faeries? Or would she follow him, clinging to the greater good. If she kept her position, she could find a way out of this! Scarlet nodded slowly.

"Yes."

Korbin grunted, smiling to himself. "Good." He moved toward the exit to the chamber. "Meet me Somensday at the Eight Stones armory. At the Late Morning bell, we will discuss your promotion."

Moments later, he was gone, and Scarlet was left in the little chamber, lit only by the light of the ever-burning flame. Her eyes darted around the room, taking in the countless number of bags on the floor.

How many times had this happened? *Why* was this happening? Her heart raced faster and faster, until she could not stomach being in the evil place further. She dashed through the door and tore her way up the stairs.

At the top of the stairs, she practically fell through the iron door, then turned to slam it closed. She gasped, letting out the sound of a restrained sob. She pressed her mouth closed with her hands. *I'm going to be sick,* she thought as she staggered forward. She heaved, then choked in another sob. Tears dripped down her cheeks like rippling streams, spilling off her chin.

"What have I done?" Her voice hit the air with a distant echo, "Oh Lights, what have I *done*?" Her head bobbed up and down as she tried to catch her breath. She panted vocally, unable to keep the horrors of what she had seen from her mind. She began to cry uncontrollably. "What have I done? What have I—?"

She ran, though she knew not where—she *cared* not where. All she wanted was to be anywhere but where she was. Run: it was the only thing she could think to do. Her vision grew black, and she lost herself in her terror. What had she become? Who *was* she?

Scarlet crashed suddenly into a wall, falling down onto the stone-cold ground, then rose again, forcing herself back into her run. She didn't care if she ran into a pit and died, she just could not handle being who she was.

The questions raced through her mind, beating her like lashes on her back. How many bags were on the floor? How many had I personally delivered to Korbin? How many Wingsdays have I been in Arelle? Why? Why would he eat them?

Scarlet collided once more into a wall, only this time she knocked something over. Snaps of breaking wood sounded, and she found herself lying on the ground with the shelving full of Exilium Prisons fallen on top of her. A rain of captured Faeries fell around her, like blood splattering on the executioner's hands.

Scarlet screamed, pulling herself free of the fallen furniture. She kicked the bags away from herself, shrieking as if she were being attacked by a hoard of wild animals. She shuffled backwards, sliding against the cold ground. Then her back hit what felt like an iron bar, and a hand clasped itself against her shoulder.

Death—Death had found her!

"Please!" she wept, "Leave me alone."

"It's alright," said a soft, womanly voice, "You are safe."

That wasn't the voice of the Death Faerie!

"I..." her voice broke, and her shoulders began to jostle erratically as she gave herself into her sobbing.

"Just cry, dear one," said the voice like an angel, "You are safe now."

Scarlet felt another hand touch her other shoulder. She leaned her head back against the bars of the cell, and the angel reached her arms through to embrace her from behind. Scarlet clutched the arms with her hands tightly, and cried until she had no more tears left.

"You..." Scarlet said at length, "You are the disobedient concubine, aren't you?"

"My name is Lola."

"Lola..." Scarlet dropped her head limply, resting her chin on Lola's arm. "You should not be showing me kindness."

"What is your name?"

"Scarlet." Scarlet hesitated, then let out a defeated sigh. "No... it's not Scarlet. It's Isabella."

"Isabella. How lovely."

Isabella sniffed, feeling another wellspring of tears rising from within. She held it back, but only just. "Well... it's who I used to be, anyway. I haven't been Isabella for a long time. She is a person of the past."

"Come now," Lola said in a calming voice, "What has happened to you? Why are you so distressed?"

Isabella shook her head, pursing her lips tightly together in an attempt not to cry.

"Isabella, you're safe here."

Isabella leaned forward, turning slightly toward Lola suspiciously. Though in the darkness, she still could not see her face. "Where is the Death Faerie?"

"I told him to stay over there," Lola replied, "He thinks he scares you."

Isabella blinked. "He does scare me."

"He's not scary," Lola chuckled, "just like death doesn't have to be scary. He likes to say that there are two kinds of death: death that leads to Death below, and death that leads to the Lights above. You do not need to fear Death after death."

"Yes, I do." Isabella said coldly. "I very much fear it. I do not deserve Light after death."

"Oh," Lola said. "Why do you say that?"

Isabella paused, feeling chilled. "I have done horrible things."

Lola nodded. "I see. Well, we have all done horrible things, haven't we?"

"Not like this," Isabella bit her lip. "You could never understand," she hesitated, "You seem too... *pure.*"

Lola chuckled, "Well, I wish that were true."

"I have done—or been a part of—things that most people would never even dream about."

"Oh," Lola paused, growing silent.

"Now you know why I fear Death, my lady."

Lola let out a melancholy sigh. "There are three things that bring us into the Light, three intertwining roads to follow."

Isabella froze, feeling the sudden conviction that she was about to hear something that might save her life. She was like a tired sailor, drowning at sea with no hope of rescue, who suddenly saw a light. "Well," she asked, as if skeptical, "What are they?"

"The Good," said Lola, "The things we do with our bodies and say with our words; the things that are as right as right be."

Isabella cringed, feeling the stabbing pain of guilt once more. Lola's words seemed to condemn rather than comfort her.

"Then there is the Beautiful," Lola continued, "which is perceived by not only the eyes, but all the senses. The Beautiful we experience with our physicality—our bodies."

Beautiful—Isabella sighed to herself—there was a time when she thought that word described herself.

"And finally—there is Truth," said Lola, "Truth is what *is*, despite what any of us might think or perceive on our own. Truth is true even if we believe a lie. And do you know what is exciting?" She paused, waiting for Isabella's response.

"What?" Isabella asked cynically.

"*You* have told me something true, Isabella."

Isabella pried herself free of Lola's protective arms and turned to face her, looking into her bright, green eyes for the first time. "What did I say?"

"You said that you have done, or been a part of, horrible things. You may have betrayed the good, Isabella, but you have not betrayed the truth."

Isabella blinked. "So?"

Lola sighed, "So, there is hope. You have not given up, have you? Do you want to do good, Isabella?"

Isabella nodded quickly, and a single tear escaped her eye. "I do."

"Then *do* it, by heavens!" Lola reached for Isabella's hand and grasped it tightly. "Please!"

Isabella burst into tears, dropping her heavy head. "It is too late for me!"

"Of course it isn't!" Lola squeezed her hand. "You have life left in you to live, don't you?"

"I don't know."

"Stop that!" Lola pulsed Isabella's hand with another squeeze. "Don't do that."

"Lola," Isabella croaked in a raspy, hopeless voice, "*How*?"

Lola sighed, loosening her grip on Isabella's hand. "Why don't you tell me about who you were before this? Before you came here to this..." she hesitated, "...place."

Isabella scoffed. "I can hardly remember."

"Of course you can!" Said Lola. "If I can remember who I was, then so can you."

Isabella shrugged, then nodded reluctantly.

"Who was Isabella?" Lola again.

"Just a girl," Isabella responded, feeling a lighter, "A girl who loved her life, a girl who dreamed of doing something important. It was a simple life; I kept sheep... and bees."

"Oh!" Lola exclaimed, "How sweet!"

Isabella chuckled. "Well, I liked it."

"What happened then? How did you get here?"

Isabella sighed defeatedly. "An opportunity came into my little world, and a calling, I thought."

"A calling?" Lola raised her eyebrows. "What sort of calling?"

Isabella paused, realizing she didn't care anymore if someone heard her. "To save the world from Somenus—at least that's what I was told I would be doing." There was silence. Isabella didn't know what Lola was thinking, she merely gazed at Isabella with her glowing, curious eyes. Isabella continued. "I joined an order of Faeries who refused to follow him."

"It sounds noble," Lola said. "It sounds good."

Isabella shook her head. "I thought it was noble, until I came to Arelle. They wanted me to find a weapon to kill the king. They wanted me to commit treason against the Faerie throne. Many Faeries died to get me into a place of influence."

Lola didn't respond verbally. She just sighed.

Isabella continued. "I helped kill many Faeries. Some Faeries willingly gave their lives to help me, some did not. And after a time, I abandoned the quest. Still—Faeries died trying to protect me, even though I abandoned them."

"Oh," Lola said, "That is *not* good."

"No."

Lola exhaled loudly. "Well...There is only one thing you can do."

Isabella straightened her back. "And what is that?"

Lola emphasized each word, "Stop killing Faeries." She gazed deeply into Isabella's face, staring seemingly at the guilt that clung so hard to her soul.

Silence filled their space once more. "Lola, I don't know what to do... I can't see a way to stop the killing."

"There is always something you can do, Isabella."

"If I do something..." Isabella shook her head defeatedly to herself, "I will probably die."

"Forget about whether or not you will die, Isabella," Lola said firmly, "Think of what the right thing to do is. *Stop killing Faeries.*"

Isabella paused, letting the words sink in. "Stop killing Faeries?"

"Stop killing Faeries."

Isabella nodded. "I need to end this."

"Yes," Lola smiled softly, reaching both hands through the bars to grip Isabella by the shoulders. "Whether it ends in death or not, it doesn't matter anymore, does it? When you know what to do, everything becomes clear."

Isabella shook her head. "I still don't know what it is I am supposed to do about my situation. I don't know how I can stop what's been happening down here...it's..." she saw Korbin's face in her mind, "It's so much bigger than me, Lola."

Lola tilted her head a little, thinking. "What would the old Isabella do if she were in your situation? That simple girl, keeping bees and sheep, what would she think?"

Isabella leaned back, blinking repeatedly as her mind was transported back to the Valley. She remembered the sky, crowded by mountains and trees; the air, full of woodsy smells; the house, lit with a crackling fire. She remembered sitting on her favorite outcropping, watching her sheep as they meandered about; and she remembered the Elf, kneeling down at her feet.

"Hades..." she whispered.

"*What*?" Lola leaned in.

"I just... I'm just remembering my old life."

"Good memories?" Lola asked, her own eyes growing distant.

"I don't... know..." Isabella shifted her position, sitting cross-legged on the ground in front of Lola's cell. "I am sure a different person than I was then. It's strange to think there was a whole life I could have lived back there if I hadn't been drawn by my brother's ambitions."

"What sort of life would that have been?"

Isabella blew air through the side of her mouth. "Well... I suppose I might have gotten married."

"Yes..." Lola whispered. "Was there someone you loved back home?"

"Not exactly," a wry smile crept up the side of her mouth.

"But there was a man, I see?" Lola clapped her hands excitedly. "Handsome?"

Isabella snorted. "He was an Elf, yeah."

"Oh! Really? From *Celestia*?"

"Elder Copse, I think. I come from the Woodlands—he came wandering through and uh... sort of shook everything up at the homestead."

"It sounds like the beginning of a good story," Lola said, gazing up toward the ceiling. "Did he propose to you?"

Isabella belted a laugh, surprising herself. "He did, yes. *Ridiculous.*"

"And he was handsome?"

"Yeah."

Lola clapped her hands again. "How fantastic!"

Isabella shook her head with a smirk. "You *do* know how this story ends, right? It ends with me sitting *here,* and him off somewhere else, never to be seen again."

"Well, the story isn't over yet," Lola said primly as she placed her hands on her knees. "Anything can happen!"

"I have a feeling the end to this story is going to be something of a tragedy," Isabella mumbled.

"Did the Elf boy have a name? Maybe I've met him!"

"I can't remember..." Isabella thought for a moment, "Clovis? *Clover?*"

Lola drew back with a look of caution. "You don't mean Prince *Trefolian,* do you?"

Isabella shook her head, "No, I don't think so. He wasn't a Prince, he was just this..." her voice turned to a mumble, "Just this simple, sincere person. *Ridiculous,* yes—but honest."

"Well," Lola smiled, "I am sure you had all kinds of suitors back in your old life, you are so pretty!"

Isabella snorted. "Thank you, but I don't really think like that anymore. I am a soldier now." Her mirth seemed to fade, and for a moment, she remembered the words of that little Faerie boy. *How many people will have to die for you before you do something about it?*

Lola reached a hand through the bars and placed it on Isabella's arm. "Isabella, don't be scared."

Isabella blinked. Lola must have seen some change in her expression. And as patronizing as the words could have sounded to her, they were comforting.

"What am I supposed to do?" she asked, searching Lola's face for answers.

"What would the simple Isabella in the Valley do?" Lola returned.

Isabella closed her eyes. Her mind raced back to the Woodlands, back to her town. She remembered meeting Clover; she remembered the town of

Nemus, full of soldiers; she remembered Korbin's presence there. Her eyes snapped open.

"I know," she muttered, "I know what I have to do."

"What is that?" Lola asked intently.

Isabella set her jaw, nodding to herself. "I have to kill Korbin."

30

— Leo —

The Question

I've got to get her out of there..."

"What was that, Leo? *Who*?"

"Huh?" I jolted back to reality. My hands were submerged in the washing basin, searching for the last remaining dishes that needed rinsing.

"Get who out?" Rowyn leaned sideways, placing her face into my field of vision.

"Uh... nothing." I smiled innocently, then fished out a cup. *Lola*. She was on my mind all the time. I could hardly think straight when I knew she wasn't okay. *Something* was wrong, and nobody around me even knew she existed! "Hey, uh... is it true that Hanz is putting together his team to get into Arelle?"

"Yeah! Isn't it exciting?" Rowyn leaned back to her station. She was scrubbing, I was rinsing.

"So... you're excited, even though Hanz is probably going to, like..." I cringed, "...*die*?"

Rowyn laughed. "You haven't heard our plan for that? With all of our powers combined, we hope to protect him when he shoots Somenus."

"Yeah..." I made a doubtful face, "Aorist thinks that's basically impossible."

"Then he hasn't heard Tristan and Riah's story," Rowyn said quickly. She refused to be discouraged.

I paused my rinsing and turned to give her my single eyebrow raise. "*What* story?"

"Don't you *know*, Leo?" Rowyn's eyes grew wide with wonder.

"Know what?"

"Tristan and Riah were there when Sol was killed. They *saw* what happened! You should ask them about it; it might make you and Aorist feel differently about Hanz' plan."

"Really? Huh." I placed my rinsed dish on a towel and turned around to face Tristan, the Faerie of Water, who was sitting on a stool peeling potatoes. "So, uh... who killed the last king, then? Did he die?"

"No," Tristan answered quietly, "He didn't."

"But..." I stared, "Was he human?"

"Yes." Tristan looked up from his peeling. There was always something so solemn about the Faerie, perhaps now I was finding out why. He had *seen* his own king die! He had seen Somenus in the flesh!

"That doesn't make sense... isn't there a curse on anyone who kills a Faerie King?" I asked as I dried my damp hands against my thighs.

"That's what we all have believed," Tristan said, "But I saw it with my own eyes: a human killed King Sol. Riah and I believe he had the protection of the Nightmare Faerie—how else could he have survived?"

"Have you..." I glanced side to side, "Have you told Momentum about this?"

Tristan shook his head. "Aorist may be a common sight to you, Leo, but he keeps away from the rest of us most of the time."

"Would you mind if I asked him about hearing your story?" I asked.

Tristan looked surprised. "Well... actually I would really appreciate that. If I am going with Hanz to Arelle, it would be very helpful to speak with Aorist beforehand, if he would see me."

"Sure, he would!" I assured him. "I'll make it happen. Anyway, I figure all of us who are going to Arelle should meet up and discuss a plan, because..." my voice trailed off as I saw Tristan's change of expression. "What? What is it?"

"You're not in the transport team, Leo. There are only a few of us going, and as far as I know, you're not one of them." His face twisted with concern.

"Oh," I blinked. Hadn't Cymbeline told me she wouldn't go without me? I was sure she must have relayed that message to Hanz! Perhaps not... perhaps I should go speak with him myself. "Oh, I am sure it will get sorted out," I mumbled, "Anyway, let me speak with Momentum about everything. I am sure he will want to hear your story."

Tristan nodded and returned to his work. I turned to Rowyn.

"Hey, I'll see you in a bit. You seen Cymbeline around today?"

Rowyn nodded. "She's with Hanz and Riah this morning, outside in the Autumn courtyard."

I left the kitchens quickly, running—as I always did—toward the courtyard. Surely this was a misunderstanding. I was definitely on the transport team! There was no way they could leave me behind. I had to go there. I had to find her!

I found Hanz, Riah and Cymbeline sitting outside in a covered garden. Hanz was talking animatedly while the two other female Faeries sat on opposite benches, listening. All quieted when I approached in my breathless, apologetic state.

"Hey guys," I panted, "What's up?"

"Leo..." Cymbeline looked at me with subdued curiosity.

"Hello, Leo!" Hanz rose from his bench with a smile. "How can we help you?"

"Hey..." my eyes shifted to Cymbeline's face. "Hey... I had a question for you guys about..." I cleared my throat, "The transport team, and the plan and everything."

Riah stood. I shifted my gaze to her and gulped. Riah, the Faerie of Illusion. She scared me, if I were honest. The woman hardly *ever* smiled, and she most definitely didn't hide her dislike of me.

"Leo," she said in a voice as soft as velvet, and as captivating as the sea, "You do not need this information. Please, leave us."

I felt my legs trying to do as she asked and lead me away. I resisted. "I, uh…" I clenched my fists and faced Cymbeline again, doing my best to ignore the intimidation, "I thought you wanted me to go with you… to Arelle. Guys?" I looked to Hanz, "Aren't I coming?"

Hanz sighed. "Leo, you have such a brave heart—a *lion's* heart," he gestured toward me proudly with a phony smile, "It is *so* admirable! But we need the team to stay small. This is a very important mission, and we can make no mistakes. You're not a Faerie, and you're not a Faerie Friend. It would be wrong of us to let you come with us. We could not guarantee your safety."

"Cym?" I looked at my friend. "Aren't I coming?"

Cymbeline shook her head.

"Right." I straightened my back, nodding to each person. "I understand." I marched away, feeling a combination of dejection and anger.

I could hear footsteps running after me as I took the path to the Winter gardens.

"Leo, wait!"

"It's fine, Cym," I said, without looking behind me, "If you don't want me there, I get it."

"Leo!" I felt her grab me by the wrist.

I turned abruptly. "Look—I get it! You don't *want* me there! I'm sorry, Cym, okay? I am sorry I think of you as a sister and not anything more. My heart is locked away in a place no one else can access it. There's nothing I can do about that!"

Cymbeline's face softened. "Leo… it's not about that, I…" she bowed her head. "This is a suicide mission, Leo."

"*What*?"

She lifted her head with renewed vigor. "I have agreed to take them there, but I am not staying. I am leaving. I don't want you there; they're all going to die."

"Why do you say that?"

"It's what Momentum told me."

"What? You... you talked to him about it?"

"Don't act so surprised," she crossed her arms, "but, yes. I told him Hanz's plans. He doesn't think we will succeed."

"Cym," I leaned closer, placing my hand on her shoulder, "What *is* Hanz's plan?"

Cymbeline cringed. "He doesn't want me to tell anyone."

I frowned.

"Fine, fine," she sighed. "I am taking him to the Eight Stones—it's the house where the Faerie King lives. From there, Riah is going to help him find the weapon, while Tristan tracks down the king. Once he is sure he has found the weapon, my presence is no longer needed; I'll leave."

"You'll come back to Winter's End?"

Cymbeline's eyes drifted to the side. "Possibly..."

"When is this all happening?"

"Next week."

"So soon?" My heart thumped. "Why so soon?"

"I don't know," she shrugged, "Hanz said he had recent communication from his sister. He wants to move."

"And who all is going?" I asked.

"Me, Hanz, Tristan, and Riah," she replied, counting on her fingers, "And..."

"And me."

"No!" Her eyes shot up at me, "Leo—no!"

"Cym, I *need* to be there!"

She narrowed her eyes. "For me?"

My face betrayed me. "Well... in part."

"Leo... it's too dangerous! Momentum thinks Hanz and Tristan and Riah are all going to *die*! HE thinks every Faerie pledged to Hanz is going to die!"

"I know..." I paused to think. If Tristan was right, perhaps they would not die! "I... I need to talk to Momentum."

"Fine," Cymbeline sighed. "But Leo, I can't take you—I don't want to take you."

"What changed your mind?"

Cymbeline pulled her lips into her mouth.

I nodded to myself. "You are trying to protect me—I get it."

"Just let me do this, Leo," she said, "Let me make this choice."

"Well," I turned my gaze back toward where I was headed, toward the Winter Wing. "I'll catch you later, Cym. I need to talk with someone."

⸎

I brought Tristan with me to see Momentum. The Water Faerie bowed his head several times as he entered the room, thanking Momentum for allowing him to come.

"Please," Momentum sighed, pulling off a pair of colored glasses as we walked into the room, "Don't upset yourself. Come and sit." He pointed with his odd, round spectacles at the chairs across from where he sat.

Tristan entered the room cautiously, as if fearing he might break something. He sat across from Momentum, and I stood behind him.

"What is this about, Leo?" Momentum asked, though he was looking at the Water Faerie with half-open, fatherly eyes.

"Tristan and Riah were there when King Sol was killed. They witnessed the whole thing," I said.

Momentum nodded. "Yes, Hanz mentioned that to me."

"There's some interesting details that might change your opinion on Hanz' plan," I said.

"I highly doubt that, but please," he motioned to Tristan with his hand, "tell me."

Tristan laced his fingers together and nodded. "Thank you for being willing to see me, Aorist. I would greatly treasure any wisdom you have to share for our venture."

Momentum frowned. "Oh, yes?"

Tristan nodded earnestly. "I would follow Hanz to the edge of the Table if he led me there," he paused, "But I also see myself as someone who is able to slow him down—to bring sense to his plans. He does not like to ask questions, but I do. If you would but share your thoughts with me, perhaps I could bring them to him in a way he could receive them."

Momentum leaned back in his chair, blowing a doubtful raspberry. "Alright," he said, "Tell me the story. What happened the day that King Sol died?"

Tristan closed his eyes; his face intensified as the memories played freshly in his mind.

"It was a Feast Day," he said, "Sol and his entire family were gathered in the Eight Stones Hall. I was there, and so was Riah; all of Sol's honored court were there. When Sol was sitting on the throne, listening to the toasts, Somenus revealed himself to be one of the guests. He began a toast to King Sol, and we all began to suspect something was wrong. Riah is a quick-thinking woman; the second she sensed danger, she threw up her protective spell, making herself invisible to all eyes. I was standing close to her, so I must have been protected too. We, and all in the banquet hall watched in silence and awe as a human pulled back Orion's Bow. Those of us who had been alive a thousand seasons ago remembered his face—and King Sol called out his name. *Somenus,* he said, *how did you come back?* There was a red wall of water behind the bowman, and Felix the Sight Faerie was standing beside him."

"I see," Momentum nodded, "The Crimson Gate."

Tristan's eyes snapped open. "Sorry?"

"It's how they got in," Momentum said with a yawn, "Through the Crimson Gate. Go on, Tristan." Momentum folded his hands together and closed his eyes as he leaned his head back onto his chair, listening.

"Sol reached for his scepter, fearing the return of Somenus, his sworn enemy. But the man had a bow, and he was quick. Without wasting a click, he shot the king, in front of us all. Sol fell to his knees, screaming."

I watched Momentum's face as it tightened with pain. What was he thinking about all this?

"Chaos ensued," Tristan continued, "Some tried to run away, and others ran to the king's side."

"What happened to the archer? He had a mirrored wound to the king?" Momentum asked, his eyes still shut.

"Yes," Tristan said, "Blood began to gush from his chest. But he did not fall to his knees as the king did; he instead began to shoot more and more Faeries, aiming first at Sol's children and his wife. We wanted to run, but we couldn't. Somenus, he..." Tristan hesitated, "His presence seemed to still us all. We found we could not leave. Riah and I watched as the archer went around, killing every one of the king's family, and all in his court. Blood filled the hall, and soon, Faeries began to turn to stone. Sol knelt there, clutching his chest and watching as Somenus murdered his loved ones. Then he fell to his back, crying out one, single word: *Aorist*."

Momentum opened his eyes. "What did you say?"

"Aorist—he called out Aorist."

Momentum lifted his head. "He..." His voice drifted away.

"He died, uttering your name. But what Riah and I found the most surprising was the archer: he did not die when the king died. Blood seemed to flow endlessly from him, but he did not die; he did not even cry out in pain."

Momentum's face turned to a scowl. "Impossible."

"It is true," Tristan said with a sigh, "We were sure he had the Nightmare Faerie's protection. But we could not stay to witness anything further. Riah managed to help me escape. From there, we fled to the Woodlands, seeking Timbre Wulf. We wanted to find you, but we didn't know where you were! It wasn't until later, when Rowyn joined the order, that we knew how to find you. But why, Aorist? Why did the king call out *your* name in the end?"

Momentum scoffed. "Well, I would like to think it was the cry of a suffering child, begging for a parent to be by their side..." he shook his head, "But it wasn't. No—he..." Momentum stood suddenly, "Anyway, I thank you for telling me this."

"Aorist," Tristan said with urgency, "I must ask you... why? Why won't you help us?"

"Haven't I said a hundred times to Hanz?" Momentum's eyes darkened. "I will not have anything to do with plots to kill or murder, especially not my king. Faeries must not kill—it is a law as old as our race. Why, Tristan, usurper or not, would I kill my king?"

Tristan grinded his teeth for a moment. "But... is he right, then? Is he right about his answer to the question?"

"And what answer would that be?" Momentum asked, keeping his eyes locked on the Water Faerie.

Tristan held Momentum's gaze. "He says that the Faeries were made to be gods of creation. The humans must not rule the land, *we* must. When they serve us, we gain power. Somenus wants Faeries owning all the land eventually. He wants to divide Raqia amongst the thousand titles, giving Faeries authority and lordship."

"Faeries the royalty of Raqia," Momentum chuckled. "How interesting."

"Is he right, Aorist? Is that why you will not move against him? Is he right? Are we *gods*?"

"I refuse to move against him," Momentum said as he sat back down in his chair, "...because he is my king."

"Were you there, Aorist?" Tristan asked with wide eyes.

Momentum glared silently.

"Please—were you *there*, Aorist? When the world was made? Were you there when the laws were written?"

Momentum held his stare.

"Aorist—why? Why were we made? Who are the Faeries supposed to *be* in the Cosmos? Was Sol right? Are we just hermits? Playing with our giftings like little street tricks to entertain passers-by? Or is Somenus right? Are we gods—deserving of the glory we see and create?"

Momentum shook his head.

"Why do you withhold this truth from us, Aorist?" Tristan's voice grew cold. "If you would just *tell* us! The Faeries are following Hanz because he fights for us, he leads us. We would follow *you* if you rose to it. Why won't you? Why won't *you* lead us?"

"I don't know what happened to the archer who killed King Sol," Momentum said blandly as he turned his face toward the window beside him, "But he would have died... eventually anyway. No one who kills the Faerie King can live. *That* is the law—written on the throne since the day it was made. Why, Tristan? Why do you think such a law was made?"

Tristan sighed. "Because..."

"Because it is *unforgivable*!" Momentum snarled, still gazing out the window.

Tristan stood. "The Faeries are lost, Aorist. We have been since the early days. No one save you remembers a time when the Faeries had a purpose. We are nomads in our own lands, without a center. Hanz offers us a calling, showing us that we can unite around a common cause, and so does Somenus, promising us we *do* belong in this world. Who is right, Aorist? *Who do we follow?*"

"All I can tell you is not to kill," Momentum mumbled, "Have no part in it. *That* is what it means to be a Faerie."

"I know there is more than that..." Tristan pressed. "Please, Aorist, were you there? Were you the first?"

"Go," Momentum whispered. "Please... go."

Tristan stood quickly. "Thank you for receiving me, Aorist. I am... disappointed."

I watched the Water Faerie leave, drifting out of the room like a floating leaf. He closed the door behind himself, and I heard Momentum groan.

I strode over, knowing I should choose my words carefully.

"I'm sorry, Momentum," I said.

Momentum, still gazing outside, made a soft chuckle. "What are *you* apologizing for, Leo?"

"Last night..." I said under my breath.

Momentum turned toward me. "Ah..."

"I'm sort of..." I huffed, "I am working through something. I am sorry I wasn't honest with you. I get other people to tell me their deepest thoughts and desires, and yet I keep my own hidden deep inside, as if no one in the world is trustworthy enough to know them."

Momentum pulled the corner of his mouth to the side. "Well? Do you trust me?"

I nodded hesitantly. "I do... I *want* to... I will... I am trying."

"What do you see in the dreamscape, Leo? It's Somenus, isn't it?" He asked with lifeless eyes.

"I do," I whispered, "I see him and... in some strange, sick way, I even anticipate it. But... that's not the real reason I go there."

Momentum cocked his head to the side. "Alright, I am genuinely curious."

"Hah... yeah..." I scraped the bottom of my shoe along the floor, making the shape of a semicircle. "No... it all goes back to when you took me through that Portal."

Momentum winced. "The Lapis Gate? What about it?"

"I felt something when I was in there... like..." I moved to sit where Tristan had been, across from Momentum. "Like I felt so many things at once!"

"I've told you before," Momentum said, "You experienced timelessness. You felt all of yourself—from conception to death—at once."

"Yes... and I felt this like," I took in a deep breath, "This *love* for somebody. This undying affection."

"I don't like where this is going."

"I am not talking about Somenus, Momentum. I am just talking about this pure, innocent affection: like a bright warmth at the thought of her name."

Momentum popped up an eyebrow. "*Her*?"

"Yeah... she's... I found her in the dreamscape."

Momentum shook his head. "Somenus is a master of deception and mirage. I am sure he is playing riffs off the memory of how you felt in the Flammarion Tunnel."

"No..." I shook my head. "I *know* she is real. She's... she's real, for sure."

Momentum stood, then pushed open the window. A gust of cool ocean air blew in, forcing his hair into movement.

"I don't like this, Leo." Momentum said in a hopeless voice.

I looked up from the armchair where I had been sitting. "Which part?"

"Everything... this... this stupid *'plan'* to kill the king."

"I can tell..." I slumped a little in my chair, relieved that Momentum wasn't asking further questions about Lola.

"It's true—I have lived longer than anyone else on Raqia," he said in a monotone, "I was there when we received our first commands. I know more than anyone why we should not kill or use others to kill." He looked in my direction. "And yet, I know just how wrong Somenus is... I know he is killing Faeries and oppressing the free nations of Raqia. But it is not for the Faeries to kill him. He is our *King*! I told Hanz I would not help him—but I don't know if that was the right call, either. There is something right about what he wants, but he is doing it the wrong way. I saw what happened to his father—poor Joel. For a time, he lost his humanity."

I sat there quietly for a bit, playing over his words in my head a few times before responding to them as I rolled one of my buttons between my fingers. "Timbre Wulf said something about the wisdom aging with time. You've walked a road that we young haven't walked yet. So surely your opinion should matter the most. It's kind of funny how with less information and experience, Hanz seems to have more clarity, and then with all the knowledge and years of experience, you seem to be more confused."

"Not confused, Leo. I just give much more pause before making important calls. It is easy to make a simple decision with little information. This issue is simple for Hanz because he doesn't know all the things I know. If he did, he would give pause, too."

"So why don't you *tell* Hanz what you know?" I asked.

Momentum snorted. "Leo—have you met the guy? He won't give ear to *anyone* who gets in the way of what he thinks is right—not even his own father! No. He doesn't *want* to know. He wants this to be simple. He is a man who does not treasure counsel. He sees questions and delays as threats, rather than as help. The wise are there, sitting on either side of him, but he won't ask what we think."

"Then what are the wise supposed to do? Shouldn't *you* be the ones making the calls?"

My master shrugged. "I made many calls, Leo, long ago, but I don't make *all* the calls. And frankly, while he is wielding that staff, Hanz can do just about anything he wants to do. Whether what he does is the right thing or not, that is another matter."

"But Master, what *is* the right thing to do?" I sat forward, grabbing the arms of my chair. "Surely it can't be standing by and letting Somenus dominate Raqia like a tyrant?"

"That's what I am trying to figure out, Leo," he replied. "Here is what I *do* know. I know that I must not kill, and I will not kill. I know that Hanz doesn't want my wisdom, nor my intervention, but I also know that he is not the leader of the Faeries. He is just one man—a human. And I know..." he sighed, "I know that if he is going to attempt to kill the Faerie King, I must be there—I must be there for what follows. I know that I must protect the Faerie throne, though I don't know what that will look like. I know this will be ugly, no matter what happens, and I know that I cannot let these Faeries who follow Hanz go there alone. I know I need to be there; that's all I know."

My mouth was hanging open. "You... you're *going*?"

"Yes, Leo," he nodded, "That is what I have decided. I cannot hide from my king, or the other Faeries any longer—that is what I know."

We stared at each other for a moment, and I smiled weakly. "I think there is one *more* thing you know—something that no one else knows."

Momentum's look of conviction faded and his face lost all its color.

"Why does it scare you so much, Momentum?" I stood, stepping closer to him. He didn't move a muscle; he stood there frozen like a pillar of stone. "Momentum, come on—it's *me*, Leo! Just tell me!" I placed my hands on his shoulders and gripped them tightly. "You said you were there when the Faeries received their first commands. Momentum—*why were the Faeries made*?"

31

—— Momentum ——

The Original Eight

At the very beginning, there were eight of us.

Over nine thousand seasons ago—we were the first of the Faeries. It was the fifth day of the Cosmos, Wingsday, that we were made. We didn't know anything yet, except that we were happy to exist. The Lights taught us who we were. We watched as they created Raqia. Everywhere, the lights of creation danced around us. The land radiated glory—the lights of creation. That glory gave us power; it drew us to different purposes. As those purposes formed, we found our titles. Steward of Moments: that's who I was back then.

Raqia was complete; from corner to corner, her lands were formed. She was the canopy over the stars. We flew to the edges of the land and looked down. There, we could see over the edge of our world, and down past the stars. We saw the lowlands. The four pillars of our table world reached down to other worlds below ours.

The next day, people were created. The humans were made, down there on your Earth, and Elves were made up on Raqia with us. All this happened before Death ever existed. Back then, everything was flawless.

Then, the words came. They were words written on the inside of our hearts, words not heard, but known. The words were laws. They told us who we were supposed to be, and why we were made. They said: *You, my Faeries, are the servants of creation. You were made to celebrate and cultivate its glory. You, oh race created on the fifth day, were made to serve the land; and those created on the sixth day were made to fill and rule it.*

Where the humans were charged to multiply and expand, we were charged to watch and help. We were made to serve you, Leo—not rule you. We, the Faeries, were the servants of all creation, made to glorify *others*, not ourselves.

It was so exciting. Here was our new world, and we were nestled at the top of it, gazing down at its beauty. The Eight of us used our gifts to serve creation. We built things; embellished things, enchanted things without magik. Together, we made the Lapis Gate. It provided a way for us to travel past the barrier of space and stars, down to the lowlands. We spent time living among the humans and serving them. After a while, we even began to bring some of them through the gate and up to Raqia. Over time, more Faeries were made, and more titles were filled. We built Arelle, the home of our people. And there, we crowned a king. Pondus, Faerie of Authority, was one of the Original Eight. Even without him asking us to, we followed him. In that time, the Faeries thrived, living according to their purpose.

Then, things got bad—*really* bad. By bringing humans to Raqia, we also brought Death. And with Death came war. It was the first of the Faerie wars, and there was division between the eight of us. That war ended with the death of our king. It was an evil, ugly time. After the dust settled, and hundreds of Faeries had been killed, there were only two of the Original Eight left. Viktor, the Faerie of Transport, and me. I cannot begin to tell you how broken we were after that war. The innocence that we began life with had died.

Pondus' infant son Sol was left with a fragile throne, and Viktor and I knew we had to protect him in order for Arelle to survive. So, we ruled the kingdom as duel regents. And I raised Sol, as if he were my son.

With the other six dead, and a young King who knew nothing about the Lapis Gate, we made a decision. We hid the Gate from the rest of the Fae. It was selfish—wrong, even—but if you had seen the kinds of evil that we had seen come to Raqia through that gate, you would know why. The portal was dangerous for the Faeries, so we sealed it off in a place only we could find it. We told ourselves that it was what Raqia needed.

Aorist and Viktor stood at the head of the throne room on either side of the king. He was standing there proudly, with a crown on his head and a scepter in his hand. The room was roaring with applause. They had done it; they had finally crowned the king.

"We did it, Aorist," Viktor whispered. He had a pure smile stretching across his face. Viktor was always smiling, but this one actually got Aorist to smile back.

Aorist agreed with a single nod. Viktor, draped in long, skydeaconesque robes, glided behind the throne and stood beside him.

"Come on," Viktor said as he elbowed his friend in the side, "Let's clap with them! Let's rejoice that Arelle finally has a king again!"

Aorist smirked, then joined his hands together in a slow, though sincere clap. Viktor whooped and cheered.

"I am relieved. Of course, I am," Aorist said casually, continuing to clap as he watched King Sol slowly leave the room. The crowds followed him, but the two Firsts remained behind by the throne. "But *Hades*, Viktor, I am tired."

Viktor lowered his cheering hands and looked at his friend with concern. "But we did it, Aorist. We saved Arelle. Look at her—she's a kingdom again!"

"A kingdom without a heart," Aorist mumbled.

"How can you *say* that?"

"She has no purpose. We cut off the lowlands from the Faeries, and now they're just..." he shrugged, "idle."

"There's plenty of humans here for them to serve, plenty of creation to cultivate," Viktor said.

"It's not the same," Aorist crossed his arms stubbornly, "It is like telling someone they are human because they have a head, but no body. We severed Raqia's ties from the rest of creation when we hid the Gate. It feels wrong."

"It only feels wrong to us because we were the ones who used to go there," Viktor lowered his voice, "And... now that our duty here in Arelle is done..."

Aorist drew back, eyeing Viktor with caution. "What exactly are you suggesting?"

Viktor leaned into Aorist's ear. "*You* are the keeper of the Lapis Gate, Aorist," he whispered, "You can still summon it. There's still two of us who remember the original call—we can still go there."

Aorist's heart began to thump with excitement. "You mean... pick up the old charge?"

"Why not? Sol is leading Arelle into a new era—an era after the war. But we are too old for new callings. Let the world move on, but you and I can go back and taste the air of the Earth." Viktor squeezed Aorist's arm tightly. "I am so *ready* to go back!"

The two exchanged sinister smiles.

"Well," Aorist bobbed his head to the side, "I suppose it wouldn't be *too* much of a problem if we disappeared for a bit."

Viktor hopped up and down childishly. "Yes, yes! Let me *travel*!"

Aorist laughed openly—something he hadn't done in a long time. "Alright, well let's get out of these ridiculous outfits and find something Earth-suited."

Viktor was already pulling him by the arm and trying to drag him out the servant's exit. "How much do you think it has changed in the last forty seasons? Will our clothes be outdated?"

"Only one way to find out!"

2500 Seasons Ago

Viktor jumped out of the Tunnel, landing onto a white stone outcropping. He stood quickly, stretching out his arms triumphantly.

"We are so lucky!" he exclaimed, pointing at the rocky Grecian coast, "— to wander here, where no other Faerie is allowed to go!"

Aorist exited the Tunnel in a rather different mood. He wore a grim look, though it was shielded partway with his stained-glass spectacles, each lens a different color. He looked around, surveying the waters, dotted with ships and colorful sails. Life on the Earth seemed to be advancing. Those ships had begun to cross oceans.

"It feels wrong," Aorist said, "that we see this every day. We get to give to creation, see its glory, taste its beauty, while every other Faerie exists up there, living without their true purpose."

Viktor sniffed, irritated by the negativity. "We saw what happened firsthand when the Faerie Kingdom had access to Earth. Our race nearly went extinct."

"Still," Aorist said, sitting down on a large boulder, "You and I are happy and free because we are doing what we were made to do."

"Well, *I* am happy," Viktor said playfully, "I wish you would stop sulking!"

"I mean it, Vik," Aorist mumbled, "It feels wrong not to let everyone serve humanity in the way that we do."

"Maybe that purpose was only for the firsts. We first Eight who witnessed the beginning. We were the only ones who ever heard the words." Viktor said, shielding his eyes from the sun as he turned to look at me, "We gave Raqia humans to watch over—not to mention the Elves. That is enough for them... but the Earth is safer this way, and so is Raqia. It is best we keep them apart."

"Maybe there is a compromise to all this," Aorist said with a sheepish smile, "I still think it is wrong that Raqia has no contact with the Earth."

Viktor stood there silently for a moment, then put his hands on his hips. "I see where you are going with this. You want to bring a little bit of Earth to Raqia?"

Aorist shrugged, though he couldn't hide his grin. "And I mean, we don't have to bring people, just culture! Think about it, our worlds don't have to be *completely* segregated!"

Viktor snorted. "Hellenize Raqia?"

Aorist laughed. "Yeah, Hellenize Raqia. We could bring back scrolls, writings..."

"Put on plays!"

"Sure," Aorist jumped to his feet, "And writings..."

"And plays!"

Aorist slammed his hands together with a loud clap. "We can be trend-setters."

"I am game," Viktor said hesitantly, "But we have to be careful. No one uses this portal except for us. Nobody comes to Earth—agreed?"

Aorist nodded soberly. "No need to ask me twice. I am never making that mistake again." He pulled off his spectacles and squinted, gazing up at the sky.

Viktor shook his head. "By the floods, Aorist! You are always so melancholy when we come out of the tunnel!"

"I know, I know. I'm sorry. It'll wear off as it always does." Aorist quickly returned his lenses to his eyes, growing suddenly self-aware.

"Well come on then, trend-setter! Let's make a plan!"

⊷———•———⊶

Yes, it felt a little cheap, giving the Faeries culture when we could have given them the world. But that was just it—we couldn't give them the world! The happy friendship between us and the lowlands had broken in that last war. We both knew it had. The sad thing was, we just couldn't let it go!

So, in an attempt to keep a shadow of that old friendship alive, we brought some of Earth's gifts to Raqia.

We brought books and plays, music and art—we even brought some plants and animals. The Faeries got a taste for Earth culture, and they drank it up. We sold it like fiction, though some of the Fae knew it had to have come from *somewhere*. Some hounded us for answers, but we were too wary to give them anything. So, Viktor and I grew reclusive. We played background roles, using other Fae as mediators to bring in the new Earth culture.

Then there was Temmy, one of our mediators. It didn't take long for her to be convinced that the Earth was a real place. She wanted so *badly* to go there, and we told her 'No' so many times. But *Hades*, try telling the only Faerie without a title 'No' when she begs you over and over again! We...we just felt bad for her. And *Hades*, we *liked* her. She was curious like us.

Viktor, Aorist, and Temmy appeared on a stone threshold, overlooking the forests beneath Chiri-San in Korea. They had built many small structures like this around the Earth, providing a safe landing place after the chaotic and jarring travels through the Flammarion Tunnel.

Viktor was beaming, holding his hands out in the air as if he were flying, just like he always did. "It is like sailing through the Lights, feeling everything you will ever feel, all at once. It is pure happiness. Even now, all I feel is love! It is *pure* happiness—do you feel it?"

Temmy smiled at Viktor, nodding, then turned to look at Aorist. He was gazing off into the distance with a melancholy stare.

"Is that how *you* feel, Aorist?" Temmy said to Aorist. She waved a hand in front of his face.

The Time Faerie whipped off his spectacles and turned to give her a moody look. "Yes, I feel love."

Temmy looked out at the Earth before her, scanning her eyes across its novel topography with eyes of fascination. "I don't think I felt any love but... I did feel something," she said, folding her hands together carefully.

"Oh yeah?" Viktor rubbed his hands together. "You've got me deeply curious now. What did you feel in the Tunnel, Temmy? You know it's a *very* special thing to go through there! Everyone's experience is different."

"Well, I think..." A smile formed on her face. "I felt power."

It all went so bad. She didn't *serve* the humans, she *ruled* them. She did then exactly what Somenus hopes to do now, only worse—she did it on the Earth! She was given the title of Moon Faerie, she would say, and so she needed to be near the moon. That, we could understand. But she became obsessed with ruling—with being a god. And *of course*, she knew we wouldn't let her. We were the threat to her and what she wanted, so the war began. We tried to catch her, and she tried to kill us. And for nearly a thousand Earth years, we chased her, trying to clean up the stupid mess we created by bringing her there.

"This is it, Vik," Aorist said, "It's a full moon tonight."

It was dusk, and the only sounds to be heard around the camp were weak coughs, silent sobs, and the scraping of rocks. The village was preparing for battle, a battle they were sure to lose.

Viktor was sitting cross-legged in the dirt, sharpening an arrowhead.

"If we had only gotten to the hills before tonight," the Transport Faerie muttered under his breath, "We wouldn't be sitting ducks here in the middle of a prairie!"

"They're farmers and young families, not soldiers, Vik. They move slow... they did the best they could," Aorist said as he lay on his back.

"Well, the least you could do is help me sharpen some more arrows," Viktor whispered, then tossed his arrow into a messy pile.

Aorist sat up and grasped Viktor by the wrist. "Hey, just stop."

Viktor shook his head. "I am not giving up. These people don't have to die."

"They are going to die, just like all the others who refused to worship the Moon Queen..." Aorist hesitated, "And so are we."

Viktor narrowed his eyes. "Temmy won't kill us."

"*Everyone* is going to die tonight."

Viktor's eyes flashed with realization. "Aorist... what do you see?"

"I see what I see," Aorist said slowly, "Just trust me. They will surround us at moon rise, and we will *all* die."

Viktor remained frozen as the chieftain approached.

"We have hidden the women and children in the central tent. The men are at their posts, guarding all sides." He held his chin high, but his face was already wearing the grief of what was to come. "Is it true, Aorist?"

Aorist looked up at the chieftain. His dark skin blended in with the night, but his brown eyes seemed to glow like stars.

"Is what true?"

"Is the Moon Queen truly not a god?"

Aorist sighed, then shook his head. "She is not a god, Whirling. She is a disobedient spirit."

The chieftain nodded. "I have put my strongest men on the four horses we have, but I do not think it will be enough."

"We will not leave you," Viktor said quickly, "We promise you that!"

"I will be honored to die alongside you, my friends," said Whirling. "Sound the alarm when it is time. Until then, I will spend my remaining hours with my family."

"Thank you, chief," Aorist said. His eyes dropped to the ground; they could hardly handle the intensity of what they saw—it was just too bright! Once the chief left, he threw on his spectacles and sighed.

"That bad?" Viktor lowered his arrowhead and sharpening stone to the ground.

"It's almost too much to bear," Aorist replied.

"I see... so, tonight *is* different."

Aorist lay back on the ground once more. The stars were coming out; he could see them better through the multi-colored lenses. "I've known this day was coming for a long time," he said, "I feel it every time we go through the Tunnel."

Viktor placed his work on the ground quietly, then lay beside his friend. He rolled onto his side, facing Aorist, and leaned his head in his hand. "Alright," he said, "I am listening—really. What is this about?"

Aorist kept his eyes focused on the stars above; down there on the Earth, they looked so still and clear. "Do you remember the first time we ever went through the Tunnel—all eight of us?"

Viktor cracked a smile. "How could I forget? It was incredible."

"You came out smiling," Aorist said, "talking about deep love and happiness."

Viktor nodded. "I knew I would always be with you. That feeling got me through the war, through raising Sol... it's gotten me through this chase with Temmy."

"Yes," Aorist sucked air deeply into his lungs, then let it out. "But it was different for me. I felt the same love that you did, but I came out feeling lost, empty, and alone. I *knew*, Vik... I knew I would lose you one day."

Viktor's smile faded. "But you said we are *all* going to die tonight."

Aorist closed his eyes. "I... I was twisting the truth." He turned his head slowly to gaze at his friend through his spectacles. "Everyone should have died tonight, but you are going to do something...I think. Viktor, you are going to die tonight, and I am not."

Viktor blinked. "You could be wrong..."

"I am not wrong, Vik. It's tonight..." his voice wavered and his eyes grew damp, "I am going to lose you. It's starting. My long years of loneliness."

"No," Viktor shook his head quickly, sitting up, "There has to be something we can do!"

Aorist closed his eyes tightly, letting the moisture stream down his face. "I knew you would say that..."

"We can think of something... we can do something! Aorist—let's open the portal... let's get out of here!"

"And leave our friends behind to die?" Aorist asked, eyes still closed. He knew what Viktor would say next.

"We can save them all! Open the Lapis Gate as wide as we can make it. Let's send them to the wastelands in the west. No one needs to know where they came from."

Aorist whipped off his glasses and threw his hands over his eyes. "This can't be happening!"

Viktor seized Aorist's shoulder and shook him. "Come on, get up! Temmy won't come until moonrise. If this really is my last night, I want to save lives, not watch them die!"

Aorist turned onto his stomach. "No," he sobbed, "I don't want this to happen."

"Come on," Viktor shook him again, "Get up, Aorist! Don't give up. We can fight this!"

Aorist sat up quickly and grabbed Viktor by the shoulders. He brought him close, clutching him tightly. "I don't want to lose you. I don't want to be alone," he sobbed.

"You won't be alone, Aorist..." Viktor said quietly, startled by the uncharacteristic display of emotion.

"You can't say that! You don't know!"

Viktor wrapped up Aorist in a tight hug, then pushed him back. "Come on, we still have time, and I will not stop fighting. Listen. You open the portal, and I will guide them through."

Aorist's head dropped into his chest and cupped his hands over his eyes, weeping. Viktor ruffled the Time Faerie's hair with his hand, stood, and called out to the camp. "Whirling! Men—to me! We will not die tonight!"

Viktor did die that night, as I knew he would. I used the Lapis Gate to rescue our little village, leading them into Raqia, and behind me, Viktor guided them through. He barely managed to save the warriors at the back and died protecting the portal as it closed. And just like that, it was over.

The pain of losing him—my last friend and brother from my first moments of existence—filled my very being. It was a feeling I had grown somewhat used to. I felt it every time we traveled between the firmaments. But when that feeling became a reality, it was too much to bear. He was dead, and my spirit died with him. The day I feared more than anything had finally come, and I was alone.

One Earth year later, I finally did it: I trapped her. I apprehended Temmy and brought her back to Winter's End. I felt no joy, no success in her capture, only pain. It was the end of a sad story that I hoped to tie up tightly and throw into the abyss. I was so empty; so lost.

Viktor was gone; *Aorist* was gone. All of those who remembered the old days were gone. Sure, I saved a small village; I saved some friends. But even they reminded me of a life which had been torn away. I had no place with them. I had no place on Raqia. I was lost—I was the most lost being in the Cosmos, and there was only one thing left that I wanted, and that was to die.

I wandered west of Winter's End, flying as far as I could, over the sea. There, at the edge of the world, I sat atop a jagged rock, clinging to the Table's edge like a stubborn barnacle. I peered down, over the edge of the roaring waters and gazed at the stars below. Down there was Death, the only comfort left for me. The sea bucketed down the edge of the world, pouring its waters off an endless cliff, into the bottomless starry sky. I wanted to be like that water, poured out into nothingness.

I knew it wasn't true what people said about the Faerie of Time—they used to say I could not die, not until I had seen all of time. No, I could die like anyone else, surely! No, I *needed* to die, because no one could live on for seasons and seasons with the kind of pain that I felt in my heart. My life *needed* to end.

"Why won't you just kill me? Just let me die!" I cried out to the Lights above, screaming with every ounce of breath I had in my body. And wind blew through my hair, and for a moment I wondered if the Lights would speak to me like they did when I was first made. Instead, there was nothing but silence.

I was alone.

"I know it is against my law to kill," I said to myself as I took a step toward the world's edge, "But this is all I have left. Please, Lights, forgive me." Then I jumped.

I fell. I fell off the face of my world, enveloped by an endless pain. I felt the pain first on my skin as it tore here and there, covering my body in thousands of miniature lacerations. Then I felt it in my bones as they snapped into hundreds of microscopic fractures. Then it went deeper; I felt it in my wings. The terror of death took me, and I flailed. My arms, legs, then my wings, thrashed, grasping anywhere for support. Why—why had I done this? But it was too late for regrets or rescue; finally, I was dying.

My wings—my six glorious wings—tried to catch me like sails, slowing my fall. Instead, they ripped into shreds in mere seconds. Nothing could break that fall through the firmaments. I was like a falling star, burning up in a blaze of pain and fire. I went crashing down toward the places that linger at the bottom of creation, the place I had sentenced others to for their crimes. Soon, I would see them myself. I was on my way to Hades.

I fell through an endless tunnel of stars. No, it was not like the Flammarion Tunnel. There was nothing peaceful or timeless about it. All I felt was pure terror.

I wrapped my body around itself, imagining I was lying in a coffin as I prepared for impact. I waited for my body to grow warm as one of the only things I knew for sure about Hades was that it was made of fire.

"My time has come—I am coming, Viktor." I whispered, "I am coming."

I fell like a star falls from the heavens. But I did not find Hades. No. Instead, my body hit dirt.

A cloud of dust and debris surrounded my tattered body. I waited for a while. Expecting my soul to leave its physical form. I don't know how long I lay there, waiting to die. But to my confusion and dismay, I didn't. I *didn't* die!

I was alive.

I sat up slowly, surprising myself by moving my aching muscles. How was I not completely broken from that fall? When I found the strength to stand, I screamed with horror—how had I lived? How had I not died? But then I heard it—I heard the voice. It told me to look.

I had fallen down into the lowlands, but I had not fallen onto the Earth, I had fallen somewhere else. There was another land, a new land I had never seen, hiding under the northwest corner of Raqia, supporting her leg of the table. That was when I realized there could be something new, there was another day after the last day of my life.

That place I called Paidion: Child. It represented to me the promise of a new life, and it gave me a new passion to invest in, even after Viktor was gone.

Yes, Leo. It is the world that Cymbeline came from, a world with no moon. After a time, I took Temmy there, knowing she would be as powerless as a human there. I spent much time in that world, learning about it, caring for it, and getting to know the unique race of humans there.

<hr>

"I was given a new purpose, Leo," Momentum said to me with distant eyes, "When I was first made, I was given the charge to serve creation—to serve the humans above and below the stars. I fulfilled that purpose. But after the war, when the rest of the Eight were lost, the purpose was lost, too." He shook his head, closing the window as the evening air grew cold.

"When I tried to return to that original calling," he said, "it brought evil and destruction onto the Earth. No, that purpose was no longer possible for me. But when I found Paidion, I realized that there was such a thing as newness. There could be new callings, and new ways of living. In the early times, the way of serving humanity meant Faeries going down to the Earth. But it can't mean that anymore, it's just too dangerous."

I sat there in my chair watching him. My hands had grown numb from my nervously clenched fists. What was there to say? I was just a small, tiny blip in this Faerie's long, important life. What could I possibly say?

"So why, Leo?" Momentum said, moving toward the chair where I sat. "Why should I be the one to answer the question for the Faeries? I have no answer! I am a failure from an old calling, an old mission. We made a mess trying to serve humanity, and we were broken by it! I can't tell the Faeries who they are if I don't even know who *I* am, Leo. I am just a lingering shadow, and echo from an old promise, spoken into the stars. What do I tell them, Leo? What do I say? Do I tell them the old calling is *dead*? Do I tell them we already failed? Is it not better for them to search and theorize, and find their own purposes? They want me to save them from their confusion, to lead them into a new age. But it would only be the blind leading the blind, Leo. Don't you see? I am as lost as they are!"

He walked toward me and placed his hand on my shoulder, looking down at me through his lenses.

"I may be the only Faerie left who knows who the Faeries should have been," he said, "but I am also the only Faerie left alive who will ever be able to taste it. It would be cruel to tell them if they cannot taste it too. It is better for them to invent a new purpose. And for that, perhaps, they do not need my help at all."

There was silence. I waited, wondering if he would say more, then watched as he turned to sit on the chair across from me. He blew out air through his lips, looking around, as if waiting for the world to end now that he had spoken of what he knew. Then, he removed his spectacles and looked at me with tired eyes.

"There," he said with a weak smile, "I did it. It is done."

I cleared my throat, then sat forward, twiddling my thumbs together. "Well," I said, "It is kind of hard to follow that."

Momentum chuckled.

"Momentum?"

"Hmm?"

"Is that why you hate Cymbeline?"

His smile faded. "What do you mean?"

"I mean, you said you don't hate her for being Temmy's daughter," I said slowly.

"Well," he rolled his eyes to the side, "That certainly doesn't *help*."

"Viktor," I said quietly, fearing wrath for speaking his name. "He... he was really special to you."

Momentum's eyes widened at the sound of Viktor's name; then his face grew dark and cold. "*Special*?" He shook his head. "Leo, it is something you could *never* understand."

I readjusted my stiff body in my chair and leaned forward, "Maybe not," I grunted, "But still... Cymbeline is the first to carry his title, isn't she? She is the second Transport Faerie. She bears his powers, his wings."

Momentum's fists formed together, vibrating like tremors before an earthquake. "*No one* could ever be worthy of that title! It was supposed to stay vacant!" His voice grew louder, "Some titles should *never* be given again!"

"Momentum," I swallowed, knowing I probably didn't have the authority to say what I was about to say, "You don't get to decide those things. You don't get to pick who is worthy, and who isn't."

Momentum scoffed, leaning back into his chair.

"Cymbeline didn't take Viktor away from you, Momentum. It's not fair to either of them for you to hold this grudge."

"Stop preaching, seminary boy."

"No!" I yelled, grabbing the arms of my chair with a sudden burst of conviction, "You keep citing laws about how Faeries can't kill—why? Because it was written on your soul by the Lights the day you were made, right? *They* told you who you are; *they* are the ones who pick the titles; *they* decide who is worthy.

So, you've got to stop blaming Cymbeline, as if she has stolen her wings from you—from Viktor. She didn't take him away from you, he *died*!"

Momentum was staring at me with wide, hateful eyes, but he had no words.

I felt an eerie chill, knowing I was way out of bounds for talking to him so directly, but instead of backing away, I pressed into my uneasiness.

"You shared this story with me," I said calmly, "Because you trust me. Well, trust me now, *Aorist*," I reached forward, daring to touch him. I placed my hand on his, which was clutching tightly to his chair's arm. "Cymbeline is a *gift* to you," I paused, breathing in deeply, "*from* Viktor."

Momentum's glossy, fierce eyes began to soften. They seemed to dance with memories and visions that only he could see. He nodded in agreement, as if hearing some inner voice. His shaking arms relaxed, and I saw him melt a little into his chair.

"No," he finally whispered in a voice as still as the sea after a typhoon, "*You are, Leo.*"

I blinked, leaning back into my chair as I withdrew my hand from his. "...What?"

Momentum rotated his stiff head slightly to look at me, then turned up the corner of his mouth into a smile. Then he rose, stretching like a cat who suddenly decided—for no reason at all—his time at your side was over. He walked across the room and placed his spectacles on his bedside.

"Uh..." I sat there still, his words dancing around in my mind.

"I'm going to bed, Leo," Momentum said from across the room.

I looked up quickly to see him lying on his bed with his arm over his eyes. "Already?"

"My eyes need a break," he mumbled.

I glanced at his glasses, then back at him. I jumped up and paced over to where he lay. "Hey, uh—Momentum?"

"Hmm?"

"What's with the glasses?"

I saw his mouth turn down into a frown. "That's personal."

I crossed my arms. "Oh, yeah... sorry for asking." He had told me that all Faeries see different kinds of lights, depending on their title. What on Earth did *he* see?

"You can go now, Leo," he mumbled.

I rolled my eyes. It was a little irritating how quickly conversations seemed to end with him, simply because he found himself *tired*.

"Hey, Momentum?"

He groaned.

"About the Question... about why the Faeries were made..." I mumbled.

He groaned again.

"Isn't it crazy how Somenus' answer to the Question was the same as Temmy's?"

There was a moment of silence, then Momentum lifted his arm slightly to peek at me with one eye.

"I mean," I continued, "She started out as a Faerie with no title, no purpose. Then, she goes to the Earth and instead of serving people, she makes herself a god. And she threatens to destroy anyone who doesn't worship her, right?"

Momentum's eye kept looking at me.

"And now, Somenus is doing the same thing. Without an answer to the Question, he is trying to use his power to rule. Somenus... Temmy... the Purple Order... even *you*, you are all lost. And without a purpose or a calling, you find yourself trying to kill: to end life, rather than preserve it. Somenus kills Faeries; Temmy killed humans; Hanz kills kings; and you tried to kill *yourself*."

His eye blinked.

"The fact remains, until that Question is answered—poorly or not—there will be more and more death—more *killing*, the one thing you are so against taking part in. You may not have the full picture, but you do have words to share with the Faeries about what was spoken back when you were made. Has it never occurred to you that by keeping those words to yourself, you're effectively doing the same thing—killing?"

He covered his eye with his arm once more, then sighed. "Leo..."

"Some bring death by things they have done," I said, "while others by what they have left undone."

Momentum lowered his arm to his side and looked at me full on.

"I'm sorry, Momentum," I said as we locked eyes.

"For what?" he asked lifelessly.

"For..." I hesitated, "For your loss. I am sorry you lost Viktor, and that you've been alone for so long. I am sorry you have to carry this weight on your shoulders that no one else could ever understand."

One of his eyebrows twitched, then he cracked a little smile. "*Out of the mouths of babes?*"

I snorted, looking away. "Yeah... fine." I turned away, but he caught me by the wrist.

"Leo..."

"Yeah?" I kept my eyes on the ground, too embarrassed to look him in the eyes.

"Thanks... no one's ever..." he sighed. "No one's ever said that to me before. Thank you—really."

"Well..." my voice cracked awkwardly, "No... problem... um..."

"Leo?" He squeezed my wrist.

I slowly lifted my eyes to look at his face. "Yeah?"

"Good night."

"Right." I made a nervous chuckle and backed away from where he lay. "Goodnight."

I tiptoed away, feeling the intense beating of my heart thump in my chest as I processed the words spoken that evening. I paused at the door, turning toward him as I opened my mouth, "Uh..."

"Good *night*, Leo!"

"Good night..." I opened the door.

"Leo..." I heard a reluctant groan as the Time Faerie turned toward me in his bed.

I looked back, forcing a cringy smile. "Yeah?"

"I, uh..." he cleared his throat with a couple coughs. "I see important moments..."

I raised my eyebrows. "You mean...?"

"Important moments are... *bright...* for me."

I smiled. "Like tonight?"

He turned away from me in his bed. "Good night, Leo!"

I couldn't help but beam with a little pride as I shut the door. "Good night!"

— Clover —

The King of Men

W ake up, Clover."

Clover clenched his eyes closed. "Two more clicks…"

"Wake *up*!" Yuma bored the toe of his boot into Clover's back.

"Stop it!" Clover turned quickly, swiping for the foot.

"Too slow," Yuma chuckled. "You've slept until the mid-morning bell—it's time to get up, really."

Clover blinked his eyes open. Yuma's large body was standing above him, silhouetted against the open door. Clover had slept on a rug on the ground of Yuma's shared room. While a little curious, the other Eagles hadn't minded Clover's presence there. If he didn't snore, they didn't care; that's what they had told him, anyway.

Yuma knelt down on one knee and reached toward Clover's body. He lifted up the little sleeping body of Thieving Scumbag and held him close to his chest.

"How sweet," the warrior grinned, "Still asleep."

Clover sat up quickly. "Give him back!"

Yuma was about to quip, but snapped his mouth closed when he saw how distressed Clover actually was. He passed the little ball-of-a-gnome back to Clover. Clover seized the little thing quickly.

"He…" the Elf stuttered, "He–he just wanted to sleep some more."

Yuma stood. "It's Mansday, Clover. We see the king today."

Clover closed his eyes.

"You don't have to say anything, Clover, just let me do all the talking."

Clover rose groggily, cradling the sleeping gnome in his hands. "What did the general say?"

"I haven't gotten an answer from him yet—he's not an easy man to read. But he did agree to walk us to the Sixth Level this morning. He's interested, at least."

"Interested in what?" Clover asked with half-open eyes.

"In going to war with Arelle."

Clover sighed. Is *that* what they wanted? To start a war?

"I don't like it, Yuma," Clover said quietly.

"I told you, *I* will do all the talking."

"No, I mean…"

"Come on," Yuma pulled Clover out of the sleeping quarters by the arm. "Let's just keep moving." Clover quickly grabbed his spear and followed.

They came out of the barracks and onto the main stretch of the Fifth Level wall. The wall tops were like main streets in the military city. And in full daylight, it was bustling with men in black uniforms. Some were patrolling, walking along the walls in circuits; some were standing still, eyeing the lower levels; and others were going about their lives, as if there were no other world but their own.

TSB roused from his slumber as they stepped into the light. He rubbed his eyes, then quickly jerked into motion. He climbed onto Clover's shoulders and looked around, scanning for danger.

"Good morning, little Thief," Clover whispered as he held up his finger to the critter. He had been particularly protective of the gnome since losing Solo.

Yuma watched them carefully for a moment, then said, "When we go into Arelle… are you going to bring him with you?"

Clover started. "*What*?"

"When you go to kill Somenus," Yuma lowered his voice, "Is he going with you?"

Clover stood there, blinking repeatedly.

Yuma rubbed his forehead. "Have you thought about what's going to happen to him... when..."

"I need him."

Yuma looked side to side. "What do you mean?"

"I need him with me... at the end." Clover said.

Yuma frowned. "You're not worried about him getting hurt?"

"Of course I am," Clover replied coolly, "And I trust you will look out for him, once I am gone."

Yuma took a sudden step back.

"Is something the matter?" Clover asked as he studied Yuma's fearful expression.

"I..."

"You are going to be there with me, aren't you?" Clover asked, growing a little pale.

"Of course I am!"

Clover nodded. "Good. Well, once it's over, I want you to protect him."

Yuma turned his head to the side.

"Am I asking too much?"

"No," Yuma looked back quickly. "Clover, what do you mean... when you said that you need him?"

"Corporal!" A voice barked. Yuma snapped to attention, waiting as a soldier clothed in black approached. Clover turned to regard him. He was tall, and heavily built. His eyes were a striking, bright blue, and his hair wispy and blonde. His stern square face peered down at Clover with suspicion. "Is this the civilian you brought up here?"

"Yes, Sir," Yuma said, still frozen in his salute.

Clover pulled the gnome off his shoulder and hid him under his cloak. "Hallo," he said, "I am Clover."

The newcomer snorted. "So, it's true. You brought an Elf up here."

"I did."

"At ease, soldier," the large man laughed.

"This is Clover, Sir," Yuma said as he relaxed, "Clover, this here is the Brigadier General of the Black Eagles."

The second-in-command grinned proudly. "General Bonyx will meet you at the Sixth Level. I am to bring you to him."

Clover gazed upwards at the man who was nearing seven feet tall. "What's it like... the Sixth Level?"

The Brigadier General twisted his face thoughtfully. "It's... a little sad... yet impressive."

"Oh?" Clover blinked lazily, "Sad?"

"Well," the Brigadier General gazed up toward the heavens, as if for support, "*Cards*, it's not for *me* to comment on how the gods live their lives, is it? I'm merely a soldier." He forced a phony smile.

"*Gods*?" Clover glanced at Yuma.

"Don't overthink it," Yuma mumbled, "It's just how Bavelonians think. They believe anyone above you in station is deserving of worship, and anyone below you must worship you."

"That, I knew." Clover sighed inwardly. Oh, how he *hated* this culture.

"We aren't here to comment on how the king lives his life," Yuma said bluntly, "We just need his support."

"So, I have heard," said the Brigadier, "Pretty bold, coming into Bavel with demands of our King."

"Not demands," Yuma replied, "Just propositions."

"Ah," the Brigadier nodded knowingly. "That does sound like something... *he* might want to hear..."

Clover groaned. "Yuma..."

"Well, the sooner the better," Yuma said quickly, sensing Clover's reluctance.

"Oh, sorry for the delay, *Corporal*," the Brigadier waved his mouth with a yawn. "How *rude* of me."

"Have *you* met the king?" Clover asked. "Is he... reasonable?"

The Brigadier belted a laugh, then did his best to steady himself, leaning heavily against the wall for support. "*Oh*, ho ho…" He shook his head and wiped a proverbial tear from his eye, "*Reasonable*? Ladies… you might have better luck *reasoning* with a whore!"

Clover shot Yuma a glare.

"Would you lead us on, Brigadier?" Yuma asked as he seized Clover by the arm. "Just be patient," he whispered to the Elf, "He doesn't take *anything* seriously."

"Fine, fine—come this way," the second-in-command marched forward, waving them into action with a flick of his hand.

"Yuma… I don't feel good about this." Clover whispered as they followed. "The king… he sounds like the epitome of what I hate about this place!"

"The Truth Faerie told us to come here, Clover," Yuma whispered back, "We just have to trust that this is the right thing to do."

"That's not how prophecy works!" Clover hissed.

"Oh?" Yuma grumbled back, "And how *does* prophecy work, Clover?"

Neither of them was listening to the Brigadiers ramblings as he led them toward the Sixth Level stairs.

"Prophecy is words of truth," Clover whispered in return, "They're not commands we must follow, regardless of their consequences."

Yuma scoffed. "Clover, the Truth Faerie said we should come here, so *that's* what I am doing! Don't complicate it!"

"I am not complicating *anything*," Clover snapped, "The truth Faerie said we should come here, but he did not tell us we should ask for war! The Truth can't be true apart from what is good and beautiful, and this place is neither!"

"Clover," Yuma slapped a hand against the Elf's chest, stopping him in place. The Brigadier General went on pacing forward, jabbering away. "This isn't a philosophical debate—this is reality! Life is messy, results are messy. Sometimes we have to ask for help from people who are less than ideal to get what we want."

"No!" Clover seized Yuma by the collar of his black tunic and pulled himself closer. "I don't care what it is we need, we cannot get good from an alliance with evil!"

"Clover!" Yuma rose to the argument, seizing Clover by *his* collar. "Wake up! You're not in the woods anymore! You can't live in this world without making hard decisions! I am not talking about allying with evil, I am just trying to save my *people*!"

"And are their lives worth the war that might arise from Bavel going to war with Arelle?" Clover raged, "Are you ready to take *that* upon your shoulders, after the Faerex is dead?"

"*Hades*, lads," the Brigadier was biting off the edge of his fingernail, "Are you quite finished?"

Clover and Yuma, both holding each other by the front of their shirts turned to look at their escort.

"Come on," said the second in command, "Let's not waste daylight, we don't know how long it's going to last, do we?" He turned and began gliding up the Back Eagles' private staircase, leading up to the Sixth Level walls.

Clover and Yuma followed silently, trying their best to keep their thoughts to themselves.

Once at the Sixth Level, the Brigadier pointed down at the Gate below. "There's the master of the Sapphire House," he said, "The general is with him." He glanced toward Clover and Yuma with a condescending sniff. "This is where I leave you, then?"

"Fine," Clover said quickly, eager to leave the man behind.

"Thank you," Yuma said, "We will take it from here."

The two of them trotted down the spiral stairs which led to the gate. Patro yelped as he spotted them and reached for his handkerchief to dab the eternal sweat dripping from his forehead.

"Ah, Clover," the round man blubbered, "I wasn't sure if you were going to—"

"Patro," Clover mumbled as he approached, "Hallo."

"Morning, Corporal," said General Bonyx; he was standing beside Patro with the presence of a monument.

"Sir," Yuma nodded his head, "Thank you for seeing us here."

"General!" Patro stammered, doing his best to bow with respect. Clover elbowed him in the side.

"That's enough from you," the Elf whispered, "Now pipe down!"

"Alright," The general called to the Eagles up on the walls, "Open the gates!"

The four of them stood at the Sixth Level gate, waiting. TSB crouched on Clover's shoulder, watching with a gaping mouth as the gates began to creak open. It turned Clover's stomach to see how much wealth sat at the top of this man-made mountain. The gates themselves were inlaid with cut gemstones, intricately depicting constellations. Above them, the hard sky was so close, they could see its texture.

"Look at that," Yuma said, astonished. Clover followed Yuma's arm in the direction it pointed. Massive cracks in the glass ceiling were jetting out from where the central castle's pointy peak hit the top of the sky, like a massive arrow head penetrating a shield.

"By the Lights," Clover whispered. "They've dug into the sky!" It gave Clover chills. Something felt very, *very* wrong about it.

The general rotated to look at Clover with curiosity, then grinned.

"An Elf?" he asked, directing his question at Yuma.

"As I told you, Sir," Yuma said nervously, "I have unique friends."

The four of them began to walk together into the Sixth Level. The only building that seemed to be on this Level was the king's Castle itself. Its architecture was a stunning masterpiece, with reflective gold plating and countless spires. It resembled a display of vertical crystals jetting up into the sky—a magnificent pipe organ, with its peaks penetrating the heavens.

Clover looked around the grounds as they walked up to the Castle's entrance. He was surprised to see, well—*no one.* Not even a single guard inhabited the place.

"Where—?" Patro stammered, glancing at Clover fearfully, then turning to the general.

"Where are the people?" The general finished his question.

Patro nodded wordlessly.

"Inside," The general said blankly.

There was an eerie silence as they walked. It was normal for a dry desert, or an empty sea to be blank and devoid of any life. But a castle? Why? Why were there no people?

The air grew still as they entered the palace. A servant passed them nervously. Finally! A sign of life!

"Where is everyone?" Clover asked, watching the servant scurry away.

"This is the Sixth Level," The general said, "Who would you expect to be here other than the king and his family? Who else is high enough?"

Patro nodded reverently. "Yes, of course," he muttered, "We are lucky to be here at all."

"Lucky?" Clover snorted.

"Yuma," The general said, stopping in his tracks. The other three stopped walking as the general turned to face them. "You are going to ask for assistance—to go to war with Arelle?"

Clover turned to look at Yuma.

"Yes." Yuma nodded to his general. "The Faerex has transgressed his authority over the free nations of Raqia. He is threatening to take over the world."

"You want to..." The general rubbed his beard. "...You want to *kill* the Faerex?"

Patro gasped. "You *what*?"

"Yes," said Yuma. "It is the only way I can save my people from imminent destruction. He's withheld food from our lands."

The general nodded. "You are a Fero man."

"Yes."

Clover didn't say anything; he watched the general close his eyes, thinking as he carved shapes into his beard with his index finger. "I...*well*, let us see what the Queen says. It might be worth our while."

"How so?" Yuma asked, looking hopeful yet cautious.

The general shrugged modestly. "There are... *riches* there... that she might desire. Arelle has been our enemy for a long time. It would be good to remind her of our power."

Clover shook his head slowly. *Riches?* This was what he feared. What would it look like if Bavel *plundered* Arelle? Is that something they would be willing to risk? No...

Yuma sighed. "Let us speak with the king."

The general coughed, looking a little uncomfortable. "Well, this way then."

The four of them began to walk again. Clover leaned in toward Yuma, whispering. "Something feels wrong. You feel it, don't you?"

"I know." Yuma whispered back. "Let's just see what the king says. It is too late to turn back now."

"Fine." Clover groaned.

The general led them to a large, gold-plated door, then turned to them to grimace before pushing it open. They entered.

The throne room was a large hall, with vast ceilings and tall, thin pillars. Long, stained-glass windows lined the outer walls, spraying colorful light into the room. There was a lengthy banquet table lining what should have been the aisle leading to the throne up ahead. They skirted it, noticing the incredible amount of uneaten food sitting atop it.

The place was silent; they could hear only their own footsteps as they approached the throne. TSB tugged on Clover's ear and pointed up. Clover peered upwards. The ceiling was like a dome—a dome of glass cut roughly into the Glassy Sea. Above, Clover spotted a workman balanced on a ladder, cutting away at the ceiling with a tiny hammer.

"By the Lights," Yuma breathed in sharply.

"Godstones," the general said, looking upward. "That is where they come from."

Clover's heart thumped with pain. "They broke the sky?" he asked, looking back at the general. The aging man gave him a skeptical look, then nodded.

"I thought godstones came from falling pieces of the Glassy Sea," said Yuma, glancing at Clover, "Didn't you tell me that?"

"Like falling stars," Clover mumbled absently.

"I am sure some do," the general mumbled, then cleared his throat as they came closer to the throne. "Now," he whispered, "I expect you to show respect. Our kings are our gods. Honor them, or I will not hesitate to kill you."

"Of course!" Patro blurted. Clover examined the short man. He was sweating, endlessly dabbing his forehead with a blue cloth.

"Your holiness," The general called out toward the throne as they approached, "I bring your honored guests! This is Patro of the Sapphire House. He brought you the gift you loved so dearly. And with him is Clover of Sapphire House, and Yuma, one of my Eagles."

Clover audibly gasped. Sitting on the throne crafted of pure gold was the Queen of Bavel, wearing her godstone-studded crown. A loosely-tied silk toga was draped messily over her shoulder, screaming mockery in the face of modesty; it seemed to reveal more than it covered, flaunting her blaring nakedness to those present. As disturbing as her clothing was, it was what she wore on her head that offended Clover to the point of sweating blood.

Into a menacing hairpiece which sat just above her crown was a set of curly, ribbed ram's horns, fashioned into a menacing crown. All Clover could do was gape, running his eyes across the perfect white swirls of keratin. He *knew* those horns—those were Solo's horns. But before he could find words to put to his rage, his gaze lowered, and he saw what lay beneath the queen.

"*Hades...*" Yuma stumbled back, covering his nose with his hand. The stench assaulted them.

Patro fell to his knees, bowing repeatedly. He couldn't think of what else to do.

Beneath the woman—the disturbingly *beautiful* woman—was a half-decayed body, crunched in half, nestled into the seat of the throne. The king's corpse acted as a seat cushion, while the head of the body was draped over the arm of the throne. Upon the king's head sat his crown.

"Welcome!" The queen moaned drunkenly, swaying back and forth. She held a goblet in her hand and splashed its deep red contents in their direction. Her eyes focused on Clover and Yuma. All they could do was stare at her in horror.

She narrowed her eyes at them, "Well," she said, pausing as she searched for the right words. "*Bow* to the king!" she finally slurred.

Yuma shifted, bowing his head, but Clover remained frozen.

"Bow." The general tapped the back of Clover's legs with the tip of his spear. Clover could not move.

The queen stared at the group with crazed eyes. She stuck out her tongue as she studied them, then slurped it back into her mouth. It was almost as if she didn't know what she was looking at. "Who gave me the goat?" she finally asked, hiccupping.

Patro trembled. "It was I, your holiness."

"What... is *that*?" she demanded, pointing an unsteady finger at Clover.

The general cleared his throat. "He is an Elf," he said.

"No!" she screamed, throwing her goblet at the general. It missed him, splattering a puddle of wine on the floor. "*That*!" She pointed again.

The general noticed the gnome on Clover's shoulders. "It is some sort of animal," he said.

"I want it!" She stood, pressing a foot into the king's decaying ribcage. More cracking sound commenced.

Clover gritted his teeth and clenched his fists.

"Holiness," the general said calmly, unalarmed by her tantrum. "These men have a question for you."

"Men..." she licked her lips. "Yes—I see them."

"Your holiness," The general raised his voice, "This is a political matter. They have a *question* to ask you."

The Queen paused, examining them once more. Then she grinned gleefully. "Yes, yes, I know what they will ask me. Come closer!"

The general hesitated, then tapped the backs of their knees, ushering them forward. Clover, Yuma, and Patro inched closer.

Patro moaned fearfully, making repeated bowing motions with his body.

"That one," The Queen pointed at Yuma. "No..." she wavered, looking confused, "No—*that* one!" Her finger swung towards Clover. "I want *that* one!"

"These are *guests*," The general reminded her softly.

"No!" She slammed her fist against one of the king's crumbling bones, "I *want* one!"

"Hear them out," the general said firmly. There was a hint of irritation in his voice.

"Queen of Bavel," Yuma said, stepping forward boldly, "We have a question." He drew in a breath, closed his eyes, then let it out. "We—"

"No!" Clover's shrill cry reverberated through the throne room.

Yuma held his breath, then turned to see Clover standing there with a body as tense as a hurricane.

"Clover?" Yuma whispered. "No—no.... No, no, no, no... not *now*!" He pleaded under his breath.

"No!" Clover bellowed, his voice pounding through the hall like a cannon blast.

The Queen gritted her teeth. "And what is this?" She gazed at Clover, half offended, half intrigued.

"*No!*" Clover's voice grew supernaturally louder, and he stepped ahead of his group, pointing his finger at the queen. "We have *no* questions for you—you disgusting, *evil* spawn of Hades!"

"*Clover!*" Patro, Yuma, and the general cried out in unison.

Clover could not hear them; Clover would not hear them. He continued, his voice as clear as a French horn, reverberating with purity as he stepped closer to the throne.

"We have no questions for you. There *are* no questions for you. We have only *judgment* for you. You—you bringer of death and wickedness. You rule a kingdom of putrid rats, devouring anything of goodness and beauty. You see loveliness and you destroy it; you see innocence and you *eat* it! You have desecrated the holiness of Raqia; the sanctity of marriage; the purity of life; and the innocence of children. There *are* no questions for you," He marched up to the throne until he was right under the Queen's nose. He was so close he could smell the rotting corpse of the half-decayed King. "You..." he hissed, "For *you*, there is only judgment."

"*Judgment*? Hah!" She barked a laugh. "Who are you to say *judgment*?"

"I am a prophet," Clover said, "I am a prophet from outside this horrific and upside-down kingdom. And this is your judgment." Clover reached forward and ripped the crown of horns from her head. He stepped back, holding them in front of her as she stared at him in shock. "You and all who worship you will *die*."

There was Silence.

The Queen began to cackle.

"*Die*?" she asked mockingly, then motioned to the general. She leaned back into her throne, kicking her legs alternatingly in the air as she laughed. Then, after a moment of heavy breathing and self-fanning, she said, "Kill them."

"*Heed my words, woman!*" Clover cried, shaking the room with his voice, "There is nothing left for you. No rescue. No help. As sure as the day," he pointed up at the dome where the Bavelonians had mined into the surface of the Glassy Sea, "This ceiling will shatter, and the flood waters from above will rain down your punishment. Not a soul who worships you will be left alive."

Yuma, Patro, and the general all eyed Clover with awe-struck, open mouths.

"Clover!" Yuma croaked. "Stop!"

The Queen's body began to quake with rage. She stepped off the throne and reached her hands toward Clover. He didn't flinch. She dove toward him and grasped him by the neck. "I said *kill* them!" she screamed.

The general started, then turned to Clover, unsheathing his sword. Yuma acted quickly, moving toward the Queen. The queen clawed at Clover's throat, digging her nails into his skin. Before Yuma could come to his rescue, the general swung the sword against Yuma's neck.

"I am sorry," the general said. Yuma froze, pulling away from Clover. "It is over."

It *was* over. With a sound like the bright clash of cymbals, one of the large, crystalline windows shattered into a million pieces. All cowered in fear as millions of glass shards rained down on them. Clover looked up, hardly believing what he saw. A great black shape, which at first resembled a massive spider, flew into the room and collided into the ground in a cloud of dust. Emerging from the misty debris were six black wings. Waiting For the Day rose from the cloud, eyeing the group with a haunting stare.

"Day!" Yuma cried, rushing to the beast. The general cowered, dropping his sword. The horse cried like the sound of a trump, leaping upward. Clover gaped at the beast who thrashed back and forth, kicking its legs violently.

"Clover!" Yuma yelled, "He says come! He will not stay here!"

Clover pulled himself free of the Queen's clutches and tucked TSB under his arm. Then, with everything he had, he bolted toward the horse.

"Come back!" The queen screamed with spit flying from her mouth. Clover did not turn around to look at her as he and Yuma climbed on Day's back.

"Hang on tight," Yuma cried. Clover snapped his eyes closed as the beast took off into the air and soared toward the broken window.

⸻ ⬧ ⸻

Clover and Yuma laid against Waiting For the Day's stomach as they gazed up at the stars' reflections.

The great black beast was sleeping with his head nestled into the grass. TSB was curled up under the horse's chin with his long billowy scarf wrapped around his little gnome body like a blanket.

Clover held Dezmund's newly-recovered bag in one hand and Solo's curly-horned crown in the other. The reunited party was resting on a private grassy hill which faced the distant city of Arelle. The Faerie city was less than a day's walk away now. They were so close, and yet—so far.

Neither Yuma nor Clover had spoken to one another since the great flight, though neither of them could sleep. As the day waned and the night covered them in its thick, heavy cloth, they gazed up at the Heavens, side by side, observing the change of colors.

"Did you see that?" Yuma broke the silence. He pointed up toward the dark sky. "Up there—to the East?"

"No," Clover responded dully.

"It was like a flash of light. A falling star, perhaps?"

Clover rolled his head to the side. "I missed it."

The two men inhaled, then exhaled in unison.

"Did you see that?" Clover said at length, pointing west.

"No," Yuma rolled his head Clover's way. "What was it?"

"Nothing," Clover mumbled, "I just wanted to see if you would look."

Yuma snorted.

"Oh," Clover gasped.

"What?"

Clover pointed at another patch of rippling star reflections. "Did you see *that*?"

Yuma hesitated. "Are you teasing me?"

"Yeah."

Yuma closed his eyes, exhaling hopelessly. "You going to open Dezmund's bag yet?"

"Not yet..."

Yuma grunted. "Well... you'll have to open it eventually."

"I know..." Clover glanced down at Dezmund's bag, then shifted his eyes to Solo's crown of horns. "Yuma?"

"Hmm?"

Clover folded his arms together. "Yuma... I'm sorry." He paused. "Sorry for what... for how that all went down."

The warrior paused before responding.

"I'm not," Yuma finally said. "You saved me back there."

Clover blinked. "I... *what*?"

"I almost..." Yuma hesitated, then looked at Clover with a resigned smile. "I am *glad* we failed."

Clover turned his head, and they stared at each other quietly.

Yuma cleared his throat, then pointed toward Arelle; she sat there glowing on the horizon. "Even though we made it this far—I am still glad we failed."

"Failed?" Clover frowned. "What do you mean: *failed*?"

Yuma blinked. "Clover, we—" he cleared his throat, "—You *do* realize what's happened, right? We can't *get* into Arelle at this point."

"Didn't the Truth Faerie say I was going to kill Somenus?" Clover asked.

"Well," Yuma paused, "Yeah."

"So, I am going to go do it."

"But..."

"I know we don't have an army. So? Nothing has changed—the truth *doesn't* change." Clover tucked his arms behind his head. "In some odd way..." he smiled to himself, "It makes sense to come against Somenus and his human army with a different kind of opposition, right? To come not with an army of strength, but just... us."

"Make sense?" Yuma chuckled. "No." He shook his head back and forth. "It doesn't make sense, but it sounds poetic."

The two grew quiet once more. Clover could hear Waiting For the Day's heartbeat thumping behind his head. "Yuma?"

"Hmm?" Yuma hummed.

"Why do you think Waiting For the Day came when he did?"

Yuma yawned, then sat forward, leaning his elbows on his knees. "I told you before... he's a prophet."

Clover placed his hand on one of Waiting for the Day's legs, stroking it. "I remember..."

"From what I can tell... He was drawn to your words." Yuma turned to look at the Elf. "Clover—why didn't you tell me you were a prophet, too?"

Clover's face flushed with embarrassment, "I'm not."

"You said you were."

"I didn't know what I was saying." He turned away from Yuma.

Yuma hesitated. "Then why did you say all that?"

"I don't know. I just had to. It was true."

"And what about that thing about the Glassy Sea flooding Bavel," Yuma poked Clover in the side.

"What about it?" Clover glanced over sheepishly. "I don't know... It just sort of... popped out."

"Well," Yuma chuckled, "It was a pretty strong visual. *Hades*, I like to imagine what it would be like if that were true."

"I..." Clover turned his eyes away, "I don't know if I would."

"You know," Yuma smirked to himself, "When Waiting For the Day burst in through those windows... and I heard that loud crash..."

"You thought it was happening?" Clover anticipated him. "My uh... *judgment*?"

"Yeah," Yuma laughed.

"Me too," said Clover. There was a moment of silence as they connected eyes, then they both laughed together; the tension broke like an egg. "I was almost disappointed when it didn't happen."

"Oh, I am *still* disappointed!" Yuma slapped him on the shoulder.

"It *will* happen though—one day, anyway." Clover said, scratching the back of his head.

Yuma looked at him with raised eyebrows, then nodded. "Oh, yeah? Thus says the prophet?"

"Well," Clover shifted, "It's what *should* happen, anyway."

Yuma bit his lip; his smile faded slowly. "Clover?"

"Hm?"

"You said you needed TSB with you... when you go to kill Somenus?"

"And?"

Yuma shrugged. "Why?"

"Why... Why do I want him with me?"

"Yeah," Yuma reached his arm across Waiting For the Day's leg and rubbed the gnome's back.

Clover leaned forward, nodding to himself. "Do you remember what the Truth Faerie said—about how to stand up to the Nightmare Faerie?"

Yuma thought for a moment. "He said you had to love someone more than you feared him, right?"

"Yeah," said Clover, "You know something I realized?"

"What's that?"

"Little Thief," Clover glanced at the gnome. "He really, really loves me. And no matter what else is happening, when I am there, he's not scared."

"Are you going to have *him* kill the Nightmare Faerie?"

"Don't tease," Clover said, "I can't even stomach the idea of him dying for me. No, I want him there with me as a symbol of courage. The Truth Faerie said that Somenus is so powerful, you cannot think about anyone but him when he is in the room; not unless there is someone or something more dear to you in your mind."

"What about your girl... Isabella?"

"Isabella is someone I love deeply," Clover said as his eyes drifted up towards the sky, "And she will help me hold my ground, but the Thief... he loves *me*. I can't help but think that if he is with me, I will be able to do what I need to do..."

"I see," Yuma studied Clover's damp eyes. "Isabella will help you shoot the arrow... but Little Thief..."

"He will give me the courage to die."

"Clover..."

Clover blinked out a tear, then glanced at Yuma.

"I'll be there too, you know."

Clover attempted a smile.

"I promise. You won't have to do it alone."

"Thanks." Clover wiped his eye on his sleeve.

Yuma lunged forward, rising suddenly to his feet. Clover watched in confusion as the warrior screamed, driving a punch into a nearby tree.

"What's gotten into you?" Clover leaned forward.

Yuma roared again, kicking the tree with his boot. "It's so *stupid*! It makes no *sense*!"

Clover rose. "What are you talking about?"

"It's not even your people who are dying! Why should *you* be the one to die? It's... it's so wrong!" The warrior whirled toward Clover, panting with fists clenched. "*You* shouldn't die, Clover! It's wrong!"

"This isn't about *should* and *shouldn't*," Clover said quietly, "It's just about what *will* happen."

"But why? It is so arbitrary! Why *you*?"

"Yuma..."

"Clover... I refuse to believe you're going to die!"

"Yuma!" Clover tensed.

"No! I refuse to let more and more of those I care about die! First the famine, then the sheep, then Solo—now you?" Yuma seized Clover by the collar. "It would be wrong of me not to fight this, Clover! Forget *truth*. It's *wrong*!"

Clover stared at Yuma's fiery eyes, only inches from his own.

"Yuma... I am not being forced to do this... I am choosing it."

"But *why*?" Yuma demanded, "Aren't you afraid to die? How can you be so calm and accepting about it? Why don't you *fight* it? Be honest with yourself, Clover. No one wants to die!"

Clover froze, his wide eyes fixed on Yuma. And then Yuma saw it: the fear.

"I..." Yuma loosened his hold on Clover's tunic, "Forget I said anything."

"I don't want to die," Clover said softly. He turned himself away from Yuma. "I never expected my life to turn out this way. But I suppose," he hesitated, "I suppose I would rather live a short, meaningful life than a long idle one." He looked over at Yuma. "Before this quest I was barely alive. Like... like... for most of my life I was a body in a coffin. After I found out I was going to die, it was like," He gazed up at the sky, "It was like I broke out of it and smelled fresh air for the first time. I don't know why, but it was like the promise of death brought me life. It's crazy... Before meeting the Truth Faerie, I was immortal. Once there was a promise of death, I suddenly had a reason to live well."

"I see..." Yuma nodded to himself. "You're not just taking the Truth Faerie's words like a fatalistic curse that you wish you could escape. You are clinging to them—as if to a gift."

Clover blinked. "But they *are* a gift, Yuma. They're the truth."

33

—— Lola ——

Imminent Death

"My spirits rose as I went deeper," Lola read, "into the forest; but I could not regain my former elasticity of mind. I found cheerfulness to be like life itself - not to be created by any argument."

Beloved was twirling a lock of her hair around his finger as she leaned her head against his lap, holding her book over her face. She lowered her book slightly to look at him; helmet or not, there was something so pleasant about his appearance. It was as if the "t"-shaped slit in his visor were some sort of expressive face, always looking at her with compassionate eyes.

"Read on," he said as he noticed her, "I'm listening—I promise!"

Lola lifted the book back over her face to read. "Afterwards, I learned, that the best way to manage some kinds of painful thoughts, is to dare them to do their worst; to let them lie and gnaw at your heart till they are tired; and you find you still have a residue of life they cannot kill. So, better and worse, I went on, till I came to..."

"Lola?"

Lola lowered her book again. "I *knew* you weren't listening!"

"No, no—I was..." Beloved seemed agitated. He looked side to side, as if trying to make up his mind. "I just..."

"What is it?"

"Would you read that last bit again? About painful thoughts?"

Lola's eyes refocused on the page. "If you wish..." she took a deep breath and read. "The best way to manage some kinds of painful thoughts, is to dare them to do their worst; to let them lie and gnaw at your heart till they are tired; and you find you still have a residue of life they cannot kill." She lowered the book again.

Beloved was nodding. "Lola, we both love coming here because it's all pretty and safe, don't we?"

Lola narrowed her brow. "Yes..."

"But it's like whenever we are together, the rest of us doesn't exist. This is merely a dream..."

"So?"

"What if," Beloved took her by the hand and made her sit up. "What if we did that..."

"Did what?" She scooted back a little.

"Admit those painful thoughts are real... let them do their worst." Beloved said as he still held onto her hand. "Lola, what if you just tell me what's happened to you. Open up about what you have been through and find that you are still standing."

She shook her head quickly, yanking her hand free of his.

Beloved sighed, dropping his head defeatedly.

"Lola, I don't want to just be a dream of yours. I want to know you—the *whole* you—I want to know the Lola who is scared and hurt, too."

"No!" She shook her head again. "No, Beloved. Let this place remain my safe place!"

"But Lola," Beloved climbed to his feet and turned away. "It means I'll just stay a fantasy, just a dream in your mind. I don't want to be your dream. I want to be real to you! I want to be a part of what's really going on!"

"I..." Lola tucked her knees into her body and hugged them. If Beloved *was* a real person, it would only be more painful to meet him! She belonged to another man! It didn't feel wrong to dream about someone she loved—but if he were real? No. If he were real, then she really *was* missing out on the life she always wanted. "There is nothing else to know about me, other than what you see here," she mumbled.

"That's not true!" Beloved kicked a feather pillow. It went flying off the temple, tumbling down a cliff. Lola stood slowly, watching as he stood there, with back turned, clenching his shaking fists.

"Beloved... can't we just keep reading?"

"No!" He kicked another pillow, then turned to face her. "No, Lola. I don't want to just sit there, reading books when I *know* something more is going on! Why won't you open up to me? Why won't you tell me about where you *really* are?"

"*I don't want to!*" Lola found herself yelling back. "This place is the only thing keeping me happy! It's all I have!"

"I don't want to just be *this place* for you, Lola!" He turned to face her. "I want you—the *real* you!"

Lola's lip quivered. "Beloved, what happened? Why are you being so cruel?"

"I'm not being cruel, Lola," he said firmly, marching right up to her. "I'm telling you how I really feel. It's not a bad thing to be angry or upset about what's going on with you! I know things aren't okay, and it's *killing* me!"

Lola's heart began to pound. It was killing her, too, but she didn't want to think about that! Not when she was here, in the safety of her own mind!

"Beloved," she whispered, "Please... let's just *be* together... I don't want to think about all this."

"I don't want to be together like this anymore!" he said, seizing her by the shoulders. "Lola, I want to come *see* you!"

"No!" She tried to yank herself away, but he held on tight.

"Why not?" He shook her. "Don't you *want* me to be more than a dream?"

Lola's eyes streamed with tears. "Beloved," she said, "I can't... I don't want you to... see me like this."

"I don't care!" he yelled, "I don't care if you're broken, or scared—or married to the Nightmare Faerie. I just want to *see* you!"

"See me now," she said, "See me as I am here—see me how I want you to see me."

Beloved let go of her and stepped back, shaking his head. "No…"

"Beloved," she whimpered, "Don't be angry with me."

"I am not just a doll that you can play with and control. I am *not* a fantasy, Lola!" His body began to fade before her eyes.

"No!" She lunged toward him, "Beloved, don't go!"

"I…" he was shaking his head. "I am sorry; I need some space."

Beloved vanished, and with him, so did her surroundings. Lola gasped, throwing her arms around herself in terror. Her world was suddenly black. Color began to swirl around her shapelessly, and she watched as ground began to form beneath her feet. In moments, she was somewhere else. To Lola's dismay, the surroundings seemed to be her old room in the Vineyard Palace, back where she first dreamed of her Beloved.

"I see…" a voice said from behind her.

Lola turned slowly, still wrapping herself in her arms, and found Somenus standing before her, with his arms behind his back. His wings were hidden, and he was wearing a simple faerie tunic, as he often did whenever they were alone together. There was no pomp or ceremony; it was just Somenus the man.

"Hello, Lolette," he said without a smile.

"Somenus…"

"It's a genius idea," he said as he walked toward her. "Hiding you inside his own dream… no wonder I couldn't find you."

Lola's eyes flashed. Did he mean… Beloved? "Somenus," she took a timid step away from him. "What are you doing here?"

"What am *I* doing here?" he raised his voice, then scoffed to himself. "You do realize that it is *I*, and not *he*, that is the Dream Faerie!" He walked just past her, then stopped, shoulder to shoulder. "Never mind him, Lola. He is merely a distraction, a thief who would keep us apart."

"Somenus... even if he weren't here, my feelings toward you would not change," she said.

Somenus nodded to himself. "Why? Will you at least tell me *why* I am so disgusting to you?"

Lola lifted her chin bravely, remembering Beloved's exhortation: The best way to manage some kinds of painful thoughts, is to dare them to do their worst.

"I cannot love you," she said, "because you are not good. To love you would mean accepting a man who kills those who will not follow you. A man who keeps the company of wretches who benefit you. A man who... who..." she forced the words from her mouth, "who rapes women who will not love you."

Somenus' eyes flashed. "Lola..."

"A man who..." she continued, her voice growing stronger as she turned to face him. "...who came out of Hades."

Somenus turned abruptly toward her, and his four black wings flashed into being. "How *dare* you?" he screamed. Lola dropped to her knees as his presence began to fill her mind. Here he was—the Faerie of Affection, unveiled! He was both beautiful and terrifying; he was all she could see and all she could hear. It had been so long since he came into her dreams, she had forgotten how hard it was to resist him when he was inside her own head! Had Beloved been protecting her from him all this time?

Lola cradled her head in her hands and began to sob. "Somenus," she cried, "Please, stop!"

"Look at me!" he bellowed as darkness surrounded them on all sides. "Aren't I beautiful? Can't you see that I *love* you?"

Lola looked up at him. Yes, he was beautiful. It was beauty without goodness; but it *was* beautiful.

"Somenus... please... just stop," she muttered.

Somenus roared, turning away from her. The darkness seemed to dissipate, and his intensifying aura began to fade.

"I don't understand," he said with back turned, "Why can't I get through to you?"

"Some boxes cannot be forced open, Somenus," Lola said.

The king paced toward her and knelt by her side. "Then where can I find the key?" He reached forward to pull loose a strand of her hair.

Lola sighed deeply. "Someone else has it."

Somenus' eyes darkened. "But I need it, Lola."

"Somenus," she reached forward and placed her hand on his chest. "You have a hole—right here—don't you?"

The Faerie blinked his wide, cautious eyes. "What?"

"A hole... a gaping hole of need: here." She tapped her finger against his heart.

His eyes darted back and forth between her two eyes. "Yes... *Yes*—how did you know?"

"You think that the love and affection that I have to give will fill it up, and that you will be whole again."

Somenus nodded. "Yes. I *know* I will."

She shook her head. "No, you won't. Somenus, your emptiness cannot be filled by others' obsession. When will you realize there is no fulfillment in selfishness? Whether I loved you or not, it would never be enough for you."

"Yes, it would!" he growled, "I *know* it would!"

"*Look* at you!" she snapped, "You are like a spoiled child, *crying* because I slapped your hand away!"

His eyes widened. "*What*?"

"Somenus!" She lunged forward, grabbing him by the shoulders. "Do you want to feel full? Do you want your needs met?"

"Yes." he whispered.

"Then do *one* good thing." She stared into his eyes. "Let me *go*!"

Somenus stared at her vacantly. "I..." he sighed, "I can't."

"If you don't let me go," she said quietly, holding his gaze, "You will kill me. Don't you see? *That* is where this goes. You will *kill* me, Somenus. I will never love you. And that will drive you to kill me."

He looked up, towards the dark sky; a tear dribbled down his cheek. "Yes..." he whispered, "yes, you are right."

Lola watched in horror as he turned to walk away from her, his head hanging low. "Oh, Lights," she threw her hand over her mouth, "You have already decided, haven't you?"

He turned back to gaze at her with a mournful look. "I don't *want* to, Lola... but... I can't keep living like this!"

She closed her eyes tightly, breathing as deeply as she could. Yes—she had known this was coming. Whether he discovered her secret or not, he *would* kill her. She had seen it in his eyes, so many times—murder. This was a man without a shred of selflessness in him. He didn't care what *she* wanted, or what *she* needed; all he could ever think about was his own desires. Wasn't that the root of murder? Selfishness? Putting one's desires over another's?

"There's still time, Lola," she heard him say.

Lola opened her eyes. Somenus was standing at a distance, watching her with his arms hanging limply at his sides.

"Time for what?" she asked defeatedly. "Time to sit around and wait for you to kill me? Time to read my book one more time?"

"Time to change your mind."

Lola bobbed her head, thinking. "And how long would that be?"

"As long as I can manage," The king sighed to himself. "I will visit you tomorrow—on Somensday. I hope that... well, I hope you will at least try to see things my way."

Lola scoffed. "And therein lies your problem, Sire, you only ever want others to see things *your* way."

<hr>

Lola sat up suddenly. Hevel was tapping her on the shoulder.

"Lola, are you alright?" he asked urgently, placing a hand on her arm for support.

She was panting, sweat beading on her forehead.

"What?" She turned to make eye contact with the Faerie. "What's going on?"

"I thought you were having a bad dream," he said as he leaned back a little, "Or perhaps you were in pain?"

"My back hurts," she mumbled, placing her feet on the ground. She rubbed her back a bit. "Thank you for waking me."

"It *was* a bad dream then?" His eyebrows twisted with concern.

Lola nodded. "Somenus."

Hevel muttered some curse under his breath, then straightened with a smile. "Well, I am glad it's over, child. How are..." he froze, studying her eyes. She seemed to be gazing above him with a look of awe. "Lola..." he drew back, rising to his feet. "I don't like what I am seeing..."

"What?" She blinked herself back to attention.

"You were looking at my wings just now." He said quietly.

"They just look so beautiful. I had no idea!" She smiled.

"No... no..." he shook his head quickly. "No, no, no," he was muttering to himself, "I have seen some survive this stage... there is still hope."

Lola sighed. "Death is coming for me... isn't it?"

Hevel shot her an angry look. "He may be coming to your door, but you've got to do everything you can to send him away!"

Lola leaned back on her arm. "Isn't it your job to *comfort* those whose time has come? You said not all death is bad!"

"Of course I will comfort you, Lola," Hevel said, holding up an admonishing finger, "But I will also fight to the very *end* to keep you alive!"

Lola chuckled—and she was a little surprised to find herself doing so. Perhaps that was the effect of being around the Death Faerie when one was so close to their end. She stood and hobbled up to Hevel, propping up her sore back with her hand.

"Thank you, Hevel," she said, holding open her arms.

The Faerie's blushed when he realized she was actually inviting contact. He bit his lip, trying to calm the anger he felt at seeing her acceptance of her eminent fate, and pulled her into his arms. Her head hit him mid-chest, and she sighed as his curtain-like wings surrounded her like a warm blanket.

"I am so sorry for what is happening, Lola... if you would but tell me why you think you are dying, perhaps I could help," he said as he held her.

"Somenus... he's going to kill me. I've known for a while. I've seen it in his eyes."

"I see," he sighed to himself. "And the pain? Has he hurt you?"

Lola squeezed her eyes closed, "Yes," she whispered, "he hurt me deeply."

Hevel's eyes snapped open. "Lola…" he whispered.

"Yes?"

"I… did I just…? Are you—?"

"Sorry to interrupt," Felix cleared his throat. "Good Somensday morning to you two."

Hevel jumped, then moved to block Felix's line of sight. "Stay back, cretin!"

"Calm down, Death," Felix tucked his hands into his pocket. "I am not here to fetch her."

Lola pushed Hevel to the side and walked forward. "Good morning, Felix. What is it this time?"

Lola wrapped her arms around herself and glided up to the bars, with her baggy robes dragging behind her. She lifted her chin to find Felix's moody blue eyes.

Felix's eyes followed her. "Somenus says you must prepare to come back to the Eight Stones today."

"Felix…" Lola said, "You know what's coming, don't you?"

Felix's eyes flashed. "What do y–you…" he stuttered, "I don't know what you… It's not like I watch when you two—"

"He's going to kill me, Felix," she said blankly.

Felix jolted. "What? No… he wouldn't…" his voice trailed off.

Lola nodded. "You know him better than anyone, don't you? What do you think he will do to someone who resists him long enough? My mere presence on this Table is a reminder of what he cannot have."

Felix's mouth opened and closed wordlessly.

Hevel appeared behind Lola and put his hand on her shoulder. "She's right, Felix," he said, "She *will* die."

"I don't see what I am supposed to do about it…" Felix hissed through gritted teeth.

"Don't you?" Hevel snapped and lunged toward the bars. Felix stepped away.

"I can't go against my king!" he cried.

"Felix!" Lola grasped the bars with her hands. "Stop acting like you're innocent to everything that's been going on around you! Don't you *see*?"

Felix raised his chin defiantly and shook his head. "Stop, Lola, your words are wasted on someone like me."

"*Felix*!" she cried, shaking herself against the iron bars, "You think that none of this evil is on your hands? You think that by simply *watching*, you're not taking part in the evil that's being done? Don't you know that your indifference in the face of evil is as good as worshiping it? You could help me! You could *do* something, Felix!"

"It's too late for me, Princess!" Felix slammed his hand against a bar as he jerked forward unexpectedly. "Don't you get it? You're right. I am no better than him. It was me—my eyes—that brought him back from Hades. Do you honestly think *I* will be the one to help you? *I brought him here!*"

"It's never too late, Felix," Lola pleaded, "Just turn your eyes up rather than down. You don't have to atone for everything you've been a part of, just change your direction: just do *one* good thing."

Felix and Lola stared at one another, their noses only an inch apart.

"Felix," she whispered, "Just *do* something. Just *one* good thing... let me go!"

Felix held his breath.

"Please, Felix. He's going to *kill* me."

"I can't, Lola," he said. He leaned back. "It's... it's too late for me."

Lola dropped her head forward until her forehead hit the bar. She sighed. "It's just as well," she said, "Death might be a mercy for me..." She sniffed. "I don't have the strength for what's coming."

Felix stared absently at her. A single tear escaped her eye. Felix watched the tear fall onto the ground. It made a tiny drop of moisture on the stone floor between her bare feet. Then came another drop... and then another. Then, a loud splash erupted as a rush of water gushed onto the floor.

Felix stumbled backwards, yelling in surprise. "*Lola*!"

Lola lifted her head quickly; her eyes were filled with horror. "No..." she swallowed. "No... no, no, no.... Not *now*!"

"Lola…" Felix lifted his hand and pointed at the puddle of water that had formed between her feet.

Lola scrambled backwards, panting. Hevel caught her from behind.

"Calm yourself, child," Hevel whispered as she began to hyperventilate.

"No, Hevel," she moaned, "I am not ready… I don't want this!"

Felix watched lifelessly. "Lola…?"

"*Get out*!" Hevel screeched. "Get out, I say!"

Felix jumped, then scurried away like a frightened animal.

Hevel lowered Lola to the ground slowly. "Oh, Lola," he sighed, "Why didn't you tell me you were with child?"

Lola's feet kicked against the ground as pain surged up her back. "I don't want this!"

34

— Isabella —

The Spider

Isabella dressed herself as Scarlet Wingsday, "one final time," she said to the woman in the mirror. She turned away from her washing table and leaned against it, thumbing her lips thoughtfully. Did she really have it in her? To kill Korbin? She had told herself it's what she needed to do in order to atone for all the Faeries she had led to the slaughter; but was it even possible?

She walked into the middle of her room and looked around. Her little room was quiet and cold; her single fire had burned into mere embers, and all she could hear was an occasional crackle. This was her last day on the Table; there was no way she was going to live past it. Whether she succeeded or failed in downing the giant, it would mean death for her.

Isabella placed her hands on her hips and pulled her back as straight as she could. Then her head dropped, and she slumped in defeat. She wiped her damp eyes hurriedly.

"No," she scolded herself, "Don't lose courage now—you know what you have to do!" She spun to face her mirror and pointed at Scarlet Wingsday. "Hanz may have led you into this mess, but it was *you* who chose to follow! I don't care if you're scared; it is time to right your wrongs! If you have anything to do with it, you will not let that monster kill one more precious Faerie!"

The room grew quiet once more, and she lowered her hand. "Well," she said with a shrug. "It's time."

Isabella forced herself from her chambers and slammed the door closed. Her hand clutched tightly at the hilt of her dagger sheathed just behind her back and concealed by her red cape.

Don't feel, just act... just move... she thought as she marched out of the barracks. Once outside, the smell of Fort Axes hit her like a punch to the face. Funny—she thought she had gotten used to that smell. Now? Now she could barely stomach it.

Movement distracted her. Isabella tilted her head to the side to see Felix of Sight bolting from the underground entrance.

"Felix!" she called as she took a couple steps in his direction. He didn't so much as look her way. "Felix!" she called again, then raced to catch up with him. Just as she approached, she fell backwards with a yelp as Felix's wings shot out beside him. "Watch out, damn you!" She scrambled back.

Felix turned to scowl at her. "What do you want, Wingsday?"

Isabella righted herself, straightening her cloak and jacket. "I... I wanted to know if something was wrong. You look—" she hesitated before finishing her statement as Felix's eyes widened threateningly. She cleared her throat.

"Mind your own business, soldier." He turned his back to her, then crouched slightly as he prepared to take off.

"Felix!" Isabella seized him by the arm.

Felix turned aside, flinging her away from him.

Isabella barely caught herself on her feet.

"*What*?" he demanded.

"Felix," she lowered her voice. "I...I found out... I went with Korbin on Wingsday."

Felix's eyes studied her as he held his scowl. "*And*?"

She swallowed. "And... do *you* know what happens to the Faeries?"

"Of course I know!" he snapped.

Isabella drew back slightly; she couldn't help but shake her head. "You knew—and you're *okay* with it?"

Felix lunged toward her. "Who are *you* to lecture *me*, Wingsday?"

"But he's—" she looked side to side, her voice growing quieter, "He's doing something horrible to them!"

"Is it any different to all the Faeries *you* killed to get here?"

Isabella bit her lip. Part of her wanted to deny Scarlet Wingsday's past, but still—it was true. She *had* killed Faeries to get where she was. "I can't be a part of it anymore, Felix," she said, "I am turning down the promotion."

Felix's face remained skeptical. "How virtuous."

"Something really freaky is going on with him, Felix...He's—"

"Who?" Felix snorted. "*Korbin*?"

"Yes! Felix, he's... he's..." she closed her eyes, "He's eating Faeries, Felix!"

Felix's flexing muscles relaxed slightly. "I know."

"*Why*?"

Felix glanced to the side. "He..." He shook his head. "I want nothing to do with it..." He turned to face her. "I've got nothing to do with *any* of this!"

Isabella shielded her face protectively as Felix sprung into the air. His four wings flapped unevenly and carried him upwards until he resembled a black bird, darting around the tops of the highest towers.

She lowered her arms with a sigh. Well, perhaps she wasn't the only one who had turned a blind eye to what was going on in Arelle.

Isabella meandered slowly toward the Eight Stones, taking in the sights. Arelle was so beautiful. Every building was unique, and yet there was a symmetry to the circular city. Some Faeries stopped to wave to her as she passed, while others ignored her. She had built a life there; it wasn't a perfect life, but it was good. If only there hadn't been a rotten core to this life; perhaps she could have continued on here.

The Eight Stones armory was at the base of one of the Palace's many towers. Isabella climbed the stairs of the tower, breathing as steadily as she could. Eventually, she came to the door, closed her eyes, counted ten clicks, then marched in.

"Ah, Wingsday!" Korbin was standing directly on the other side of the door, so Isabella walked right into him and yelped in surprise.

"S—sir!" she stuttered, looking down at her shoulder to see his hand massaging it.

"Hello!" he said cheerily. She stared up at him—*way* up at him. It was like gazing up at an Elder Giant tree. Most unsettling of all, he was grinning.

"Sir," She shook her shoulder free of his clutch with a scowl, then pushed past him into the room. "Now, about my promotion." She looked around. It was a simple room with a table and chairs at its center, and the bolted armory door at the back.

"No questions?" Korbin turned slowly, peering in her direction as she rounded the map table and stood by the vault. "You just *accept* everything I do? You ask *no* questions?" He made a sound that resembled giggling.

Isabella scoffed. "Would you answer them if I asked?"

Korbin lumbered in her direction, walking in a crooked line. He stopped at the table at the center of the room and leaned against it with his hands, grinning. "Yes, I would."

She blinked. Should she ask him something? This whole conversation made her uncomfortable, as all conversations with him did. "Well," She crossed her arms, "Why do you eat them?"

Korbin smacked his lips, as if remembering their taste. "I wouldn't call it eating," he said, "*drinking*, perhaps."

Isabella scowled. "Why?"

"Because I need to," he said, tapping a finger against the table.

Isabella paled. "*Why*?"

"I helped the king get what he wanted, and so now he helps me." His eyes shifted. "It's all very above board."

Above board? Isabella kept her mouth shut.

He shrugged, then straightened up to full height. "Any other questions?"

"Yes," she snapped. "When do we see inside this vault?" She hoped that in an enclosed space, she might have a better chance at attacking him.

Korbin chuckled, nodding. "Always so straight to the point, Isabella."

"Well?" She gestured toward the armory door.

He nodded politely at her, then walked over to the door. After shoving a key into the lock within, Korbin unbolted and opened the entrance to the armory. Isabella gulped. Something felt off—what *was* it? Korbin stepped into the room, then turned around to hold his hand out to her.

What felt wrong? There was something she was missing. She stepped in. Looking around, the armory was less impressive than she had imagined it would be. It was a small, square room lined with weapons and shields.

She paced down its length, until she came to its end. There, mounted on the back wall was a single bow without arrows or quiver.

Isabella walked toward it and picked it up, examining it closely. It looked quite simple. It was made of wood, polished tenderly, with a leather handle. Set into the leather were three stones resembling stars. Those were godstones; she was sure of it. She ran her fingers across the wood. Could *this* be Orion's Bow? She turned to face Korbin who was standing in the doorway, leaning against the frame with his arm. He was hunched over, like a large stick snapped in half, barely able to fit.

"Sir..." she said slowly, looking up at him. "Is this the bow that killed King Sol?"

"Very good, Isabella," he said. She couldn't make out his expression when he was backlit inside the dark room.

"I—" She stopped short. *Isabella*? He called her Isabella! Korbin chuckled as the horror formed on her face. "But!"

"Why are you surprised? Don't you remember meeting me all that time ago?" he asked mockingly. He stepped into the room. She felt as cornered as she was, standing at the end of the little vault.

"B—but," She clutched the bow tightly in her hands.

"Did you really expect me to forget that pretty face?" He gestured toward her with his long fingers.

"But... th—there was a spell!" she stammered, trying to remember what Hanz had told her about the spell.

"Ooh," he nodded, stepping closer, "A spell. How sly!"

"I..." She pulled the bow closer to herself. What could she possibly say? "How long have you known?"

"Known what?" He tapped his chin, taking another step closer. "That you were in the Purple Order?" Isabella's mouth dropped open as she stepped away, backing herself against the wall. "That you were looking for my bow? Or..." He pulled his long arms behind his back and clasped his hands together, leaning down toward her face. "That you were the child of the great Pilgrim... or that you were my loyal servant who will do everything I ask?"

Isabella scowled. "*What?*"

"Do you deny it?" He grinned through his teeth. "Do you deny that Isabella, that pretty little forest girl, has done everything I have asked? You have made a remarkable soldier. Do you deny it?"

The words hit her like a slap in the face. She gritted her teeth, letting her anger kindle. "No. No, I don't deny it."

He nodded. "You will not fail me," he said, "You are mine. You passed my test." He reached forward and brushed her cheek with the tip of his finger. "I couldn't be more proud."

"No." She slapped his hand away. "I will *never* listen to you again." She reached behind her back and pulled out her dagger, pointing it up at him. Korbin glanced down at it.

"You will not kill me," he said calmly. "You are my loyal servant."

"I don't care if I die here tonight!" she screamed, surprising herself with her volume, "But I will never listen to you again."

"You will not kill me," he said again. He did not move; he did not even *try* to take the dagger from her. He stood there, bent over, staring at her in the face. She could smell his decaying breath from where she stood and closed her eyes for a moment.

"Oh Lights—*help me,*" she prayed, then shot her eyes open and swiped the dagger in his direction.

A stream of blood splattered across the room. She gasped, covering her mouth. She had slit his throat. Korbin straightened, looking down at himself. He touched his neck. Blood gushed from it. He looked at her, making no noise, then fell forward, collapsing directly on top of her.

Isabella screamed, thrashing beneath the massive corpse. He was so heavy!

"Get off!" she cried, panicking. It took as much strength as she could muster to push the body off of herself. She pulled herself out, collapsing to the side of it. She panted, feeling the adrenaline course through her body like a drug. She stared at Korbin. He was perfectly still. She dared to place her hand on his back.

There was no heartbeat.

The only sound she could hear was that of her own breathing. He was dead. He was *dead*! She fled the room, collapsing onto the ground as she freed herself from the vault. She turned around, looking into the room. His twisted feet were sticking out through the door. She sighed, mustering up some courage, and marched back to the door. It wasn't easy shoving his feet back into the room. The man was so *heavy*! She worked quickly, shoving him out of sight as if he were a dead spider, haunting her with his crooked state. Isabella slammed the iron door shut, then pulled the bolt over it.

Isabella whirled around, throwing her back against the door. She panted, clutching Orion's Bow in her hands. Was he *really* dead? How was that so easy? Did he *really* think she wouldn't do it?

"Well," she muttered, "There's no turning back now... and there is no rescue for me. Time to wait here... and die." She closed her eyes and fingered the bow in her hands. Her eyes snapped open again. The beacon! Hanz had given her a beacon! Since Korbin already knew who she was, she had nothing to lose by summoning her brother and dispelling the magik veil on her face. If her brother really had connected with the Transport Faerie, perhaps they could get her out of there! Perhaps she wouldn't die, after all!

Isabella yanked off her leather glove. She looked down at her arm. *Where* was that mark? *How* did she activate it, again?

Isabella's legs buckled beneath her as the charge of adrenaline cooled. The rush was leaving her. She collapsed onto the ground and leaned against the iron door. She placed two of her fingers on her arm, where she thought the hidden mark was, closed her eyes, and whispered,

"Hear me, Timbre Wulf." She opened her eyes, wincing as a purple light burst from her arm. The light filled the room and grew until she could no longer see. Moments later, the light was gone. "Well," she said with dry lips, "It's done."

35

—— Leo ——

The Beacon

I was lying on my bed that Somensday morning, reading the little brown book that Momentum had given Benji.

"Rasselas," I snorted, "What a weird book."

There I was, still undressed and in bed, sulking. For the first time, there in Winter's End, I had no desire to get up, or do anything. I had forced myself awake early that morning, abandoning Lola so that I could spend some time alone in my thoughts. What a stupid idea; all I wanted now was to see her again! But no—she wasn't in love with *me*, she was in love with some fantasy of which I played a part! But the fantasy wasn't real; it was a distraction from reality. *But surely,* I thought to myself, *fantasy has a role to play; fantasy can grant beauty in a place of darkness!*

I rolled onto my stomach and placed the open book on the bed.

"Fantasy does have a role to play," I said as I turned a yellowing page in the old book, "But it shouldn't replace reality; it should *augment* it."

My eyes glossed across the page in front of me. Was I only reading this book because it made me think of Lola and her little romance novel?

I groaned to myself, reading lazily. "She had lost her taste of pleasure and her ambition of excellence; and her mind, though forced into short excursions, always recurred to the image of her friend." I snapped the book shut, sighing loudly as I turned onto my back. "I'm so pathetic."

I closed my eyes, and I saw her face. That lovely, beautiful Lola, her green eyes, her bright hair, her warm smile. My eyes snapped open.

"This is ridiculous," I jumped out of bed, "I am not going to lie around pining all day. If she doesn't want me to be real, I have got to let her go!" I scanned the room for any sense of inspiration, then melted into another sigh. I was just like the character in that book, diverted for a moment, then enraptured once more by thoughts of my Lola.

"I need a distraction," I said to myself. I dressed lazily, pulling on some black trousers and a plain white tunic. "Right," I said to the Leo in the mirror, "Time to handle this a *man's* way!"

⸺ ✦ ⸺

"Please, just spar with me a little?" I pleaded. I was sitting on one of the countertops in the Autumn kitchens.

"Leo," Flagon grunted, thrusting his cleaver through a thick vegetable. "Can't you see I am busy here?"

"Come on!" I picked up a loose carrot and bit the tip off, chewing loudly. "You're the Faerie of *Skill*! You could help me learn to fight!"

"Can't you just appreciate my skill in the kitchen?" Flagon leaned back, placing his knife on the chopping board to look at me. "Besides, I don't see you as much of a..." he coughed, "...a fighter." He was large and burly for a Faerie, with combed brown hair and a thick mustache. The kitchens were bustling with about six different Faeries who were preparing for dinner that evening. It had become the custom for us all to eat together, despite the fact that we could all just feed ourselves from the gardens if we so wished.

"Leo, why don't you ask Hanz," another Faerie asked. It was Seily, the Faerie of Roads. "I am sure a human could teach you best how to fight."

I blinked in her direction, then turned back to Flagon. "Flagon, can't *you* do it?"

"I don't want to," he picked up his knife again and began to hack away at a parsnip. "Listen to Seily. Ask Hanz."

"I don't," I nibbled my carrot nervously. "...I don't know."

"What?" Seily wiped her hands against her apron, "He's one of the greatest warriors of our age! I am sure he would be glad to spar with you!"

I snorted.

"What is it, Leo?" Seily asked, walking up to me, and peering at me closely with her wide, green eyes. She was a petite little Faerie with brown hair tied up into a thick braid that ran down her back like a rope.

I huffed, crossing my arms protectively like a kid forced to apologize. "I don't—well, I don't think Hanz *likes* me very much."

"*What?*" A third voice piped in. Rowyn stood there with her hands on her hips. "Leo! Everyone likes you!"

I laughed.

"It's true!" Seily said, turning to Rowyn who had just walked into the kitchens holding a basket of brown eggs, straight from the hen house. "I can't even imagine someone not liking you, Leo!"

I blushed. "Well," I glanced at Flagon who was grinning at me through his mustache. "Still."

"Leo, why do you think Hanz doesn't like you?" Seily pressed. "Hanz is wonderful. He loves everyone!"

"Plus, you're both Faerie Friends!" Rowyn added, placing her basket on a table. "You share so much in common. I am sure all you need to do is spend some time with him. You should ask him to spar with you!"

Those words stung. Yes, Hanz was a Faerie Friend. Me? I was not. Was *that* why I didn't like Hanz? Was I just jealous? Most people still just assumed I was Momentum's Faerie Friend, and Momentum never denied it in public. Maybe he felt bad for me.

"I don't want to bother him," I mumbled.

"Tristan," Seily turned to a fourth Faerie in the room. It was Tristan, sitting in the back of the kitchen as he always did. I cringed as she drew him into the conversation. "Tristan, does Hanz dislike Leo?"

Tristan was sitting on a stool silently peeling his potatoes, bristling slightly from the attention. He looked at me, then back at Seily and smiled. "Dislike?"

"Yes. Leo thinks Hanz doesn't like him, so he won't go speak with him."

"I didn't say—!"

"Quiet, Leo!" She held up her palm to me, keeping her eyes on Tristan who leaned back, dropping a potato into a barrel.

"Well, I am not sure."

"Don't *you* like Leo?" she asked, placing her hands on her hips.

Tristan nodded, smiling weakly. "I do."

"Guys," I fidgeted, growing increasingly more stressed by the constant battering of attention. "You don't need to do this. It's not like I am insecure about it."

"Yes, you are!" Both Seily and Rowyn said in unison.

Flagon chuckled, hacking away loudly with his cleaver.

"Look," I hopped off the counter, throwing my carrot end into the discard barrel. "Don't worry about this. I just wanted to kill some time..." I glanced at Tristan. We held eye contact for a moment, then broke away in unison.

"Leo, what's wrong?" Rowyn stepped closer and tapped my arm. I shot her a defensive look.

"Nothing!"

"You seem upset."

"I'm not," I said as I backed myself toward the door. I had only come to the kitchens to try and get Flagon to teach me to fight so I could work through my fight with Lola in a *manly* way. The last thing I wanted—or needed—was a couple of girls hounding me about my *feelings*!

"Is this about you being left out of the rescue party?" Rowyn made a sympathetic face.

"*What*?" I flushed. "No!"

Tristan glanced up from his peeling, then back down again.

"That is..." I cleared my throat. "I don't *want* to go, anyway!" There I was, lying to them and to myself. Of course I wanted to go. I was just stuck licking my wounds after Lola told me she didn't want to meet me. I was trying to respect her by staying away... but how stupid was *that*?

"Why don't you just ask Hanz about it," Rowyn said, "We might be willing to go with—"

"Guys!" I held up my hands, breaking the tension in the room with a wide smile. "You can all calm down! I'll talk to Hanz, alright? Would that make you all happy?"

"Very happy." Flagon muttered.

I shot him a look.

"Good!" Seily clapped excitedly. "I know you two will get along swimmingly once you *try*!"

I glanced at Tristan who was peering down at his potatoes, looking doubtful. *He* knew; he knew Hanz wasn't my biggest fan. I sighed. Well—why not at least *try* to like him?

I skipped through the kitchen, stealing a roll from a basket and waved goodbye as I passed into the hallway. I yelped as I almost came crashing into someone.

"Oh, sorry!" I threw myself backwards awkwardly then looked up to see Momentum standing here. "Momentum?"

He straightened up. "Leo... Hallo."

"Hey," my eyes shifted side to side. *Should I say something? Should I wait for him to say something?* We were both nursing vulnerability hangovers from the night before. "Just, uh," I began to walk past him.

"Leo," he turned, following me with his eyes.

"Yes?" I hesitated. "Oh, were you looking for me?"

"Yes." He crossed his arms.

I blinked. "Oh. Yeah? What is it?"

Momentum began to walk, so I followed along with him, listening expectantly.

"Leo," he said, "...about last night."

"Oh!" I jumped. "Momentum, I promise I won't tell anyone."

"I know, I know," he waved away my reassurances with his hand, "I wanted to tell you that speaking with you gave me some clarity."

"It did?" I asked, feeling surprised that not only was I helpful to him, but that he was *telling* me that I was.

He nodded. What was going through his head right now? This man was so hard to read.

"Are you... going to tell me what it was?"

He shook his head, then shrugged. "Leo, thanks for everything."

That sounded ominously like a goodbye. I raised my brow, then pulled the corner of my mouth to the side. "Momentum?"

"Yes?" he asked, plain-faced.

"Can I go on the rescue mission? You know—To Arelle?"

Momentum raised his eyebrows, looking surprised. "Why?"

I sighed. "I feel like I need to be there. You know, for Cymbeline and stuff."

"I'll be there for Cymbeline," he said. "You should stay."

"But I—"

"This isn't about Cymbeline, is it, Leo?" he said, locking eyes with me. "This is about *her*."

I blushed. "Uh..."

"Leo," Momentum dropped his head with a sigh. "It's not—"

"I'm not compromised by Somenus, I promise!" I jumped in. "You can trust me, Momentum!"

"I *do* trust you," he said blankly, "Now I want you to trust *me*. Stay home."

"You... you trust me?"

He nodded.

"How do you know I am not...like," I bobbed my head to the side, "All obsessed with Somenus?"

"Are you *trying* to make me suspicious?" he smirked.

"No! I just... aren't you afraid I'm... I don't know... under his influence?"

He shook his head. "I see more than you realize, Leo. I know you're being honest with me."

I wasn't sure how to respond to that. Was he referring to his powers as the Faerie of Moments—to what he *saw*? "Momentum... are you trying to keep me from going because you think the mission is going to fail?"

Momentum nodded.

I swallowed. Perhaps this *wasn't* the time to try and meet Lola. I would hate to wrap her up in all the danger! By butting in uninvited, I could be making things *worse* for her!

"Hey, um..." I clicked my heels together. "Have you told Hanz that you're joining him on the mission?"

"Yes."

"How did he take it?"

Momentum's smirk widened. "He took it fine."

We shared a smile. "Hey, you seen Cymbeline?"

"I think she was with Hanz," Momentum fanned a yawn.

"Right," I nodded to myself. Well, perhaps it was time to please everyone and go talk to him.

"Well," Momentum nodded once at me, "Good morning."

I watched him walk away.

"Alright," I said to myself as I marched toward Hanz' chambers, "time to go suck up my pride and befriend Hanz."

Hanz had moved into my old room when I relocated to the Winter Wing. Really—it was the best room. As I approached the door, I could hear voices within. I stopped just outside and waited, counting breaths as I tried to figure out what it was that I wanted. Did I want to go? Did I want to meet Lola when she clearly didn't want me around? Did I want to try to understand Hanz' perspective and somehow make friends?

I sighed, hovering my hand over the doorknob.

"No! Aorist can't know about any of this... you know how he feels about killing." Hanz' muffled voice said from the other side of the door. I withdrew my hand from the knob and listened a moment longer. What on Earth were they talking about?

"How are we supposed to do this if he is coming with us, then?" Riah responded. Even through the door, her voice was so soothing.

I smiled inwardly. As I suspected, Hanz wasn't thrilled about Momentum joining his party.

"When we arrive, our teams can split. I'll take care of this, while you and Tristan find the king. Once you find the butler's hall just outside of the Throne room, stay there and watch the Time Faerie. Don't let him out of your sight."

"And Orion's bow?" Riah asked.

"I have some ideas," Hanz replied, "But until I find it, Beatus will serve me."

"Be sure to take a quiver," Riah said, "The bow will be pretty useless to you if you don't have any arrows."

"Right. Adding that to my list," Hanz mumbled. I could hear some scribbling on paper. "Now... What about the Vineyard Palace?"

"That's where Somenus keeps his entertainment."

"Women?"

"Yes."

"Then we should take care of them, too," said Hanz.

"Any women he copulates with are taken to the Radiant Palace to join his harem—I don't think you'll need to worry about the Vineyard Palace."

I heard a pounding noise, like a fist hitting a table. "Riah, there can be *no* loose ends! If a *single* heir of Somenus survives, the throne will remain locked to his bloodline! We won't be able to crown a new king."

"I realize that," Riah said, "But Somenus is aware of this fact too. That's why he keeps his women close—in the *Radiant* Palace."

Hanz sighed. "Fine. I'll head to the Radiant Palace first, then I'll go to the armory. You said that's where the king keeps legendary weapons?"

I was holding in a deep breath as I listened. Were they *really* saying what I thought they were saying?

"Yes. It will be the safest place for such a weapon, unless Somenus himself carries it," replied Riah.

"Right," Hanz coughed, "Well—until I return with Orion's bow, I want you to stay in the Butler's Hall. Don't do anything until I arrive. We have to take out the possibility of heirs *first* before we take him down, that way we can crown someone immediately.”

My heart thumped with rage. They were! They *were* talking about killing Somenus’ concubines! I backed slowly away from the door. I had to get out of there before they knew I was listening. Then I realized that no one was talking. There was total silence on the other side of the door.

What do I do? I panicked. *Do I knock and pretend I only just arrived?* I held my fist to the door, then paused. I could see purple light streaming from the small crack under the door by my feet. I stepped back. What was happening?

“I don’t believe it,” I heard Hanz exclaim. “She’s... she’s done it!”

“That was Isabella’s signal? You’re *sure*?” Riah asked urgently.

What? Hanz’ sister had found the weapon? *Now?*

“I couldn’t be more sure!” Hanz said excitedly. “Riah—we can do this! We can actually do this!”

“Let’s gather the party,” Riah said quickly. I could hear the ruffling of papers. “Isabella might be in a compromised position. We need to hurry.”

I jumped, then scurried into the lounge. I hid behind a chaise and watched as the two of them went bolting through the room.

“Oh damn,” I whispered, “*Damn, damn, damn...!*” I shook nervously. “They are going to Arelle right *now*! And... and... Hanz is going to—!”

I ran after them.

⸻ ⬩ ⸻

I blazed into the Winter Wing and scanned for Momentum. Where was he? I had to tell him what Hanz was planning before they left! I ran room to room, shouting for him.

The Winter Wing was empty, so I found myself in the solstice. There, I saw the back of Cymbeline’s head as she marched into the Summer Wing. I chased after her.

“Cym, wait up!” I called. She turned for a moment to see me jogging toward her.

“Why are you following me, Leo?” she asked, not slowing her pace.

“Cym,” I panted, “Where are you headed?”

"To the armory," she stated as she ran, "It's time, Leo, the party is assembling."

"Cym, listen—I need to come along!" I said.

"No, Leo. How many times do I have to tell you?"

"But there's something I need to—!" I halted as Cymbeline and I passed under a stone archway. This was a room I had only visited a few times. There in the Summer Wing, Momentum had a fancy armory. The weapons and suits of armor that lined the room were so shiny and ornate, I would have thought they were props. Had *any* of these things seen battle?

"Cymbeline, glad you're here!" Hanz said from across the room. "Come on, suit up."

"Hallo, Leo," said Momentum. I turned to see him sitting on a padded bench, fastening an armored boot. "What are you doing here?"

I widened my eyes at Momentum in warning, then said, "I... I have something to say, before you guys leave!"

"Quiet, Leo," Hanz barked. "The team has a lot to discuss to prepare for the transport, I am afraid it is time for you to leave."

I frowned as Tristan, Riah, Cymbeline and Hanz all gathered in the armory around Momentum. Did he really just *silence* me like that? I opened my mouth, but nothing came out. What was I supposed to say? Why was it so hard to say it? I knew Hanz planned on killing Somenus' concubines, I shuddered— and that included Lola, *didn't it*?

"Alright," Hanz stepped forward, pounding his staff against the marble ground; it created a reverberating snap. "Isabella gave the signal. This means she has found Orion's bow. I will be the one to go retrieve it." Tristan and Riah nodded in agreement. "Aorist?" He turned to Momentum, "You stay with Tristan and Riah. Wait for me in the hiding spot Riah leads you to. We will not engage with the king until we are all together. Understand?"

Everyone nodded but Momentum, who was still absently focused on fastening his boots.

"Cymbeline," Hanz said, "Are you sure you will not stay with us? We might need you when the time comes."

"I promised to take you there," she said coldly, "But I will not stay. This isn't my war."

Hanz glanced at me, then said, "Very well. There is a landing tower at the top of the Eight Stones, Riah will guide you to transport us there."

"Guys!" I blurted. I *had* to tell them what I thought Hanz was planning on doing!

"Quiet, please," Hanz held up his palm to me, without even giving me so much as a glance, "Aorist, if your wing cannot stay silent, please have him leave."

"Wing?" I frowned. Wasn't that something they called valets in Raqia?

"Leo," Momentum looked at me, "Just be quiet for now."

"We," Hanz raised his voice in a bright, inspiring, tone, "Are setting out on the most important quest in Faerie history. Because of us, a good king will sit on the throne. Because of us, Somenus' terrible reign will come to an end! We may die, but it will be in the service of a cause greater than ourselves. We are the Purple Order, and we are doing a *good* thing here today!"

Silence fell upon the room.

"This is a terrible thing we are doing," Momentum said, "Terrible."

Hanz shot the Time Faerie a look. "War is terrible, indeed you are right, Aorist. But we must brave this terrible thing in order to bring about good for others."

Well, it was happening; no matter what I did, it was happening. Even if I spoke out now about what Hanz planned on doing, would anyone believe me? Besides, he was the one with the weapon that could kill just about anyone in an instant. If I tried to stop him now, would he just kill me? If he was prepared to attack defenseless women who stood in the way of his cause, I was sure he wouldn't hesitate to silence *me*. What was I supposed to *do*?

"I am coming." I said quietly. The others in the room turned to look at me. Hanz snorted.

"No, you're not," he said.

"Yes, I am," I looked at him.

"Leo," Momentum sighed.

"*I am coming*!" I bellowed, my voice growing as loud as a trumpet. All in the room seemed to stir, watching both me and Hanz.

"Why?" Hanz frowned.

"It doesn't matter," I shot him a hateful glare, "I am coming! Right, Cymbeline?" I turned to her.

Cymbeline studied my face with a raised eyebrow. "Yes, Leo," she said carefully, "I suppose you can come."

"Very well, Leo," Hanz said darkly, "But we cannot protect you from what is to come. Without proper preparation for such a venture, it is likely you will not survive."

"Fine!" I yelled. The quest seemed doomed, anyway; prepared or not—I was going!

"Alright," Momentum sighed, "Let's not waste time, then," he looked at me wearily, then offered a weak smile. "We should suit up and go."

Inside the little armory was all the equipment the rescue party had set aside for when the time came to transport. I watched as everyone shuffled around quietly, fitting themselves with armor. Hanz donned himself with the black, shiny suit of armor that once belonged to Timbre Wulf. I wasn't fond of Hanz, but I still got chills of admiration whenever I saw him in that sleek, menacing black armor. Riah cloaked herself, and once she did, I had a hard time looking at her, as if my mind wanted to think about anything else in the room. Before long, I forgot she was there altogether. Even Cymbeline began to armor herself in a light, silvery chainmail suit.

Momentum pulled his own suit of armor off the wall. I watched reverently as he clasped the shiny maroon plate greaves over his legs, sitting on his little bench. He wasn't planning on being a part of any attack, so why was *he* putting on armor?

"Leo," he said, looking up at me from the bench as I watched him suit up. "You going to just go like that? You'll be killed in seconds if there is a fight."

I looked down at myself. "I—" I stammered, "I'm not a fighter or anything..." I heard Hanz snort behind me at the comment.

"Go on," Momentum said with a parental smile. "Put something on."

I turned around and looked at some of the plate suits which were displayed gloriously behind me. "Well," I mumbled to myself and walked up to one. I pulled the breastplate off and it immediately came crashing down onto my foot. "*Gah!*" It hurt.

Hanz laughed, stepping up to me. "Here," he said, placing a simple, unornamented helmet in my hands. "See if you can lift *that*."

I looked at the thing in my hands, surprised at how much I liked it. I put it on my head, trying it on for size. The view through the visor felt alarmingly familiar. I turned to look at Momentum through it.

Momentum straightened up from his bench, now wearing a full suit of reflective maroon armor. He wore no helmet, but his silvery hair now had a red tint to it, and somehow that completed the look. "Well," he chuckled. "You don't look too bad."

"Thanks," I said, my voice muffled from the helmet. "Where's the rest of the suit?"

"Come on," Hanz said, "It's time to go, and we are not going to wait around for two bells while you try to figure out how to put on a suit of armor."

"Fine," I put my hands on my hips Peter-Pan-style. "Let's *go* then!"

I could see Hanz's look of frustration through the slit in my visor. Why did this all feel so familiar?

"Alright, Cymbeline," Hanz said as the six of us formed a circle together. Hanz held his massive black staff into the center of the circle. "Are you ready?"

"Sure," she said. Glancing her way, I realized she was looking at me. I offered her a little smile, forgetting that my face was covered.

I felt Momentum place an arm on my shoulder. He leaned toward me. "What is going on with you?" he whispered.

"I'll tell you once we are there," I whispered back.

Cymbeline closed her eyes, concentrating quietly. Then, my skin prickled with a familiar sensation as sparkly blue veins of lightning began to form around me.

I'm coming Lola, I thought to myself, *Whether you like it or not—I am going to find you.*

—— Felix ——

The Siren

Felix sat on his spire, looking over the face of the Raqian table world. He could see everything from up there. If felt good, feeling separated from the rest of creation. When he was up on his spire, at the highest point in Arelle, he felt like he wasn't really a part of everything happening down below. He was just the watcher; the observer; the witness of all things. He felt the wind blowing through his four bat-like wings as they stretched themselves out freely.

So—Lola was pregnant. Somenus got his child, and he didn't even know it. Would it be a boy? It had to be. It was the first child of a king. It would be a boy. He *knew* it would be a boy.

Lola. She was pregnant. Yes, she was right. She was going to die the second she delivered that baby. Once Somenus got what he wanted, he would discard her like old laundry. He would finally have a person who could fill him with all the love and affection he desired—for a time, anyway.

Lola. Oh, how he *hated* her. Her eyes; her face; her words. He hated that iron hand of hers that knifed its way into his steel-cased heart. She clawed her way in there, screaming life into emotions he had long destroyed. She made him feel pain. She was an enemy to all he believed in—to all that he was. She was a siren; a ghost from Hades who called to him, reminding him that he still has places in his soul which hurt—which felt.

Lola. Oh, how he hated her. At least—that's what he told himself. What other way could he tolerate this—this disrupting *villain*. Hate—it was the closest thing he had to love. It obsessed; it gnawed; it infiltrated his most inner core.

Lola. Oh, how he loved her. Felix closed his eyes. Tears. Tears streamed down his face like acid, torturing him with guilt.

"Why?" he begged, looking up toward the horizon; toward the edge of the world. "Why did she have to come into my life?" He bowed his aching head, cradling it in his hands. "Lola."

He remembered the first time he saw her. Somenus' new watchman, spying on the various kingdoms, it was an easy job. All he had to do there was sit, watch and report back to Somenus. He watched Celestia closely; those Elves wanted nothing to do with the new Faerie monarch. Somenus became obsessed with learning their secrets. Who knew his most powerful asset would be his only daughter, Lola? She was so innocent, so pure. Her body glowed like a sun when Felix first saw her. Something woke up inside him that day, something new.

But, like the hound he was, he relayed the information on the beautiful daughter to Somenus. And just like that, the one beautiful thing left in Felix's world was torn away. What would have happened if he had never seen her; if he had never told the king about her?

Well, it was a fitting end to this twisted story, wasn't it? He would see her die. And with her, that last, torturous part of his heart that still breathed—still gasped for life—would die as well. He rubbed his bleary eyes with his palms. "Lola!" he croaked.

He saw her face in his mind, as clear as the day. He heard her words. *Just do one good thing.*

Felix dropped his eyes to the horizon. "It is too late for me," said his weak, defeated voice. Then his vision focused on something... unexpected.

37

—— Momentum ——

The War of Fours

I n the beginning, there were eight of us.

We eight formed a council of leaders, overseeing the calling we had received to watch and aid those made on the sixth day. We were the foundation stones placed in Arelle, making a place for all the other Faeries who would be made after us.

First, there was Pondus, the Faerie of Authority; he was eventually our king. Then there was Pneuma, the Faerie of Life; Viktor, the Faerie of Movement; Witness, the Faerie of Sight; Grey, the Faerie of Power; Rest, the Faerie of Affection; Honor, the Faerie of Skill; and me—Aorist, the Faerie of Moments. We were the Council of Eight.

Together we built the Lapis Gate, the greatest of all Faerie creations. With water given to us from the Glassy Sea, we made a portal that could pass through the barrier between us and the Earth. I was made the keeper of the Lapis Gate. With the gate, we were able to travel and observe anywhere and anything.

As other Faeries were created on Raqia, we tasked them with caring for the Elves in our world. The Eight of us, however, watched over the Earth as it began to fill with humans. We watched them; we visited them; we aided them. That was our purpose: to serve.

Together, we made decisions and trusted each other's wisdom and insight. And so, together we decided to bring humans up to Raqia. We wanted to share our world with them as they shared with us. Sometimes we took humans who we thought would die from wars; sometimes we took humans who inspired us. But before long, there was chaos in our own land. The humans multiplied so quickly; they grew by the thousands! But they had no government. We didn't want to lead them—we were supposed to serve them!

So, together we decided they needed a leader. We watched the Earth and we looked for a man who would make a good king. There was a man down there; he was a good man, a farmer. Together, we decided to bring him up to Raqia. His name was Pilgrim. Pilgrim took up his mantle to lead the humans on Raqia with pride and formed villages. He was a rural man, so he led in a rural way. He was a simple man and he led in a simple way, traveling between villages he founded and leading the scattered humans through example rather than force. He was a good man.

Then, something happened down on the Earth that broke our minds; it broke our understanding; and it broke our bond of unity. The spirits got involved. All the time that we had lived up on Raqia, the bodiless spirits from before we were made dwelled among the stars, watching. Some of the stars fell— crashing down into the lowlands—and gained wills of their own; wills that defied what they were made for. Instead of watching, they partook. They took bodies, and with those bodies they took women. Their children were like the Fae—part flesh, and part spirit—but they were different. For one thing, they *could* kill. And kill, they did. They became warlords and heroes on the Earth, ruling in a kind of way we had never seen before.

One of these warlords was a man named Orion. But Orion was so much more than a warrior: he was a leader. He rallied the humans together, building cities and great wonders. His rule was fierce but strong. We had never seen anything like it. That was when we started to disagree.

Honor, the Faerie of Skill, was mesmerized by him. He proposed that we bring him to Raqia. The eight of us discussed it, but we were divided. Some of us wanted to bring him up, believing he could lead far better and bring greater influence to Raqia than Pilgrim did, while others of us thought it would be unwise. He was such a wild card, and there was—well there was something *wrong* about him. So, without a unanimous decision, we chose not to bring him through the Lapis Gate.

But the disagreement festered amongst us. Four of the Original Eight could not let it go. Honor of Skill, Witness of Sight, Grey of Power, and Rest of Affection, who we now call the Faerie of Dreams, were convinced that Orion was someone we needed up here. I still don't know how or why, but he seemed to capture their loyalty in a very deep and unshakable way. So, they betrayed the Council of Eight. They made their own portal. Without all eight of us, it was a lesser, weaker portal. They could not use holy water from above without it being gifted to them, so they made a portal from the waters below, straight from the seas of the Earth. It was the Crimson Gate, and Witness was its keeper.

Through the Crimson Gate, they brought Orion, and made him a king. Well, no—he made *himself* a king. Orion became a fierce conqueror on Raqia, and after seizing so much of what Pilgrim built, he built his own city. He built Bavel, the great city of men. Grey, the Faerie of Power, enchanted the city so that Faeries could not enter it. That was when the segregation of humans and Faeries on Raqia began. Orion knew we were called to serve the humans, not rule them, so he pushed us away. Then, things got worse.

He continued to drive a wedge into the Council of Eight. Before long, the four who supported Orion began to ask for a new Faerie King. Horrified by their treason, Pondus banished them from the Counsel of Eight. That's when the first Faerie War started: The War of Fours. The council had divided, four against four.

It was horrible. By this point, not a single Faerie had ever died. We didn't even know we *could* die! All we knew was that we could not kill. Humans, however, could kill. So, Honor, Witness, Grey, and Rest formed a great weapon. They made a bow. With Grey, the Faerie of Power—or Magik, really—they were able to make a bow of unending power: a bow that could kill anything and anyone.

After they gave it to Orion, I cannot even begin to describe to you the amount of death we saw on Raqia. We became a blood-stained world, just like the Earth. It was so horrible. They killed King Pondus, but his infant son, Sol, lived. Viktor, Pneuma, and I did everything we could to hide him and keep him alive. It was only a matter of time, though.

With Orion's bow, we knew they would soon kill us all.

And so, I did what I swore I would never do. I created a killer. I went to Pilgrim and begged him for help. He was our only hope. Viktor, Pneuma, and I made our own weapon. We made a staff, and we called it blessed: Beatus. It wasn't as powerful as Orion's bow, but it gave Pilgrim unimaginable strength. And with Pneuma's blessing, Beatus would protect anyone who wielded it from dying. Other Faeries who were still loyal to the king blessed it, too. And so, the last of us Fae who stood against Orion made our own abomination.

We made Timbre Wulf.

With Timbre Wulf, Beatus, and the Lapis Gate, we stood a chance. That final season of the War of Fours was something out of a nightmare. There was so much death. We killed so many of them, and they killed so many of us. We killed the Faerie of Dreams; we killed the Faerie of Sight; we killed the Faerie of Skill; and we even managed to wound Orion enough to take his bow and kill the most powerful Faerie who ever lived, the Faerie of Power.

By then, Viktor and I were the only ones left from the Council of Eight. Pneuma, Faerie of Life died. No, she wasn't killed—at least not by a bow. She just died. I suppose the fault of her death must lie with me. I killed her because of what I made her take part in. I was a villain back then, Leo. I was a horrible, horrible person for doing what I did to Pilgrim—by making him a weapon.

In the end, the only problem that remained was Orion. What were we supposed to do with him? We didn't know what to do with a Spirit—could he even die? So, we used the Lapis Gate to banish him to the only place we believed could hold him. We sent him and his evil bow into Hades, the realm of Death, way down under the Earth. Finally, he was gone.

We rebuilt Raqia slowly. Many of the original Thousand Faeries had died, and so marriage was introduced to our people. We were given a way to rebuild our numbers. Slowly, more Faeries began to populate Raqia. However, thanks to Orion's hate of the Faerie kind, we were hated and hunted by the humans. So, most of the Faeries scattered, either hiding in Arelle, or living as hermits in remote places. Our purpose—our calling to serve the humankind—was abandoned. How could we serve those who hated us? They hunted us; they killed us.

We won the war, but we also lost. After the War of Fours, we were a broken race.

Pilgrim hid away after that, ashamed of what he had become. The Faeries hated what he represented, and the humans wanted nothing to do with the man who killed their king. He became an outcast, a hermit, living in the woods.

I wish I could say we left him alone. But too many Faeries had pledged themselves to him, believing he was their savior. He lived on. Two thousand seasons ago a new Faerie of Dreams, Somenus, rose up to try and take the throne from King Sol. And it was like the War of Fours all over again, but this time, I was more prepared.

King Sol summoned Viktor and me back to Arelle, and we took part in another bloody, hateful Faerie War. When Somenus' endeavors failed, Viktor and I didn't want to kill him—by then, I had sworn never to kill again. So, we sent him where we had sent Orion five thousand seasons prior. We sent him down to Hades.

I can only imagine that during his time there, Somenus found Orion's Bow and brought it back with him. How else could that cursed thing have returned to us after all this time?

38

—— Clover ——

The Gates

Clover and Yuma walked together, side by side, toward Arelle. She was so close now, that she was towering above them. Clover had no idea her walls were so high. Like Elder Giants, they seemed to disappear into the sky.

Clover used his spear as a staff as he walked; with his free hand, he cradled Dezmund's bag.

"When are you finally going to open him up?" Yuma asked.

"Once we are inside," Clover said, "I'd hate to worry him needlessly."

Yuma chuckled. "I can't imagine he would be thrilled about approaching the gate of Arelle without an army."

"Besides," Clover added, "He said he has limited magik. I am sure a four-hundred-day season would have drained him a lot. Let's wait until it's absolutely necessary."

The grass beneath their feet made swishing sounds as they walked, then Clover's spear made a snap as it hit stone. The two of them looked down.

"Here's the road," Yuma said. His eyes followed the road to its destination. "Look, the bridge is just up ahead."

"It's called the Pleasant Way," Clover said. "It's supposed to have really beautiful views."

Yuma snorted. "Clover, how can you be thinking about views at a time like this?"

Clover turned his horned head toward Yuma. "Why wouldn't I be thinking about views?"

Yuma chuckled. "Speaking of views—why are you wearing those horns? You look ridiculous."

Clover reached up to adjust his crown. "I don't know. I suppose it's my way of bringing Solo with me. It looks ridiculous?" Clover dropped his arm limply, crestfallen.

"It looks fine. Wear your crown, Elf," Yuma said, then laughed when TSB popped up on Clover's shoulder with a smile. "Never mind. You look ridiculous."

"Not as ridiculous as you," Clover pointed, "With your *one* arrow!"

"Hey," Yuma pulled his single arrow from his rucksack. "This is special."

"Well," Clover said impatiently, "I'm about to die. You might as well tell me what's so important about it, now!"

Yuma rolled the arrow between his fingers, studying the arrowhead fondly. "It's an heirloom, passed down to me by my great uncle—the last Fero general."

"Did it kill someone important?" Clover asked.

Yuma shook his head. "When my uncle gave it to me, I was just a boy. He said that to be a warrior is to protect, and only kill when you must." He glanced up at Clover. "Our ancestor, Chief Whirling, held this one arrow in a battle long ago. It was a battle destined to be lost, and his people had so few weapons, that this was all he had. In the end, he never used it. My great uncle, when he passed it on to me. said that holding this arrow reminds a warrior to think about who he is killing, and what their absence will mean to the world. When the famine started, I swore to myself I would kill Somenus with it. Now?" He smiled, "Now I will pass it on to *you*, Clover, when the time is right."

Clover looked down at the arrow. Its red ribbon, tied to its tail, flicked around in the breeze. "Well," he said, "If and when we find the bow that can kill Somenus, I guess we are going to need it."

Clover lifted his boot to walk forward, but Yuma held him back by his arm.

"Clover," he said, "Wait."

Clover turned curiously.

"You..." Yuma cleared his throat nervously. "You've been a good friend."

"Thanks."

Yuma's eyes looked everywhere but at Clover's face. "Well," he coughed, "glad that's sorted."

"You, too, Yuma." Said Clover.

"Well," Yuma charged forward. "Enough of that! Let's go!"

⸺ ⬥ ⸺

Clover and Yuma walked slowly across the Pleasant Way. It was a long, white bridge that stretched over the gap between the gates of Arelle and the grasslands to the south. They could never be more conspicuous, crossing that bridge. Yuma glanced up toward the high walls of the Faerie City, grimacing at a splatter of four black bat wings sticking out of one of the spires, like a massive crane fly.

"Clover... They are going to see us," Yuma said.

"Of course they are," Clover said nonchalantly. He was strolling confidently; the long bridge spanned out for nearly a mile ahead of them.

"They'll probably shoot us before we even get to the gates," Yuma said, rubbing the tip of his arrowhead.

"Don't be ridiculous," Clover said, exasperated, "No one shoots down visitors before they know who they are!"

Yuma sighed. "Fine. They will shoot us as soon as they find out who we are."

TSB sat on the top of Clover's head, finding that place the most desirable to nest since Clover began wearing Solo's horns like a crown. Clover didn't seem to mind, but constantly had to brush hair away from his eyes every time the gnome resituated.

"You still look ridiculous." Yuma muttered.

"So do you," Clover said, glancing to the side, "and you don't need a gnome to complete the look, either."

It seemed to take ages before they arrived at the foot of the gate. The two of them peered upward at it. Yuma cleared his throat.

"Do we knock?" Clover asked, turning to his burly traveling companion.

"How should I know?" Yuma crossed his arms. "You're the one with the plan."

The two of them jolted as a shadow suddenly appeared over them. They looked upwards, backing away slowly from the gate. The crane flew down slowly toward them.

"Well," Yuma muttered, "Get ready to die."

"He's a Faerie," Clover whispered. "He can't kill us."

"Then get ready to die *soon*," Yuma moaned.

The Faerie landed in front of them with his arms dangling to his sides. He wore a deep blue tunic and had four black wings. Four wings? He must have been a second-generation Faerie! Clover didn't even know any of those were left, other than Somenus.

"Who in Hades are you?" he asked, his unruly black hair hanging over his eyes.

"I am Clover of the Elder Copse," Clover said, placing his hand on his heart. Then he gestured to Yuma, "And this is Yuma of the Fero Lands."

The Faerie snorted, crossing his arms. "I am the Faerie of Sight—Arelle's watchman. Why have you come?" His eyes narrowed as he spotted the Exilium bag under Clover's arm.

Clover folded his arms behind his back and cleared his throat. "We have come to kill the Nightmare Faerie."

There was an eerie silence as the Faerie of Sight stared at them in astonishment.

"I'm sorry, *what*?" the Faerie of Sight finally asked, stepping back.

"We," Clover stepped closer, "Have come to kill the Faerie King."

Wind seemed to pass between them at the most poetic moment. The three stared silently at each other as their capes rustled in the breeze.

The Faerie stepped away from them, nodding. "I see," he said. Then, he flew away.

Confused, Clover and Yuma gazed up at him, watching his flighty figure float over the walls like a loose feather caught in a gale. They watched for several clicks, until they were sure he was not coming back.

"Well," Yuma turned to Clover. "That was—"

The two of them started at the sudden sound of creaking. Then, like an old book at the start of a good story, the gates of Arelle opened.

Clover and Yuma raced into the city, their hearts pounding. Clover didn't stop to ask why things seemed to be working in his favor, he just pressed onwards. They ran through the cobblestoned streets, which wove through the city in symmetrical swirls. They stopped at an intersection to pant.

They stood under a pergola, attached to a few stony pillars. Tiny vine tails and colorful flowers cascaded down around them, providing shade from the blinding light of the city. The city—it was so white! Everything was reflective and vibrant. It was like walking through a kaleidoscope of mirrors, sprinkled with splashes of color as the various hanging gardens curled their way around the buildings and streets.

"Beautiful," Clover remarked.

"Forget the views, Clover," Yuma quipped, "We don't know where we are going!"

"Oh!" Clover started, then nodded. He stood quietly for a moment, thinking, then reached for the little sack on his belt. Opening the now dusty-looking bag, Clover carefully pulled out Dezmund.

"Dezmund," Yuma said, making quick eye contact with Clover. It was concerning; Dezmund was so pale now—so colorless—he didn't even open his eyes! "Dezmund, wake up!"

"Dezmund?" Clover asked, poking the Faerie's body with his finger. "Dezmund, please wake."

Dezmund, the Faerie of War, lay there lifelessly. Clover and Yuma looked at each other hopelessly. He wasn't going to wake up.

Clover raised his eyebrows in excitement. "Wait!" he said, "He's a Faerie."

"No kidding, he's a Faerie!" Yuma barked.

"I mean—he gets power from things. He's the Faerie of War, right? What do you think he gets power from?"

Yuma's eyes flashed, then he nodded with a wry smile. He drove his fist into Clover's face. Clover's feet flew over his head in a display that left Yuma cackling. The Elf sprung back quickly, fists drawn.

"Hey, hey!" Yuma pushed him back. "Careful or you'll hurt Dezmund!" Yuma held the little Faerie in his hands. Dezmund was sitting there, crossed legged, with a weak but satisfied smile.

"Nice," Dezmund nodded approvingly. "Again."

"Dezmund!" Clover leaned down toward Yuma's hand. "Dezmund, look where we are!"

The little Faerie of War looked around with half-open eyes. "Arelle," he said, then stopped to yawn.

"Where do we find Orion's bow?" Yuma asked, cutting to the chase.

Dezmund laid back on Yuma's palm, closing his eyes. "I..."

"Dezmund, please. Just tell us where to look," Clover pleaded as the Faerie began to snore softly. Clover huffed, then drove his elbow into Yuma's ribs.

"Ow!" Yuma grunted, glaring at Clover.

Dezmund's eyes snapped open at the sudden, though small burst of power.

"Where do we look for Orion's bow?" Clover urged.

"Eight Stones," Dezmund said through another long, drawn-out yawn. "There's a weapons vault there—it's where I would look."

Clover and Yuma looked at each other quickly, then back at Dezmund.

"Look for the," he stopped to yawn once more, "—the tower."

Clover didn't wait another second before he slipped Dezmund back into the bag.

"Look," Yuma pointed northwards where a Faerie seemed to be sitting on the roadside. "I bet she can tell us where the Eight Stones is."

"The Eight Stones is the king's house," Clover said smartly.

"Fine—do you know where that is?"

"No..."

Yuma motioned with his chin toward the Faerie. "Go ask her!"

Clover jogged up to the Faerie. "Hey," he said, stopping a few paces away from her.

The woman looked up in surprise. She was covered in, well—dirt, though her hair was delicately combed and styled as if she tried to look presentable. She was crouching by a bit of turf that had been uprooted partially, with a little pile of conspicuous black soil dashed onto the cobblestone road. "Oh," she said slowly, "hallo!" There was a worm in her hand.

"Hi," Clover said awkwardly. "Do you know where one could find the Eight Stones?"

The woman nodded then pointed her dirt-stained index finger up toward the center of the city. There was a concentration of spires, clinging to the front of the mountains that Arelle bordered. Clover and Yuma didn't stop to wonder who she was; they took off toward the city center.

"The city," Yuma said through heavy breaths as they ran, "It's so empty!"

"It's a Faerie city," Clover returned, "There's not many Faeries left these days."

"Really?" Yuma shook his head in disbelief, "I figured this place would be full of them."

They passed a group of soldiers who eyed them suspiciously.

"Quiet," Clover said as they approached a long flight of stairs. "Let's try not to draw too much attention."

Yuma scoffed. "Any second now, we are dead," he said as they began to climb the stairs up to the inner city.

"We will be fine," Clover said, "Let's just keep moving."

At the top of the stairs, they found the king's Palace. A fleet of guards loitered about. Yuma glared sidelong at Clover. "What *now*?"

"Look," Clover pointed, "They're moving away!" They watched in astonishment as the guards rushed off. "Something is drawing them away."

"Perhaps it's that purple light over there," Yuma said, pointing to one of the nearby palaces. Purple lights flashed between distant pillars. The guards seemed to be running toward the commotion.

"No time to wait," Clover said determinedly, "Let's go!"

He ran forward into the Eight Stones side entrance, just below its largest tower.

"The tower," Yuma mouthed, "right." He followed.

Clover crashed through the door at the top of the tower and stopped to look around. Yuma practically fell on top of him as he came colliding into his back. The two fell in a heap on the floor. TSB scurried off into a corner, scared off by the commotion.

"Look where you're going! Now you've gone and scared him!" Clover snapped, watching as the Yuma found his balance.

Yuma frowned, looking around. "Is that the vault?" He pointed at an iron door that was on the wall opposite from where they had come in. A large map table sat at the center of the room. They circled it, parting on opposite sides. Both froze as they saw what was beyond the table.

A woman sat on the floor, leaning against the vault door. Dressed like one of the other Arellian soldiers, she was curled into a ball with her head between her knees. Her hands clutching tightly to a bow.

"Is she... dead?" Clover whispered.

"Hello?" Yuma said in a raised voice. Her body jolted, but she didn't look up.

"Woman," Clover said dryly, "We aren't going to hurt you. Just..." he huffed, "can you move out of the way?"

The woman, wearing a red cape and a tidy top knot, slowly raised her head.

"What?" she asked, sounding confused. Her eyes focused on them.

"He said *move*," Yuma barked, pointing at her, "So move!"

Clover's mouth gaped open, and he froze like a statue.

"Who... who are you?" she asked, recoiling under Clover's intense gaze.

"We—" Yuma cut himself off, watching as Clover began to step toward the woman in slow motion. "Clover? What are you doing?"

The girl pulled her knees closer to her chest fearfully, clutching the bow tightly with gritted teeth. "Stay back!" she hissed. "I'm not afraid to use this! It's Orion's bow—the bow that killed King Sol!"

"Clover!" Yuma whispered, "Did you *hear* that?"

The girl shook violently, shrinking further as Clover continued toward her, approaching in slow motion. He began to crouch lower, holding out his hands out to her as if she were a scared animal.

"I said stay back!" she screeched, visibly trembling as Clover knelt on one knee beside her. "Stay *back*!"

Clover said nothing as he reached forward and took hold of the bow.

The woman stared at him with wide, terrified eyes, but released her grip on the weapon. With a quick sweep of his arm, Clover threw the bow away from her. It slid across the floor and bumped into Yuma's boot.

The woman sat there, quaking in terror, with her eyes locked on Clover's face. She shook her head, muttering to herself.

"I've gone insane now," she sputtered, "Oh Lights—I've lost my mind."

Clover reached toward her with both hands. She cowered, tightening her eyes closed. He placed his hands firmly on her shoulders, then knelt down on both knees beside her.

"Isabella," he whispered, his voice as gentle as ripples made by rain. She froze, then opened her eyes, gazing back up into his face. The two looked at each other in pure silence and stillness. Clover's face was so calm—so peaceful. Isabella gazed into it, awe-struck. Then her lip quivered, and she blinked quickly, tears escaping from them in little streams.

"Clover?" her weak voice croaked.

Clover leaned forward and kissed her on the side of the mouth. She drew in a sharp breath. Then he kissed her again, on the forehead, and rather than resisting him further, she closed her eyes.

39

—— Isabella ——

Orion

Isabella felt the tension leave her body at Clover's embrace. She felt his arms pull her up off the ground, as if she were weightless, and toward his chest, tightly wrapping his arms around her. She didn't understand why he was there, or how in Hades he had found her, but one thing felt true: she was safe.

"Are you..." she whispered, "How did you...?" What could she possibly say? "How did you *get* here? How did you find me?"

"Isabella," Clover whispered, tucking her head tightly under his chin, "I love you."

Isabella drew in a sharp breath, then jolted, trying to pull away. "No!" she muttered weakly. Clover didn't let her go; he held onto her tightly, as unshakable as the foundations of the cosmos. "Clover," her voice shook, and her body grew limp again, dead-weighting in his arms. "Clover—you fool. You don't even know who I am. I am not the kind of girl that..." she sniffed, "I am not someone deserving of your love." Finally—she admitted it to herself. It was *she* who didn't deserve *him*.

Clover sat down onto the floor with a grunt, pulling Isabella's numb body up against himself as he leaned back against the vault door. She clung onto his shirt with her hands, suddenly fearing he might let her go.

"Isabella," he sighed, "Nothing will shake me. Just let those fears drift away."

Isabella drew air into her chest tightly, processing his words. "What? No... you don't understand."

Clover placed one of his hands on her head, holding it firmly in place. "I love you, Isabella. I am so glad I got to see you... one last time." he said in a steady voice. She felt a drop of moisture fall on her cheek. Was he... *crying*?

Isabella grew silent, closing her eyes. She would not fight him, not anymore. In that moment, all that mattered was that she wasn't alone. Finally, she wasn't alone. Perhaps one day he would find out what she had done, but at that moment, he was not turning her away.

Clover and Isabella sat there quietly, holding each other in a tight embrace, breathing. As Isabella's blood began to return to her limbs, she relaxed her body and gazed up at Clover. She could see one of his eyes from her perspective under his chin. It was looking down at her.

"Clover?" she asked.

"Yes?" he said.

"What did you mean when you said... *one last time*?"

Clover held his breath for a moment, then his body locked itself around her like a steel trap. Isabella screamed as their bodies flew across the room.

Isabella's world was dark for a moment. She first felt a cold, flat surface pressed on the side of her face, and then—she screamed—the familiar feeling of being trapped under a dead body. She wiggled, trying to pull herself loose from Clover's lifeless embrace. He didn't move, but his muscles no longer held her in place. She managed to yank herself free.

"Clover?" she cried out in confusion. She scrambled away from his body, her eyes darting around as she tried to figure out what in Hades had happened! There was Clover, lying on the ground with a misshapen iron door on top of him. From here, all she could see was the side of his head, and a single hand sticking out from under the debris. A small pool of blood leaked onto the floor beneath him.

"*Clover?*" She threw her hands over her mouth. Just like that—he was *dead?* She turned slowly, daring to look back toward the vault, where they had been sitting moments before.

Standing in the open doorway, where the iron door once stood, was the figure of a crooked giant, rising like a roused bear. His arms hung at his sides with fists clenched, and he appeared taller than he had ever been before.

Korbin.

"No!" Isabella shook her head, stumbling backwards as he marched toward her with the uncanny speed of a spider, leaping upon its prey. Isabella screamed as he hooked his hand around her neck and drew her up into the air with an inhuman growl. Isabella kicked her legs gracelessly, clutching onto his hand as she tried to strain for breath.

She felt her back hit a wall as Korbin, who was apparently *not* dead, drove her body against the side of the room. She felt something crack in her shoulder. Isabella gasped in pain, her eyes snapping open as she dared to look into the face of her attacker. It was as if she had never seen his face before; it was the most terrifying thing Isabella had ever seen. Across his neck was a dried trail of blood; how had he *survived* that? With eyes filled with the lust for violence, and teeth grinding with the hunger for blood, he dared to smile.

"Isabella," he said, "My loyal servant."

"No!" she croaked, her eyes searching the room for help. Clover's body remained lifeless under the iron door. And where was that other man? No, no one was here—no one but Korbin. He filled up her field of vision.

"Did you really think you could *kill* me, you little worm?" he hissed through his teeth, "Did you truly think the greatest of all men could be destroyed by a little knife?" He tipped his head back to bellow a deep laugh.

Isabella tried to wiggle free, but he tightened his grip. She froze, barely able to breathe. "Please," she pleaded, her voice barely audible, "Please let me..."

"Let you—what—*live?*" He cackled, "Of course you will live, my little disciple! You will live on and on, until you no longer know the difference between my will and yours. Then, my revenge will be complete. The innocent daughter of my enemy will be as if one with me."

Her eyes widened in horror. She shook her head.

"Yes," he tightened his grip even more, cutting off her air supply. She coughed, straining for breath. "You cannot resist me, little wench—no one can. For I am not a mere man," he loosened his grip enough for her to breathe again, and she gasped in air quickly. "I am protected by the Fae," he pushed her higher into the air until her head hit the ceiling. "Did you really think you could kill the one who had the protection of the Faerie King *himself*?" Korbin threw Isabella across the room.

Her body came crashing into the map table. Before she could recover herself, she was lifted up into the air once more, this time by her hair. She squealed in pain as Korbin set her onto the map table like a little toy.

"You're a *Faerie Friend*?" she asked, touching her aching throat with her hand. She shook her head. No wonder he hadn't died! It would be impossible to kill this man!

"I am so much more than that," he scowled, stepping up to her again as she pulled her legs away from him, tucking them into her chest. "Haven't you figured it out?" His voice was booming, "Isn't it obvious?"

Korbin stepped back, roaring like a lion, and shaking the room like an earthquake. "Don't you know who I *am*?" He locked his snakelike eyes back on her again. Isabella shook, tightening her body into the fetal position as he lunged toward her, grabbing her by the neck once more and pulling her up above the map table. It looked as though she was floating in the middle of the room. "I *am* Orion, you fool! I am the last of the living gods—Did you *really* think you could kill me—Or trick me with your *pathetic* spells?"

Isabella's mouth dropped open. She had no words.

"Don't you see, oh daughter of Pilgrim? I killed King Sol and lived—even the old Faerie curse couldn't kill me." Korbin pulled her up to his face, until her nose touched his.

Isabella coughed, "That's impossible! No one could survive—"

"I am only *half* flesh, woman!" He shook her, "My human flesh may have suffered a mortal wound from killing the last Faerie king, but my god-side kept me alive. With the help of that slave Somenus, and the food he gives me, I eventually contained the wound." He cackled.

It was clear to her what he meant; the Faeries he ate—they were somehow sustaining him.

"*Eventually* contained the w-w-wound...?" she stuttered as her imagination began to fill in the gaps. "The b-blood covering Fort Axes..."

"...is mine," he grinned.

"You called Somenus your slave... does he...?"

"I released him from Hades with a price. If he went free, so did I," his smile turned upside down. "He owes me his throne, and he knows it."

"Oh, Lights." She shook her head in disbelief, "So as long as he is King... you will make him feed you Faeries?"

"Yes." His eyes flashed. "You see, I am the keeper of the bow, not him. If he disobeys me, or stops protecting me, I will not hesitate to drive my arrow through *his* heart."

"You monster..."

"Yes, oh, daughter of Pilgrim. And soon, you will be 'monster', too." His laugh gurgled in his lungs.

"Why do you keep calling me that?" she demanded helplessly.

"That fool will regret ending my reign of Bavel—he will deeply regret it when I steal every ounce of innocence his dear child has." His tongue ran itself lustfully along his lips.

Isabella shook herself violently. "Please, let me go!"

"Don't you see, Isabella? You are mine."

40

—— Leo ——

Upriver

We appeared on a platform in the sky. I looked around as the physical world came swirling back around me. We must have been at the top of a tower. I checked for the others, half fearing I was the only one there. Hanz, Riah, Tristan, Momentum, and I all stood around in a circle. Momentum stood still, drawing me in with an unconvincing smile.

"But where's...?" I muttered. Momentum's eyes led me down to the floor. There, where Cymbeline should have been standing was a note.

"Come on," Riah said. "Time to act." Everyone seemed to be moving quickly, talking to one another, and launching into action; meanwhile, I was just frozen, staring down at the envelope.

Hanz dashed down the stairs of the tower quickly, breaking away from the rest of us. Momentum looked around at the rest of the group.

"Alright, everyone stay close to me," he said, "We are Faeries—save Leo— If we go slow and act confident, most will just assume that we belong here. With any luck, we can avoid the gaze of their watchman. So, let's try to stay indoors as we make our way toward the throne room. Alright?" He made eye contact with each one of us, then nodded. Everyone began to move toward the stairs which led to the bottom of the tower.

I hesitated, then knelt down to pick up the letter. I turned it over. "Leo," it read. I sighed.

"Well," I said, "She did say she wasn't going to stay..." I tucked the letter into my pocket, then looked up. I gasped, overcome by the view.

This was Arelle—the Light City! I had seen paintings at Winter's End but seeing it for real was like hiking to the top of a mountain for the first time. The view was paralyzing! White spires from various towers and palaces jetted out across the cityscape at different elevations.

Then I saw something: a bright flash of purple light down below. Purple Light? That was Beatus! Hanz was moving so quickly! What was I doing dilly dallying around—there was a *reason* I came here!

Just before I broke myself away from the enrapturing view, I saw something else. Atop one of the tower spires was a black shape, with big wings waving in the wind. It began to glide off of its perch, moving toward the palace where I saw the purple flashes of light.

"Oh, hell..." I stammered, stepping away from the edge of the tower. I had to hurry!

I began to descend the tower, running as fast as my feet could carry me. Then the adrenaline hit. It was like I was walking on air! *Lola's out there*, I thought. *I can't let him find her—I have to stop him!*

Well, I honestly didn't know what I was going to do when I found him; I was just an ordinary human in a steel helmet! It didn't matter though—I was determined. I had to find him. I had to stop him!

Once I landed at the bottom of the tower, I gazed around, feeling confused about where I was now that I was at ground level. Where had I seen that purple light? Momentum and the other group were nowhere to be seen. I was falling behind; this wasn't good.

I began to run through a courtyard, looking side to side for another flash of purple light. For a time, I felt like a mouse in a maze: wandering aimlessly, expecting to find cheese at the turn of every corner.

"Damn," I cursed when I came to the end of a street. There was a little house there with a single Faerie sitting on the bench just outside it, looking confused. "Hey!" I stepped toward him, pulling off my helmet for a moment.

"Oh," the man started, spilling a couple drops of tea from the little cup he held to his lips, "You're a human!" He was *scared* of me!

"I am Leo," I bowed my head, "Please can you tell me," I searched my memories for a moment, "Where the Radiant Palace is?"

"Why?" He leaned back for a moment, then sighed to himself. "It's that way," he said dryly. "Back where you came from. It's just beside the Eight Stones."

I followed his gesture to see a large building not far behind me. Thank the Lights! I grinned at him, thrusting my helmet back over my face. "Thanks!" I said, then darted away.

As close as I thought the Radiant Palace was, it took me what felt like ten minutes to begin ascending the steps to its main doors. Once at the top of the stairs, the courtyard around me looked a lot like the Parthenon; a massive rectangular roofless building surrounded in fat, ribbed pillars. I could see purple light flashing up ahead inside where the courtyard turned into a covered indoor palace. My heart filled with dread as I began to see dark figures dotted around on the courtyard floor. Bodies.

"No, no, no..." I ran through the paved empty center which seemed to stretch out as far as a football field. I cursed repeatedly, my eyes grazing across the ground that grew increasingly more and more covered in bodies.

A couple of them were Faeries, but most looked like human women, wearing blood-stained white robes. As many as twenty people lay dead in that courtyard. Had Hanz done all this? How could he kill so many people so quickly? I ran to one body, then another, checking for a pulse.

"Dead... dead... dead..." I muttered to myself. I turned one red-haired woman onto her back, fearing what I would find. She was dead too, but she wasn't Lola.

"I am so sorry," I whispered to her as I closed her eyes. "Please, rest now." I laid her body down carefully, gazing forward. I couldn't check everyone; not if

I wanted to catch Hanz! But it felt so wrong to leave so many fallen behind. I would come back for them, I promised myself, once I caught up with Hanz!

I muttered a prayer as I stepped inside the palace, scanning the lobby. A line of bodies trailed up the main set of stairs. I covered my mouth, feeling the urge to vomit. Once again, I checked a few bodies, looking for survivors, but no—Hanz had done his work well, mostly aiming for throats.

I cursed, pressing forward, and hoping there were at least *some* ahead I could rescue. If I could just catch up with Hanz! How was he killing so many people so fast? I saw the purple lights flashing like a strobe light ahead of me. I ran.

I made it up the stairs to the second level of the Radiant Palace. Part of me wished I had never gone there—*Hades*—I could hardly fathom what I saw. To witness dead soldiers on a battlefield would be horrific in its own right, but what I saw there was much, much worse. *Dozens* of bodies—over a hundred—lay strewn across the palace floor, and all of them unarmed women. I was too late.

"No!" I screamed, my voice reverberating through the halls. I ran through the Palace, desperately hoping to find *someone* alive! I raced person to person, feeling their pulses and checking for breaths.

The dead surrounded me; my *failure* surrounded me.

"Please—*no!*" I knelt beside the body of another red-haired woman. She lay there crookedly, holding a book in her hands as if she hadn't even known that she had been struck. "What the hell? How could he do this?" I turned her over, feeling sure it was Lola. Once again—it wasn't. After muttering a prayer for her, I stood and walked through the place limply like a zombie. "Is *anyone* alive?" I cried, pulling off my helmet as tears formed in my eyes.

"Help!" a weak voice called. I gasped, rushing toward it.

"Who said that?" I called. I did not find the source of the voice until I came to the very end of the main hall where an open-air balcony provided an overlook of the rest of Arelle.

There on the ground lay the body of a Faerie, lying on a tangled mess of broken wings. I rushed to his side, cringing at the amount of blood I saw on his face. I felt for his pulse; it was weak. I checked his body for wounds. He looked as though he had been pummeled to the ground, but there was no fatal blow on his abdomen. But his face...

I ripped off a piece of my tunic and placed it over his eyes. He gasped at my contact, shaking violently. His hands waved around, searching for me.

"It's okay," I said, growing calm as my old training kicked in. "You're going to be ok. I am here now. Just stay calm."

"Who *are* you?" The Faerie finally found my wrist and gripped it tightly, "Why have you come?"

I sighed. "Let me bind your eyes. If we stop the bleeding we can keep you alive."

"Forget about me!" he croaked, pushing my hand away. I ignored him and placed the rag over his bloodied face. "My eyes are gone—I'll die anyway." He clawed at me with his fingernails.

"Stop fighting me!" I yelled. "Just let me save you!"

"You can't!" His voice was filled with sorrow. "Save *her*!"

"Calm down!" I scolded, "People can live without their eyes!" Why had Hanz killed everyone but left this Faerie alive? It didn't make sense to me.

"I saw Timbre Wulf," the Faerie said. He trembled violently. He was in shock. Even without his eyes, I could see how scared he was. "He had Beatus— he killed everyone with it. It was..."

"That wasn't Timbre Wulf," I said, "It was someone... else."

"He took my eyes," the Faerie gritted his teeth, "So that I would die a slow death. If I cannot see, I cannot get power."

"Oh..." I sat back, bowing my head. "You are the Faerie of Sight?" I observed his wings; crooked as they were, I made out four of them. He was the successor of one of the Original Eight!

"Please!" He reached for me, searching blindly with his arms. I leaned forward, letting him take me by the shoulders. "He will find her!"

"Her? What? *Who*? Find who?" I stammered, leaning forward.

"He went to the Eight Stones—he thinks she is there—but it will not be long before he finds her."

"Please," I gripped his hand in mine, squeezing tightly. "*Who*?"

The Faerie froze. "Are you going to kill her?"

"No, dude!" I yelled, "What do you think I am *doing* here? I'm trying to stop him from killing anyone else—Who *is* it?"

"Somenus' favored concubine," he croaked, "She is with *child*! Please—don't let him kill her!"

"With—" I gaped, "*What*? Where is she? Please! Tell me, and I might be able to save her!"

The Faerie reached for his collar, groping helplessly for something. He took hold of a small chain around his neck and yanked it free, breaking the chain. Attached to it was a monocle of sorts with a long, ornate handle.

"Take this," he said, reaching out for my hand. I took it, and he wrapped his hands around mine. "This is part of me, it will open the cell."

"Your Imperium?" I asked, raising my eyebrows. "I can't take your... you'll die much quicker if you don't have this!"

"Forget about me," he squeezed my hand as tightly as he could, "You can't save her without it. She is in the prison beneath Fort Axes—please—don't let Timbre Wulf kill her! Please, save Lola!"

My heart stopped beating in my chest.

"W—what did you say?" I stuttered.

"Find Lola, damn it! *Hurry*!" he cried, pushing me away. I stumbled backwards in shock. *Lola*? She was... with *child*?

"Does Hanz—erm—*Timbre Wulf* know this? Does he know about the baby?" I asked quickly.

"He knows Somenus has a favored concubine—one of the women here told him before he killed her. I tried to stop him—I was too..." The Faerie of sight sniffed. "I was too late!"

"Lola..." I said. "Right... Where is Fort Axes? If I go now, I should be able to find her before Hanz does!"

"Here," The Faerie grasped the imperium in my hand and held it tightly. It flashed with light, then he cried out in pain. "There... look through the lens; it will take you to her. But please, hurry!"

I stood, fueled by my pounding heart, and placed the helmet back on my head.

"Thank you, sir," I said, "Die believing that you saved her—I'll do everything I can!"

—— Lola ——

Out from the Blur

Lola lay on the cell's cold floor, panting. Sweat dripped down her forehead, sticking her unkempt hair to her face. The pain in her back seemed to be growing worse, though she had moments of respite between the intense episodes of what she was sure were labor pains.

It had been some time since her water broke—at least a few bells—and while the pain grew worse and worse, she had no idea how much time she had before her child would no longer be something she could hide from the king. And what did it matter anyway? Felix would have told Somenus by now that she was pregnant. Soon, the king would come for his child, and she would be dead.

"I don't want this..." she moaned, "I don't want this to be happening!"

Hevel stood beside her nervously. He had tried offering assistance once or twice but had only proved to be a nuisance.

"You're doing well, child," he said softly. "Your child is coming... let that give you joy!"

"It's not my child!" she screamed.

Hevel flinched. "It's your child as much as it is his..."

"Stop saying that!"

"Lola," Hevel knelt beside her, "Children are beautiful—this is a *good* thing that's happening to you..."

"Hevel," Lola said between pants, "You don't need to keep saying that."

"Alright," he said nervously, "It seems it might be best if I gave you space, then?"

"I don't know what's best!" she screeched. Hevel jolted, stepping away from her. "I'm sorry," she sighed, "I don't feel like myself right now."

"I am sure you don't," he mumbled under his breath. He gasped slightly as Lola began to moan again, gritting her teeth as she crawled away from him into the darkness. He looked in her direction, sighing defeatedly. "Lights help me," he said to himself. "I'm good with death pains, not *life* pains! Oh, Lights..." He gazed upwards, as if begging for help. "Help me—I'm *useless* here!"

Lola breathed as best she could when the pain came screaming back like a riptide, swelling with intensity. She counted breaths, then lost count. This was miserable—and it was sure to get worse!

Was it really time? Was it really happening? Yes. It was, and there was no stopping it now. After about a hundred clicks or so, the pain ceased, and she gasped in relief. Lola fell onto her side.

For a moment she thought she could hear Hevel calling her name. But no—she could not think about others anymore. Her mind was too focused. Everything else in the world turned into a blur, and the only thing she could even see were her hands on the ground in front of her. This pain! It was so intense— so *raw*! How had it not completely *broken* her yet?

"Rest until the next one," came Hevel's voice. "Go. Go make sure no one comes through here. Guard the hall, and yell to me if you see anyone coming." No, that wasn't Hevel's voice. It was someone else.

"Felix is coming? Wait, where did you get that monocle?" *That* was Hevel's voice.

"Who?" said the other voice, "No... Not Felix... someone far worse. Go—watch the entrance and alert me if anyone is coming! We can't move her when she is like this." There came a pause. "Damn—this baby is coming *now*."

Lola was too focused to discern whose voice it was, but it sounded hauntingly familiar; surely it wasn't Somenus! Had he come to witness the birth of his child?

Before she could even turn around to ask Hevel whose voice it was, the pain hit her again. This time, the breathing was not enough; this time, the pain overwhelmed her. She screamed as something as hard as a rock seemed to drop from her belly into her pelvis. It was like nothing she had ever felt before.

"Hevel!" Lola screamed, gasping as the pain ceased suddenly. She plopped herself on her backside, turning to search for her cellmate. "It—It's time! It's coming—I don't know what to do; I don't know what to do!"

A man stepped toward her. It was not Hevel. He was too short to be the Death Faerie. He was standing far enough away that she could barely see him. Anything further than her arm's reach seemed to be a swirling blur.

"Who—who *are* you?" she asked. "Where is Hevel? Please... it's time." Her words grew weak.

The man stepped forward into her radius of clarity, as if he were stepping out of a dream into a reality. Lola gasped. No—perhaps it *was* a dream. This was her beloved! There he was, standing in a simple, bloodstained white tunic, wearing his steel helmet.

"Lola," she heard him say, his voice shaking, "What have they done to you?"

Lola watched, frozen in suspense as he stepped forward, removing his helmet. The man knelt down in front of her, casting the helmet aside. It was a face she had never seen before: a kind, handsome face. Unruly ringlet curls dropped down over his brow as he smiled at her. There were tears in his eyes.

"Lola," he held out his hand to her; tears dripped down his cheeks. "My God—What have they done to you?"

She wanted to answer—she reached out her hand to him—then she yanked it away as the pain came crashing in. She felt nothing short of fire beneath her, and she began to scream.

"Well," she could hear Beloved's voice speaking loudly over her screams, "Let's do this!"

Lola was too stunned, too helpless to send him away. She wanted to respond but found herself crying out instead.

"If it makes you feel any better," Beloved said in a jovial voice as he lifted up the bottom of her tattered, wet robe, "This isn't my first time doing this."

Lola gasped as the pain suddenly ceased. "*What*?" she finally asked.

Beloved was smiling warmly. He placed one of his hands on her knee and glanced down between her legs. How? How was he so calm in a moment like this?

"Why," she panted, "Why does it keep stopping? Why won't this just *end*?"

Beloved nodded. "They're contractions—like waves of pressure. They're working for you, not against you, Lola."

She whimpered. "I don't want this... I hate this..."

"Don't fight the pain, Lola," he said, taking her hand in his. "Let it come—let it do its worst, and then you'll find you still have life it cannot kill."

She gazed into his smiling face. "You... you really *are* him."

"Lola," he released her hand and leaned back. "Listen to me."

Lola managed to keep her eyes on his face. "Yes?"

"Rest until the pain comes, but when it does come, I want you to go for it—push as hard as you can. Do you hear what I am saying?" He enunciated every word.

Lola shook her head. "No," she said with a quivering voice, "I can't... I don't want—"

"Lola," He grasped her knee. "There is *nothing* you can't do. I'm here, okay? You can do this, and you *do* want this. The pain is coming, no matter what. So don't fight it; ride it! Just watch... you'll see."

Lola nodded, then gritted her teeth. Her eyes grew wild. "I think... I think it's coming."

"Okay," Beloved grinned, "Get ready Lola. Get ready for the best moment of your life."

The pain came again. *The best moment of her life?* How could this be the best moment of her life?

Lola screamed. She could hear Beloved yelling commands, but all she could do was force her entire body into tension. A surging pain scorched her like fire, and then she felt it—she felt something move through her. Then the pain halted, if only for a moment.

"Oh, my God, Lola!" Beloved laughed, "You're nearly there! I am looking at 'im right now!"

Lola whimpered and shook her tear-stricken face side to side.

"This is it," Beloved was removing his white, blood-stained tunic. Bare chested, he flipped it inside out, then placed it in front of him on his knees. "This next one will be easy, alright? Just ride the wave, okay? It's the last wave—then you're there."

Lola nodded quickly. Tears mixed with sweat streamed down her cheeks and dripped off her chin. She was so scared, but the pain came anyway. With one final cry, she pushed with all her might, and then came a sudden release of pressure. She gasped.

Beloved whooped, then laughed. Lola watched as he quickly began to wrap something up in his tunic. Dazed, she watched him rub the little bundle gently with the cloth.

"Whoah!" He jolted, "—*wings!*"

Lola turned her face away quickly. A Faerie—it was a Faerie. Then, the strangest sound began to echo through the cavernous dungeon. It was crying.

She whipped her face back to look at it, then reached out her hands without thinking. Beloved looked up at her. He was crying, too.

"Lola, you did it," he said as he inched closer to her, "Here is your baby."

She held out her arms weakly, forgetting anything in her life that happened before this moment. Beloved leaned the baby closer, into her view.

"W–what..." she stammered, looking at the little face. The child was wet, covered in white, chalky slime. Was it *supposed* to look like that?

"Here," said her Beloved, scooting close beside her. "Let's get it warm. Why don't you open up your—*erm*—you know," he coughed, "the front of your shirt—er—*Dress... top... Damn.*"

Lola nodded, pulling open the neck of the cross-over robe. Her Beloved took the soiled shirt off of the baby then laid its bare body, stomach first, on her chest. She gasped as four small, wet-looking wings began to stretch themselves out from his back. The two wings on his right side were white, feathery and luminous, while the two on his left side were dark and spiny, looking quite a bit like his father's wings. She pulled the sides of her robe around him, shielding his skin from the cold, then closed her eyes as she felt his body move against hers. It was a feeling unlike anything she had ever experienced. It was beautiful.

Lola's arms were shaking; she was so tired. There was no place to rest her head in this dreary prison, and just as she was about to fall backwards onto the cell floor, her Beloved scooted behind her, catching her against his chest. She felt her tense muscles relax.

She had done it; she really had done it! She could feel the heartbeat of her Beloved behind her as he wrapped his warm hands around her tenderly. This child in her arms made her feel, well—she wasn't sure *what* she felt. The child was much like her Beloved. She felt deep affection for a person who, in reality, she had never met, and yet her soul felt externally bonded to in a way she couldn't explain.

"There's," she said, realizing her voice was dry and crackly. "Something weird is hanging off him."

Beloved chucked. "That's the umbilical cord. Have you never heard of it?"

"Oh," she said, "I didn't realize... It's..."

"Yeah, it's still attached to your insides. Uh, just don't worry about that right now. It'll come out and all. I'll cut it loose in a minute."

Lola drew in a deep breath, then let it out.

"Beloved?" she asked weakly, tightening her arms around the baby.

"Yes, Lola?"

"Is it a boy or a girl?"

"Oh!" he laughed, "Didn't you see?"

"No."

"Look!" He reached forward and lifted the side of her robe slightly. "It's pretty hard to miss."

"A boy?" she asked in surprise.

"A prince!" Beloved squeezed her arm. "He's so amazing, isn't he?"

Lola smiled. "Yes. He's perfect."

"What's his name?" he asked, wrapping both his arms around Lola and her baby once more.

"Oh!" she breathed in sharply. "I don't know!"

"Don't you?" She felt him chuckling. "Come on—give him a name!"

"You seem to think you already know what I'll pick," she said. Was this man *really* the one from her dreams? How was that even possible?

"I have a pretty good guess," Beloved said.

"What is it?" She asked, holding her breath.

"Why, the character from that book you're always reading to me! Come on—Anodos?"

Lola's heart swelled within her chest. This *was* her Beloved; this *was* the man who visited in her dreams. *How?*

"Yes," she smiled, a tear rolling down her cheek. It was a perfect moment—indeed—the best moment of her life. "Anodos."

"I think I know which Faerie Anodos is," Beloved said. He reached one of his fingers gently toward the child, brushing it against one of the feathered wings. "There is only one Faerie in the world who ever had wings like this."

"*Really?*" Lola wasn't sure what to make of a baby with wings! "Which Faerie is he?"

"Well," He said, "You can tell that he is the second of his kind because he has four wings. Right? So, first generation Fae have six; second have four, and everything else after have two."

"Amazing!" Lola gazed in wonder at her son. Was he really someone so special? "You..." she hesitated, "You are human, aren't you?"

Beloved laughed. "Uh—yeah."

"How do you know so much about Faeries? How did you get here?" Her heart began to race as the questions flooded in. "Why did you come here? How did you find me? Beloved!" She tensed. "Do you have a *name*?" After all this time, would he actually *tell* her now?

He laughed heartily. "Man. Slow down. We will get it all figured out. My name is Leo."

Lola sat quietly for a moment, thinking. Leo. His name was Leo! "Leo," she mouthed the name. "Leo..."

"Yeah. And as for how and why I got here," his voice trailed off. She could feel tension in his body as he held her. "Lola. Down here one of the most beautiful things in the world just happened. But upstairs, up in Arelle, horrible things are happening. There is a plot to kill the king—*erm*—your husband."

Lola sighed, holding tightly to her baby. "I am not sure how to feel about that. I did know someone was involved in a plot to kill him—but I didn't think it would actually happen."

"Really? Who?"

"A girl... a soldier, I think."

"You must have met Isabella," Leo said. "How strange."

"Yes—that was her name! Have you seen her? Did she kill Korbin?"

"I—I actually don't know. I am not really a part of the whole plot-to-kill-the-king thing, I..."

"You came to find me?"

"Hah... sort of. I guess, yeah."

"Even after I told you not to...?"

"Yeah... sorry."

"What am I going to do, Leo?" she asked, surprising herself as the sound of his name came from her mouth. "Somenus will kill me when he gets his hands on Anodos. I—I can't let him take him away from me!"

Leo let out a long, deep breath. He held her tighter. "Lola... *damn*. This is the worst. You really think he would kill you? Why?"

Lola hesitated. "He... he wants me to love him in a way I just can't love him; it's driven him mad—mad enough to kill me. Once he finds out I gave him a child, he will finally have someone to raise—someone to share that deep affection with. He won't want me there, pulling his child away from him."

"Damn... This is the *worst*!" Leo tensed.

"Yes..."

"I can't believe *Somenus* is your husband. *Damn*! It's not fair!"

Her heart sank. "I am so sorry... I wish I..." She sniffed. "I wish I was free to... to..." She bit her lip.

"Lola. Never apologize to me ever again," he said firmly, yet as gentle as a breeze.

"I..."

"You must never—and I mean *never*—apologize to *anyone* ever again."

"Leo..." she blushed.

"Lola," there was a hint of anger in his voice. "I will protect you from Somenus, whatever happens."

"Can you do something like that?"

"Um... I am not sure what I can do. But I know that the wisest Faerie in the world is up there confronting him right now. He will know what to do. I promise, Lola; no one will take Anodos away from you."

Lola closed her eyes, feeling finally safe. Her body still hurt somewhat, and she was growing cold in the damp cell, covered in her own blood—but she was safe.

In an instant, she felt Beloved's body tense. "Who—who is there? Hevel?" he called, "Hevel, is that you?"

Lola opened her eyes weakly. Her eyes scanned the room. The cell door hung open—she had not noticed that before. Down the long passageway through the underground dungeon, she should see the silhouette of a man walking toward them. He carried a staff which glowed with a soft purple light at its peak.

"No," Beloved jolted. "*No*! No, please! Stay back! Stay the hell away from us!"

"Leo?" Lola's weak voice asked timidly. "Leo, who is that?"

42

—— Leo ——

The Friend of the Fae

L ola," I whispered as I slid Lola's stiff body off of mine, "Stay back... just—try to stay out of sight." I pointed to the back of the cell, where the dim light didn't reach. She scooted back as I turned to face Hanz.

"Leo—what are *you* doing down here?" Hanz's black armored faceplate appeared as he stepped up to the cell's door, illuminated by the one torch in the room. "Where's your clothes?" There was mockery in his voice.

"Hanz!" I stood in front of Lola, holding my arms out to my sides as a barricade. "I saw what you did—I went to the Radiant Palace. You can't *do* this, Hanz! It's murder!"

Hanz walked through the cell door, then placed the butt of his staff on the ground with a clank. He pulled off his helmet, then tucked it under his arm. Then he looked to the side, blowing a loose lock of hair away from his face. "Leo... I don't expect someone like you to understand the intricacies of what is going on here."

"Are you—are you *serious*? I know exactly what is going on!" I shouted, "You're trying to kill anyone who might be carrying one of Somenus' heirs!

You're killing defenseless women—and Faeries, Hanz! Why are you killing Faeries? You swore to protect them!"

Hanz gave me an unimpressed glare. "Leo, this is a war we are fighting. I have done my best not to kill Faeries today, but I don't expect *you* to understand the nuances, and nor do I need to explain them to you."

"And what about Hevel?" I pointed down the hall, where I sent Lola's cellmate to watch for intruders.

"I am not going to needlessly kill Faeries. Leo—" He stepped toward me, "Why won't you *trust* me?"

"*Trust*?" My voice cracked, "You killed *dozens* of women up there! I will never trust you again! I don't care about the throne—or whatever plan you have for it—it's *murder*!"

Hanz took a step closer to me.

"Stay back!" I screamed, taking a step toward him.

Hanz raised an eyebrow. "The last concubine... she's in here, isn't she?"

"No!"

"Leo... I've been to the Eight Stones already. They *told* me she was here." He leaned over to gaze past me. "I smell blood."

"And who did you have to threaten to find that out, Hanz? How many more did you kill?" I demanded.

"I did not come this far to be slowed down, only to have to listen to your felling sermons. Step aside, Leo—I know she's in here." Hanz pointed his Beatus staff at me. The purple glow swirled, then took shape into the blade of a halberd.

"She's dead," I said quietly.

Hanz stepped closer. He hovered the purple blade just over my navel. "Leo," he said softly, "Let me pass."

I cringed as a faint noise began to echo from behind me. Anodos—he was crying. Hanz's face tensed into a lustful scowl. "I knew it..." he hissed, "There *is* a child."

"Hanz!" I cried, "I am warning you—stay back!"

"*Warning* me?" Hanz snorted. "Leo..." His eyes danced across my unimpressive body, "Please... don't make me kill you."

"You *can't*!" I blurted.

Hanz twisted his head amusedly. "Oh?"

"I am a Faerie Friend—just like you! I have the Time Faerie's protection, remember?" It was a weak lie, but it might buy me some time.

Hanz shook his head. "I *know*, Leo."

I blinked. "You..."

"I *know* you are not Aorist's boy. Cymbeline explained your sad story to me, how you were mistaken for Aorist's boy." He tutted with a shake of his head, then lifted the halberd's tip up to my heart. "You will die the second my blade touches your pathetic, *useless* body."

I sighed. "Fine," I said, "I'm just me—and I know I am not a fighter, or a Faerie Friend," I hesitated. "But I will gladly die if I can buy that baby one more minute of life. I can only hope that my death might sting your conscience just enough to keep you from killing that boy." I closed my eyes and exhaled. Then I snapped my eyes open again, letting my rage kindle. "But I am going to fight with everything I have left—I'll *kill* you if I have to!"

I pulled my arms toward myself and formed my hands into fists. I had no idea how to fight, but I knew I couldn't just stand by and let him murder Anodos and Lola! But who was I kidding? Hanz had the protection of over a *hundred* Faeries!

"Leo," Hanz groaned, sliding his helmet back over his face, "This is just sad."

"Stay back!" I howled. "I will not let you hurt Anodos!"

"Oh please," Hanz scoffed, "You *named* the bastard?"

"Stay *back*!" I leapt toward him, doing my best to dodge the blade. Hanz slashed his weapon, and I found myself frozen in place. An unimaginable pain filled my body.

"Beloved!" I heard Lola's scream echoing around me. "*No!*"

Hanz withdrew the blade from my chest. I coughed, dropping to my knees with a horrifying splash into a puddle of my own blood. I looked down at myself, observing a gaping wound that ran from my shoulder to my navel. I tried to open my mouth to speak, but nothing came out. Then, my world grew white.

I collapsed forward onto my hands. I blinked my eyes open. The pain had ceased! I pushed myself up into a kneel and looked around.

"This..." I said aloud to myself, "This is Lola's temple!" It was the place I had made in my dreams—a safe place, tucked away in my mind, meant to make her feel safe. I had crafted it from my own imagination, and led Lola into it, to keep Somenus from visiting her in her sleep. What was I doing there *now*? Was I *dead*?

I jumped to my feet and looked around. "Lola?" I called. Was she dead, too? Well—if I was dead, it would only be a matter of time until she was, too.

"No!" I cried, directing my voice out toward the mountainous view. "She can't die!"

"Well," A skeptical voice said from behind me. "What sort of trouble have you gotten yourself into *now*?"

Turning, I was surprised to find Momentum—of all people—standing in my hidden temple.

"Momentum?" I exclaimed, "What are *you* doing here?"

Momentum looked around. "You took me to your safe place..." he said absently, "It's quite developed."

"M–my—?" I stuttered.

With hands on hips, he sauntered towards me, shaking his head with disapproval. "I *knew* this would happen if you came along, you know. I *knew* you would go and get yourself killed."

"I—" I blinked. "Am I dead?"

"Not yet," Momentum rubbed his chin. "*Hades*, Leo... look at the state of you! This is going to take a lot of power." He pointed at me.

I peered down at my bare chest, then choked. There was the wound, gaping open, and yet somehow not dripping any blood onto the floor. I shot my gaze back up at him.

"How am I not *dead*?"

Momentum rubbed his mouth. "Right... about that..."

"Momentum..." I raised my eyebrows. "Are you...? Am I...?"

He groaned. "It was stupid really," he said, "Trading Benji for you. You're going to cost me a lot of magik trying to stitch this up." Wait... he had made me—*me*—his Faerie Friend?

"Momentum..." I said suspensefully, stepping closer to him, "Are you telling me... that you are going to heal me?"

"Eventually."

"No!" I snapped, seizing him by the shoulder. "Now, Momentum—*now*!"

"I..." He yanked his shoulder back, "Leo, I am about to face the king! I need to conserve magik! I'll heal you enough to keep you alive, but you'll be passed out for a while."

"No!" I grabbed him by both shoulders this time. "Momentum you need to wake me up *now!*"

"Leo..." His eyes studied me carefully, "What is going on?"

"*Hanz* killed me!"

Momentum blinked himself backwards in shock. "*What?*"

"Hanz has been murdering Somenus' concubines!"

"*What?*" His face darkened.

"Somenus has a son—a baby! He was seconds away from killing him when I—I—!" I stammered, "Momentum you've got to wake me up!"

"Damn!" Momentum stomped. "Why didn't you say something sooner?"

"Momentum, now! It might be too late!"

"*Damn!*" He slammed his hands together. "Why didn't I see this coming?" Light began to fill the room, until my vision turned white once again. "I'll do what I can for you... but this won't be easy..." I heard his voice echo around me. Then, to my great dismay, the pain came charging back into my body.

⸻ ❦ ⸻

I was lying on my face. A sticky wetness coated my body. I turned my head, laying my cheek against the ground. I tried opening my eyes, but blood clouded my vision. Moving...it hurt too much. I wasn't going to be able to save her, was I? No—I had to try!

I pressed myself up on my hands, my head spinning like a top. Defying the pain, I sat back, kneeling in a reflective red pool. I slid my arm across my eyes, then blinked repeatedly as my vision returned. I listened; I could hear something. Crying! I could hear someone crying!

I strained my eyes, looking further back into the dark cell. Hanz, dressed in Timbre Wulf's chilling black armor, was holding his weapon high over his head. Below him was Lola. She was lying on the floor, curled onto her stomach, shielding her baby with her body.

"You don't have to die, woman," Hanz's dark voice growled, "Just give me the child."

"Please!" she sobbed, curling herself into a tighter ball.

I forced one of my feet to the ground, then tried to stand. The world around me kept spinning, but I strained, as if pulling myself from a pit of tar. I finally stood; my body swayed back and forth.

"That's the Nightmare Faerie's child!" Hanz howled, "It's cursed! This is your last chance. Give him to me, or die with him!"

I took a step forward, then slumped forward, gasping for strength. I was sure I was going to vomit. The pain—it was too much. I pulled my other leg forward. In a sort of dream-like way, my mind seemed to float above my body, controlling my limbs like a puppet as I shuffled forward. I held my arms out in front of me, partway in an attempt to balance myself, and partway reaching for Hanz's weapon.

I moved drunkenly up to his rear, forcing my lungs to fill with air, despite the torturous pain ripping through my chest. Hanz held the halberd behind his back, ready to swing it forward onto Lola's body.

"I can't," she whimpered, "I won't give him up!"

I came right behind Hanz, then without thinking, I grabbed hold of the shaft of his staff. I yanked as hard as I could. Hanz, thrown by the blindside, lost his balance and crashed onto his rear with a yell. Seizing my opportunity, I pulled the staff free of his hands and flung it across the room. The purple light, which seemed to fill the room with its faint color, suddenly vanished. The scene went from an eerie purple to a gloomy blue.

Hanz' menacing helmet turned to look at me. I didn't need to see his eyes to know he was shocked. Then, as if possessed by a rageful spirit, I leapt on top of him. My legs straddled his waist, and I yanked his helmet from his head.

"Leo!" Hanz gasped. His eyes ran down my chest. I didn't stop to observe how much of my blood was spilling down onto him; I drove my fist into his face. Then again; and again; and again. I beat him until his eyes rolled back into his head, and his head dropped backwards.

I paused, holding my clenched hand above my head, and watched as his body slumped onto the floor. Hanz was limp and lifeless. I stared at him, straining to catch my breath. He did not move.

"Leo," Lola's weak voice called from behind me. "Leo—you're *alive*?"

I slid off of his body and caught myself on my hands before collapsing onto the ground. I heard Lola shriek.

"Leo," she cried, "Are you alright?"

With great effort, I turned my head toward her.

"Lola," I said in a voice as coarse as gravel. "Are *you*... alright?" I scrambled to my feet, as if in slow motion, and hobbled toward her.

She was pushing herself up from the ground, holding her crying baby to her bosom. Her face was white as she gazed at me. "L–Leo... your body..." She pointed a shaky finger at me. "You look like a... a shade!"

I paused to look at myself; my skin was as white and colorless as snow. Half of the wound still hung open, while the other half seemed to be closed. I could see my flesh slowly sewing itself together.

"Don't worry about that," I slurred, "We've got to get out of here before he wakes up."

"He's still *alive*?" Lola shrunk.

"He's a Faerie Friend," I said as I knelt beside her, "He can't be killed—not by me—and not without killing a lot of other Faeries first."

Lola choked on a sob, then clutched her baby. "Leo..." she cried, "He... he almost..."

"No," I said firmly, "No time for crying, Lola, we have to leave *now*! He *will* wake up, just like I did."

She dropped her head and wept bitterly.

I looked beside me to see Hanz's staff lying lifelessly on the floor. Momentum had told me it granted many powers to the wielder—even protection from death. I seized it. Instantly, my body seemed to warm. While the pain still radiated through me, it didn't seem to paralyze me as before. I was weak, and yet, I felt strong. I leaned down toward Lola and pulled her into my arms.

"Come on," I said, "Let's go."

"Leo," she sniffed, "There's something..." she gasped as something wet slipped out from between her legs. Blood gushed onto my lap, and then a mass of flesh. Lola screamed.

"Don't worry," I said slowly, still feeling drunk, "It's just the placenta. Come on, pick it up," I tried to lift Lola up.

"What—*that*?" Her white face grew even more pale.

"Come on," I snapped, "I can't carry everything. Pick it up!"

Lola reached down and picked up the sack of blood attached to the end of Anodos' umbilical cord. She dropped it into her lap, then held onto Anodos with a shudder. I managed to get a solid hold on her body, while still clutching to the Beatus staff, and stood. Somehow, I found the strength to carry both myself and Lola. I tucked the staff under my arm, then plodded out of the cell.

Lola curled up in my arms, trembling. She was soaked in afterbirth and blood, just like I was. We both smelled—and looked—a mess. She nestled her sticky head under my chin and closed her eyes. I had no idea what would come next, but for the moment, she was safe.

I walked down the length of the underground prison. I passed a lifeless body which lay on the ground. I stopped to look down at Hevel, the Faerie I had met when I found Lola; he turned his head slightly but did not wake. Well—at least he was alive.

I kept walking until I saw light where the stairs exited the dungeon.

"Where are you taking me, Beloved?" Lola finally asked. She squeezed her eyes shut as daylight made contact with her face.

Beloved—she still called me that. I turned my gaze down to look at her face. There in the natural light, I could finally see her clearly.

"Man, you're beautiful," I said.

Her round green eyes drifted open. She smiled at me.

"Lola," I sighed, "I am taking you to the Eight Stones."

Her face filled with horror. "What? No!"

"Don't worry," I said, "My friend Momentum, *erm*—Aorist—is there. He's going to make everything right."

"He is?"

"Well," I hesitated, "I don't know... chances are, we are all going to die. But Lola, what else can we do? Our best option is to face this problem head on. I don't know... maybe we can convince the king not to kill you."

Lola's face twisted with sorrow, then she buried it in my chest. I listened to her cry as I reached the top of the stairs. I looked around at the Fort. The courtyard was littered with the bodies of fallen soldiers.

"Keep your eyes closed," I whispered. I walked through the silent courtyard, then found the main road to the Inner city.

Really, there was no hope. I was walking us both to our death. But what else could I do? The only savior left in my mind seemed to be Momentum. If I could just find him, he might know what to do!

43

—— Momentum ——

Petition

Momentum's eyes snapped open. He was sitting on the floor in the Butler's Hall, a small room adjoined to the throne room by a discrete side door. Riah had managed to keep anyone from entering by putting up a shield around them; it kept others from thinking about the room, and so far, they had been undisturbed.

Tristan, who was standing by the door, turned to make eye contact.

"Aorist," he asked, "Is something wrong?"

Momentum held a glare. "You idiots."

Riah appeared out of the corner of the room and stepped into Momentum's field of vision. "Have a nice nap?"

Momentum jumped to his feet. "You *idiots*!"

Tristan jumped, then glanced at Riah. "What's going on?"

The Illusion Faerie narrowed her eyes at Momentum. "Good question."

Momentum gnashed his teeth silently.

"Riah...?" Tristan backed away from the Time Faerie.

"Killing women? *Children*? I thought Hanz was looking for Orion's Bow, not causing a *massacre*!" Momentum bellowed.

"Quiet!" Riah hissed. "Are you trying to tell the whole world where we are?"

"Riah..." Tristan, the Faerie of Water, stepped beside Riah and placed his hand on her shoulder. "What is Aorist talking about?"

Riah turned up her chin. "I have no idea."

"Liar!" Momentum screamed. "I have *had* it with you lot." He pushed past Riah and moved toward the door.

"What are you doing?" Riah leapt toward him and seized him by the arm. Tristan took him by the other arm.

"I am going to do what I came here to do," Momentum said, "I am going to petition my king!"

"You'll ruin *everything*!" Riah pulled against him as hard as she could.

Momentum dragged himself toward the door, pulling the two other Faeries behind him.

"You've already done that!" Momentum snapped, "The second you decided to use murder to further your cause. I won't have it! I won't let you murder my king!"

"Traitor!" Riah cried, "Loyal to the Nightmare Faerie all this time?"

"Let me go!" Momentum freed the arm held by Riah, and Tristan released his own grasp. Momentum spun to face them. "Listen! I want nothing to do with your sick plan."

Tristan eyed Riah. "What is he talking about, Riah?" Riah only glared at the Time Faerie.

"While we have been sitting here, Hanz has been murdering Somenus' wives!" Momentum said.

Tristan's face said everything; he had no knowledge of that part of the plan. "What...? Is this *true*, Riah?"

The three of them cowered as a nearby bell tower began to ring.

Momentum sighed. "They've sounded the alarm. The king will know something is wrong." He moved to open the door.

"Please!" Riah yelped. "Just wait for Hanz—he will be here any minute! We cannot face the king without Orion's bow!"

Momentum shook his head. "You coming with me, Tristan?"

The Water Faerie was still frozen in shock. His mouth hung open.

Momentum sighed, then opened the door and entered the throne room.

He made his way down the central aisle, holding his breath. Somenus sat on his throne, watching. The king's four black wings sprung out from behind him like a black-lit star. He drummed his fingers on the arm of his throne, watching as the Time Faerie approached.

Momentum stopped at the foot of the steps leading up to the raised throne, then knelt and bowed his head.

"Sire," he said, "It is I, Aorist, the first and only Faerie of Moments."

Somenus stared at him.

"And I," a voice said from behind Momentum, "am Tristan, the XI Faerie of Water." Momentum glanced back to see Tristan kneeling, just behind him.

"And I suppose it's the Faerie of Illusion wandering around back there somewhere?" Somenus' booming voice asked skeptically. "I am the Faerex, you know. I can identify any title."

Momentum lifted his head. "I've come... to petition you."

"*Petition*?" Somenus scoffed. "I know what you have come to do, Aorist! You've come with your felling bodyguard to come and kill me—just like last time!"

"I have not come to kill you," Momentum said calmly, "And I did not enlist Timbre Wulf."

"Then why have I heard reports of him storming Arelle—*killing* my men? My *women*!" The king was holding his scepter, tapping it rhythmically against the arm where his missing hand should have been.

Momentum eyed the scepter; it was the imperium that let him kill anyone in his presence instantly. He knew Somenus would not hesitate to use it on him.

"I could not stop him," Momentum said, "I did try; but he has Beatus."

Somenus leaned back in his seat. "Fitting, isn't it? Timbre Wulf attacks here with Beatus, while my warrior defends with Orion's bow. We both know one of those is more powerful than the other. Orion's Bow was blessed by the

Faerie of Magik—it has no limits. You know, Aorist," he chuckled, "You *know* who is going to win here. It is only a matter of time."

"I am not here to win," Momentum said, "I am here to submit. I am sorry it took me so long, but I have come to bow to you, as you see."

Somenus studied the Time Faerie skeptically. "Then you know how this is going to end." He lifted his scepter and pointed it at Momentum.

"If that is what you choose," Momentum said, then narrowed his eyes, "But I compel you to first listen to what I have to say."

Somenus frowned, pulling his scepter back onto his lap. "Fine," he said, "What is it?"

Momentum stood, and so did Tristan, following his lead. The Time Faerie cleared his throat, and joined his hands behind his back. "Somenus, as the last of the Firsts, I find it is my responsibility to correct you. You have sought to answer The Question for the Faeries—and I truly admire you for that—but as someone who was there when the laws were written, I must tell you that it is wrong."

Somenus groaned. "And how long did it take you to come out and say this? The Fae have waited for thousands of seasons to hear the answer. If it is true that you have it, why wait until now?"

"Because I am a coward," Momentum replied. "And I deserve the judgment that is no doubt coming for me. But still—I must speak the truth now, before it is too late."

"Fine," Somenus yawned, "What is *your* answer, Aorist?"

"Like the spirits," Momentum said, "We were made before the humans and the Elves, and yet—like the Spirits—we were put below them in authority. We were made not to rule, but to serve."

Somenus blinked. "That's it? *That's* the answer everyone has been waiting for?"

"There is much history lost to Raqia that I still remember—there are reasons why we forgot and abandoned our calling to service Raqia, and her inhabitants. But I will tell you that history, if you ask it of me. I compel you, Somenus, be a *good* King. Be a king who listens to his people and considers the words of those who came before him. I may only be your subject, but I am also your elder. It would be wise to hear my counsel."

"I have others on my counsel," Somenus said darkly, "Even Faeries older than myself, like the II Faerie of Sight. Aorist—it is too late for you to come here, giving me your words of wisdom. You're an old Faerie, from an old time. Your answer for the Faerie's calling is outdated. I am giving them a new purpose."

"Sire!" Momentum raised his voice. "It is *wrong* for a Faerie to rule over a human—it is wrong for them to be worshiped like gods. We were not given such great powers in order to save glory for ourselves. We were meant to glorify *others*."

"Aorist..." Tristan whispered from behind. "Is this *true*?"

Momentum kept his eyes on the king. "It was wrong of me to hide this from the other Faeries, but I have been as lost as everyone else. I may remember the original calling, but I have not had the strength to face it. You... you are a strong king, you could lead us back into it! You could help the Faeries find their purpose again, without dominating the Human and Elf kingdoms!"

"You are right," Somenus said coldly, "I am a strong King. I do not need whispers from the past to lead this world, I have a new vision, a vision that finally raises up the Fae to a place of honor where we belong! The Faeries are glorious beings, with immense power. We should not be hiding in the shadowy corners of the world, ashamed of our existence, we should be shining lights—like the stars in the seas!"

Momentum glanced to his side, noticing that others had begun to creep into the room. Curious Faeries gathered in the wings, watching and listening. One Faerie ran to Somenus' side and whispered into his ear.

"Sire," Momentum could barely make out the man's words. "Felix is down, as well as many soldiers." He stole a glance at Momentum. "Timbre Wulf is sure to get here soon."

"And the Faeries?" Somenus asked, still keeping his eyes on Momentum.

"They are all gathering here for protection," whispered the Faerie, "They're scared... Timbre Wulf is here."

"Where is Korbin?"

The Faerie hesitated, "Not sure, Sire."

"Well," Somenus straightened in his chair, "Tell everyone not to worry, Endring. Korbin will soon put this whole situation to rest."

"Sire," Endring leaned closer, "Fort Axes has been laid waste."

Somenus' face filled with horror, then he gritted his teeth. "So," he barked, "You say you come in the name of peace, and yet—you come with swords, killing my soldiers... my *women*!" Sweat beaded his forehead. Momentum studied him; something seemed to really upset him. What was at Fort Axes that concerned him so deeply? Orion's Bow?

"I told you," Momentum raised his voice, "I am not with him! I hoped to stop his bloodshed. Somenus, he is here because you have been killing Faeries who will not submit to your rule! He represents over a hundred Faeries who believe your rule is tyrannical! Listen, Somenus, your people are suffering! Hear their voices!"

Endring, the Faerie standing at Somenus' side, turned his head to regard Momentum with a look of stupefaction.

"S–Sire," he stammered, "Is that... *Aorist*?"

Momentum held his breath as more Faeries poured into the room from behind. He heard frightened whispers and gasps.

"Somenus," Momentum said, "Please—listen! Your people will follow you. Lead us well! Please, listen to my words. Put an end to the Faerie Rites!"

Mutters of shock reverberated through the room.

Somenus stood, holding his scepter out at Momentum. "I have heard enough," he said, "Aorist... do you really think I would take counsel from the man who imprisoned me a thousand seasons ago? Do you really expect me to show mercy to the man who condemned me to a fate worse than *death*? Even to this day, I am held prisoner by one of the torturers. Even still; I suffer!"

Momentum felt a stabbing pain in his heart. Yes, he *had* done that. He had condemned Somenus to a fate worse than death. He had locked a Faerie away in Hades, in the name of mercy. He dropped his head in defeat.

"I am sorry," he said, "I did what I believed was best at the time. I begged King Sol not to kill you, as I beg you now not to kill anyone else." He lifted his head. "I should not have sent you to that prison... but do not let that wrong lead to other wrongs. I was there when the laws were written, Somenus. We must not kill!"

"You are right," Somenus returned, "Faeries must not kill, aside from one. Early on, the king was given the authority to kill. For me, it is not wrong."

Momentum held his breath. Somenus was right; he hated to admit it—but he was right.

"Please," Momentum pleaded, "Listen! The Faerie Rites are wrong. We are not gods! We are not above the Humans and the Elves, we were made to *serve* them!"

The room burst into chaos. Over a hundred Faeries, all loyal to Somenus, were now present. Some whispered in confusion, while others shouted in anger.

"Sire, is this true?" Endring asked, "*Is this Aorist?*"

"Get down!" Somenus hissed at the Faerie beside him. Endring shrunk back and melted into the crowd, until Somenus was the only one standing on the raised platform. He took a step forward, aiming his scepter at Momentum.

"I am only going to ask this once," The king said darkly, "Where is that human?"

Momentum raised an eyebrow. Human?

"Where..." Somenus grinded his teeth venomously, "Is my *hand*?"

"I don't have it," Momentum said blankly.

"Well, Aorist, allegedly *First* Faerie of Time—Your time has come." The scepter glowed faintly.

Momentum closed his eyes.

More than a few clicks passed, and his eyes were still closed. There seemed to be no noise, no movement. Not even a whisper sounded in the great hall. Momentum waited.

Finally, he thought to himself, *I will join you, Viktor.*

Still, nothing happened. Momentum blinked his eyes open. He wanted to look up, but he found his head would not move.

"What in Hades?" Somenus cried from his throne. "What is happening?"

Momentum tried with all his might, but neither his head, nor his limbs could budge even an inch. Somehow, he was about to move his eyes, but his body was effectively petrified like a statue. Apparently—Somenus was also petrified. And apparently—so was everyone else.

Then, Momentum heard a sound. It was the sound of shuffling. Someone was approaching down the aisle from directly behind him and Tristan. Suddenly, he inhaled the scent of sweat mixed with blood. Then he sensed him, the person to whom he had bonded his soul.

"Leo?" he said through teeth that remained clenched shut, "Is that *you*?"

44

— Leo —

The Son of Somenus

I knelt a couple meters behind Momentum, with Lola curled up in my arms and the Beatus staff propped up before me for support. A long, sticky trail of blood tailed behind me, but finally, my wound seemed to be mostly closed. There was nothing conscious about how I used the staff, it seemed to work *for* me, as if on its own. I didn't ask it to freeze everybody in the room, it just seemed to know that that's what I wanted it to do. It held powers and abilities from other Faeries—including Viktor, the First Faerie of Movement. It was like Viktor himself stepped in to help, washing through the room with a stilling peace.

No one moved, except those in my little sphere of protection. Lola kept her eyes shut as she clutched Anodos against her chest.

I lifted my eyes to the throne, then instantly regretted it. There he was— Somenus, the source of all my nightmares. He was as beautiful and intoxicating as I remembered him, only instead of a dreamy impression, I was seeing him in the flesh. His glory seemed to burst around him; no matter what I did, I could not stop looking at him.

His glowing hazel eyes were locked onto me. Vengeance swirled around them. Oh, how he hated me. My arms started to shake, and my hand's grip around the staff began to weaken.

"You..." Somenus hissed through his teeth, which were also clenched shut. "It's *you*!"

"Leo..." Momentum said, "How are you *doing* this?"

"I have Beatus," I muttered, though my eyes couldn't look away from the Dream Faerie. Our eyes were fused to each other, like an unbreakable bond.

"Beatus isn't powerful enough to restrain the king!" Momentum said under his breath, "*No one* has enough power!"

"Uh..." I remembered the baby, "I think *someone* does..." Could it be? Could *Anodos* be powering me and my staff?

Somenus finally released my eyes from his hold, and he looked downward, scanning the woman in my arms. His face flushed with indignation.

"Lola!" he hissed, "You will not take her from me!"

Lola's name shook me from my trance. I gazed down at her. She was quaking in terror.

"I'm not *trying* to take her from you!" I shouted.

Somenus' eyes flashed. "W–who..." He grew pale, "Who is *that*?"

Lola squeezed her arms around her child.

"It's your son," I said.

Somenus remained frozen, but his body began to tremble like a quaking volcano about to erupt. "I have... a *son*?"

"Leo...!" Momentum said, "What are you *doing*?"

"Hanz was trying to kill him!" I said, "I didn't know where else to bring him!"

"Release me!" Somenus demanded, vibrating with rage, "Release me now! Bring me my *son*!"

"Leo!" Momentum raised his voice as best he could. "Do *not* release him! He will kill us all!"

I looked up at the king, and then I myself was paralyzed. How could I say no to his man? He was the king—he was Anodos' *father*!

"I..." I felt tears welling up in my eyes. "I can't hold on... I can't refuse him."

"My son!" Somenus' eyes dripped tears. "Let me hold him! I see now. I see him! The Faerie of Magik has come to me..."

"*What?*" Momentum's voice seemed to screech like a hawk, "That's impossible!"

"Give him to me!" Somenus demanded. "Bring me my son. Bring me my wife!"

"Leo!" Momentum said urgently, "Don't let go—if that really is the II Faerie of Power, he can hold Somenus back indefinitely! *You* just need to hold on!"

Somenus' face; his beauty; his being—he seemed to fill my mind until he was all I could think about. His voice rang through my head like a reverberating bell. "Bring me my son." I could sense everything. I could feel his overwhelming joy. He had a son—*finally*, he had a son!

"Leo," Lola's voice crept into my mind. I blinked, then looked down. Her sweet, innocent face was peering up at me. "Please, don't let go."

Somenus' voice seemed to drift away into the background, and soon all I could think about was her. Lola—my sweet, *perfect* Lola.

"King Somenus," A bold, echoey voice bellowed from behind me. "Listen to what I have to say!"

I started. Someone *else* had come into the room; someone who was not bound by the spell of stillness.

"Leo," Momentum muttered, "Who in Hades is *that?*"

I cranked my head to look. A man in a black tunic, with warm brown skin and long silky hair stood there, holding a bow at the ready.

"It's..." I turned back to look at Somenus; the king's eyes widened with terror. "It's an archer... he's holding an arrow at the king..."

"How dare you come in here with that weapon!" Somenus seethed. His focus targeted the archer, and I felt a sudden relief of tension. Whatever intimidation had been focused on me was now tormenting the man, and I knew he probably wouldn't last long.

"I am Yuma, General of the Fero People: I demand that you cease the persecution of our nation!" The archer declared in a quaking voice.

"*Demand*?" replied the king, "How dare a human come to Arelle and demand *anything*! Beloved—release me this instant!" Fear coated his words like a heavy snow. I was sure that I wasn't the only one in that moment who was surprised by Somenus' name for me. That said, no one questioned it.

"I ask you one more time," the archer said, "Return prosperity to our land. End the famine. Cease your persecution, and I will let you live."

Somenus shifted his focus back to me. "Beloved," he seemed to whisper in my mind. "Listen to me." Why? Why did *him* calling me 'Beloved' feel so comforting? My hand started to loosen its grip on the Beatus staff. "Beloved," Somenus said again—much softer this time, "Release me."

Somenus gasped, just as I dropped the staff. He stumbled backwards, clutching at his chest. A red ribbon fluttered around him. He fell to his knees.

"Aorist," he whispered, "Help!"

Momentum, now freed from his stasis, rushed to the king, just in time to soften his fall. The room remained eerily silent. The Faeries who had witnessed the scene while frozen in place remained still, even though the spell had been lifted. They watched in horror as their King's clothes grew stained with blood. Momentum laid Somenus' back against his chest, and placed his hand over the king's pierced heart.

"No!" Momentum's voice cracked, "Sire!"

I heard a crash, then turned to see the archer lying on his back. A dark pool formed beneath his body. It was as if he had suffered the same blow to the heart! A little critter seemed to be running circles confusedly around him. Some nearby Faeries peered down at him, but no one dared to touch him; no one even knew who he was!

Momentum pressed his hand against Somenus' wound.

"It won't do, Sire," he said with squinting eyes, "I can't stop the—*augh*!" Momentum snapped his eyes shut and tossed his head back and forth. "It's too much!"

"Beloved," Somenus croaked, "Please... bring him to me!"

I hesitated. Lola squeezed my arm. "Do it, Leo," she whispered. Poor Lola, her body was still shaking. Requiring its strength, I picked up the Beatus staff and lifted Lola from the ground. I lumbered up the steps to where Momentum was holding the dying king. Momentum's eyes were still clamped shut, as if in pain.

I knelt by the king, and Lola leaned over to look at him in the face. I watched as he reached out a hand and touched her jaw. I hated the man more than anything, and yet still—my heart ached with sadness for him.

"Lola," Somenus whispered as a trail of blood dripped from his mouth, "I *loved* you."

Lola snapped her eyes shut, then dove back into the comfort of my arms. I held her tightly—protectively. Somenus moved his finger to touch the baby's head.

"My son," he said. "My legacy will live on... my reign... will not end."

—— Clover ——

The Ancient Evil One

A massive weight pressed Clover to the ground. He forced his eyes open. The iron door from the vault lay over his back; he was crushed beneath its mass. Thankfully, none of his limbs seemed to be trapped under it, though more than one broken rib screamed out in pain. He tasted blood. What had happened? How had he been knocked unconscious?

Clover pulled himself free of the door and stood, swaying slightly as he regained his equilibrium. His heart began to thump urgency as his eyes focused on what stood at the center of the room. A giant, at least seven feet tall, with thick tree-branch arms, gripped Isabella by the neck. She was floating in the air over the table at the center of the room, dwarfed by the size of her enemy. Her legs dangled helplessly as she clutched his wrist.

Clover didn't know who the man was, or where he came from, but it didn't matter—he was hurting Isabella. He snatched his crown of horns from the ground and placed them on his head. His spear Venture had rolled into a corner. He plucked it up and held it over his shoulder, aiming for the giant.

"You!" he called, "Unhand Isabella!"

The giant slowly turned his head, like a ship's hefty rutter. He focused his predatory gaze on Clover and smiled. He opened his claw-like hand and Isabella dropped gracelessly onto the table. The giant turned toward him and joined his hands behind his back.

"Do you have any idea how many men have tried—and failed—to tell me what to do?" He glanced at Clover's golden spear. It looked about as impressive to him as a wooden sword.

"Who are you?" Clover shouted, tightening his grip on his weapon.

"Clover, run!" Isabella cried. Clover stole a glance at her; she was crying. "He's *Orion*, Clover—he can't die! *Run!*" Orion? The bow's original owner? Clover glanced side to side; where was the bow? Where was *Yuma*?

"Leave Isabella alone," Clover said firmly, "And I will not kill you."

Orion laughed. His voice shook the room. "Isabella is mine."

That was all Clover needed to hear. He threw his spear, and it hit its mark, impaling the giant through the heart. Orion gasped, stumbling back. Isabella screamed, then shielded her eyes. Clover watched in horror as the giant grasped the spear with both hands and pulled. He yanked it free, and a river of black blood followed. Moments later, the wound closed up, and Orion coughed up a congested laugh.

Clover scowled. A wound healing itself like that—he must have a Faerie protector!

"He can't die, Clover!" Isabella shouted, "He's got Somenus' protection! *Run!*"

"Never!" Clover bellowed. He raced toward the giant, tipping his head down to point his horns at his chest. Orion grinned and stepped forward as Clover barreled into him. It was like throwing a pebble at a dam. Nothing happened. Orion took hold of Clover's cape by the back and pulled him into the air. Clover dangled like a fly in a web, swinging his fists in futility.

Orion threw him at the wall. Clover felt multiple cracks on impact, then sunk into the floor.

"Clover!" Isabella screamed. He could hear her sobbing. He pulled himself to his feet, cradling his aching chest with his arms. He spotted Isabella's black dagger on the ground and scooped it up. Before he could adjust his grip on the weapon, he was yanked from the ground once more.

"No!" he cried as he flew through the air against the opposite wall. His face met the ground cruelly. More than ribs snapped this time. He tried to push himself up on his arm but dropped back onto back on the ground with a cry of pain. "*Damn*," he cursed. His dominant arm had been dislocated. He thought he could hear Isabella calling for him, but the sound seemed to distort into nothingness.

He would not last much longer now, but he couldn't stop! Clover used his left arm to prop himself up, then clambered to his feet. He gripped the dagger with his only usable hand and shuffled toward Orion. The giant stood by Isabella, cackling at the sight of the broken, blood-stained ram.

"Back for more?" Orion taunted. When Clover shuffled close enough, the giant seized him by the neck. Clover gritted his teeth as he felt himself pulled up into the air.

"You will not have her," Clover said in a raspy, breathless voice. Orion tightened his grip, cutting off Clover's air. The Elf's eyes bulged and his legs thrashed violently.

"Clover!" Isabella sobbed, "No! Stop—*please!*"

Clover stared at Orion, growing still. Then he managed a smile.

Orion twitched, then loosened his grip. "Why do you smile?" He growled.

"I am smiling because I know you will die," he wheezed, "Evil always dies."

Orion snorted. "Boy—I have lived for..."

"I don't care how long you've lived, you roach!" Clover snapped, "I am telling you—as sure as the coming of morning—you are going to die. Today, Orion," Clover narrowed his eyes, "You are going to die *today*."

Orion's eyes widened with fear. It was as if he actually believed him! Then his terror turned to rage. "Even if I were to die today," he tightened his grip, "*You will die first.*"

"Works for me," Clover choked, then opened his mouth like a fish out of water. Orion squeezed, and Clover's lungs stopped pumping. His legs fought for a few clicks, then weakened into motionlessness. His head filled with unimaginable pressure, and then his ears clogged with moisture. His arms dropped limply to his sides, then his eyes drifted sideways, down at Isabella.

She was just as lovely as he remembered. How lucky he was, to have her face be the last thing he saw.

Orion released his grip on Clover's throat. The Elf crashed to the ground.

The giant staggered backwards until his back hit a wall.

To Clover's surprise, he was still alive. He lifted himself up on his wobbly legs and looked up to see Orion's mouth dropping open, just as lifelessly as Clover's had only moments ago. Then he saw it: blood suddenly poured forth from Orion's chest wound Clover had given him. Not only that, but the slit across the giant's throat split open like a weak seam. Orion's eyes rolled back into his head, and he moaned nonsensically.

Clover retrieved Isabella's dagger from the floor and limped toward Orion.

"Like I said," Clover said, "Evil *must* die. And now, in the name of all that is good, true, and beautiful—" he held up his dagger, "*Die.*" He swung his arm in a clean, swift stroke, and Orion's head dropped to the ground with a mighty thump. The giant's body toppled over, like a felled tree.

Clover panted heavily, and the dagger clanked onto the floor. He then reached for his throbbing shoulder with his working hand and groaned.

"Well," he said to the lifeless corpse, "Try coming back from *that.*"

Clover collapsed onto his backside, then, with spinning vision, laid down onto his back. He gazed at the ceiling and laughed.

Isabella's face leaned over him. Her expression started off worried, then softened into a smile.

"Whoa..." Clover mumbled, "You're so pretty."

She shook her head, then reached forward and parted his hair from his sweaty forehead. "Clover," she said, "You never cease to surprise me."

"Well," Clover grinned with blood-laced teeth. "I do what I can."

Isabella's deep brown eyes dripped tears. She pulled a handkerchief from her belt and wiped Clover's mouth.

"Don't cry, Isabella," Clover said. "Let our last moments be happy ones."

Isabella dove toward him, and their lips met. Clover closed his eyes, reveling in the taste of her passion. He lifted his working arm and took hold of her waist, pulling her closer. Isabella cupped his face with her hands amorously, then shot back.

"Clover," she gasped, "What do you mean: *our last moments*?"

Clover glanced to the side. "I... There is one last thing I need to do."

"What are you talking about?"

Clover studied her face. "I... I came here to kill the Nightmare Faerie."

Isabella's eyes shot wide. "The king?" She shook her head. "You can't! You'll die!"

"I know... I have to." Clover forced himself to sit up, groaning as he moved. "The Truth Faerie told me... he told me I was going to..."

"The *Truth* Faerie?" Isabella drew back, shaking her head in disbelief.

"Where is it?" Clover scanned his eyes across the circular room.

"Where is what?" Isabella jumped to his side for support.

"*Ow*!" Clover recoiled as she pulled his dislocated arm over her shoulder. "Orion's bow—didn't you say you had it?"

"*You* took it away from me!" she snapped, "Maybe your friend took it."

"My friend...?" Clover mouthed, then he remembered. "*Yuma*! Where is Yuma?" In all the commotion—seeing Isabella again, then fighting that giant— he had completely forgotten about him! Then it hit him. "No!" he screeched, "No! No, no, no..."

"Clover, what is it?" Isabella asked hurriedly as Clover tried to shuffle towards the door. She did her best to support him, hugging closely to his side.

"Where's Somenus! You've got to take me to him!"

"He's downstairs..." Isabella said cautiously. "Clover, if you kill him, you'll—"

"He's going to try to do it himself!" Clover barked, "Take me to him! *Now*!"

It took some time to get the limping Clover down the stairs. Eventually, they found themselves barging into the throne room. Already, there was a dry streaky trail of blood stretching down the aisle. Whose blood was this? Clover gazed about. The hall was filled with Faeries, crowded together on the sidelines.

At the back, down where the throne sat, a cluster of people were gathered together around the king. He had been shot! Clover directed his focus to the center of the room, then screamed.

"No!" He pushed Isabella away from himself, then staggered forward. Yuma lay, flat on his back, at the aisle's midpoint. He threw himself by Clover's side, grabbing him by the collar. "No, no, no, no—Yuma! What have you *done*?"

Yuma's eyes drifted open. He rotated his head slightly, then his mouth cracked into a smile.

"Clover," he muttered, "You came."

"Yuma," Clover moaned; tears painted his cheeks, "*Why*?"

Thieving Scumbag poked his head out from under Yuma's hair. His eyes brightened with familiarity, then he hopped onto Clover's lap.

Yuma closed his eyes tightly, wincing from pain. Clover pressed his hand on Yuma's chest where a deep wound gushed. Yuma gasped, then shook his head. "Clover, stop! It's over—it's done!"

Clover withdrew his hand, then dropped his forehead onto Yuma's chest. "Please..." Clover, wept, "Don't die."

Yuma lifted his hand and placed it on the back of Clover's head. He rubbed it unevenly.

"It's done, Clover—I shot him."

"It was supposed to be *me*!" Clover moaned.

"No," Yuma said, "You needed to live."

Clover lifted his head and looked Yuma in the eyes. Yuma was smiling. "I did it Clover—I shot him. Even though the Truth Faerie said I couldn't... I *did* have someone I loved more than myself."

"Oh yeah?" Clover sniffed as he endeavored to smile. "You had little Thief with you, then?"

"Little Thief was there to remind me of who really mattered." Yuma's smile weakened. "*You*, Clover—I thought of you."

Clover's lip quivered, then he released another sob, dropping his head onto Yuma.

"I knew you would come," Yuma said softly, "You'll sit with me, won't you... until it's over? Like Andrew—You'll stay with me?"

Clover leaned back, looking into Yuma's deep black eyes. He nodded, restraining his weeping long enough to pull Solo's crown of horns from his head. He then placed the crown on Yuma and smiled.

"Of course I will," Clover said softly. He felt Isabella's hand on his back. She knelt down close beside him silently.

Yuma's eyes drifted toward Isabella. "This is her, isn't it?" He smiled faintly, "You found your girl."

Clover nodded quickly.

"You will stay with him, won't you?" Yuma said to her, "You will do your best to deserve him?"

"I..." Isabella glanced at Clover, then nodded.

Yuma's face twisted in agony. "Clover," he gasped, clutching his chest, "I don't want to die!"

"Help me," Clover cried to Isabella as he tried to pull Yuma into his lap with only one arm. Isabella dove forward to help. She and Clover dragged Yuma up so that Clover could lean him against his chest. The Elf cradled him up in his arms and held on tightly, swaying back and forth as Yuma struggled to breathe.

"You did it," Clover said into Yuma's ear. "You saved your people, and you saved me."

Yuma broke into a sob, and then—with no warning whatsoever—he gasped his final breath and fell limp against Clover's body.

"*No!*" Clover screamed, shaking Yuma's body in rage, "Not again!"

He slumped over Yuma's body, falling into a sea of tears. Isabella leaned over his back, wrapping her arms around him as he cried.

46

—— Leo ——

The Throne

Momentum laid the king slowly onto the ground. Lola and I watched as Somenus weakly closed his eyes.

"Aorist," The king whispered.

"I'm here," Momentum cracked an eye open. As if gazing at the sun, he looked Somenus in the eyes.

"Don't let them... hurt my son." Somenus exhaled but did not inhale. The time had come. He was dead.

"*No!*" A voice screamed from behind. "Not again!"

I looked up to see two others surrounding the fallen archer. "They died at the same time," I observed.

"Somenus," Lola squeaked, "He's... *dead*?" She pulled Anodos against her and whimpered.

"I'm sorry, Lola," I said. What else could I say?

Momentum's eyes blinked. Then he squinted up at the perfectly silent audience of stunned Faeries.

"The king..." he belted, "is dead." He turned his gaze back to Somenus and pulled the crown from his head. "Rest now, if you can," he said to the body, "This burden is no longer yours to bear."

"What's happening?" I asked, pointing my chin at Somenus, "He's turning gray!"

"His body will become stone soon," Momentum said as he rose to his feet. "All Magik has left him."

"Somenus has been killed," Momentum said to the room. Faeries finally began to look around at each other. "It is over."

"It's not over yet!" A voice called from the back of the room.

Voices muttering in anticipation swirled around the throne room as Timbre Wulf charged down the aisle, side stepping the fallen archer with a sneer. He paced up to the throne, then turned to face the crowds.

"Finally!" he cried, "Somenus the Tyrant is dead!"

Momentum shot him a glare, then hid the crown behind his back.

"I am Timbre Wulf, the head of the Purple Order. My Faeries and I have come to Arelle to end this Faerie's reign and begin afresh!" He pulled a sword from his belt and pointed it at Anodos. "But his reign cannot end until everyone in his bloodline has been exterminated!"

Lola huddled closer to me. "It's him!" she cried, "He's the one who tried to kill me!"

"I know," I whispered, holding my glare on Hanz. It did get a *little* satisfaction as I noted his blackened face. Despite how little he thought of me, I still managed to give him a hefty beating.

"This cursed infant must die!" Hanz declared.

"I don't know if this has occurred to you or not," Momentum said coolly, "But this is a Faerie throne room. We do not need *your* leadership here, Hanz."

Murmuring rippled through the crowd, but no one spoke out. These Faeries may have served Somenus, but it was under a reign of fear and domination. Now, here was *another* insurrection. How were they to respond?

Hanz turned toward the crowd. "Listen," he said loud enough for all to hear, "The Faerie throne is still tied to Somenus' bloodline. You are Kingless until we can crown a new King!"

"You will not kill my baby!" Lola screamed, startling more than just myself with her volume.

"That's Lola," one Faerie said from the sidelines, "She was one of Somenus' concubines!"

"Somenus had an heir? We knew nothing about this!" Another Faerie declared.

"You need a King," Hanz cried, pointing at Momentum, "and here he is! The oldest Faerie—you can have him." He looked at Momentum, "You can be King, Aorist—once the child is dead."

"Is it really Aorist?" A female Faerie voice called. "Has he returned to finally lead us?"

Momentum gritted his teeth. "Did you honestly think such an offer would tempt me?" he said to Hanz, "I don't want to be king, and we are not killing this—!"

"Fine!" Hanz turned back toward the gathered crowd. "I didn't think it would have to come to this, but I am afraid there is only one path forward." He placed his hand on his heart.

"Oh, you've got to be kidding me," I mumbled.

"There is one person here who has gained the loyalty of over a hundred Faeries, and *without* oppression!"

"What?" Momentum balked. "Hanz—you can't be serious!"

"The Faeries are clearly incapable of ruling themselves! They are without a purpose, or a calling—you wander, leaderless and aimless through this world, wishing for someone to answer your questions! Even Aorist here," he pointed at Momentum, "will not tell you who you are meant to be! The time for Faeries leading themselves into darkness has ended. Finally, a human can show you the way!"

"This is madness!" Momentum raised his voice; his eyes were twitching alternatingly. "A human cannot rule from Arelle! This is a *Faerie* Kingdom!"

"We asked you to answer the Question," Hanz whirled to face Momentum, "and you refused! Stand down, Time Faerie, if you have nothing useful to offer!"

"*Fine*!" Momentum's voice boomed through the halls. All grew quiet. "Fine," he said again, "I will tell you!"

Even Hanz was stunned into silence as Momentum took center stage.

"I know," he said with a look of grief, "I know what we were made for. I was... I was there... at the beginning." He paused, waiting for the murmurs of shock to die down. "In the beginning, Raqia was made as a canopy over creation, like a watchtower over a city. On the fifth day, the Faeries were made. We were given the task to watch and serve, like creation's gardeners. On the sixth day, the Elves were made up here on Raqia, and humans were made in the Lowlands below the stars." He waited as another burst of gasps resounded. "We were told," he continued, "That it was our job to bring the glory of creation to those made on the sixth day—to serve them and support them. We were *not* made to be gods or rulers, but caretakers and friends."

Hanz took a step back as he processed Momentum's words. I could see the wheels spinning in his head.

"Once, there were ways of us traveling to the Lowlands," Momentum said, "And some humans made homes here on Raqia. After a time, we were cut off from the Lowlands, and it became harder for Faeries to play their roles. After the War of Fours, all of the Faeries who remembered the calling to serve the world of the mortals had died. All, save me. I'm *sorry*!" He raised his voice, "I kept the truth from you because... because I didn't want to do it anymore. I am as broken and leaderless as the rest of you!"

"So, what do we *do*, Aorist?" One Faerie stepped forward from the crowd. I recognized him as the one Somenus called Endring. "If you will not lead us, who will?"

"A human can't lead us," Momentum said, turning to Hanz, "A human cannot sit on this throne. We may not rule over humans, but we definitely rule ourselves. A king was given to the Fae at the very beginning, and I refuse to give up this throne to a murderer like *him*!"

"Don't listen to this liar!" Hanz snapped. "It is so easy to claim to be Aorist—to be a First—when you *never* show your wings! Why should any of us believe anything you say, if you have *lied* to the Faeries all this time?"

All eyes turned to Momentum. He looked around. "I am sorry I kept the truth from you," he said, "But I have never lied to the Fae. I *am* a First."

"Show us your wings," Tristan, the Water Faerie, stepped forward from the crowd. "If it is true—just show us your wings!"

Momentum dropped his head.

"Don't listen to Hanz!" I shouted, rising shakily to my feet. "Aorist is who he says he is!"

"Stand down, boy," Hanz hissed at me, "Before you hurt yourself."

"Show them, Momentum," I said, turning to Momentum. "It's okay: just show them who you are. You don't have to hide anymore. Just let them *see*!" I turned to the crowd. "If he showed you six wings, would you believe him?"

There was a humming sound emanating from the crowd, but no unified response.

"I will believe you, Aorist," Tristan said, "Please... show us!"

Momentum gazed vacantly at the crowd, then nodded.

Then, like parting curtains, a light began to form behind Momentum, revealing what had been hidden from sight all this time. The light seemed to fill the entire hall in glittering rays. How big *were* his wings? Or rather—how big *had* they been? Once the illumination finished, all that anyone could see were a few black stumps, jetting from his back like broken dead branches. He turned, showing his back to the audience. Six black roots seemed to jet out from his back. The wings had been all but destroyed—but there *were* six.

Momentum completed his turn, facing the room once more.

"I am but a shell of what I once was," he said, "But I am a First. I am sorry..." a tear dropped from his eye, "I am sorry I kept myself from you. I... I am lost." He turned and pointed to Somenus. "He wasn't a good man, but he was *our* king. Kings are given, not made. I don't *care* what this human says," He shoved a finger into Hanz's face, "We are not going to kill his child!"

Momentum turned to look down at Lola. She recoiled at the attention. He knelt down and took her by the hand.

"Rise, your highness," he said. I helped Lola's weak and exhausted body to her feet, and stayed by her side as Momentum walked her to the throne. "None of us Faeries need to be told we cannot kill," he said as he sat her on the throne, "This law is written on our very souls. But when we use humans like Timbre Wulf to do our killing for us, it is like taking a weapon into our hands. And in doing so, we destroy both ourselves, and them." He glanced at Hanz.

Hanz was huffing and puffing with restrained anger.

"We will not kill," Momentum said to the crowd, "We will not kill our little king." He looked down at Lola and whispered. "What is his name?"

Lola blanched. "He is... Anodos."

"Please, highness," he said gently, "Show them Anodos."

I felt a little defensive of Lola being the center of attention while she was still barely recovered from labor and drenched in her own blood. But I was surprised to see her strength, even now. She smiled softly, then lifted naked Anodos out from his hiding place within her robes.

Once exposed to the cold air, Anodos started to cry, and his little four wings stretched out in protest.

Momentum smiled widely, then raised his voice to the hall. "Arelle—this is Anodos! Bow to your king!"

I watched in awe as everyone bowed. Who was going to refuse when the oldest Faerie alive was standing there, commanding them? Momentum may not have wanted to be King, but he sure looked the part. No one could have been surprised at the one person in the room *not* bowing.

Hanz shook his head in disgust. Lola pulled Anodos back to her bosom and wrapped him up warmly against her skin. I dashed to her side and placed my hand on her back.

"He's upset," she whispered to me.

"You're doing great—he'll be fine," I whispered back.

"And what *now*?" Hanz thrust a finger at Lola. "Who will lead you now? A baby? An Elven *whore*?"

Without missing a beat, I stepped forward and swung Beatus, decking Hanz right in the face. He flung backwards, feet over head, and toppled off the raised platform. Some gasps erupted, but Momentum slammed his hands together, drawing the attention back to himself. I watched as Hanz clambered to his feet. Riah rushed to his side, and moments later, I forgot all about them.

"Listen, Arelle!" Momentum cried. "It is the Queen Mother's responsibility to select a Faerie regent—someone to rule until the prince comes of age," he paused, holding up his finger. He leaned down to Lola and whispered, "A *Faerie* Regent."

Lola shot Momentum a confused stare, then shook her head.

"It's alright Lola," I whispered, kneeling down at her feet. She looked down at my face. "You can always change your mind if you want, just pick someone."

Lola sighed, then gazed forward, scanning the room with her eyes. She bit her lip, and her eyes seemed to glaze over. This was too much for her—should I just tell her to pick Momentum? Suddenly, she brightened with a look of recognition.

"I know," she said in a soft voice, "I know who it is."

"Yes, highness?" Momentum asked as he leaned his ear down her way.

"I choose," Lola raised her voice, "Him!" She pointed at the back of the crowd. Commotion stirred as the gathered Faeries peered around, parting until one tall Faerie stood out from the rest of the crowd. "Hevel," Lola declared, "I choose Hevel!"

More gasps. Momentum restrained a laugh, rubbing his mouth. "Alright..." he mumbled, "Are you sure, highness? He's the *Death* Faerie, you know."

"I know," Lola shared a smile with the Death Faerie. "He is a good man. He will be the regent until Anodos comes of age."

Hevel raised an eyebrow at Momentum.

"Well," Momentum threw up his hands, "Alright—I suppose that seems right. Come up here, Hevel!" The murmurs of concern grew louder as Hevel approached the throne. "Listen well, Arelle!" Momentum cried, "Death watches over this throne! Now—if anyone ever mentions laying a hand on this prince again, they must answer to him!" He pointed at the Death Faerie as he took his place by Lola's side.

This silenced the uneasy crowd.

"It is a dark day," Momentum said, "Today, our king has died. But thank the Lights, he had a son. The Faeries have been given hope in a dark time. I know it will not be easy finding our way in the coming seasons, but we have *hope*!"

"Hear, hear!" Hevel cried, slamming his hands together in a slow clap. "Now, Arelle—join your voices with mine as we welcome in a new reign. Long live the king!"

"Long live the king!" a chorus of voices—some jovial, some hesitant—responded.

"Long live the king!" Hevel cried again.

"Long live the king!" I joined my voice with the crowd's, looking up at Lola with a smile. She gazed around in astonishment, holding Anodos to her heart.

"Long live the king!" Momentum echoed along with the voices as he placed the crown over Anodos' little body.

"Now," Hevel walked over to Somenus' body and plucked up an object that lay by his side. He held up the scepter for all to see. "With the authority given to me by the Queen Mother," he declared, "It is time to release the prisoners. Bring me those who have been exiled—in the wake of Somenus' death, I declare all prisoners free!"

"Sir," a female voice called from the crowd. Hevel turned to see one of Somenus' soldiers stepping forward. I recognized her as one of the people who had been mourning the archer's death. She was trembling as she knelt before the new regent.

"Isabella," Hevel said quietly. "We meet again."

"I..." her voice wavered, "I am guilty of taking part in the deaths of many Faeries. General Korbin—"

"Child," Hevel raised the scepter slightly. "You will not be punished for serving under the laws of King Somenus—be free."

Her tear-filled eyes widened, then she nodded. "Thank you, Sir," she said, then reached for her belt. "I have been asked... to bring you this." She held out an Exilium Prison.

"Put him there," Hevel said as he pointed to the ground in front of him. Isabella placed the bag on the ground, then stepped back.

Hevel bounced the specter in the air, saying, "Be free." In a sudden burst of light, a Faerie suddenly stood above the bag, looking stunned. His eyes met Hevel's, then he drew his fingers through his slick white hair, straightened his red, double-breasted coat, and said, "Ah—Hevel. This is a surprise."

"Hello Dezmund," Hevel smirked. "Alright, come on," he called to the crowd, "I know there's more! Go get them!"

Hevel began to rally the room with his contagious excitement, and one by one, the exiled Faeries were summoned and brought to him.

All the while, Lola sat there with her eyes half open. I knelt before her, marveling at how strong she had been, despite everything that happened. I reached forward and took her hand in mine, squeezing it.

"Hey," I whispered, "Can you believe it? We did it. You're safe!"

Lola's tired eyes drifted over to my face. Then, like a glorious sunrise after a dark night, she smiled at me.

"Yes," she said, "We did it."

"Lola, you are so amazing," I said quietly as the commotion continued around us. "You just blow me away."

She blushed. "Oh, Leo," she shook her head.

"So... you've picked a regent—I doubt anyone expects you to do anything else right now. You just gave birth! Let's say we get you out of here?"

"Oh!" she nodded earnestly, "That would be wonderful! *Please!*"

"And I bet we could find you a nice bath or something." I grinned. She nodded again. "And a nice big nap with Anodos?"

"Oh yes," she squeezed my hand, "Yes, *please!*"

"Great," I smacked my lips, looking around for Momentum. I was sure that he could help me track down a place to bring Lola to rest.

"Leo?"

"Hmm?" I snapped my head back in her direction.

"Somenus... he's dead."

"Yeah," I blinked.

Lola bit the side of her lip, then the corner of her mouth turned upwards into a wry smile.

My cheeks grew hot. "Lola?" I asked. "Are you... are you thinking what I am thinking?"

She shrugged, and her smile widened.

"You're free from Somenus now?"

She nodded quickly, growing flushed.

"So..." I held my breath. "Can I kiss you then?"

She nodded again.

So, I kissed her.

THE END

Epilogue

I laid on my back with my eyes closed. My arm had fallen asleep, but I didn't care. I wasn't going to make Lola move for anything in the world. After a busy stretch of her and Anodos' various needs being tended to, they finally let me see her again. She was staying in her old room, next to Somenus' quarters.

The bedroom was a sanctuary of tranquility and comfort. Soft lighting cast a warm glow across the space and the walls were painted in a calming shade of light blue. A large, luxurious bed with soft linens and fluffy pillows was the centerpiece of the room, while natural elements like plants and flowers provided balance and harmony.

As I laid there, indented in the soft bed, I felt the stress of the day melting away. The peaceful haven provided a respite from the insanity that followed the attack on Arelle, and I finally felt I could fully relax and recharge.

Only seconds after sitting next to Lola on her bed, she plopped Anodos into my arms and fell asleep. It was a slice of paradise, reclining there with Lola sleeping on my arm, and Anodos in my lap. The maid had left the window open, and a soft, cleansing breeze was moving through the room.

I slid my hand into my pocket absentmindedly and was surprised to find a piece of paper tucked inside.

"Of course!" I muttered, "Cymbeline's note!" I fished the paper out of my pocket and frowned. They had washed my clothes for me while I was bathing, and now the ink seemed to be bleeding through the paper. I cracked open the letter and squinted. It was nearly impossible to read.

"Dear Leo," I mumbled, "I am sorry for—*something*—but I think you will... *something, something...*" My eyes scanned for anything legible. "Ah!" I found a paragraph that seemed to have been spared some moisture. "A father I should have had; a brother I never had; and a..." I blushed, "A lover I couldn't have. But I will always remember you as," my eyes began to water. This was a goodbye. "As the best friend a person could ever hope to find. I hope you will remember me fondly as I go to find..." I grunted. The rest of the letter had been washed away. "Damn," I lowered the letter. Just then, something small slipped out from between the papers.

I picked up a little woven ring. "Ah, man," I smiled. It was the ring she nearly gave me, back when she tried to tell me how she felt. "I won't forget you, Cym," I said, then tucked the ring in my pocket.

There was a faint knock on the door. I lifted my head enough to see Momentum creeping into the room. He shook his head at me, then stood by my side.

"Sleeping with an unmarried woman?" he smirked.

"Don't you dare!" I slapped him with my letter from Cymbeline. "This is a beautiful, *innocent* moment!"

"*Sure* it is," he bounced his eyebrows at me.

"Get out of here!"

"They've asked me to come find you," Momentum said casually.

"What for?"

"Do you know..." his eyes shifted, "...Where Orion's bow is?"

"Uh..." I shook my head. "Did it go missing?"

Momentum studied me. "How about the Beatus staff?"

"Uh, *hah, hah,*" I smiled virtuously, "No idea!"

"You're a terrible liar, Leo."

"Mm," I closed my eyes, "I am super tired, Mo. Maybe we should resume this conversation another time."

"Oh, don't worry," he said, "We will."

The trilogy continues in…

Castling

and

Sky Fury

and more to come in…

A Series *of* Frigid Fragments

Dᴇᴀʀ Rᴇᴀᴅᴇʀ,

I wrote this trilogy within a stretch of six months. It was the year I lost the ability to swallow and was processing the fact that I might be dying. In the midst of severe pain, constant starvation, and intermittent hospitalizations, I took to writing. I wanted to leave something of beauty behind in this world. These books mark a very meaningful time in my life; I was suffering, and yet I was writing. I found solace in making these stories, and through them, I grappled deeply with the questions that spawned from my isolating predicament.

My world seemed to be nothing but pain and death. And yet—a whole world of fantasy was born out of it.

I've since learned that my disease isn't terminal, but it also isn't curable. I will be dealing with pain and a steady decline the rest of my life. This reality does not make me want to give up on life. It drives me, and it drives my creativity. The Tempest Trilogy deals with some dark and seemingly hopeless situations, but I'm writing about them in order to prove that—like my own trials—they are not hopeless. They are not meaningless. Beauty can spring from the seeds of loss, failure, and hopelessness.

The Tempest Trilogy and the world I've built there is my gift to the world. And as long as I have working fingers, I will continue to write stories in the land of Raqia.

Thank you for reading my work. May you find hope in the midst of your own battles.

Natasha Kennedy

About the Author

Natasha Kennedy is an author and illustrator based in Seattle, Washington. Natasha deals with a painful and debilitating connective tissue disease, and her writing reflects her belief that suffering and hardship can bring about beauty and richness. Her interests in ancient Near Eastern and Medieval Cosmology have inspired her to combine truth with symbolism in the fantasy world of Raqia.

Natasha has produced a variety of works throughout her career as both an author and an illustrator. She is best known for her illustration work in a children's book line called the FatCat series, produced by Lexham Press.

Earlier publications, combining story-telling with illustration, include:

Where I Go When I Sleep, a bedtime series written for her own children,
Maia of the Forest, a fantasy retelling of Thumbelina in coloring book form,
Reklas Abandon, a graphic murder mystery novel, her first work, and
Tempest: Volume One, the beginning of a graphic novel series released in 2020.

In the years following the release of *Tempest V.1*, Natasha developed a debilitating disease which made her rethink the graphic novel series. Realizing it would take too long to complete the story in graphic form, she chose to compose the entire narrative as a fantasy novel. That novel became *Firmaments*, and it led quickly to books 2 and 3 as *The Tempest Trilogy* came into being.

After finishing the trilogy, Natasha began working on a collection of smaller books, eight in number, which take place after the events of the *Tempest Trilogy*. This will be called *A Series of Frigid Fragments*.